THE
CASTLED
LANDS

Sea of Jundria

Farlendish Islands

THE EAST

TUNDA~HOST

Dawnwood

Myn-lak

Lost Plains

Yarm R.

TUZANCHIM

Here R.

Tekura R.

LAN~HOST

Esterwood

Lan-ta R.

EMPIRE

Near Valley

Lan-kan R.

Bloodberry Hills

Sea of Tears

Tears R.

Shitan Mts.

SHOHAN

Tamchizu Desert

Wester Hills

Red dunes

Sea of Esterlan

Anstel Mts.

Chompra Mts.

Thorn Wood

PECHON

ZANCHOR

TIRSUD

Flood Lands

Shaumwood

40 KINGDOMS of ESTERIAN

DURHEIM

ESTERSUD

DROKU

ROCHAN

IMEWAR

SUDLENDISH ISLANDS

CHASING FATE

A
Snowdragon's
Odyssey

A Novel

GORDON LAZARUS

ISBN: 978-0-9907199-1-5
Library of Congress Control Number: 2014951496
Edited by: Angela "Penny" Scott
Cover Design: Sean Alexander Ghobad
Interior Design: John Sibley, Rock Solid Productions
Graphic Design: Gina Murphy

All characters, places, people, maps, and symbols were created and designed by author, Gordon Lazarus.

This is entirely a work of speculative fiction. Any resemblance to persons, places, or other things of the past, present or future is strictly coincidence.

Published by:
Knowledge Power Books
Valencia, California 91355
www.knowledgepowerbooks.com

Printed in the United States of America

To all my readers and believers,
who helped make this chase possible.

gánsi méni to Kathy, Bobbie, Phyllis,
Mary, Peter, Linda, Susan and Gabriel

Barry, Lynn, Michael, Dahlia, Jessica,
Anne, Vernon, Ralph, Patrice and Howard

Shwranda, Blaine, Kathleen, Angela,
Bruce, Leigh, Gina and the Rossmangos

Extra *gánsi* to Willa Robinson
For her faith and perseverance

Front cover art by Sean Alexander Ghobad
Back cover & spine design by Gina Murphy
Back cover art by the author

Table of Contents:

FOR THE CURIOUS

1: The Hatchling

Outside, the clouds began to break up—a bad omen for the event at hand. Even with partial sun, the air stayed below freezing, normal for this area in mid Thrice-month. Low, slumbering hills buttered with snow and ice cradled a jumble of deformed, thatched stone huts, all looking as if waiting to be washed out to the grey sea, sleeping a stone's throw beyond. Fishing, trading and crafts sustained the village of Tiefenbo, a base for Tundrite hunters at home in the arctic, plus a score of short, robust Delfinian craftsmen. A handful of Delfinian merchants from the Stonelaw, an alpine realm to the west, also made regular visits. Only thirty people lived here year-round, as did the snowdragon, Serukeeba. She kept hall under the village, forcibly protecting it from all manner of evil.

Emerging from her home, Serukeeba craned her neck to look back. From just inside, an elderly voice scolded, "Go. Call on everyone, but don't run. Patience. It could be many hours yet—if at all. We Álukois give plenty of warning before we finally hatch."

"Promise you'll roar to wake the dead if there's any sign," demanded Serukeeba, her scales sparkling in the sun. Like all Álukois, what the snowdragons called themselves, she possessed huge, black, wide-set eyes, a modest snout and small, expressive ears—all capable far beyond human reach, and extra alert on this day.

"I promise," said the old voice. "Pace yourself, young lady. Once your joy hatches, you may not get a full night's sleep again for years. And you look thin—nothing close to a healthy five tons, or filling that polished doorway of yours. So you promise, too!"

Nodding like a human, Serukeeba turned to begin her errand. A pained "yoih!" from inside bemoaned that influence. Ignoring it, she walked lightly in the snow, her tail gently swishing from side to side but never touching the ground. Even moving slowly, she called on the whole village in five minutes. Everyone had been waiting for her summons to the hatching party.

From head to tail, Serukeeba stretched sixteen feet long, six feet tall at the shoulders, and just over four feet wide in the ribs—except after feasting. Like all Álukois, she did not weigh half what her bulk implied. Álukois lacked wings, but could traverse any type of snow, ice, or rock at impossible speed, and swam just as well. A ridge of sharp crystal spikes, sparkling and glowing translucent like amethyst, stretched from the top of her head to her tail, reaching its zenith at the middle of her broad back. The end of her short tail held eight massive spikes, for splitting stone, ice or enemies. All the rest of her hide dazzled like white quartz.

Serukeeba ushered everyone into the solarium, her home's largest room. Two old Álukois had journeyed far to help at this crucial time. As the mother of two healthy, grown Álukois, Palitéa brought priceless experience and luck. Rokímba was the oldest, most revered seer among the Álukois. Both assured Serukeeba that her hatchling-to-be would turn out fine. Yet they worried, like the human guests. The women, children and elders of five Tundrite families, ten Delfinians, including a seer, plus a tall sorcerer and his assistant visiting from the lowlands all smiled patiently, feeling her anxiety.

"Please eat," Serukeeba urged them. "Hours may pass before my joy arrives."

"It all looks very tempting," said the Delfinian seer, smiling.

The guests began snacking on an assortment of cakes, breads, smoked nuts and cheeses, dried fruits, and spiced tea laced with spirits. Honored by the invitation to this rare event, all kept glancing at the pine branch nest in the center of the room. Silently praying for success, they spoke softly about neutral things. None dared mention the ruthless Tuzanchim horde advancing from the east, the invincible Tierdragon of Monz pillaging the Stonelaw and the Castled Lands, or the plague ravaging its southern realms. Instead, they complimented Serukeeba on her hospitality. As hosts, the Álukois knew no equals on the Continent. And there was no greater safety than within the hall of a rock-armored, diamond-clawed snowdragon.

Serukeeba kept putting an ear to the hefty, pale grey egg, praying for any sign of life. Everyone listened with her. Every ten minutes, Palitéa or one of the seers also checked. After many hours, they all showed the strain, despite efforts to hide it. This was supposed to be a hatching party, but as day turned to night, most of the guests left with excuses and apologies, giving hopeful, yet empty words. Still, Serukeeba thanked them.

After three more sleepless days and nights, she suddenly rounded up everyone again, hoping one last, all-out effort could will her egg to life. She absolutely could not bear another loss. Her beloved Golármon had recently died battling the Tierdragon of Monz. Álukois mated for life.

Two years earlier, her egg was sterile. Two years before that, her hatchling died in the shell. Two years prior to that, she over-hibernated, producing no egg at all. Such was the luck of the Álukois, and before Serukeeba's time, the main cause of their decline. Now she poured all hope into this one last egg, wishing it held a life to love. All her village hoped with her.

"Could it possibly be too cold—for the hatchling?" asked the lowland sorcerer, struggling to keep himself warm.

"No!" Serukeeba growled, "Not cold enough." She reached to extinguish a torch.

"No, just right," said Palitéa, the experienced mother, taking it back from her.

"May I try again?" asked the Delfinian seer. Serukeeba nodded. Gently touching an ear and both hands to the egg, the short, stocky man closed his eyes to listen. Álukois hatched on a known due date, never more than a day early or late. Knowing this, people's last hopes had vanished. Yet the man smiled. "This one's a sleeper for sure. Can't be rushed. He'll cause great mischief soon enough. The cold air is fine, but too quiet for his nature. We should talk, laugh or make music for him."

"Him—you know it's a boy?" Serukeeba asked. "Will he hatch soon?"

"Late tonight," the Delfinian nodded, smiling. "Very late, I'm sure."

Both visiting Álukois exchanged a hard look.

"He is not Álukoi. He can know little of these things," said Palitéa, looking between Serukeeba and Rokímba.

Sensing problems, the Tundrite women rhythmically waved their spirit dolls overhead, chanting good fortune upon the egg.

Swallowing hard, Palitéa continued. "Serukeeba, I am sorry, but your child is four days overdue. If life still waits inside the egg, we must bring it out now. Sometimes the shell must be cracked from the outside to start a new life."

"But those rarely live past a year," warned Rokímba, the old seer. "It's already too late for that. We are all sorry."

Serukeeba checked her egg again, before exiting the room, to hide her despair. As night arrived, people again found excuses to leave. Yet all demanded to be told the instant she had "the great news." Palitéa, the sorcerer and both seers retired to their guest rooms. Alone in the dark, Serukeeba gazed at her last hope gone cold, wondering how she could bear another loss. Exhausted, she lapsed into sleep. But her mind refused to surrender.

She dreamt of Golármon and cherished memories of great mountains and halls, then of having a son who caused much trouble, yet brought infinite joy. Her last dream found her arguing with several Álukois, regarding her five-year-old son! Then she woke—long enough to be reminded that she would never have children.

But at dawn, she was gently awakened by purring sounds and a tiny, wet nose insistently nuzzling her ear. Hatching at that hour foretold a life filled with adventure. Opening the door, Serukeeba viewed a low grey sky promising snow—and horrific battles for her son. But she was far too overjoyed to notice either omen. Her long awaited son had finally arrived, impossibly overdue by Álukoi standards, yet strong and healthy.

Within seconds, her joyous shouting jolted everyone awake. Three hours later, they celebrated with a feast. Serukeeba rolled out a huge barrel of ale and enough food for two villages. All ate their fill and then some. The Delfinians played fiddles, pipes, harps and drums, while everyone but the snowdragons danced or sang. The hatchling's ears never stopped wiggling, straining to make sense of all the competing sounds. His eyes struggled to focus on anything so soon. Already he smiled. An hour later, he giggled. Palitéa lauded such promising signs of early development. Then the seers went to work.

"*Nómesang gu?*" asked Rokímba. "How will you call him?"

"Lorgámon, after his father, Golármon," said Serukeeba, beaming.

"Has a solid ring to it," said the Delfinian seer. "Finely thought."

"Well chosen." Palitéa smiled. "It will give him added strength."

"With the bonus of sounding Delfinian," cheered Jinva, Serukeeba's closest friend, a stout Delfinian woman of forty-five years with wavy red hair and round freckled cheeks.

"Well I think it sounds Lendish, which is always good," said the sorcerer, a tall, wiry Lendishman. "Yet may his name bring honor and good luck."

"The kudos all ring like Delfinian toasts, but the name sounds more like a mighty Álukoi to me," laughed Weliben, Jinva's husband. Except for being five years older, he looked so much like her that people referred to the couple as Tiefenbo's "official bookends."

"Thank you all," beamed Serukeeba.

"Now to the shell," began Rokímba. "Hard and thick, so he will be strong! Yet too many internal lumps…Oh, my! The break lines so…random…tortured…unique," the old seer frowned. "What impossible…challenges. The inside colorations, without pattern or any relation to the breaks…Oh, no!"

Stop fussing and start celebrating," ordered Serukeeba, gently nudging Rokímba away from the abnormal shell to end her scrutiny.

"You must have seen it too," pressed the old seer. "Considering just how deformed the inside of the shell is—"

"Enough with the shell!" snapped Serukeeba. "Can't you see how perfectly my Lorgámon turned out?"

"He will draw much blood, of many types, over his lifetime. He will…not bring happiness to the Álukois, but…" Rokímba trailed off, frowning and looking to the ground.

"What? How can you say that!" roared Serukeeba. "Just look at my beautiful baby. Already he brings hope and joy to our whole village. Savor the present; see the good!"

"I am sorry, but the shell clearly tells otherwise," began Rokímba. "Knowing and accepting fate will help keep you from making it worse. There is more, but you are not ready to hear it."

"What say our wise and worldly sorcerer from the distant lowlands?" asked Serukeeba, turning her back to Rokímba. She sought a better report from the man, regardless of how unreliable it might be.

"As he was born—hatched—at dawn," began the sorcerer, speaking slowly, "at mid-March, or what you call *Thrice-month* in this region, he will have a most…interesting…challenging life, and outlive most of his peers."

"Wonderful! And what say our esteemed Delfinian seer from the Stonelaw?" asked Serukeeba, impatient. As he was the only one to predict a healthy child, she put the most stock in the kindly man's words.

"Well," he sighed. "Your son will fight many battles, travel far and long. He may both cause and prevent tragedy. A careful upbringing can prevent the former—"

"No! It cannot," barked Rokímba. "In fact, this child will bring doom to his own people. The end of the Álukois. Clearly written in his shell. You must take him far away and never let him return to the Stonelaw, for everyone's sake."

"What kind of seer are you, trying to rob me of my one joy in life?" Serukeeba roared.

"The most experienced of our people. I give only the shell's truth, however kind or harsh that fate must be."

"Then I reject your fate. We will make our own much better," Serukeeba laughed, with anger and fear mixed in her voice.

"You cannot. I warn you Serukeeba," groaned the old seer. "You *must* keep him away, or your son will be the death of us. That is now your sacred duty. I hate being the one who must tell you. But the shell has spoken—screamed—with inescapable clarity. It must be. It is our way."

"No more!" Serukeeba curled her tail as if ready to strike a blow with it. "Go. Take your *doom* and be gone from this place. You are no longer welcome here."

"We will discuss the shell and your…situation…at the next Winter Gathering," said Rokímba, already backing away. "The Council of Elders can decide what is best for you."

"NO!" yelled Serukeeba, advancing toward her. "Can they bring back my Golármon, or defeat the Tierdragon of Monz, stop the plague or make peace with the lowlands?"

"That has nothing to do with your baby."

"Then you will have nothing to do with him either!"

"His shell speaks his fate. It is our way. You must accept what has been—"

"Never!" With both forepaws, Serukeeba ground the shell to

powder before anyone could stop her. The other two Álukois gasped, that Serukeeba broke ancient traditions. "There. The shell speaks no more. Our way has not served us well either. I say goodbye to both. If you were so wise, you would, too. Nothing more for the elders to ponder but your word and memory, which will be a good ten months old by the next Winter Gathering."

Both visiting Álukois turned to leave. Palitéa ached to stay and help Serukeeba with her baby, but Rokímba was getting old and needed help in traveling back to the mountains of the Stonelaw, the Álukoi homeland. Shocked, the villagers immediately rallied around Serukeeba and her new baby. They felt blessed to have a new snowdragon in their midst. And so Lorgámon began life as an outcast from his own race, but loved beyond measure in Tiefenbo.

2: Envoys and Omens

That year, Serukeeba shunned the annual Winter Gathering. She was far too busy raising her son and bracing her hall against tierdragons, hordes, plagues and natural disasters. Just out of his shell, Lorgámon weighed twenty-eight pounds. By Solstice (June) he could run, swim and climb. At nine months of age, he began carving simple pictures in the dirt or ice with his fore-claws, and could use heat vision. Lorgi would softly growl or purr in his sleep, yet belch louder than the worst lowland pub dwellers. On his first Hatching Day, he weighed 100 pounds and beat Aterwak, the strongest human in Tiefenbo, at tug of war.

Lorgi voiced his wants in three languages, which he often mixed and confused. At home, he spoke Álukop, the snowdragon language. With Delfinians he spoke Lendish, and Tundrish with the Tundrites. Copying human children, he used selective comprehension, depending on whether adults were scolding or rewarding him at the time. By his second Solstice, Lorgi had reached 200 pounds. He discovered endless ways to get into trouble, every hour of the long, warm days.

Two new Delfinian traders, one tall and one short, arrived with many vital goods, selling them all in an hour. They also gave Serukeeba a letter from the Álukoi Council of Elders, artfully brushed in Álukop on a parchment that had been sealed for privacy. But in Tiefenbo, anyone's business became everyone's in minutes. Gathering all to hear, Serukeeba gingerly scratched the wax seal off with a thumb claw, and unrolled the letter, taking care not to touch any of it with her claws.

"What does it say, mother?" asked Lorgi. "It's making you unhappy."

She translated into Lendish, the common tongue of the lowlands, but also known to the highlands, meaning the Delfinians, Volpings and Álukois of the Stonelaw. The village's Tundrites also knew it as a second language. She spoke with deliberately slow clarity for all to hear. "Dearest, honored Serukeeba. Congratulations on your new baby."

"Now that he's over two years old," said Aterwak. Some people shook their heads. Others sighed or frowned.

"This is the first chance we've had to trek here," said the short trader. "At great risk, with so many bandits, and the Monz Tierdragon risen again."

"Its hunger grows daily," added the tall one. "Now, no path is safe."

"Please know that we thank you traders for everything, even this note," said Serukeeba. "Our rub is with the Stonelaw." She read on. "May this letter find you in good health and cheer, no matter when it arrives! You were sorely missed at the Winter Gathering, even by Rokímba, whose prophecy sparked anger. But Palitéa spoke well of you, and all is calm. Let us help each other." Serukeeba looked away, her ears twitching with alarm. "I don't believe it."

"What's wrong, mother?" Lorgi stared up, his own ears twitching.

"Sounds like the mayor of Landrake spewing smoke," said Glomin. Tall and lean for a Delfinian, he had traveled much of the lowlands, and could almost pass for a lowlander—what the Álukois called a *hyúlem*. "I heard him speak once. A real master of sawdust, as you'd expect. But to get such from the Álukoi Council of Elders?"

Serukeeba read on. "The Tierdragon of Monz now seeks the Stonelaw's halls, preying on them one by one, ending any life it finds in them. It burns our crops, and those of the lowlands. It raids castles, towns and cities, devouring any humans or livestock within reach. Nothing can stop it, as you know only too well from Golármon's valiant attempt."

"How dare they torture you, still grieving!" shouted Jinva.

"Thank you. I had best finish reading while I still can," said Serukeeba. "Most lords in the Tierdragon's reach now pay tribute—while their people starve. Any who delay suffer her fire. Against all honor, we too have offered tribute. But that monster seeks to annihilate us. Only an all-out effort, using every fit Álukoi, can defeat the Monz terror."

"What have they not tried against it already?" asked Weliben.

"Here's the last of it," moaned Serukeeba. "The Stonelaw will send fifty crossbowmen to guard your village while you are away. All must sacrifice if we are to kill the scourge."

"By what plan will they achieve that?" asked Weliben.

"None, based on their history," said Serukeeba. "Yet they ask me to throw my life away, like Golármon and so many others."

"NO!" yelled Ubwan, the senior Tundrite woman of the village.

"Guard Tiefenbo?" asked Aterwak.

"Fifty crossbows won't stop any real foe," said Glomin.

"Did the Council mention the Tuzanchim Horde?" asked Jinva, scowling at the traders.

"They will only call it a potential threat—until it arrives," said the short one.

"And the plague?" asked Serukeeba.

"They say it still afflicts only kingdoms far to the south," said the tall one.

"What of my son? By avoiding his name, the Council shuns us, and they've never met him." Furious, Serukeeba snapped her jaws. "Speak plainly, fair traders. Will they ever accept Lorgi?"

"They long to see you both," said the tall one, stepping back.

"Can Rokímba admit her error, recant her doom prophecy?" asked Serukeeba.

"She did say mistakes are possible. She and Palitéa demand a full account of how you and Lorgi are getting on, once we return to the Stonelaw."

"Thank you, gentlemen." With a large reed pen, Serukeeba brushed her reply on the back of the parchment. Once the ink had dried, she handed it to the traders. "Please deliver this to Ónegin Hall, or wherever that inept Council hides. Until they guarantee Tiefenbo's safety, and recant Lorgi's shell prophecy, we stay home."

"They need many kinds of help, besides fighting the Tierdragon," said the short trader. "At least go and find out before you decide. One day that demon may even burn *this* village."

"Ha! Dragon fly long way for nothing," said Ubwan. "Winter too cold, summer too wet for burn." Many laughed.

"Stay put, as you said. Have nothing to do with that Council," said Jinva. Everyone agreed.

"Tiefenbo is well outside the Stonelaw," said Weliben. "They are under no oath to help us."

"Has anyone ever?" asked Kamwa, a young Tundrite man.

"No," said Aterwak. "But we always help each other. All your friends are here, Seri."

"That cooks it, said Weliben, smiling up at Serukeeba.

"Thank you all," she sighed. "Let us speak no more of this ill summons."

Frowning, the traders nodded defeat. Yet Serukeeba sent them away smiling with fifty gold pieces, deliberately flouting the Council's law forbidding Álukois to trade in that metal. Her reply noted one coin for each promised soldier she knew would never arrive.

* * *

The Delfinians gave the Stonelaw its only year-round government, the Council of Chieftains. For millennia, its leadership had rotated among twenty-eight members. The Delfinians had always shared the alpine realm with a few hundred widely-dispersed Álukois and thousands of small Volpings huddled in a score of compact towns. All three peoples called themselves highlanders, but only the Delfinians had shown any talent for governing the vast terrain. The Álukois gladly left that chore to them. Because the Álukois had become too few to even pretend to guard the Stonelaw, the Delfinians shouldered much of the realm's defense, as well.

Still, the Álukois kept their own leadership, the Council of Elders, which usually met only in winter. What semblance of order and purpose they mustered, they owed to Delfinian and Volping influence. Yet the Álukois Council of Elders imposed the no-gold law on its own kind, hoping to make the Stonelaw less tempting for bandits and other evils. Limited in authority, they elected a new leader at each Winter Gathering. The roster changed as new members reached the qualifying age of 200 years, and others departed for the spirit realms. In Serukeeba's time, the Council had been shrinking by about one member every decade. All peoples living in or near the Stonelaw knew of the Álukois' decline. None had any idea how to reverse it.

* * *

Fall passed without news. Snow. Ponds and lakes turned to marble, each night stealing more time from the brief day. Serukeeba and all who stayed had long since packed Tiefenbo with what they needed for the arctic winter. The others left. They were lucky. Lorgi grew deadly sharp teeth, claws and back spikes, all of which caused much damage and got him into constant trouble. At the most awkward growing stage for a "cub," he often injured himself, sometimes even drawing his own glowing, turquoise blood. His soft, white belly became crisscrossed with cuts and scratches.

Serukeeba could not leave Lorgi for a minute. Never finishing half of what she tried to do, yet always exhausted, she wished Palitéa had stayed to help with the "little avalanche." Nightmonth (December) saw Tiefenbo under six-foot snowdrifts, enduring the winter in the company of a clumsy, 260-pound toddler having boundless energy. People urged Serukeeba to take Lorgi to the next Winter Gathering so they could get a reprieve.

"Not unless the Council sends a glowing reply or their fifty crossbows," she said one night, before Weliben or Jinva asked again.

"Doesn't Lorgi need to be around, well, other Álukoi children, to learn Álukoi ways?" asked Jinva.

"It *would* help," Serukeeba agreed.

"Once you know he'll be accepted," added Weliben.

"Can't know 'til you go," said Jinva. "Awkward at first, but Lorgi will win them over."

"I cannot risk him being hurt," said Serukeeba. "He's still innocent. How long can anyone keep that in this world?" The Council waited two years to send word, yet shunned Lorgi's name. Pure insult. Like some lowlanders, they only correspond when they want something. Sure as Sun they did not care for my reply."

"What did they expect?" asked Jinva.

Weliben shook his head. "Hold to your principles, Seri. They'll come 'round."

"Will they ever understand what they have done to me, to Golármon, and to my baby?"

"In time," said Weliben, hugging Jinva as both nodded.

Serukeeba focused on making improvements to her hall. Golármon had always helped when at home, yet much of the time had been far away, battling the Stonelaw's enemies. Serukeeba was left to design, build and decorate most of the hall herself. While less luxurious than some, hers grew more *hospitable* each year. By Lorgi's third year, it rivaled many lowland castles and palaces. Every Álukoi hall sought acclaim for something. Ónegin Hall hosted the most books and ancestor skulls. Zorakímba Hall sat on the highest mountain, yet held the most traps for looters. Áksilon Hall boasted the fiercest war trophies. Alukeeba Hall dazzled the eye with crystals and stained glass. Those famed halls ranged from 500 to more than 5,000 years of age.

Inspired by a human artist who had been stranded in Tiefenbo one winter, Serukeeba began painting the walls and ceilings of every room and hallway with maps, murals, landscapes, skyscapes, or whatever inspired her. The solarium and the three next largest chambers owned 20-foot-tall ceilings. Every room had one at least nine feet above the floor at the walls, giving Serukeeba plenty of space to indulge her fancy. All rose dramatically to the center by various arches or a single, grand dome. For contrast, the library and pantry ceilings used simple, Laskomian style A-frames. Serukeeba would win praise for her young hall by its artfully-painted walls and ceilings.

Thricemonth brought Lorgi's third Hatching Day. The villagers rejoiced that he had finally outgrown his chewing, clawing, screaming, stumbling and crashing stage. Yet the children missed Lorgi's past months as a toddler. At 300 pounds, with new, sharper claws, teeth and spikes, Lorgi had become far too dangerous to play sports with. To celebrate the occasion, Serukeeba made a vegetarian feast for everyone. Due to snow, she held the event in her hall, extravagantly lit by a hundred candles.

"So much in storage?" said Ubwan, as both a statement and a question.

"By now, most folks are running low, praying for an early spring," said Aterwak, brushing his thick, black hair back off his leathery face.

"Yet you still have enough for two winters," said Jinva. "Why?"

"She's got the fastest growing boy in town to feed," replied Weliben.

"I save for Summer, when our village may be severely tested," said Serukeeba.

"Tested how?" asked Weliben. "The Tuzanchim? Bandits? Plague?"

"Not the river flooding again," moaned Aterwak.

"I don't know yet," said Serukeeba. "We must keep extra fit and prepared. The moment the signs gel, I will call a town meeting. Wish the stars I'm wrong."

"Are you sure of this?" asked Jinva, already knowing the answer.

Serukeeba nodded like a human. "Blessing or not, foresight has become one of my…attributes. It grows a bit stronger each year."

Fearing disaster, everyone worked tirelessly to store extra food, and repair any defects in their homes, tools, and gardens. By Summer, all were exhausted. Ever more anxious and protective of Lorgi, Serukeeba reinforced her hall's entrance to rival the strongest lowland castle gates, and stockpiled enough food for an army. She even added supplies that only humans used: clothing, blankets, small tools—and weapons.

People began to worry more about Serukeeba's mind than any outside threat, feeling that they had to root out what drove her. Whenever people decided that "someone must do something," the task always fell to Weliben, Tiefenbo's reluctant mayor. He never saw to any vital matter without Jinva beside him. On a rainy day in mid Solstice, the couple shared a rum-soaked, spice cake with Serukeeba, coaxing her to spill her troubles.

"Two fears gnaw at me," said Serukeeba. "I have not hibernated since Lorgi arrived. At three years, he's due for his first, too. An Álukoi only needs about two weeks, ideally at summer's peak. Without it, we risk over-hibernating in future years—a danger for old Álukois."

Then you will hibernate this year!" Jinva ordered. Weliben vigorously nodded. "Sunfire (July) is the hottest 'round here, unless it rains. Still have three or four weeks to prepare. Is that enough time?"

"Were it only so simple," said Serukeeba. "Once upon ancient times, Álukois hibernated by calendar alone. But enemies learned. *Hyúlem* dragon slayers always strike in summer, like the tierdragons and balkotars of old. Picking a time is a steeper gamble each year, as evil becomes too clever. The hottest weeks are only safe in the most remote areas."

"What could be more remote than Tiefenbo?" asked Weliben.

"My second fear. All winter I've had a nameless dread, but no proof of it to show anyone. It grows daily. I keep alert for signs until my dread takes form for all to see."

"Will our village be attacked?" gasped Jinva.

"Why? We've got nothing here." Weliben shook his head.

"Someone covets what we seem to have," guessed Serukeeba. "They will attack when I hibernate and the village has no defense. I must find them first."

"That Council of Elders could help by sending a friendly reply—and their soldiers," said Jinva.

"Who needs empty words?" Weliben sighed.

"Still, it flatters that they thought of Tiefenbo," said Jinva.

"Drawing attention we don't need," said Weliben.

"Keeping hidden has been good for Tiefenbo," mused Serukeeba. "Only a few traders' maps even bother to show it. Pray none ever fall into Tuzanchim hands."

"As we speak, they pillage Laskomia, not far away by their reach," said Weliben. "And the Council would send only *fifty* men!"

"An insult, but pray they never do," said Serukeeba. "That would force me by honor to answer their call against the Tierdragon. One cannot refuse and remain Álukoi."

"But haven't you done so already?" asked Jinva.

"Nearly," said Serukeeba. "For years, I've lived away from my own kind. Broken taboos. Expelled Rokímba! But I promised to return with Lorgi—when the Council recants his prophecy and delivers their soldiers. If I renege, we will be banished from the Stonelaw. All for the Tierdragon of Monz. It destroys even beyond its terrible reach."

"Don't tierdragons hibernate, too?" asked Jinva.

"For years, sometimes even decades," said Serukeeba. "Then suddenly emerge to wreak destruction for a few years before vanishing again. And they can live 500 years."

"Here's a thought," Weliben smiled, opening a jug of Delfinian smoked whiskey. Pouring a half-cup each for Jinva and himself, he emptied the rest into a gallon-sized "snow cup" for Serukeeba. "May the Tierdragon catch the plague, over-hibernate, and burn itself to death all at once."

"Oh, Weli!" laughed Jinva, shaking her head as if scolding him. "Ever the distiller's view, no matter the crisis."

* * *

No soldiers or letters came from the Stonelaw. No screaming Tuzanchim horde from the east. No lowland plague from the south. But an omen visited Serukeeba in her sleep, something the Álukois and most ancient peoples took very seriously. In her dream, a pale falcon appeared every time Serukeeba and Lorgi left her hall. When she took him along the shore, into the hills, up the river, or into the woods, it followed. Always it circled a few times and flew away, only to return, ever focused on her son.

Serukeeba feared a lowland noble wanted her child, either for a live pet or a dead trophy locked in a treasure vault. The next day, she refused to leave him for a second, even knowing that he weighed more than 300 pounds and could defend himself against most creatures. Because she had confided in Jinva, by noon the whole village knew every detail of her nightmare. Serukeeba did not mind. All gave their support, even if the dream made no sense.

In three days, a real falcon appeared, circling on warm updrafts above the village. Taunting, it hovered just at the edge of arrow range. Twice, the most skilled Tundrite hunters nearly hit it. If they could just bring it down, Serukeeba would learn much about its master, from the scent alone. If not, then someone would have to follow it to its source. But the falcon waited until dusk before flying away south, leaving no landing marks, scent, or feathers for Serukeeba to study. She ached to slay the threat, but dared not leave her son.

That night, she rounded up everyone for one of Tiefenbo's long-winded town meetings. Following Tundrite custom, every adult and child in turn spoke their thoughts on the omen, but always in Lendish so that all understood. After that, Lorgi and the other children went to bed. Then, any adult wanting a second turn got it. With luck, a majority could agree on how to deal with the threat. If not, they would have to meet the next night and repeat the custom until they did agree.

"Forcing debate, it could just be coincidence," said Glomin. "Meaning no disrespect, but with Seri lately on edge—needing to hibernate…"

"What if she's right?" posed Weliben. "How many warnings do we need? Enemies hate to announce themselves. We're lucky to get one sign."

"If bird come back, not chance," Ubwan said in her best broken Lendish.

"That was no arctic bird," said Aterwak, shaking his head. "Why is it here?"

"We'd better post lookouts," said Weliben. "And prepare for attack."

"Some of us must fish far from Tiefenbo," said Kamwa. "Fish every day now or starve next winter."

"Of course," agreed Serukeeba. "But everyone else stay close by and keep alert for anything unusual."

"Tiefenbo has four good horses," said Glomin. "I can ride south with three others to look for signs, or find where the falcon rests."

"Put a few long-eyed boys on the mill's roof as lookouts," said Jinva.

"But not Lorgi," said Ubwan. "Then no roof!" Everyone laughed, including Serukeeba, painfully aware of her son's destructive powers.

"Lorgi can help me make javelins. Tipped with my own spent claws, saved up over the year. I can split and re-sharpen them to cut through any foe. Pray we never need them."

"But I want to be a lookout," said Lorgi.

"Later," smiled Serukeeba.

The next day went as agreed upon at the town meeting. The Tundrite men fished as usual. Weliben planned a defense, while six boys took turns as lookouts. The rest of the people stayed in or near the village, mostly tending to supplies. Glomin and three others rode south, looking for the falcon or any signs of an approaching enemy. Near sunset, they returned with nothing to report.

Toward the end of that night, Serukeeba's dream called again, with the falcon landing on the shiny grey mandible of a giant, cold-weather *balkotar*. The falcon told all it had seen just by glaring into the giant arachnid's eight cold eyes. At dawn, Serukeeba woke everyone up and herded them into her hall for a second meeting.

Exactly what is a balkotar?" asked Glomin, still yawning.

"Spawn of Hell," Weliben cursed. "Ugliest of all creatures. Look like greasy tarantulas, but can grow big as Laskomian haystacks."

"Hatched, small as a human hand, yet already lethal," added Serukeeba. "Every one of them holds poison enough to kill a thousand men. By day, they see clear as humans, but all around at once. They think on a par with slower humans."

"By legend, balkotars were the Continent's first hunters," said Aterwak. "I thought they had vanished ages ago."

"Not quite," grumbled Weliben. "The largest have jaws to crack even a snowdragon."

"Balkotars carry two kinds of venom; no antidote exists for either," said Serukeeba. "They can use their jaw venom twice a day, but hunt using the hundreds of dart-sized quills on their back pairs of legs. They throw these like daggers, singly, in pairs or bunches, with horrific speed and accuracy over a hundred yards. New quills grow in to replace those in a week. Just one kills anything in seconds. Those from giant balkotars can split wood or pierce shields. Dead balkotar quills remain potent until burned in a good fire or rotted six months in damp ground."

"A team of mounted knights and two score of crack bowmen might have a chance, if they struck first," said Weliben. "But what arms have we? No shields, armor or longbows. Just a few axes, knives and tired old swords. We've some crossbows for hunting."

"Which take far too long to reload," added Glomin. "We could never defeat a balkotar. Probably not even with mighty Serukeeba. A war we must never fight."

"Tundrites have never warred on anyone or anything," said Aterwak. "We don't even have a word for it in our language."

"My dream becomes my battle." Serukeeba met all eyes as she spoke. "I must find and slay the balkotar before it finds our village."

That night, her dream returned, again just before dawn. When she awoke, she slapped her belly hard all over, thinking it strong enough to turn away any quills, because a balkotar would aim for her softest area. As far as Serukeeba knew, only an Álukoi, a tierdragon—or other balkotars—could ever dare war on one. She prayed that before Lorgi grew up, such horrors would no longer exist.

After a third town meeting, Serukeeba and four Delfinian riders marched south to hunt the rare beast. Though everyone dreaded the balkotar, the Tundrites feared winter more. No matter what trials awaited them, they fished, hunted and gathered every day, regardless of weather.

Yet on this day, they placed their children and elders in Serukeeba's hall. Delfinians kept watch over the village, while devising ways to defend it. Summer now gave twenty hours of light, but low clouds dulled visibility and showed no signs of clearing. Serukeeba sent the four riders back to help in the village while she continued her hunt. She had to find the balkotar of her nightmare. If she triumphed, she would win respect from the Stonelaw and bolster her claim of Rokímba's error. But Serukeeba also knew that she would have to battle whatever demon her omen foretold—alone.

3: Balkotars

The land rose gently, but the day grew long as Serukeeba trekked south away from the coast, over muddy ponds and tiny hills strewn with lichen-crusted boulders, deformed black spruce, and countless wild flowers. Six miles inland, these gave way to ever larger hills. Taller, thicker pines became a forest, hiding myriad streams bursting with snowmelt. Serukeeba kept telling herself Lorgi and Tiefenbo were still safe. Slaying the balkotar would keep them so.

She snacked only on what edibles lay in her path, and lost no time from her hunt. When too tired to continue, she slept in the open, because humans, balkotars and even tierdragons only hunted by day, when they could see. Two more days tracing the river upstream still brought no signs. If any emerged, Serukeeba would hunt all night and all the next day, not resting while there was any trail to follow. The best human trackers would do no less. A sorcerer could do no more, without that mysterious falcon.

"If only I had such a scout," she murmured, from atop a hill with a long view. She still picked up no signs of the bird, yet sensed its master lurking nearby. "A balkotar capable of training a damn bird, of *hyúlem* wizardry? Only in my nightmare!"

Serukeeba rued not getting a pet silverhair when she had the chance. Many Álukois had them. Eons before any people knew bronze, the wheel, or the crudest writing, when ice still buried half the Continent, Álukois tamed the silverhair, a rare type of wolf. Faithful and sharp, they cut tracking time by half, guarded halls and children, made the purest friends, and kept human guests warm when fire could not. They also kept them frightfully wide awake, as much by their keen alertness and curiosity as by their great size. When Golármon died, friends urged Serukeeba to get one, but she was too grief-stricken. At Lorgi's hatching, Palitéa and Rokímba nagged her about it. "Yes, we *will* go to the next Winter Gathering," she told herself. "If only to obtain our very own silverhair cub. Lorgi will be almost four by then—old enough for the honor of naming our pet, and learning to help care for it."

Whenever Serukeeba faced a crisis or danger alone, she spoke to Golármon in her mind. She had done this often when he was alive because he had been gone so much. She hated the Stonelaw for every stolen minute. Even dead, Golármon sent her courage, solace and wisdom. She also used imaginary talks to "walk in the snow prints of others." Wondering how Lorgi might view the Stonelaw, Álukois and the Winter Gathering, Serukeeba foresaw endless explaining.

"You'll make new friends, play all day, feast every night, wishing the Gathering would never end!" she imagined telling him. "If any ask about your hatching, change the subject. Too many fun things to do to waste a second on that! But do ask all about your father. Golármon was a great champion. Be proud of him, as he is of you. We can still learn from him. The dead have much to say."

"Brogan says most Álukois keep skulls in their homes," said Lorgi. "That's too ghouly."

"All peoples need ways to honor their ancestors, son. We honor ours by hosting their sacred skulls. They bring wisdom, energy and pride to the halls they grace. And strong luck. When the living face hard choices, they ask the dead. Even some *hyúlem* cultures have like ways. Álukoi skulls find endless purpose helping the living, most often in the halls where they had once spent much of their time in life."

"Then why don't we have father's?"

"We will demand it at the Gathering," said Serukeeba, knowing Lorgi would ask. "I can only guess the Council keeps Golármon at Ónegin Hall because we live outside the Stonelaw, or they want him in a grand hall, with other great ancestors. Mostly, I think none expected him to have heirs. You are a miracle, Lorgi."

"Why is the Stonelaw so important?" Lorgi asked.

"Our people have lived there for over 10,000 years."

"Where were they before that?"

"No one knows."

"Why don't they find out?"

"Good question," answered Serukeeba.

"Why don't people just all speak the same language?"

"The Continent is too vast. Learning other tongues makes one smarter. You are lucky to be from a village that speaks three."

"Am I really lucky, Mother?"

"Absolutely!" Serukeeba imagined nuzzling him. "You are the luckiest child."

"Then why did Rokímba say bad things when I hatched?"

"You were so late to hatch, and she clings to old ways. But you bring a new era and better luck. You have already done so for Tiefenbo. Last summer was bountiful, and winter mild for our human neighbors. Thanks to you, we all have a lucky, new friend." Serukeeba envisioned Lorgi beaming with joy, his questions answered.

"Then why don't we have my shell? Brogan says Álukoi parents save hatchling shells the way humans save baby shoes—for good luck and memories."

"You spend too much time around Brogan."

"What about my shell, Mother?"

Even in her imagined talk, Serukeeba's throat tightened. Every time the question echoed in her mind, her answer dissolved. She dreaded the day Lorgi asked, guessing it would come before his fifth Hatchling Day.

Just then a breeze slapped her with pungent balkotar scent from a nearby stream, jolting Serukeeba to the present. She wanted to bolt downhill to slay the beast, without falling into a trap. Scanning with eyes and ears, while stopping to feel any ground vibrations with her paws, Serukeeba picked up nothing. Yet the next breeze revealed two distinct balkotars: one twice the size and age of the other. Suddenly, she felt both relieved and terrified to at last reach her enemy. The dream had not warned her to expect two of them.

Balkotars did not spin webs, lay eggs in their victims or drink blood. They ate only freshly killed prey—including their own kind—one limb at a time, grinding up all but the hardest bones and shells in their jaws. To deal with natural enemies like dragons, whose blood was poisonous to them, balkotars simply fought for territory. They spun a thick, tough rope from their coarse hair, using that tool for many things. They also dug tunnels to breach castle walls or to reach dragons asleep in their lairs. For the largest game or foes, balkotars made pit traps, lined with stakes and hidden by camouflage. All these things they learned from humans.

Serukeeba prepared herself by conjuring Golármon, asking "What would you do here?"

"First, know your enemy," he answered in that youthful voice. "Preempt their moves. Seize the advantage."

"But I can't see them. I only smell them, waiting."

"Let them wait, Seri. Go slowly, alert for traps. Avoid level or disturbed ground between trees, and large, round, flat patches. Some balkotars grow clever with age."

"The woods should be roaring with birds and insects, yet all is still," said Serukeeba. "Now I smell three balkotars downstream, fouling both water and air. Best to slay them quickly while I have the chance."

"Wait!" shouted Golármon. "First, clear your mind. Set all fears, angers and motives aside. You can ponder those after the battle. Guard your belly. Keep your jaws shut. Maximize your best skills to avoid leaning on your weakest."

"Now I smell five—all giants, and all wet. Why?"

"They use waterways to hide their tracks," said Golármon. "But it really slows them down. Your game of Castle, Seri."

"I could never beat you at that! Now I smell ten of them!"

"You almost beat me many times, Seri. Remember, you need not move every piece. And you are to be feared, even by giant balkotars! Perceived force often gains more than applied force. Pace yourself to finish what you start, or they will return stronger to hunt you again."

Treading downhill lightly as a cat, she kept alert for ambush, especially in low spots or clearings. Only the rocky stream dared make sound. The balkotars still might feel her approach even if they never heard her coming. While their other senses rivaled those of humans, balkotars had poor hearing. An hour before sundown, Serukeeba reached the confluence of her stream and the Yazutak. Both yawned wide and shallow as they merged. Here, the river stretched thirty feet across, beginning a long 'S'-shaped curve down its next half-mile. Along the outside bends, the woods reached to within a dozen feet of the rocky, moss-covered banks. The opposite banks held sandbars and meadows, from which the forest retreated up to fifty yards. Serukeeba knew this favorite part of her domain completely.

"Huge boulders, too round and smooth, half-submerged," she told Golármon. "Where the stream joins our river. Each year alters a few details, but this? Still, I have not been to this spot since…"

"Stop! You found them. Plan your attack."

"They cannot sit there long, numbed by icy waters. Making them slow, easy prey."

"Then for once, fate smiles on us. The balkotars did not expect you so soon. This is your land, your move, not theirs. Great luck, my love."

Now Seri counted twelve balkotars of varying size and age. With cat speed, she might slay half before they escaped the river. But she would stay in, keep her mouth shut and her belly submerged to avoid their lethal quills. After dark, Serukeeba could easily hunt down the rest, using her night vision. Hating the task before her, she took a long breath. Who but Golármon had the courage and stamina to carry such a battle, she wondered.

"Stop it!" he shouted. "Marshal all your strengths. Banish fear. Plan your battle, Seri."

She inhaled slowly. "I must kill the largest first. If need be, I will retreat upstream."

"Take another look all around. Any change, anywhere?"

"I ache to sound a war cry and claim this battle for you, my love."

"Not this time," warned Golármon. "Dire necessity trumps custom. You must surprise them. Besides, war cries only work on *hyúlems*."

So she whispered, "For my late Golármon. For our son, Lorgámon. For Tiefenbo. For good people everywhere. Sun and Moon, let me rid the Earth of these balkotars, that they never kill again."

"Well said, my love. Now to victory!"

But she hesitated while the frigid water taxed the enemy. Suddenly, a clump of eight obsidian eyes as large as eggs rose a few inches above the current. Forced to act, Serukeeba charged, pouncing on the nearest balkotar. The impact smashed the top of its main body shell, paralyzing the beast. Serukeeba slashed all of its eyes and jumped away, barely escaping giant mandibles. She did the same for all she could reach before the rest fled the river. If a leg came within reach, she lopped it off at one of its segmented joints. If a balkotar rose too high above the water or listed, she flipped it over and gutted it, slicing through its thinner, lower shell with ease.

Serukeeba had to keep moving, never opening her mouth. On land, that could make her overheat. But in cold water, an Álukoi could fight hard for a very long time. Struggling to keep beyond reach of their mandibles, she tried to blind or cripple as many of them as possible. This gave her far better odds than having to fight off every fit balkotar in turn.

"Already six float downstream, gutted and waiting to sink," she told Golármon. "Four run blind in tight, spastic circles on one bank. Only two medium-sized balkotars remain fit and ready to fight on the other. One of those has thrown all its quills. Luck will be ours this day!"

"Good. Finish while you hold advantage! You better the world by your work today."

"Thank you, my love. But why don't those two flee? I weigh as much as both of them together."

"They can't be alone. Seri, step back and scan the whole battlefield."

Suddenly, hundreds of much smaller balkotars, none over 400 pounds, issued from the surrounding woods, blocking any escape by land. In seconds, hundreds more waited upstream. Linking themselves together by their mandibles and a single, arm-thick rope, they became a living net across the river. The current pushed them into an ellipse floating downstream toward Serukeeba. A second, third and fourth living net formed behind them with alarming efficiency. On the hard ground framing both banks of the river, thousands of balkotars in four long lines appeared, copying the largest human battle formations.

"Golármon, what can I do? They wait everywhere, ready to kill a hundred Álukois!"

"You must retreat."

"Where? They mean to battle by land and water. How can they be so clever?"

"Keep what distance you can, 'till you find a way out."

When the front net came within ten feet, the balkotars unlinked, paddling toward Serukeeba. Killing three of them, she learned their plan. One got past her forepaws and managed to climb onto her back while Serukeeba was busy fending off others. Before she could brush it off, it deliberately impaled itself on one of her back spikes. Christening her with oily, purple blood and gelatinous guts, the balkotar left 300 pounds of dead weight squarely in the middle of Serukeeba's back. Alone, the sacrifice meant nothing. But scores of them came within seconds of doing the same. Suddenly, the Álukoi's mighty back spikes had changed from a superior defense to a unique liability.

She swam for her life downstream, 200 yards away from those in the river. But two giant balkotars, each larger than she, waited just ahead, on rocks framing a narrow bend in the river. In their mandibles they held the ends of a massive net, made from balkotar rope to catch an Álukoi.

All along both banks, the spider army scrambled to bar any escape. Serukeeba forced herself to a stop, refusing to swim into a waiting net. She scanned all around to guess the weakest points in their lines and how she might inflict the most damage before they vanquished her. Like a human knight, she required an honorable way to die—slaying as many foes as possible.

For an instant, the falcon circled high above, then flew away. Four more balkotars impaled themselves on Serukeeba's back. Nearby, two giants waited with the net. Sensing the time had come, the whole army charged, swam, crawled or fell over each other in an all-out effort to reach the prey, like a million ants. In the sudden frenzy, some even drowned or were trampled by others. Diving for the river's center, Serukeeba threw off the carcasses with all possible speed. Yet the instant she resurfaced, twice as many spiders gutted themselves on her back.

"My own hide, used as a tool to drown me! How did they think of that?"

"Only a *hyúlem* could brew such evil," said Golármon.

"What can I do? How to discourage them?"

"Nothing can deter them from their lord's will. When you found them, which way were they headed?"

"Downstream. To Tiefenbo. I must warn them!"

"You cannot," said Golármon. "But you can still foil their plans."

"How, with so many of them, and so organized?"

"Stop doing what they expect of you!" Golármon shouted. "Clean your back, take a dragon's breath, and move like one! Swim hard upstream, right through them, quick as you can. By the time they adjust, you will have slain many more of them and gained position."

Gulping a huge breath, Serukeeba dove just in time. The Yazutak had a depth of eight feet in the center at this point, just enough room to swim clear under the second living balkotar net. But as she reached the third, the river bottom rose to only five feet. Turning on her side to try and keep them from skewering themselves on her back spikes, Serukeeba cut her way through. Dozens slid over her belly's marble smooth surface. None could grab onto that. But the river grew too broad and shallow for her to keep swimming, handing advantage back to the enemy. Serukeeba had to stand and try to fight her way out, an impossible but worthy task.

She called Golármon again, but got no answer. How long before anyone learned of her fate? Tiefenbo had no chance. Fighting her way upriver until she found a *real* boulder midstream, Serukeeba stood up on it with just her back legs and tail. Stretching her neck and body to her full height, like a bear, she gave herself a clean view twelve feet above the water. A hailstorm of quills, enough to fell a human army, bounced off her hide. Most were no larger than crow feathers.

For her last stand, Serukeeba picked a hill that reached down to a bend in the river. To draw the enemy away from her goal, first she exited the river on the opposite bank. Pretending that she had chosen to fight to the death there at the water's edge, she roared. Instantly, the whole army lunged toward the spot and that side of the river. Many drowned in their frenzy to cross, pushed down by others scrambling over them. Serukeeba gutted or cut the legs from the first dozen balkotars to reach her, but had to keep moving as the mass got thicker.

"Champion work, Seri!" cheered Golármon. "Keep them guessing."

"I'm too winded to keep this up any longer."

"So are they. You must not give them time to adjust."

Leaping back into the river, Serukeeba swam hard for the river's bend with the two giants. Surprised by her illogical moves, the whole army froze in place. The giants held out their net, as if Serukeeba wanted to swim into it. Each outweighed her by at least 400 pounds. Both would have to be lured into the river before she dared fight them. From the newly cleared bank, she splashed them with plenty of water to make the rocks under them slippery. Agitated and dazed by her ploy, they squatted down on their bellies. Their hair suddenly pulled tight against their backs, making them appear smaller. The giants raised their huge mandibles to shield their eyes. By instinct, they wanted to attack. Only a very potent spell kept them to their duty. They held their net too high, its bottom barely touching the water—exactly what Serukeeba wanted.

Gambling her life, she dove back into the river, straight between the rocks. As she did so, the giants remembered to lower their net. Though Serukeeba swam underwater, it caught on her back spikes. Yet these proved too sharp for even the thickest balkotar rope. Suddenly downstream of the torn net, she immediately recoiled to grab it. Bracing herself with her tail and back legs against rocks on the river bottom, she yanked hard. Tug-of-war had always been a popular Álukoi sport. Serukeeba felt her confidence return, along with her second wind.

One giant lost its end of the net. The other hung on, but fell into the river with it. Serukeeba cut the legs off of that one, dove underwater and gutted it. By the time she emerged, only seconds later, hundreds of small balkotars lined both banks, while others floated downstream towards her. Several reached her and impaled themselves on her back spikes. Despite all this, she felt hopeful of surviving the battle.

Suddenly, the one remaining giant leapt, impaling itself on Serukeeba's largest center back spikes. The impact submerged her, with a splash that cast any nearby spiders aside. She never imagined her enemy would sacrifice its most prized giant. This left her with a grim choice: being crushed and drowned, or being crushed and smothered to death. With all her might, she could barely pull herself up out of the water. In spite of her lungs screaming for air, she dared not open her mouth. Hundreds on the bank waited to launch quills. Serukeeba clawed her way to the nearest hill, as small balkotars piled on top of her. The sheer weight, fumes, and heat from their oozing bodies finally brought her down.

In dusk's final light, the once pristine river ran with the blood, filth and innards of 400 balkotars. The trees, banks, meadows, even the boulders all suffered, and would have to endure the stain for years. No one would ever guess that Serukeeba lay under that mountain of dead spiders encasing her. Purple blood and grey slime seeped out from the greasy, putrid mass of hair, quills, and broken shells. Hundreds of bodies twisted in every position on land, as scores of others floated upside down in the river until they absorbed enough water to sink.

"How will my baby survive?" thought Serukeeba. "If only I could breathe—even just a little. NO! How did they trap me so easily? Curse the heavens, who made these creatures!"

Just as she lost consciousness, a distant war horn sounded. All the balkotars scrambled to the opposite bank. Once assembled, they marched north, toward Tiefenbo.

4: The Battle of Tiefenbo

On that long morning, low clouds held the sky, as if wanting a quiet day. Yet Tiefenbo roared with industry beyond its grandest dreams, fearing imminent attack. Every hand set to work, regardless of age or condition, dreading Serukeeba's omen. Before leaving with the four horsemen, she had put Jinva in charge of her hall and Weliben of Tiefenbo's defense. He was the village's only other living soul—human or snowdragon—who had ever seen a balkotar.

The Tundrites built four huge pit traps. The Delfinian women stocked Serukeeba's hall or made thick leather shields and crude armor to stop balkotar quills, while their men built rock and earthen walls linking the village's 20-odd structures. A few long-eyed boys kept watch from the mill's rooftop, while the other children, the elders and anyone not already busy with other chores all began digging a long trench, or dry moat, around the village. Even with Lorgi's help, they made uneven progress, due to areas of permafrost.

If an attack came, Serukeeba's hall would be the keep. Built to house seven Álukois and fifty humans for a month under siege, its defense amounted to closing the door and hoping no enemy could break in. She had carved and polished the foot-thick round door from a single block of *gritstone*, designed to be movable by four strong men from the inside. Serukeeba had always been Tiefenbo's champion, but if ever she was away, men would defend her hall with their lives.

"The riders are back," screamed Brogan, running to the village center. A Delfinian boy of ten, he had a stout frame, strawberry-blond hair, freckles and sky-blue eyes.

"Isn't your watch over?" asked his mother.

"But I saw first. I have the longest eyes."

"And the loudest shout," said his mother.

"Our horsemen return!" yelled Nuwak from atop the mill, Tiefenbo's highest structure. "My turn now." Six months younger than Brogan, he already stood an inch taller. A Tundrite, he had a leaner frame, straight black hair, dark skin and black eyes with sharp epicanthic folds.

"And Seri?" asked Weliben, emerging from the town lodge.

"Not with them," said Nuwak.

Aching for news, people gathered in the "village square," an open space defined mostly by the mill, Weliben's home and the lodge, Tiefenbo's largest above-ground building.

"Back before noon?" Weliben asked as the riders dismounted. "Where is Serukeeba?"

"She fired us," said Glomin. "Would not be distracted by fearing for us, too. With porridge for a sky, we could hardly see to track, anyway."

"When can we expect Seri?" asked Jinva. "I want to have a fine meal ready when she gets back."

"Swore she'd only return after slaying the beast," said Glomin. "Certain it waits for her. Insisted she could best deal with it alone. No use arguing when she gets like that."

"Did any of you find anything?" asked Weliben.

"No bird, no feathers or tracks," said Glomin. "No disturbed branches, leaves or grass. Not even a sound. Strange."

"Did Seri pick up anything?" asked Jinva.

"Nothing but her frightful dreams," said Glomin. "With her not sleeping, too long without hibernating, still mourning Golármon, and at odds with her own kind, maybe—"

"She always keeps a sharp mind, no matter life's trials," said Jinva, "If that's where you're fishing."

"She has over sixty years by now," said Aterwak.

"Make that seventy, which is nothing for a snowdragon!" Jinva shouted. "Like to thirty for a human—a right blessed one at that. Álukois can live to be 300. No, Aterwak. You can't row a boat with that one."

"After all her sorrows, I don't know," said Aterwak. "Not everyone can stay sharp through life. Grief ages the mind."

"Since Lorgi came to us, Seri's never been happier," said Jinva. "When have her dreams failed? Stop doubting and keep working, before her nightmare arrives!"

"How Tiefenbo has grown today!" exclaimed Glomin, looking around. "So organized. So industrious! Weli, how did you do it?"

"Simple," said Weliben. "People had me tell them what to do. How do you like Tiefenbo's new walls?"

Glomin frowned at him.

"Gives a castled look, as if we villagers are seasoned in the ways of war. An enemy will think twice before—"

"But it is just a look, Weli," said Glomin. "Only impressive from a distance."

"Still far better than doing nothing in that department. Pray our quaint country walls are never tested. If a real enemy appears, we'll put the women and children in Seri's hall in a blink."

"And the men right after them," laughed Glomin.

"About five minutes after," said Weliben. "To say we put up a fight."

"Has anyone besides you and I—and Serukeeba—ever been in one?"

Weliben shook his head. "The walls are our wish that it never comes to that. Hope it won't be so obvious to an enemy."

By late afternoon, Tiefenbo boasted a short wall, a shallow dry moat on its west and south flanks, and a patchwork of thin, secondary walls linking most of the village's structures. Weliben insisted on these, saying it was part of how the great lowland castles rendered themselves unconquerable. Nothing yet guarded Tiefenbo from the ocean shore, a stone's throw to the north, as it seemed the least likely approach by the monster in Serukeeba's dream.

By then, people grew anxious, exhausted and hungry. All but five lookouts gathered in the village center for a hot meal. Serukeeba had been gone all day. No falcon or any other sign appeared. A few people expressed doubts. Inevitably, someone complained.

"Big talk meeting keep up half night," Ubwan shouted, in broken Lendish, looking around the room while glaring at no one in particular. As the village's oldest Tundrite, she held great respect. "All run 'round. Look all next day for nothing. More big talk meeting. Move everything. Dig monster trap. Make wall. Turn town upside down, make ugly. Big waste work."

"But Seri's dreams always come to pass," warned Jinva.

"Dream bird came, but long gone now," said Ubwan. "We all lose two longest days good work! Maybe not enough food store by next winter, because all this."

"Remember the flood, years ago?" asked Jinva. "If not for Serukeeba, none of us would be here to argue."

"The spring the Yazutak overflowed," said Kamwa, a young Tundrite man. "Washed the whole village away, an hour after our most stubborn finally left for higher ground."

"Where Tiefenbo stands today, but near enough to the ruins to remind us," said Weliben.

"Serukeeba still had her Golármon then, so her thinking flowed free, not pained by grief," said Aterwak. "He gave her balance."

"Seri predicted the falcon. It came the next day!" said Jinva. "She's been hinting at trouble and quietly bracing for it all year. Now it's our turn and we'd better have the stomach for it."

"Well said!" cheered Weliben.

"What does Seri predict after the balkotar?" pried Glomin.

"I predict long, hard winter and cold, hungry people," warned Ubwan.

"Arctic summers are short," said Aterwak. "How long can we put off needed work and prepare for an enemy we can't see?"

"Until the threat passes," said Weliben. "Seri's dreams always play out quickly. We've no time to argue."

"Of course, there is always a first time for her gift to fail," said Glomin. "Lorgi, has all been fine...er, usual, at home?"

"Stop it!" scolded Jinva.

"My mother just says to be ready for evil," answered Lorgi. "So she stores extra for everything. Did we dig the moat deep enough?"

"Yes, and you did a fine job digging half of it yourself," said Weliben.

"Those pit traps are too dangerous to keep live indefinitely," warned Kamwa. "Anyone, especially a child, could forget and fall into one of them."

"Yes, I know," said Weliben. "In a few days, we'll have to mark them only too well to snare a real enemy. Pray that our mighty Serukeeba returns victorious before then."

He eyed the heavy sky as weary people got back to work. The air felt cool, damp and lifeless, until a breeze carried a faint but sour odor into the village. A terrible queasiness gripped Weliben, then a shock of adrenaline when he recognized the scent. Reading her husband's fear, Jinva bustled off to Serukeeba's hall, herding women and children on the way. Weliben knew Tiefenbo could not defeat a giant balkotar, no matter how much they prepared. But, could they possibly discourage one enough to drive it away? Everyone depended on him. Determined to give his best to the end, Weliben put all hope in Serukeeba's return, before that happened.

"Dream bird!" shouted Nuwak, from the mill's roof, as the pale grey falcon glided in from the south. It circled four times high over the village before flying back the way it had come.

"See where it goes," yelled Weliben. "We need fresh lookouts. Now!"

"We got it," shouted Brogan.

He and two other boys scrambled up to replace the lookouts. But Nuwak refused to give up his post, having finally spotted something important at the end of his turn. He vied with Brogan for the distinction of which boy had the longest eyes in Tiefenbo. They excluded Lorgi because Álukois could see much farther than humans. Ubwan signaled for her stubborn grandson to get down, but Nuwak pretended not to see her. She called up to him, but her small voice got lost in all the sudden noise coming from the village center.

"Have our riders follow the bird and hunt it down," shouted Kamwa.

"Impossible," said Glomin. "Our horses are about spent. We'll try that tomorrow."

"All must stay in town now," said Weliben. "No arguing 'til all our work's done."

"Dream bird returns!" shouted Brogan and Nuwak together.

"Put meat for bait," yelled Ubwan. "Catch damn bird and wring neck! No more bad omen."

"I wish we could, but it seems too clever for that," said Glomin.

"The falcon is only a spy," Weliben moaned. "As Seri warned, our real enemy is a giant balkotar. Forget the sky and look to the land."

"Dream spider monster!" screamed Nuwak, terrified. "Huge, hairy gray spider-crab. Big as four horses."

"Mind your prophetic words, Weli!" snapped Glomin. "Next time, say something good and it may just happen."

"Brogan, do you see it, too?" asked Weliben.

"Slow, but so big and heavy," Brogan called down. "Making straight for Tiefenbo."

"Wish it into one of our traps, Weli," shouted Kamwa.

"Two of those are not finished," said Aterwak. "A one-eyed grandmother could spot them, but they might still work on a beast."

"Balkotars are sharper than that," said Weliben. "Our moat could only stall its arrival for a sneeze. It's starting to look too massive to be delayed by our walls either. Men, ready every weapon. Pray they're sharp, hard, and fast enough. Take your posts but keep down behind our walls. One quill will kill you, and they fly like Dunhala arrows. Everyone else into Seri's hall."

"Wait!" shouted Nuwak.

But he could not be heard above the screaming adults running every which way. In the panic, the ladder had fallen away from the roof, leaving him stranded on top. Unable to get anyone's attention, he turned to look at the distant beast. Suddenly he felt its eyes lock onto him. Doubly terrified, he could no longer move, or even speak.

Trails of abandoned food, clothing, and supplies all led to Serukeeba's hall. A chorus of hysteria railed from within, while the men outside eyed the half-closed door with dread. Those inside had just enough strength to shut the door, but perhaps not to reopen it. Only an Álukoi or its equal could open such a door from the outside, as long as it was not locked from within.

"We need time," said Glomin. "I'm riding out—to confuse the scourge."

"Have you been drinking, or did you fall and hit your head during your ride?" gasped Weliben. "Didn't you hear what Seri and I said of the balkotar?"

"Someone has to see the beast's methods and the range of its quills," said Glomin. "I intend to stay well away from it. But just close enough to be a distraction. Yesterday folks made us some crude armor for just that purpose."

"I cannot let you risk it. Your horses need rest. And Seri may return in time."

"Before it destroys our village?" said Glomin. "Seri can't always fight for us. She's away; the beast is here. Someday she may need *our* help."

"Then we had best live long enough to give it," said Weliben. "If only we had some real armor about."

"This will have to do," said Glomin, putting on a rough leather, padded coat. "We also have shields of wood and boiled leather."

"What about your horses?"

"Only the best for them, too," cheered Glomin with false bravado, pointing to the horses, as men were covering them in metal-studded plates of thick, cured leather. "If we can hurt the beast with our crossbows...we'll spread out, confuse it, give it too many targets to let it focus on one."

"Don't be fools! It has eight, totally independent eyes. Eight stout legs and looks to weigh even more than Serukeeba. A gallant, but futile suicide, gentlemen. I will not allow it."

"We all must do what we can," said Glomin. "Even as slowly as it goes, the thing will be standing right here in five minutes. What then?"

"Maybe you're right," said Weliben. "But respect it like a square of a hundred veteran longbows. When it has spent most of its quills, that is your chance to strike. But only while it is busy inflicting death and destruction elsewhere."

"Agreed. But how will we know when it has used most of its quills?"

"Can't say," said Weliben. "But know this. Our soft boggy ground must be slowing it down. Always keep plenty between you and the beast. On hard, dry land, it can run! And mind the pit traps. Wembrish good luck to you."

Each rider carried an ax, shield and crossbow. Two rode out about four hundred yards to the right, and two to the left of the balkotar. They kept moving and shouting, but none could distract the giant, all its eyes on Tiefenbo.

Forty yards from the village wall, the balkotar stopped. Slowly it stretched all but its back pair of legs. Leaning forward, the beast dug its huge mandibles into the ground, as if to anchor or brace itself. Then it stretched its largest pair of legs—the back ones holding all the quills— out to the sides.

"This is it!" yelled Weliben. "Stay down and hug the walls. You'll hear the quills fly like darts. Damn quick ones. Balkotars need a half-minute yawn between salvos, but no more. Usually they don't have to throw twice."

Suddenly the beast whipped its left back leg forward in a looping motion, hurling a dozen quills at the nearest wall. One whirred just over it, striking a shield with a hard knock. Six inches long but thin as a feather shaft, the shiny black dart vibrated from the impact.

"That was just a test," yelled Weliben. He saw Kamwa reach for the quill and grabbed his hand. "Stop! The slightest scratch ends life, and they're sharp all over."

Reverting to its normal walking posture, the balkotar let its eyes scan independently. It focused two of them on Nuwak, still on the roof, and the rest on various points along the wall. Only by forcing all his will did Nuwak free himself of the beast's mental hold on him. He barely scrambled to the opposite side of the roof in time to escape a hail of quills. Most of these lodged deep into the thatched roof. But a few sailed over and into the village center. There, a Delfinian man working to restring a bow was hit in the ankle. He let out a pained scream, but froze, dead, standing with his eyes and mouth wide open.

"Komlar!" cried Weliben, looking back and seeing the result.

"We cannot possibly fight a beast so huge, so quick!" yelled Aterwak.

"Time to lock ourselves in Seri's hall," said one man.

"First the balkotar must answer for Komlar!" yelled Weliben. "Now be glad we built the walls."

"Only twenty yards away now!" yelled Nuwak, still on the roof.

"Get down and to Seri's hall this instant!" shouted Weliben.

"I need the ladder!" cried Nuwak. "So many quills everywhere. Look out, it's ready to throw again."

"At least stay out of sight until we can get you off of there." As Weliben shouted, a hundred quills flew, striking everywhere at once. Many into the wall, but others into dwellings and roofs. Three barely missed Nuwak.

"Now it's only ten yards away!" he screamed.

"I told you to get out of sight!" Weliben shouted.

"How?" cried Nuwak. "The roof is full of quills. There is no place for me to walk or even jump without stepping on them!"

"He has no chance," gasped Aterwak. "We must act!"

"It looks ready to attack the wall," guessed Nuwak.

"When it throws again, we hurl our first salvo, fast and hard as Tuzanchim devils!" ordered Weliben. "The surprise may give it pause, or at least a bruise. Then we duck and try once more."

The beast launched another scattered volley.

"Attack!" shrieked Weliben, jumping up to hurl one of Serukeeba's claw-tipped javelins. Axes, arrows and stones flew, most of them bouncing off the monster's hard shell. But a few became lodged in the thick, greasy mat of hair covering the top of its main body. The balkotar lost an eye and part of a leg. In three places, its hair sizzled where flaming arrows stuck. Yet it would not quite catch fire. Nothing pierced its armor.

Enraged, the balkotar stepped up to and *through* the wall. Seeing that, the four riders drew close enough to fire on it. For their bravado, they had to endure the next volley of quills, which the beast otherwise would have used on the fleeing men behind the wall. Many of those quills stuck in the riders' leather armor without piercing it. But one found an unprotected spot on a horse's leg and it collapsed, dead in seconds. Despite the loss of another eye, the balkotar still had 360-degree vision, and could throw in any direction with accuracy. The rider of the fallen horse barely positioned his shield in time.

Fearing a breach in the wall from the start, Weliben had insisted on building a number of secondary walls connecting the dwellings behind it. That way, losing one segment of the main wall did not surrender the whole. Built in haste, all of it was weak. Still, the effort proved that the lowland art of warfare had reached this tiny, remote village. But once a few of these secondary walls fell, the defenders would find themselves exposed in the village center—or fleeing Tiefenbo altogether.

"So much for our walls," scoffed Aterwak. "A day's labor broken in a sneeze."

"They gave us vital minutes and took hundreds of quills," said Weliben. "Now thank our secondary walls. And our riders."

"Only Álukois could dream of battling such demons," said Kamwa.

"Or fools like us," cursed Aterwak.

On firmer ground now, the balkotar charged straight ahead as men dove for cover behind the nearest wall or building. It halted, just inches from a secondary wall, confused by the scattered humans almost surrounding it. When it hesitated to launch more quills, the boldest men taunted it from several directions. The beast turned one way, then back, all its eyes moving, as if trying to decide where to charge next. All knew the standoff could not last long. Then the real slaughter would begin.

"I can't take this any longer," moaned Aterwak.

"We have no choice," said Weliben.

"Kamwa, I need your coat," Aterwak demanded. "Weli, your ax."

"No!" gasped both.

"Just help me, quick."

"What do you intend to do?" Weliben asked.

"Cut the beast down to size," said Aterwak.

"NO!" cried Weliben, but Aterwak nodded. "Doesn't anyone heed my *no* anymore?"

Donning the coat and taking the ax, Tiefenbo's strongest man crawled behind the balkotar, staying too low for its eyes to notice him. He had come within inches of its terrible back legs, each as long as a man, without being detected. Just as he prepared to strike, the falcon passed overhead, emitting an ugly shriek.

Knowing that he had been found out, and so had no chance of surviving, Aterwak stood and swung the ax with all his might, as if trying to chop a limb from a tree in one blow. He aimed directly for the narrow junction between the upper two segments of a leg, a vulnerable gap in the beast's armor. His first blow crippled the leg. Immediately he swung again, the second blow severing the leg.

The balkotar let out a choking sound, then a long hiss. Quills flew everywhere. Aterwak died instantly, before the beast trampled him. Only Weliben's shouts kept the men from fleeing. Every ax, arrow, stone and javelin flew at the monster.

"Finish the demon!" he screamed. "For Aterwak! For Komlar! The monster has lost far more than a leg. It bleeds. It holds no more quills to throw at us."

Staying clear of mandibles grabbing at the air, men hacked at the balkotar's legs with swords and axes until it had none, With a dozen torches and kindling they set the oozing hulk ablaze, shouting victory.

"Glomin and Yonte return, but both on one horse," yelled Nuwak, still on the roof.

"Where are the other two riders?" asked Weliben, shouting the same question to Glomin as he reached the village.

"A new monster appears!" screamed Nuwak. "Also from the south."

"Earth Mother, no," Kamwa moaned.

"It looks about a third smaller than the first one, but faster!" yelled Nuwak.

"We can beat it, just like the first one," urged Weliben.

"We lost two men, a horse, and our walls are broken," yelled Kamwa. "Now we have to be very careful where we step. Those quills are all over the place."

"Don't you see?" Weliben snapped. "They mean to kill us all, and Seri too. We can't just hole up and wait for that."

"Another monster, from the east!" Nuwak shrieked. "Same size and speed."

"Classic lowland tactic," said Weliben. "No balkotar thought of that!"

"No use, Weli," said Kamwa. "We barely fought one of them."

"I know."

"Wait, it fell," shouted Nuwak. "Into one of our traps!"

Weliben held a hand to his mouth, begging silence. He heard a faint gasping, then a long hissing sound. From this he knew the beast had impaled itself on the sharp but hefty stakes waiting at the bottom of the pit.

The balkotar marching down from the south made straight for the break in the wall, apparently oblivious to the legless, burnt carcass of one of its own kind, smoldering in plain view.

This smaller balkotar proved just as deadly. With a single quill, thrown from 100 yards away, it shot the horse out from under Glomin in the middle of the village, before anyone knew what was happening. Another merely grazed Weliben's right thigh. It drew no blood. But in seconds it paralyzed his whole right leg. In too much agony to even speak, all he could do was nod and gulp air to avoid screaming. Everyone assumed that he would die in seconds.

"Another monster, from the west!" screamed Nuwak. "Someone help me down. Hurry!"

"It's no use. Everyone into Seri's hall!" shouted Glomin, as he propped the ladder against the mill's roof. Nuwak scurried down fast as a cat.

Kamwa hoisted Weliben onto his back and carried him to the hall. The smaller of the two arriving balkotars began to ransack the village, as if searching for something. The other trudged after the men fleeing into Serukeeba's hall, yet threw no quills. Kamwa and Weliben were the last to arrive, barely a yard ahead of it. Four men waiting inside heaved to shut the massive door. Despite all their force, it would not quite close. A huge balkotar mandible and front leg wedged in the round doorjamb. All who saw it screamed, certain the beast would gain entry.

"Stop screaming and start hacking!" yelled Weliben.

"You're still alive!" gasped Kamwa.

"And mean to stay that way. Keep pushing the door; don't give it an inch more. Glomin, Rauben, chop off the beast's limbs."

Glomin swung his ax down on the leg, with a resounding crack. Aiming for the same spot, Rauben followed up with his sword and severed the giant limb. Loud gasping, then hissing sounds answered from outside, as the balkotar withdrew what remained of a front leg.

"One fine trophy for us, and a limp for the beast!" Cheered Glomin.

"Now do the same for that huge claw so we can shut the door," urged Weliben.

"We're giving our all!" yelled Rauben. Sparks flew from his sword with every blow. "My blade is too dull. It won't even chip that thing."

"You're just getting tired," said Weliben. "Give another man a turn with the sword. Yonte."

Trading places with Rauben, Yonte swung hard with both hands. His second blow did make the mandible's armor chip. But his third broke the sword in two. Glomin hacked away at the same spot with his ax, causing tiny chips to fly off both the mandible and his ax. His fifth chop broke the wooden handle. Defeated, he stepped back in horror.

The four men straining to hold the door gave an all-out burst of energy. Forcing the door hard against the mandible, they brought it an inch closer to being shut. For all their gasps and tortured muscles, they could do no more. An iron hard mandible, long as a man's whole leg but much thicker, kept the door open. At this point, it seemed that the beast could not withdraw the appendage from the vice even if it wanted to.

Ten seconds later, the balkotar ended the stalemate. While the first mandible twisted a quarter turn, a second one appeared above it. Together, both suddenly jerked the door open two inches, then two more. Many people inside screamed in terror. With nowhere to escape, they knew the end had come.

As the women and children fled the room, the men gathered all of their remaining weapons, broken or not. Squatting behind barricades of furniture and blankets, they braced to fend off the beast at the room's three hallways. Once the beast cut through any one of those, there was no stopping it—or other balkotars waiting to enter the home. The four men still held the door, but they were exhausted. The beast gave another jerk, forcing the door three more inches open.

"My turn!" shouted Lorgi, running to the door. Putting his mouth over the second, higher mandible, he unleashed the full force of his jaws, for the first time in his life. Audibly crunching between Lorgi's diamond teeth, the mandible oozed purple blood. Both mandibles and Lorgi retreated from the door, amid human gasps and balkotar hisses. With a final burst, the men slammed it shut and collapsed on the floor. Lorgi spent the next five minutes spitting the acrid spider blood out of his mouth. For once, he received praise for his destructive powers. Now nothing could get into or out of Serukeeba's hall, unless its defenders wanted it so.

5: Under Siege

Carved deep into a mossy hill framing Tiefenbo on the west, Serukeeba's hall had grown over the years, into a veritable palace. A narrow entry hall, only five feet long, shaded the front door. This opened to the solarium, the largest room in her entire home. It had round, pink marble walls, wrought iron sconces, and a high domed ceiling. A yard-wide glass *sunpiece* crowned its zenith, drawing in natural light. Just before leaving, Serukeeba had shut its cherry wood eyelid. Her hall also boasted a library, pantry, brewery, its own underground spring, separate cellars for wine, cheese and mushrooms, and a hibernation room. Only one of its five guest rooms was designed for Álukois. Children played hide-and-seek throughout the home, while new visitors became lost. Like any Álukoi hall, it was built to last five generations. That could mean anywhere between 400 to 1,000 years, depending on who wanted to know, and which Álukoi answered.

"I'll never doubt her again," swore Glomin. "But her door! A few pounds heavier and…"

"Don't even think about it," said Kamwa.

"Before Lorgi, it weighed another 500 pounds," said Jinva. "Seri has trimmed it down to two tons, 'give or take an ounce,' as she likes to say. Polished its floor groove to royal perfection, so four able men can shut it *efficiently!*"

"We all did our best," said Glomin. "Our enemy pummels it as we speak."

"May they break their demon bones on it!" snarled Weliben. "Don't all look at me like that! I'm in far too much pain to die from it, but that barb has left my leg useless."

"I'll ice the pain," said Lorgi. With his rough, grey tongue, he licked Weliben's outer right thigh where the balkotar quill had grazed it.

"Stop, Lorgi—poison!" yelled Glomin, lunging at him.

"The damage is done," said Weliben. "I've not been able to move my leg at all, even the toes, since that damned quill nicked me. At least now it doesn't hurt anymore."

All eyes returned to Lorgi.

"I do this all the time for children. Mother showed me how."

"Well, get to it, Lorgi," said Jinva. "All the men have cuts and scrapes needing your magic."

"They're really pounding the door now," said Kamwa. "How long can it hold?"

"Built to stop a tierdragon," assured Weliben. "When Seri first carved it, I was so young, only Kamwa's age. 'No hinges, chains or any other *hyúlem* flimsies for my door,' said Seri. From outside, none can guess how thick or stubborn her door and its casing truly are."

"Part of its charm," said Jinva. "Like Seri, humble outside, mighty tough inside."

"But these balkotars fight like lowlanders," said Glomin.

"What does that mean?" asked Kamwa.

"They may just wait, try to starve us out," said Weliben.

"Not with Seri on the hunt," said Glomin. "They'll dig, pound, or force their way in anywhere they can, quick as they can."

"Giving their lowland best," sighed Weliben. "Kamwa, have children set bowls of water on the floor in every room, dead center. Hang something light by a yard of string, from the middle of every ceiling. All must take turns looking for any wobbles to these. We need folks watching in key spots all night. Quiet sleeping quarters for them by day. Jinva can assist you."

"But my hands are too full already, managing the hall," she protested.

"Sorry dear; war trumps all," said Weliben. "Let Ubwan do some of that for you."

"We need a plan to deal with a breach," Glomin whispered in Weliben's ear.

"We need Serukeeba," he answered. "Plans wash to sea the instant a balkotar crashes in. But thick granite shields us. May take them days to find a weak spot. Hope they grind their choppers to stumps before that. Should make them easy work for Seri on her return."

The balkotars pounded the door for an hour, before turning to the granite framing it, and what they guessed to be a weak point on the hill itself. Despite finding even harder rock just inches below the surface, they never stopped. Hours later, people began to detect vibrations. The sounds grew louder. Closer. The pace of digging seemed to get faster. Children cried. Adults shook with fear. People debated what to do.

"I don't want to be eaten by them!" said Nuwak.

"The children must not suffer," said one mother. "If all becomes hopeless—"

"Stop it, everyone!" shouted Weliben. "It will be days before they can break in. Save your energy. Put faith in Seri's work."

"Then what?" cried the mother, hugging two children at once.

"If they make a breach, we seal off that room as best we can," said Weliben. "And fight like Tuzanchim to hold it."

But at dusk, a war horn's long call halted the mining. Silence. For several hours, smoke seeped into the hall. Everyone knew Tiefenbo had been burnt to the ground.

In the next two days, all became experts on balkotars, weapons, sieges and traps, and the details of every room in Serukeeba's hall. Men repaired weapons or crafted new ones, plus shields and other tools for defense. Women tended the injured, mended clothes, and prepared meals. Lorgi and the other children watched and listened for any signs of a breach, or helped the adults in any way they could. Jinva and Ubwan took a thorough inventory of the hall's food stores. All kept busy every hour they were awake.

Weliben tried everything to revive his right leg, which had no feeling below the quill's mark. He feared losing the limb unless he could coax it back to life. All he could do was to elevate it, massage it, and limp about on crutches. Keeping his mind busy with the hall's defense, he had children take turns sounding the walls near the door and in a few outer rooms where vibrations had been detected. He was organizing a practice drill when Glomin stopped him.

"Given how clever our enemy has proven to be, it only makes sense that they'll be listening, too," said Glomin. "We'd best not make any noise they can use."

"You're right. We must keep quiet from now on," said Weliben. "Pray they're not that sharp."

"They coaxed Serukeeba away, made a coordinated attack and

burned the village," said Glomin. "They've trapped us down here and now try to sap their way in—in several places. "

"No balkotars thought of all that. They must have human help," said Weliben. "But who would do such a thing?"

"I've heard tales of lowland sorcerers doing all kinds of ugly things."

"Something is wrong with Lorgi!" yelled Brogan, running into the solarium.

Bounding in after him, Lorgi shouted, "I have to go out! Mother needs me. Now!"

"Of course she does, just as you need her," said Jinva.

"Not like that," snapped Lorgi. "She needs help. My help."

"Serukeeba needing help?" Blinking her eyes, Jinva forced a smile. She put her hands behind her back so that Lorgi would not see them shaking.

"She needs me now. I just know."

"Has she ever needed help before?"

"No. Not like this," said Lorgi.

"We don't have a rat's prayer," muttered Glomin, "if Seri needs our help."

"Ever the optimist, Glomin," Jinva scolded. "Please! One disaster at a time."

"She really needs me," cried Lorgi. "I have to go out to her. Now."

"Where could she be?" asked Jinva.

"Miles up the river," answered Lorgi.

"How can you know?"

"I don't know how. I just know. That's all."

"Like your mother knows?"

"I guess so. I just have to go out now!"

"Nothing doing," said Weliben. "I'm sorry, Lorgi, but Serukeeba will have to wait. You're staying inside. Alive. We need your help, too. What do you sense about our enemy?"

"Hundreds of them, waiting."

"Where will they break in?" asked Weliben.

"I don't know yet," said Lorgi.

"Well start sniffing and use your *know* to find out."

Lorgi pressed an ear to the door, walls of the solarium, and five storage rooms, but picked up no signs. Running back to the solarium, he stretched his neck up to sniff, wiggled his ears and pointed to the ceiling. Before anyone could stop him, he opened the sunpiece's wooden eyelid, revealing the chamber to the world above. People yelled for it to be shut. But Lorgi refused. He could no longer endure being a prisoner in his own home, without his mother to comfort him. The instant Jinva closed the eyelid, Lorgi pulled the lever back open and sat against it. Nothing could entice him away from his spot.

"Your mother shut it for good reason," scolded Jinva. "What will she think of what you're doing now?"

"Why, Lorgi?" asked Weliben. "Please close it again."

"You asked about the monsters," said Lorgi. "They came to the sunpiece. To trade."

All eyes met Lorgi's, then fixed on the glass pouring daylight into the room. Suddenly, the two missing horsemen rolled onto it, both of them completely bound up in spider rope, with only their heads exposed. Huge mandibles placed them face down against the glass, to stare into the solarium. Amid gasps and screams, a white cloth appeared at the glass's edge. A long old hand—gnarled, burned and scarred—limply held it.

"What was that?" asked Kamwa.

"Hand of lowland sorcerer," said Ubwan. "Hand did many bad thing, many time."

"At least now they seem willing to talk," said Weliben. "What can they want?"

"Me," said Lorgi.

"What?" gasped Jinva.

"NO!" yelled Ubwan. "Sorcerer want train, use Lorgi, like spider monster."

"How did you arrive at that?" asked Jinva.

"Ugly hand, train bird and monster," said Ubwan. "Seri's omen."

"The falcon spied Lorgi in her dream," cursed Glomin.

"What about our poor riders?" cried Jinva.

"We had better show our own white flag, and quick," said Weliben.

"What if it's all just a trap?" asked Glomin.

"We're already in it!" moaned Weliben. "We need time. But also must learn what our foe is about. We'll have to parley with him."

Because the glass sunpiece was too thick to transfer sound, Weliben wrote a large note on a white cloth, holding it up for the hostages to read to their captor. The Sorcerer's reply: "Send one above. Now!" Mandibles yanked the prisoners away. People screamed or pressed hands to trembling mouths. Some debated who should go, or if it was all just a ruse to open the hall's door.

"Stop!" shouted Weliben, hobbling to the door. "Think what Seri would do. Everyone out of the solarium except armed men, ready to fight. When I say, open the door just enough for me to squeeze through and close it right behind me. If this is just a trick, then close it *on* me!"

"No, Weli, please," begged Jinva.

"Maybe the sorcerer can cure my limp," he sighed, hugging her. "He should know how; he gave it to me."

"Wait," Glomin seized his arm. "Not you, Weli. You're our leader."

"Any other time, I'd think you wanted something," Weliben laughed, to hide his fears. "Like a bottle of my smoked whiskey."

"I'll gladly accept one for going in your place."

"Listen to him, Weli," pleaded Jinva.

"Seri's away, maybe in trouble of her own," said Glomin. "We have two dead. Two others are hostages. We lost the village, our horses and half our weapons. All we have left is the hall and our mayor. We cannot risk either."

"Weli best peace talker," said Ubwan. "He can make deal."

"Glomin is just as adept," said Jinva.

"And quite ready," he agreed.

"Can you limp like me?" asked Weliben.

"That's just it; you're in no shape to—" Glomin began.

"I'm perfect for this. Who else will need so much time? It may irk our foe, delay his plans—a value in itself."

After a quick round of Tundrite good luck chants, Delfinian prayers, and farewell hugs, Weliben stood at the door, looking grim but determined. Only when all the women and children had left the room, did he let it be opened, just enough for him to squeeze through sideways.

Taking a huge breath, Weliben used a full minute just to exit and reposition his crutches. He took seven more to crest the hill over Serukeeba's hall.

There waited a tall, lean, grey-bearded sorcerer with pitted, blotchy skin and long, repellant features. Clad in dark grey robes and a traveler's hat, he carried an old sword showing signs of much use. He sat mounted on a spotty grey horse, whose hateful expression matched his own. On either side of him squatted a balkotar as big as an ox. Before these lay the hostages, bound so tightly that they had trouble breathing.

"Your pathetic struggle is over," sneered the man. "Take a long look around, so that you make a wise choice."

"That I will," said Weliben, fighting not to shake from fear. "But release these poor gentlemen. They cannot possibly delay your plans, whatever they are. We all know how deadly and quick are your balkotars."

"You are in no position to even ask."

"Even you do not hold all the cards," said Weliben.

"Look before spouting idiocy," growled the sorcerer.

Weliben saw no sign of Aterwak, Komlar or the horses. Tiefenbo had been burned to the ground. Hundreds of small balkotars formed a ring, or siege line, around the base of the hill over Serukeeba's hall. Dwarfed by the sorcerer's giant guards, each spider in the line still weighed between 200 and 500 pounds. Each held hundreds of quills. Weliben could not hide his terror or shock, which delighted the sorcerer. Still, he found the nerve to ask, "Where is your falcon?"

"One of these shot him," spat the sorcerer, pointing to the hostages. "They should feed my guards. But to make peace, we will return them to you...in exchange for something."

"We?" asked Weliben. "Are you some kind of displaced royalty?"

The sorcerer only gestured to his army of spiders.

"Where are the men your beasts killed?" demanded Weliben. "We must give them a proper burial."

"I did nothing with them. But my army grew hungry after marching down to this rubble you call a village. They are still hungry. Ravenous. Four horses, two short men and a bird can hardly satisfy a score of them—the smaller ones at that—let alone 600."

"You have 600 of those things?" gasped Weliben.

"Enough of your dribble!" barked the sorcerer. "My command…has its limits. All the more reason for you to stop dallying and help me get them out of here!"

"This is the domain of a mighty snowdragon, soon to—"

"We felled that pile of quartz two days ago. While you had a skirmish, we had a war! Nothing ever put up such a fight. Slew my best giants. Costly. Glorious! But history. You have what I want. Hand over the dragon child by noon, and these two live. We will leave at once, and never return to this…" he waved his hand and sneered, "*place*. Noon. Or we will dig you out and eat all of you. Go. Make your backward little friends understand."

"We love our dragon child," Weliben gulped. "What can you possibly want with him?"

"That is not yours to even ask."

"Lorgi is everyone's concern," said Weliben.

"If you must know," moaned the sorcerer, "I will make him into a servant and bodyguard. Go back to your rabble and decide. By noon. Go."

"We need more time that than to decide so grave a matter. A full day at least."

"Noon!" yelled the sorcerer. "Must we resume digging to persuade you?"

"One more thing."

"What?" barked the sorcerer.

"The antidote. I also have limited control of my side, and need all my limbs. If the mother dragon recovers, everyone must flee her revenge."

"As I already told you, we killed her," moaned the sorcerer, "and there is no antidote for balkotar poison."

"You carry it, or you'd never be in their company. If we are to reach any agreement, you must keep true words, or face the Stonelaw's revenge!" Weliben yelled back, red-faced, stepping forward on his good leg and alarming the balkotar guards nearby.

Impressed, the sorcerer fought back a smile. Pulling a small flask from a pocket concealed in his robe, he handed it to Weliben.

"It will sway the vote if you release your captives."

"Noon. Exactly. Not a second late. Surrender the dragon child, your friends live, and we leave."

"My people will have questions before they can agree."

"NOON!" screamed the sorcerer, angrily waving him away. "Go. But words alone will not convince you." He signaled a few of his guards to resume digging. They began at once, despite their bleeding, eroded mandibles.

"No digging or no deal!" shouted Weliben, still refusing to go.

The sorcerer clapped his hands and his guards halted, returning to him.

Certain that he had pushed his foe to the limit, Weliben began gently hobbling back down the hill. Irked by the slow pace, the sorcerer yelled after him: "Drink it now, fool, or you will always need crutches."

Weliben halted, opened the flask and sniffed. Ever so slowly, he tasted a drop. If it contained poison, masked by the sweet alcohol, then he would never take it into the hall. Waiting to feel any possible effects, he stood silent. This infuriated the sorcerer.

"Idiot! You must drink more than a taste to do any good!"

Weliben swallowed a spoonful, but still refused to enter the hall until that amount had a definite effect, good or ill. His right leg slowly regained feeling. He wiggled his toes, stretched the entire leg, then walked on it without the crutches. By the time he reached the door, it felt whole again.

"Mother Earth, you were gone long!" said Kamwa. Everyone cheered. Jinva embraced her husband so tightly that he squeaked.

"Yes, but it makes no difference," sighed Weliben. "He won't budge on his deadline—noon. Lorgi was right. The sorcerer demands him, or his spiders will dig us out and…"

"What?" gasped Jinva.

"That devil throws all he has into this enterprise. Pray Seri returns before noon."

"Just how many balkotars does he have?" asked Glomin.

"He said 600. Some no bigger than a sack of potatoes. Plenty of those. But others are older and so much larger. Nothing close to the haystack we killed. But…" Weliben swallowed hard and glanced at Jinva.

"He claims...claims to have slain our champion by the river."

"Where Lorgi says she is," cried Jinva. "Do you believe him?"

"He'd be wicked at cards," Weliben cursed. "I can't know."

"Why noon? What's his hurry?" asked Glomin.

"He must have grander targets elsewhere that won't keep" guessed Weliben. "He was enraged by my slowness, but hardly worried about Álukois. Wish I had Seri's gift right now."

"Lorgi shows signs of it," said Glomin. "He might be able to—"

"No! We cannot risk him," snapped Jinva.

"We already risk everything," said Glomin.

"Where our two riders?" asked Ubwan. "You promise bring back."

"The sorcerer will only trade them for Lorgi—at noon. Or he will kill them and...and..." Weliben broke off, shaking his head.

"We'll think of something," Jinva calmed him.

"We have nothing to fight with," said Glomin.

"This is all about time," said Weliben. "How long will it be before they break in?"

"Depends where they dig, I'm sure," said Jinva.

"The two biggest ones by the sorcerer must be the same as Nuwak saw coming," said Weliben. "And have ground their mandibles to stumps. But hundreds wait to replace them."

"If only we could have sent for help," said Kamwa.

"If, nothing! We're alone here, as usual," said Glomin. "With only two horrible choices."

"And less than two hours to decide," said Weliben. "Everyone must think hard, and return to the solarium by half before noon to vote. I don't know what else to do."

People cursed or cried. Some slumped into chairs or recessed benches, which Álukoi halls provided for human guests. Others just collapsed onto the floor in shock. Totally spent, Weliben sat down in the solarium. Many wanted to speak with him, but he needed time alone, so they left the room. Jinva leaned against him, quietly supporting him. Lorgi sat on his haunches, inches in front of the couple, knowing they always found solutions.

"What's that?" Lorgi asked, pointing to the flask.

"The antidote," said Weliben.

"Smells sweet. Does it work?"

"Yes, and I only used a spoonful."

"Let me see," asked Lorgi, reaching for the flask.

"No, we must save it." Weliben shook his head. "Your mother or someone else may need it as I have."

"Just let me sniff it."

Jinva nudged Weliben and he held out the flask. Lorgi sniffed it all over like a dog, then sat back on his haunches.

"Well, Lorgi, what did you get from that?" asked Jinva.

"Sick, old man. Hates people. Many enemies. But thinks power will make him happy."

"Lorgi, he said he will...destroy...everything, unless we give you to him," Weliben stammered, holding back tears and looking to Jinva.

"No, he said he would eat everybody if you don't hand me over to him."

"We took care to keep that from your ears, Lorgi," gasped Jinva. "How did you find out?"

"From the sorcerer himself," said Lorgi. "You can hear great in the kitchen. Put your ear to the fireplace to hear on top of the hill. And when you're up there—"

"Heavens, no!" yelled Weliben, putting a hand over Lorgi's mouth. "Jinva, get people out of there!"

"Done," she said, already scurrying down the hallway.

"Glomin," called Weliben.

"Coming," he answered, entering the solarium.

"Get men and arms to the kitchen, silently but quickly. I'll explain later."

"We've another problem, Weli," said Kamwa, jumping out of his way. Glomin and Rauben came right behind. Finding the room empty, Weliben sighed relief, but kept them all out of it. He refused to speak until they followed him to another room. "What other problem, Kamwa?"

"One of Seri's javelins is gone," muttered Kamwa.

"Yes, we checked everywhere and thrice over," added Rauben. Both looked ill from reporting the bad news.

"We broke seven on the monster," said Weliben.

"And recovered only six," said Kamwa.

"Now our foes will have a diamond to dig with, once they think of it," said Glomin.

"You can be sure they will," cursed Weliben. "But I see no use in alarming the others."

"Not much time until noon, anyway," said Glomin.

Weliben nodded. "Lorgi, do you think you could dig your way out of this home?"

"Why would I do that?"

"Alright. How long would it take you to dig your way in?" Weliben squinted. "Just pretend the door was broken and shut, but you just had to get in. How long would it take you, and where would you dig?"

"An hour—from on top of the kitchen or the solarium," guessed Lorgi.

"Earth Mother!" gasped Ubwan, entering the room.

"All the balkotars of the world—which seem to be right over us— will still need far longer than Lorgi to dig their way to anything, even by the softest route," assured Weliben. "Time to bring everyone back to the solarium."

That room's water clock showed twenty minutes before noon. People quietly entered, all looking grim, horrified and totally spent.

"Before we vote, you must know that the sorcerer claims to have defeated Serukeeba by the river," said Weliben. "He admitted that she slew the largest balkotars in his army before…before she fell." Jinva hugged him firmly. Barely recovering himself enough to continue, Weliben added: "He claims to still have 600 of them. He would train Lorgi, like a balkotar, to carry out his will."

"They say you cannot spell an Álukoi—immune to magic and evil," said Glomin. "Better to surrender Lorgi for the moment, than for all to perish."

"No!" yelled Jinva. "We cannot give up Lorgi. He is not for bargaining."

"Maybe sorcerer want kill us all anyway, after take Lorgi away," posed Ubwan.

"If Lorgi says his mother needs him, she must still be alive, but in some monstrous kind of trouble that won't keep," said Jinva.

"Brace Lorgi for whatever that madman above has in store," said Glomin. "Lorgi can thwart him just by being himself. The rest of us can help by cleaning up the mess, getting a search party up river, and word to the Stonelaw."

"Shameful, but maybe our only chance," said Weliben. "We can do nothing locked up in here. Pray that Lorgi emerges from the ordeal unharmed. Or we may face an Álukoi's revenge. Even the smallest children must vote on this. Our lives ride on the choices forced upon us now."

"Ask Lorgi before deciding what's best for him—in his own home, no less!" scolded Jinva. "Seri asked me to keep charge and all. But with her away, Lorgi is master of this hall. Give him the last word."

"I'm master of the hall?" mused Lorgi.

"Do you understand what the sorcerer wants?" asked Jinva.

"As well as anyone."

"How can you, child?" sighed Weliben.

"I'm almost three-and-one-half, already! You don't have to baby me. This will be my first adventure. You can be proud of me when mother and I return."

"We're proud of you now," cried Jinva, with tears running down her cheeks. Weliben clasped her hand, as both nodded to Lorgi.

"Can I go with him?" asked Brogan, echoed by Nuwak and Sirwan, Lorgi's closest friends. Brogan's mother grabbed all three children in her arms and told them to be silent.

"Almost noon," said Lorgi. "I had better go out. Goodbye, everybody."

"Wait," ordered Weliben. "First a quick snack and farewells. I'll go up and stall the old bastard."

Still hoping to negotiate, or at least to delay the terms, Weliben used a grandfather's pace as he hiked to the top of the hill, with all the bravado he could muster. The sorcerer stood waiting in the same spot as before. On the ground before him lay the two hostages. Only a few feet away slept the two largest balkotars, their mandibles ground down to useless, bleeding stumps. A dozen small balkotars stood within a lance's reach.

"You are late, which carries a price," snarled the man.

"What is your hurry?" asked Weliben. "I am here to say that a narrow majority of the villagers agreed, so you will get what you came for. We will surrender the dragon child."

"My reputation demands punctuality!" laughed the sorcerer. "Have you ever seen a balkotar feed?" A sour grin came over his face. "Fascinating—but far from pretty!" He waved a hand while snapping his fingers. Two balkotars quickly unbound one of the captives. The other spiders perked up, drooling and working their jaws, which made gurgling sounds.

"Stop, or no deal!" Weliben shouted.

"Then get on with it, fool!" yelled the sorcerer, clapping his hands four times in rhythm. Instantly, the balkotars froze. "Produce what I require—now! I've no time to waste here."

"It is not quite as simple as that," said Weliben. "Here are my people's terms: Send all but two of your monsters back where they came from. You and those two big bloodied ones must wait 100 yards south of the hall's door. Not an inch less. We will post a far-sighted lookout on this hill to relay your progress. Release these two gentlemen to us unharmed, as a sign of peace. Only when all that has been done, will you get the dragon child."

"You are in no place to state terms to me." The sorcerer laughed.

"That depends. Nearly half of my people would rather fight to the end than surrender our child. They will see him dead rather than in your custody, and mean to carry that out when the time comes. You must give a sign to show you are indeed less wicked, and more reliable than they think."

"You'd be a worthy opponent in any game." The sorcerer mounted his horse. "Very well. If you can bring your lookout now—without delay—we shall begin moving our forces out. These two may return with you."

Raising a large, cured bone war horn to his craggy lips, the victor drew a deep breath to sound a long blast, then two quick staccatos. His army began moving south. After freeing the captives, the two giant guards rewound their ropes into compact, foot-thick balls, which they put on top of their backs, well behind their eyes. Without any means of fastening, the great balls of rope stuck perfectly to the balkotars' mat of dense, coarse hair. They also looked more like ammunition for siege engines than rope.

The instant the two guards had finished, the sorcerer led them to the bottom of the hill, then 200 yards south of it, to deprive Weliben any further excuse for delays. Slowly removing his hat, the man swept it out to his right, until holding it straight out with his arm fully extended.

Weliben could not be certain if the sorcerer meant to show that his army had gone, or where Lorgi needed to follow. Relieved to have saved the two hostages, he staggered back to the hall with them, all their nerves shattered. Seeing the price for their lives and freedom waiting at the door, all wept. Nuwak slogged out ahead of Lorgi to be the lookout. But as Lorgi turned to march off, Weliben stopped him.

"Wait, Lorgi," said Weliben. "A last thought. You need not do this. Take a good long breath on it first."

"I understand," Lorgi assured him, nodding like a human.

"What will happen to him?" cried Brogan.

"My first adventure," said Lorgi. "Tell you all about it when I get back. Don't worry about me. I'm lucky."

"Spin all the luck you can, my little avalanche," ordered Jinva, sobbing. "Get away from that devil and his crew the first chance…"

"And you don't exactly have to mind him either," added Brogan.

"Just be careful, Lorgi," said Weliben. "Don't push the bastard too hard. Bit by bit each day. Wear him down while we send for help."

Lorgi tried to smile. "I'll be like a knight on a quest. When I bring mother home, we must celebrate with pies and cheese and cakes and cider."

"That we will!" Jinva smiled through her tears.

"Wish I knew about sorcerers," said Lorgi.

"I'm afraid you're about to find out, in the worst way," said Jinva.

"Stay close to him," said Weliben. "Eat only what he does himself. Mimic him, but don't seem too smart. Delay him. Take long with every tiny thing. Learn what you can without falling under his spell."

"Maybe I can learn some magic and put the sorcerer under one of his own spells!" cheered Lorgi.

"No, far too dangerous," said Jinva. "Better not dabble in any of his madness. Just always be careful."

"Too late for that," said Lorgi. "I just have to be lucky. More than ever, to make things right. And to make my own destiny."

6: A Sorcerer's Nemesis

Undaunted and determined, Lorgi marched straight down to the waiting sorcerer. Only Nuwak could see him from atop the hill encasing Serukeeba's hall. Weliben stood in the doorway at the hill's base. Everyone else huddled inside, sobbing. Many wanted to go out and see for themselves, but Weliben refused to allow it. Nuwak relayed Lorgi's progress down to Weliben, who then told everyone else. Straining for hope, both voices wavered.

"The sorcerer's two biggest spiders try to tie up Lorgi like our riders," said Nuwak. "They work fast, but he cuts through their rope faster than they can bind him. They try to hold him with their mandibles, but Lorgi wiggles and squirms free. He catches one in his jaws, snaps it in half! That balkotar hisses and spits at him."

"No, child!" moaned Weliben, shaking his head.

"The sorcerer steps between it and Lorgi, signaling about twenty small spiders," said Nuwak. "He coaxes Lorgi aside. What? The small ones attack the big one with the broken mandible."

"To keep it from murdering Lorgi," gasped Weliben.

"They just killed it. Ugh! They're all eating it, one part at a time."

"Where is Lorgi?" cried Weliben.

"The sorcerer led him away. He tries to hypnotize Lorgi, but can't hold his attention. Lorgi droops his eyes and ears, giving his sleepy, dumb look. Candy is offered, but he won't take it."

"Good, Lorgi," muttered Weliben.

"The sorcerer just cut his hands trying to open Lorgi's mouth," yelled Nuwak.

"Don't shout," warned Weliben. Only then did he relay all that had transpired to everyone waiting inside.

"One down!" cheered Kamwa. "One less for Seri to hunt."

"Quiet in there!" hushed Weliben. "If the sorcerer hears, he'll smell deceit and not honor his terms."

"Nobody plays dumb better than Lorgi," said Nuwak. "Uh-oh!"

"What now?" asked Weliben.

"He finally took the candy, but threw it at two balkotars fifty yards away. They start towards him. The sorcerer stops them. Oh, Lorgi! He walks up to one and flips it over onto its back. Its legs flail at the air. It looks helpless until it can right itself. Now the biggest one grabs Lorgi."

"Moon's Pox!" cried Weliben. "Don't tease death, Lorgi."

"He just bit one of its mandibles in half!" yelled Nuwak. "Purple spider blood all over Lorgi. Now the sorcerer keeps all of them away from him."

"Lorgi pushes luck past death itself," moaned Weliben. "Our fault for encouraging him."

"The sorcerer calls back the one with a broken mandible. You won't believe this!" Nuwak stopped, his mouth open but silent.

"What, already?" demanded Weliben.

"It jumped, killing itself on Lorgi's back spikes. It has to be four times Lorgi's size. Barrels of purple blood and slime everywhere. I can barely see Lorgi, smothered under it all."

"The sorcerer must have lost all patience," said Weliben. "Seems the only way to keep Lorgi stationary—and alive. But all that dead weight crushing down on him."

"The sorcerer gets back on his horse…and rides toward us! Ten balkotars chase after him."

"No doubt furious with Lorgi and all our delays," said Weliben, starting to hike back uphill. "What will he demand now? Nuwak, run back down to the hall. Quick!" Weliben reached the hill's top only a step ahead of the sorcerer.

"You will make that spoiled, wiggling, pile of quartz obey me!" shrieked the sorcerer.

"He is far too young to understand any of this," said Weliben. "He only minds his mother—half the time. Many would gladly take his place as your hostage."

"Idiot! That gem-studded brat is the only thing of value within a thousand miles. Get it to mind, or watch it die—along with your people!"

"I'll do my best," said Weliben. "But no one can guarantee, with such a young child. So innocent. So simple. You ask the impossible. I had thought a man with all your worldly knowledge—"

"Hurry up with it, you over-fed, hen-jabbering dwarf!"

Ignoring the insult, Weliben walked down to Lorgi, smothered under the balkotar's dead weight. He refused to begin scolding the child until the huge carcass had been removed. Yet Weliben still hesitated, with the sorcerer listening over his shoulder. He had only heard the man speak Lendish, free of any particular accent. If Weliben risked using Delfinian, a language closely related to Lendish, then the sorcerer would probably understand. Weliben wanted to use Álukop, but did not know enough of it himself for this critical situation.

Gambling on Tundrish, the arctic nomads' unwritten tongue, Weliben greeted Lorgi with his back to the sorcerer. He also clapped his hands and stretched them out to make a big circle in the air, an Álukoi greeting. Lorgi sat back on his haunches, answering in kind. Looking over his shoulder, Weliben smiled at the sorcerer, still mounted on his horse.

"Enough with the hellos!" snapped the sorcerer. "He only left you a few minutes ago."

"I must keep his trust," Weliben said in Lendish. "One just cannot rush these things."

"Even to save your life," quipped the sorcerer.

"Lorgi, my careless young friend, take great care," Weliben said in a low monotone.

The sorcerer strained all his senses trying to pick up any meaning. From the look on his face, he did not succeed.

Both villagers' eyes lit up when they sensed the sorcerer got nothing. Weliben smiled, gambling everything on his next words. "Speak only in Tundrish with me. Never talk to sorcerer horse-piss in Lendish. Ignore him when he uses it. Keep playing dumb. The only safe thing to do."

"Nuwak saw me; I heard him," said Lorgi. "How is my adventure going so far?"

"We all nearly died of fright! Never be so bold. You must take care to stay alive."

"Make that insolent bundle of rock know your lives depend on his obedience to me!" yelled the sorcerer. "If I must return again, all will pay."

"That I will," said Weliben. "But you must understand him as if he were a human child. A four-year-old, but a slow one. He has limits. You can only move him so far in one day."

"You had better hope he is not too slow to learn," warned the sorcerer.

"He responds much better to rewards than threats."

"That remains to be seen," growled the sorcerer. "For the lot of you. Now get on with it before I exterminate your whole village."

"Lorgi, try to remember every detail about where horse-piss takes you, to help get back home when this nightmare is over."

"Álukois always know how to get home. No need to remember. We just know. Only humans get lost."

"Note the details anyway," said Weliben. "Every kernel may help later. Find out how horse-piss brews his evil. But take care! Never antagonize his spiders again, or touch their quills, even if you find one on the ground. Turn your back and make like a turtle if you think they might throw them. Make horse-piss think you are dumb, yet trainable in small ways. You know our hopes. We all carry you in our hearts and pray for your safe return. Sun and Moon protect you."

For the sorcerer's benefit, Lorgi gave his dumb look, with eyes half shut and ears drooping.

"Are we finally done?" moaned the sorcerer.

Weliben nodded.

"Then back to your rat's nest. If you have accomplished what I asked, we'll never meet again. Go!"

"We should never have met at all," said Weliben. He staggered back to the hall, tears streaming down his cheeks, as the sorcerer led his forces south away from the ruins of Tiefenbo.

Once beyond sight or sound of the village, the sorcerer had another large balkotar impale itself on Lorgi's back. The army kept marching right past the carnage, oblivious to the sacrifice. The sorcerer's two largest guards wrapped up Lorgi so tightly in rope that he could not take a deep breath. Unable to move even a thumb claw, let alone see, he whined, growled, roared, then cried, but could barely hear himself inside the miles of balkotar rope spun around him. Painfully insulated, he grew too hot to do anything but sleep, a very unhealthy state for a snowdragon.

An elite corps of twenty mid-sized guards, the same that had stayed near the sorcerer during his parleys with Weliben, now took turns carrying the immense bundle encasing Lorgi. To any observer they would have looked like a team of slaves from the ancient Sudlish Empire, hauling a giant stone slab destined for a temple or fortress. Taking no chances, the sorcerer kept his prize tightly bound and guarded for the whole week-long journey. He also led his army home by a longer route, a mile east of the river, so that Lorgi would not sense any of the carnage on the Yazutak, which included his own mother.

* * *

The sorcerer lived in a thatched house, hidden atop a ridge between two cone-shaped, limestone bluffs, on the western fringe of a vast, ageless forest called the Dawnwood. A dozen pine trees, many boulders, a few large outcroppings, three storage sheds and a water well occupied all the level space crowning the ridge. Like a matching pair of miniature volcanoes, the bluffs rose 400 feet above the woods blanketing the surrounding, hilly landscape. From his perch, the sorcerer could spot foes or his next victims well in advance. With such a natural fortress and an army of balkotars, he could repel any attack. At home, he felt invincible.

Upon arrival, most of his army vanished into hundreds of small, shallow caves dug high up into the bluffs. But the twenty special guards tending Lorgi followed the wizard directly into his house and down into his basement laboratory. Even after they unwrapped him, Lorgi was far too sleepy and over-heated to care about where he was or anything else.

"Wake up, my little rock-head," laughed the sorcerer. "Maybe that should be your name. Rock-head."

Lorgi gazed back with half-open eyes and drooping ears. Seconds later, his ears pointed straight down for sleep. His eyelids closed.

"Enough! You slept all week, the entire journey, ate nothing and refused even water. Perhaps you are ill. Open wide. *Ahhh*. Like this. *Ahhh*. Say *Ahhh* for me."

"*Ahhh* for me," Lorgi mimicked him.

"Slow, eh?" the sorcerer glared. "Keep that jeweler's mouth of yours open. Say *Ahhh*."

"Say *Ahhh*," Lorgi answered.

The sorcerer touched Lorgi's tongue. "Hot, dry as chalk, grey as ash. Not looking well, my sleepy rock-head. Dragon's fever. But I can treat that with ease."

The man clapped hands and made quick signals with them. Two of his guards carried Lorgi back upstairs. What the dragon child needed most was to cool off. The sorcerer brewed an herbal tea, made palatable with milk and honey. Lorgi sniffed the steaming liquid but refused to drink. Guessing distrust, the sorcerer assured him by tasting it himself. Waiting until the man reached to take the drink away, Lorgi downed it all in one gulp. Instantly he began to revive. Surprised at how well the medicine worked, he focused on the man's eyes.

"Good," praised the sorcerer. "At last, I have your attention. Time for my best magic. Watch my hand." Holding a tiny disk in the palm of his hand, he spun it rapidly. To Lorgi, it seemed nothing more than a brightly painted toy. It also looked a bit like an Álukoi's pupils at the instant of switching between different light and distant focusing: snow and wood, moon and cave, or long and short eyes—all at the same time.

All the special guards stared intently at Lorgi, whose great eyes reflected the sorcerer's hypnotism only too well. Having no sound language, the balkotars communicated by visual signals, making them acutely susceptible. After many frustrating minutes, the man found his intended subject all too alert, but his elite guards out cold. They would remain so for hours, no matter how anyone tried to wake them. Until this moment, the wizard had never found a need to break the spell, so had never developed one.

Suddenly it occurred to Lorgi that with enough effort, he could achieve the same thing, using only his eyes. He recalled once overhearing his mother describe the ancient, rare Álukoi art of *spinning*, and how she had never been able to develop it herself. Maybe Lorgi could learn something of use from the evil man, after all—even if Jinva and Weliben had warned him not to.

"Perhaps the old myth holds true, or you're just too dull for my spells to work on you."

"Say *Ahhh, Ahhh* for me?" said Lorgi.

"No," sighed the man, shaking his head.

"No," sighed Lorgi, mimicking him. Having sat quietly for twenty minutes—his daytime record—he assumed the wizard had given up on spells and would move on, hopefully to things that did not involve Lorgi. Homesick and famished, he eyed the door. But first, he needed to fortify himself with a good snack. Ever reliable, his nose led him to the kitchen.

"Where do you think you are going, rock-head?"

Suddenly too hungry to care about anything else, Lorgi ignored him. Until the man tried to inhibit his search for food.

"What are you doing with that?...No...Put that down...That is not for you...Stop!"

Lorgi found a stack of dry, crispy flat bread in a wooden box on the counter. He nibbled one to make sure it was edible, but wanted something tasty to go with the bland staple. His nose led him straight to a large round of smoked cheese, waiting in a floor ice box under the counter. Lorgi nudged the protesting man aside just enough to open it. The sorcerer resisted, but Lorgi already had more than twice the human's weight and a dragon child's strength.

"No!" shouted the man. "No."

"Nóshul!" (snack) Lorgi chirped in Álukop, tasting the melon-sized cheese.

"So you're finally hungry," laughed the sorcerer. "But dragons and other mighty beasts do not eat cheese. They eat meat. In great quantity. I'll get you some mutton. Maybe even spoil you with seared mutton."

"Syaz mústar?" asked Lorgi, hoping for mustard or another spread to go with his flat bread and cheese. *"Ánter syaz?"*

"So you do speak, if only in dragon gibberish."

"Hábev yúni syaz? Mak góbo nóshul!" When no sauce appeared, Lorgi resigned himself to eating his snack dry. In three bites, he devoured the entire round of cheese and all the flatbread.

"That was enough for five men! Out! Get out of my kitchen. Go. Bad dragon. Go!"

"Góbo nóshul!" (good, satisfying snack). Parched after the dry morsel, Lorgi sought a beverage. Returning to the floor box, he hoisted a barrel of ale up onto a chair, ignoring the man's rants and gestures.

"NO!" yelled the sorcerer.

"*Góbo nóshul!*" said Lorgi with an innocent, yet firm tone, expecting the man to understand. He drank a gallon of the ale before letting the barrel roll and spill all over the wood floor. Cocking his head and pointing his ears forward, Lorgi gazed at it, enjoying the sound it made as it rumbled away from him.

"You'll pay for that, rock-head! Once the ale takes effect."

Still hungry, Lorgi opened every drawer and cupboard in the kitchen, oblivious to the sorcerer. When the man's shouting got too loud, Lorgi shut his ear lids, reducing the angriest human tantrums to muted whispers. In a cupboard too high to reach, two delicacies that no Álukoi could resist vied for Lorgi's attention. A large jar of honey and an even bigger one of pine nuts; both called with rich, sweet aromas.

"Now what? No! Leave the table alone! Stop! Let go!"

Lorgi pulled what looked like a solid, new table—and the sorcerer along with it—across the room with his forepaws, until it rested directly under the prized cupboard. To make sure the table would prove sturdy enough to hold him, Lorgi slapped the top of it three times with a forepaw, also enjoying the sound that made.

"No, not the honey!" begged the man.

"*Zeeblut yi nuts—góbo nóshul!*" sang Lorgi in a joyful child's voice.

As he climbed onto the table, Lorgi severely gouged and chipped it. Standing up on just his back legs and tail, he easily retrieved both jars. Setting them on the counter, he jumped down off the table. Before Lorgi, it really was new. Now it looked like it had endured a sandstorm. Normally, even a three-year-old Álukoi would have known to mix ingredients in a bowl. But Lorgi felt that in an enemy's house no rules of civility applied. All should be broken in short order, and he intended to have fun with the concept.

Emptying all the nuts and what his patience allowed of the honey onto the stone counter, Lorgi mixed them with both forepaws, taking no care to avoid scratching the counter with his claws. The sorcerer heard them scraping, gouging and ruining his counter. The table looked ready to collapse. Lorgi would have loved cinnamon or nutmeg to complete his dessert, but had no more patience to search for those treats.

"You'll pay for that too—turning my table into firewood."

"*Góbo nóshul!*" Lorgi burped. In the next moment he ate all the nuts and most of the honey. Holding the jar upside down over his head, Lorgi set his tongue to work on what remained inside of it.

"That was enough to last three months," said the sorcerer, his face growing a darker red every minute. He shouted ever more dire spells, threats and curses until Lorgi finally gave up on the jar. Enraged, he struck his wizard's staff down with bone-shattering force. It snapped in two on Lorgi's back spikes with a hard, loud crack. If the blow had struck anywhere else, it might actually have injured him. Pretending not to even have felt it, Lorgi turned to leave the room.

But the sorcerer blocked the way. Lorgi motioned four times for the man to let him pass. When the sorcerer refused, Lorgi threw a half dozen, lightning cat scratches from both forepaws. The man jumped back, screaming in pain, his arms and legs all bleeding, as his ransom exited the kitchen, then the house.

Lorgi would have fled right then, but suddenly caught a hint of his mother's energy on a small balkotar resting near the door.

He prodded the beast. It retreated. Lorgi followed, pestering it all the way. When the spider could endure no more, it punched Lorgi in the face with both mandibles, eliciting an "ow!" Immediately, Lorgi returned the insult, pounding the spider on top of its main shell with both forepaws, crushing its armor and its brain. He still had no concept of his own strength.

Lorgi studied the dead balkotar until a live one came by, also with a trace of his mother's energy. That one he chased twice around the perimeter of the house before it stopped to fight, with the same result. Running to the storage sheds, then up and down the spider paths ringing the bluffs, Lorgi picked up traces on many of the balkotars. As he approached, they ran, climbed, jumped or fell, just to stay clear of him. In seconds, all stood guarding the entrances to their caves, their jaws dripping venom, ready to kill if Lorgi got too close.

The sorcerer lurched out of his house, despite his pain and bleeding, knowing he had to retrieve his prize at once. Using one of his many clapping signals, he sent all his spiders back into their caves. Only very slowly did he coax Lorgi back inside the house, offering a peanut-sized caramel. Recalling Jinva's warning, Lorgi only pretended to enjoy it, storing the sweet in one side of his gums. Quickly the sorcerer gave him a second candy.

"Good little dragon," cooed the man.

"*Góbo nóshul!*" answered Lorgi.

"Three of those will keep a bear asleep all day," said the wizard. "You drank enough ale to flatten four swordsmen." Scowling at Lorgi, he shook his head. "Yet look more awake than ever. Ah, but you are such a hefty, vexing little rock-head. Better have one more."

Lorgi yawned, but kept them hidden under his tongue. With a fourth, the sorcerer coaxed him to a bare corner of the main room, where he wanted Lorgi to sleep. Once the candies seemed to be taking effect, the sorcerer went to the other end of the room to treat his many cuts. Silently, Lorgi deposited whatever had not dissolved of the four candies under a rug, before putting his head down on top of it to sleep.

Shaken by his pain and the repeated near loss of his prized ransom, the wizard could not steady his hands enough to bandage his own wounds. Fearing the spiders' revenge if their master became incapacitated, Lorgi shuffled back to him, using his tongue to heal the cuts he had inflicted on the man. At once, those stopped bleeding, as a cold numbness took away the pain.

"Amazing! You have the gift of healing. But why so destructive, my dragon rock-head?" The sorcerer looked at his wounds, then toward the mess in the kitchen.

"*Góbo nóshul?*" Lorgi asked with pretended innocence, the way only a child could. He cocked his head and wiggled his ears.

"Now I see that your village got much the better end of the bargain. They must still be celebrating your departure. After all you ingested, how can you still be awake?"

"Ahhh for me?" Lorgi chirped.

"Ah, indeed!" The sorcerer narrowed his eyes and shook his head. "Between you and that slow-talking Delfinian..." Pointing, he added, "back to your corner."

Lorgi did so and pretended to fall asleep. He sensed the man's stern gaze, until the sorcerer gave a long exhale of relief. Finally, the man went down into his basement laboratory, closing the door behind him as quietly as possible. Though sleepy, Lorgi felt compelled to learn what he could by exploring the house—starting with the kitchen. Taking care not to make noise, Lorgi found two jars of dried fruit. Before launching into these, he also discovered a barrel resting in a dark corner on the floor, filled with thousands of the sleeping candies. He decided to make good use of them in his escape. But by now, all the ale and what Lorgi had tasted of the candies made sleeping very difficult to postpone.

Suddenly, balkotar eyes studied him through a narrow window, jarring him awake. Grabbing a few candies from the barrel, Lorgi stored them in his mouth. Silently he went to the front door. Opening it, he found two balkotars roughly his own size guarding it. Eager to test the candy, Lorgi tried giving it to them, but they backed away. So he set it on the ground, went back inside and shut the door.

At once he heard a brief struggle outside, just as the wizard's labored footsteps began ascending the stairs. Scurrying back to his corner, Lorgi curled into a ball and shut his eyes. In seconds, he and both spiders guarding the door all fell into a deep sleep.

By the time he awoke, the sun had sailed two hours into the next morning. Too groggy and afraid to go outside without the sorcerer, Lorgi saw what he could from the safety of the house's narrow windows. Hobbling from the injuries Lorgi had given him the day before, the man was making an inventory of his army that might take all day. After counting the eyes, limbs and especially all the quills for each balkotar, the sorcerer wrote in a large tablet. When he and his twenty special guards disappeared into a large cave, Lorgi gave up watching for them.

Returning to the candy barrel, it occurred to him to make his own inventory. The hefty container seemed to hold more than enough for the whole army. But Lorgi had to know for certain. Once he began counting, a better idea came to him—finding the source.

Checking all the windows again, he saw no sign of the wizard or his guards. Lorgi found the basement door secured by a metal padlock. Bored, anxious and frustrated, he began gnawing on the lock, which proved no match for his snowdragon jaws. In a few minutes, it broke, freeing the door. Charging down the stairs into the laboratory, he wanted to find or make enough candy to put the whole army asleep for a very long time.

Closing the door behind him, Lorgi smiled. "Time to play wizard. And leave a royal mess for him to clean up! So much fun. Nuwak and Brogan and Sirwan would be jealous. Tiefenbo will be proud."

Endless rows of cupboards and shelves lined three walls from floor to ceiling. Myriad glass and pottery jars, all meticulously labeled, sat on these, as well as strange little tools and scores of books. Several long tables held tools for cutting, grinding, measuring, mixing, heating or distilling, amidst a vast array of powders and liquids. Everything waited for clever hands to make magic with them.

"Gems and rainbows, where should I start?"

The fourth wall held four levels of deep, long shelves, each divided into compartments, all numbered and labeled. Only the top, furthest left of these was empty. All the rest held hundreds of apple-sized eggs, covered in a pungent, yellow mucus. The sight and smell of these made Lorgi pinch his nostrils and pin his ears back.

He knew he had to demolish this balkotar hatchery soon, but then the sorcerer might let the spiders kill him. *This certainly is not that day*, he thought. Lorgi would just play in the laboratory, leaving the eggs alone. Donning a neck scarf and a tall, wide-brimmed traveler's hat from a wall hanger, he could not help cutting both in the process. But a child just had to play and have fun.

"I'm a wizard now!" he cheered aloud. "I am the Grand Sorcerer...Konzor...Zongkor? Zongula...whatever. Now let us make a fine concoction. I wonder what this is. Looks like some kind of berry juice."

Lorgi sniffed a beaker half full of a thin red liquid. "How can the wizard be sure what this stuff is when it has no smell?"

Gingerly, he picked up an empty glass tube, taking care not to let his claws scratch it. He used this to mix a spoonful of the red liquid with about as much of a blue one. It bubbled for a moment, turning pink. Hardly satisfied with the result, Lorgi chanted an imaginary spell to empower his new concoction. "Uga Pazuga Machuga!"

Adding more of each liquid only got the same reaction. With

Delfinian drama, Lorgi threw a paw-full of yellow powder into it, chanting "Wampa Chonka Mazigula!"

Instead of turning orange, the liquid suddenly fizzed into a hot, foaming purple mess that expanded, overflowing the glass tube and giving off a strange, volcanic odor. "Great Snows! You can sure smell it now," said Lorgi. "Being a sorcerer is a lot easier than I thought."

Cooling down, his new purple mixture lost the fizz and burnt odor. Still, Lorgi thought he had better get rid of it before the real wizard came back. Reaching for the back of one of the shelves holding the balkotar eggs, Lorgi poured where he thought the mess would be least noticed. Instantly it began dissolving the eggs. Dozens of translucent baby spiders broke through their shells, writhed in quick death spasms, then froze. Suddenly, Lorgi was not playing at all. He had to repeat his experiment, for the good of all. Yet hide the growing evidence of his mischief.

Pouring more of the blue and red liquids into his adopted beaker, Lorgi added the last of the yellow powder. But it was not enough to make the brew heat up and fizz like before. Unable to find any more of it anywhere, he substituted a beige powder. Getting no reaction with the new mix, Lorgi tried adding a green liquid to it. When this failed to show any reaction, Lorgi poured a black powder over it all. This only made the whole mixture solidify into a hard, brown clay.

Having tired of the whole experiment, Lorgi turned to leave when he noticed a silver flint lighter waiting by an oil lamp. Only wealthy lowlanders owned such magical things. At home, Lorgi was forbidden to play with fire or even go near the fireplace. But no rules applied here. At first, the tiny *hyúlem* device proved frustrating for his clumsy forepaws. Yet within minutes, he worked the tool like a favorite toy.

"Lightning!" cheered Lorgi, borrowing a word used by human teens. "The most lightning thing in this whole, ugly place. Sure to get me or any child in trouble at home. But anybody would love to use it."

He lit the oil lamp, then every candle in the lab. Inspired to try one last experiment, he lit the solid brown concoction now filling his beaker. It nearly exploded, shooting out a white-hot flame. Startled, Lorgi jumped back, knocking over the table behind him. As it all hit the floor with the thunderclap of heavy wood and a great shattering of glass, Lorgi managed to retrieve what looked like a very welcome glass of water. Throwing this liquid onto the fire only made it ten times worse, setting the whole long table before him and everything on it ablaze. With his mightiest breath, Lorgi tried to blow out the culprit.

Spewing a foot-long flame as it went, the beaker rolled off the table and across the floor, all the way to the wall holding the shelves of eggs, igniting everything in its path. With the whole laboratory in flames, Lorgi fled upstairs. Knowing his experiment would quickly engulf the entire house, he rolled the barrel of sleeping candy out with him, hoping to bribe any angry spiders he encountered. Missing its lid, the barrel gladly shared its contents. Slipping free of Lorgi's paws, it began to tumble downhill with increasing speed, spewing candy as it went.

The sorcerer and his guards tried desperately to put out the fire or salvage what they could from the house. Lorgi raced after the barrel, but could never catch up to it, as hundreds of balkotars pursued him. Within minutes, he left them all far behind to fight over the candy. In a few more minutes, Lorgi had run too far ahead for any of them to ever catch up with him.

But he also ran straight into an old trap, set in a narrow clearing between four trees. With a snap and a whoosh, Lorgi suddenly found himself hanging upside down, dazed, confused and too exhausted to cut his way out of a thick balkotar net. Some minutes later, an ash-covered sorcerer and his special guards arrived. They wound Lorgi tightly in enough rope for a ship and rolled him back up to the bluffs. All along the way, they passed hundreds of sleeping balkotars. Smoke billowed up from the ruined house. Inside his cocoon, Lorgi could only smell it. But he wished the smoke could be seen all the way back to Tiefenbo

7: The Wind from the East

Klimgu scanned the panorama with raven, far-sighted eyes, framed by sharp epicanthic folds. Halting his scouts on reaching the choice hilltop, he drank in a deep breath, savoring the view. Compact and hard like all Tuzanchim warriors, these wore plain woolen clothes, leather coats and boots. Some wore close-fitting leather hats, while others used headbands. None wore any armor or helmets. Each carried a slightly curved sword, a small round shield, a powerful composite bow and a quiver of arrows. Their packs held only a dozen small tools, dry food, a few gems, but no gold. Weight reduced an item's worth.

The Tuzanchim had never ventured so far from their bleak homeland, thousands of miles to the southeast. They had raided many lands, but none like this, what the few locals called the Tunda-Host. With absurdly long summer days and short nights, it held a dazzling variety of wildflowers bursting from even the harshest rocky and frozen places. It offered fine, sweet grasses for the horses, superior game, yet such relentless mosquitoes that even the hardest warriors yearned to leave this northern extreme of what they called the Exotic West.

"Why stop here, when it is still morning?" Bungtai yelled at his leader. "Push hard west and south to our goal, the Castled Lands."

"I see no method to this day's wandering," said another man, brushing long, black hair out of his face. "Find us a village with meat worth eating—or taking!" The other scouts laughed.

"Tezanjo!" yelled Klimgu. "Connect your tongue to your mind, or I will have to remove it."

"Why lose time here while others gain?" sniped Bungtai, scowling at his leader. "Nothing here but hills, woods and hordes of giant mosquitoes."

"Nothing for the blind or the hasty," Klimgu chided him. "Let us surprise our foes, not the reverse."

"Only crumbs for the slow or the timid," Bungtai fired back.

Klimgu took a deep breath to wash away the insult, an old

Tuzanchim saying. As leader, he constantly worked to keep some warriors on task—and mindful of his rank. He hoped to finally prove Bungtai wrong on this day, but gripped his sword, all the same. Having toiled to earn the respect of all under his command, Klimgu also knew that a rare few only respected the swords that finally cut them down. Chotzan, his loyal Second-in-command, sensed trouble and put himself between the two riders.

"This will be a very long summer day," Chotzan yelled at Bungtai. "We must water and rest the horses before fools like you ruin them."

"We found a good stream just north of this hill," shouted Ziteng, a more reliable scout.

"Of course you did," laughed Klimgu. "Even Bungtai can hear the river."

"Also some huge bear tracks," said Ziteng. "A dead smell, too."

"Show me," ordered Klimgu, signaling all to follow Ziteng to the stream. "So massive! But triangular claws? This was no bear. And these over here look like tail marks."

"Who cares? Even a fool will think not to stay here," said Bungtai.

"No one cares what Bungtai thinks," said Klimgu, looking to his Second. "Probably a giant reptile. What do you think, Chotzan?"

"It must weigh at least four horses," said Chotzan. "Could have a taste for them, too. Maybe humans as well."

"Arrows won't stop such a beast," warned Ziteng. "It will defend its land to the death, and have no patience for intruders like us."

"Perhaps it can teach Bungtai a little respect," said Klimgu. "How I wish to meet such a rare creature—yet survive the encounter."

"Bringing ruin to our expedition," laughed Chotzan.

"Or the finest trophy," said Klimgu. "The Gran Vazuk loves the exotic, and rewards any who can deliver it."

"Or punish those who fail!" yelled Bungtai. "Stupid waste of time, tracking monsters when we could soon be plundering the Castled Lands, just days to the west."

"Ah, the lure of the Exotic West!" Klimgu shouted and laughed. "Stop fretting like Esterlan cowards. Those prints must be a week old, their mighty owner now far away, patrolling its vast domain. But they ensure that no other large predators dare roam for many miles around."

"What about the dead smell?" asked Ziteng.

"Leftovers, scraps from the monster's last kill," guessed Klimgu. "Chotzan, take all but these to my left back up. Keep lookout atop our hill until I call you. Bungtai, Ziteng, Otwaje brothers, Kibak, Tezanjo and I will scout down to the river."

"Why?" asked Bungtai, irritated.

"Bungtai will lead the way, so that he waits for no one," said Klimgu, smiling and gesturing for the rebellious scout to do so. "Let his questions be answered first."

Surprised, Bungtai nodded slightly to thank his leader for the honor.

"Big as four horses," mused Klimgu. "I would give as many just to glimpse such a creature."

The stream and tracks led the seven riders to Serukeeba's last stand by the Yazutak River. All of these warriors had seen and caused much destruction. Until now they had assumed that only humans truly knew pain, cunning, and organized war. But the Tuzanchim studied every battlefield they found. Despite the horrid stench and billions of insects digesting the carnage, they resolved to learn from what had taken place here.

"Wait," said Klimgu. "This is too alien."

"Cowards wait," said Bungtai. "Heroes discover."

"We know nothing of what lies here. Wise to observe everything, before disturbing anything." Klimgu stayed on his horse, yet the others dismounted and began walking about.

"What ugly creatures," spat Bungtai.

"Like something from a nightmare after eating too many bloodberries," said Klimgu. "Perhaps a war for territory between rival clans of those beasts. The river will have marked the boundary. We can only guess, but it seems the battle ended in a stalemate."

"No matter, but a fine tale for our children," laughed Bungtai. "Spiders as big as sheep. A few even bigger than yaks! I will choose a perfect specimen. After showing one of these, people will believe whatever I tell them about the west." He grabbed a mid-sized balkotar by one of its back legs. Opening his mouth wide with pain, he froze rigid, falling over on his side. Klimgu shook him, poured water on him, yelled in his ear and slapped him. But the scout lay stiff as wood, with three quills stuck in his hand.

"Aih! I can't move my arm!" yelled one of the Otwaje brothers, clutching his left arm with his right hand. Klimgu applied a tourniquet, but already too late. All the men crouched around him, gripping their swords as their eyes darted in every direction.

"Bows, circle out—touch nothing," barked Klimgu. This time, no one questioned his order.

"Ambush?" guessed Tezanjo.

"A snare for curious fools like us," said Kibak, the lead scout.

"Feels like a curse," said Ziteng.

"A battlefield," reminded Klimgu. "Warring monsters of the Exotic West. Ziteng, bring Chotzan and all but four down from the hill. After you make them know *not* to touch anything!"

"It must be those barbed darts," said Tezanjo. "Look anywhere. On the ground, in the trees, even sticking through the eyes of some of those things. Sharp and dripping with poison."

"Grand news, Tezanjo," said Klimgu. "At long last, you start to think."

"Armies of giant spiders whose quills are their arrows," said Kibak. "But if we can find a way to safely remove them and tip our own arrows with them…"

Every warrior's eyes widened at the idea.

"Wind must have given us this terrible, new weapon," yelled Klimgu. "But first, we honor our dead—the blind and the hasty. Learn from their folly. Then take what those spider demons hold, with motherly care, and leave this place forever. It wants no living thing to disturb it."

The moment Chotzan and the others arrived, Klimgu spoke to convince them all of what he thought should be done. The Tuzanchim liked to decide things after quick, spirited debate. They would rather suffer the consequences of quick choices than lose precious time weighing details. Brave foolishness, in spite of lives lost, still carried dignity and potential. Timid caution offered nothing. Luck and bold, clever leadership made a conqueror.

After a third casualty, the men learned how to safely extract quills from the spiders' back legs and fasten them as arrowheads. They were able to do this by covering their hands with crude gloves, made on the spot from strips of leather or wool cut from their blankets. In a few minutes they learned that only quills from the largest beasts proved hard enough to pierce what they considered to be armor—Tuzanchim hard-cured leather coats, or balkotar shells.

"Thousands litter both sides of the river, to an arrow's range in any direction," said Chotzan. "It will take days, even weeks, to harvest this war treasure."

Nodding, Klimgu shouted, "Kibak!"

"I'm busy getting quills," answered the lead scout. "I have forty choice ones already."

"But I need you busy getting two swift riders to go back with you," yelled Klimgu. "Bring every glove and scrap of leather in camp. And all our warriors, waiting with the main horde. So we can do this well."

"Picking quills?" asked Kibak in disbelief.

"Yes!" laughed Klimgu, slapping him on the shoulder. "But you will wait in camp. Once our group is on its way here, you will ask Twarejik to join us with his. He must not be denied this new weapon."

"What? I thought he was your rival—friendly or not. I don't understand."

"One day you will," said Klimgu, smiling. "Invite Twarejik. Insist. Then he will owe us a whole herd of favors. Giving to him makes us richer. Besides, his scouts are bound to find this place quick as crows anyway. Especially with the main horde camped so close to the east."

Kibak nodded with a muted grunt. In half a minute, he and two friends left to ride back to the main horde, wondering what their leader really hoped to gain by the offer.

Before Klimgu's main force could arrive to help, his scouting party had gathered many of the largest, hardest quills. They avoided the mountain of spider corpses piled on top of a giant black rock monster. Yet here the largest spider of all, bearing the choicest quills, lay buried under many smaller beasts that formed the pyramid. After some debate, scouts carefully removed enough of the carnage to reach the prize.

Finally, they stopped to rest, making their leader nervous. He feared what harm they might get into, without a challenging task to keep them busy.

Scooping out a balkotar eye, Tezanjo sniffed to guess if it might be edible. The Tuzanchim considered the pickled eyes and various parts of many creatures to be delicacies. All watched to see what would happen. Klimgu walked over and knocked the spider eye out of Tezanjo's hand with a lightning slap. The scout glared, but Klimgu smiled, tapping his own forehead with his left index finger. He pointed to the three fresh graves. Tezanjo nodded, to thank his leader for his concern. Others began to laugh, but Klimgu's scowl silenced them.

"Never dismiss the arms of the west—human or otherwise!" shouted Klimgu. "Tezanjo, share your new wisdom with all. Let no more fall to poison. I make this your special duty. When the others arrive, you will be busy!"

"Far too much when thousands will arrive all at once," said Tezanjo.

"Kam Otwaje will assist you."

"He grieves for his brother!"

"Refer skeptics to him," Klimgu yelled with a sweep of his hand. "Remind all that nothing edible or benign lies here. Nothing."

In spite of all the material rotting on top of Serukeeba, her tail spikes lay exposed, glinting in the sun even with dried, blackened spider blood coating them. Few humans anywhere had ever seen either type of creature, now dead at the feet of these warriors. Chotzan reached a gloved hand for one of the snowdragon's tail spikes, in order to study it. Fearing the worst, Klimgu instantly yanked the hand back. A dozen paces away, Tezanjo smiled.

"Don't be greedy, my friend," said Klimgu. "Sky, Earth, Sun or Moon gave us a deadly new tool. Which has already cost three lives. We take it, but leave this…stone spirit, giant lizard, rock-bear?"

"Rock dragon?" posed Chotzan.

"Rock dragon," nodded Klimgu. "Well-shot, my friend. That name fits best."

"A long-dead rock dragon," noted Chotzan.

"For luck and respect, do not even touch it. The Castled Lands will pay more gems than we can carry, anyway. That black crystal luring your eyes may just be more poison, itching to sting the first curious hand."

"This battlefield holds more venom than all the snakes of Esterlan," said Chotzan. "What if we run into a live group of these things?"

"A glorious but fatal mistake, my friend," said Klimgu. "It looks like our rock dragon did just that. We had best not stay too long, ourselves."

"With so many dead here, in one place, thousands must dwell in this land."

"It will explain why we have seen no locals in four days," said Klimgu. "Not that anyone wants to see us, either."

"Do you think those spiders eat people, too?" asked Chotzan.

"Why not? I think we have just reached the Exotic West. Savage beasts for savage lands."

"Then we must plan how to fight them."

Frowning, Klimgu agreed. As leader, that became his burden. Choosing a safe spot away from the others, he leaned his shield against a tree. Cutting off a hind leg from a smaller balkotar, he held it by the safe, upper end with gloved hands. He tried plucking, then throwing single quills at his shield, with no usable result.

Frustrated, he merely loosened a few quills, yet left them still partly attached to their holding cases. Swinging the leg overhead like a spear-thrower, Klimgu hurled the ready quills forcefully as the best knives. Several stuck hard against his shield, though none pierced it. Having tested the spider's weapons, he tried their armor, confirming that the larger the beast, the harder its shell.

"Yahai!" he shouted, gathering everyone. "Replace only half your arrowheads with quills, but keep your best iron ones."

"But the quills are better for both hunting and war," said Tezanjo.

"Not for armor, or killing these beasts if we meet up with them," said Klimgu. "But first, all of us must hollow out two whole shells, big enough to cover your chest and back."

"Why?" asked Ziteng.

"Because you are too slow for me to explain why!" yelled Klimgu. "The shells are remarkably strong for their weight. Unlike your brain."

"That will take far too much time," said Ziteng.

"It will take no time to die if we meet these things in battle."

"We need not fight the spiders if you get us out of here," Ziteng yelled back, gesturing for the group to leave.

"Then waste no more time arguing with your leader."

"Skinning beasts is slave's work, beneath warriors. A needless risk."

The others agreed.

"Warriors must be clever, able and tireless in any situation, especially honored, advance scouts like all of you!" yelled Klimgu, raising his hands and looking disgusted. But he smiled instantly, tapping his head to inspire thought. "Must I do all your thinking for you? Help is far away."

"As we should be also," said Ziteng.

"How do you know a band of spiders, maybe a whole army of them, does not wait a few hills away, eager to hunt us?"

"Because they all died here fighting the stone monster?"

"Wager your life on it?" Klimgu asked. "What is your plan if they attack—to flee like rabbits and be struck down at their leisure?"

"I think they would not need long," said Chotzan, to support his leader.

"Well?" Klimgu stepped back, spreading his arms wide to invite response. Quickly, he met eyes with everyone.

They had to accept his order or suggest a better idea—which obligated a leader to consider it at once. If he rejected it, he would have to explain also, to keep their trust in his leadership. The way of the Tuzanchim. But when none spoke up, Klimgu merely nodded, and they all got back to work.

"Good choice." A patronizing laugh with his words often held off their next challenge by an entire day. When reason failed—or was not to be attempted—Klimgu drew on simple fear of the unknown to bring them back into line.

"Fire!" screamed one of the lookouts, riding down from the hill.

"From?" asked Klimgu.

"South and a spit east. Fresh!"

"Long?"

Not even twelve miles, but hilly country that way," yelled the horseman, as fast as he could speak. "A whole day at worst, but three hours best luck."

"What kind of smoke?"

"Sweet! Small, but rich village. Hurry!"

"How did Twarejik beat us again?" shouted Klimgu, angry.

"Not today, our turn scouting out front," the lookout yelled back with equal vigor. "Not Twarejik, not Tuzanchim. Must be locals warring on each other. Lead us there now!"

"I must see for myself," yelled Klimgu, mounting his horse, "before taking a young fool's word."

Cresting the hill, he laughed at the sight. "We're certainly done here!" For the Tuzanchim, smoke went with their favorite activity—pillaging. Klimgu had to lead his scouts to the source quickly, or they would never forgive him. Gathering them all in one spot, he shouted, "Take only what you already have packed and leave the rest." For the second time this day, none argued with him. All were mounted before he asked.

Those who had wasted no time arguing the need to hollow out spider shells now held rare trophies for their efforts: frightful armor, as well as souvenirs to later impress families and friends. The rest still had plenty of quill-tipped poison arrows, but no shells for protection or camouflage, if the scouting party met live specimens of the monsters.

"Chotzan, take those five men lacking shells," ordered Klimgu, pointing them out as he shook his head. "Make the fools quickly do what I had asked. When our main force arrives, bring all to us with the greatest speed. Twarejik and his group will just have to find us later."

Without another word, Klimgu threw his left arm overhead, as if hurling a stone in the direction he wished to ride, and led most of his scouting party away. As soon as they left, Chotzan saw Klimgu's warriors approaching from the east. He rode hard to catch up with his leader, leaving the five to direct the main force to follow after him. All ignored the battlefield anyway, charging south for the smoke. By midafternoon it had vanished, but the Tuzanchim had discovered its source. And once they found something, they either seized or destroyed it.

* * *

Having sown many enemies, the sorcerer feared at least one must have eyed the fire as a rare chance to strike back. He did everything possible to reduce the smoke. Most of his army lay in a drugged stupor, forming a long, haphazard trail downhill. Nearly all his equipment had perished in the fire. By the smoldering ruins of his house waited his special guards, entirely coated with ash and soot. They protected the massive rope cocoon holding Lorgi, but were too exhausted to do anything else.

Posting eighty still-wakeful spiders in strategic points around the bluffs, the sorcerer determined to mount the best possible defense, should enemies attack. Beyond that, he could only wait. At best, the sleeping candy would take hours to start wearing off—for balkotars who had only consumed one piece of it. Fearing a night attack, the man rested by his special guards. Just as he fell asleep, Lorgi woke him.

"Let me out! Get me out of here!" growled Lorgi, through his teeth, unable to even open his mouth under the binding. Desperate, he had spoken in Lendish. But so much rope encased him that nothing discernable reached the sorcerer's ears.

"What was that, rock-brat?"

"*Nóshul?*" squeaked Lorgi.

"What?" snarled the wizard.

"Say Ahhh?"

"Go with the nóshul, you scourge!"

"*Góbo nóshul?*" Lorgi wiggled violently enough to roll his cocoon back and forth a few inches.

"When I've finally wrung some use from you, you can make a *góbo nóshul* for my elite guards. I'll sell your hide to the best gem cutters to recoup my losses. In a full year, my worst enemy could not match the destruction you have caused today. Not even the mother dragon, many times your size."

"Say Ahhh for me?" tried Lorgi.

Livid, the man cupped both hands around his mouth and pressed against the ball of rope, to make certain Lorgi heard him. "Idiot! We killed your mother. We burned your village. We will go back and eat all your friends."

Lorgi could see nothing from inside the smothering layers of balkotar rope. Repeating Jinva's words, he refused to believe those of the sorcerer. Yet he wondered why his mother had not rescued him. What if she *had* died fighting the balkotars? Serukeeba had never spoken of it in front of Lorgi, but he already knew that most Álukois ended life in violence. His father had perished fighting a tierdragon before Lorgi even hatched. Now he guessed his fate would be to die fighting the mad sorcerer.

"What do you have to say now, rock-brat?"

"*Góbo nóshul?*" murmured Lorgi.

"Dimwits. No wonder the snowdragons are vanishing! I have no use for a worthless, 500-pound idiot!"

"You idiot!" Lorgi shouted out clearly.

"Idiot, indeed!" growled the wizard, surveying his losses. "I'd love to burn you alive in that cocoon of yours right now, but it would markedly reduce the value of your hide."

Four small, fast balkotars suddenly scrambled up to the sorcerer, all of them frantically gesturing at once.

"No, no," the sorcerer spoke aloud, while gesturing back in their balkotar sign language. "There have been no rivals in these parts for thousands of years. You are the last of your kind, yet also the first, as we grow and conquer better lands."

"These are not like us; they are foreign," gestured one, with a hiss, showing extreme agitation. "Not of our bluffs. Imposters!"

"No. They just struggle to wake from my sleeping candy, though far sooner than I had hoped. Which is good news, indeed," explained the sorcerer. "Rock-brat emptied the whole barrel in his bid to escape."

"The foreigners have weak back legs," gestured another of the four. "They have to crawl, dragging back legs."

"That is what happens if you eat too much candy," gestured the sorcerer. "Let that be a lesson to you."

"They have no quills," gestured the same balkotar.

"They must have thrown all of them at rock-brat," said the man. "A miracle that he still breathes."

"But each has one very long quill, loose on one front leg," gestured the third balkotar. "We told you they are foreign."

"All are mid-sized," added the fourth balkotar. "They come from all sides. And they are many."

"I'd better see for myself," the sorcerer gestured. "When all has finally been rebuilt, I must refine the formula for my sleeping candy, and make an antidote."

From far below, scores of lethargic balkotars crawled up toward the bluffs, dragging their back legs. At such distance, the sorcerer could not tell if their back legs lacked quills. Yet they seemed to be wearing boots. The instant the sorcerer saw the ruse, an arrow whipped past his right ear, hitting the trunk of a pine tree with a loud knock. Grabbing his war horn, he sounded the alarm loud and long. Only then did he fetch the arrow to determine its source.

"Tuzanchim!" gasped the sorcerer. Seeing that it had been tipped with a very large balkotar quill, he ducked behind the nearest boulder and reached for his traveler's vile of antidote. But he had given it to the village's leader. "Boiling oil for the scheming dwarf! I swear to see him eaten by my guards, if it is my last dying act!"

One of the four messengers suddenly ran back up to the sorcerer, again frantically gesturing. "Fifty enemy false-balkotars on the trail up to your nest. Many more scattered all around. Thousands of humans with horses close behind them. They kill our sleeping balkotars before they can wake. They gut them and put on their shells to confuse us."

"How did those savages ever think of that?" the sorcerer asked.

The Tuzanchim quickly discovered that opposing spiders used neither venom nor quills when battling their own kind. Instead, they wrestled, clawed, cut or ripped at each other using their feet and especially their great mandibles, struggling to dismember or gut their foes. But they wasted no poison. Brute force, speed and cunning had to decide contests between balkotars.

When Klimgu's pseudo balkotars learned just how strong and quick those mandibles could be, his men almost gave up the battle. So he grouped them into teams of five that were only to advance and attack against individual spiders. Every few minutes, another man screamed in pain, and it seemed that the invaders would be driven off. Yet, downhill from the struggle, several more warriors fitted themselves with shells and crawled up to join the fight, as another of the sorcerer's spiders hissed in pain. Ever so slowly, the Tuzanchim were driving them up the bluffs. By now, most of the sleeping balkotars had been slaughtered.

"How wasteful, how foolish I've been," cursed the sorcerer, poking his head up to glimpse the battle. "Who could have guessed the Tuzanchim were so close? If only I had waited for them to sack that village, then attacked when their guard was down. What discipline, speed and skill they have! How could those barbarians become so organized, so determined?"

"Tell us what to do," gestured the messenger.

"We cannot defeat them today," the sorcerer answered. "But we must frighten them away quickly, or they will destroy us. It may take every quill we have."

Even under a mountain of rope, Lorgi smelled the man's fear, and heard some of his words. Whoever warred on the sorcerer must surely be Lorgi's friends—even if they were also the dreaded Tuzanchim of the east. Bound so tightly that he could not move, Lorgi strained every muscle, desperate to work himself loose. He needed five minutes just to open his mouth, plus five more to gain enough range of motion to start chewing his way through it all. Despite his powerful jaws, Lorgi found the rope surprisingly tough and resilient. It tasted like rancid grease, yet smelled of human sweat and adrenaline. Suddenly, Lorgi knew that the same tool that now restrained him had also been used to trap humans—perhaps as food for balkotars.

Rallying his elite guards, the sorcerer devised a plan for counterattack. Along with them, he saw the cocoon begin to wiggle and expand, but was far too absorbed in surviving the battle to waste a moment on Lorgi. Arrows flew everywhere, most with iron tips or flaming tar. Yet once in a while, a choice one meant only for the sorcerer came tipped with a balkotar quill. He dared only peek at the course of the battle. Each time he did so, more arrows flew at him.

By Tuzanchim standards, Klimgu's warriors moved with extreme caution as they systematically reduced the wizard's army, one spider at a time. But even at that rate, in an hour the sorcerer would have none left. Suddenly, hundreds of new warriors arrived, kicking up dust as they rode headlong up the bluffs to join the battle. Ignoring screams and frantic signals from Klimgu and his warriors, the first 400 of Twarejik's riders charged right up towards the center of battle, guessing it nearly won.

The eight closest balkotars—those directly in the path of the charge—threw all of their remaining quills. Felling half the riders and horses in one flash, the volley suddenly brought the attack to a stop. Klimgu called a temporary halt to the fighting. Following custom, Twarejik handed command of his whole force over to him for the battle.

Despite the psychological impact of his balkotars' volley, the sorcerer saw his forces hopelessly outnumbered. He guessed the enemy knew that as well. From his coat pocket he drew the same white cloth used to parley at the village. But the instant he raised it overhead, two arrows ripped through it. Unlike peoples of the west, the Tuzanchim rarely negotiated, once a battle had begun. Only victory mattered to them, no matter the cost. Either they left a place untouched and at peace, or utterly destroyed it.

Following custom, Klimgu planned to leave only after taking or burning everything of value and killing every spider to be found. He hoped to do so with minimal losses. Such a victory could only add to his status, and perhaps his wealth. But losing too many warriors or horses would hurt his standing. He summoned the captains to motivate them and get their help in planning a final assault on the bluffs. He also needed to reaffirm his leadership.

"If those suddenly dead had heeded my orders, they could still be fighting, ready to share in the spoils," Klimgu scolded them all. "We face a unique enemy. Do we die like fools, retreat in everlasting shame, or adapt to win?"

All eyes focused on him. Praying to the sacred Wind, Klimgu risked one quiet, deep breath. To his surprise, none would deny him this silent moment. Then he gave his plan. Typically, captains debated or modified orders before agreeing to carry them out, but this time fear kept them all mute. Klimgu greatly valued quiet when he could get it. Yet here it almost unnerved him.

For the third time on the same day, no one argued against his orders. The captains had just put all their faith in him, as if he were the Gran Vazuk, supreme ruler of all the Tuzanchim. For another silent, long breath, Klimgu dared imagine wielding the power of such a man. The power to order quiet, thought, or even peace.

"The shaman ties a parchment to a spider's front leg," yelled a scout.

"Sweet," laughed Klimgu. "A rich shaman's terms!"

"No terms!" yelled Ziteng. "Bad luck."

"But the note may be useful, if any can read it," said Twarejik. "Do you have someone, Klimgu?"

"It will not be in Tuzanchim," said Chotzan. "Now that we approach the west, it will be in Laskomian or Lendish."

"Good; you can read it then," said Twarejik.

"Oh, no," Chotzan laughed, shaking his head. "About forty of us can speak Tundrish. A few have picked up some Laskomian. But I know of no one who reads—in any language."

"So how will we decipher it?" asked Twarejik, disappointed.

He joined Klimgu, Chotzan, Kibak and Ziteng to decide what to do about the sorcerer's note, soon to arrive. Ancient Shohaneze scholars had once devised a written form of the Tuzanchim language, used now only in Uxanda and villages on the Tekurs River. The only "writing" these or most warriors knew was drawing battle plans in the dirt with their swords.

"We should have brought those two fat Laskomian monks, instead of locking them up inside their own temple to starve," said Chotzan.

"We could learn to read much before that happens," joked Kibak, the lead scout. The others looked silently at him and each other, shaking their heads. Kibak shrugged.

"We can free them on our return," suggested Chotzan. All but Klimgu gave him scornful glances. "Or we could fetch them to read for us—very useful in conquering the west."

"Getting back to the parley note," grunted Twarejik.

"Who needs to read anything?" laughed Klimgu. "We can guess what it asks."

"Shamans are too clever," warned Kibak. "He may use magic to kill us with his writing."

"How can his spells sting those who cannot even read them?" asked Klimgu.

The chosen spider waved the same white cloth, now much tattered, as it crawled slowly downhill towards the leaders. Scores of warriors in balkotar shells scrambled aside, clearing a wide path for the messenger.

When it finally reached within a dozen feet of Klimgu, it removed the parchment and laid it on the ground, gesturing for someone to take it. The balkotar's eyes worked independently, studying all five men at the same time, to try and guess which one was the leader. None of them would pick up the sorcerer's note. So the beast did. Again it laid the note on the ground, this time a foot closer to the men, gesturing for one of them to take it. Klimgu eyed Ziteng, then the parchment. Taking the cue, Ziteng picked it up and started to hand it to his leader.

"No. Look at it first," snapped Klimgu in a hoarse whisper. "Then hand it to Kibak."

"What am I supposed to do with it?" Kibak whispered from the side of his mouth.

"Look at it!" barked Klimgu. "The way a leader would. At least pretend to understand it."

"But it's just writing, delivered by a hideous, goat-sized…bug!" said Kibak, no longer whispering.

"We lost over 200 men and horses in a blink with such lack of thinking," said Twarejik.

"Enough, let me see it," said Klimgu, grabbing the parchment. He held it so that Chotzan and Twarejik could see as well.

From atop the ridge, the sorcerer squinted hard, trying to guess which of the three viewing the note would prove to be the horde's leader, and what they were thinking.

"Just pictures with writing," said Chotzan.

"Arrows, there to here," Twarejik pointed. "Fat pony in a great bundle of rope, up there, to come down…here. *That's* his offer?"

"A poor country knight wouldn't settle for that!" scoffed Klimgu.

"No, it must be something else, something rare and valuable," said Chotzan. "Perhaps the shaman knows of our Vazuk's trading in exotics. The writing may explain."

"Good work, Chotzan," said Twarejik. "Now tell us about the writing part."

Chotzan glared back with a silent "No!"

"The messenger beast gestures," said Ziteng, eyeing the others. "I think it expects a reply."

"Of course," said Twarejik. "Chotzan should write it, don't you think, Klimgu?"

"Write with what, blood?" asked Chotzan.

"The beast motions again," said Ziteng. "I think it's holding one of those bamboo straws, the kind they paint with in the Well-East."

"Looks too much like one of the beast's quills," said Klimgu. "Use a strip of leather to take it, Ziteng."

"It really is a writing pen from the east," said Twarejik, studying it.

"So you have been all the way to the Well-East, my friend?" Klimgu smiled at him.

"Well, as far as the Near Valley," said Twarejik.

"Still a tall mountain range away from it. But since you went so far, you should do the honors here," said Klimgu.

"Chotzan already volunteered," said Twarejik.

"What is our reply?" asked Chotzan, glaring at him.

"Simple," said Klimgu. "Arrows pointing away from the bluff, calling off our siege."

"Of course," nodded Twarejik, as if he had already thought of it. "But you cannot mean that?"

"First we must see what the old shaman offers," said Klimgu.

Chotzan drew the reply and handed the parchment to Twarejik. It relayed from Klimgu to Kibak to Ziteng, who laid it on the ground just in front of the spider messenger. It retied the note to the same leg. Rather than turning about, the spider walked backwards, all the way to the top of the bluff, keeping the same slow pace.

All knew the sorcerer was trying desperately to wring more time for himself. Borrowing Weliben's tactic, he delayed several moments before sending four of his choice guards down, carrying a huge, wiggling ball of thick, grey rope, over six feet in diameter. Reaching within a yard of the seven men, the spiders suddenly halted. Dropping their load as if it held the plague, they scrambled back up to their master at full speed. Three men began to cut the ropes away when they discovered that Lorgi was fast chewing his way out, from the inside.

"Ahhh for me," Lorgi yawned, tired after his efforts.

"Did it just speak?" Chotzan asked, startled.

"Say Ahhh for me," Lorgi tried again.

"I think it just sounds that way when it yawns," guessed Kibak, helping to remove the rope. "But it may be able to learn some words if we talk to it enough. My best horse knows forty words."

"No, but your bowels hold as much as his," laughed Chotzan, shaking his head. "If you must speak to our new beast, at least speak truth."

Offended, Kibak turned his back and walked away. But all other eyes widened with joy at the sight of Lorgi, sparkling in the sun as he stretched his limbs and looked about. A deafening round of cheers welled up, because the warriors knew their prize would bring a staggering price in any market.

"Hello," Lorgi tried in Lendish, then Tundrish. "Does anyone here know Tundrish?"

"Klimgu, You must have heard that," gasped Chotzan. "It can speak Tundrish!"

"Then for once, the Gran Vazuk will be truly pleased," laughed Klimgu. "Beyond rare. An albino form of that giant, black rock dragon we saw at the river."

"I want to go home," Lorgi said in Tundrish.

"Your prize owns a voice," warned Chotzan. "How can we justify selling or gifting him?"

"Everyone's prize, for which we paid dearly—250 men and as many horses!" Klimgu yelled back. "If this creature really has a voice, then use it to draw information. Like how to rid this land of the spider shaman."

"But he has a voice and a home."

"Perhaps, but regardless, we present him as our gift to the Vazuk. That will enrich my status, and make life better for all under our command. We've suffered enough."

Swallowing, Chotzan nodded, hating to go against his leader or the group's sudden good luck. He sat beside Lorgi, while Klimgu and Twarejik left to preside over a very slow, careful withdrawal from the bluffs. News of the talking dragon child reached every warrior in minutes. All the handful of Tundrish-speakers descended upon Lorgi. With a truce in effect, extreme curiosity trumped any orders they had. In minutes, every warrior knew of Lorgi's struggles, the sorcerer's attack on his village, and his need to find his mother. All took an instant liking to him. None had the heart to tell Lorgi what they had seen at the river.

"Klimgu!" yelled Chotzan, running to him. "Our prize owns more than a voice. Sharp as swords. In one minute, he has learned a dozen Tuzanchim words. He speaks Tundrish faster than a mother-in-law. He only wants—"

"His wants weigh nothing against the needs of 5,000 warriors and their families!" shouted Klimgu.

"He has a name: Lorgi, and—"

"Then all must call him that," Klimgu interrupted again.

"He is a very young child for his kind. Yet he fought the sorcerer in his own way. His fire brought us here, and he put most of the spiders to sleep for us."

"And we are grateful to him."

"He is no less than a young, warrior-to-be of the frozen north!" exclaimed Chotzan. "He has pride, honor, and customs. A soul. Every warrior senses it. We cannot gift him like some pet or slave. He has a home. He asks to return to it."

"That had to be his mother by the river," sighed Klimgu. "The spider shaman must have burned his village, too. Best that Lorgi never see either."

"That is not ours to decide for him," said Chotzan, shaking his head.

"You said he's a child. What home awaits him now? The Vazuk can provide the most luxurious. No one is ever to speak of what we saw by the river, while Lorgi travels with us."

Twarejik walked up to them. "Everyone is satisfied, and ready to leave."

"I'm not," said Klimgu, eying the top of the bluffs. "The sorcerer has only twenty good beasts left, holding few quills. Did you notice how they sacrificed much to guard that large cave, high on the east side of the bluffs?"

"We were all too busy ducking quills or fighting," said Twarejik. "You think the shaman is still hiding his best from us?"

"Of course!" shouted Klimgu. "Why leave without it?"

"Because we already hold the shaman's finest treasure," said Chotzan. "Why spend lives for things of lesser value?"

Twarejik frowned at Chotzan. "A good warrior must take calculated risks, and be thorough."

"Which means not leaving an enemy intact," added Klimgu. "Otherwise, he could return and bite us like a snake."

He sent ten men in balkotar shells crawling back up towards the prized cave. As a dozen spiders raced to stop them, Klimgu launched an all-out assault. The sorcerer's "NO!" could be heard for miles. Blowing his war horn and frantically gesturing, he led a spirited defense until an arrow struck him.

In one moment, every quill flew, 200 more men fell, and every last balkotar died. Inside the choice cave, eight giant but defenseless, egg-laying balkotars smoldered as they bled to death. Warriors destroyed every egg, while riders combed the surrounding woods for any surviving spiders. Nothing escaped them. The way of the Tuzanchim.

Before Lorgi could turn his back or "turtle" into an impervious, armored ball, a huge balkotar quill pierced his leathery abdomen. This was the only place it could have broken his skin. Suddenly collapsing on his side, he blinked his eyes and endured searing pain. He stayed awake, but the poison had already begun to stiffen him. Chotzan spoke to Lorgi as Kibak knelt by his side and removed the quill. Both glared at Klimgu.

Only later would everyone debate the wisdom of the final assault on the balkotars and their shaman master. Long minutes passed before Klimgu dared to look upon the stricken prize. Everywhere else, angry eyes shamed him for his greed and poor judgment. Sensing that Lorgi's fate and his own had become linked, Klimgu assumed both would die in the next moment.

8: Serukeeba

When his search party rounded the river's next bend, Weliben shrieked, dropping to his knees. Serukeeba lay stiff, coated in many layers of decomposing spider blood, amidst hundreds of rotting balkotar corpses. Even on that grey afternoon, long after her fall, all her spikes still glinted beneath the ink. The party's three Tundrites launched into a sacred chant, while the five Delfinians said their own prayers and farewells. When all ceremony ended, none knew what to do with Serukeeba's massive body.

"She belongs to Tiefenbo," said Kamwa. "She was its soul, as well as its champion."

Weliben nodded. "By Álukoi tradition, her final resting place should be in her own hall, though it is far from the Stonelaw."

"Stonelaw never did her no good," said Birentak, Kamwa's uncle and the oldest one present. Pulling his long, grey hair back, he put on a headband. Tears flowed down his high, brown cheeks. "Much work to do. Even Seri should not have hunted on her own. We failed her."

"But who was going to stop her?" asked Kamwa. "You know how she is…was." He also broke down and wept. His uncle put a hand on his shoulder.

"No use kicking ourselves," said Weliben. "Bad as things are now, what if Serukeeba had been hibernating? Then the sorcerer would have struck with total surprise. We'd have lost everyone, including Seri and Lorgi."

"We did lose both of them!" yelled Birentak.

"That remains to be seen," said Weliben.

"You're seeing the remains now."

"We must bring her home, mourn her properly."

"With eight tired men, no wagon or horses?" asked Glomin. "Impossible."

"Álukois are actually much lighter than they appear," said Weliben. "Seri always told the curious that she weighed 'four tons, give or take an ounce.' So at least we know that."

"Lorgi said she weighs five," said Glomin.

"Can't take a child's word over that of his mother."

"You'd better this time. If only we still had horses, not to mention a wagon and more tools."

"We've got each other, our axes, and the Continent's best wood."

"You're not suggesting that we *build* a wagon to cart her home?"

"We owe it to her, to Lorgi, the whole village. And to her own kind."

"Crafting a wagon, however crude, will take too long." Glomin shook his head. "We can't lift her. We'll shred all our ropes, just trying. While we exhaust ourselves here, what happens to Lorgi? And Tiefenbo?"

"We could make a great funeral pyre," said Kamwa. "How we Tundrites honor the dead. If we can't move her, then build it around her."

"Far from Álukoi ways, but the best we can do," said Glomin. "Lorgi is our top priority now. We'd best get on with it. As Seri would want."

"Not so hasty," said Weliben. "First, we absolutely must wash all that muck off of her. Restore dignity to our late champion. Then retrieve her skull—clean, intact and unburned."

"We have neither the stomachs nor the tools for that!" cried Glomin.

"Skulls are sacred to the Álukois," said Weliben. "We must honor their ways, no matter how awful the task."

"Wait," said Kamwa, wiping away tears as he looked around. "What if all that spider blood is poison, too?"

"Say, why so few quills anywhere, for all the hundreds of carcasses?" asked Glomin. The others joined him in scanning the whole battlefield. "Seem to be only small quills, in spite of some huge balkotars. Why?"

"Because we were not the first to see this horror," said Birentak.

Taking great care where they stepped, the men traversed the battlefield. Anywhere they looked, they found horse tracks and human boot prints leading everywhere. Birentak had discovered them, but was the first to lose interest. After filling his water bags, he poured some on an area of Serukeeba's hide, alternately scrubbing with pine needles and rinsing. With persistence, this removed all the dried spider blood.

"What we should be doing." Weliben pointed to Birentak. "The rest can wait, because we are quite alone here. Just be alert for stray quills.

The sooner we clean up Seri and get out of here, the better for all."

"But what if the spider blood is also poisonous?" asked Glomin.

"I already cut myself twice on Seri's hide, and I'm still here," assured Birentak. "Any of you going to help me, or just watch and talk?"

Nodding, the others joined him, using anything they found that was not already stained with spider blood or tainted by quills. Despite working slowly and carefully, all cut themselves on Serukeeba's hide. But none attended to these until done cleaning, out of respect. Only then did they make a fire, dry themselves and thaw their hands and feet. Even at the height of summer, the Yazutak's water ran icy cold. As they worked, the sky grew dark with thick clouds. Yet Serukeeba's hide sparked like new.

"Sun's truth, she looks spectacular for being dead so long," said Weliben.

"Almost just like sleeping," said Birentak.

"Amazing, still no sight of decay," said Glomin. "Certainly a bit thinner, but all her armor shines like new." Holding up bandaged hands, he added, "And still sharp as ever."

"That's the snowdragons—excuse me, the Álukois—for you," sighed Weliben. "Built to last, and never show their pains."

"Quiet!" ordered Kamwa, bending over close to Serukeeba's head.

"Company?" whispered Glomin. Everyone grabbed a weapon.

A faint breeze diluted the battlefield's stench, tossing a few wildflower petals before the Álukoi's snout. It teased and stopped. Kamwa drew his knife, holding it an inch from her nostrils. "Serukeeba!"

"It has been a week, Kamwa," said Glomin. "If any life yet stirred in her, all our scrubbing and dousing—"

"Quiet!" snapped Kamwa.

"She is long gone, son," said Weliben, putting a hand on the youth's shoulder. Kamwa angrily brushed it off. All looked to his uncle for support. But Birentak went to the river and refilled his water bags.

"We're done washing her, Birentak," said Glomin. "Tend to your nephew."

"Not done at all." Birentak returned, only to empty both his bags onto Serukeeba.

"Weli, we may be losing more than time here," murmured Glomin, grabbing his arm while pointing toward Kamwa and his uncle.

"Don't ask me to nurse minds, even at home," said Weliben.

"Wait...yes, this time I'm sure!" shouted Kamwa.

Water vapor finally appeared on the youth's knife. Glomin thought he saw a paw twitch. Weliben saw an ear wiggle. Everyone stepped close.

"Back away, give her air," said Birentak, doing so himself.

"She must have fallen into a dragon's coma, under all that tar," said Weliben. "But she had better start breathing a whole lot deeper, if she is to live. Douse her with enough cold water, and she just may!"

"I'll be damned!" shouted Glomin.

"Tell us something we don't already know, thank you," laughed Weliben.

For half an hour, they drenched her with all they could deliver, while Birentak and his nephew collected medicinal herbs. They had returned and were brewing a tea when a faint, but horrible sound broke their hopes. The sorcerer's war horn. Terrified, all looked to Weliben. He just shook his head.

"The old bastard won't be back for us. We've nothing left that anyone could want. Said so himself. But he has found others who do— and they'll suffer for it."

"How I would love to kill him!" shouted Glomin, echoed by the rest.

"Another day, Gentlemen," said Weliben. "Seri fights for her life."

"South," yelled Birentak. All of them stared at him for what seemed an irrelevant comment. Even his own nephew opened his hands in a gesture begging explanation. "The war horn came from the south, maybe twelve miles."

"Maybe Lorgi got away from the sorcerer," guessed Kamwa. "He's quick and clever enough."

"Then we had better revive Seri quickly!" said Weliben. "We must not be out here if the old bastard comes chasing after Lorgi."

"Somebody open Seri's mouth so we can give her the tea," said Birentak.

"Locked shut!" huffed Glomin, pressing his hands hard against her jaws. His arms shook from the effort, and his hands bled."

"What about the gums?" asked Weliben. "I've seen medicine served that way to stubborn patients, human and otherwise."

"Even those won't budge," said Kamwa, his hands also bleeding.

"Don't be so gentle—this is an emergency!" shouted Weliben.

"We're not!" said Glomin and Kamwa together.

Prying Serukeeba's gums open with a knife, Birentak finally delivered the medicine. Kamwa fanned her with aromatic vapors, while the rest strained to move her tail back and forth for circulation. Shouting got no reaction because her ear lids were shut. Just as they all sat down around her to think what else to try, the war horn sounded twice again.

"Someone is giving him trouble," said Kamwa.

"Gem of a thought," sighed Glomin. "If only that were possible."

"Moon's melt, how could I forget?" shouted Weliben, holding up the sorcerer's antidote. Before he could administer it, Birentak stopped him.

"Week too late," said the old Tundrite. "No poison in her now. Save it for us."

"What else can we try?" asked Kamwa.

"Nothing," said Weliben. "Now it's up to Seri. If she wakes, we'll be quite busy helping her. In the meantime, we should make camp."

The war horn sounded again, but cut short after a second. All waited in silence, expecting to hear more. After a patient minute, they looked to each other.

"Perhaps the old snake broke his damn horn," said Glomin.

"Or somebody broke it for him," said Birentak.

"Lorgi!" Kamwa blurted out. The others cheered his thought.

"Again, a fine wish." Weliben smiled, yet shook his head.

"Oh, come on, Weli," said Kamwa. "Lorgi can break anything. Who has not seen proof?" All of them laughed nervously, masking their pain.

Suddenly, Serukeeba's eyes flashed wide open. Everyone shrieked, gushing tears of joy. Gasping cavernous breaths, she thundered many violent coughs and growls to clear her throat. At first, she could only lift her neck and tail. After several faltering attempts, she managed to gain a sitting position. Forcing herself to stand on shaking limbs, she needed all her effort to keep from falling over or collapsing. She took only a few tiny, wobbly steps before sitting again. This repeated many times. Dehydrated, malnourished, but most of all distraught, she begged for news with haunted eyes.

Weliben explained, but Serukeeba already knew. Turning away, she gazed at the southern horizon. Everyone gave sound reasons for going home first, sending for help from the Stonelaw, and fortifying what remained of Tiefenbo. But Lorgi had just called to her. Weliben gave her a worried eye. Yet a moment later, without knowing how, he understood her. Once she could walk, she staggered about, studying the myriad human and horse tracks overlaying the spider prints.

"We ignored them to help you," said Weliben, walking beside her.

"Horse tracks new," said Birentak, walking beside them. The others followed close behind. "What can your dragon sense tell about them?"

But Serukeeba did not respond.

"And all the boot prints going with them?" asked Kamwa.

"Her mind is far away," Glomin whispered. "The ordeal still tortures her. Look how she staggers in confusion, lost and unaware."

Nodding, Weliben stepped right in front of her, blocking her path. "Seri...Serukeeba. Are you alright?" He shook his head. "Of course not. I'm sorry. Who could be?"

"Seri, can you hear us?" shouted Birentak.

"What can we do for her?" asked Kamwa.

"Say something, anything, Seri, so that we know your mind still lives," begged Weliben. "Blink your eyes or shake your head."

"Find where the horse tracks lead," she gargled. "Their riders can help us."

"But those are Tuzanchim!" gasped Birentak.

"I know," coughed Serukeeba.

"They won't help us!" said Glomin. "We'd be lucky if they don't kill us on sight."

"We need them," groaned Serukeeba. "Now we need them."

9: Laskomia

 Lorgi woke to find himself the sole passenger in a roofless, crudely-made wagon, rumbling east by southeast on four-foot diameter wheels. Two huge Laskomian war horses pulled the vehicle far faster than it wanted to go. The wagon popped, roared, wailed and jerked as if being tortured, making so much noise that Lorgi half-shut his ear lids.

Squinting, the white-bearded driver frowned with clenched teeth. Ten yards behind, a second wagon carried three equally grim-faced women with braided grey hair, their mouths also tightly shut. One drove as two others struggled to prepare something looking like tea, despite a ride so brutal that all gripped the rails to keep from being thrown out of that wagon.

Sixty yards in front rode a pack of 200 warriors. Two hundred more rode behind, while just as many rode on either side of the wagons. The space separating the four groups often dissolved, as some riders moved between them to converse. Combined, the force totaled just over 800, but seemed much larger, from its ill-defined shape and the clouds of dust it generated. To all but Tuzanchim eyes, all rode in perpetual chaos.

Struggling to focus, Lorgi saw about thirty women and adolescents in each group, many leading extra horses with tethers. But most of the warriors looked to be seasoned men. A dozen scouts rode far to the front and sides of the whole. Every person carried a sword, knife, rope, a taut bow and a full quiver of arrows. Even the wagon drivers and the women making tea all wore swords. Just as Lorgi noted this, all the warriors checked their weapons, as if *expecting* to be using them within the hour.

Guessing the balkotars had sent these Tuzanchim fleeing, Lorgi yawned, stretched, whipped his tail, and snapped his jaws, like a grown Álukoi before battle. Yet he also practiced the "make like a turtle" move his mother had taught him. Shaking his head, he blinked his ear and eyelids to rouse his senses. But this only made him recall the balkotar quill's searing pain just before it had knocked him out. The tiny scar it had left still hurt, even with Lorgi not yet fully awake. His sudden activity drew all eyes to him. The leader of the whole, ever-shifting swarm rode up to the left side of Lorgi's wagon, smiling at him.

"Yahai!" shouted Klimgu, raising his left hand. The entire mass halted. "Our rock dragon lives! Kibak, where are you?"

"Right behind you. How far ahead do I scout? Five miles?"

"Two," said Klimgu. His lead scout nodded and turned to ride off with ten others. "Wait Kibak! Take care. Dead scouts help no one. I want details, no matter how trivial they seem."

"Take care what you ask," yelled Kibak, riding away.

"Wagoners, see to our rock dragon," barked Chotzan. "Ziteng, get Porzan back here where he belongs." Two women from the other wagon climbed aboard Lorgi's with a pot of strong, herbal tea. Grabbing hold of Lorgi's mouth, they tried to force it open, only to cut their hands.

"That's too hot," Lorgi said in Tundrish, shaking his head. He and the women backed away to opposite ends of the wagon's hold.

"Chotzan, see to that," said Klimgu, motioning toward Lorgi. "Someone get Porzan!"

"Sijun, Temsuji, rock dragon is in your care," said Chotzan, pointing to the women with the tea.

"Too hard to handle," yelled Sijun, a short, but remarkably fit old woman. Lorgi reached to lick her cut hands, but she backed away. "This one will grow quickly into a man-eater!"

"He's only a cub," said Chotzan. "Wait a yawn and try again. By now he must be thirsty, if not also very hungry."

"Better he not get hungry," said Temsuji, looking just as fit, but slightly younger than Sijun. "See his teeth—and our hands? How dare you put women in such danger. Shame to you, Chotzan!"

"Our rock dragon refuses any meat," said Chotzan. "Perfectly harmless."

"So you need Porzan's healing too, for your soft head," sniped Temsuji.

"His health is yours!" warned Chotzan, glaring at both women. "Be glad he is awake. Keep him so until we harness fresh horses to the wagons. Once we're moving again, he cannot sleep. Then you may relax."

"Relax?" yelled Sijun, angry. "Awake, he will destroy the wagon by sundown. See what he has done in just a few minutes. Where is Porzan?"

"Porzan!" shouted Chotzan.

"Here," called a grey-bearded man, the only person without a sword, riding up to the wagon.

"While you are healing rock dragon, see to our bleeding hands," demanded Sijun.

"I'll do what I can," assured Porzan.

"And use your powers to calm this beast," yelled Temsuji. "Then you must help Chotzan, who hurt his head, and can no longer think."

"I'll do what I can," said the healer, smiling at Lorgi and all of them. Glad to be included, Lorgi smiled back.

"And make these two ornery old mares stop pestering me!" shouted Chotzan.

"I'm a healer, not a Vazuk!" Porzan laughed, 'but I'll do what I can."

"I'll do what I can," Lorgi mimicked him in perfect Tuzanchim. Pleased by everyone's stunned reaction, Lorgi wiggled his ears and smiled again.

"What?" gasped the healer.

"Good work!" laughed Chotzan. "Between Porzan and our wagon babblers, Lorgi should be speaking Tuzanchim in no time. Good work."

"Good work!" shouted Lorgi, imitating words he caught on repetition.

"Better than any talking bird," said a young man riding close by.

"Back to your group, pony!" barked Sijun. "And pray rock dragon is not a *Karmchugtai.*"

"What is that?" asked the youth.

"I knew, by your age, because I listened to my elders."

The youth turned to leave, not wanting a lecture.

"A *Karmchugtai* is a large animal possessed by a ghost intent on revenge," Porzan told the young man. "Older warriors fear that our Lorgi might only be a host for a dead Laskomian knight, or some other foe we cut down on our way. But meet his eyes, even for a second, and you will know he cannot be a *Karmchugtai.*"

"*Karmchugtai,*" said Lorgi.

"No one is to use that word again!" ordered Chotzan.

Anyone riding within earshot moved closer, jostling for a clear view, straining to hear more from the talking exotic, regardless of superstitions.

"But what can his talking mean, Chotzan?" asked Porzan, with an outstretched hand.

"Chotzan!" shouted Lorgi, pointing with his right forepaw. Turning to the healer, he cheered, "Porzan!"

Fearing non-human intelligence, most people fell silent. A rare state for Tuzanchim.

"He speaks Tundrish," said Chotzan. "Actually, better than anyone here. He hails from some frozen realm, far to the west and north. Our gift to the Vazuk."

"Why did none tell me?" Porzan scowled at Chotzan, as he climbed aboard the wagon. "What else have you kept from me, to do with him or your other discoveries in the West?"

"We were all far too busy—my apologies," said Chotzan. "None thought he could live, after taking a spider dart. He is a child of only three years. Treat him thus. Judging by what we saw before our battle at the spider bluffs, he will grow to twelve times his present size. He has a shaman's ears, but a warrior's heart."

"Thank you for finally telling me," said Porzan. "But one does not make a gift of a warrior."

"Try arguing that with Klimgu—and most of the others," said Chotzan. "They expect to gain much from his scheme, blind to what they may lose in turn. In Lorgi, they see new boots, swords, ropes, jackets, blankets. All the jerky, flatbread and liquor they can carry. Praise from the Vazuk and a great feast for the whole quiver. Something to brag about. They do not see a child taken from his home."

Porzan nodded. He needed to touch Lorgi to guess his temperature, but hesitated on seeing the women's cut hands. He dared not tend to any human needs until certain the dragon child was stable. Unlike most Tuzanchim, Porzan had a gentle manner that he was not afraid to show. It had a calming effect on those near him. Lorgi stared intently into his eyes, sniffed his face and hands, then emptied the contents of his medicine bag to sniff them as well. Smiling at all this, the healer calmly observed his exotic patient. Taking an instant liking to Porzan, Lorgi gave him a dragon's toothsome grin. When he guessed the tea cool enough, he reached for the pot, but Sijun pulled back. Chotzan shook his head and glared at her. Lorgi studied both of them.

"Sijun!" yelled Chotzan. "Just give it to him, already."

"My job to make him drink, but my teapot he will break."

"Then I will get you a better one," said Chotzan.

"What can you know of such things?" barked Sijun.

"Enough, but less than Sijun will know of pain, if she keeps needling me."

"Stop it, stop it, both of you!" Porzan scolded, shaking his left hand.

"Stop it, stop it, both of you!" Lorgi mimicked him perfectly, also shaking his left forepaw.

The whole group erupted with laughter. Though quite wobbly, Lorgi stood on his hind legs and tail to enjoy the moment. Leaning his forepaws against the wooden rails, he made a slow circle, studying them all. As people met his gaze, they fell silent. But with the slightest motion, Lorgi eroded the wagon, whose bed already seemed to have weathered a sand storm. The rails looked to have survived the thick of a battle.

"I take back my estimate," Sijun crowed at Chotzan. "Awake, rock dragon will destroy his wagon in an hour, if he chooses to stay in it."

"Then we will use the other wagon," said Chotzan.

"And after that?" asked Temsuji.

"Then Chotzan will wish he had listened to us the first time," Sijun nodded to her.

"Wagoners, your duty is to keep our rock dragon healthy and inside his wagon," shouted Chotzan. "Everything depends on that."

"Impossible!" yelled Temsuji. "Easy to order, but you try doing that."

"Temsuji!" yelled Chotzan, glaring at her.

"Temsuji," said Lorgi, smiling and pointing to her. Pointing to the other woman, he said "Sijun." Both stared at him in shock.

"There, he's made you his friends," Chotzan laughed. "An honor. Perhaps he can be a good influence on you."

"My patient needs care, not arguing," said Porzan. "He is dehydrated. Starved. Barely awake after being out for days. Riding hand-close to death. Poison may still linger in him."

"Then you should have ridden by Lorgi, not with the scouts, picking herbs and flowers," said Chotzan.

"He was in a coma," said Porzan. "Nothing could be done until he came to. All I gathered went into his tea. Now I can treat him, but cannot promise his recovery. We know nothing about him."

Lorgi focused intently on each speaker, guessing their quarrel had to do with him. While they had acted poorly by shouting in anger, he had been good. At home, such adult drama in front of well-behaved children always brought tasty rewards, forthwith. He looked expectantly from Chotzan to Sijun, Temsuji, Porzan, then back to Chotzan, who seemed to be in charge. When no treat was offered after a reasonable wait, Lorgi felt disgusted and let down.

"I want to go home," he spoke in clear Tundrish, followed by the Tuzanchim verb for 'go,' shouting "*guyat!*" When spoken forcefully, *guyat* became a command.

"What?" gasped Chotzan.

"He wants you to go—leave us alone!" Sijun yelled, shaking a fist at Chotzan.

"I hate all your arguing," said Lorgi, to Chotzan because he understood Tundrish. "I want to go home. *Guyat*—home." Almost instinctively, he gave Chotzan his sad eyes to compound the guilt. But it also tugged at everyone close enough to see Lorgi's face. The technique had always worked at home.

"Drink your tea, Lorgi," Chotzan stammered in Tundrish. "Please be careful with the teapot. Sijun thinks you might break it."

"Why would I do that?" asked Lorgi, offended.

"Well, see what you have done to the wagon?"

"Delfinians make better wagons and teapots. They also take great care of children, always giving snacks, hugs, cheers, rewards and tasty treats. Especially lots of snacks and treats."

"Of course they do," Chotzan frowned.

"But your people are far better riders."

Using his right forepaw, Lorgi gently took hold of the pot's handle with only the soft pads of two digits. He took a moment to study it, guessing the vessel held just enough to quench his thirst. Slowly, he emptied a quart of sweet tea into his parched mouth. The healer tried in vain to glimpse Lorgi's throat as he drank.

"*Aaaeioh*," sang Porzan, opening his own mouth as wide as he could, pretending to yawn. Gesturing for Lorgi to copy him, he yawned again.

"*Aaaeioh*," Lorgi answered, with the same pitch, inflection, tone and volume of the man's bear-like yawn. His paw gestures mirrored Porzan's hand motions.

All who witnessed this cheered. Porzan smiled, so Lorgi did too. At last, the group's prize seemed to be healing. People assumed he would please the Gran Vazuk, bringing rewards to Klimgu's entire *quiver* of warriors, their families and servants. Klimgu led Ziteng and five captains up to the wagons. Lorgi recognized them all from the battle at the sorcerer's bluff. They smiled and gestured to him, which he mimicked. Yet this time, none laughed. Their adrenalin and sweat told him to be afraid.

"Welcome rock dragon to our quiver, or part of it. Congratulate him on his lucky recovery," Klimgu nodded to Lorgi, gesturing for Chotzan to hurry and translate.

"Welcome to our herd," Chotzan told Lorgi in Tundrish. "Glad you are feeling better. The wagoners treat you well, yes?"

"I'm hungry," said Lorgi. "I want to go home. *Guyat.*"

"Later, my friend," said Chotzan.

"Explain that we still have fierce enemies on these plains," said Klimgu. "If they attack, it will be our battle, not his. Lorgi must stay hidden in the wagon, until we are past the threat."

"We are in a bad place, Lorgi," said Chotzan. "We must get away from here before any of us can go home. Be good to the wagoners. They try to help you. Keep down and be gentle on the wagon. See what you have done to it already."

"Sorry, I didn't mean to," chirped Lorgi.

"Of course not," Chotzan swallowed, a knot in his throat. Looking down and away, he hoped no one saw his weakness. Yet Sijun and Temsuji smiled knowingly to each other.

"*Guyat!*" shouted Klimgu, raising his left hand high and signaling forward.

"Guyat!" Lorgi copied him, ducking below the rails as Klimgu scowled. Once the leader glanced away, Lorgi popped his head back up to see where they were all going.

The group set off at a fast, but quiet trot. Most rode in silence. What few words aired came in harsh whispers. At first, Klimgu and Chotzan rode beside the wagons, but ignored Lorgi and the wagoners. All eyes scanned the horizon. Once Porzan felt that Lorgi would remain conscious, he bandaged the women's hands and left the wagon for his own horse. While riding, everyone checked their weapons again, and stretched their muscles to prepare for battle. In ten minutes, the group caught up with Kibak and his scouts.

"Yahai," hissed Kibak, with a pushing down gesture of both hands.

"Yahai," Lorgi mimicked him, instantly ducking below the wagon rail. Ignoring his driver's scolding, he carved a peephole in the wagon's left side wall with his fore claws.

"Chumga, keep it down in there!" Klimgu snapped at Lorgi's driver. "What is rock dragon doing, eating the wagon? Chotzan, see to that."

"Lorgi, we are in danger," whispered Chotzan. "You must be quiet."

Turning to his lead scout, Klimgu asked, "What do you have for us, Kibak?"

"Laskomian tracks. Enough to give anyone pause."

"Of course," nodded Klimgu. "We must find them first."

"Then we must be lucky—and more subtle," whispered Kibak, glancing at the wagons.

Klimgu put his left fist in the air, then slowly lowered it to the side. All dismounted and the group walked in silence. Curious, Lorgi poked his head above the rails. The wagoners begged him to stay down, but he grew restless, wiggling about and making noise. Frowning, Chumga put his left pointer finger to his lips with a barely audible "shh," which Lorgi mimicked. Sijun and Temsuji whispered to Lorgi, but he did not understand most of their Tuzanchim words.

"Chotzan!" hissed Temsuji in a hoarse whisper.

"What now?" he asked.

"This cannot work. Neither Sijun nor I speak Tundrish or know how to train bears. What are we supposed to do with rock dragon?"

"Return to your wagon," said Chotzan. "But keep ready if Lorgi needs help."

A minute later, a scout rode up and spoke with Klimgu. Then both rode off at a gallop. Lorgi gripped the wagon's front rail with both forepaws, standing tall. Sensing danger, he had to see, too. Sijun, Temsuji and Chumga all begged, motioned, and pushed, trying to get Lorgi down and out of sight. Porzan climbed back aboard and did the same. None of them spoke Tundrish, so Lorgi ignored them. He knew very well what they wanted, but in his experience, doing as told had failed to keep him safe.

"Chumga, Lorgi must not be seen," hissed Chotzan, angry with the driver. "Do whatever you must to control him. I don't care how. I cannot stay by the wagon."

"I'll do my best," promised Chumga, as Chotzan rode off.

"I'll do *what I can*," Lorgi corrected him, with a raised forepaw and an emphatic nod. The wagoners could not help but smile at each other.

"You can get your big fat head down," Chumga scolded him.

"You can get big fat," answered Lorgi. Covering their mouths and shaking, the wagoners muffled their laughter. Lorgi mimicked this too, bringing them to tears. Pleased, he repeated the special new phrase, "You can get big fat."

Smiling, Lorgi refused to keep down. When begging, pulling, pushing and even spitting failed, Chumga slapped him hard on his snout. This only made Lorgi twitch his ears and cock his head in surprise. All nearby heard the resounding slap. Some even winced, guessing the pain.

"Aiii!" yelped Chumga. He held up a throbbing, bleeding hand, and glared at Lorgi and any laughing witnesses. "May you all freeze in winter, or die of thirst in summer."

"He speaks no Tuzanchim and wears a hide of rock," said Temsuji. "Why even try to discipline him?"

"Chotzan's order," wheezed Chumga, in agony. "How can he be so hard all over?"

Instinctively, Lorgi treated the injury with a few soothing, cold licks of his tongue. The driver gazed back in wonder. Discarding their bandages, Sijun and Temsuji thrust their cut hands at Lorgi, demanding his healing magic. Guessing that made all well, Lorgi stood back up to see all around. Like any warrior, he had to know. The wagoners urged him down, but he shook his head like a human to say "no."

"What are all of you so afraid of, anyway?" Lorgi asked in Tundrish.

"Shh!" they all hissed at him.

"You can get big fat," said Lorgi.

Expecting giant balkotars or rival hordes to spring up on the horizon, Lorgi scanned it like everyone else. Yet he viewed only scattered rolling hills amid flat grasslands. Tall, sweet grasses undulated in a clean wind, sparing this day from growing even hotter. Small patches of woods dotted the landscape, especially in low places where rain water might gather in abundance. Promising forests loomed in the distance, both to the northeast and southeast.

But due east, the land grew ever more flat and pale. An anemic river threaded between former hills, ending in a vast lake called Gabriska. With his long eyes, Lorgi spied whitecaps, heralding stronger wind on the lake. An endless herd of cumulus clouds gave both sky and land an artist's dream of light and shadow on this late morning. If it could just be cooler, Lorgi knew this would make a perfect day for racing, playing, feasting or exploring—not battling or fleeing.

"Can we stop?" chirped Lorgi, with a stretch that cut deep gouges into the wagon's floor bed. "Stop. Enough. *Yahai!* I'm hungry. And thirsty. And now I have to go, too."

"Shh, get down!" urged the wagoners. Ignoring them, Lorgi focused on warriors riding nearby. He already knew who among them spoke Tundrish or held rank, focusing on those.

"Hello!" he yelled, waving a forepaw high and wide, the way humans did to get attention. "*Guyat.* Me—*guyat.*" All noticed, yet ignored him. A few came close beside the wagon, only to order silence. Turning back to his driver, Lorgi said, "Me *guyat*, now. *Yahai*, Chumga. *Yahai!*"

The wagoners kept repeating their "shh's" and gestures for him to keep down and quiet. Twitching his ears, Lorgi wondered if these were the horde's "slowest arrows," relegated to the wagons for good reason. Impatient, he climbed over the rail and fell off the wagon. Suddenly the whole group stopped. While people debated in harsh whispers, Lorgi did what he had to, then climbed aboard the other wagon, seeking food and drink.

"No!" hissed many voices. But none tried to stop him.

"Give him some of the sweetened flatbread," wheezed Chumga.

"Not that," Sijun balked. "A luxury for captains and leaders, only."

"Rock dragon is our luxury, now," said Chumga. "Give just enough to coax him back into my wagon."

"Speak gently to him, like a toddler or your favorite horse," said Porzan. "Sweet as honey, if you want results."

Lorgi knew exactly what they needed from him, but held out for a larger bribe. At home, other children had shown him this simple technique. It worked best on Delfinians and visitors. But not on these Tuzanchim. They made just one offer, and were about to retract it altogether. So Lorgi jumped back into his own wagon with a thunderous crash. For that, he got a hand-sized wedge of honeyed flatbread, a steppe delicacy. Very generous by Tuzanchim measures. But Lorgi found it a scant appetizer. He still felt cheated that none had rewarded him after all the arguing he had been forced to witness.

"Good!" Lorgi nodded to Sijun. "Cinnamon would make it perfect."

"We have none," laughed a Tundrish-speaking captain next to the wagon.

"Where are we?" demanded Lorgi, already sounding like a warrior. "And where are the children? But first, what is your name?"

"What?" gasped the captain, surprised at Lorgi's aggressive tone. "Whisper. We near a terrible foe."

"More spiders?" Lorgi's eyes widened; his ears pinned back in fear.

"No, praise the Wind!" said the captain. "We slew them all."

"How?" asked Lorgi.

"With your help, and our leader's cunning. Now we face an old enemy."

"My only enemies are those spiders," said Lorgi in a loud voice.

"Whisper," hissed the captain.

"Why? People kept yelling all morning."

"No one yells now."

"What's your name?" asked Lorgi.

"Ganjaset, lead captain and Third-in-command of the whole group," he nodded to respect an aggressive equal.

"Ganjaset," said Lorgi. "Sounds a bit like *gánsi*, or *thank you* in my language. So where are all the rest of your people, your families?"

"With Twarejik's group. Only Klimgu's best ride with us now, your escort to the Gran Vazuk."

"The only place I want to go is home, and we're going the wrong way."

"It is a great honor to see the Gran Vazuk. You are quite special. He will be delighted to meet you."

"Then why do you all look so grim and smell afraid?"

"The Laskomians wait somewhere, perhaps in those woods," Ganjaset pointed with his sword. "One of our oldest, toughest enemies."

"Why are you enemies?" asked Lorgi, with a child's eyes, expecting a logical answer.

"It never matters why."

"Then why don't you make peace with them?"

"Because we are their enemy," said Ganjaset, no match for an inquisitive child.

"But why? Do you even know why?"

"It is never a warrior's place to ask why. Not even a lead captain, like myself."

"That is stupid!" snapped Lorgi.

"It is our way, and you should respect it," whispered Ganjaset. "But you are foreign beyond foreign. From the far end of the earth. Perhaps you could ask the Gran Vazuk, yourself."

"I will," chirped Lorgi.

Klimgu returned, ordering silence for the whole group. A quick, forward jerk of his left arm put them back to a trot. Fifteen minutes of this brought the expedition within a mile of the lake's west shore. Klimgu slowly pulled his left fist down to the side. Everyone dismounted to walk in silence. Half a mile from the lake, he raised a hand and they halted. All kept quiet, so Lorgi did as well. He peered above the wagon rails, just high enough to stare at the leader. After locking eyes with the dragon child for five long breaths, Klimgu had to yank himself out of a trance, as if Lorgi had been trying to put him to sleep. Shaking his head as if to combat a strong liquor, he turned to his Second.

"Chotzan—peace before blood," said Klimgu, locking eyes with him. "Time to clear the mind for battle. Make peace with our wagoners, especially Sijun and Temsuji."

"Now, not just a little later?" asked Chotzan, looking irritated.

"Now. This place feels like a rotten tooth, even more so when I look to our rock dragon."

"I'll bet his teeth never wear out," said Chotzan.

"Or his eyes. Beware—they could swallow you whole. He has the eyes of ten shamans. May they bring us grand luck instead of ruin. The next hour will decide our fate."

"Where are ten shamans who could possibly know that?" Chotzan shook his head.

"I cannot explain; I just know from his eyes," said Klimgu. "So much blood, and I must make the best of all the bad choices here. You can only help with a clear mind. I need your absolute best. Can you forego a little pride for that?"

"For you, anything. But those two old mares?"

"Let them win this one. Today may be our last—or theirs. They also need clear minds, to help with our rock dragon and too many other things."

"Of course, they won't see it that way. And they have yet to be of much—"

"Chotzan! Let it go," Klimgu snapped. "We can debate later, maybe over Laskomian ale. Gather the captains."

Hand signals instantly rippled throughout the whole group. In seconds, all the captains, which included half the Tundrish-speakers, formed a circle around Klimgu. Suddenly guessing that knowing two languages made one sharper and more likely to increase in rank and status, he swore to learn Tundrish if he survived this day. "Ask all to bury any grievances, so that they give their best. Many will not outlive this day. But be quick. Time is against us, so long as we tread Laskomian ground."

Fearing for his own safety, Lorgi studied the leader and captains, especially those who seemed to have the most influence. Still, the wagoners vied for his attention. Chumga begged him to lie down quietly, handing him the last piece of sweet flatbread as a bribe. Imitating Lorgi's "turtle" move, the driver would have brought the whole group to laughter, if not for the danger at hand. Sensing danger, Lorgi complied with his request.

Thankful for the unexpected cooperation, Chumga nodded, smiling with genuine delight. He offered a prized Tuzanchim snack, a strip of spicy beef jerky. Frowning when Lorgi refused it, the driver instead offered an egg-sized ball of dried, sweetened yogurt. Though inhaling it in a second, Lorgi kept licking his chops until he got another one. Risking his good hand, Chumga very gingerly stroked Lorgi's hard, but relatively smooth front neck. He spoke slowly in gentle tones, making his passenger's ears and nostrils twitch in surprise.

"*Gánsi*," said Lorgi. "That's how we say 'thank you' in my language. *Gánsi*."

"*Gánsi*," echoed the driver, guessing the meaning. Lorgi, Chumga, Sijun and Temsuji all exchanged a few nodding rounds of "*gánsi*," until Chotzan rode up and ordered silence.

When a scout called Chotzan away, Lorgi shot up, refusing to miss anything. Like any warrior, he hated waiting for news. Klimgu saw him poking his sparkling head above the ever-eroding wagon rails, but had no time to worry about him. As Lorgi had seen many times before, the leaders debated which way to proceed.

Even at this early age, Lorgi's *paháphkoltam*, or "middle-finder," told him that he was hundreds of miles south, and more than twice that distance east of home. He wondered why fish, birds, bats, reindeer and so many others always knew their way, yet humans constantly became lost, in spite of all their maps, tools and clever ways. But Lorgi dared not strike out on his own just yet. His whole body shook at the thought of balkotars. He was still not ready to abandon these Tuzanchim, even if they did not know where they were going. All Lorgi knew was that they raced across vast grasslands, home to an ancient foe waiting for any chance to slaughter them.

10: The Battle of Lake Gabriska

 With Chotzan at his side, Klimgu met Ganjaset and Kibak on their return from scouting part-way around Lake Gabriska. Kibak had followed the more expansive north shore, and Ganjaset the shorter but heavily wooded south shore. Neither route looked safe or fast to the leader. Yet avoiding the lake entirely meant trekking through forests to the north or south, either of which might hold a Laskomian army. Hating his choices, Klimgu sweated more than anyone, but Ganjaset, Kibak and their scouts worried nearly as much, knowing their leader's decision must ride on their reports. A wrong choice could end many lives, as well as the high standing Klimgu had toiled for decades to build. All supported him, very glad not to be the leader just now.

"The Laskomians have the most feared cavalry in all the west," said Klimgu. "They wear the hardest armor and ride the grandest horses on all the Continent."

"But a few months ago they proved no match for us in open country," Kibak reminded him.

"Which Lake Gabriska and its woods are not," said Klimgu.

"Then we can expect their revenge here," said Ganjaset.

"Kibak, your best arrow on the north," asked the leader, with false calm.

"Long, mostly flat, open ground, sandy shores. Few good hiding places. Could be a few swamps, but you gave us no time to reach them. Large, abandoned camp about half-way around, many tracks, but—"

"Thank you," said Klimgu. "Ganjaset, what of the south?"

Narrowing inscrutable eyes, Ganjaset knew his penchant for caution diluted his influence. "Long stretches of sandy banks trade with strands of trees reaching for the lake. It may prove shallow enough to wade through at those points. But you left us no time to reach any of them, either. No Laskomian tracks."

Klimgu nodded. "What I most needed to hear."

"But if I were the enemy, all my force should wait there."

"Yet no tracks," said Klimgu. "Kibak, how much longer by the north?"

"I, we…well," stammered Kibak. "No way to know without—"

"Guess! The longer we stew here, the more arms the Laskomians can mass in one place."

"Six hours?" mumbled Kibak. "A full day or more with swamps. But no enemy will dare strike, if they think we precede the main horde. Pretend that and frighten them away."

"All 800 of us," Klimgu grimaced. "Very well, by which route?"

"South. Leave Gabriska quickly," urged Kibak.

"Ganjaset?" asked Klimgu, already knowing his answer.

"North. If Laskomians still camp there, cut them down on our way through. But we must clear the lake by sundown, and before they learn of our treasure or tiny numbers."

"Well shot," Klimgu nodded. "But why fear a route lacking enemy tracks?"

"For that very reason," said Ganjaset. "It feels unlucky."

"Kibak, why not the north way?" asked Klimgu, growing annoyed.

"From a distance, the camp looked too foolish. Or strangely artful," said Kibak. "If only you had given us more time to reach it…"

"So after two hours of scouting, we are no wiser," moaned Klimgu, shaking his head. "Chotzan?"

"South—with care," he nodded grimly.

"South it is," ordered Klimgu, signaling to proceed.

Now he rued his choice not to bring the entire quiver. The Gran Vazuk's order for Twarejik to hunt down the missing Laskomian army had caught up to him en route to the sorcerer's bluff. Aching to ride with Klimgu, he also wanted his fair share of credit in *gifting* Lorgi to the Vazuk. Both leaders knew that Twarejik would require maximum force when he found the enemy, while Klimgu needed only a strong escort for the prize, as he rode swiftly away from danger. So Klimgu loaned most of his warriors to Twarejik, the latest in a long history of favors between the two quiver leaders. Gazing at the huge lake, Klimgu recalled their last conversation, near the spider bluffs:

"You do me so many favors that I can never hope to repay you," said Twarejik. "How will I ever balance my ride?"

"You have done much for me, and never failed me," said Klimgu.

"Thank you, but this…is far too generous, when we still have only rumors about that last remaining Laskomian army," said Twarejik. "Where it waits, if it exists at all. How will I ever repay such a grand favor?"

"Don't grind your teeth over it. Just do me the ultimate favor, my friend."

"It will be my greatest honor to die in your place in battle," nodded Twarejik.

"No. Back me if I must rebel against the Gran Vazuk."

"What?" gasped Twarejik. "Do my ears trick me?"

"Never," laughed Klimgu. "You hear better than a young wolf. Well?"

"Some say the Vazuk's habits would disgust anyone. Yes, he has never ruled with an even hand. But it is by far the strongest hand on the Continent. How can revolt ever come to be?"

"What seems impossible may also prove absolutely necessary. A warped hand and ill habits cannot rule an empire for long. Well? Do you need time to think on it?"

"Yes, I mean no," stuttered Twarejik. "I always knew you were bold, but *this*?"

"What about you?" Klimgu asked. "Yes or no? I will respect any clear answer."

"Yes. I ride with you, only for you," nodded Twarejik, shaking his head at his friend's audacity. "And it will be the death of me."

"Not one word to anyone—even your best horse. Just be ready when I ask."

On that day, a mile from the smoldering ruins of the sorcerer's house, Twarejik did more than politely offer a formal "yes" with a nod. By also grasping Klimgu's hand, he thereby swore an oath witnessed by the Tuzanchim Gods: Sky, Wind, Earth, Sun and Moon.

* * *

Moving at their famously quiet, brisk trot, the expedition reached Lake Gabriska's west shore in minutes. The southern forest stretched a thin arm to within a dozen yards of the water. Calling a silent halt, Klimgu sent a dozen scouts running out on foot past the group on three sides. A hundred yards out, each pressed an ear to the ground for a full minute before reporting back. Only then did Klimgu send four others riding to the nearest wood's edge. These returned before he would allow the whole group to advance. Minutes later, they entered a spacious half-moon swath of open ground stretching out for nearly a mile. There, a slightly thicker wooded arm met the lake itself, forming a decisive obstruction, ideal for an ambush. The other captains began criticizing Ganjaset and his scouts, but he vigorously defended their efforts.

"*Yahai!*" Klimgu silenced them. Whirling his sword in a circle overhead, he shouted, "*Guyat par hatok!*"

The whole group suddenly transformed. Lorgi popped his head up to view all of it. Women, adolescents and horse tenders placed themselves by the wagons. The rest spread out in a defensive battle formation, bows ready. Alarmed, Lorgi pinned his ears back and twitched his nostrils, refusing either to sit still or keep down. Preparing for battle, the wagoners put on helmets, war gloves and chain mail hauberks, none of which had been made by any Tuzanchim. Despite having nothing in common with Lorgi, they knew what he was thinking.

"Be calm," said Chumga. "This is not your battle."

"Why does there have to be one?" Lorgi managed to ask in Tuzanchim. "My mother says most battles don't help anything. They just destroy all that they touch."

"Perhaps you are too clever or lucky to be forced into war, unlike the rest of us," laughed Sijun, from the other wagon.

"Why do humans laugh when most afraid?" asked Lorgi. "Why are only you wagon people putting on armor?"

"Too confining and heavy for riders—makes them slow, easy targets," said Chumga. "But since wagoners already make the easiest prey, we collect the best armor whenever we can, as part of our war spoils. This mail coat has saved me twice already."

Lorgi cocked his head and wiggled his ears, struggling to understand.

All watched as Chotzan led the front group of 200 out to the natural barricade, treading the wood's edge. Most nocked their luckiest arrows, expecting to be firing them in seconds. When no enemy materialized, some warriors showed frustration, even anger. Yet others, especially the women and youths, looked relieved. Never had Lorgi smelled so much adrenalin. This scenario replayed twice within the hour, eroding nerves. Beyond these obstacles lay a two-mile stretch of soggy meadow, trying to become a swamp. The Tuzanchim eschewed any such type of slow ground as a fool's trap. Just past that, they reached a slightly thicker tongue of woods lapping at the shore, forming an even better place for an ambush.

"Chotzan, you must go through first, again," ordered Klimgu. "Everyone else, keep ready arms and eyes. We are a quiver of the Tuzanchim Empire, not some tired caravan!"

As quickly as possible, Chotzan led the forward group over the driest turf he could find—that nearest the woods—before stopping by the lake on the other side of the budding swamp. If the Laskomians waited for this, then at least they could not attack the whole group at once. Klimgu threw Ganjaset a scowl for his poor reconnaissance.

"You gave us no time to scout this far," said Ganjaset.

"You must grow swift and bold, to gather facts before they sour," said Klimgu.

"I start now. Have me lead the advance group next time."

"Not today." Klimgu frowned, keeping his eyes on the woods where Chotzan's group had gone ahead. "I hate risking my Second every time, but he has a gift for exposing ambushes. Your turn will come all too soon, and I will not like risking you then, either."

"But we ride home, and may not battle again for months."

"Home. What is that, beyond a scrap of land? A cruel, false labor of hope, begging to be attacked. Do you own it or does it own you? Whether a possession or just a state of mind, I will have none. One never has to wait long for battle, home or not."

"Why so bitter, when the warrior's path keeps bringing you higher and higher standing?"

"Standing?" mused Klimgu. "It can double instantly with good fortune. Or vanish quick as arrows with bad luck, or one critical mistake. Enough ill words by foes may even grind a mountain of it down to a stump. And yet the best standing grows only very slowly, by earning praise from many friends. It can dissolve if one stops to nap when bolder souls ride ahead."

"Your standing shines like a great sword," said Ganjaset.

"Right now, all we have that shines is our albino rock dragon. Whether a champion or a runt among his own kind, he is still a unique treasure for us, hard-won in battle. Now we will have to fight to keep him, and what fleeting status he may bring to us. I can smell the blood already."

"Sorry I asked," said Ganjaset, also frowning.

Yet by midafternoon, the ambush-weary 800 reached Lake Gabriska's last obstacle, with still no sign of the Laskomians. Just beyond, endless miles of flat, open country beckoned. Klimgu chided the scouts for their slowness. Chotzan lectured all the rest for getting sloppy with defensive procedures. Yet even the Tuzanchim could not keep up such intense alertness all day, constantly ready to fight, with no enemy to be found. Most assumed that the Laskomians had fled a day or more ahead of them to avoid battle. Now, the warriors thought only of making camp, resting their horses, and enjoying a good meal.

For the last time, Klimgu sent Chotzan ahead to secure this final obstacle. But the rest slackened, tired of keeping up a fighting stance. Most held their bows down loosely at their sides, while conversing about trivial things. As Chotzan neared the last strand of trees touching the lake—the last hindrance between the whole group and their natural environment—the wind turned.

Lorgi's nostrils twitched, picking up many new scents. He caught a glimmer of light bouncing off metal in the woods. Switching to his heat eyes, Lorgi detected many soldiers hiding all through the woods framing the meadow. In an instant, he knew a battle was about to erupt, because the Tuzanchim were practically surrounded. Still, he hoped to avert it.

"I see them. I smell them. Many, so many, all around!" growled Lorgi in a course whisper. Nudging his driver, he pointed to tight scores of soldiers hiding in the woods only fifty yards from the shore, but Chumga shook his head. "Listen to me! Look right there! See? I should have sensed them earlier. We must go back."

"Ganjaset, calm our rock dragon until we're past the lake," ordered Klimgu.

"Look at all the metal in there!" Lorgi jabbed with a forepaw.

"Can you see anything, Chumga?" asked Ganjaset, himself squinting in that direction.

"Nothing; I'm too old," the driver shook his head. "What about you?"

"No, not by the water, Ganjaset. Look over there!" yelled Lorgi, pointing fifty yards away from the lake. "Armor, men, horses. So many."

His eyebrows knotting up, Ganjaset focused exactly where Lorgi asked, but also shook his head. "Are you sure, Lorgi?"

"How can you not see them?" asked Lorgi, angry.

"I do not, and I am said to have long eyes."

"Not long enough," said Lorgi.

"Wait," said Ganjaset. "Something just moved. Metal. Klimgu!"

"We are but one arrow's flight from clearing this lake entirely," murmured the leader.

"Too late. They all start to move," warned Ganjaset. "Many, as Lorgi said."

"How many?" demanded Klimgu.

"Three thousand," said Lorgi. "But more may be hiding behind those."

"How can you know?" asked Ganjaset.

"Turn back!" yelled Lorgi. "Get us out of here. They want blood!"

"Hatok banchugit!" shouted Klimgu. Instantly the main group fanned out to make a staggered, zigzag formation, expecting an enemy charge from any part of the woods framing the crescent-shaped meadow occupied by the Tuzanchim.

"Guyat!" yelled Lorgi, whirling a forepaw overhead, to urge the group back, away from danger. Captains glared at him. Warriors shunned him. Most wanted to punish him for his recklessness, for breaking one of their most critical rules of conduct. But no time. A sudden whooshing and rustling jostled the foliage of the wood's edge, all the way around the meadow, while the Tuzanchim kicked up sand and dust, scrambling to form a defensive position. Alone in the eye of a human storm, Lorgi felt

the most compelling urge to bolt from the wagon, dive into the lake, and escape, even though it would hurt his new friends, the wagon people. He was about ready to jump when the storm broke.

Five hundred skull-splitting Laskomian arrows suddenly volleyed from the woods. Whistling through the air in a high arch, they looked almost like spears. As with all their tools of war, including men, horses, swords and shields, the Laskomians used the largest possible arrows to ensure their effect. These measured half again longer than their Steppe counterparts. In a surprise for the Tuzanchim, the volley did not aim for the warriors nearest to the woods and the enemy, but for the wagons and the center of Klimgu's force. In a cruel illusion, the volley appeared to lose momentum during its ascent, only to suddenly gain it back with a vengeance on impact.

"Answer them!" yelled Klimgu. Directly, half his warriors fired their own stout Tuzanchim arrows into the hostile woods, but with no clear targets, these had little effect. Only a dozen muffled cries escaped the wood, immediately followed by thunderous cheers from the bitter foe within. And a second volley.

"Kibak!" yelled Klimgu.

"Never before have the Laskomians dared such a bold gambit," gasped Kibak. "Either their archers have by some new magic doubled their firing speed, or they are willing to sacrifice them for the wagons."

"Now we will have to spend much blood to keep our prize," yelled Klimgu. "Make Chumga drive his wagon toward Chotzan, and Sijun take the other in the opposite direction. Our only choice, for now."

The Tuzanchim scattered, whirling in pretended disorder to confuse the Laskomians and deprive them of stationary targets. Few arrows found a live mark, but another volley launched every quarter of a minute, proving that this enemy had indeed improved its rate of fire. Chotzan's group struggled to inch forward against foot soldiers hiding in the narrow tongue of woods by the shore.

As others spread away from them, the wagoners found themselves even more exposed, riding in circles before Klimgu's order reached them. Chumga cursed and his wagon let out pained squeals as it made tight, uneven turns. One arrow split a rail on the other wagon. A second effectively nailed its driver to the back of the wooden seat, despite his wearing a chain mail hauberk, killing him instantly. A third grazed Sijun's helmet with a loud ring, just as she took the reins. Lorgi whirled about, fearing she had been hit.

"I'm fine, just deaf after that!" she yelled, smiling and nodding to Lorgi for his concern.

"Sijun, drive your wagon back the way we came," yelled a rider sent by Kibak. "Chumga, take our prize to Chotzan."

"But they look hard-pressed at the shore!" yelled Chumga, squinting. "And one of my front wheels seems ready to break!"

From the other wagon, Sijun quickly eyed both calamities, frowning with doubt. Only half-nodding to the messenger, she squinted at Chumga. In her view, a previous order from Chotzan to stay with Lorgi held far more luck and logic than one to ride off as a decoy.

"Klimgu's order!" yelled the rider, guessing both drivers doubted him. "Sijun, only you can draw the enemy away from our rock dragon. Chumga, your best hope, your only hope is to reach Chotzan. Keep our prize down and safe until then. Good luck."

"Impossible," said Chumga. "He has the will of a Vazuk!"

"Vazuk?" Lorgi repeated.

"Down!" snapped Chumga, pushing on Lorgi's snout, cutting the same hand again. "I said down!"

"No!" yelled Lorgi, springing back up. "*Guyat! Guyat* us out of here!"

"In that case, you can help drive our limping wagon, now that you make me less able to do so. Watch...like this...see?"

"I'm the prize?" asked Lorgi. "What is that supposed to mean?"

"Here," barked Chumga, handing Lorgi the reins. "Watch...see? Like this...no. Not that way...here...like this, see?"

"Like this?" Lorgi asked, trying his best.

"Almost. Lightly, because we have a bad wheel. So we must go slow or we won't go at all."

"How am I doing now?"

"Better. Good. You learn fast, thank the Sky."

"*Gánsi!*" Lorgi saw through the smile on his driver's face. Chumga did not expect to survive this battle.

"*Gánsi* to you, too. May your quartz hide save us both today."

* * *

Fierce resistance met Chotzan's group where the woods reached the shore. Archers shot from the foliage, paired with swordsmen to protect them. To bar any Tuzanchim from escape, a tight formation of Laskomian heavy infantry held the soggy, narrow patch of sand dividing wooded land from water. Their huge shields and pikes rendered them immune to any mounted charge.

Beyond desperate, Chotzan risked all by splitting his group. Half dismounted and charged on foot, not at the impregnable infantry waiting for them on the shore, but into the adjacent woods. The Laskomian swordsmen held their ground, but amidst the foliage, the shorter, lighter Tuzanchim swords quickly began to tell. The archers who had been hiding in that patch of wood fled, as their sword-bearing protectors were cut down. Dividing the remainder of his group, he kept half on the narrow ground between the wood's edge and the shore.

Gambling on the water not being too deep—as Ganjaset had suggested—Chotzan led the rest into the shallows of the lake immediately adjacent to the shore, in order to outflank or push back the enemy facing him. Although his riders were able to maneuver their horses through the shallows, the task proved treacherous. The enemy pikes could walk faster, even on the mushy sands between the woods and the lake. If Chotzan's impromptu foot warriors had not routed the archers, his whole group would have perished.

Wading in water that reached almost to their saddles, gazing up at a wall of shields, pikes and helmets on shore, Chotzan's riders took aim wherever a crack in that armor appeared, however briefly. A handful of his warriors on foot also began to shoot at the same formation from the woods. The tight clump of pike men outnumbered Chotzan's whole group by two to one, but now he could fire on them from three sides. For all the arrows launched, few actually struck anything but iron, and then only an occasional arm or foot.

At first, only a few of Chotzan's warriors thought to spend their poison arrows, but this made all the difference. The Laskomian armor held firm, yet they had trouble shielding themselves on three sides at once. The slightest gap in that iron wall of shields insured death for the one so exposed. Suddenly undone by the same tactic their army was using against Klimgu's force overall, the infantry formation broke and fled. Arrows, then mounted swords cut down most of them. A lesson that most enemies of the Tuzanchim learned the hard way.

Just as his group shouted cheers for their small victory, Chotzan saw not one, but two enemy reserve companies rushing in to fill the breach he had risked all to create. No escape this day. Chumga's wagon began to lumber towards Chotzan, and the Laskomians roared. All their eyes turned to Lorgi, as if he were the Tuzanchim leader. Rather than continuing to just hold the Tuzanchim in the meadow and keep showering them with arrows until only a handful of them survived, the Laskomians changed tactics.

A final volley launched, timed just after 1,000 mounted, superbly armored knights emerged from the segment of forest parallel to the lake. They formed a single line stretching a mile wide. Holding their lances vertically, this heavy cavalry waited motionless for three breaths, as if to make certain they were clearly noticed before launching into a charge. With the last volley halfway to its destiny, the Laskomians unleashed their famed cavalry charge, far earlier in the battle than any on either side had expected. They also threw every foot soldier they had into the battle.

Gambling all their resources at once, the Laskomians strived to broadside the Tuzanchim, swiftly drive them into the lake, and massacre all of them in a single coordinated attack. They had suffered and waited centuries for this moment.

Four hundred armored foot soldiers in tight formation, wielding spears, battleaxes, and heavy shields marched out to block any retreat to the west. The exact counterpart to what Chotzan faced on the east, it strived to not only contain, but also compress the battle, forming one side of a giant vice to crush the Tuzanchim. Scattered throughout the crescent of woods framing the battle, the surviving Laskomian archers emerged and began to act like Tuzanchim, firing at will, but only at clear, single targets.

Lacking maneuvering room or any escape route, the Tuzanchim found the cavalry charge doubly impressive, giving most of the warriors pause for the first time in their lives. Looking invincible, the Laskomian knights wielded long, sturdy war lances and heavy shields. Tall and muscular, they wore iron helms with towering plumes, the hardest chain mail known, and bright green and white surcoats, making them appear like giants.

Klimgu's warriors feared their lighter swords and arrows might not pierce such robust Laskomian metalwork. Without room to get out of the way, in minutes the cavalry would run them all down. Chotzan's group began to falter and retreat, pushed back by 400 fresh enemy soldiers with pikes and battleaxes. The rest of the quiver fared no better.

"We're caught in a noose!" yelled Kibak, riding to his leader.

"I know. Just find us a way out!" shouted Klimgu.

"They force us to fight by their method—boxed in," yelled Ganjaset.

"All see that too!" shouted Klimgu. "Both of you have failed me!"

Desperate, Klimgu raced to Lorgi's wagon, leapt from his horse and stood atop the corroded front rail for the most complete—and foolhardy—view of his disaster. Sijun drove the second wagon up alongside and both stopped. Klimgu scowled at her, but had no time to argue. He could only guess that she never received his order, or had chosen not to follow it for a good reason. Shrieking and waving his sword, he ordered everyone to retreat to the banks of the lake. Not knowing what to do after that, he prayed for ideas. With the Laskomian charge already begun, his retreat would buy only seconds.

"Klimgu!" yelled Sijun. "Spend our advantage against theirs."

"What advantage?" Klimgu grimaced.

"Forget the knights. Fell their charging horses with our spider arrows."

"Of course! *Gánsi!*" yelled Klimgu, leaping back onto his horse and riding away.

He gathered his surviving captains to give final orders. An exhausted, blood-drenched Chotzan was the last to join them. All looked resigned to death. But the leader cleared his throat, spat out blood, and smiled. None cared for his false bravado.

"Poison arrows only," Klimgu shouted. "But waste nothing on armor. Aim only for legs and horses. *Guyat!*"

"Spider arrows to their legs and horses!" yelled the captains, racing back to their warriors.

But Ganjaset turned to Klimgu, shouting, "Someone must slow the Laskomian charge, or at least distract them from the wagons. I am proud to ride with you. Now I will earn your respect."

"I need you to command a unit, not commit suicide!" yelled Klimgu.

"After my poor scouting, none will take orders from me," said Ganjaset. "So I can only direct myself. Let my fate help save the group."

"We need you in our formation," urged Klimgu.

"Others can do that. I will slow the enemy down, maybe even cut a hole in their line, and die happy."

"Mend honor and ego tomorrow," yelled Klimgu. "Today is only about survival. You must not go off on your own."

"Watch me," jeered Ganjaset, sending his horse into a gallop against the very center of the Laskomian charge.

"Grand luck," Klimgu shouted after him, but shook his head.

Despite laughing at the solitary fool, the Laskomian knights hated his gambit to disrupt their perfect line, however fleeting it would be. This had the desired effect of slowing the charge, yet only for a breath. Their leader barked orders and the line split in half. In seconds, a twenty-foot gap appeared, leaving ample room for Ganjaset to ride through without stalling even one knight in the charge. He could only assume that they intended to let archers or foot soldiers deal with him on their way to "mopping up" after the charge had done its work. Once past him, he knew the line would reform into a single, unbroken chain. A thousand lances to impale somewhat less than 800 warriors.

"Even the enemy has no respect for me!" he cursed. "None will even take the smallest trouble to kill me. Must I beg them for a combat, a respectable way to die?"

As if responding to his words, the closest knight approaching on either side of the line suddenly lowered his war lance, while the rest kept theirs high. Veering slightly from the charge, the two aimed at Ganjaset, in order to impale him. A skilled warrior or foot soldier could at least attempt to turn one lance with sword or shield, but never two lances at once. Suddenly, the next order from their commander made the two knights turn their lances sideways, as if to form the arms or a gate or bridge that Ganjaset would not be allowed to pass. That way, they could knock him off his horse without even slowing down their charge, or dulling their lances.

"Very well. Your mistake, not mine," said Ganjaset.

With cat speed, he jabbed his sword back into its scabbard. Freeing his left foot from its stirrup with a quick jerk, he raised that leg up, while putting most of his weight on his right side, as if about to dismount. Grabbing the saddle with both hands, he shouted to his horse: *"par choyuts."*

Reacting to the sudden obstacle, as well as the order, his stallion lowered its own head, slowing from a gallop to an easy run. At the same instant, Ganjaset leaned hard over to his right, hanging onto his saddle with both hands and legs, using a technique known only to the Tuzanchim. Barely a second later, both lances whooshed harmlessly overhead, though only by inches, as Laskomian curses emitted from the knights holding them.

In a breath, both Ganjaset and his horse had regained a normal position. Yet the knights were already fifty yards away. Those Tuzanchim who could see him all cheered Ganjaset's riding skill, causing him to smile for the first time this day. But his efforts made no difference to a battle approaching the endgame. He could never hope to catch up to the charging lances before they struck. Still, he raced after them, as Laskomian foot soldiers chased after him.

Most of the Tuzanchim already waded in foot-deep water, only seconds ahead of the charge. All chose a favorite, quill-tipped arrow, while waiting to dodge a freshly sharpened war lance aiming for their chest. A knight of Laskomia, or any land further west, might sacrifice his own horse to save himself from being impaled by a war lance. Yet no Tuzanchim would risk such eternal shame. They might jump or fall, sword in hand, but never make their *own* horse suffer a weapon intended for humans. That sin brought the most horrible punishment in the afterlife. And yet, the taboo did not apply to enemy horses.

In the next minute, many lances fell just short of their marks. Most of the rest impaled human targets. Desperate sword combat followed in the shallows of the lake. Laskomian infantry from both east and west pushed in, further compressing the battle as archers came out of the woods. Sijun's idea came too late to turn the battle, but assured that it was not over.

* * *

Eager to capture Lorgi and end the whole struggle, two knights charged towards his wagon, now hopelessly separated from the rest of the Tuzanchim force. One knight rode up on either side of the vehicle. The first took a powerful chopping swing at the driver, as the other aimed for his exotic passenger. Just in time, Lorgi tackled Chumga to block the first sword with his back spikes. The impact chipped the sword with a resounding ring, and forced both dragon and driver to yelp in surprise, if not pain. But it drew no blood.

Shocked by Lorgi's natural armor, the knight drew back with a pained grunt, his whole arm stung by the force of his own blow. From the wagon's other side, the second knight also struck at Lorgi's mid back. His sword aimed for the exact same spot, in case the first blow had weakened it enough for a second strike to make the difference. Instead, the impact broke his sword directly at the point of contact. Undaunted, that knight produced a mace.

"*Gánsi*," wheezed Chumga, dazed and bleeding under Lorgi.

"*Guyat, guyat!*" Lorgi screamed at the knights, swiping at their weapons with both forepaws.

"To where?" gasped Chumga, suffering under Lorgi's weight.

"Anywhere!"

Enraged and revived, Lorgi growled, bared his full arsenal of teeth and prepared to lunge. The mace-wielding knight pulled back four paces, riding alongside as the other knight seized control of the wagon's horses. Taking quick turns, they baited and retreated from Lorgi, while turning the wagon about. They began to lead it south toward the thickest part of the woods, where a reserve company of twenty cheering foot soldiers waited. Lorgi saw their game, but dared not leap to attack either knight, for fear the other would kill Chumga.

Klimgu only glimpsed the struggle, because he fought his own against a mounted knight who was proving more than his equal with a sword. Every time Klimgu blinked or allowed even the quickest thought about anything other than the knight's superior weapon, it nearly killed him. Perfectly anticipating every move that Klimgu tried, the knight also refused to tire, despite wielding much the heavier sword in the dual. Blocking out everything except his own immediate combat, Klimgu finally managed to cut his adversary's sword arm, just below the elbow. Like so many other things, he credited that tiny success to luck, not skill.

The knight let out a pained gasp, but only for an instant. Refusing to give up, he bludgeoned Klimgu with his hefty shield. In the seconds before Klimgu could recover enough to strike back, the Laskomian deftly traded hands for his sword and shield. Wasting no time, the knight immediately attacked with his sword, now held in his left hand. Incredibly, he did so with equal force, speed and skill.

By the time Klimgu won or more probably lost this individual combat, his whole group would be cut down. Against this rare, ambidextrous knight, suddenly he felt strangely, acutely inept. With his own force encircled and greatly outnumbered, he felt doomed.

"Chotzan! Ganjaset, Kibak, anyone!" shrieked Klimgu. But even his mighty voice drowned in the battle's din.

If anyone heard, none could help. Every warrior engaged in his or her own desperate combat. Some even fended off two swords at once—the sign of doom. Never had the Tuzanchim fought such tough or skilled foes. On this day, the Laskomians did not war for lives, lands or respect lost to the Tuzanchim. They just wanted blood.

Suddenly the knight chopped into Klimgu's small Tuzanchim shield with his unrivaled sword, cracking the shield dead center and nearly breaking it in half. A numbing pain shot up Klimgu's arm, but he could not tell if he was bleeding. Amazed that he still had an arm, he assumed it would be useless now. By luck, the sword had become firmly lodged in the shield, neutralizing both tools.

Instantly, Klimgu reached to attack with his own sword, but the knight proved even quicker with his shield, again using it as an offensive weapon. The impact made the shield ring like a huge bell and Klimgu grunt from having all the air knocked out of him. It also threw Klimgu off his horse, leaving him dazed, weaponless, but painfully alive. By cruel irony, the indignity saved him from a Laskomian arrow, which struck down the too-skilled knight instead.

* * *

Harried by his own clever foes, eager to plunge their swords into him, Lorgi yanked on the wagon reins with a resounding *"Yahai!"* The horses jerked to a stop, digging their hooves into the ground. They refused to move, surprising both knights. With that success, Lorgi smiled at two easy targets.

But a third knight joined the struggle for control of the wagon. The biggest man on the field, he also wielded the largest battle-ax, the loudest voice, and an ego to match. Gesturing to his comrades that only *he* had the requisite brawn and skill to deal with Lorgi, he claimed the knightly privilege of killing him. With that boast, the champion knight halted squarely beside the wagon as the first two backed away, trying to warn of Lorgi's armor and speed. Yet the third knight smirked at them, brushing their words aside with a refined, condescending wave of his hand.

Lorgi sensed the man had a bear's strength, yet an ox's brain, placing his horse in a defenseless broadside, not even sword-length away. Twitching his ears and nostrils in disbelief, Lorgi wondered if the brute thought Álukois were made of glass, light as feathers, slow as slugs, or dim as stone-drunk humans.

"What can this idiot expect?" Lorgi asked Chumga, still bleeding and grimacing in pain under him. He knew the old Tuzanchim could not understand him, but Lorgi felt compelled to express himself anyway. "Chumga?"

"Gánsi," wheezed the driver, looking resigned to death.

Lorgi already knew a little Tuzanchim, but not enough for what he had to say now, so he spoke in slow, clear Tundrish. "Chumga, I must fight this idiot. I have never...killed a human before."

Despite Lorgi's foreign words, Chumga met his eyes with sudden recognition. In equally clear Tuzanchim, he answered, "You will be a great warrior. I am proud to ride with you."

As the huge knight raised his battle-ax, Lorgi shouted to his driver, "I am proud to ride with you."

"Gánsi, Lorgi," smiled Chumga. "Now *guyat!* Run. Our war is not

yours. Flee this trap. You were made for so much better than this. *Guyat, guyat, guyat!*"

"You can get big fat!" yelled Lorgi. "I'll do what I can."

Just as the knight began to swing, Lorgi sprang at him with catapult force, knocking the man off his horse. The knight struck the ground head-first, breaking his neck with a loud snap as Lorgi crashed on top of him. Chumga wiggled desperately as one of the other knights alternately thrust or swung at him with his sword. The other led the wagon towards the woods.

"Yahai!" Lorgi shouted again, stopping the wagon. Before the second knight could react, the dragon child yanked him off his horse.

But this one landed intact. Immediately he struck with his mace, hitting Lorgi on the tip of his snout with a stinging smack. It made him yelp with pain, yet still drew no blood. Emboldened by a perceived injury to their enemy, screaming foot soldiers charged out from the woods to assist the knight. Sensing imminent death, Lorgi finally let go with the full force of his claws, for the first time in his life, shredding arms, armor and finally severing the head of the knight, all in a matter of seconds. Directly, the last knight met the same fate. Quick as rabbits, the foot soldiers ran back to their woods and beyond, quitting the battle altogether.

Three more knights suddenly found themselves close enough to challenge Lorgi. Seeing the result of his rage, they all fled rather than answer his gaze, because he had already felled the Laskomians' best knight. After that, none dared face him. In the center of the storm, he had become an obstacle that had to be avoided. Jumping back onto his wagon, he began to lick Chumga's many cuts, most of them inflicted by Lorgi himself.

Red squirted, splattered, gushed, dripped, and ran everywhere, including into Lorgi's mouth, nose, ears and eyes. He tried to dodge, shake off or wipe it away, but became drenched in it like everyone else: 4,000 screaming, murdering *hyúlems* and all their hot, salty blood. Metal fought metal, arrows cursed the air in search of meat, the stricken cried out, bones snapped, flesh ripped, people and horses choked on their own life fluid or showered others with the currency of violence. Screams of rage, agony and death tortured any un-dead ears.

Overwhelmed, Lorgi's ear lids slammed shut, and he heard almost nothing more of the deafening struggle. He could still see and smell it all, but only through a deep crimson film. The lake's shallows turned burgundy, as corpses or parts of them floated or sank therein. The stench, the cries, and the sight of it all made Lorgi nauseous, but his stomach had been empty since long before the killing started. He wondered if the Tuzanchim had unwittingly or deliberately conveyed him to the *hyúlem* spirit world—Hell.

* * *

Suddenly, from the safety of the woods, signal horns called retreat. Open spaces appeared between combatants, rapidly growing all across the battlefield. The Laskomian knights fled en masse, almost as swiftly as they had charged. Their foot soldiers could not escape as quickly, and many fell to poison arrows before they could reach the woods.

While the Tuzanchim watched the Laskomians dive back into their forest, Lorgi studied Klimgu. Grabbing Kibak by the arm, the leader muttered something in his ear. Grunting "Yahai!," Kibak shook his head and frowned, trying to pull himself away. But Klimgu gripped him by both shoulders and spoke forcefully to him. After several deep breaths, the lead scout nodded.

The Tuzanchim pumped their arms overhead, shouting hurrahs that filled all but Lorgi's ears, yet it hardly masked their sense of defeat. For the first time, they did not pursue a retreating enemy. In choosing the southern route, Klimgu had stepped into a rare trap, losing nearly half of his warriors and many horses. Disgraced, he hung his head and slumped his shoulders, guessing that only his dragon prize might dissuade the Gran Vazuk from ordering Klimgu's execution.

"Lorgi!" yelled Klimgu, running to him. "Crows! Where are you *not* bleeding?"

"*Guyat!*" Lorgi spat out human blood, his only injury a mildly bruised snout.

"Porzan!" screamed Klimgu.

"Our prize is too covered in blood for me to even guess his wounds," said Porzan. "Sijun, help me wash our rock dragon."

"No! Porzan, you help her!" yelled Lorgi, pointing to Sijun. She kneeled, wailing, rocking back and forth, grasping a pale, limp Temsuji in her arms. Thinking to heal with his tongue, Lorgi approached. But then he saw that nothing could help.

"Sijun!" yelled Porzan, glaring at her.

"Leave her be," said Klimgu.

"She is one of the few not injured," said Porzan.

"You of all people should know better. See first to Lorgi, then captains, scouts, warriors. Porters last."

The healer nodded, but ignored the order, treating anyone with the most serious injuries first, regardless of rank.

"Yahai, Lorgi," Porzan called after him. "Where are you going?"

Running to the shore, Lorgi dove into the lake. The cool water revived him, but all the blood and filth in it sickened him. He swam hard for clean, deep waters. Four of the best human swimmers tried to follow. Reaching over a hundred yards out, Lorgi made a wide arch to the west, before returning ashore. Having washed the human blood off of himself, Lorgi ran back to the wagon to check on his friends.

"You sure know how to help—and hurt," said Chumga, wincing as Lorgi licked his many wounds again. "You fought like a lion. I owe you my life. *Gánsi*, Lorgi."

"Who would have thought he could swim like that," said Klimgu, walking away. "And fight like that!"

"We must deliver him to the Vazuk at any cost," said Ganjaset, limping up to Klimgu.

"Yes, but not you or I. Once we tend our dead and wounded, the captains must reform the leadership. You understand."

Ganjaset nodded with a low grunt. Both men looked to the ground.

Regardless of exhaustion, all who survived the battle intact had to help "send up the dead" before treating minor injuries. The Tuzanchim believed that any who delayed this sacred duty faced a hideous afterlife. They built a huge funeral pyre for slain warriors, yet left the Laskomian soldiers and horses to rot where they had fallen, bitter over their first defeat. To avoid any further bad luck, they took no spoils from this battle. From its first volley to the last arrow, the entire struggle had lasted only twenty minutes. The warriors needed hours to tend to its aftermath.

When they were almost done, Klimgu faced his most dreaded chore of all, gathering Chotzan, Ganjaset, Kibak and his surviving captains.

"We must confer away from Lorgi, not worry him," said Ganjaset.

"What can we keep from him?" posed Chotzan, tilting his head and casting his eyes to the right. Fifty yards away, Lorgi stared at them, looking strangely offended.

"Let us calmly walk a hundred more paces away from him before talking," said one captain. "In case Lorgi turns out to be a *Karmchugtai*."

"Get Ziteng; he knows most about such things," said Klimgu.

"He's dead," said two captains at once.

Klimgu nodded and looked down, stung by the loss of a friend and a superb scout.

Thirteen men walked east along the shore, to get away from both Lorgi and the carnage. None wanted to believe that their prized rock dragon could be a *Karmchugtai*, possessed by a vengeful spirit, but this battle's rare bad luck implied otherwise.

Sniffing fresh trouble, Lorgi followed them, ignoring all pleas and commands to stop. Yawning, wiggling his ears and working his jaws, he tried to reopen his ear lids. But after all the trauma his sensitive ears had endured, their lids refused. Without working ears, all Lorgi could do was focus on anyone talking at the meeting. If they had been speaking Álukop, Lendish or Tundrish, then Lorgi might have caught much just from reading their lips. But he stood no chance in this new language, Tuzanchim. At the moment, all he could gather was who spoke, how much, and in what order. He would have to make sense of that information later.

"Ganjaset, go help Chumga occupy Lorgi while we confer," said Kibak.

"What?" said Ganjaset. "I am lead captain, Third-in-command!"

"Were," said Kibak.

"I have ridden with this quiver as long as you. Who will support me staying?" Ganjaset looked to the others. None dared meet his eyes, but none disputed Kibak. So the former lead captain left to do as told.

But Lorgi refused to let anything distract him from their meeting. He knew it was deadly urgent.

Powered by his first success, Kibak tried a second, much bolder move. "Time to regroup, pick a new leader and a safe route home."

The captains guessed Kibak would emerge in that role.

"You ride ahead of yourself," said Klimgu, looking offended.

"I hope not," Kibak answered. "We have just seen that result."

"Here comes Lorgi," shouted Ganjaset. "None can get through to him. The battle must have destroyed his ears."

"Or he is no longer possessed," said one captain. "No more *Karmchugtai*, just a big, dumb animal, now that his demon has completed its revenge."

"Never call Lorgi that again!" yelled Klimgu. "And nothing is completed. The Laskomians will see this battle as a draw—and return in force. You must be gone by then."

"You?" asked Kibak, feigning surprise at Klimgu's resignation.

"I will stay and tend the doomed, too injured to ride. If you try to carry them, they will die anyway. But first they will slow you down, inviting a massacre."

"No, Klimgu!" yelled Chotzan. "Ride with us."

Shaking his head, Klimgu raised his left hand. "I will hinder the Laskomians if I can, to give you time. Learn all you can about our prize on your way home. When gifting Lorgi to the Vazuk, tell of my sacrifice. Let no one suffer his anger for my mistake. Go now."

"My scouts and I will assist you," said Ganjaset. "Our mistake too."

"No!" yelled Klimgu, smacking him on the shoulder, but eying Kibak. "Chotzan, you must lead. Kibak and his scouts did their best, as always. Yet like me, he chose the wrong path. But make him your Second anyway. May his nerve bring you grand luck. For balance, make Ganjaset your Third. His caution would have saved us today, if only we had listened. All who can still ride must leave at once, and never return to this cursed lake. But that alone will not keep you alive. Expect the Laskomians to give chase, or wait again at some point east of here. Good luck to you all. *Guyat!*"

11: Words, Winds & Fires

Chotzan led the surviving 400 east at a brisk trot, but their pace steadily sagged. By sunset, exhaustion forced a halt. Knowing it would use half their remaining food, he insisted that all eat a good meal. Like Klimgu before him, he gambled on a few small supply sources cropping up along the way home. Full stomachs kept limbs fit for battle, minds sharp, and a leader popular, at least until hunger returned. If not for Kibak shadowing him, Chotzan might have rationed the food. He eyed his new Second like the horizon—a source of both trouble and hope. Like most, he thought Kibak should have waited for Klimgu to offer his own resignation before requesting a new leader.

Wondering how things might have turned out if Kibak had scouted the south side instead of Ganjaset, Chotzan envisioned the latter as his loyal Second, and a shamed Kibak with no rank at all. Ganjaset had more leadership and battle experience, as well as tact. But Kibak's superior scouting and boldness had saved him on this day. Yet not even he could have scouted far enough to have found the Laskomian trap before it was too late.

Much preferring a reserved Ganjaset to an impulsive Kibak, Chotzan began pondering ways to neutralize or rein in his ambitious new Second. Kibak's greater openness, confidence and boldness made him more popular among the warriors. Yet Kibak could not speak Tundrish with Lorgi. Anything else that might humble the new Second greatly appealed to Chotzan, still grieving over the loss of many friends in the battle, Klimgu's sudden fall, and struggling to adjust to his new responsibility as leader of the whole quiver. Chotzan had enough to worry about without Kibak nipping at his heals.

At sunrise, Chotzan woke with a leader's headache, dreading some of the tasks before him. Sensing that pain, Lorgi cured him by spinning his dragon eyes. Too curious to mind his own business, Kibak stepped close beside his new leader and fell under the same spell. Happy the new skill seemed to work better each time he tried it, Lorgi smiled, forcing all who looked at him then to do the same. Mesmerized, both men fought a potent urge to sleep. Struggling to rouse himself, Chotzan finally yanked himself away from the healing dragon eyes, shaking his head and stretching his sore limbs. In the next moment, he forced everyone up. Still fearing a Laskomian attack, none argued with him. Twenty minutes later, the group left at a fast trot.

The handful who knew any Tundrish hovered by Lorgi, speaking what they liked to call the *ice tongue* or *dragon-speak* with him all day. While enjoying the attention, he really just wanted to learn more Tuzanchim, guessing he would have to travel with these steppe warriors for some time. Ganjaset and Chotzan easily conversed in Tundrish with Lorgi, raising their status in the group daily. Jealous and desperate, Kibak employed an old, little-used Tuzanchim custom to "rebalance his ride." Downing a full cup of a highly distilled liquor, he approached Chotzan and Ganjaset, neither of whom seemed eager to talk with him at the moment.

"Ganjaset, my friend, I have a stallion of a favor to ask," said Kibak, smiling.

"We can smell your fortitude," laughed Chotzan. "But will you remember any of it when the liquor departs?"

Ignoring the slight, Kibak smiled harder. "Ganjaset, teach me Tundrish, and I will trade ranks with you." Kibak extended a hand for him to grasp and seal the agreement.

"What?" gasped Chotzan. "We should honor Klimgu's last wishes."

"He stalls death. We ride to success," said Kibak.

Stunned, the two men stared back, begging explanation.

"Well, I just hate being left out! I want to be able to talk with Lorgi, too. Teach me Tundrish, tongue of the magic rock dragons."

"Can it be worth so much to you?" asked Chotzan, surprised.

"Yes." Kibak nodded. "Yes."

"How much did you drink?"

"Why are you making this harder for me?"

"Are you sure about this?" Ganjaset finally asked.

Kibak nodded, smiling but impatient.

"I will gladly teach you, when I'm not speaking to Lorgi myself."

"*Gánsi!*" shouted Kibak, grabbing and shaking his hand.

"But you need not trade rank for this favor," said Ganjaset.

"You already agreed, so it is done," nodded Chotzan, eying both of them.

"Now I am happy!" laughed Kibak. "It will be well worth it."

"It will be interesting," laughed Chotzan, fighting to contain his joy.

The shrunken group of about 400 traversed the heart of the Laskomian Plains. Swarms of mosquitoes, grasshoppers, and tiny, nameless pests harassed them near any water, be it a pond, stream, or well. Typical of summer in this area, the sky grew violent thunderheads swelling to monstrous heights. Darkness prevailed as clouds took possession of the sky. The heat made Lorgi ill, barely able to stay awake.

"Walled town to southeast!" yelled a returning scout.

"Out of our way, but with any luck, it may stall our hunger," said Ganjaset.

"Or satisfy revenge," said Kibak. "Close enough to have supplied our foes at the lake."

Agreeing with a silent nod, as Klimgu would have, Chotzan led the group swiftly to the landmark. What the scout had discounted as a town actually proved to be a walled city of at least 10,000 people. Warriors only used the false diminutive to remind each other of greater challenges faced in the past. Miles of ripe grains surrounded its pale grey walls and twelve towers. The group halted—in battle formation—only 500 yards before the city's main gate. Chotzan sent warriors to open it, scouts to circle around the walls, and volunteers to scale over them and test the city. Still smarting from Lake Gabriska, none debated his caution.

"Too strange," said Ganjaset. "No banners. Silence. A burnt smell, yet all seems intact. Possibly they brace for the storm."

"Tuzanchim never touched this place," huffed Kibak.

"We will be wise to leave it so," said Chotzan.

"Another Laskomian ruse?" posed Kibak. "We need Lorgi's shaman skills."

"Lorgi, over here," Ganjaset waved vigorously to him. "He looks bad again, maybe from the angry weather. I doubt he can help just now."

All three men strained to smile, as Lorgi walked up to them, twitching his nostrils.

"You want something," said Lorgi.

"What can you sense about this city?" asked Chotzan.

Stretching to his full height, Lorgi scanned the panorama, sniffed every inch he could reach of the huge wooden gate and the stonework near it. Pounding the gate's center, he then pressed an ear to the ground for a full minute. Everyone kept silent twenty paces behind him, and many of them also put an ear to the ground. After Lake Gabriska, all had great respect for his sensory, as well as fighting skills. In fact they studied everything he did, down to the slightest twitch of an eye, ear, his tail or nostrils.

"Most of the people left two days ago," said Lorgi. "I think the last of them fled yesterday, burning what they could not carry. You won't find anything useful in there."

"You can tell all that?" gasped Chotzan, shaking his head.

"I'm an Álukoi. I could tell more if it were not so hot and a storm coming."

"Like I told you," said Ganjaset, nudging Kibak in the arm.

As warriors pried open the gate, volunteers returned only to confirm Lorgi's "shamaning." Everyone swarmed Chotzan, shouting opinions on what to do. Mindful of his tenuous new position, he dared not cut any of them off the way an esteemed leader might have. Turning to Kibak, he asked: "Why did they leave their city intact, including their fields?"

"Could be they had no time to burn, fleeing only a day ahead of us," said Kibak. "We might be able to catch them."

"We have no time, either," said Chotzan. "A Laskomian force still wants our blood."

"Then burn it all right now and move on. Fire brings starvation, the ultimate revenge."

"Telling the enemy we are here?" laughed Chotzan. "No. Let us ride straight to Uxanda before something else goes wrong."

"We need to burn something, to help get over Lake Gabriska."

"How stupid!" yelled Sijun. "Nothing will make up for that."

"Go tend Lorgi and the wagon horses," snapped Kibak, only to catch Lorgi staring straight at him with huge, sad eyes. Suddenly ashamed, Kibak bowed to both with arms folded, muttering a Tuzanchim apology.

"The spider shaman burned Lorgi's village," said Sijun. "We are nearly out of food. Some of those fields look ripe. I say harvest what we can today. Leave tomorrow with full bellies."

"Stallion of a plan!" said Chotzan, nodding to her. "*Gánsi*, Sijun."

"*Gánsi*, Sijun," echoed Kibak and Ganjaset."

"*Gánsi*," she smiled back.

"Why is everybody saying *gánsi* when it's not Tuzanchim or even Tundrish?" asked Lorgi, cocking his head while staring at her.

"You already know," laughed Sijun.

"Because it's easier to say than *tekursedim*?" guessed Lorgi.

"And holds better luck," said Sijun. "*Gánsi* for the word and its magic, Lorgi."

Twitching both his ears and nostrils, Lorgi studied the group as a whole. The battle at Lake Gabriska had shaken them far more than the one at the sorcerer's bluff. Having lost many things, they were gaining some traits that Lorgi liked. Though they still quarreled too much, it was less often, and less severe. What few provisions they still had they always shared equally. Despite their wounds, hunger and other hardships, they found more reasons to say *gánsi* each day.

"We are all hungry enough. But this whole empty city could be just another trap," yelled a captain. "We should leave now."

"Walls are easy to defend, and a welcome break from that stampeding wind," shouted Kibak. "It's getting too loud even to argue. Rest our wounded in shelter and comfort. We can torch the city when we leave."

"We can debate that later," said Chotzan.

"Perfect weather for a Devil's Broom," said Ganjaset. "Expect it."

"Enough with your weather," jeered Kibak.

"Enough with your fires," said Ganjaset.

Suddenly the sky's debate rendered any on the ground pointless. Furious, swirling clouds turned charcoal as they wrestled each other. Yet the air stayed hot. Lightning bolts shook the ground, spooking the horses. Sporadic volleys of hard rain pelted the land unevenly. The wind tripled in force, spinning a huge Devil's Broom in the west. Its funnel reached down to the ground, growing longer and more violent as it whipped east, devouring all in its willful path. Barely a minute ahead of it, the group poured into the city. Anything left behind became food for the wind monster. The tornado hit with a deafening roar, ripping the city's hefty wooden gate to shreds that vanished up into the monster. Again, Lorgi's ear lids slammed shut.

"Ganjaset was right," said Kibak, echoed by others.

"Again," said Sijun. "He has grown longer and wiser eyes—from talks with our magic rock dragon."

"*Gánsi.*" Ganjaset smiled, his status beginning to return.

Vanishing as swiftly as it had come, the beast left a zigzag swath of destruction. The group narrowly voted to stay the night. Chotzan allowed only twenty warriors outside the city at a time. All returned with full sacks of grain. Able or not, the rest took turns guarding the walls. At dusk, any food was divided and half of it consumed. Most slept in peace.

But at dawn, Chotzan met his first resistance since taking command. Some warriors ached to scrub the city, or utterly destroy it, no matter how long that would take. Those who had been against stopping at all now advised leaving it intact. Half favored burning just what came within easy reach as they left. For Lorgi's sake, Chotzan argued against any destruction, but put all choices to a vote. When it was done, he turned to pack his things, but Sijun stopped him.

"Vital decisions must never be left to tired warriors, especially when too many of them are men," she scolded. "Chotzan, you should have pressed your rank instead."

"I'm too new to press anything," said Chotzan.

"I'm too old to give bad advice," said Sijun. "Count the dents on your shield, your battle scars, the worry lines on your face, all hard-earned in serving Klimgu. Now exert yourself and lead!"

"I'm exhausted," said Chotzan. "Let them burn, if it will help them to get over Lake Gabriska, as Kibak says. The Laskomians have abandoned this city anyway."

"What about Lorgi?" asked Ganjaset. "No one asked him."

The three looked over their shoulders to find Lorgi right behind them, his head cocked and his ears high, expecting something. Kibak turned and gazed into the dragon child's eyes.

"Change my vote," said Kibak. "No fires. Stupid idea. Just leave this place now."

"Too late!" yelled Sijun. "But fools always gallop to disaster."

Just as a warrior reached to set a roof ablaze, Lorgi pounced, seizing the torch in his mouth. Immediately he spat it out, stomping out the flame with his paws. Chasing anyone wielding fire, he shouted "*Yahai!*" and punished all who ignored his call. Kibak and some others followed his example. Broken ribs, dislocated shoulders, myriad cuts and two severed hands finally earned Lorgi some enemies. Frantically, Chotzan herded everyone out of the city.

Yet seven hours later, they could still see a mile-high plume of smoke to the west. All that day, weary eyes interpolated columns of enemy lances far off among the high grass. Before the heat inevitably drove him to sleep, Lorgi also kept his eyes on the horizon. But like everyone else, he was too hot, tired and anxious to think, thus making the expedition ripe for another Laskomian surprise attack.

* * *

Klimgu survived the battle with only minor scrapes, but had lost half his warriors, horses—and his command. He comforted the dying until he became exhausted. Half of them expired that night. The next morning he tended the dead before treating the living, then fished the lake with no luck. All afternoon he laboriously moved survivors a scant mile away from the battlefield, always keeping weapons close and senses alert. The next day, his charges limped three miles, tracing the shore west and around to the north. A day later they made good use of the Laskomian's false camp. In a week, they began to recover. The enemy did not return. Seven bandaged warriors had Lake Gabriska all to themselves, and felt ready to leave it behind.

"I ride west to Twarejik," said Klimgu, to spur thinking.

"He will get a summons, just like others," said one man.

"Once my failure reaches the Vazuk," said Klimgu. "If I were to save him the trouble of chasing me down, and find him in good humor on that day, he might spare me. But make my life a tortured one."

"Will he make you a slave?" asked another man.

"Perhaps, but more likely just a shamed warrior," said Klimgu.

"Forever barred from rank or standing. No voice, no vote, invisible."

"There are worse things," said a third.

"After leading a full quiver—of the Empire's very best?" Klimgu muttered. "Assuming the Vazuk does not just execute me. No! Count my days as a Tuzanchim by how long it takes his summons to find me."

"A whole moon to reach Twarejik or any in the west," said the first man. "Maybe longer. If the Laskomians can ambush 800 of us, they certainly can stop a few couriers."

"What will all of you do?" asked Klimgu.

"Try to catch up with Chotzan, of course," said one.

"Far too late for that," Klimgu sighed.

"We have to try anyway," said the same man. "Good luck, Klimgu. All wish things could have ridden better for you, and for all of us."

"*Gánsi*, my friends, as the rock dragons say." Klimgu smiled, nodding to each man in turn. "Good luck to you all. But if things don't ride well for you, then journey west. Seek me out."

"What are you saying?" asked one.

"Fate has made me the Vazuk's enemy. If he becomes yours too, join me. But if you still serve him when we meet again, you will find my sword sharper than ever!" Mounting his horse, Klimgu added, "now to retrace the steps that brought us here."

"Take a new path," said one. "Why torment yourself?"

"Many reasons," said Klimgu. "To build, to find something…"

"What?" asked all of them.

"Ask when we meet again, when you tire of the Vazuk. Much could be better than what we know. I seek that, and you should, too. And you will not find me alone!"

12: Journeys

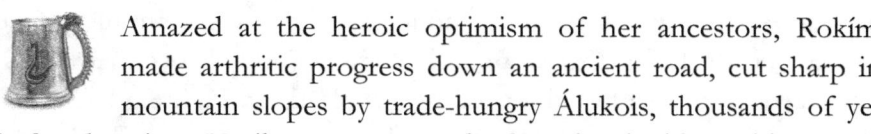 Amazed at the heroic optimism of her ancestors, Rokímba made arthritic progress down an ancient road, cut sharp into mountain slopes by trade-hungry Álukois, thousands of years before her time. Until ten years ago, the Stonelaw had kept this east-west route in passable shape. But the seer found this once-thriving artery broken or dissolved where erosion chose to focus. Another decade of neglect would erase all but its memory. Lately, adventurers, traders and even Álukois avoided the road, due to marauding packs of lowland thugs. Yet it was the only direct way to Rokímba's goal. She resolved to keep alert and sidestep whatever deadly *hyúlem* snares awaited the unwary.

Three more twists in the path finally brought her within sight of her goal—an ancient traveler's hollow, carved into the mountainside, half a stone's throw above the trail. A one-room cave, it made a fine place for a snowdragon to rest and cool down, or humans to take shelter in cold weather. A younger Álukoi would have completed Rokímba's trek hours earlier, but she had lived over 250 years. If she hoped to reach 300, she should avoid such arduous travel, especially in summer. Yet Serukeeba cried out for help. Tiefenbo still lay a good ten days east, but Rokímba began rehearsing her introduction, dreading the encounter. She had not spoken with Serukeeba since her disastrous first visit for Lorgi's hatching.

"We...everyone...I miss you," Rokímba said in a sweet voice. "Why move so far away? What if you have an emergency? Like now. Foolish pride. Oh, why couldn't I swallow my prophecy, or at least honey it like the others? Let mother and son enjoy a few years of bliss, before fate catches up with them. Why did Seri have to pick Tiefenbo, of all places?"

"It rests, apart from the world," Rokímba guessed her answer. "I love Tiefenbo; it loves me back. Golármon often said the same."

"Seri, we've both suffered enough! Forgive me. In spite of all, your son began life well, though his shell screamed doom." (Spirits, I hope he stays well.) "Come home to the Stonelaw, to civilization. Meet the Council of Elders. So many empty halls ache for a loving hall maker like you to bring one back to life. If none suit you—which I cannot imagine—then we'll all help you carve a new one. At least visit, so Lorgámon can see the Stonelaw. You owe him that."

Suddenly, Rokímba saw the hollow's door had been shattered. Inside, the headless corpse of a young adult, six-ton Álukoi in his prime sprawled, nearly filling the room. All of his claws had been extracted. Crystallized, turquoise blood coated the whole floor. Fighting back rage and nausea, Rokímba sought clues. She knew of this rare crime only in the far west. Human blood, hair, skin, rags, iron chips from weapons, and a horrid stench all screamed *lowland bandits*. Now the seer would have to delay her mission to deal with the crime. She longed for her old travel companion.

"Palitéa, I sorely miss you! Your comfort, solace, wisdom—and brute strength! How can I accomplish all the grim labor our ways demand, at my age?"

"One step at a time, no matter how you cut it," she imagined Palitéa's response. "Who was the victim?"

"With no head, we can only guess," said Rokímba. "I'll try to make imprints of his forepaws, but they have been so mutilated, who will recognize them?"

"No need. With so few of us about, we can guess. Who might be in the area?"

"Yómgolin?" wheezed Rokímba, rolling the stiff corpse onto its side so she could make the imprints. "No, this one's too heavy even without his head. I remember Zortríton wanted to hunt the spider wizard said to be brewing in the Dawnwood. If so, he did not get very far. A young champion, slain by lowlanders, while trying to help lowlanders."

"Don't think like that," Palitéa scolded.

"You have the best heart. Why didn't the plague take me instead? I have no family, and fifty years on you. What is fair in this world?"

"The quilt of the world is not yours to mend," said Palitéa. "Just do your best, and good will bloom. Serukeeba waits for you—a mend worth all your effort."

"No stores. Bandits picked this hollow clean. Now I'll have to scour the slopes for food, delaying me even more. Seri calls to me even as we speak. Her village cries out for help, too."

Fearing the killers might return, Rokímba barricaded herself inside for the night, filling the entrance with boulders. At daybreak, she buried the hollow and its victim forever with a rock avalanche. Álukois passing by in future would know the sign and not stop, lest ill spirits follow them, or tragedy repeat itself. Exhausted, she slept an hour in the shade before resuming her trek to the "Recluse of Tiefenbo," as Serukeeba had become known in the Stonelaw.

The next day, Rokímba descended the trail until it dissolved among gentle forested hills and glens. Every sound and sight called her east to the tundra and Serukeeba's village. But *hyúlem* scent reached her, matching what had defiled the traveler's hollow. Shadowing a stream south led the seer down to a pack of thirteen ruffians. As expected, she found them sitting around a campfire, arguing. A yard from the flames, Zortríton's severed head lay on its side, both eyes and all his teeth gone. The long, tapered jaw, yet wide-set ears told Rokímba it must be him. With only a few hundred snowdragons living at the time, all knew each other well. All but Serukeeba lived within the Stonelaw. Most attended the annual Winter Gathering every year.

"Zortríton was to be the next Golármon," said Rokímba. "And I will have to tell his father, his sister…and…and…"

"Everyone else," Palitéa added in her mind. "I'm sorry, Roki."

"Justice demands swift revenge, by any witness," muttered Rokímba. "Those *hyúlem* dregs must have surprised him. If they could slay a young champion twice my size, they'll make quick work of a withered old seer like me."

"You must strike first, like an avalanche," urged Palitéa. "For the next hour, you must be Golármon!"

"Absurd, but I know you're right."

Retreating upstream from the camp, Rokímba refreshed herself with a long cold draught and stretched every muscle for battle. Imagining herself transformed into one of the Álukois' greatest champions, she resolved to make every swipe, lunge, whip, bite, and roll count, and not rest until the crime had been avenged. Taking a huge breath, she charged into the murderers' camp. Ignoring all else, she cut their horses loose and sent them running.

"For Zortríton," she roared, slicing a man's head off with a forepaw. Amid frantic *hyúlem* screams, she kicked up enough dirt to squelch their fire. Encircling her, they pounded away with swords, axes, and maces. But Rokímba had already deprived them of what they most needed— surprise, mobility and fire. A steady barrage of iron struck the Álukoi's back. Yet by keeping her mouth shut and her vulnerable belly flat on the ground, she made it impossible for them to harm her.

Any man straying within reach of her tail paid with his life. The pack's leader held them together as long as he could. But when six lay dead, the others fled like rats. Chasing four down, Rokímba crushed them. Two others climbed adjacent pines. Though bleeding from cuts earned in their frantic ascents, those promised to hang on for a long time. Unable to pursue, the seer waited for them to fall or give up. Only the leader had escaped.

Duty, honor and justice required her to slay them all. Just then, Seri and Lorgámon called to the seer, and each other. Tiefenbo screamed to the Stonelaw for help. As the only one trekking in their direction, Rokímba *was* the Stonelaw, torn between duties impossible to fulfill. She could not punish all the bandits and reach any of the good people needing her in time to help even one of them.

The men in the trees held no weapons or tools. Rokímba made sure they would find nothing usable on the ground. She had never been any good at throwing, either for sport or need, but hurled stones up at them anyway. Each try seemed to reach closer, drew frightful cries from the thugs and made them climb higher. But Rokímba never hit either of them. Whining in Lendish, they begged for mercy, swearing to lead exemplary lives and never trespass dragon lands again, if only she would let them go in peace. Just as Rokímba gave up trying to hit them with stones, a gust of wind swayed the treetops. One man lost his grip and fell.

"One dead!" Rokímba shouted in Lendish. "One to go."

"Have mercy, noble dragon," pleaded the other, shaking and sweating. "I can pay much for it."

"Only with your blood. Do the world a favor. Fall. I have far nobler errands than tending *hyúlem* garbage. Fall. Or suffer and then fall."

"My cries will bring other thieves," he said.

"I think not," Rokímba laughed. "But you chose well. I may have to wait long to see you dead."

"You spoke of nobler errands. You will have to wait long indeed for me."

"Then I will hunt down and slay your kin, the whole plague of your line, until I meet you again and dance on your flat, red corpse."

"I have no living kin," said the man.

"Nor will you ever!"

Enraged, Rokímba considered felling the tree, a crime among the Álukois. But a sudden twinge of pain in her right side reminded the old seer of her limits. Returning to the camp, she dug a deep grave for Zortríton's head. After laying it to rest, she let out a long, high wail. She capped the grave with a huge boulder, on which she carved his name, the date according to the Álukoi calendar, and words of praise for the young champion. Severing the *hyúlem* heads, she set them atop their own swords in a circle, to remind both friend and foe that justice still walked the earth.

All during the grisly task, Rokímba kept wishing that the surviving bandit would flee, and urged him to do so with all the force of her mind. But this one proved either too clever or cautious. When all her other tasks had been done, Rokímba found him still gripping the top branches of the pine that had saved him. With a final curse, she had to walk away.

* * *

Serukeeba wobbled about, sniffing myriad hoof prints crisscrossing her battlefield. Her rescue party knew those had been left by Tuzanchim horses, but hoped she would not notice in her current state. All begged her to regain her health before seeking Lorgi, recalling the seer's doom prophecy. Without Serukeeba, her son would forever remain an outcast among his own kind. The villagers would do their best, but only Lorgi's own mother could raise him as a true Álukoi, teaching him what he must know to live as one. Finally, she acquiesced.

Ten minutes into what promised to be a slow, painful return home, the rescue party heard many horses rumbling behind them. Seconds later, a company of 200 Kitrian knights appeared atop the fateful hill. Only their blue and white surcoats revealed them as such, because their shields bore no insignia. No plumes, feathers or even the simplest ornaments dared adorn their helmets, scabbards, or any part of their gear. They carried no supplies. Whoever did so for them trailed far behind. All wore new helmets, chain mail and wielded the finest lances, swords and crossbows, but carried no other weapons or tools. Only knights so lightly equipped could ride with such speed.

"They must be on a desperate quest, indeed," guessed Weliben.

"Or seek immediate blood—revenge," said Glomin.

Suddenly the 200 charged. Serukeeba tried to stand to her full height, but her limbs refused. In no condition to argue with anyone at the moment, she sat back on her haunches, pretending to relax. Exhausted, her rescue party could only salute the knights, ask what they wanted and try to accommodate them.

"Weli, you had best speak for us," said Serukeeba. "Both my head and body feel soft as pudding. Pray those Kitrian knights are friendly."

"My specialty." Weliben smiled, raising a hand in greeting.

"Halt!" barked one in Lendish.

"We're not moving," said Weliben, surprised.

"Explain this," demanded a second knight, dropping the point of his lance barely a foot from Weliben. "Speak quickly! We ride on an urgent mission."

"So do we—and take mother's care with that!" shouted Weliben, jumping back. Half of a small balkotar shell dangled from the lance's tip. Only one back leg remained, still holding twenty moldy quills. All the Kitrians stared at Serukeeba, even when speaking to Weliben. A third knight dismounted. He reached for the shell, as if seeking to remove it from the lance.

"Don't touch it, anywhere!" yelled Weliben. "Poison in every quill to kill a horse."

"We know only too well," said their captain. "Do you also know what valiant fools dared battle these things, just upriver?"

"Yes, and she will take long to heal from it," said Weliben.

"What marvelous creature is this?" asked the captain, pointing to Serukeeba.

"I'm a person, not a creature," she wheezed back.

"Our beloved champion—she who dared," said Weliben.

"Impossible, even for a beast so grand," said the captain.

"Not for an Álukoi, but how is beyond figuring," said Weliben, shaking his head.

"We saw hundreds of these," said the captain, pointing to the balkotar shell. "Or pieces thereof, scattered by the river. Their tracks lead north, yet countless horse tracks lead south. Explain. Speak truth, and quickly."

"Álukois and their friends always do," said Weliben.

"I had best speak for myself now," Serukeeba coughed. "If the spiders had not outsmarted me, I might have slain them all."

Every knight rested his lance, opened his visor and saluted. Normally hiding all expression, they gazed in child-like wonder, shocked by their first encounter with non-human intelligence. Most knew Álukois only as myth. The Tundrites in Weliben's party had never seen knights of the lowlands, and studied them with nearly equal intensity. The villagers asked about the kingdom of Kitria to the southwest, while the knights asked all about snowdragons. All shared what they knew of the spider sorcerer.

"They took my baby!" moaned Serukeeba.

"We shall mourn him and avenge your loss," swore the captain. "The sorcerer's demise is our quest."

"My son lives, but the sorcerer ransomed him away," said Serukeeba.

"Then spare not a second," said the captain. "Though new, this one already owns a gruesome reputation, timing his deadlines to the last grain in an hourglass. Cruel as he is prompt, he carries out his threats and ultimatums in the most hideous ways."

Weliben's whole party glared at him for his stalling of the sorcerer. "Well, how was I supposed to know? We must have had Lorgi's miraculous luck, is all."

"We must be quick and lucky beyond stars, to see your son again— alive," warned the captain. "What were the madman's terms?"

"None. He means to turn my sweet baby to his evil will," moaned Serukeeba. "My Lorgi is so young, so innocent, so fragile."

"He does weigh nearly 400 pounds. His claws and teeth will cut through armor like it were buckskin," Weliben nodded as he told the knights. "Lorgi can outrun a wolf, dig like a bear, see like an eagle—"

"He is just a baby," said Serukeeba. "He has never tasted blood. My highest wish is that he never will."

"How old is your…child?" asked the captain.

"Only three," moaned Serukeeba.

"Making devil's work even quicker," sighed the captain. "We may be too late already."

"Some say an Álukoi cannot be spelled," said Glomin, looking to Serukeeba.

"But we face the most clever and wicked of sorcerers!" she yelled back at him, before turning to the captain. "This one moves his spiders like a general of the best lowland army."

"He destroyed Tiefenbo with his siege," said Glomin.

"Please, you must save my son. He answers to 'Lorgi' and speaks perfect Lendish."

"If we can defeat the sorcerer, we will return Lorgi to you," said the captain.

"You will be sweetly rewarded," promised Serukeeba.

"Great luck to all," shouted the knights, saluting her.

"And to you," she returned, echoed by her party.

"Wait—can you spare any of your Tundrites?" asked the captain. "I hear they make the best trackers."

"Not today," said Serukeeba. "Just follow the horse prints stampeding south. Even a drunken lowlander can track them."

"Seri…," murmured Weliben, raising an eyebrow.

"Oh, sorry, excuse me," she covered her mouth with a forepaw. "I meant no offense."

"None taken. We're all frightfully sober," assured the captain. On his signal, the whole company turned as one and rode south, kicking up plenty of dust and noise.

"They're no match for what they seek," said Glomin.

"Right now, we're no match for anything," added Serukeeba.

"Good luck if enemies do not find them first," said Birentak.

"And if we get home before evil finds us," said Kamwa.

"I say we're done with bad luck," shouted Weliben, with a firm nod and a stern look to the others. "We do our best and good will grow."

"Now you sound like old Palitéa," said Serukeeba.

"Don't try to cheer us up without smoked whiskey to fortify your words, Weli," scolded Glomin.

"He owes us a round just for that," said Birentak.

"My pleasure," laughed Weliben. "We'll pour it the minute we return, if they left us any."

* * *

Hours later, the Kitrian knights reached a massive funeral pyre below the sorcerer's bluff. Scattered everywhere leading up to the bluffs were hundreds of dead balkotars of varying sizes, many missing their upper shells, and most missing a few legs. Halfway up a trail leading to the top of the bluffs lay over 200 dead horses, mostly crowded together, all frozen in agony and terror. With their eyes bulging and mouths screaming, they seemed to have just fallen in a battle still raging on higher ground. Near the ashes of a house on top, the Kitrians found a solitary, mangled old human corpse, missing both ears and all of his fingers. At first the knights laughed that barbarians had done all their work for them. But a closer look revealed Tuzanchim arrows.

"Those villagers have no chance if the Tuzanchim find them, even with their dragon in tow," said one knight. "Not that we would either."

"Look. Prints just like a small version of the great beast," said another. "The Tuzanchim must have carried her baby off to the east."

"From what the villagers said, he might slow even the Tuzanchim," said the captain. "But whatever those barbarians take, they keep. And they will be far away by now."

"What can we do?" asked the first knight.

"Rejoice that our enemies fought each other," said the captain. "The Tuzanchim must have fled this place after heavy losses. And yet the Spider Sorcerer and his army have been broken. Sir Benek, be so good as to cut off the bastard's head. We can present it to the king along with any other proof of our adventure that is not poisonous."

"What of our promise to the mother dragon?" asked Sir Benek.

"Impossible," shouted another knight. "Look about, sir. Thousands of barbarians took her son. Tuzanchim!"

"Our first and last duty is to our king," said the captain. "That burden includes not starting a war that could only destroy Kitria."

"Then we never should have promised anything," said Sir Benek.

"True—had we known," said the captain.

Once the knights had gathered enough souvenirs for both themselves and their king, they left the way they had come. When they later rejoined their porters, the company made west for Kitria with great speed, inspired by an unspoken fear of the Tuzanchim. Unable to keep their word to Serukeeba, all of them muttered that Kitrian knighthood had lost its luster.

* * *

Lorgi awoke to a cloudless, brutally hot day on the vast Tuzanchim Steppes. Only the constant wind saved anyone. The Tuzanchim worshiped it in summer, and the sun in winter. Sparse clumps of gnarled, former hills gave eyes the only relief from an endless sea of blond grass perpetually bowing to the wind. The grass looked as if it had been here since the beginning of time, and would stay—unchanged—to the very end of it. To Lorgi, the reality stinging his eyes hardly qualified as land. Yet what horrified him gave the Tuzanchim joy and calm, welcoming them home—a rare treat for most of the warriors.

Fortunately, Chumga had installed poles and a tarp on his wagon to shade his unique passenger. Porzan and Sijun sat hunched over Lorgi, their faces wrung with concern as they kept applying wet rags to him. When these dried up and grew warm—a matter of seconds—they replaced them with freshly soaked rags. No matter how carefully applied, all disintegrated by the third or fourth time on Lorgi's hide. Chotzan, Kibak and Ganjaset rode beside the wagon.

"He looks bad," said Kibak. "Can the quill venom still be in him?"

"Porzan, have you really tried everything?" asked Chotzan.

"Everything possible here, which amounts to nothing," said Porzan.

"We're running out of things to put on his back," said Sijun. "Getting low on water, too."

"Porzan, have you finally learned what ails him?" asked Ganjaset.

"I can only guess: plague or some other horrible disease of the West. I do not know how to treat him."

"Treat him like a sick human," said Kibak.

"We have," said Porzan. "Nothing has worked so far."

"Then treat him like a horse," said Ganjaset.

"What?" gasped Chotzan. "We cannot leave him, even if he dies. Keeping him will bring no worse luck than we have already suffered."

"No, I did not mean just any horse, or to purge our luck," said Ganjaset. "We should treat him like a favorite horse. The one who knows your heart. The one you keep no matter what."

"We pampered him that way too," said Sijun. "But he is nothing like a horse."

"Then treat him like a favorite yak," said Chotzan.

"And we tried that too," said Porzan. "He just won't cool down. If Lorgi were human, he would die of his fever this hour."

"Is that how plague kills?" asked Chotzan in a low voice.

"That, or you start coughing up blood, or bleed from sores everywhere," answered Porzan. "Either way, a very painful and degrading way to meet death."

"Will others catch it from him?" asked Chotzan, looking ill himself.

"Perhaps, but that should have happened already. I know so little of the West's countless ailments. And of course nothing about Lorgi, so unlike...anything, east or west."

"He feels human," said Chumga. If a captain or leader had said that, it could be taken as a sign of weakness. But the old driver had no status to lose.

"He's going out again," shouted Kibak. "Can't you keep him awake?"

"We're trying!" yelled Sijun.

"Yell, jostle him," urged Kibak. "Lorgi, wake up!"

"Lorgi," shouted Chumga. "Lorgi want yogurt ball?"

"He ate the last of those yesterday," said Sijun.

"I know," sighed Chumga. "I just said that to wake him up."

"I'm not hungry," Lorgi mumbled. All looked at him with new foreboding.

"But you're always hungry, Lorgi," said Kibak, pasting on a false smile.

"No more. Heat makes me sick. Take me to a pond, a river, some woods, mountains, any place cool. I'll die if we stay here."

"He's right," said Porzan. "Whatever else ails him, Lorgi has a roaring fever. We must quell it very soon, or—"

"He's out again," said Sijun.

"Shake him," ordered Chotzan.

"We do every time," said Sijun. "See our bloody hands? And it never works anyway."

"*Yahai!*" shouted Chotzan, signaling the captains. Immediately they came to him. "Our prize dies unless we make haste for kinder land. We must escape this heat."

"Higher ground just north of here" said Ganjaset. "Hills with a few trees and cooler wind. A river too, if I can find it. I will scout, yes?"

"*Guyat*, quick!" nodded Chotzan. "We will follow as best we can."

"What of the Gran Vazuk, whose courier found us this morning?" asked a captain. "He will be expecting our gift to be brought to him with all possible speed."

"Let him wait!" yelled Kibak. "I have seen the Vazuk; there is nothing grand about him. He just sits in his palace, counting his plunder, belching venom and lunacy, tormenting his concubines and all the servants. He eats so much that he can no longer ride. If Lorgi dies, we dare not venture within a thousand miles of him. He would roast a chipmunk for dropping an acorn."

"Then we have no use for him!" yelled Sijun. "Let us ride west like a Devil's Broom—and slay any that pester us!"

Kibak smiled. Chotzan and many others laughed.

"Do we agree that our prize requires an urgent detour?" asked Chotzan.

"Not all will see it so," warned Sijun. "Many expect to arrive at the Vazuk's palace quickly. Idiots who cannot wait for rewards."

"Any who abandon our expedition forfeit its rewards," snapped Chotzan. "Let any who would debate me first take a beating from Sijun."

She nodded at the compliment. The captains chuckled nervously.

Chotzan led the group northeast toward higher ground at a fast trot. Kibak hovered close by Lorgi, monitoring his care. When the wagoners ran out of water, Kibak handed Sijun his own water bag. Seeing this, many others did the same, though fearing the whole group would run dry. If that came to pass, then Lorgi would only be the first of many to die. Porzan feared Lorgi had already gone beyond any hope of recovery.

Yet Ganjaset soon returned like a great hunter. He had found the river, and led the group straight to it. The instant they reached it, all immersed themselves to cool off, while the wagoners doused Lorgi with many gallons of cool water. When this failed to revive him, men hoisted Lorgi out of the wagon and into the river. In spite of wrapping their hands and arms in leather strips, most suffered cuts from their effort.

Stretching, laughing and splashing people with water, Lorgi seemed to recover. Yet he babbled in Tundrish and bits of Álukop about going home to his mother, friends, and village. He mumbled half-sentences about favorite foods, games, snowball fights, blizzards, swimming under the ice in winter, and a host of things far removed from the present reality. He did not focus his eyes or ears on anything, and seemed totally unaware of everything around him.

"Porzan," yelled Chotzan. "Lorgi suffers from a new delirium. Can he recover from this?"

"Probably, slowly, perhaps never fully, but—"

"Give me a simple straight answer for once."

"For once let me finish!" yelled Porzan, one of the few Tuzanchim not given to raising his voice. "It took Lorgi many days to get this bad. When a human becomes too hot or cold for too long, the mind breaks. We must keep him cooled for days before even guessing at recovery."

All that Lorgi tried to see kept changing forms, or vanishing and reappearing. For a moment, he saw warriors on horseback change into giant balkotars. Then men slowly approached on foot, focused on him. They kept talking, both to him and to each other, but Lorgi could not understand the words. He wondered if they planned to abandon him or worse. Might they try to slay him for his diamond claws, as lowlanders had been known to do? Suddenly fearing another gruesome battle at hand, he bounded up to the wagon and leaped into it with a loud crash.

"*Guyat!*" Lorgi shouted, rearing up and waving his forepaws. "Stay away, all of you!"

"But Lorgi, we are your friends," pleaded Kibak.

"What friends would take me away from home, to a land of death?"

Several men slowly approached the wagon. Lorgi bared his teeth, spread his claws, and whipped his tail high from side to side, ready to strike anyone that got too close. Knowing his prowess at the battle of Lake Gabriska, all of them backed away. The instant Lorgi looked at him, Chumga handed over the reins.

"I'm leaving this oven now! No one try to stop me. When Klimgu returns, tell him he should have taken me straight home in the first place."

"Our prize has gone mad after all," said Ganjaset, echoed by many others.

"Perhaps not," said Chotzan. "I wish Klimgu could return."

"If we do not present Lorgi to the Vazuk, and soon, then he will want our blood as well as Klimgu's," warned Ganjaset.

"The Vazuk can wait, as Kibak said," shouted Chotzan. "Everyone, follow Lorgi quietly at a safe distance. If he becomes amenable, humor him. If not, give him all the room he wants."

Lorgi fought for equilibrium, but the horizon kept tilting, undulating or warping. It shrank or stretched, pulling on his limbs, his tail, even his ears. Any sounds entering them took long to arrive, echoing, distorting and spinning around at wildly different tempos. They competed with frightful alien howls and low, rolling thunder. Visual images fought similar struggles, unable to keep anything close to their original forms. Lorgi only knew he was quite ill, and that little or nothing he sensed at the moment was real. Frightened and ready to pass out, he handed the reins back to Chumga.

"Please just take me north, up river to someplace high. Or shady. Or cooler."

"Of course," Chumga forced a smile. Looking over his shoulder, he saw Chotzan's nod of approval. "I am proud to help you, my friend. But Lorgi, please try not to fall asleep."

"Actually, I am trying to wake up from a terrible dream."

"Then don't close your eyes."

"I have to," said Lorgi. "It hurts too much to see."

With no one to cool him off, Lorgi quickly overheated and passed out. Chumga slowed down so the other wagoners could jump aboard and resume caring for Lorgi. A minute later, he seemed to revive, but did not recognize any of them. He growled, bared his teeth, swished his tail and waved his forepaws, threatening to strike if they did not leave his wagon. Most warriors stayed away from him, guessing the fever had at last cooked his brain, like a rare, diseased horse gone mad. The Tuzanchim had no remedy but to end such an animal's suffering. Finally, several men made the suggestion to Chotzan.

13: Tiefenbo Reborn

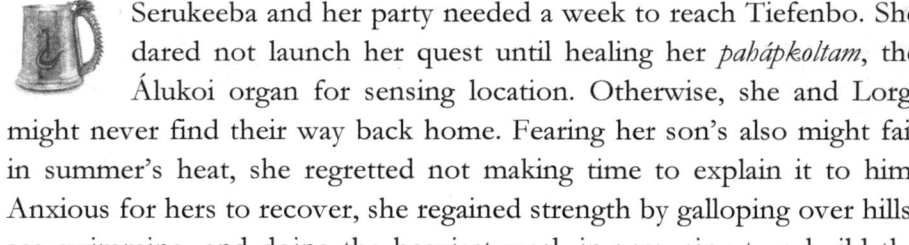 Serukeeba and her party needed a week to reach Tiefenbo. She dared not launch her quest until healing her *pahápkoltam*, the Álukoi organ for sensing location. Otherwise, she and Lorgi might never find their way back home. Fearing her son's also might fail in summer's heat, she regretted not making time to explain it to him. Anxious for hers to recover, she regained strength by galloping over hills, sea swimming, and doing the heaviest work in preparing to rebuild the village. Yet she refused to dull her claws.

Nature had designed them for traversing rock and ice. But since the dawn of writing, Álukoi claws had been used most often for war. Guessing hers could never be sharp or hard enough for the quest before her, Serukeeba took a break from her angst to survey the "new Tiefenbo." In two weeks, a high stone wall encased what aspired to become a major town—at this point no more than a large swath of level ground. None yet agreed on what to build where in the next incarnation of Tiefenbo. While others debated, Serukeeba took stock of her dwindling supplies.

"We still have enough to last the winter, right?" guessed Jinva.

"Not a long one, or another siege. The sorcerer erased years of work. I have no spent claws left to trade, and must keep all that I have sharp for enemies."

"Then how will you reward those Kitrian knights if they find Lorgi?"

"Gold, but hardly enough to outweigh an insult, considering."

"You said the Álukois had stopped trading in gold long ago, because it drove Lowlanders mad." Jinva looked confused.

"By law," huffed Serukeeba. "An easy one to obey, once the Stonelaw ran out of gold. Ask me again after we repay the Kitrians."

"Most villagers envy your wealth and your powers."

"Now I know how a typical castle lord feels. Buried in troubles, short in reach, ever in peril from forces beyond control. Yet envied by the naïve."

"The naïve need your help to break their impasse on how to rebuild. What to put where, and why."

"Not my debate. Please confine it to the solarium. Pour my best when all agree. Nothing but water before. I'm leaving at dawn."

"Are you really ready?" asked Jinva.

"Still too wobbly," said Ubwan, entering the pantry. "Need week more for heal."

"Yes—no!" said Serukeeba. "I only know that waiting any longer will just make it harder to find Lorgi. But *gánsi* for your concern. Good night."

"And great luck to us all," said Weliben, joining them. Once Serukeeba retired, he brought Jinva and Ubwan back to the solarium. "We're still in a snail's rut with it all."

"We must agree on something before she goes," said Jinva. "And build it true before she returns. Or we're all no better than royal leeches draining her hall of its stores."

Late the next morning, Serukeeba made her farewells. Some begged her to wait; others wanted to go with her. Politely refusing them all, she made everyone promise to rebuild Tiefenbo before she returned. This seemed impossible to most, who expected her back in weeks. Only Glomin thought she would be searching for months or even years. Marching off, Serukeeba had not gone more than 500 yards when an old voice called in her native Álukop.

"*Vat*, Seri—stop!" shouted Rokímba, just emerging from a strand of dwarf spruce a few hundred yards to the west of the village. "*Vat pyar Íye, komenónda myit!*"

"I must leave now—and quest alone," Serukeeba answered in Lendish, so that all understood. But as she faced the old seer, children raced out, surrounding both Álukois and welcoming them back to Tiefenbo.

"Can *now* wait just a moment longer, especially for one who has trekked so far to help? You, Lorgi, all Tiefenbo called to me, pushing me onward. Only tragedy delayed me."

Serukeeba froze, her ears and nostrils twitching with dread. Rokímba could only slow her down and spark conflict with anyone they met, due to the seer's loose tongue. But Rokímba had just fought a real battle, and recently lost several close friends. How Serukeeba knew, she could not say. At last, the two held common ground. Ignoring the past, she bounded over to the seer, the first adult Álukoi she had seen in three years. They rubbed muzzles, the snowdragon equivalent of a human hug.

"Seri, forgive my ill prophecy," asked Rokímba. "A mountain of apologies."

"You remembered."

"I forget only lesser things. So much has happened, mostly bad. Ten days ago I found Zortríton—ripped apart by bandits! Don't even ask. Palitéa died of the plague."

"But Álukois do not get plague," said Serukeeba nervously.

"They caught this one, so bad that most lowland kingdoms have not warred on each other this whole year."

"We had war enough here."

"They say a new sorcerer terrorizes lands all too close to here," warned Rokímba. "We must act before—"

"He's already been and gone," cursed Weliben. "Took Lorgi with him."

"NO!" gasped Rokímba. "How? Where? Why? How old is he now, three?"

"And four months," added Serukeeba.

"Is he healthy?"

"Fine, the last I saw him. Days before, I had nightmares of a falcon targeting him—for a giant balkotar. All Tiefenbo set to arms. I fought a whole army of them. But in the end…"

"How hard is his back?" asked Rokímba.

"Superior for his age. I guess that means he will be small as an adult."

"Never mind that now. What of his claws and tail spikes?"

"Everyone can vouch for their destructiveness," said Serukeeba. "But he is just a baby. How can he survive without me?"

"Together, we will find him sooner. But I'm far too exhausted, today. May we start tomorrow?"

"I travel much faster alone," said Serukeeba. "You cannot help that way."

"Maybe you're right," admitted Rokímba, with a slump. "But I'm good with planning."

"I've no time for that either."

"Spend a little now or waste much later," warned the seer. "Your path is clouded. I must help you sift through it. Tell me everything. Then tomorrow all will become clear."

Though leery of the seer, all the villagers agreed with her on this point. They said nothing, but Serukeeba read it in their eyes.

"Alright," she sighed. "You can watch over Tiefenbo, oversee its rebuilding, and reward the Kitrian knights if they bring back Lorgi."

The two Álukois spent the afternoon in Serukeeba's library, talking and studying maps and books. Everyone took part in a farewell dinner, after which Ubwan served mint tea, generously graced with honey and spirits to ensure that all slept well that night. She gave a cup to every adult villager, while Jinva and Weliben served gallon-sized mugs to the Álukois.

But Rokímba sipped only half of hers before excusing herself to step outside. More than nine hours past noon, the sun still gripped the horizon, in no hurry to end a long summer day. Rokímba limped to the top of the hall's hill, oblivious to a dozen worried villagers trailing after her. Standing to her full height to sniff the air, she scanned the landscape.

"What's the matter?" asked Nuwak, scowling at her.

"Don't worry," Rokímba smiled. "I do this often."

"Just tell us," demanded the boy. "We'll find out anyway. If something bad is going to happen, the sooner we know, the better."

"What is it?" asked Serukeeba, with the same tone.

"Do you sense anything new, different?" asked Rokímba.

"No, thank the Skies! The last time I did, terrible things...." Serukeeba broke off, swallowing and shaking her head like a human.

"Expect a visitor," said Rokímba.

"No!" shouted Serukeeba. "They bring only bad fortune."

"Visitor from where?" asked Kamwa, joining them atop the hill.

"By land," answered the seer.

"And...?" prodded Kamwa, whipping the air with his hands.

"From the east, or maybe the south," said Rokímba.

"That certainly narrows it down," said Glomin, joining them.

In a minute, the whole village arrived at the top of the hill, all of them suddenly looking to the south and demanding to know what the seer foresaw.

"Not yet," laughed Rokímba. "Tomorrow."

"What can this ill-timed visitor want?" asked Serukeeba.

"He seeks…something," pondered the seer.

"Whether the fool is a lost traveler, a prince or a thief, I expect you get rid of him the minute he's fed—outdoors," ordered Serukeeba. "Don't let him near my hall."

The next morning, all turned out to see their champion off. Serukeeba made a quick, group farewell, fearing she would pay dearly for the slightest delay. Yet once again, she marched only 500 yards before halting. Scanning the hilly southern horizon, she eyed a tiny speck slowly making its way down toward the village, and stood up to her full height for the best view. Rokímba hobbled to her side. Unable to stand as tall or see quite as far, the old seer could not find what worried Serukeeba. But a minute later, a lone rider came into her view. When he reached fifty yards closer, all Tiefenbo saw him. The two Álukois glanced at each other, their ears twitching with pure curiosity.

"Your visitor has arrived, only too promptly," huffed Serukeeba.

"So now he's *my* visitor?" asked Rokímba.

"You predicted him; he arrives. Next time, predict Lorgi galloping home."

"I'm a seer, not a sorcerer!"

"With a limp and creaking joints. In no shape to quest."

"I strained my whole body pretending to be Golármon. Be glad I got here at all. Same with *our* visitor. And you'd be foolish to reject any help offered, even from a flea."

The last rider Tiefenbo had seen was the spider sorcerer. This one controlled his horse with nothing but a quiet voice most of the time. Both rider and horse looked smaller, yet vastly more capable than the sorcerer and his steed. This pair moved lightly, as one. Keeping his telltale bow and a full quiver ready for immediate use, he also rode like a Tuzanchim. More than 1,000 yards away, he could not be mistaken for anything else. A lone barbarian warrior, traveling at anything less than a gallop, made no sense to anyone in Tiefenbo or any point west of it.

"Neither a lost traveler nor a thief," said Rokímba.

"He is both," huffed Serukeeba.

"Tuzanchim," gasped Weliben. "Why?"

Everyone ran to join the Álukois.

"Pure trouble, and we've already had our fill here!" growled Serukeeba.

"He has his own woes," said the seer. "Yet fate brought him here."

"What can he possibly want—directions?" Serukeeba pointed her snout at the intruder. "We have nothing here but a wall. Maybe all he has is the plague."

"Seri, please give him a chance," asked Rokímba. "No one say a word. Don't even move for the next minute. I'm getting something from him."

"I'll get something from him! If he knows anything about my baby."

"He does, but it will be long work to get it out of him."

"I'll squeeze it from his breaking bones in a minute!"

"Seri!" Rokímba scolded her. "He does not even speak a language we understand. He has traveled quite far. And lost much, too. Be glad he has even reached here alive."

"How can you know all that?" asked Serukeeba.

"I'm an old seer, remember? Trust me and be patient. Truth needs time."

"What if Lorgi does not have all this time?"

"That rider has met your son," Rokímba grabbed the mother's forepaws in her own. "We need him—healthy. He holds much that you need to know. Help us to work with him."

"But I don't want to work with him or any other savages. I just want my Lorgi back."

"As we all do," said Rokímba. "That man will help."

Klimgu made a very awkward introduction, only able to speak Tuzanchim. For a long, tense moment, the villagers scanned the southern horizon, expecting a barbarian horde to suddenly descend upon the village. With clumsy pantomime, smiles and nods, Klimgu tried to show that he came alone, in peace. Assuming Serukeeba to be the town's leader, he presented her with a necklace made of leather and bear claws. For the

Tuzanchim, such a gift spoke courage, strength, and generosity, conveying great honor to the recipient. Yet anything made from animals could only horrify an Álukoi. Despite Klimgu's smiling and nodding, Serukeeba was slow to respond. Only after much prodding from the villagers did she accept the gift. Directly she handed it to Weliben.

"Thank you," Weliben said to the warrior.

"Tang...ju," Klimgu tried to respond. "*Tekursedim?*"

"Thank you," Weliben repeated.

"Tang kyu," Klimgu struggled to improve his pronunciation.

"You're welcome. Welcome to Tiefenbo, or what's left of it."

"Welkim?" Klimgu half-asked, puzzled. Turning to Serukeeba, he nodded. "*Gánsi.*"

Both Álukois twitched their ears in shock. Everyone gasped, wide-eyed, looking to Rokímba for explanation.

"Patience," she implored.

"What else does he know?" asked Serukeeba. "Where is my Lorgi? LOR-GÁ-MON?" Holding a forepaw four feet off the ground, she stared hard into Klimgu's eyes, barely a foot from her own. "You...see...Lorgi?"

"Lorgi...*hai!*" he answered with a smile, a vigorous nod and more pantomime.

"Don't forget I told you so," nudged Rokímba.

"Maybe he also knows about the sorcerer," said Glomin.

All Tiefenbo vied for Klimgu's attention, straining to describe the sorcerer who ransomed Lorgi. Outmatched in the frenzy, most of the children quietly watched. Klimgu tried to see and hear everyone shouting at him, but gave up, shaking his head. All he got from their efforts was an image of a tall, old, bearded man on a horse—nothing remarkable by itself. Only when Nuwak produced a balkotar shell did Klimgu begin to understand.

"*Yahai!*" he shouted with raised hands.

Grasping the dull beige wool of Brogan's shirt, Klimgu then brushed the mane of his horse, to suggest its color. Gesturing to Weliben's graying hair, Klimgu pretended to paint spots on his horse to better describe the one belonging to the sorcerer. He pantomimed a terrified old man stroking his beard. Grabbing his quiver in one hand, he pointed to the arrows with the other. Holding up both hands, he flashed all his fingers four times, then rolled his hands around each other and flashed all his fingers once again (a Tuzanchim signal for 40 times 10) and pointed to the balkotar shell, to show 400 of the beasts.

"What about them?" asked Serukeeba, motioning with a forepaw.

Klimgu pantomimed fire and smoke.

"The beard-man, what of him?" asked Weliben, gesturing.

Klimgu lifted his bow in response.

"Dead?" asked Glomin, acting the sorcerer's demise by arrow.

"Hai!" smiled Klimgu, nodding. All but Serukeeba cheered that news.

"He knows too much to be innocent in Lorgi's regard," she said.

"We must work with him, Seri," said Rokímba. "Fate sent him."

"Only after he's had a bath," said Jinva.

"Thank you, Jinva," said Serukeeba.

"Thank you—*Gánsi*," said Klimgu, smiling at his success. The villagers applauded.

"Hold just a moment," shouted Serukeeba. "Before blindly offering hospitality, think what the Tuzanchim are best known for, beyond superior riding skills." She paused long enough to make eye contact with everyone. "They steal horses by the thousands. They fight to the death, taking no prisoners. They pillage and burn without mercy. And they commit another crime that all human women and their loved ones dread. The Tuzanchim produce nothing. Help no one. There is no good in them. They just take all they can carry and destroy the rest. Be mindful what evil you welcome into our village."

"This is just one tired, desperate man," said Jinva.

"A scout," warned Serukeeba. "He must not see anything of value. He can sleep outside."

"BIG meeting tonight!" shouted Ubwan.

Everyone would have to decide which of Tiefenbo's three languages Klimgu should learn—Tundrish, Álukop, or Lendish with a Delfinian accent. Like most warriors, he remained illiterate. Sorely missing his Tundrish-speaking captains, he still recognized that language when he heard it. Now more than ever, he regretted never having taken the time to learn any. At the town meeting, he gestured, pantomimed, and drew pictures in the air. Yet people garnered very little from all his efforts, except his frustration. Because this concerned everyone, even the children voted, resulting in a tie between Lendish and Tundrish. After a short debate, a second tally earned the same result. Jinva, Ubwan and even Rokímba suggested sleeping on it, but Serukeeba refused.

"Who can spend the time needed?" she asked, angry. "Look at him. He cannot even write his own name! He will be the slowest pupil, and we have no time for that."

"Then we best waste no more arguing," said Jinva. "Change my vote back to Tundrish. At least the sound of it seems familiar to him. Curious."

"Change mine too," said Weliben. "Jinva know best."

"Fine!" snapped Serukeeba. "And who can have such motherly patience? Whoever can suffer the thankless task, let her—or him, or all who try—let them choose the language."

"If nobody else offer," said Ubwan, "then I teach him Tundrish." Smiling at Birentak, she added, "You can help. But how teach wild horse man? How make nice so learn?"

"Leave him to me," said Jinva. "My rolling pin works on the best of them. We can also show him some manners and hygiene."

Tiefenbo exploded with laughter. Children mimicked Klimgu's pantomimes. The whole village had a round of fun at his expense, yet he resolved to weather the insults. An impossible feat for a warrior, but Klimgu kept smiling. He never planned to spend much time in the strange village anyway. At this point, he felt strong enough to tolerate anything that brought him closer to his goal. But it pained him to think what might become of Lorgi, Chotzan, Ganjaset, Sijun, and everyone in his former quiver. He also marveled at how this tiny, defenseless village at the end of the world managed to survive. Its people seemed to know nothing of war, famine, drought, plague, horses, or the rest of the world. Yet every one of them spoke at least two languages. And they had something not to be found in Klimgu's world. Peace.

Within days, Klimgu no longer missed the dry wind, bleak diet, constant moving, battling and arguing of his homeland. All could see the change in his face, as the lines softened and he smiled more and laughed.

Once he let go, Klimgu began to pick up the new language much faster. To boost his progress, everyone agreed to speak only Tundrish while Klimgu stayed in Tiefenbo. Rokímba did not know that tongue either, and so was forced to learn it as well. Despite the seer's advanced years, all assumed she would acquire it much faster than a human, especially an illiterate barbarian. Klimgu proved them wrong. All but Serukeeba cheered his progress, as well as the old seer's eagerness to take on a new challenge. Gathering everyone in the solarium after breakfast one morning, Serukeeba stood by the entrance. All guessed her words.

"More than a week has passed, two people are quickly learning Tundrish, and all of us are healed from what physical harm the world had thrown at us," said Serukeeba. "This morning is perfect for travel, so I'm leaving. Now. Please let no one try to stop me."

"Wait," begged Jinva.

"I've done far too much of that already," said Serukeeba, stretching her limbs for what she knew would be the longest journey of her life. The whole village tagged along as she began marching south. Yet again, only 500 yards into her quest, a new voice called her to a stop.

"Wait. Stop. *Yahai!*" shouted Klimgu. "You need me scout."

"No, *tang-ju*," huffed Serukeeba, mimicking his accent.

Jinva frowned, shaking her head, with hands on hips, as if to say *"Shame, Seri."* Rokímba slumped, with her ears drooping. Everyone looked disappointed in Serukeeba.

"Many bad wait for you, to east. Bad land, bad water…bad people," warned Klimgu, scowling and shaking his head.

"Of that, I have no doubt," laughed Serukeeba.

"Many more danger wait you," Klimgu said in his still-broken Tundrish. "Any go there need help. Even whole army. Even big you! So I be your scout. Best scout. Find Lorgi much faster."

"No," huffed Serukeeba. "I do not trust you."

"You need me!" Klimgu shouted, outraged, yet fearful at the same time. Shaking his head, he scowled at the ground, before glaring at Serukeeba. The budding villager within him struggled against the warrior. Refusing help, especially on a perilous journey, was a great insult among the Tuzanchim. It could also bring terrible luck to the traveler.

"NO!" roared Serukeeba. "We do not need you. We only need our Lorgi back home."

"Not find him without me!" yelled Klimgu, in a firm voice that none in Tiefenbo had heard from him before. "Only fool throw away help on danger hunt. Fool not live long in bad land."

"So now we have threats and insults," said Serukeeba. "Only proving that you can take the savage out of the Steppe, but you can never take the Steppe out of the savage."

"I want to help you, help Lorgi," implored Klimgu. "Much, much bad to east. I ride, I live long in east lands, bad lands. I know them best. Without know, land kill you. Yes, even big you!"

"He's right, damn it," said Weliben. "None of us trust him either, Seri. But we need every helping hand, and don't care what else he may be up to, so long as we get Lorgi back. The Stonelaw is never going to come through. The last time you went off alone, look what happened to you. Buried in balkotars and a doll's thread from death."

"Seri, at least give him an hour to pack," asked Jinva. "In fact, two might save you a whole day down the trail. Best yet, plan your route today and leave tomorrow at dawn."

Serukeeba blew a long, hard breath through clenched teeth. "All right. One hour. Not a blink more. And not one word from anyone to delay me after that."

Yet Klimgu had what he needed in minutes. Impressed, Serukeeba rallied Tiefenbo for yet another round of farewells. Just as the Álukoi and her scout turned to leave, Jinva thought of something Klimgu might need and ran back into the hall to fetch it. That made others do the same. Thanking everyone with a smiling "*gánsi*," Klimgu politely refused most of the items they suddenly offered. He had to spare his horse the weight, and whatever remained of Serukeeba's patience. The pair finally left at noon.

"Wait!" shouted someone.

"Do *not* look back; pretend to be deaf," ordered Serukeeba.

Klimgu nodded, unsure what she really meant. But he dared not ask.

Suddenly Brogan caught up with them and ran around in front of Serukeeba to stop her. In an instant, Nuwak stood beside him, followed by Sirwan. Gasping for air, Brogan asked, "Weliben wants to know who will be in charge of what."

Turning around and sitting back on her haunches, Serukeeba pondered her best answer. Seeing this, the whole village charged out towards her. Laughing but frustrated, she shook her head like a human. "Very well. Jinva's in charge of my hall, as always when I'm away. Put Glomin in charge of rebuilding; it will be the best thing for him and the village. Have Ubwan be in charge of meetings, Rokímba for warnings and visitors, and Weliben of everything in general. I'm in charge of leaving. Good bye."

With that, Serukeeba turned and began marching south once again. Voices called out, but she closed her ear lids. She and her guide walked in silence until well beyond sight of Tiefenbo. Only then did she reopen them. She began conversing with Klimgu in Tundrish, not out of friendship, but the need to teach him the language. That much Klimgu knew instantly.

Yet as understanding grew, Serukeeba's animosity shrank. This warrior had traveled countless miles to find Lorgi's home. Since the moment he had arrived, Klimgu had shown nothing but respect for Serukeeba. Yet he refused to be intimidated by her. He expressed a consistent, genuine desire to help her find Lorgi. Once Serukeeba grasped this, she accepted him. Neither of them could foresee the consequences of their budding friendship.

14: Uxanda

 A wind-whipped sea of tall, yellow grass stretched to the horizon in every direction. Teasing the eyes, it never ceased rippling, tossed one way, then another by fickle air currents. Scattered remnants of ancient hills broke the monotony in places, but flat ground defined this land. Bunches of low, twisted shrubs, every one of them holding countless tiny berries, gripped the dying hills. Crimson sparkling in the sun, the famed bloodberries of the Steppes called to anyone bold or foolish enough to try them. Yet thousands of stinging needles guarded the tart-sweet hallucinogen. No trees, large animals, or water could be found anywhere within eighty miles. Only the steppe grass thrived here, ever whispering to the wind, oblivious to all but fire itself. From this, Uxanda magically rose like a flat, rust-red island, out of a golden sea.

Five miles away, the ancient Tuzanchim capitol revealed her armor. Massive sandstone walls, twenty-five feet tall and five miles long, formed each side of a giant square. Rising fifteen feet above all that, Uxanda's towers held pointed gold tile roofs, huge blood-red banners, and sharp crenellations looking like angry teeth waiting to devour whatever came too close. Twelve Great Towers soared twice as high, four of them anchoring the city's corners, the rest standing in pairs to frame the four Grand Gates of Uxanda. She needed a thousand guards to defend her long flanks. But a natural oasis, the city asked nothing of the land. Since her birth some 1,200 years before, Uxanda had never fallen to siege. None had dared to attempt it in over two centuries. Whoever ruled here also ruled the Steppes, the Continent's middle, and east-west trade.

Despite Lorgi's state and everyone's suffering, Chotzan dared not try entering Uxanda without permission. Stopping his parched group three miles northwest of the city, he stood atop Lorgi's wagon, aching to see a rider issue from one of Uxanda's Grand Gates. Sijun found Chotzan's stance and expression all too much like Klimgu's, atop the same wagon during the battle at Lake Gabriska—a bad omen. Yet she smiled when he noticed her concern. This unique city always sent a courier out to any visiting quiver, large or small. With luck, in an hour or two, the same courier would return bearing an imperial clearance, allowing that group to enter the capitol. Humbled after twelve empty minutes, Chotzan stepped down to meet with his captains.

"How long must we wait?" asked Ganjaset. "Do their sentries sleep in the towers, or do they ignore us, as if we are hostile foreigners?"

"It debases any capitol when it invites such questions," said Kibak. "I do not care for Uxanda. Nothing but brick, depravity and insult."

"It seems not to like us, either," said Ganjaset.

"No matter. All must take great care while we are here," intoned Chotzan. "Everyone listen well. When they finally *do* send a rider, we are a united quiver. Speak nothing of our poison arrows, what few remain. Only Ganjaset, Kibak and I will meet the Gran Vazuk—at first. Sijun, Chumga and Porzan can present Lorgi. All others must hold back, yet show pride in our triumph."

Ganjaset shrugged. "What of Klimgu, the spider shaman, the Laskomians?"

"Say only that we fought hard to bring our prize home to His Greatness," said Chotzan. "Ask nothing until he receives Lorgi. Discuss what draws his curiosity. Only then do we air our needs, unless the Vazuk asks first."

"He won't. He doesn't care," said Kibak. "We must explain Lorgi's needs at once, before the old yak can dismiss us."

"The old yak?" snickered Ganjaset.

"Put a grey beard and coat on a yak, take away the heart, the dignity, and you will have our current 'Grazuk,' the most absurd ruler of our time," said Kibak, with a quizzical nod. "But alas, how long can such a wonder endure?"

"You taunt death itself!" gasped Chotzan. "Why?"

"Forget my words," said Kibak, "that we all may live longer."

"Messenger," yelled Sijun, pointing to Uxanda.

"Good! Let us meet him half-way," shouted Chotzan, signaling the group. "Everyone smile. Ride tall; show pride. We have achieved a great deed!" He tried to lead by example. Yet in a somber tone, he added, "But hold quiet while I greet the Vazuk's courier."

"Very strange, nothing like the couriers I remember," said Sijun. "Surely not one meant for us."

"We'll know in a minute," said Chotzan. "Ganjaset, Kibak, ride with me twenty paces ahead of our group."

"What is it—the sister-in-law from Hell?" asked Kibak.

"An apparition, a nightmare from eating too many bloodberries," laughed Ganjaset. "Bad bloodberries."

"Behave yourselves!" scolded Chotzan. "We must deal with...*it?* Human or not. Our success depends on good will. Maybe it is not riding to us at all, and we are only in its way."

A pale, bald-shaven man in his 30's rode up, stopping barely a yard from the three dust-covered leaders. An anemic mustache and a perpetual smirk stood out on his bloated face. He still rode like a Tuzanchim, but could not be mistaken for one. Wearing perfume and lavish garments of imported silk, he carried no bow, yet a quiver filled with tightly-rolled parchments, proving that he really was some type of courier. For show, he wore an untested, or "virgin" sword. But his round shoulders, soft hands and plump belly told that he could hardly defend himself against an angry farmer, let alone a warrior of any realm on the Continent. Holding his chin absurdly high, he looked down upon everyone and everything around him with disdain. None in Chotzan's group knew what to make of him until stung by his first question.

"I am Zikurjam, the Gran Vazuk's special envoy. What runt of a quiver is this?"

"Part of Klimgu's as you well know," said Chotzan.

"Then where is he?" sneered the envoy.

"Lost, fighting the Laskomians at Lake Gabriska, as you also know."

"We know now, but who might you be?"

"Loyal warriors of the Vazuk, and no other!" yelled Chotzan, irked by childish questions. "We bring the rarest of gifts, a living treasure for His Greatness. Like him, we pride ourselves on efficiency, and wish to—"

"So what," laughed the envoy. "Everyone brings gifts to curry favor. You must wait your turn. Camp here. With luck, the Vazuk will summon you in a few days."

"We cannot wait."

"Then you cannot see the Vazuk."

"He will be extremely interested in our gift," said Kibak.

"Not without Zikurjam!" The envoy laughed, rolling his eyes. "First you must interest *me*."

Opening an empty pouch on the right side of his saddle, he threw a contemptuous glance at the leaders. Chotzan breathed hard, gritting his teeth the way Klimgu did to contain his rage. Ganjaset's round, dark face and hard, narrow eyes hid all emotion, except for his tendency to squint when angry. His eyes nearly shut when studying the envoy. In contrast, Kibak expressed himself openly, even at his own peril, and so developed the closest bond with Lorgi. Despite the envoy's affronts, Kibak rode close and leaned over, curious to see what "interest" might already be in his pouch. Lorgi would have done the same. Kibak felt a sudden urge to spit into it, but had to say something first.

"Why take orders or insults from parasites?" growled Kibak, gripping his sword, turning to face the others. "Did we come all this way, giving the blood of 400, only to suffer this pampered mosquito? Look what has bred in the unnatural confines of Uxanda. I say we put this oily, plagued runt out of—"

"Kibak!" warned Chotzan, barely stopping him in time. Trying to appear angry at his Third, the leader clenched his teeth again, but only to hold back a smile. Directly, he nodded to Ganjaset, signaling for him to explain.

"Envoy, our gift is priceless, yet cannot tolerate heat," Ganjaset shouted rapidly. "He must be put in some place cool this hour, or he may die. We gave much blood and labor to keep him alive."

"He?" sneered the envoy. "We already have fifty princes and half as many princesses—from all over the Continent—locked up for ransom. Who cares if your royal wilts in the heat? Dare not waste the Gran Vazuk's time on that! Time is revenue. Only revenue can interest me. Only I can interest the Vazuk."

All eyes cursed the envoy, but none could move him. Fearing that one of his warriors might suddenly make an error fatal to all, Chotzan raised both hands for calm. Yet Kibak would not let go of his sword or back away from Zikurjam. Many warriors also gripped theirs. A dozen held their bows at their sides. Pretending to scratch necks or adjust hats, a few eager hands hovered inches from arrows, and seconds from firing them at the insult. Outwardly unfazed, the envoy redoubled his smirk. Kibak glared back, but only to decide the best way to cut him down.

"No blood today," said Chotzan to calm his Third, inwardly thankful for Kibak's display. "This fool may only be doing his job, however badly. The Gran Vazuk would be fascinated to learn how Zikurjam's interest must precede his own. If our gift dies, we can watch the Vazuk strangle this idiot with his own hands."

"Idiot...fat hands," mumbled Lorgi, waking up.

"What is that?" asked the envoy. "A parrot to go with your beast in the wagon?"

"Enough!" shouted Chotzan. "Every one of us has killed more than a hundred foes apiece. No warrior with a grain of honor has time for you. Now, while you still breathe, take us to the Vazuk!"

"Take us to the Vazuk!" mimicked Lorgi. "Take me home."

"An albino, a talking bear?" laughed the envoy. "Novel, indeed. Perhaps entertaining. But still not worth an audience with the Gran Vazuk. Even such lowly mongrels as you should know better than to threaten *me*."

"He is no bear, you idiot!" yelled Kibak. "Look in the wagon. See for yourself, while you still have eyes to feed the mush rotting between your ears."

"What is it, a giant, overfed lizard?" sneered the envoy, looking up and shaking his head.

Lorgi yawned, twitched his ears and nostrils as he stared back down. Nothing about the envoy made sense to him.

"You're no warrior," burped Lorgi. "Are you an idiot?" Everyone burst into laughter. Enjoying the reaction, Lorgi added, "You can get big fat! Idiot fat hands."

"I will inform the Vazuk at once," snapped the envoy, red-faced and eyes smoldering. He rode away fast as the most urgent courier, while the group cheered Lorgi. Any who still had water gave it to him.

"Inform what, that we came to trade insults?" chuckled Ganjaset. "Lorgi did not help. Or Kibak. Right as both were."

"Both helped a great rain!" yelled Sijun.

"We're burnt anyway," said Kibak. "Lorgi just shot the last arrow. He's too good for the Vazuk. I say we ride west and ride hard. Find Lorgi's home, find Klimgu and Twarejik, then…"

"Break the Empire?" guessed Chotzan. "First care for today, Kibak. Always riding ahead of yourself. Let us camp three arrows from Uxanda and prepare for a much-deserved welcome!"

"What about that…*thing?*" asked Ganjaset. "We refused to bribe him. What reply can we expect?"

"The best, just for that!" laughed Chotzan, looking more confident. "We won't mention his graft unless he fails us. But if we ever meet him again, and he has not reformed, then we take joy in his demise."

"I think not," said Kibak. "How could he live so long? Rare wonder he breathes now. That should tell you what reigns in Uxanda."

After some debate, Chotzan led his group to a spot 1,500 yards diagonal from Uxanda's northwest corner, to make the ride just as long for riders issuing from either of the two nearest gates. Ganjaset and Kibak nodded their approval. Yet as the group began to set up camp, Zikurjam returned with an armed escort.

Still livid, the courier tried to appear as if he were leading the party of forty mounted guards, when in fact he merely rode next to their captain. Only when the detail arrived did Zikurjam finally let the red drain from his face. Puffing up his chest and raising his chin, he put on his most satisfied smirk. Waiting a few seconds, he ordered the captain of the guards to bring Chotzan, Ganjaset and Kibak to the Vazuk's palace at once—on foot and unarmed. Everyone including Lorgi smelled treachery, besides one of the worst Tuzanchim insults.

To prevent blood, Chotzan asked his people for calm. With raised hands and a smile, he promised to make them happy within the hour. While speaking, he met eyes with all, including the captain and his guards, but not Zikurjam. By this, Chotzan imparted a small but well-deserved slap—and a subtle warning—to the courier.

"I go alone, unless the Vazuk will receive his gift from our whole group."

"No! But those two must go as well, especially him," sniped the envoy, nudging the captain of the guards and pointing at Kibak. Far more interested in Lorgi and the wagoners, the captain shrugged the flabby hand away. His detail also ignored the envoy. All in Chotzan's group focused on the captain, wondering what he would do.

"They only serve me, and extremely well," Chotzan nodded to him. "I serve only the Vazuk."

But the captain also ignored Chotzan. Suddenly, all eyes followed his to the wagons.

"Sijun!" he yelled, beaming. Dismounting quickly as a warrior, he ran to embrace her.

"Jinwak!" cried Sijun. "Look how you've grown. So tall, you could be mistaken for a Laskomian."

"Hardly, but you fed me well enough. None take me for a Tundrite anymore."

"Such pride you bring, my heart will burst!" shouted Sijun, forming tears. "For one born foreign to become captain of the guard—in Uxanda!"

"Well, captain of *this* guard, all forty of us," said Jinwak.

"Captain of *this* guard," mimicked Lorgi, looking straight at him.

Jinwak darted his eyes between the woman who had raised him, and Lorgi.

"Yes, our exotic talks," answered Sijun. "We learned him some Tuzanchim on our way, but his home language is Tundrish. Imagine that! Smart as a shaman, sweet as the best horse. You will like him very much, as we will miss him."

"And who might this be?" Jinwak pried with a raised eyebrow and a wide smile, pointing to Chumga. "A fine prize. Are you not going to introduce me?"

"What? Oh! No, we're not like that!" gasped Sijun.

Smiling, Chumga vigorously shook his head while the whole group laughed. "We both work the wagons. But no, we're not like that!"

The envoy tried in vain to get Jinwak's attention.

"We're not like that!" shouted Lorgi, pointing a forepaw and shaking his head at the envoy. The whole group roared with laughter.

"Enough, catch up later," snapped the envoy, his face contorted in anger. "Captain, you have a ransom and suspects to deliver. At once! You will carry out my orders—immediately!"

"You can get big fat—immediately!" said Lorgi, mimicking him. More laughter.

Jinwak waved his right hand down twice to try and deter the envoy.

Yet Zikurjam persisted. "Fail to carry out my orders and you will be punished, too, captain. I said immediately!"

"I said immediately!" yelled Lorgi. "Idiot at once immediately!"

"You have a big nose," Jinwak snarled at the envoy.

"What? I have a rather small nose, and no time for—"

"You will have none when I cut it off!" yelled Jinwak. His own men laughed.

Standing up for a moment, Lorgi pointed to the envoy, shouting, "Take us to the Vazuk. Idiot fat hands. I said immediately!"

As laughter seized everyone else, the red-faced envoy bolted again, fleeing to the city's west gate. When the laughter subsided, Jinwak turned to Chotzan with curious eyes. "How much did you bribe Zikurjam to get such a quick audience?"

"Nothing," said Chotzan. "He insults life itself, and will get nothing from us but his own blood, unless someone deprives us of that scant compensation."

Jinwak gave Chotzan a long, deep nod of respect. "Years have I waited to meet such warriors! True warriors. Please honor me by riding beside me. Bring your living treasure, along with your Second and Third. By some miracle, the Vazuk will see us now!"

"What was all that about suspects, unarmed and on foot?" asked Kibak.

"Yak dung," Jinwak shook his head. "Something must be done about Zikurjam, like so many pests. With luck, any decent warrior rides far from here. Uxanda fevers with many ills of its own making. Take mothering care if you must speak of Klimgu or Twarejik. And please do not repeat my words. The Vazuk fears revolt from every quarter, but from those two most of all. He says the exotic, barbarous west can be the worst influence on a warrior."

Looking somber, Chotzan nodded to thank Jinwak for the advice. Except for blinking, Ganjaset showed no hint of his thoughts. Kibak slapped a hand over his mouth to hide his, but his eyes gave him away. Only Sijun and Lorgi read all three leaders.

Together, Jinwak and Chotzan led. Next came Ganjaset, Kibak, the wagon bearing Lorgi, Chumga, Sijun and Porzan, followed by the forty guards, through Uxanda's massive West Gate. Tower guards saluted them all as they passed. Lorgi saluted back. City dwellers, mostly women, children and old, battle-scarred men—half of them missing fingers or limbs—waved and cheered, thinking these must be heroes returning from yet another victory. While Lorgi enjoyed the attention, he far more liked seeing other children and people who were not warriors.

The procession made its way down a wide cobblestone street lined with hearty fruit-bearing trees. Every ten yards or so, narrow streets or alleys met the main boulevard at right angles. All of them held row upon row of three- and four-story buildings, made of brick or stone the color of sand, and all compounding the sun's deadly heat. Trees lining the main street and potted plants on windowsills provided the only greenery. Lorgi guessed this main street to be the least overheated place in Uxanda, yet it already felt ten degrees hotter than the surrounding grasslands. He took an immediate dislike to this, the first city he had ever seen. On reaching the palace gates, he passed out. Nothing could revive him.

Chotzan demanded to be taken directly to the fountain courtyard. With many cuts, scrapes and bruises, palace guards put Lorgi in the fountain pool to cool off. Sijun, Chumga and Porzan stayed by him, while Jinwak and four honor guards escorted Chotzan, Ganjaset and Kibak to a spacious hall. A large tent had been set up inside it, to imply that the Vazuk had not lost "the ways of the warrior." Kibak covered his mouth to keep from laughing. Ganjaset squinted in disgust. Too drained to care, Chotzan just accepted the absurdity, and anything else that confronted his weary senses.

All three knelt, rising only as Jinwak introduced each to the Gran Vazuk, supreme ruler of all the Tuzanchim and the largest empire the Continent had ever known. Yet all knew he wanted even more land. Like any Tuzanchim, the Vazuk wore locally made boots and a sword in a plain leather scabbard. But he also wore silk garments imported from the Kingdom of Shohan, far to the southeast, and covered his bald head with a jeweled crown like a king of the west. Gold rings weighed down all his fingers. Most Tuzanchim abhorred jewelry as symbols of waste, sloth, and pacifism, worn only by peoples who needed to be conquered. Yet by flaunting such incongruous tokens, the Vazuk fancied himself a wise and worldly despot.

All three visitors were struck by the Vazuk's resemblance to Zikurjam, only taller, older and much fatter. Suddenly, one of Lorgi's favorite Tuzanchim phrases, 'You can get big fat' began echoing in Chotzan's head. He fought to smother it, yet marveled how it fit the "old yak" only too well. The Vazuk's first words, like those of his envoy, primed to insult.

"Why did your quiver take longer than elders to reach us?" growled the Vazuk. After a thunderous belch, he added, "We expected better from veteran warriors. Are you all still cubs?"

"We battled the Laskomians, and other things, Your Greatness," said Chotzan. "Having lost our quiver leader, we had to regroup."

"Klimgu—how do you know he is dead?" rasped the Vazuk, between snacks.

"Because of how the Laskomians fought at the battle at Lake Gabriska, Your Greatness," said Chotzan, in a monotone.

"But you did not see him die!" shouted the Vazuk. Following another monstrous belch, he added, "I say he lives, and insults me by not riding with you to honor me."

"He was too ashamed of his error to return, Your Greatness," said Ganjaset. "So he chose to stay with the dying. But for his sacrifice, not one of us would have survived to bring our prize to Your Greatness."

"Enough with greatness!" burped the Vazuk. Clapping his hands, he shouted, "Fresh wine! Bread, rolls, more snacks. Enough for five…No, ten, or…who else is with you?"

"Four hundred parched, hungry warriors, camped half a mile outside the walls," said Kibak.

Chotzan shot a quick, stinging glare at his Third, praying Kibak would take the hint.

"What is your wish, Your Greatness?" chirped a sun-deprived eunuch, pasting on a false smile the instant he entered the room.

"Bring an afternoon feast for…say, twelve—that sounds lucky," laughed the Vazuk. Another belch. "Ah, now I can think." Jinwak allowed himself to smile and relax his shoulders, but the three visitors could not. Their tension began to make even the Vazuk notice. Finally he asked, "Oh, those other three with the beast, are they important?"

"Very, as are all the people in my quiver," said Chotzan.

"Well shot!" cheered Kibak, forgetting himself. While Chotzan and Ganjaset studied the floor, the Vazuk scowled at Kibak.

"How did you become leader, and where is the rest of your little group?" rasped the Vazuk.

"Klimgu resigned and named us," Chotzan nodded toward Ganjaset, then Kibak. "Our shrunken group voted on it. We came as quickly as possible, given the delicate nature and priceless rarity of our treasure."

"Treasure can wait," burped the Vazuk. "Now, where is the rest of your quiver?"

"With Twarejik, fighting the Laskomians," said Chotzan, before he recalled Jinwak's warning. Suddenly Lorgi's question, 'Are you an idiot?' started repeating in his head.

"I think not," snapped the Vazuk, tilting his head up, while scowling at Chotzan. "They forget what I can do for them and the Tuzanchim. My great goal will bring order, prosperity, and at long last peace to all the Continent. Destiny begs for it to be ruled from here, its very center. Do you see? If Twarejik or Klimgu stray, you may have to choose between them and me. I need you. The whole Continent needs you. A grand destiny. Join me and drink on it, all three of you.

"We serve only Your Greatness, and no one else," recited Chotzan. Ganjaset and Kibak echoed his hollow words. The Vazuk nodded only minimally in response to Chotzan and Ganjaset, but ignored Kibak.

"Swear on it," demanded the Vazuk, spraying all three of them with food particles, his mouth half full. Thrusting out his flabby left hand, greasy and wet from constant snacking, he ordered, "Kneel. Kiss my rings, as you swear it on your lives."

Kibak recalled Lorgi's phrase 'idiot fat hands' as he eyed the most repulsive hand on the Continent. It was also the most powerful, by far. Swallowing hard, then clearing his tightening throat, he dared to protest.

"But that is a custom of the savage west—the Castled Lands. Not the Tuzanchim!"

"So what. I like it," burped the Vazuk. "We embrace good ideas from any land. Soon, all will be forced to take our ways. So we take a few of theirs too, because I am a wise emperor."

Eager to be done with the exercise, Chotzan gulped down a full cup of wine, kissed all the Vazuk's rings, then swore fealty in the same groveling manner as some pathetic western vassal, hating being treated like a pet or a slave. Lorgi's phrases kept echoing in his head: 'Idiot fat hands…You're no warrior…Are you an idiot?' Struggle as he did, Chotzan could not make them stop. Every thought of Lorgi, the Vazuk, or his envoy brought them out. Stifling a deadly powerful urge, Chotzan dared not meet anyone's eyes, for fear of sparking uncontrollable laughter. Ganjaset, then Kibak immediately followed in the ritual. Thanks to Lorgi's words, they had to wrestle the same fatal urge.

"You all look suddenly ill. Swearing fealty to me should not make anyone so."

"It is from our trials in procuring this treasure of the west, Your Greatness," assured Chotzan.

"Yes? What riches have you brought me?"

"Rarest of the rare, a living gem for Your Greatness. The Laskomians gave their finest blood in a desperate bid to steal him from us."

"Not another royal," moaned the Vazuk. "We already have too many, most of them as worthless as old concubines."

"A unique albino rock dragon child of the frozen Tunda-host to the far west and north, Your Greatness," said Ganjaset.

The Vazuk's eyes lost focus, as he resumed snacking and burping.

Ganjaset continued, though his own eyes narrowed in disgust. "All our group respects him. He learns to speak Tuzanchim faster than any human child. Before the first snow, he will surely become your close friend, as well as your favorite possession."

Sensing none of this was having the desired effect, Kibak took an opposite approach. "Know that our gift to you can never fit in a corrupt envoy's pouch."

The Vazuk stopped snacking, raised his left eyebrow, and focused on Kibak with more intensity that any of his staff had witnessed in years.

Taking a huge breath, Kibak shot his verbal arrows. "Never mind that your prize also happens to be the Lord Gamon of Tiefenbo, a rock dragon prince of the frozen north. Yes, another royal, but like no other. Never mind that he fought for you, though only three years of age! Or that his mother weighed twelve tons and could have broken Uxanda, no matter what anyone employed to stop her!"

"Kibak!" snapped Chotzan.

"Let him finish," said the Vazuk, his eyes suddenly gleaming. "I will hear all of it."

"*Gánsi*, I mean thank you, Your Greatness," said Kibak. "Know that our gift is unique. He can cure—or kill—faster than you can devour a plate of the tastiest snacks. You will never meet another Lorgi if you live to be a thousand. Only the very long-eyed, the good mothers and the true warriors of this world need value such wonders. For riches easy to count, look no further than that perfumed, pig-faced leach who claims to be your special envoy."

The Vazuk, two palace guards, Jinwak and his four honor guards, and even the eunuch all gasped, raised eyebrows and looked to each other to verify the unprecedented flood. Chotzan and Ganjaset swallowed hard, again staring at the floor before glaring at Kibak. They agreed entirely, but did not want him gambling their lives along with his own. Undaunted, Kibak held his head up, glad that he had been able to say all that he wanted to—a rare joy for any Tuzanchim. A tense silence followed, during which the Vazuk scowled at Kibak for daring to expose a long-silent truth, then at all the others for not doing so. Finally he gave a subtle nod to Kibak.

"Jinwak," shouted the Vazuk. "Arrest Zikurjam."

"With pleasure," Jinwak nodded, then vanished.

"Now… show me this exotic beyond exotic," grated the Vazuk, gesturing for the three to lead him to the fountain court. There they found Lorgi asleep in the pool, his head leaning over the tile rails, his mouth open and his tongue hanging out to one side. Sijun and Chumga sat by him, pouring water over his head, as Porzan flapped a giant, royal fan to help cool him. Lorgi's breathing remained shallow, while both his eyelids and earlids stayed tightly shut.

"Exquisite, unique…but hardly alive," scoffed the Vazuk. "Couriers say the worst plague ever rages in the west. No friend of the Tuzanchim would bring any victim of it—man or beast—to Uxanda or My Greatness. You are either fools or traitors!"

"Neither," said Chotzan. "At first we did fear plague, or the poison he suffered, but—"

"You bring poison as well as plague?" shrieked the Vazuk.

"Neither!" Chotzan shouted. "Remember, we speak of an exotic of the far west, a strange, savage realm. You should have seen the forests, the mosquitoes."

"Forget that," snapped Kibak. "Tell of the giant spiders."

"Yes, but later," said Chotzan. "Great noble Vazuk, our gift to you is this young rock dragon. All he needs is a little cold, and gently negotiated…supervision. But he can die from too much heat. Beware his claws, his teeth, his tail and all his spikes. Actually his whole hide."

"He has a child's humor but a warrior's heart," added Kibak.

"No doubt a rare animal, but nearly dead," said the Vazuk. "Hardly a living treasure."

"He can literally smell truth or deception," said Ganjaset. "He always speaks truth, and draws it out of others, like the best warrior. Having the keenest senses, he will make the ultimate scout."

"And he will bring grand luck to anyone who deserves it," promised Kibak.

Again, Chotzan and Ganjaset swallowed hard and eyed the floor, digging frantically for words to neutralize those of Kibak. Finding none, they kept silent.

"You speak as if he were a person," laughed the Vazuk. "The hardships of your journey have shortened your eyes."

"Not so; just the reverse," said Kibak. "Clever as kings, your prize can speak four languages. He has a monk's heart, but a lion's jaws, eagle eyes, and shaman powers."

"Silence!" yelled the Vazuk, raising a hand. "Though unique, your gift is not practical. We have no place for dying beasts, no matter how fine or rare. Bring back Klimgu and Twarejik. Or stamp out the last of the Laskomian resistance. Then you will be greatly rewarded. Jinwak can see to your supplies. You leave at dawn."

"We are only 400, exhausted and hungry after a long, hard ride," Chotzan protested.

"But loyal Tuzanchim, sworn to me," said the Vazuk. "Worry not. Many thousands will join you in this quest."

"Klimgu is dead," said Kibak. "And Twarejik has done none of us ill."

The Vazuk glared at him a full, silent minute. No one else dared breathe, let alone blink or move the smallest muscle. Chotzan and Ganjaset both wondered if Kibak could live long enough to learn how to tame his words. After a long breath and another belch, the Vazuk smiled, which could bode good or ill. "Then you may bring those two back to me dead or alive, as you like, to explain themselves. A grand reward waits for you. Can you do this, what your Vazuk, the whole Continent, and Destiny itself humbly ask of you?"

"Of course, Your Greatness," assured Chotzan, eyeing Ganjaset and especially Kibak.

"Good. Good." The Vazuk nodded to Chotzan. "I formally place you in command. Food and supplies will be brought out to you. Your servants tending the beast are excused. Obviously, Uxanda has its own, who are far more skilled at such things."

"But those three know Lorgi—your gift—the best," said Kibak.

"Again, worry not," replied the Vazuk. "We will keep him in the fountain courtyard, certainly the coolest place in all the Steppes now."

"Jinwak returns with Zikurjam," announced a guard entering the room.

"Fine," burped the Vazuk. "Have them meet me in my favorite tower." Just then the eunuch returned, carrying a huge tray, bearing an assortment of enough snacks to feed twenty people. "Take that away," ordered the Vazuk, waving his lesser, right hand. "You three return to your group at once to prepare. You leave at dawn."

"Wait!" shouted Chotzan in a plain, hard voice. "We are starving."

Too tired and hungry to care if he offended anyone, Chotzan

grabbed the eunuch by the arm before he could exit the room. Seizing the tray, Chotzan signaled for Ganjaset and Kibak to join him as he gulped down some of its food. Four palace guards anxiously clutched their swords, their eyes darting between the visitors and the Vazuk. Jinwak and his guards all looked ill. To eat in front of the Vazuk without his consent was an insult. Like everyone, Ganjaset feared a swift, fatal answer for the affront, yet still presented his stone face, "resting" his dominant left hand on the palm of his sword. Both he and Kibak inhaled the first items on the tray within reach, immediately washing those down with quick, deep draughts of the Vazuk's favorite, imported rice wine.

"No warrior, or a whole army, gets far without food or rest," said Chotzan. "Give us what we need, so that we can carry out your will."

"What are you smiling about now, Third?" demanded the Vazuk, again scowling at Kibak. All eyes locked on him, fearing what else he might volunteer.

"Leadership," Kibak cheered with gusto. "This fine leader serves you better than any other, and I am more proud than ever to serve him. Why isn't everyone smiling with me?"

Another tense silence. All eyes burned on Kibak, but he kept smiling.

"You should go far—so long as you don't let your tongue race ahead of you," laughed the Vazuk. For once, he inhaled deeply without burping. "Fair enough. Rest. Care for your horses. Leave only when you are ready. I know the needs of a warrior."

"*Gánsi*," said all three visitors at once, out of recent habit.

"What?" asked the Vazuk.

"Dragon-speak for *thank you*, Your Greatness," said Chotzan.

"Wait, what will become of Lorgi—our gift to you?" asked Kibak. "We lost 400 people and horses to bring him to you."

"Practical or not, your gift honors my heart," nodded the Vazuk. "The king of Shohan has a fierce interest in exotic beasts. In trade, such a rarity may hold the value of many horses. But your loyalty is the greatest gift of all. Go now and share my glorious blessing upon your whole group. *Gánsi* them all for me."

With that, the Vazuk and any guards present all exited, leaving the three visitors alone in the room—a mild affront. Chotzan and his delegation gave farewells to an unconscious Lorgi. The eunuch had to escort them out of the palace, so that they would not get lost in its maze of halls, corridors and walkways. Having anyone but a respected warrior do so amounted to another affront, but Chotzan let both pass. Just as they finally exited the palace, a messenger called after them. In no hurry to even ponder the Vazuk's orders, Chotzan happily waited for the man to reach him.

"His Greatness invites you to watch justice, as a gift of satisfaction," said the breathless young man, also bald-shaven like the envoy, yet with a healthier moustache. "His Greatness understands that Zikurjam offended you."

"The Vazuk is wise; we are tired," said Chotzan. "Thank him, but we need not watch. We have seen more justice in one day than you may see in a lifetime, if you are lucky. We only require the food and supplies promised to us. But we need water right now."

"All will be brought soon," said the messenger. He nodded and vanished.

Chotzan and his people walked slowly down the boulevard towards the west gate. Halfway, they suddenly heard tortured screams emit from one of the palace towers. The cries seemed to echo throughout the city. Just as the visitors returned to their camp, the same messenger who had stopped them before came riding out to them.

"Do you wish the corpse or any specific parts thereof, as tokens of justice or satisfaction?" asked the rider.

"We only want the food, water and supplies that we have asked for so many times today, and we need them now!" yelled Chotzan.

Startled, the messenger nodded and rode back to the city.

"More proof that Lorgi brings people what they deserve," sighed Kibak.

"Lorgi had nothing to do with the mosquito," Ganjaset scolded him. "But your loose mouth nearly ended our luck here."

"What luck can grow in Uxanda?" asked Kibak, stretching his arms out for emphasis. "Deprived of wind in summer and sun in winter, it casts ill on any who stay too long. We should never have brought Lorgi here. And our reward? Guilt and bitter fortune to haunt us."

"Then we'd best leave quickly, and have no more to do with Uxanda," sighed Chotzan.

"As I had suggested earlier, remember?" Kibak nudged him.

The sun set before the promised goods arrived. These proved to be of inferior quality and not half what 400 people and their horses actually needed. Thoroughly demoralized, Chotzan, Ganjaset and Kibak began to discuss their course under the circumstances. One by one, all the captains joined in. Sijun, Chumga and Porzan entered the fray all at once, out of concern for Lorgi, then everyone in the whole group demanded to be heard. Frenzied debate engulfed the entire camp. Though arguing about many things, they all were disgusted with the Vazuk and Uxanda.

For the Tuzanchim, favors, good deeds, acts of valor and gifts all required prompt, generous responses. Debts had to be repaid, justice delivered, and recognition bestowed with efficiency. Personal relationships and tangible actions counted far more than verbal oaths of fealty or other rituals.

Unlike the Castled Lands of the west or the hopelessly crowded realms of the Well-East, in the Tuzanchim Empire, fortunes rose or fell quickly by personal effort. Warriors saw rank, status, wealth and good luck as seasonal harvests, resulting from hard work and wise choices. By adopting foreign customs at odds with these ways, the Gran Vazuk alienated Chotzan's group.

"Our 'Leader's Leader' has forsaken the ways of the warrior," huffed Ganjaset. "Uxanda rots from within. Both insult our ancestors. No empire can endure such ills."

"If only Klimgu had lived…" wished Sijun. "He would know what to do."

"We should join with Twarejik," said Chotzan.

"A fine leader, but he is no Klimgu," sighed Kibak.

"Then we must forge him into one!" yelled Chotzan.

"No," Kibak smiled. "But as Klimgu said, 'beware the arms of the west,' Remember?"

"Beware your mouth nearly costing our lives!" yelled Ganjaset. "Easy to praise Klimgu now! You were the most eager to replace him. Remember that?"

"I only did what he asked of me," said Kibak. "While we argue, he builds. We must do the same, and join with him."

"What?" asked many all at once.

"Then why did we suffer to trek all this way, risking Lorgi and everyone?" gasped Chotzan, seconded by many others.

"To reach our gut's limit, while Klimgu gathers force in the west," said Kibak. "All part of his plan. You will see. But he can explain far better than I."

"If he yet lives," said Chotzan, "he will be risking life to explain himself to us!"

End of Part I

15: Traded

An unseasonably cool wind reached into the fountain courtyard, bending the corn-high geyser in its center first one way, then another, trying to whip it like the steppe grass. A round, knee-deep pool, twelve feet across, cradled the fountain. The exquisite wavy pattern of blue and gold tiles lining its sides gave the water an alpine lake's rich hue, while the fountain kept its surface agitated. Like frosting on a cake, a polished white marble bench surrounded the pool, inviting anyone to sit, gaze at the liquid, with its ever dancing reflections, and forget the harsh lands waiting beyond the city walls.

As falling water hit the surface, its spray often rode the air beyond the pool, tickling Lorgi's nose and rousing him from a perpetual slumber. Weeks without food had left him with no strength or even his voice. This time he resolved to stay awake long enough to meet his needs—by force if necessary.

Two feet away, on the pool's marble bench, sat a thin, despairing young lady in a sleek, knee-length, blue silk dress with gold trim. Like everyone Lorgi had met on his journey, she had straight black hair, epicanthic folds framing her dark eyes, and a serious manner. But those eyes were fresh, soft and begging for a friend. As Lorgi stretched, the girl became more alert too, reseating herself four feet away. She seemed to have been waiting hours for him to wake up. Now that he had suddenly done so, she was unsure of just how to deal with him.

Whether from anger or fear, her blood carried adrenaline. As Lorgi focused on her, she scooted another two feet away. Yet the young lady murmured to him in the most gentle, sweet voice, one too quiet even for Lorgi to make out any words. By her tone alone, he knew she wanted only peace and friendship. He appreciated her company but missed Chumga, Sijun, Porzan, Kibak and many others. Between her legs, the girl held a terra cotta bowl, overflowing with premium dates. The first person in Uxanda to offer Lorgi something other than meat, she also seemed the only one who spoke to him in a sincere voice. Her smile, as well as her posture and scent all spoke pain and dread, yet hope. Taking an instant liking to this new person, Lorgi halved the distance between them, determined to help her, whether she was afraid of him or not.

"Those are for the rock dragon, not you," shouted a tall, obese guard, scratching his grey beard. His uniform strained to hold all his girth, and differed from Jinwak's. Lorgi guessed he had not ridden in years.

"Fine," said the girl. "I'm used to starving. Unlike you, I do not take what belongs to others, or tell them what to do."

"Take royal care, you Shohaneze slut!" yelled the guard. "Feed the dragon, or be fed *to* it."

"Fine again," she answered. "Still better than being had by a fat, old yak with rotten breath and a heart of dung. Either way, I will die bravely, unlike you."

"Keep your brainless death wishes to yourself."

"I overheard those who gifted this exotic. Real warriors—not lazy guards. They say he brings people what luck they deserve. So I have no need to fear him, unlike you."

"Worthless concubine, stop your mindless chatter. Hurry up and feed the beast!"

"With nothing to gain or lose, I cannot be rushed." She threw the guard a sarcastic smile.

Starving, Lorgi put himself between the arguing humans. The act of standing on his back legs and scowling drove the bully ten paces back. Then Lorgi could focus on the nice lady with the food. She finished de-pitting the dates while studying him for as long as he could sit still—one minute. As though feeding a wild predator, the girl set one date on the ground two yards away from both of them. Confused by her behavior, Lorgi twitched his ears and nostrils, then cocked his head. What she offered amounted to almost no snack at all, for anyone larger than a prosperous rodent. Snorting at the affront, Lorgi walked over and inhaled it anyway. As he turned back to face her, the girl held up a second one in her left hand, unsure of what to do with the treat.

"Get on with it, while you still have hands to feed the dragon!" yelled the guard.

"I'm thinking," said the girl. "You should try it some time."

"Slaves don't think, if they wish to live."

"A guard like you has no idea what the word means," laughed the girl. "But know this, if you can know anything. Each time you yell at me, it delays my task. Is that your intent?"

"If you were my slave, you would be in great pain or your task done by now."

She squinted at the man, the way Ganjaset did when angry or disgusted. "They say warriors who ride the west no longer take slaves, and they are the best."

In no mood to tolerate any more delays, Lorgi whirled around, flashing his teeth at the guard. He wanted to yell *"Guyat!"* but still had no voice. A few more dates, a gallon of spring water and ten minutes could remedy that. Lorgi mouthed the word anyway, but neither human noticed. So he sat down with his head between his forepaws, resigned to waiting out the argument before his own needs were met.

"The beast hungers," shouted the guard. "You are to feed it, not tease it."

"Be patient. The gifters said this exotic is an orphan, one who has already endured many trials in his short, tragic life," said the girl, tears pooling in her eyes.

"What can a fool like you know about him or anything else?" sneered the guard.

While the bully hurled more insults, three other guards suddenly appeared, stumbling through the courtyard, ogling the girl with intense longing. The bully shoed them away, but they returned in seconds. All this told Lorgi the young lady must be quite beautiful to other humans. Her accent, mannerisms and scent revealed that she was not a Tuzanchim, but a foreigner herself. This greatly pleased Lorgi, making him even more curious.

"This rock beast is a poor eater, refusing every kind of meat in Uxanda," sighed the girl, tilting her head. "Some terrible disease of the West still ails him. He will not even take bone broth. He might even be a vegetarian, like a monk from Shohan or one of the Esterlan kingdoms. Imagine that—a holy dragon child."

"Then you may be a holy idiot," growled the man, scowling at her. "If he dies, so will you."

"Your words mean nothing to me, or anyone else, I'm certain. Keep them to yourself. But I will have to win this child's trust, make it a game to get him to eat anything."

"They say the Vazuk rejected you, no doubt for your own lack of meat, as well as your vinegar tongue," jeered the guard. "So you lost that game."

"At least I played. How many women have dared wrestle the Gran Vazuk?"

"Far too many, and the rejected ones all died within a moon," laughed the guard. "Pray this beast accepts you. Otherwise, His Greatness will send you back to Shohan, where failures like you are thrown to lions."

Certain that nothing could save her anyway, the girl grew bolder in her feeding approach with each date. Making sure the guard could see, she extended her right arm, offering one in her open palm, gambling that Lorgi would take it without harming her. When he gently did so, she smiled. Immediately, Lorgi gave her an Álukoi's toothsome grin in return. For an instant, the girl held her breath in fright. Gazing into his huge eyes, she saw only the courtyard and several guards reflected in them. To her, Lorgi seemed an innocent cub, yet with all the tools for hunting and devouring the largest game. Relieved that he preferred dates to human flesh, she let out a sigh. So did her audience. Lorgi cocked his head and wiggled his ears, making the girl smile again.

Other guards flocked to see, so she decided to entertain them while feeding Lorgi, tempting him with a date on her outstretched right forearm. He gently but quickly took it. Deliberately pulling up her dress, the girl held her next treat between her knees. Using extreme care to avoid cutting her soft skin, Lorgi slowly retrieved it with just his tongue. Something about it made her wince, but now she dared not back away even an inch from what she fancied to be her exotic new friend. The next date she placed between her thighs. Lorgi took it with equal care. "Ahh!" gasped a dozen guards now watching the show. The girl gave them all a bright smile, knowing she had just earned a potent ally and some admirers.

"You live boldly, especially for a Shohaneze!" said one guard.

"Worthy of a Tuzanchim," cheered another, hoping she would notice him and answer his smile. Or at least place the next date even higher up between her legs.

"What choice do I have?" she asked, keeping her eyes on Lorgi.

"To take great caution with this beast," warned the first, "said to have the jaws of ten lions, with a temper to match."

"And a cat's speed," said the other. "He slew four Laskomian knights in a matter of seconds."

"I heard five," said a third.

"Seven or eight is what I heard," said another.

"I will die soon enough anyway, caution or not," said the girl. "Thank you all for your concern, but it never matters what I do. Fate despises me."

Like a matching set of pearls, twin tears rolled down her cheeks. Her audience sighed, inching closer with every word. Sensing pain, Lorgi nuzzled up to help her, twitching his nostrils and ears with concern. Seeing no blood, swelling or bruising, he could not guess what ailed her besides malnutrition, so he sniffed her all over for clues. Wondering if the girl just had a headache, Lorgi licked her forehead, then the tears off her face, for what they might reveal about her. Fearing that the exotic was about to try and eat her, the guards drew swords, ignoring their superior's order not to interfere in the trials of a failed slave.

"Aiy! So cold," she winced. "He has a block of ice for a tongue."

"Aiy," Lorgi managed to squeak out.

"Aiy?" she gasped, turning to the guards. "Did you hear that?"

"Hear me," Lorgi barely coaxed out of his swollen, parched throat.

"He's trying to talk!" shouted the girl, placing her entire right hand in his mouth with the next date.

"You're trying to die, one way or another," laughed the bully. The twelve men under his command protested, hating him for trying to discourage the girl's show.

When she hesitated, Lorgi gently nudged her with a forepaw, craving more dates. She feared what he might do when those ran out. To prolong the feeding game, she tossed one high in the air. Jumping after it, Lorgi caught the prize in midair. While the guards cheered, the girl smiled.

Picking the largest date in the bowl, she said "careful," to Lorgi before placing it between her outstretched lips. Again, he gently retrieved it using just his tongue. While the girl beamed her widest smile yet, a loud chorus of "Ahh's!" sang from the guards. Their superior ordered them back to their posts. None moved. The girl fought to contain her joy, but her eyes betrayed her.

Gambling, she threw a date high over the fountain to the other side of the pool. Lorgi plunged in, displacing a third of its water onto the surrounding walkways. Drenched, the guards yelled in protest, so the girl tossed her next one the opposite way, well away from them. Chasing it, Lorgi smacked into a stone column, leaving hundreds of scratches, chips and a few cracks in it. Upon impact, Lorgi merely shook himself, inhaled the date, and bounded back to his playful new friend, ready for more treats. That column would have to be replaced.

Putting two dates in her lap, the girl studied Lorgi to see if he had hurt himself on the column. She reached to touch him on one side of his head. But Lorgi shied away, to keep her from cutting her hand on him. Placing another date between her legs, she drew him close again. As Lorgi carefully took the treat, the girl managed to pet him near the ears, only to let out a surprised "ouch." Before she could back away, Lorgi instantly healed her cuts with his tongue.

To show friendship, he presented her with the pad of an upturned forepaw, one of the few areas on his body that was safe for humans to touch without hurting themselves. As the girl put her hand on his left forepaw, Lorgi deftly retrieved a date from the bowl with his other, offering the treat to her. Gazing into Lorgi's huge eyes, her own grew wide. She opened her mouth to speak, but for a long moment, could not.

"Here," wheezed Lorgi, thrusting the date within an inch of her mouth. "Your turn."

"Wha…what?" she stuttered.

"For you. This is the best one."

"Why?" she stammered.

"They taste great," chirped Lorgi. "And you need them even more than I do."

The shock of meeting non-human intelligence and friendship all at once was too much for the girl. Everything but Lorgi disappeared from her watery field of vision. For five more seconds, she held her breath. A world she had never deserved suddenly cracked open. Then she broke. Tears poured from her eyes. Her mouth hung wide open, the corners of her lips drew down and far apart, as her jaw wobbled. She sobbed uncontrollably, from a long, searing history of wrongs. Gasping with frightfully loud, tortuous breaths, and doubled over on her knees, she wept so hard that at first Lorgi feared she might die from the intensity of her emotions. Only once had he seen humans cry like this—the day the balkotars attacked his village.

"I'm sorry; what happened to you?" he murmured. "Let me help." But no matter how gently he spoke, his words only seemed to make the girl worse. With his ears drooping and his nose twitching, Lorgi sat himself close by her side and kept quiet. Taking great care to use only the soft pads of a forepaw, he patted the sobbing girl on her back, as gently as a human grandmother, to try and lessen her pain.

"Enough!" yelled the guard. "Keep silent or I will beat you." Hurling epithets at the girl, the bully stepped toward her.

Lorgi's ears shot up, then pinned back at the man's absurd challenge. Standing up, he turned to the guard and yawned long and wide, in order to frighten him away. But the man ignored what Lorgi understood to be a universal warning. Stretching his limbs for battle, he repeated his yawn. But the guard continued to spout abuse. So to make his threat even more clear, Lorgi shook his head from side to side while snapping his jaws and whipping his tail.

Incredibly, the guard would not stop, so Lorgi took four steps toward him. If this last threat failed, he would have to flatten the man. When the guard held out his poll ax to ward off the dragon child, Lorgi feigned a sideways retreat. Before the man could react, Lorgi sprang at the weapon, snapping it in half with a quick bite. Only then did the guard jump back and keep quiet.

"No, no. Please come back," the girl called to Lorgi. He snapped his jaws at the bully once more before returning to his new friend. Sitting on his haunches just inches from her, Lorgi again offered her one of the treats. This time she took it, whispering *"tekursedim."*

"You're welcome," said Lorgi. "And *tekursedim* to you, too."

The girl smiled at Lorgi, then her admirers.

More "Ahh's" echoed through the courtyard as they smiled back. Scowling, their superior berated them for not coming to his aid. But the dragon child had merely broken his weapon, after being provoked. To the others, such folly was not theirs to mend. Unless blood were spilled, they saw no reason to take their eyes off the heavenly girl, especially when she seemed to welcome an audience.

Afraid of sparking Lorgi's anger, the bully drew back and kept mute. Yet he snapped his fingers while motioning for the girl to hurry up with the feeding. She ignored him. He also ordered his men back to their posts. None moved. Pressing her sudden advantage, the girl threw her next date over the pool, so that Lorgi could splash the men again. Despite their protests, she hurled the last date even further, with unfortunate results.

"Reckless fool!" yelled the bully, as the guards scrambled to avoid Lorgi's charge.

"Sorry. Look out!" yelled the girl.

"*Guyat!*" squeaked Lorgi.

In his zest to snatch the treat, he charged, leapt, then skidded across the drenched tile floor, faster than anyone had thought possible. He crashed into one guard, knocking the man down and cutting him up badly in the chest. His comrades found no broken bones or other serious injuries. The victim remained conscious, yet dazed and windless from just having been tackled by a compact snowdragon child.

Squeaking out a barely audible "sorry," Lorgi reached to apply his healing tongue, but others instantly dragged the stricken guard away and would not let Lorgi near him, unaware that he wanted to help.

They all began talking at once. Shouting epithets, their superior lumbered over to the girl. She kept apologizing to everyone, from the start of Lorgi's charge up until the instant the bully slapped her hard across her right cheek. As she fell back in pain and shock, Lorgi whirled about. With a cub's angry growl, he bounded up to the guard.

Weighing close to 300 pounds and standing six feet tall, the ranking guard towered over Lorgi, but held only a useless, broken weapon.

Hoping to frighten the dragon child away, he snarled like some large, vicious, but not very intelligent dog.

"Shame to you!" wheezed Lorgi, in perfect Tuzanchim. "Stay away from my friends. This will teach you." He reared up and decked the man with one swat of a forepaw. Even in his weakened condition, Lorgi held back, using almost none of the force within him on this day. He merely wanted to make the bully "play fair" and stop tormenting the girl. Yet Lorgi's gentle slap knocked the brute senseless, made his eyes roll, his mouth hang open, and his body collapse. When the man's bloodied face smacked the brick floor, his whole frame shook like a fallen pine when *hyúlems* chopped it down. Nothing could bring him back to life.

"*Yahai!*" shouted the crying girl. "Everyone please just stop."

"*Guyat!*" Lorgi yelled at the guards, sitting back on his haunches and waving both forepaws.

"That's right," said the girl. "Leave us. Leave us alone. *Guyat!*"

Unaware of what he had just done, Lorgi turned to heal the girl's cheek with his tongue. In frantic whispers, the guards hissed about ways to coax him into a cage waiting outside, and arrest the concubine at the same time. Only after finishing that and cleaning up the room would they dare report the incident and let the Gran Vazuk decide what to do with both foreigners. The guards prayed aloud for an unlikely outcome, wherein the Vazuk did not vent his lethal anger upon them as well. Four guards vanished, to obtain tools for dealing with Lorgi, as the rest encircled and taunted the pair.

Two held out strips of dried meat, calling softly in absurd, falsetto voices to distract him as others reached for the girl. Determined to keep them all away, Lorgi pinned his ears back, shook his head, snapped his jaws and swished his tail high from side to side, ready to fight. When all had returned and their whole group stood ready, they rushed in from all sides, with ropes and spears.

In seconds, all found themselves ducking behind columns, seriously injured and bleeding from many deep cuts. Shreds of rope, clothing, broken spears, and many splattered trails of human blood littered the courtyard, its floors mutilated by thousands of claw scratches. What water still remained in the fountain pool had turned red. To help finally clear his parched throat, Lorgi forced himself to drink from it anyway. Following up with a good long yawn and a grunt, he felt his true voice return. Knowing the guards would try again, Lorgi resolved to do whatever it took to frighten them away for good.

Rearing up on his hind legs and tail, Lorgi stood nearly as tall as a man. After snapping his jaws while shaking his head from side to side, he inhaled a whale's breath. As a final warning, he forced all the air out of his lungs, trumpeting the grandest roar of his life. Though lasting only five seconds, the "call" reverberated for many more as it rang far down palace hallways and corridors. Surprised by his own success, Lorgi could not help but wiggle his ears and smile. He only wished that his mother, friends and all of Tiefenbo could have been there to hear it. And yet he guessed the sound of a three-year-old Álukoi trying to roar like an adult could only bring smiles, laughter, or cheers from anyone who witnessed it—snowdragon or not.

Cute as Lorgi's first true roar might have sounded at home, the totally alien throttle alarmed the weary guards. It sang from an unknown beast that had just killed their superior, as well as the biggest man among them, in one lightning stroke. This exotic would surely cost them their jobs, if not their lives. Scrambling desperately to outmaneuver the girl and what had in effect become her new pet dragon, the guards dared not call for help.

Yet help quickly arrived, as Lorgi's roar echoed throughout the palace. Ignoring all warnings and commands to stay away, everyone just had to come see the revived exotic for themselves. In the next minute, the Gran Vazuk himself arrived, escorted by a dozen of his personal guards. 500 pairs of eyes—most of the palace staff—studied Lorgi with all possible intensity, only glancing at the much-damaged room, and its bleeding guards. Everyone had something to say about it all, in hushed whispers.

"Silence!" thundered the Vazuk. "So! My present from the Far West returns to life after all. Perhaps those mangy, flee-bitten dogs who brought him to me were right." Shaking his head at the guards, he added, "I'll deal with you idiots later."

"I'll deal with you idiots later," Lorgi mimicked him.

Most people covered their mouths. None dared smile, let along laugh. For a dragon's yawn, Lorgi and the Vazuk eyed each other with mutual suspicion. This was only the second tall or obese Tuzanchim that Lorgi had yet seen. The first lay dead a few feet away. A nod from "His Greatness" sent two fresh guards reaching for the girl. Lorgi decked both with a single whip of his tail, killing one in the process. That was not his intent, but Lorgi refused to let anyone near his new friend.

The Vazuk threw a quick hand gesture and the other guards backed away. Snarling one of the same insults that the bully guard had used earlier, "His Greatness" motioned for the girl to step aside, away from the dragon child, so that guards could arrest her. Lorgi would have none of it, and repeated his warning signals.

Terrified, the girl nudged to within inches of her champion, expecting each breath to be her last. Thinking his new friend would cut herself deeply on his back spikes, Lorgi scooted himself a foot to the side away from her. Doubly terrified, the girl moved too close again, making him step aside a second time. All present marveled at this. Some began to murmur. A few even let out muffled, anxious giggles. Most showed fear in their eyes, wondering whose blood would spill in the next instant.

"At last, Wenji has found a use!" laughed the Vazuk. "The rock monster fears her, as my worthless guards fear him. How can this be?"

"It was all a tragic accident, Your Greatness," Wenji cried, lunging forward and prostrating herself at the Vazuk's feet. "I did not mean for any of this to happen."

Lorgi drooped his ears, eyelids and pursed his nostrils, repulsed that his innocent friend should suddenly grovel at the feet of "hog man," as he labeled the Vazuk.

"All was my fault, Your Greatness," cried Wenji. "I beg your mercy and wisdom. The guards did no wrong. Please do not punish them for my error."

"So a fool and a nag, as well as a lion tamer," chuckled the Vazuk. "Who could have guessed such talents in little Wenji? I'll deal with you later, too—unless you can control this budding monster and get it into the cage outside." Shaking his head, the Vazuk surveyed the blood-spattered courtyard, with half of its thousands of tiles scratched, cracked or broken off, and several columns damaged beyond repair. Two guards lay dead. A dozen others would be of no use for months. "This gift has brought anything but the joy promised. It is not lucky for us."

"Only the king of Shohan could make use of such a beast," said an advisor.

"Get Satungke," yelled the Vazuk, clapping his hands. "Now, you idiots!"

"Get Satungke," mimicked Lorgi, clapping his forepaws. "Now, you idiots!"

Every human mouth slammed shut, gripped by a censuring hand.

"Those west-tainted mongrels will pay for their animal tricks!" cursed the Vazuk "Get Jinwak. He can bring them back quickly."

"Not practical, Your Greatness," stammered an advisor, looking more fearful of his leader than of Lorgi. "Chotzan's group left a week ago."

"What does that matter?" growled the Vazuk.

"They are a small, veteran group, known for their speed," said the advisor. "They carry almost nothing, and have seen more of the west lands than any other Tuzanchim. By now, they could be anywhere."

"Jinwak is most needed here," said another advisor.

"Get Jinwak, get Satungke," repeated Lorgi, clapping his forepaws. "Now, you idiots!"

For a long, awkward moment, he kept a fighting stance as Wenji knelt before the Vazuk. Most of the palace staff now lined the courtyard. All who could do so tried to cower behind the undamaged columns. But regardless of personal safety, all jostled for a clear view of the dauntless, talking rock monster.

The Vazuk dared not show his own terror by retreating behind guards or columns, or by flinching at Lorgi's insults. Almost any reaction, other than fearless calm, would only give enemies within the Vazuk's own palace something to use against him later. Instead, "His Greatness" proudly smiled, keeping his eyes on the exotic, pretending to exude confidence and lack of fear. A moment later, a tall, lean Shohaneze nobleman appeared beside the Vazuk.

"Satungke, my esteemed friend," said the Vazuk, forcing himself to grin. "We need your view on our newest living acquisition. But please ignore the damages for the moment."

"Why, when they add to his value?" laughed Satungke, the Shohaneze ambassador, smiling to mask his own dread at having to stand only ten feet away from Lorgi. He politely nodded to the Vazuk, but kept his eyes on the dragon like everyone else. Lorgi took an instant dislike to the nasal-voiced man.

"Have you ever seen anything at all like this one?" asked the Vazuk.

"Exquisite!" said Satungke, shaking his head. "But what exactly is it?"

"An extremely rare exotic of the far west and frozen north—perhaps too exotic," laughed the Vazuk, hiding his own retinue of dread. "Maybe only the king of Shohan can tame it."

Backing away from the Vazuk, Wenji hovered beside her champion, whispering "Thank you" to him. Lorgi nodded back like a Tuzanchim warrior.

Having proved himself, Lorgi guessed none would challenge him now, so he sat back on his haunches. While no one in the room could relax, he came the closest to doing so, and used the sudden calm to study everyone and everything in the courtyard. His new posture allowed most to surmise that the violence had ended. Due to the Shohaneze ambassador's presence, all hoped that none would suffer further for whatever drama had just taken place.

"As you well know, my king collects exotics from all over the Continent," said Satungke. "Especially rare fighters for his arena. The more violent and destructive, the better. I can give you fifty prized horses or their worth for this one. And spare your palace at the same time."

"For so unique a prize as this? Please! That does not even rank half an insult," the Vazuk huffed. "This gem hails from the Continent's most savage wilderness, the northern extreme of the far west."

"I enjoyed your introduction the first time," smiled Satungke. "A hundred."

"In that case, you can leave before insulting me again!"

"Very well," said the ambassador. "Two."

"Too little," the Vazuk chuckled, turning as if to leave the courtyard.

"I meant 250," said Satungke, warming to the challenge.

"No, you meant ten. Ten hundreds."

"What? That is absurd!" Satungke shook his head.

"Then we are even," the Vazuk snorted, lifting both hands as if to beg calm. "No more insults or absurdities. We are friends. You can have him for eight. I should have said that at the start, but we all know how the Shohaneze love to bargain. I did not have the heart to deprive you of the sport, though I will never understand it, myself."

"Three, which I can hardly afford," moaned Satungke.

"Please! You are one of the richest men in all Shohan. Seven. You can have him for seven. Anyone else must pay ten. My sacrifice." The Vazuk put a hand to his chest and gave a pained expression, as if loathe to part with Lorgi.

"What sacrifice?" asked Satungke, looking suspicious.

"Four hundred warriors and 400 horses died to bring this exotic here," rasped the Vazuk, trying to sound as if he had taken part in the expedition himself. "So he is worth more than all of them together. Yet I give him away at a loss. But only because you are my friend."

"Four—my last offer! Far more than any single beast could possibly be worth. But only because you are my friend."

Smiling back at him, the Vazuk paused, gently shaking his head. Satungke took four deep breaths, making a show of his aggravation. Again the Vazuk turned as if to leave.

"Alright! Five. No more! Period. Five or nothing. Five hundred horses for this…what do you call it?"

"For five hundred horses you can call it anything you like!" the Vazuk roared, slapping the ambassador so hard on his back that he stumbled. Though jostled, Satungke laughed nervously with him. Almost everyone in the room did as well. Both men presented tight half-smiles while shaking hands on the transaction.

Lorgi cocked his head, twitched his ears and snorted. Fearing the worst, Wenji kept darting her eyes between the traders and her champion.

"Wait, Your Greatness," begged an advisor, cupping his hands to the Vazuk's right ear.

"You can get idiot fat hands!" huffed Lorgi, sitting on his haunches, disgusted with all of them.

"He speaks too?" asked Satungke, delighted.

"He mimics, at least," said the advisor. "As with the most clever birds, take care what you say in front of him. Mostly, he sleeps, suffering from the heat. But he has a king's temper, as you can see."

"For five hundred horses, he had better!" said Satungke.

"But we take no responsibility for what may happen once this unknown exotic leaves our care," warned the advisor. "Of course we will help you as best we can, and provide an escort when you transport him."

"And you can take this worthless concubine with him," added the Vazuk. "We have never found any use for Wenji here."

"Oh?" asked the ambassador. "She was not to your liking?"

"Look at her," said the Vazuk.

"Many men would be—" began Satungke.

"Look at me," laughed the Vazuk, gesturing to his ample girth. "Next time, bring bigger concubines."

"We are sorry," bowed Satungke, feigning concern. "Of course, you are aware of my king's...*procedure*, for rejected ones."

"Do we bore you with our details?" the Vazuk scolded him.

Satungke smiled, bowed and shook his head. The two men grasped hands again, sealing the transaction and Wenji's fate. Like everyone else, Satungke found the Vazuk's hand wet and greasy from constant snacking. The Vazuk found Satungke's reptilian. Yet they slapped each other on the back like best friends.

"We are great men of the Continent, you and I," said the Vazuk. "What are the pointless troubles of a few slaves and animals compared to our grand enterprises?"

"The...girl seems to have a way with the beast," noted Satungke.

"Present her as his trainer, and it may please your king," said an advisor. "With her life riding on such a duty, she can only succeed! Having helped everyone concerned, you will emerge quite the hero."

"As always, I leave wiser than when I arrived." The ambassador bowed, giving his least sincere smile yet.

* * *

Wenji had to coax Lorgi into a large, iron cage that formed the hold of a wagon. It still smelled of a large carnivore, even though it had just been washed. She only succeeded by first entering it herself. For maximum drama, she insisted on shutting the door and closing the lock herself, trying to appear more afraid of Lorgi than of anything else. Foolishly, the Gran Vazuk allowed her to leave Uxanda in such a manner, further eroding his reputation.

Despite sitting in a locked cage, the pair found themselves comfortably transported, in a wagon far better than what had brought either of them to Uxanda. The team of two drivers had put a burlap canopy over the cage for shade, and pillows inside for Wenji. Twelve warriors rode behind the wagon, while twenty Shohaneze knights rode in front of it. In the middle of the knights rode Ambassador Satungke, whom Lorgi had dubbed "Smiley-mouth." Scores of riders led countless horses, plus a treasure-filled wagon, in the opposite direction, kicking up a wall of dust. All in the transport held cloths over their mouths and squinted until the cloud had passed.

"The Vazuk grows too extravagant—and foolish—selling off two rare jewels," said one warrior. "Such a waste."

"If only he were more extravagant with good thinking," said another. "But every leader has flaws. The way of the world, from its first sun to the last."

"A true leader shares prosperity," said the first. "He does not send yet another angel to her death, especially when many of his own palace guards have no mates. Is our leader's leader blind or feeble? He knows not the worth of what he trades."

"Four hundred warriors died to bring the rock dragon to Uxanda," said a third. "They knew his worth."

"You forget, the Vazuk has gained incredible wealth in trade!" yelled another.

"But look what has been lost," shouted the first. "Is he blind?"

"They say a rebel in the west has long eyes and wastes nothing."

"If you believe that, then your hat is too tight," jibed the first.

Curious, Lorgi eyed the knights in brightly painted leather coats riding in front, but they spoke an alien tongue. Having a rare gift for languages, even for an Álukoi, Lorgi already understood much of what he heard in Tuzanchim. While he followed the discussion behind the wagon,

Wenji listened to the knights in front. They spoke in Esterlan, the language of Shohan and all the other kingdoms of the Well-East.

Tiring of that, the caged pair turned to confront each other. Wenji reached to pour water from a two-gallon leather bag into a bowl for Lorgi. Gently but quickly, he stopped her, lifted the bag and drank half its contents in two seconds. Months of sporadic deprivation had taught him to behave like a warrior.

"Hey, wait! Stop that!" cried Wenji.

"Here." Lorgi thrust the bag at her.

"What?" she stammered.

"Drink," Lorgi burped.

"That container has to last us a long time. How can I make you understand?"

"I'm Lorgi; what's your name?" he rolled out in slow but perfect Tuzanchim. "Why are you surprised?"

"They said you have lucky powers. And a magic healing tongue. But I did not think you could have your own name, like a real person."

"Thanks a lot!" huffed Lorgi. "I am a real person. Real hot, thirsty, lost and confused."

"I'm sorry. They will not know what to do with you in Shohan, or probably anywhere else. Not knowing makes people afraid—and dangerous. We must be careful."

"We better start over," giggled Lorgi, shaking his head like a human. Gesturing with his left forepaw, he spoke with painfully slow clarity. "I...am...Lorgámon. What...is...your...name?"

"Wenji," she smiled, thinking that a clever friend—human or not— might help her far more than a trained beast. She allowed herself to wonder what kind fortune this magic creature might eventually grant her, if only she could help him. "I am Wenji. My name is Wenji."

No "w" phoneme existed in Álukop, Lorgi's native language. Like any Álukoi, he struggled to pronounce the foreign sound. Only recently had he mastered the opening "W" in Weliben. Before that, the best he could do was "Beliben," "Veliben," "Yeliben," or just leaving the "W" sound out altogether for "Eliben," none of which Weliben much liked, but had always tolerated.

"Benji?" Lorgi tried to say her name.

"No, not Benji! I'm Wenji."

"Venji?" Lorgi stretched his ears to the side, as a question.

"Wenji." She pronounced her name slowly. "Wenji."

"Ubv...Be...Wenji!"

"Yes, Wenji. That's right," she smiled.

"Wenji, Wenji, Wenji," Lorgi practiced. "I am happy to meet you."

"And you are Lord Gamon?"

"Lorgámon," he emphasized the accent, raising a forepaw for emphasis. "But my friends call me Lorgi."

"What...I mean, where are you from?"

"Tiefenbo," he chuckled, as if expecting her to know. "I'm Lorgámon of Tiefenbo. You are Wenji of...?" When she did not answer, Lorgi gestured like a human to spur a response."

"I'm only Wenji, or whatever my next master tells me to be. But you! Little Lord Gamon, dragon prince, lord regent monster of Tiefenbo!"

"I don't know about all those things where I come from."

"Then you are lucky indeed!" cheered Wenji.

"We do have monsters, though. And most humans complain about our weather—lots of rain and snow."

"Do you think we can help each other?"

"Of course," Lorgi yawned. "I want to go home, but don't even know how any more. But we must get out of here." Eying the cage's iron bars, he guessed it would take hours to cut through any of them. Reaching to try his teeth on one, he asked, "Why do you have to have a master?"

"It is never up to us," she laughed, but looked angry. "Lorgi, I am so very sorry for what happened at the palace. Why did you have to get mixed up with me? If only I had not..."

"We did nothing wrong. They should be sorry to us, give us rewards, get us out of this stinky cage and take us home."

"Please don't be offended, but...what are you?"

"I understand. You have never seen people like me before, because where you live its too hot."

"People?" asked Wenji, looking confused.

"Álukoi people. My mother says just to tell human people that I'm an Álukoi—a snowdragon. She says we come from the mountains, but I still have not been up to see them. Snow, ice, cold rivers and lakes are good for us. My mother and I live in a human village by the Tunda-Sea, or what some call the ice ocean."

"Why do you live in a human village?"

"The people there are nice—unlike here. They really know how to laugh and play and be good to each other. And especially how to eat! I'm starving here."

"You are a snowdragon," stammered Wenji. "What is that?"

"Me, I guess," Lorgi giggled.

"Because you sparkle like snow?"

"I think because of where we live."

"How did you get here?" asked Wenji, shaking her head.

"That's a long story!" moaned Lorgi.

"We have a long ride ahead of us. Please tell me. It will keep our minds off our fate."

"I will make my own fate. You should, too. I'll help you."

"Make fate? Is that what you said?" stammered Wenji. "You better speak slowly so I understand. My Tuzanchim is not yet fluent."

"It's a mountain better than mine," cheered Lorgi. "But first, I want to know all about you."

"That only makes me cry to think about any of it. Please do not ask."

"You need to get back to your family too, right?"

"You are lucky to have one." Wenji's eyes formed tears.

"You lost your family?" Lorgi's ears drooped at the thought.

"I never had one. I warned you not to ask."

"Then we must find some of your friends."

"You are my only living friend."

"Then come home with me, to Tiefenbo! Everybody is your friend there. My mother can adopt you and you can be my sister."

"Your mother—adopt me?" Wenji laughed. "I'm sorry..." She covered her mouth, but started laughing harder. Recovering at last, she dared ask, "Just how big is your mother?"

"I don't know my numbers yet. Much easier just to show you."

Lorgi tried to see the dimensions of the entire wagon, drawn by four horses, but the cage limited his view. Frustrated, he began pawing the cage's bars, but found no weaknesses. Eyeing the padlock securing the door, Lorgi hoped to chew through its thinner metal. But he could not squeeze his thick paws through to reach it. Seeing his dilemma, Wenji reached to help, but then withdrew her hand.

"Help me, Wenji. Don't you want to get out of here?"

"After what has been paid for us, they cannot allow the slightest chance for us to escape. And our punishment for trying will be brutal, to say the least. Of course, sooner or later they always find an excuse to torture slaves and prisoners anyway."

"You did nothing wrong," said Lorgi, skaing his head. "Maybe I did, but they started it."

"I started it," said Wenji. "But it never matters who starts. Or what I do, or not do. Hard luck always follows me. They say you bring good fortune to the deserving. Do I, Lorgi?"

"Of course. Thanks, but I don't know about that. Good fortune would see us home, playing with friends and munching on tasty snacks. Not out here, so hot, thirsty, starving…or lost, thousands of miles away."

"I'll help you," said Wenji. "You fought for me, my champion! You saved my life today. No one has ever even spoken up for me before. You are the first true friend I've ever had. My 'knight in shining armor,' as they say in the Castled Lands, or what we call the Far West."

"Thanks, I guess, but I never want to be a knight. My mother says most of them cannot read, and generally don't live very long."

"You can read, too?" gasped Wenji.

"Not yet! I'm only three and a half," said Lorgi. "My mother will start showing me how, maybe next year. She says by the time I'm twelve, I must be able to write in Álukop and Lendish."

"Then you had better get clear of me," sighed Wenji. "I only bring doom."

"Someone once said that about me. But I'm not supposed to know," giggled Lorgi. "My mother says we will make our own good luck. And I'll make you the biggest, bestest wagonload, too."

"Thank you, but do you have any idea what awaits us?" Wenji shook her head. "We had better make some of your magic luck before this wagon and these soldiers are done with us." Reaching her slender hand through the grating, she pulled the lock close. Lorgi tried to bite it, but could not quite bring it within range. Determined to get around this, he began gnawing on the grate nearest to the lock. "Stop before you destroy your teeth, Lorgi," gasped Wenji. "That is solid iron."

"Yes, but it is only so thick. "I'm an Álukoi. If I break a tooth, I can grow another one."

"We only travel from one evil to another. You will need all your teeth for fighting."

"We just need to unlock this cage." Within minutes, Lorgi began spitting out metal flecks. When he finally cut through, he used all his strength to bend the metal out of the way so he could reach the padlock.

"Those riding behind the wagon are starting to notice your work."

"Took them long enough," said Lorgi. "They must not be very sharp. Probably the slowest arrows in the quiver, as Kibak would say."

"Have you no fear?" asked Wenji, shaking her head. "Lorgi, it is a wonder that either of us still breathe. Please, you must know that anyone else—any human, even one of the highest rank—would have been executed for what you said to the Vazuk."

"I should have said much more to *hog man*." Suddenly Lorgi broke the padlock in his jaws. "Done. Now we are free!"

"Free to be punished, in the most sadistic ways."

"They won't dare. Smile, Wenji. We're worth 500 horses." Throwing the cage door open, Lorgi yelled "Stop!" As Wenji begged him not to, Lorgi climbed on top of the cage for a better view, bringing the transport to a halt.

"What are you doing up there?" she asked. "You've torn the canopy; now we will have less shade."

"You asked how big is my mother. About the size of this wagon, or all four of its horses put together. She is really nice. But nobody tells her what to do."

"What did he say?" asked both terrified drivers.

"To be nice to him or his mother will come and squash you some day," Wenji told them. The Shohaneze knights laughed. But seeing that their Tuzanchim escorts did not, the knights quickly stopped. Either from fear or respect, the warriors all nodded to Wenji as she turned back to look at them. Lorgi smiled at everyone. Only when he had scanned the full horizon did he get down.

"Most likely, this exotic will go to the king's arena, madam," said Satungke. "This is your one chance. So long as our rock monster wins, and you can control him, you may prosper. If not..." the ambassador shook his head, frowning.

"He is a healer, not a fighter," protested Wenji. "Just look into his eyes. Big, kind baby eyes."

"Too bad. You must make him understand, for everyone's sake, especially your own," said Satungke, glaring at her. "My fortune purchased this beast, not the king's. But we all gamble on the king's favor. He values exotics, fighters and loyal servants. He has no use for poets or critics—human or otherwise. Are we clear about it all?"

"Painfully," sighed Wenji.

However, with an unlocked cage, everyone suddenly treated Wenji and her dragon very nicely, fetching water and snacks or stopping for a stretch whenever she asked. But they still trekked on the Steppes in late summer. Again Lorgi grew ill from the heat. Satungke frowned with rare, true concern for the survival of his investment. The journey lasted several more weeks, but Lorgi remembered none of it. The heat had long before shut down his *pahápkoltam*, so he could not sense where he was in relation to Tiefenbo. Worse, because he had slept most of the way, Lorgi could not even retrace his path. Without help, he would never be able to find his way back home.

16: The Wind from the West

Klimgu swore to retrace every step of Lorgi's journey, and reunite Serukeeba with her son. The two reached the Sorcerer's bluff with ease. But when they struck southeast onto the Laskomian plains, the heat thrashed Serukeeba. All she could do was rise by dawn and collapse at noon—on a good day. Once revived, she pushed Klimgu onward until he could see no more. Each morning she woke him before either of them had gotten enough sleep, and the pair forged on. Until nearing Lake Gabriska, they found remarkably little to argue about. Yet where Klimgu had once grilled Kibak and Ganjaset over the safest way around the lake, he now debated Serukeeba. Only the heat made her agree to the longer but cooler northern route. With sunset nearing, Klimgu sought a fit place to camp, something of no concern to an Álukoi.

"Can we stop at that third sandbar with the stunted trees?" he asked.

"Even crawling, we'll be there in half an hour," said Serukeeba. "I expected more from a Tuzanchim warrior."

"Riding, not walking in summer's heat."

"Moon's melt!" she cursed.

"What is wrong?"

"My traveler's curse! By the time we reach your campsite, so will they."

"Who? Where?" Grabbing his bow, Klimgu scanned in every direction.

"Twelve." Serukeeba pointed due east along the shore. "Looking lost or trying to become so. Remnants of your old group? Slumped over, ragged and hungry. Hardly riding to glory."

"Twelve dots?" gasped Klimgu, squinting. "And they say I am long-eyed!"

"For a *hyúlem*, yes. But half my village could match you. There, all speak two languages. Many can read and write as well. How many warriors can say that?"

"*Gánsi*, that makes me feel so much better." Klimgu laughed at the put-down, knowing he still had work to do before earning her respect.

"You can feel better when your debt to me has been paid."

"I long for that day more than you can know, mighty Serukeeba."

"Pox! Your renegades have seen us and debate what to do about it."

"How can you even guess at such distance?"

"I'm an Álukoi. Why must they intrude here, now?"

"They could be scouts for a whole quiver, a few miles back."

"Conveniently on the lake's north side—which you insisted on."

"Since you see and know all, Seri, can you spot anything else on the horizon?"

"Never use my shortened name. Only family and friends may do so."

"I want to be your friend."

"Perhaps in time. But those twelve are certainly friends of yours."

"They will have to be much closer for me to even guess. They do start to look more like renegades than scouts. Could be riding west to desert the horde, just as I did."

"So you arranged to meet them here?"

"Impossible!" yelled Klimgu. "You paint me as a Vazuk, master of all the Steppes."

"If I am not careful. Your Tundrish grows too swiftly for a pretended simpleton, especially with a little needling."

"A little?" he winced. "Not half the speed of your Tuzanchim. But to what use?"

"Anything to help find my son. With any luck, your renegades will know of him."

"*My* renegades?"

"One woman, eleven men. She seems to be in charge. Unusual for savage, lowland *hyúlems*."

"They are just people, not savages," said Klimgu.

"That would be refreshing. I don't care, as long as any of them can speak Tundrish."

The woman leading the group kept her raven hair in a ponytail, her clothes neater than the others, and her head level as she looked ahead, an expression of hope on her striking face. Even her horse seemed more confident, as well as better groomed. All of them kept bows ready, yet showed no eagerness to part with their arrows. A hundred yards away, the group halted. After a few words amongst themselves, they waited while she rode up to meet Serukeeba and Klimgu.

"I am Baqwam," she nodded to Klimgu, but immediately focused on Serukeeba.

"I am...Klimgu," he stammered, shamed by his own name.

"We thought so," she smiled, keeping her eyes on the Álukoi.

"But this is mighty Serukeeba, Queen of the rock dragons, from the frozen northern extremes of the exotic Far West," said Klimgu. "We seek to retrieve her son—from Uxanda and the Gran Vazuk!"

"What rubbish are you spewing about me?" asked Serukeeba.

"The dragon speaks!" gasped Baqwam, wide-eyed.

"Tundrish, not Tuzanchim," said Serukeeba, anxious to enter the conversation.

"So do I," smiled Baqwam, nodding. Turning to her group, she yelled "Gurjik!" Directly, a stocky man with short hair and a round face rode up beside her, also smiling and nodding.

"Good," said Serukeeba. "You two can be my translators."

"What became of your group? Where do you ride?" asked Klimgu, pained that he would have to answer the same questions in detail, over and over.

"Better not to ask," said Baqwam, signaling the rest to join them. "And yours?"

"Never mind your petty clans," said Serukeeba. "Who among you has seen my son, Lorgi? Lorgámon. Lor-gá-mon?"

"You *do* speak Tuzanchim!" smiled Baqwam, looking up to Serukeeba.

"Hardly, but I intend to learn quickly. Have any of you seen my son?"

Looking to each other, then back to Serukeeba, all mutely shook their heads.

"Do any of you have news of him?"

Their blank eyes seemed to beg her for explanation.

"Who among you knows anything of Álukois—snowdragons?"

"Please, you must tell us," said Baqwam, nodding to Serukeeba.

"Gladly, on our way to your Vazuk, to retrieve my son. A most honorable quest. We can learn much from each other on the way."

Gurjik faithfully translated for the others, but his face betrayed profound disbelief.

"I guarantee your safety," promised Serukeeba. "Who would challenge an Álukoi?"

"Only the Gran Vazuk himself," said Baqwam. "With his nearest 10,000 warriors and every possible weapon."

"No matter," huffed Serukeeba. "I will find my son and reward all who help. Know that I alone carved a fine and spacious hall from solid granite—by paw. That would have taken a score of men decades. My hall can rival some of the grandest castles and palaces in the lowlands. I once slew 400 balkotars in one day. Only my foes have anything to fear. Baqwam and Gurjik must come with me for certain."

Gurjik laughed nervously. Baqwam looked as if given a death sentence.

"What is so terrible about your Vazuk?" demanded Serukeeba. Closing her eyes and shaking her head, she added, "Never mind. I don't want to know."

"Know that we are here...because we oppose him," said Klimgu, carefully eyeing the others for support. "Our presence may hinder your quest when you near the capitol, Uxanda."

"Spare me your ambitions, Klimgu," warned Serukeeba, raising a forepaw. "I hold you responsible for Lorgi, and expect you to do everything possible to help me. Then we may part as friends, despite what else you may do."

Gurjik translated for the others.

"Western chivalry!" muttered one man. "Could Tuzanchim ever be so patient, forgiving or generous?"

"These stone dragons must bring powerful luck," said another.

"Then the Vazuk will never give up her cub," added a third.

"Serukeeba, we assumed you were dead when we found you by the river," said Klimgu. "With no mother or home for Lorgi to return to, I thought it best to place him with the Vazuk. Best for Lorgi, and, yes, best for me and my quiver as well. Getting him back will require force. Great force."

"As I feared from the start," she huffed.

"Thirteen warriors and a rock dragon against the Gran Vazuk?" asked Baqwam, shaking her head in disbelief.

"Certainly we will gather others on our way, enough to make a respectable quiver," assured Klimgu. "We can start planning while we make camp."

"Not before dusk," said Serukeeba. "Anyone sleeping past dawn need not follow. I will march as long and far as I can, every day, straight to the Vazuk. Surely, anyone clever enough to become master of the Steppes will respond to reason. But if not…then you and he will learn the meaning of great force!"

"Um, Serukeeba…first we need to make a slight detour," Klimgu murmured gently as a Delfinian.

"Not I, and you must keep up with me to keep your life," she snapped. "My kind know revenge better than forgiveness. Yes. It is one thing I have to admit that we hold in common with *hyúlems*. Do not push me."

"Not even half a day to the south?" begged Klimgu. "There wait two very clever men that we need for the quest."

"I need but one reliable, efficient guide, which has yet to appear."

"Even you will need a great host against the Gran Vazuk!" shouted Baqwam.

"Before finding Lorgi at the sorcerer's bluff, we pillaged a Laskomian temple," said Klimgu, hanging his head.

"And you'd do it again in a blink if I were not here to stop you," huffed Serukeeba.

"Not so!" shouted Klimgu. "We only raided the place. No one was killed—that day. We just locked up two monks in their own temple and stole their food. If they still live, and can be found, we need them."

"You need all the best spiritual guidance to be found on the Continent! But your first moral obligation is to me, Lorgi, and Tiefenbo. No matter the risk or hardship. I need no monks, warriors, seers or renegades to slow my quest. If I must find Lorgi without your help, you will pay my revenge, no matter where you hide on the entire Continent."

"But you, of all…people…will like these monks. They read and write, they think, and create all sorts of useful things."

"So you locked them in their temple to starve!" huffed Serukeeba.

"We may not be able to retrieve Lorgi without their help."

"Then lead us to your monks, but quickly."

"*Gánsi,*" smiled Klimgu. "You are wise."

"Someday, when your grandchildren are old, I may earn a few crumbs of wisdom. For now, we both are desperate fools trying to right horrific wrongs. Save your false charm for dull men."

"Save your venom for the Vazuk," said Klimgu.

When Serukeeba finally let the group make camp, the men talked amongst themselves while Baqwam grilled Klimgu about recent events. Neither Gurjik nor Baqwam shared any of it with her. Angered at being excluded, the snowdragon pounded the ground with her tail, demanding that every word be translated immediately into Tundrish. From then on, all conversation proceeded very slowly. Guessing the Vazuk might sell Lorgi for enough horses, the men avoided Serukeeba's eyes. Smelling deceit when Gurjik failed to translate something, she picked him up with both forepaws.

"Censoring truth is an insult, anywhere on the Continent!" she growled, shaking him lightly before setting him back down. "Share it all or speak nothing!"

"Yes, noble dragon," stammered Gurjik, wincing from cuts and bruises on his chest and back.

"Stop grimacing. I held you gently enough," scolded Serukeeba. "Out with it."

"They say the Vazuk...gives up on conquering the west." Rubbing his chest, Gurjik had trouble taking a deep breath after the Álukoi's grip. "Now he covets the Well-East...expecting those kingdoms to fall...one by one...for lack of a cooperative defense."

Scowling, Serukeeba twitched her nostrils and pinned back her ears, knowing it should have nothing to do with her quest. Yet Klimgu's look told otherwise. "What?" she glared at him.

"Foolish beyond measure," he said.

"Why?" asked Serukeeba.

"Like ants, the Well-East peoples are too numerous to count!" laughed Klimgu. "They cannot fight, organize or even ride like

Tuzanchim, but we could never conquer them. Still, the Vazuk's ambition may help us, by leaving Uxanda lightly defended."

"What of *your* ambition, Klimgu? How will that help find my son?"

"What if the Vazuk has sold Lorgi to the king of Shohan?" asked Gurjik, looking between Baqwam, Klimgu and Serukeeba.

"Then it may be too late already," said Baqwam.

"What? Why?" yelled Serukeeba.

"Though old foes, the Tuzanchim Empire and the Kingdom of Shohan trade," said Gurjik. "Via Shohan's ambassador, Satungke."

"And the Vazuk's nephew, Puchakta," added Baqwam. "Both men take huge profits from it. The Vazuk will trade anything for horses, despite already having the most and the best. He also craves eastern luxuries and decadent foreign ways. Every summer he buys a new 'litter' of Shohaneze concubines, on the off chance one might please him. He sends many back, to a horrible fate."

"How do you know all this?" Klimgu asked in disbelief.

"I can read and write, unlike most Tuzanchim, so they made me an imperial *accounter* in Uxanda Palace," said Baqwam, pulling a bamboo pen from her pack. "I tallied so many wicked things, my eyes could stand no more. But one does not freely leave such a position. I only escaped with my life."

"What of Shohan's king?" asked Serukeeba.

"He trades for exotic beasts to expand his collection," said Baqwam. "He has many vices and a deranged mind. Whatever slaves the Vazuk returns to him end life as meat in the king's Great Arena, a spectacle lower than scorpions."

"What is that?" demanded Serukeeba. "Explain."

Baqwam hesitated until the Álukoi reached to pick her up and shake her like Gurjik. Nodding with outstretched hands, Baqwam answered. "The arena is a huge, open structure. A place of gambling, of savage judgment. A theatre where people and animals from all over the Continent meet death. I am sorry."

"I cannot endure this!" moaned Serukeeba, pacing.

"Who has seen this arena?" asked Klimgu.

None answered.

"Which of you has met one who has?"

Silence.

"Who has even set foot in Shohan?" Klimgu gestured to them, but looked to Serukeeba. "Then do not alarm our dragon friend with myths."

"Not even the king of Shohan would waste anything so fine and rare as a stone dragon," said Gurjik, but without conviction. The others nodded.

"Enough talk!" yelled Klimgu. "Let us gather what force we may en route to Uxanda, where we will find Lorgi as we left him—by a cool fountain, munching the finest treats on all the Continent. Gurjik, get a cup for Serukeeba."

"What?" snapped Serukeeba. "I don't need your charm or some silly ritual. What good can that do?"

"A toast to our quest, if only with water!" cheered Klimgu. "May Grand Luck itself ride with us, with Serukeeba, and her noble son. May our foes crumble in fear, our friends bring strength, and our efforts bear fruit, before the moon regrows in the sky."

"So Weliben has got to you," chuckled Serukeeba. "Now you sound like a Delfinian. After too many toasts."

* * *

Dawn found all but Serukeeba asleep. Roaring and pounding the ground, she roused them in seconds. While she paced and snorted, the humans scrambled to eat and break camp, needing half an hour to become travel-ready. Apologizing for their slowness, Klimgu vowed to get them back into fighting shape. Just as the group left, Serukeeba felt her curse return.

"Eight scouts in formation, a mile to the west!" yelled Baqwam, with fearful eyes. "Real scouts, not..."

"Deserters," huffed Serukeeba. "I don't care."

"You should," said Klimgu. "This will be either grand or terrible news. We must know which way they ride—for or against the Vazuk."

"I leave now," said Serukeeba. "Klimgu will live much longer by fearing me more than his Vazuk. Gather rabble on your own time, not mine."

"Two scouts ride to us, but the rest go back!" yelled Baqwam, wide-eyed. "Not a good sign."

When they arrived, both looked young, unproven, and expendable.

"For whom do you scout?" Klimgu shouted.

"Twarejik," yelled one. "And you?"

"Her, in search of her son," Klimgu pointed to Serukeeba.

"Not the Vazuk?" asked the scout.

"You ride too far west to ask that question."

"Who are you? Whom do you serve?" demanded the scout, gripping his sword.

"The Wind itself often asks me," Klimgu smiled. "Now, I serve…myself."

"Truth distilled!" huffed Serukeeba, shaking her head like a reproachful human.

"Can Twarejik return Klimgu's favor?" Klimgu shouted. With a quick nod, one scout rode off, as the other dismounted and began asking all about Serukeeba.

She set out once more, walking as far as her traveler's curse allowed—500 paces. Suddenly, a dust cloud blurred the lake's shore to the west, as Twarejik and his entire force charged to meet Klimgu. Directly she felt the spell he cast over them. Every hand reached for his. Twarejik called him a "leader's leader." Even with both her translators beside her, Serukeeba struggled to get a tenth of what was said to or by Klimgu.

"My great friend, please forgive my new scouts," said Twarejik, grasping Klimgu's hand high and out to the side. "They only joined my group weeks after we fought the spider shaman. Is this the mother of your gift to the Vazuk?"

Serukeeba's eyes glowed, her nostrils flared, and her ears pinned back in rage over that question. But she clenched her jaws shut and kept still, pretending not to understand anything being said until Baqwam or Gurjik offered it to her in Tundrish. Rokímba had warned her not to interrupt truth, no matter how painful, for the sake of her son. 'Lorgi before revenge,' she kept telling herself.

"Yes, but now I ride for the rock dragons against the Vazuk," said Klimgu. "Join us, Twarejik. Help mighty Serukeeba reclaim her son. And rid our land of a rotten Vazuk."

"Honorable quests, indeed, but what does Klimgu seek for himself?" asked Twarejik.

Staring intently at him, the way only an Álukoi could, Serukeeba inhaled deeply to draw his scent. Looking surprised, she wondered if Twarejik would prove to be very clever or just the opposite. As she expected, Klimgu avoided his friend's question.

"First, a half-day ride south to retrieve those two Laskomian monks I had told you about, remember?" said Klimgu.

"A pleasant chore for elders, my friend," laughed Twarejik. "We have far greater tasks. Why trouble yourself over foreigners, especially monks?"

"Because I am learning how long, full and rich a life can be. We wronged them. Now we need their help."

Serukeeba reared her back, blinked at Klimgu and twitched her ears in surprise. A moment earlier she had wanted to kill him.

"Monks or not, they are Laskomians," said Twarejik. "Nothing could persuade them to help us."

"I have been humbled many times, in many ways," said Klimgu. "I ask all to give what help they can for our cause. Are you ready?"

"Moons before you asked."

"Stay with Serukeeba on her way to Uxanda. I need only fifty warriors. We can rejoin you in a few days."

"No!" roared Serukeeba. "We stay together."

"I agree," added Twarejik, wondering if the dragon already understood everything without translation. "Listen to her, Klimgu."

"No one will run off to pillage during my quest," said Serukeeba.

"I am through pillaging," swore Klimgu.

"Just as well," said Twarejik. "Because there is really nothing left to pillage in Laskomia, anyway."

"I would like to be remembered for something besides that," sighed Klimgu. "Let us find Lorgi and a new Vazuk before snow, no matter the cost. And make a better empire, where one can grow old to enjoy life's sunset."

"Are you well, my friend?" pried Twarejik, darting his eyes between Klimgu and the presumed source of his ailment, Serukeeba.

"Yes, for the first time in my life," said Klimgu.

Rearing her neck back in surprise, Serukeeba twitched her ears and nostrils. She also blinked both her ear and eyelids several times to make certain those senses were working as they should. Glad that she had not lost her temper with Twarejik's first words, Serukeeba heaved a long sigh of relief. Suddenly, Rokímba's nagging advice had come to life. Had she predicted this moment?

Nothing would do but to bring the entire quiver, more than 5,000 warriors, on Klimgu's errand. He devised a canopy, held aloft by six riders bearing long poles, enabling Serukeeba to walk all day in shade. The sight of a dragon, under what looked to be a floating tent, leading a small army, made the group infinitely more impressive. Whoever saw it could not resist joining. By the time they reached the Laskomian temple, an hour before sundown, the group had added a thousand more warriors. Rumors of them swept the empire faster than locusts.

Unable to hide on the Laskomian Plains, the small but immaculate, white-washed brick temple rose above a dozen crumbling structures huddled close by it. Charred walls and fences surrounded the tiny village. Well-tended farms had sprung to life around it in the two months since Klimgu's raid. His mouth open in shock, he gazed at the miraculous recovery, thinking he had not found the right place. Scratching his head, he ordered all but Serukeeba to wait while he scouted ahead. A mile closer the odd pair halted. Stretching to her full height, while Klimgu stood up in his stirrups, Serukeeba met his eyes for confirmation. He nodded.

"I see two men and a child working," he said. "There were no children here before."

"I see nine people, but smell more," stated Serukeeba. "Two men in their prime, four women, one old and three young, plus three girls of different ages." The instant she finished, the temple's bell started ringing. Terrified villagers scrambled over the fences and into the structures.

"We must keep our group away from this place," warned Klimgu.

"Your group, not mine," said Serukeeba.

"The alarm inspires them, like waving raw meat before wolves. You know what they can do."

"Not around me!" shouted Serukeeba. "Use your charisma, or I will use my teeth on them."

"If I can just retrieve those two monks before…"

"Go. Do your best while I tame your pack." Serukeeba waved him away with a forepaw. But as he rode off toward the temple, she turned and charged after him. Twarejik put the army into a battle formation, expecting another Laskomian ambush.

"Stop, Klimgu. *Yahai!*" yelled Serukeeba. "You have no chance."

"You're right," he yelled, turning back. "I cannot speak one word of Laskomian. But someone in our…my, I mean Twarejik's group must."

"As do I. Summon the captains. Keep the rest back. Far back. Make them all sit on the ground, before I start slicing off limbs!" Serukeeba tailed Klimgu as he began carrying out her demand. The captains seemed angry, while the rest looked confused.

"Are we not wasting time here, out of the way?" asked Twarejik. "That village smells too sweet not to be a trap."

"Klimgu knows what he needs," said Baqwam.

"No more talk!" yelled Serukeeba. "Look hard into my eyes, all who claim to have honor, who call themselves warriors." She stopped to sniff and scowl at each captain in turn, before resting on her haunches. To make certain all understood, she shouted one sentence at a time, pausing for Baqwam and Gurjik to translate from Tundrish to Tuzanchim.

"Everyone keep your eyes on mine until I have done, or lose yours for the insult. None of you will go near that village, hurt unarmed people, burn or pillage during my quest. I know the face and scent of every captain, and hold each responsible for all under him or her. I will find and slay any who break my rules. Any who cannot accept this must challenge me now."

Despite their fears, the captains had to debate her edict, like everything else that had ever been presented to them.

"You ask far more than any leader has ever dared. Far too much," warned Klimgu.

"You should know," huffed Serukeeba. "But I ask what is right, not what is merely to my advantage at the moment."

"Are we sheep to be herded by some monstrous exotic, not even human, let alone Tuzanchim?" yelled one captain. "My warriors go in now to take what little this place holds for us. It has always been our way, our destiny."

"NO!" screamed Klimgu.

"Fools!" Serukeeba pushed a dozen men aside to reach that captain. Directly, he felt himself suffocating between her forepaws. Everyone expected her to kill him. Instead, she raised him to eye level, bit off his dominant left hand, then threw him ten yards away, screaming in pain. Spitting the severed hand into the face of its owner, Serukeeba turned toward the other captains. "Destiny! Who else must learn the value of a hand, an arm, or perhaps a life?"

"The sooner we leave here, the better," Klimgu murmured to her.

"Now that *your* group has been cowed, we may attend to *your* errand. Bring two who can speak Laskomian."

"Done," said Klimgu. But as his delegation approached the village, he voiced doubts. "Much has changed, been rebuilt here, since…"

"You pillaged it," huffed Serukeeba. "Do you even have a word for remorse in Tuzanchim?" She asked in Tundrish. Baqwam had difficulty translating.

"This village reminds me of Tiefenbo," said Klimgu. "Both survived overwhelming assaults. Yet those monks must have gone long before now."

"Stop!" warned Serukeeba. "Six crossbows aim from the temple windows—held by children. Two men in the bell tower with longbows. Two more in the rubble, but those hide their weapons. Wait here. I will sort out the mess you made."

"No. This was my idea," said Klimgu. "I must take the first step."

Dismounting, he walked twenty paces, and slowly put his weapons on the ground. Gesturing his wish to talk to the villagers, Klimgu sat down, cross-legged, to wait for a response. Five minutes elapsed. The temple hummed with activity as terrified women and children inside prepared to defend themselves, knowing they stood no chance against even a handful of Tuzanchim.

Finally, a lean monk climbed over a low spot in the defensive rubble adjoining it. Klimgu recognized him instantly, despite the man having lost ninety pounds. The hungry Laskomian marched up and sat himself down only three feet away, facing him with a cold, fearless hatred. Klimgu nodded and smiled, motioning for his translators to join him.

"No!" barked the monk. "I have learned to speak your crow-cursed tongue, and your ways. What can you possibly want now, that you have not already stolen or destroyed?"

"I am Klimgu, leader of many thousands of warriors."

"I am Lutyam, a simple monk, leader of starving peasants."

"We ride east, with our mighty ally," Klimgu smiled, waving back at Serukeeba. She lowered her head almost to the ground, drooped her ears and blinked her eyes, mortified to be associated with the Tuzanchim.

"Please, let no one delay you," said the monk, gesturing to the east. "May your ride be swift and carry you thousands of leagues away from here."

"What has been done can never be undone," Klimgu nodded with his hands stretched out to the sides to show humility. "I am not the same man who...rode over your village months ago. I will not let that ever happen again."

"What? Are you saying you are sorry?" gasped the monk, wide-eyed.

"Since then I have found wisdom and powerful friends," said Klimgu. "I would turn enemies into friends, here and now. Join us on a new ride, unlike any other before!"

"Ride? I don't understand," Lutyam shook his head.

"We ride on Uxanda!" shouted Klimgu, smiling with a raised hand and a vigorous nod.

"You ride back to Uxanda?" Lutyam tried to paraphrase. "Good."

"No. We ride *on* Uxanda. To war on the Vazuk."

"What? I don't understand you," said Lutyam.

Klimgu waved both his translators to join him. They repeated the crucial statements in Laskomian, but Lutyam still shook his head.

Responding in Tuzanchim, the monk said, "I hear your words, but miss their intent. You cannot mean what I just heard. Let me call someone to help. Moshal!"

Another Laskomian hobbled over the same low spot in the rubble. Recognizing him as well, Klimgu swallowed hard. Though thin, Moshal did not appear quite as hungry or bitter as Lutyam. Klimgu guessed this second monk might prove more agreeable if approached with care. Smiling and nodding, Klimgu nudged his translators to do the same. He struggled to convince the monks of his quests to find Serukeeba's son and to overthrow the Vazuk. Then he had to explain why and how to wary ears. With the sun about to set and no agreement reached, a very impatient Serukeeba joined them, nearly frightening the monks away.

"Meet our siege engine," boasted Klimgu. "Nothing can stand against her."

"Amazing, but Uxanda has never been taken," said Moshal. "No water, nothing edible. No trees for a hundred miles around it, by what I've read. With walls too high and thick, even for your—"

"You would either die of thirst in summer, or freeze to death in winter, before breaching Uxanda's walls," said Lutyam.

"We do not wait for either," Serukeeba said in Laskomian, grabbing the monks' eyes.

"But you said you only have a few thousand warriors," said Lutyam. "Plenty to terrorize small villages, but no match for Uxanda and the Gran Vazuk. We could not help you even if we wanted to."

"We will triple our numbers before reaching Uxanda," assured Klimgu.

"Ridiculous," Lutyam shook his head. "You cannot take such a fortress without many siege engines, and there is no wood to build them for hundreds of miles. The ground there is too hard to tunnel under the walls. So Uxanda cannot be taken by force, period. All the Continent knows this."

"Of course, with enough rope, they could all grapple over..." Moshal trailed off as Lutyam glared at him.

"See! I told you they would be useful," cheered Klimgu, smiling at Serukeeba.

"We are needed here, to defend the shattered remnants of our village against such as you," said Lutyam. Sweeping his arm east, he shouted, "for the best rope, go to Shohan."

"Wait, Brother Lutyam," said Moshal, leaning over to whisper in his ear. "They invite us, offer us a chance to help remove the Tuzanchim from Laskomia. The very fate of the West, maybe the whole Continent, may rest in our hands."

"I agree," Serukeeba moaned in Laskomian, surprising the monks with her superior ears.

"Nothing escapes her, in any language," said Klimgu.

"Please help me find my son," asked Serukeeba. "And tame these snarling Steppe savages."

Both monks nodded and smiled with her.

"We are agreed, yes?" Klimgu smiled, starting to get up.

"Not without compensation," said Serukeeba, pressing him to stay seated.

"None has been hurt, or even threatened," said Klimgu. "What more do you want?"

"This village will suffer without their labor," said Serukeeba. "Give three horses to make up for the monks' absence."

"Four," barked Lutyam.

"No, six—but we'll bring all the rope we have," said Moshal.

"Well struck!" laughed Serukeeba. "Your company will make my trek with these warriors far more tolerable. *Gánsi*....Thank you."

At dawn, the army set off at a human walk, because the monks were very poor riders. Sensing their presence would cripple the expedition, Serukeeba thought to reject them—or the whole group—to prevent further delays. Seeing her desperation, Baqwam nodded to the snowdragon and immediately took it upon herself to teach the monks how to ride like warriors. Fortunately, they proved to be quick, eager learners. With each hour, their pace increased. Lutyam seemed the more athletic of the two, but Moshal the more personable, agreeing with every word Baqwam said about anything, making her smile. Baqwam's initiative helped to keep the budding rebel army together, while elevating her standing in it.

The group hounded Serukeeba with endless questions about snowdragons, the "exotic" or "barbarous" Far West, the "frozen north," and the Stonelaw. Then they had to know about her home village and its "short people," the Delfinians. Most of the Tuzanchim men feared that Tiefenbo's gentle ways might dangerously soften a warrior, yet agreed it would make an ideal place to settle in old age, when one could no longer fight or ride.

Gurjik did all the translating, as Baqwam was busy teaching the monks to ride. After two hours, he began to lose his voice. Tired of answering questions without getting answers to her own, Serukeeba refused to talk further. Still, curiosity held the group so firmly that Twarejik had trouble getting volunteers to ride out and recruit more rebels for the group. Both Serukeeba and Klimgu had misgivings about his sending out any at this point.

"A hundred?" gasped Klimgu. "I'd only feel better about sending scouts after we had another thousand warriors."

"One must sow if one would harvest," remarked Twarejik.

"So now you're a farmer, too?" Klimgu liked to tease him.

"We are only gamblers here, and must take chances our great foe will not expect."

"Well shot!" nodded Klimgu.

"What if all this harvesting frightens the Vazuk away from your capitol, taking my son with him?" asked Serukeeba.

"The fire is long lit," said Twarejik. "Let the Vazuk choke on his own smoke."

"Well shot again!" cheered Gurjik, after translating.

"The Vazuk must attack, or fortify himself in Uxanda," said Klimgu. "But he dare not retreat from rebellion. As we speak, he will be summoning forces from the east with all possible haste. We must strike long before those can arrive, no matter the odds already against us here."

"Never mind your odds," said Serukeeba. "What if you manage to overthrow your Gran Vazuk? What then, Klimgu? Who will fill the void you are all so eager to create?"

Klimgu shook his head, staring at the horizon. People close by focused hard on him with wrinkled brows.

* * *

Every day, the rebel horde progressed southeast toward the capitol, but in a zigzag pattern, both to gain recruits and confuse the enemy. Expecting the Vazuk to strike back at any time, they always set up a defensive camp, posting guards around its perimeter from dusk to dawn.

Yet each day, the army gathered force and confidence without detecting signs of their foe. By the time Uxanda loomed on the horizon, Klimgu found himself leading a respectable horde, more than 17,000 strong. His new army was comprised of the most skilled, experienced and efficient warriors that the Continent had yet spawned. All of them began calling Klimgu the New Vazuk.

Feeling he was only an average general, though a better gambler, Klimgu found no skills or desires within himself to become a diplomat, administrator or builder, and certainly not the Gran Vazuk. He thought of himself as a follower in search of a worthy leader—one that did not seem to exist. His original goal had been to simply oust the Vazuk. After the battle at Lake Gabriska, he had told himself that he just wanted to find the rock dragons, survive that encounter, then retire somewhere in the west. Klimgu would adopt the language and ways of any people who could accept a former warrior, and try to forget his past. But then he found Serukeeba and her village.

Tiefenbo made him want so much more. In a few weeks he had been transformed from a simple guide into a "New Vazuk." Once the real Vazuk's scouts had spotted the rebel horde, Klimgu knew there was no turning back for anyone. He must lead them to victory or die fighting in the attempt. Feeling strangely alone, with thousands of warriors behind him, he gazed silently to the east, where Uxanda glowed like a long, low island on the horizon at sunset. The question posed by Twarejik and Serukeeba gnawed at him, but his defeat at Lake Gabriska haunted him. Many times, captains riding close by asked what Klimgu was thinking, but Twarejik always cut them off.

"Don't disturb when he is planning!" Twarejik would hiss at them. "We are lucky beyond stars to follow such a great leader. Let him think, so that we succeed."

Hearing such praise, Klimgu fought back a smile, but at his core beat a tortured heart. All had questions for him, but no answers for the ones he dared not ask. If he could not retrieve Serukeeba's son alive, she was obliged to carry out blood revenge against all connected with Lorgi. Most rebellions anywhere on the Continent quickly failed. All left massive bloodbaths in their wakes. Klimgu and others knew this from Lutyam's nightly history lessons. The Vazuk still had about 80,000 loyal warriors in the eastern half of the empire. Most of what passed for the western half now rode with Klimgu. Often, he wondered if he could lead his rebels to anything but doom.

17: Trials of Shohan

When at last they reached Shohan, Lorgi and Wenji were transferred to a new wagon. After weeks on meandering roads, and over countless bridges, rivers, and widely varied terrain, they finally arrived at the king's Summer Palace. Like the Vazuk's, it claimed the center of a thriving city, yet behind walls standing only nine feet high and three feet thick at the base. The Tuzanchim would have called them "pony," or "grandmother" walls. But the Summer Palace of Shohan dwarfed all others on the Continent. The host city, while barely half the size of Uxanda, held profound advantages, sitting beside a roaring river and just below lush, pine-forested foothills in the mountainous north of the realm. Even though it was still high summer, Lorgi felt better due to cooler, moister air. He hoped that the gentler climate would produce nicer people.

Instead, he and Wenji were thrown down into a pit cage, one of many next to a large round training field. Only by luck did Wenji land on her feet, without injury. The pair felt as if they had just become the least desirable addition to the king's zoo. A stone masonry floor and walls eight feet high and nine feet across formed their cube-shaped prison, topped with an iron grating. Its sole virtue was respite from any heat above, at ground level. Wenji begged the guards to bring cold water and food—other than meat—for Lorgi. They ignored her, but an hour later, zoo keepers dumped a bucket of rotting fruit into the cage. Those also vanished without a word. Ravenous, Lorgi inhaled an orange, a few apples and a bunch of grapes, but set the least damaged fruit aside.

"I'm saving the best for you," he said as he ate.

"Why bother?" sobbed Wenji. "They are just going to..." she trailed off.

"What? What are they going to do?"

"No point in even talking about it," said Wenji. "Why are you so nice? Aren't you furious about it all, as well as starving?"

"Both, ever since I left home, and so are you." Lorgi thrust an apple to within an inch of her mouth. "Here. This is the best one."

"No thank you. I cannot eat now."

"Yes you can. Look. This side is perfectly good. See? You're very weak. I can tell. So you must eat something or you will get worse, and fast."

"Ever perceptive, as well as gracious," Wenji forced a smile, to be polite.

"Thanks. Be sure and tell my mother when you meet her. She is teaching me proper highland manners."

"Highland manners," mused Wenji. "What are those?"

"The ways of the Stonelaw," said Lorgi, cocking his head as if expecting her to know.

"The word *Stonelaw* sounds harsh, primitive."

"Stone is natural. *Iron* is harsh."

"What isn't?" sighed Wenji.

"My mother says the Stonelaw is the most civilized place on the whole entire Continent. Some people say it is the only civilized place on it—and some of those are humans. Others just say it has the nicest manners."

"We are locked in a cage, waiting our turn against death. Maybe one of several turns until it takes us. I'm sorry Lorgi. But you will never need manners again."

"Oh yes I will. My mother is on her way."

"You still believe she will come and rescue you?"

"Us!" chirped Lorgi. "Of course. But why wait? We're not helpless."

"Look where we are. Think how we got here, Lorgi. Our fate is in the hands of evil men. The type who enjoy watching others suffer. Or die. We have no say in any of it."

"I make my own fate! So can you."

"Who made this?" Wenji swept her arms out wide.

"You know Shohan, its ways, the language. I know a few things, too, besides how to fight. We can get out of here. Some of the Tuzanchim— the ones who brought me to Uxanda—called me a warrior. You even said I was your champion!"

"That you certainly are, and much more." Wenji fought back tears. "A true champion, like no other."

"My father was a great one. I want to be like him."

"You will have to be, to survive here."

"No. We just need to leave. We can survive on our way home."

"Dream on," said Wenji, shaking her head.

"Here come some very bad people."

"That is normal and constant anywhere you go in Shohan."

"These will be special. Extra spoiled bad."

"Special? We can't hear or see a thing from down here. How can you know?"

A blubbery man with a repulsive face, in his late 30's, arrived with twenty fat, bejeweled officials, all clad in silk. Laughing and talking incessantly, they showered him with praise, while snapping at each other. They could never approach the Tuzanchim in volume, intensity, or aggressiveness, but these Shohaneze nobles seemed to carry real venom in their words. Lorgi sensed it even without knowing their language. They sneered down at the pair as though observing insects in a jar.

"See what I mean?" huffed Lorgi. "Their leader is even uglier than the Vazuk. Does that funny hat make him king?"

"Yes, and if he could speak Tuzanchim, we would be put to death at once. Please, Lorgi. You must guard your words from now on. This is Shohan, a kingdom of horrors."

"A bunch of smiley-mouth liars," said Lorgi, sitting back on his haunches. "They all need a good spanking. That's what Jinva would say."

"A flogging, at the very least," said Wenji. "Or be burned at the stake, like in the Castled Lands. But that's probably still less than some of them deserve."

"How can they stand up there laughing, with you down here crying?"

"Just hope they take pity on us, though it is not in their nature."

"Watch this," smiled Lorgi. "It even works on my mother, no matter what I did wrong." He sat back on his haunches, gazing up and trying to melt them with his most lovable *baby eyes*. But neither innocence nor tears could move those above. They scowled down with both dread and distain, alarmed by a talking beast. None of them understood Tuzanchim. But once they guessed that Lorgi was speaking in it, most could not wait for him to die in the Great Arena. Blabbering more excitedly than ever, they lobbied the king to that end.

"We've done nothing at all. Why do they hate us?" asked Lorgi.

"The nobility hate everything—the innocent most of all," sighed Wenji. "But really, I think it is because we speak in the language of their enemy."

"The Tuzanchim have lots of those. Don't they know we're not Tuzanchim?"

"Yes, of course," said Wenji. "But we must not behave like Steppe warriors in any way. Not here. We must be very careful. It won't take them long to fetch an interpreter."

"Oh." Lorgi got down on all fours, silently resting his head on his forepaws. Wenji also sat and kept quiet. In a moment, the chatter above calmed down as well. But it never stopped. After a few minutes it grew louder and more exited again.

"What are they saying about us this time?"

"Right now they are just trying to think of a name for you," she sighed.

"That's easy—Lorgámon of Tiefenbo!" he said with pride, sitting up on his haunches.

"They have no interest in *your* name. Only what kind of...beast...they say you are. I am so sorry, Lorgi. How could you understand, child of a fairytale realm? Here, only the rich and powerful have personal names."

"Where I come from, all have their own names, whether they can voice them or not," said Lorgi. "Every beaver, elk, stream, pond and tree. All the hills, mountains, and every other living thing. In the Castled Lands, some nobles think they have to have very long names. But every single person owns a name."

"Not here," said Wenji. "I am just *slave*. But to those who know me, at least I am Wenji the slave. Depending on who owns me, I become Wenji the nanny, Wenji the scullery maid, the launderer, weaver, shepherd,...concubine. Or now the dragon tender—by far my best assignment."

"Not hardly," said Lorgi, eyeing the walls and grating of the pit cage. "What's a concubine?"

"You're not even four," Wenji shook her head.

"You don't have to baby me! I'm three and a half already. Which is practically four. I have traveled far and had perilous adventures and fought battles and made many friends and learned many things. Am I your champion or not?"

"Indeed you are, and do me great honor," Wenji nodded like a Tuzanchim, forgetting the nobles above. "My point was this: I must be whatever my current master tells me to be, and do whatever he or she orders, no matter how...objectionable."

"Is that the concubine part? Is it like cleaning up stinky rotten things?"

"Yes, and please just leave it at that." For an instant, Wenji looked nauseous.

"Sorry," said Lorgi. "There should be no such things."

"Sometimes, a new master will even change my name—those are always the worst. But when one has the decency to ask, then at least I can be Wenji, the name I was born to. My sole possession. Lately, I seem to have no value, except in trade. Like knights, slaves do not live long. But *you!* Little Lord Gamon, dragon prince regent, crown of Tiefenbo, son of a mighty rock dragon! How lucky you are."

"Lucky? I'm just a hungry little boy, too lost and far from home to ever find my way back. But we can't stay here. No one can."

"Nothing ever stays in one of these cages for long," cried Wenji.

"What are all those smiley-mouths blabbering now?" asked Lorgi. "They cackle like chickens, and make less sense!"

"They still debate what to call you. This could be important for us. The old man on the left wants to name you a stone leopard. His wife says crystal dragon sounds better. Forgive me, but I agree."

"Why do they have to make up names when I already have one?" asked Lorgi. "They should just ask me."

"Quiet, please, so I can hear all that they say," asked Wenji. Again the pair sat in silence for a moment. "The king says you cannot be a dragon without wings, from what he has read of the savage realms—the Far West. His physician thinks you are more like a giant lizard, but he wants to see you grow some before making up his mind. Pray long and hard that the king takes his advice."

"Tell them to call me an Álukoi."

"Absolutely not!" gasped Wenji.

"But I *am* an Álukoi. So what?"

"Is that what you really call your kind?"

"Yes. We are the Álukois," Lorgi smiled with pride. "That's our real name."

"I must never tell them that!" she shook her head, terrified.

"Why not?"

"It means *vegetarian* in our language," Wenji moaned.

"Good! Because we're that, too."

"They will laugh at us. Then throw us to the king's lions."

"What's a lion?" asked Lorgi, wide-eyed.

Her mouth open, Wenji slowly shook her head as she stared at him.

"Since they got here, they have not stopped laughing at us."

"Not good," said Wenji, blinking and swallowing. "But there is nothing we can do about it."

"Tell them we're just decent people and they had best treat us nicely," Lorgi shouted, stomping all his paws. "Tell them we did nothing wrong and they better get us out of here, now! They have no right to cage us."

Shaking her head, Wenji smiled in wonder at her naïve friend. "After all your travels, you would have me say that to them—or anyone in their position?"

"Then tell them this is wrong, they are bad and will be punished if they don't," Lorgi groaned, suddenly in a voice beyond his years, squinting like an angry Ganjaset, or a wolf ready to defend its territory.

"Right and wrong mean nothing in Shohan," said Wenji. "Who can say what does? This is an ancient, wicked realm."

"Say that I will bring them terrible luck unless they free us."

"The Shohaneze are not superstitious like the Tuzanchim. They only believe what they can measure, like blood and gold. I am sorry, Lorgi."

"Then say that my people do not tolerate wrongs, and would never treat anyone this way. Tell them my mother weighs five tons. Make that ten. No—twelve. Have them measure that! She can move a whole pine all by herself. She carved out her whole, entire hall by paw. She has many Álukoi friends. They will all come and demolish that farting hog's palace, and squash anyone in their way, unless those *smiley-mouths* free us and are nice to us!"

"I cannot tell them any of that either. But it sounded quite impressive!"

"Well, what can you do?" Lorgi burped as he ate more fruit. "We were better off at the Vazuk's. Why did you let them bring us here?"

"I didn't *let* them; we had to come here. I have no control over anything."

"Well, I have to go home, but don't even know how, any more. And we cannot stay here with these snakes."

After deciding to call Lorgi a "glass dragon," the king quickly lost interest in his latest acquisition. Satisfied with that name, he and his group waddled away to other cages. An hour later a guard and ten keepers holding lances appeared. Opening a small section of the grating, the guard lowered a long, narrow ramp, ordering Wenji to exit. Shaking her head, she sat down next to Lorgi. Yet after a brisk exchange with the guard, Wenji stood up, crying.

"What did he say?" asked Lorgi. "I'll flatten him like the Vazuk's guards. He'll never insult you or anyone else again!"

"I have to go now," said Wenji.

"Good," chirped Lorgi. "It's about time they let us out of here."

"Not you, just me. I'm sorry. It has been ordered for you to stay here. The guard says they will put me in a different jail by night, and bring me back in the morning for your training."

"Training? I don't want training!" yelled Lorgi. "I want to go home!"

"We have no say in the matter. Next week you are to be tested in the arena! We have only that long to prepare for the challenge. That is all the guard will say. Orders from the king, himself. I am sorry. Try and get as much rest as you can. Good night, Lorgi."

"Horse poop on their orders! I'm going with you."

But as Lorgi tried to follow her up the ramp, sharp lances poked at his neck and belly. While he struggled against these, the guard and a keeper plucked Wenji, screaming, from the cage. As the metal grating slammed shut, Lorgi sounded a mournful howl, making the wolves in a nearby cage answer.

A dozen yards away, Wenji fell to her knees, sobbing. The guard tried to yank her up by the arm, but she went limp. Yelling threats and epithets, he kicked her, but she still refused to cooperate. A second guard had to help him drag Wenji to the dungeon and throw her into a cell with three other women. Suspecting the worst, the other prisoners cursed the guards and spat at them for whatever had been done to Wenji. The jailor promised to feed all of them to hungry beasts in the Great Arena at the earliest opportunity.

Lorgi tested every inch of the floor and walls of his cell that he could reach, seeking a weakness. But equally hard masonry confronted him everywhere. With time, any adult snowdragon might carve an escape from this cage, but it proved beyond Lorgi's current abilities. He dared not spend his claws in the effort, fearful of what the Shohaneze meant by tests, challenges and especially contests. In the west, that usually meant combat—to the death.

Late the next morning, four guards opened the entire grating as a dozen slaves lowered a much larger wooden ramp into the cage. They brought torches, chains, ropes and poles to deal with an obstinate beast. But Lorgi bounded out of the hold before they were ready to extract him. Behind the guards, Wenji stood waiting. The nearby grounds she escorted Lorgi to was nothing more than a giant, round version of his cell, but more than 200 feet in diameter, with a dirt floor sprouting grass around the edges, ringed by a 12-foot-high stone wall. Scattered groups of two or three people stood lazily behind the wall conversing, leaning their hands on its top while gazing down at the pair.

"Everyone up there is gawking at us," said Lorgi, surveying the grounds.

"They are curious to see how you will fight," said Wenji.

"This is nothing but a horrible place, full of bad people."

"Welcome to Shohan," snapped Wenji.

"You mean Hell!"

"Never mind. You must exercise, to keep strong," prodded Wenji, looking guilty. "Our lives depend on it. Nothing else we can do."

"Every day lost here can only weaken us. You are from Shohan. Look what it has done to you, fragile and helpless as a baby doe."

"My condition is not important. Only your strength and speed are. I'm so very sorry, Lorgi. Please run, jump, pound the ground, roar, play. I don't know. Do whatever you normally do."

"Play?" yelled Lorgi. "Does this place also rot the mind?"

"Please don't argue, Lorgi. We must prepare."

"You mean leave. This ramp will help!" Lorgi began a tug of war with the slaves over it. With no incentive to risk their lives against an unknown beast, they fled, despite threats from their overseer. More worried about unattended slaves than beasts, the guards chased after them. Suddenly, Wenji and Lorgi had the whole grounds to themselves, just as he wanted.

"What are you doing?" asked Wenji.

"Preparing," chirped Lorgi, dragging the ramp to the center of the grounds.

"Stop, Lorgi. Please." begged Wenji. "This is no game."

"You said to play. Now you can help," cheered Lorgi. "Where is the best spot to jump over?"

"You can't do that!"

"The wall is not too high, only about twelve feet up."

"Only?" gasped Wenji. "From down here it looks far too high. And how can you know?"

"I'm a vegetarian, remember?" he giggled. "A grown-up Álukoi can measure by sight, exactly. When I'm older my mother will show me how. All we need right now is a low spot."

"No. The sooner you accept our reality, the better our rather slim chances of survival. You cannot jump twelve feet in the air."

"I don't know, but thanks to this ramp, we don't have to."

"Impossible," laughed Wenji. "Even if you could, it is not allowed."

"What are they going to do about it, put me in a cage?"

Scores of people began to take notice, amused until he propped the ramp against the wall at a steep angle, then retreated twenty paces. None suspected Lorgi's capabilities until he charged, using the tool to escape the grounds. Any spectators fled the walkway surrounding it, bounding away like rabbits. Soon enough, a half-dozen keepers ran about within the training grounds, yelling and waving their arms to spread the alarm, scrambling to gather ropes and weapons to deal with an escaped beast. Wenji stood at the foot of the ramp, in shock.

Though high above the training pen, the walkway raised only a few feet above the ground level of the king's zoo and gardens. Looking north, to his left, Lorgi spied row after row of pit cages like his own, all nestled close to the training pen. He knew they were only temporary holding cells, but not what that meant. Each contained a different type of animal, generally carnivores, but some held large herbivores. Most of what confronted Lorgi's senses proved alien and painful, but he struggled to interpret it all anyway. Some cages housed up to five animals, like the one with the wolves. A few looked empty, but one could only be certain by walking right next to each one. Heart-wrenching calls welled up from most of them.

Yet to Lorgi's right, the most beautiful gardens beckoned every living thing. Towering, ancient trees, all teeming with birds, promised enough shade for an army. Red squirrels, dwarf deer, exotic fish, and other rare creatures inhabited the gardens. The nearest of many waterfalls, streams and ponds sang to Lorgi as sweetly as the best human voices of Tiefenbo. Even without a working *pahápkoltam,* he traced the sound to a point through the trees and miniature hills of the artificial heaven to his right, directly opposite the hell on his left. He wanted nothing more than to dive in and cool off.

"LORGI, STOP!" shrieked Wenji.

"Why are you screaming? All I did was jump up here. You said to play."

"Please. You must not run away from me," she sobbed, kneeling on the bottom of the ramp, her forearms trembling against the wooden incline. "We have to stay together."

"Then stop crying and get up here," said Lorgi. "You look like a rabbit."

"Please try to understand. You must stay by me. My life is in your hands."

"You mean forepaws."

"I am supposed to be your trainer." Wenji shook her head. "If I fail to control you, they will execute me!"

"How long do we have to stay here?"

"No one can know that," said Wenji. "Just please do not leave me."

"You left me alone in that stinky pit all night," said Lorgi. "I'm not going back."

"I promise to do all I can for you, Lorgi, but please…"

"Alright. But I have to cool off, first. I'll come right back."

"NO! Please!" yelled Wenji. "Only people can be up there."

"I *am* people!" Lorgi growled, insulted. "An Álukoi people."

"Only humans are allowed up there," she yelled, panicked.

"Then I will make like a human. Easy."

"Lorgi."

"Well stop whining and get up here. I can't wait any longer. I'm too hot, thirsty and starving. And so are you. Too many good things in that garden to ignore."

"No, Lorgi, please…wait! Alright. I'm climbing. Wait. This is hard. Lorgi?"

By the time Wenji managed to scale the steep ramp to ground level, Lorgi had vanished. A dozen keepers and a few guards scrambled about, inside the great pen behind her, still missing the tools they required to deal with Lorgi. Their blundering gave Wenji a moment. Despite her dread, she could not help admiring the vast gardens to her right, considered one of the Eight Wonders of the Esterlans (the Well-East). She drank in one sweet look with a deep breath, before two guards and a keeper approached her. Certain that her end had come, still Wenji pasted on a "smiley-mouth" for them.

"Calm down, I will find him for you," she quietly assured them, fighting to keep her voice from cracking. "He is perfectly harmless. Cute as a baby, as long as none provoke him or attempt violence in his presence."

"They say he killed ten at Uxanda palace," barked the keeper.

"I heard it was twelve, at least," said one of the guards.

"More like twenty," said the other.

"No matter. What do you expect with Tuzanchim barbarians?" said

Wenji. "They taunted him and paid for it. But you certainly know better than that, yes?"

The men nodded.

"Good. Just tell everyone, especially our guards and keepers, to always smile and humor Lorgi as if he were a crown prince, yet keep their distance. So simple. No need for anyone to get hurt."

"What of your own safety?" asked the keeper. "You lost control of him. We should go with you."

"I am the only one with any sway over him, though it is limited. And, no, your presence would only keep him from returning. Leave the exotic to me and all will end well. Could you please check the other cages. He may have gone into one of them to visit other animals."

"Thank you. We didn't think of that," said the keeper, nodding as he and the guards turned back in that direction.

Wenji buried her panic with a smile until they left.

Guessing Lorgi's destination, she walked as quickly as possible without drawing attention, alert for trampled underbrush, paw prints, severely scratched stone or wooden walkways. Or people screaming and fleeing. Wenji traced a painter's trail over stepping stones meandering over a bed of moss framed by flowering shrubs, then through a strand of tall trees to an artificial stream, waterfall and pond teaming with brilliantly colored fish. A handful of people either stood on a delicate bridge or relaxed on shaded benches. All gazed into the water, refusing to notice anything unless it disturbed the hypnotic liquid. By the calm on people's faces, only a charging Tuzanchim horde might stir them.

Lorgi waited on a bench set apart from the others, atop a fairy's hill but deep in the shade. To an oblivious passerby, nothing more than a very short, wide woman, in a purple silk coat sat there, motionless. The "lady" faced away, with a small white parasol covering her head. Approaching quietly, Wenji saw how the coat was soaked, and irreparably torn down the middle from Lorgi's back spikes.

"Good morning, madam," she murmured to Lorgi.

"See, I'm making like human," he giggled. "How do you like it?"

"Do you have any idea what danger you put us in, trespassing the king's imperial gardens?"

"No, and let's get out of here, already!"

"You know we can't," said Wenji.

"Of course we can." Lorgi suddenly reared up on his hind legs, sniffing the air. "Whoa! I've never been so hungry. Come on. Lots of great food over there. Then we can leave."

"Lorgi," Wenji hissed. "Look to your right, in the bushes."

"What, the old lady spying on us?" Lorgi giggled.

"That's not funny, either!"

"Everyone spies on everyone here anyway," said Lorgi. "It seems to be a big stupid game they play. But I just want to eat. Follow me."

Lorgi pointed with his left forepaw, because most of the people he had observed in the east were left-handed. Ignoring Wenji's protests, he quickly tracked the delectable aromas over baby hills and glens, across brightly painted bridges over streams and ponds, by waterfalls and through stands of trees until reaching a huge, open-air pavilion. The hexagon-shaped structure overlooked a pond, set in a tiny glen framed by pines. Three long conference tables, each groaning under a mountain of food, patiently waited to be relieved of their burdens. Lorgi's eyes swelled at the vision. Wenji's tiny stomach finally demanded attention.

"Told you," Lorgi giggled, planting himself at the apex of the dessert table. "Sweets always make great appetizers."

"This is not ours to take," said Wenji, laughing at her own words. No force could deprive them now.

"We are not theirs to starve, either," said Lorgi. "It all looks good to me. 'Fit for a king,' as we say back home. Eat!"

"This king will have us executed when we are caught."

"No, because we're leaving, remember?" burped Lorgi, already gorging himself. "But first you'd better eat up. It could be a long time before we get this lucky again."

By chance, the cooking staff had retired into the kitchen when the pair arrived. In two minutes, Lorgi inhaled a nut cake, a fruit pie, a dozen spiced apples, and half of a giant basket's assorted muffins. Tired of sweets, he moved on to the vegetable table just as the master chef arrived, screaming. Unfazed, Lorgi shut his ear lids, waved, then gently pushed the enraged man aside.

Eating a platter of savory greens and one of fried pastry rolls stuffed with sautéed vegetables, he then devoured the table's flagship entree, a mountain of noodles laced with tofu, cashews, pea pods, basil and roasted peppers, all bathed in a divine mushroom-onion gravy. Enough for twenty famished humans. He washed it all down with two large jugs of rice wine.

Seeing he could have no effect on the dragon child, the chef turned to yell at Wenji. That reminded Lorgi too much of the guard at Uxanda. Placing himself between her and the man, Lorgi growled and raised a forepaw, ready to strike him down.

"No, Lorgi, please," shouted Wenji, but the chef had already vanished. "We must go back if we want to live through this day."

"I'm just getting started here. You better hurry up and eat, too."

Flanked by two assistants, the master chef sallied out of the kitchen armed with his largest meat cleaver. Lorgi reared up, showed his teeth, and roared, frightening them away. Returning to the dessert table, he enjoyed another dozen fruit tarts, a cheese cake and a pie. He avoided the third table because it held meat dishes, but everything else competed for his attention. Wenji kept begging him to stop, trying every possible line of reasoning, knowing from the start that it was useless. Finally, she allowed herself to eat.

"Even a starving bear has a limit," gasped Wenji. "What is yours?"

"I've never eaten half this much. My stomach hurts, but it was all worth it."

"Getting sick from gorging?"

"I'll be fine in an hour," Lorgi yawned. Stretching his limbs, he rolled out a thunderous belch as long as a king's full name. "That was grand! Did you get enough to eat?"

"No matter. We must go now."

Lorgi still "wore" what was left of the silk coat, draped over his back in tatters. Satisfied, he kept licking his chops as he trudged away. Terrified, Wenji nervously trailed close behind her champion.

Alone and unarmed, the master chef returned to survey the damage. He marveled at how the exotic had devoured enough for twelve of his most voracious customers, yet had been miraculously dainty, careful, and selective—far more so than many human guests. Whatever Lorgi had chosen, he totally consumed, yet left nearby dishes undisturbed. The chef found very little to clean up, but urgent need to replace what had been eaten, especially from the dessert table. Fortunately for the chef, Lorgi had avoided the table holding the most prized and expensive dishes, the meat and fish entrées. Looking back at the second table, the chef suddenly felt strangely, deeply slighted—wounded that a very hungry monster had passed over several of his best dishes.

"Stop! That's my coat!" shouted one of the first banquet guests to arrive, a profoundly corpulent woman. "Guards! Where are those useless guards?"

She attempted to lead a dozen guards, but was unable to muster anything faster than a slow waddle. Lorgi and Wenji vanished, but struggled to avoid other guards, zoo keepers, and curious eyes. The same woman, the master chef and his assistants all convened in the pavilion, joined by several 'smiley-mouths' from the king's entourage. Using his long eyes, Lorgi spied them all chattering away, from a position he took up behind a bush a good quarter mile away.

Silently, he guided Wenji on a remarkably discrete but efficient flight through the garden's back ways and underbrush. At first, she struggled to keep up as Lorgi sought escape from the human environment. But he slowed down as the wine began to take hold.

"Are you all right?" gasped Wenji, catching her breath. "Your eyelids and your ears are drooping."

"I've never felt so…heavy…and sleepy…and wobbly."

"I tried to warn you. You drank enough wine to flatten ten men!" Lorgi plunked down on his stomach, yawned and shook his head. "No, Lorgi. You must get back up."

"I…I can barely stay awake."

"We must keep moving, or—"

"Why is everything moving when I'm not?"

"Lorgi! You must not let yourself fall asleep. Get up! Wake up!"

Wenji tried shaking his ears and screaming into them, but could not rouse him. Lorgi dreamed of grand banquets in cool mountain palaces, of returning home with his new friend to a joyous welcome, and retelling all his adventures to the villagers. But he awoke—alone—in his pit cage, the late morning sun of the next day already making him uncomfortably warm. Fortunately, he did not have a headache from the wine, or a stomachache from all the food. Yet he had a monstrous thirst. Never had he felt so abandoned or far from home and civilization. Lorgi feared what could have become of Wenji, and dreaded whatever punishment the authorities intended to exact upon both of them.

18: Justice in the Arena

No one visited Lorgi all the next day. At noon on the second day, a rather old keeper lowered a bucket of water down to him, but no food. Like all the others, this man refused to speak, no matter what Lorgi said to him. No one else even came near his cage. Forsaken, Lorgi growled, roared and screamed, demanding attention. That only made animals in nearby cages do the same, raising a chorus of protest. But it drew no human reaction. When at last keepers arrived to remove him on the third day, he could not wait to get out.

They loaded him into the caged hold of a small, much abused wagon, every inch of it bloodstained and reeking of carnivores. Pulled by an old draft horse, the wagon rumbled across the training grounds, through a gate, up a ramp, then down a cobblestone street. Crying, Wenji sat next to the driver, her hands tied behind her back and her feet bound together. She could only turn partway around to glimpse Lorgi out of the corners of her eyes. Unable to reach either binding through the cage's grating, Lorgi immediately set his teeth to work on the metal.

"No!" barked the driver. "Stop or be whipped."

"Idiot, they are going to kill us anyway," shouted Wenji.

"Idiot," said Lorgi. He knew that word in five languages.

"Lorgi, I am so sorry," cried Wenji. "I tried everything. But none will listen to a slave, or take pity on a condemned one. Especially a former concubine. But they fear you, like all good things."

"No talking," barked the driver.

"How can you be so cruel?" asked Wenji. "Leave us alone or join us in the arena. Rats like you make Shohan what it is today."

"I have orders," he muttered. "Nothing I can do. Please stop the beast from chewing the cage, or I will suffer for it. My family too."

"He is a prince, not a beast!" shouted Wenji. "He will say and do as he wants and knows to be right, until the very end, unlike you. And he has a family, too. One day, you and all Shohan will regret this."

"Idiot," said Lorgi, spitting out metal shavings. "Idiots have orders."

"I am sorry beyond anything, Lorgi," sobbed Wenji. "I tried to speak for you, but they just laughed. Kept calling me *meat* and said dying in the arena was my only value. Yet they demanded silence, and slapped me when I kept shouting at them. You would have been proud of my efforts."

"I am proud to ride with you, as the Tuzanchim say," chirped Lorgi. "But they too must answer for letting us be brought here like this. And what about that smiling snake who paid 500 horses for us? Where is he?"

"Probably far away, selling more concubines to the Vazuk," cried Wenji. "So much to say, and no time."

"Time is ours," said Lorgi. "Someday I will show you Tiefenbo, and many new friends. You will love it there. But first, we must think like warriors, to get out of here!"

"Far too late." Wenji shook her head. "Our lives are over." Crying, she turned as far as she could to see Lorgi. "They slapped me, ridiculed me. I thought they would do worse, but they were pressed for time. In Shohan, no matter what else falls behind, blood always spills on schedule."

"There!" huffed Lorgi, breaking through the cage's grating. Directly he cut Wenji's feet loose. "They could not do any of those things if I had been with you. Wish I could reach your hands."

Immediately he set to work on another part of the grating further up. To discourage this, the driver yelled and began slapping his hand hard against the grating. On the last slap, Lorgi poked his sharpest claw through. Screaming in pain, the driver snapped up his hand, a fountain of blood gushing from a hole clean through the palm. Even Lorgi's tongue could not heal such an injury, and he was in no mood to help the man.

"You will pay for that!" yelled the driver.

"No. Idiot can pay for that!" shouted Lorgi. "Idiots have orders."

"Lorgi, we are to die in the arena! Now!" cried Wenji. "By what means, no one knows. The king always likes it to be a surprise. I wish he would die in his own arena, or choke on something at one of his banquets."

"Why? Just because we ate too much of their food?" gulped Lorgi.

"Hardly. Shohan is a land of plenty, or could be if those in power were fair about any of it."

"The only thing they have plenty of here is bad people—and idiots."

"You have no idea how right you are. Breaking rules brings punishment anywhere, except maybe in your land. In Shohan, the smallest offense invites death. Only here, they throw you into the arena to watch you fight for your life. They drool when you bleed, laugh when you fall, and cheer when you are ripped apart by something hungry with big teeth."

"We did nothing bad. They did," said Lorgi. "Why do they hate us?"

"You speak Tuzanchim and have proven capable of escape. The court dreads you more than the plague or barbarian hordes. Worst of all, we were traded from them, making us suspect from the start."

"They never gave us a chance," shouted Lorgi.

"We were only brought here to die for their entertainment."

"I thought we were worth 500 horses."

"Me, too."

"Land of the barbarians," muttered Lorgi. "This place should not exist. Someday, I will return and destroy it."

"Lorgi, for us there can be no someday. This is it."

The pair kept eye contact as the wagon delved into an underground tunnel, through two gates and into the Great Arena. As Lorgi roared and battered the cage, four hefty slaves took Wenji away and strapped her into a chair. They suspended it loosely by ropes between four poles reaching ten feet high over the arena's center. With rare luck, whatever monsters the king had chosen would not be able to reach her. The contest planners used an endless variety of such contrivances to tease audiences, predators and victims alike.

Before Lorgi could react, the same four men dumped him out of the wagon and vanished with it through a gate, with virtuosic skill and efficiency. Only now did he fully understand his mother's warning: *hyúlems* really were capable of anything—at least anything bad.

The arena grounds were composed of dirt, generously sprinkled with a mixture of fresh leaves, bark and flower petals around the edges, so that the capacity audience of 50,000 would smell that first. But to Lorgi, the overwhelming scents of human blood, sweat and terror saturated every inch of the arena and blotted out all else. It looked just like the training pen he had escaped from, three days prior, only double in size, ringed by a huge stone amphitheater, surrounding it like the walls of a canyon.

A giant, muscular black man with tight curly grey hair stepped up to the podium at one end of the Great Arena. The biggest man Lorgi had ever seen, he stretched his arms wide as a condor's wings, shouting with a bear's voice to demand silence. All eyes kept glancing at him and the slender, helpless bait dangling above the slaughter ground's exact center. But mostly, they focused on the unknown. Most had watched countless humans and beasts of all types kill each other here before. None had seen anything close to the sparkling creature now sitting on his haunches in Wenji's shadow. Resigned to her fate, she translated the announcer's words for Lorgi.

"Welcome to the Great Arena of Shohan," shouted the giant at the podium, in the most compelling human voice Lorgi had ever heard. Waiting just long enough to catch a deep breath, he continued. "Friends and visitors from all parts, near and far, welcome. Or welcome back! Give now your full attention, that you grasp the rare drama about to unfold before your eyes, for your utmost pleasure and profit."

The crowd hushed as the Arena's natural acoustics helped the announcer's mighty voice ring in every ear. To ensure the greatest possible clarity, he spoke at a slow, measured pace, inserting a slight pause between many words, and after each sentence. He punched his consonants, substituting "p" for "b," and "t" for "d," as well as "v" for "w" in most words. Favoring long vowels, he also rolled every "r" and sounded each word with intense force. Exaggerating the rise and fall of his voice, he added grand arm gestures, facial expressions and stepped about while speaking, to achieve maximum drama. He did everything possible to ensure that his delivery could be appreciated even at the Arena's furthest reaches.

Using his long eyes, Lorgi noted how the man smiled with his mouth closed and breathed hard through his nose whenever not speaking. Throwing all possible energy into his hammered oratory, he strained every muscle in his face, neck, and even some in his gut and back. Lorgi wondered if so much effort caused pain. The announcer demanded such attention, exuded such power in his delivery that many in the audience could not help but turn their eyes to him, even though none had ever seen an Álukoi. To Lorgi, the man seemed like a proud rooster who might crow for a very long time before tiring of his own voice—or saying anything of value.

"Today, we give you the fruit of a most costly, perilous transaction with those barbarians of the Steppes...yes, the dreaded Tuzanchim!" Nodding theatrically, the announcer paused while his audience gasped, muttered or shook their heads, exactly as he wished them to do. Having made his point, the man raised his hands again for quiet.

"We present to you this gem, rarest of beasts. An albino, a young glass dragon cub. Plucked from the most savage, frozen reaches of the Far West. A land where monsters fight for territory, even *beyond* death. Where beasts still outnumber men—and dine on them regularly."

The announcer took a practiced step back and to his right. Bowing, he swept his left arm out towards the center of the arena. As Wenji finished translating, Lorgi twitched his ears, cocked his head and shook it in disgust.

"I'm not made of glass, not a cub or albino, and certainly not a dragon! I *am* an Álukoi. Why is he making up things?"

"Lorgi, they don't want facts, only blood and gold," cried Wenji. "This is Shohan—an ancient, corrupt land. Truth does not last a day here."

"Then how does Shohan?"

"Great question. I wish it would crumble."

"The announcer insults me with his lies."

"He's probably just getting started, only doing what they demand. But you really are quite rare, Lorgi. What is important is that you know the truth, and by some miracle survive this contest. Then truth lives even in Shohan."

"And now more lies from the rooster man," huffed Lorgi.

"Today we bring you a highly trained team of the king's own, his four best giant war dogs," shouted the announcer. "Starving for blood, ravenous for a kill, they cannot wait to maul, shred, crack, crush, strangle, rip apart, and devour this worthy dragon and his only friend, the girl."

"These people are worse than I ever imagined," gasped Lorgi.

"No, they are infinitely more evil that that!" cursed Wenji.

"War dogs usually win," heralded the announcer. "This team *always* wins. Now look hard upon this exotic cub and his beautiful, young trainer. Have pity on them, for in five minutes, they become dinner!"

Growing more afraid with every word, Lorgi checked his claws and tail spikes, glad he had not spent any trying to dig his way out of the pit cage. Stretching, yawning and snapping his jaws to prepare, he also practiced his "make like a turtle," guessing he would have to both "turtle" and fight like a cornered bear, to survive the ensuing contest. His every move fascinated the crowd. Thousands of whispering voices charged the air and refused to subside. The announcer held his arms out, as if inviting them to debate.

"I just hope they snap my neck first," said Wenji. "Then at least I won't feel all the pain."

"Wenji!"

"Maybe I can work myself free of my bindings, fall headfirst and break my neck myself. That would be best. It may draw the dogs so you can flee. But I must be quick for that to work."

"Wenji, stop it!"

"Listen to me, Lorgi. You must run and not stop for anything, no matter your thirst, hunger or pain. Run to escape this whole, worthless kingdom and never look back. Remember me, your friend. That is all I ask of you. Promise me."

"Like good people anywhere, Álukois do not leave friends in danger," shouted Lorgi. "I'll take care of the war dogs. As long as they can't reach you, you'll be safe."

"For about three of my sneezes or one of yours. These are the fastest killers known."

"Not after I'm done with them! My mother says already I have the hardest crust for my age. And the sharpest claws and spikes. All my village says I'm the most destructive living thing they have ever seen. So you just be patient and I'll show you—and everybody."

"Ever the champion," she smiled, shaking her head. "Your mother or someone close fed you too many knightly tales of the west."

Cocking his head, Lorgi twitched his ears as he looked up to her. "You mean like *right is might* or *truth always finds the sun?*"

"Yes, and I admire all of that—though it will do you no good here."

"Thanks, but I don't know that," Lorgi shook his head like a human. "I never want to know that. We just need to know how to get out of here."

"There is no way out of this, Lorgi. But please do me one last favor."

"We can make it through this."

"No. Just please get them to announce our names, or they will steal even those from us."

"Steal our names?"

"Please, I don't want to die nameless. Real names demand respect and remembrance. People owning them live long and well. Perhaps real names will even conjure your fabled luck. Please hurry, Lorgi. No time to argue."

"I still think we can survive this."

"Lorgi!" shrieked Wenji. "You must run to the announcer or it will be too late even for names! Please!"

"Alright," Lorgi reared his neck back. "I'll go tell the big-mouth rooster man right now. He can tell everyone else. But we are not going to die. And you please remember that I'm an Álukoi and your friend."

"So long as I breathe."

He marched across the arena, right up under the podium, set just above the protective wall. The announcer inhaled to trumpet more fiction, but stopped himself when the unknown approached. In spite of all the horrors he had seen, the man felt Lorgi tugging at his heart—what was left of it after years in the arena. The crowd's chatter welled up until the announcer motioned for silence. Most of them saw Lorgi as an 800-pound ball of quartz, visibly hard on his back, perhaps strong and agile enough to survive a different type of contest, but far too slow, young and soft in the belly to last a minute against a team of giant war dogs.

Both the exotic and his trainer looked too green, innocent and beautiful to be put in the arena at all. Even for the most sadistic spectators, such an obvious mismatch hardly qualified as entertainment. It only showed incompetence and waste by the arena planners, which included the king himself. An increasingly shrill audience began to complain. Mimicking the giant, Lorgi stood up on his back legs and tail, motioning for silence with his forepaws. Some laughed, but most did as he asked. The announcer looked up and to his left where the king and his entourage sat in a luxurious box to view the contest.

"Mr. Herald!" shouted Lorgi, hoping he could be understood with his month-old grasp of the local language. "Speak-man. HELLO!"

"What? You can talk?" gasped the announcer.

"Yes, but not like you," yelled Lorgi, thrusting out his left forepaw for emphasis.

The crowd roared with laughter.

Again mimicking the giant man, Lorgi shouted his loudest, so that as many people as possible in the crowd could hear. "Tell our names. I am Lorgámon. Lorgámon of Tiefenbo. My friend is Wenji. Lady Wenji of no land. And I'm an Álukoi, not a glass dragon. Did you get all of that?"

Swallowing, the man nodded, then turned to the king.

"Stop encouraging him, fool!" snarled the king, scowling.

"I'm not, Your Majesty," protested the announcer.

"Stop, fool!" Lorgi mimicked the king, who glared back in shock. Instantly Lorgi tried to spin him, but the coward pulled his eyes away.

"I want that girl in my dog's bellies in five minutes, and this talking freak gutted and ready for my taxidermist in ten!" growled the king, shaking his fist at the announcer. "Stop wasting my time."

"I would not dare, Your Majesty," said the announcer, slowly bowing to him. "But I use only what time is needed to maximize your profits. Even you must be amazed by this intelligent exotic."

Rattling his left index finger in the direction of Wenji, the king barked, "Not at all. She is only here to spy for the Tuzanchim. The *exotic* works for her, fool. Delay justice for either of them and you will require your own."

"Stop, fool!" yelled Lorgi.

Both men had sweat beading up on their foreheads. With a pained expression and slumped shoulders, the announcer turned back to Lorgi. Suddenly the man looked ten years older, and did not appear so large or important. He opened his mouth and took several deep breaths, but at first could not make himself speak. Lorgi already knew his answer, but not how the man would phrase it.

"Lord Gamon…I am sorry beyond words for you and Lady Wenji." The giant spoke gently, but not too softly while gazing down at him. Due to the natural power and clarity of the man's voice, many nearby heard them, as he intended. The names rolled through the crowd. "But the king says that Lord Gamon and Lady Wenji cannot have names in Shohan. Lord Gamon and Lady Wenji are to die now for offenses, though I know not what they are. That is the king's final word."

"Here's mine," shouted Lorgi, flaring his nostrils and pinning his ears back in anger. He took a long yawn and shook his head as a warning. Sitting back on his haunches with his forepaws holding his sides, Lorgi adopted Jinva's scolding posture. Unable to find the words he needed in Esterlan, the language of Shohan and the kingdoms of the East, Lorgi hurled his salvo in Tuzanchim. The few who understood it instantly translated for the rest.

"Tell that stinky, mean, coward, idiot hog-man I'll pounce on him right now and shred him finer than those noodles he keeps stuffing in his ugly face—unless you tell everyone our names. Nobody can stop me."

In various, rough translations, Lorgi's slap quickly rumbled throughout the audience. Years had elapsed since they had enjoyed such novel or bold entertainment. The king wiggled nervously in his seat, red-faced, as his own interpreter struggled to give him a false version, without bursting into laughter herself. Dignitaries surrounding the king covered their mouths in supposed shock, but really to help squelch laughter. The further away people sat, the more openly they laughed.

"I see no harm in giving names, Your Majesty," stammered the announcer. "In the end, just empty words, forgotten even as they are spoken. But their novelty may add to your profits, and the offenders will die in seconds, anyway."

"Idiot!" barked the king. "You have already aired them three times."

"Three times idiot!" shouted Lorgi. "Idiots have orders."

In spite of his advisors' assurances to the contrary, the king feared that Lorgi could indeed accomplish a leap into the stands. If so many Tuzanchim guards had failed to subdue him, then certainly no Shohaneze could stop him. After a moment of teeth-grinding, the king nodded. "Alright, but hurry up with your stupid names." Leaning to his right, the king wheezed to an advisor, "Subversive little monster. You'd think he was a crown prince or a general."

Regaining his full posture, the giant raised his hands to calm an expectant audience. Most already waited in silence, wishing they could be privy to the debates by the podium. "Friends of the Arena," shouted the announcer. "We have a rare, fine creature before you in this glass dragon child. He calls himself the Lord Gamon of Tiefenbo. Champion to the beautiful Lady Wenji. Nothing has yet been able to pierce his rock armor. But know that he is an…*Alukoi*."

The word drew instant laughter, boos and moans of disgust. Backing away from the podium, Lorgi glared at many in the crowd. Whoever met his eyes suddenly fell silent and looked away. None wanted him to remember them, in case he should win the contest. The announcer shouted them all down with his angry bear's voice and a huge gesture of his arms. When he launched into his next description, Lorgi bristled, sensing more fiction.

"Though a mere herbivore, he has killed men and beasts—many times in many places!" the giant intoned with foreboding. "Taken from his mother so young, he has had adventures far and wide, leaving an endless trail of blood in his wake. After burning one sorcerer alive, he ran with Steppe hordes, taking part in their savagery." Fearfully curious, the audience held silent. With arms raised to keep them so, the announcer made them wait eight seconds before saying more.

"While pillaging with the Tuzanchim, this dragon child also took part in their massacres. He fought seventeen or more of the most powerful, superbly armed Laskomian knights, mounted on huge, Laskomian war horses—the grandest steeds in the known world! Yet he slew them all in mere minutes, in a fit of dragon's fury. In another outburst, he killed thirty guards, maiming and crippling twice as many others at Uxanda Palace. How many other men has he slain in his short life? We can never know."

Running back to Wenji, Lorgi asked, "What is he saying about us?"

"You don't want to know, but what does it matter?" said Wenji. "Remember, this is Shohan. Truth, kindness and mercy are never welcome here."

"Not even the Gran Vazuk's elite guards could stop him," shouted the announcer. "Only the uniquely skilled Wenji—a Shohaneze—holds any sway over him. This dragon child is slow to anger. But three days in a cage without food have made him furious. And when he becomes so, he kills! A worthy bet, my friends. Think on it quickly and place your wagers, if you dare!"

The giant rang a bronze bell and turned over a huge, five-minute sand timer, sparking a deafening frenzy throughout the audience. As Lorgi's ears twitched and his eyes darted about in bewilderment, Wenji explained what the audience was doing.

"See all the uniformed slaves combing through the audience?" she asked.

"Selling little slips of paper?"

"They take wagers," cried Wenji. "Spectators can bet either for or against the arena, in almost any amount. Some prefer to bet against each other, while others do both. My guess is that some older, experienced gamblers will hold out for more predictable battles to follow, and refuse to bet on either a child or an unknown exotic. Of course, most of the crowd will bet on the war dogs."

"Bet on what?" gasped Lorgi. "Who will survive a contest?"

"A favorite pastime for the evil, idle and wealthy—which are invariably one and the same in this realm. Proof that Shohan is not civilized and never will be. A kingdom that should not exist. If by some miracle we do prevail, then anyone foolish enough to have bet on us will leave the arena suddenly rich."

"How can you know all this?"

"One of my masters made me and several other newly purchased slaves go with him to the arena," cried Wenji. "To remind us of what could happen if we ever displeased him. Once was enough. I became the best little slave anyone could want, working myself to exhaustion every day. But it made no difference."

"If I ever get my paws on him..." said Lorgi.

"Actually, you came within a dozen feet of him."

"Satungke? The *snake man*?"

"Sold me to the Vazuk, along with seven other girls," said Wenji, nodding. "About three months before the fateful day I met you in the fountain courtyard."

As the sand timer finished, the announcer rang his bell hard twice.

"What?" gulped Lorgi, running back toward the podium. "Wait. Stop. Yahai!"

"No more bets!" thundered the man, ignoring Lorgi. "No more debates."

"No more contests!" yelled Lorgi, making the announcer blink. Yet the man dared not respond, fearing for his own survival at the hands of an angry king. "Stop, fool!"

"Now commence this battle of life and death," shouted the announcer. "Let victory prove innocence or guilt. Good luck to all combatants, and those who support them in wagers. Let this contest be done!" Looking back over his shoulder for approval, he saw his king busy chastising an advisor. Seizing the moment, the announcer leaned forward and met Lorgi's eyes. Before anyone took notice, he spoke softly but quickly. "Keep your belly to the ground and your back against the wall—your only chance. Good luck, my friend."

Lorgi saw a crew of slaves ready to open a gate at the arena's far end. Fearing the evil waiting to spring from it might reach Wenji before him, Lorgi ran back to her. He hoped the war dogs would prove less fearsome than promised. Struggling to loosen her bindings, Wenji flashed her eyes between Lorgi and the chosen gate, squeaking to open. He could smell her adrenaline, pain and helplessness. Sheer terror had finally dried her tears.

"I'm scared too, Wenji. But have faith in me. Remember, I'm an Álukoi. The Tuzanchim didn't call me a rock dragon for nothing."

"Thank you for saving our names. I am so very sorry for all this. Please just cut me down. I will run toward the dogs as you flee. You must not try to fight them. You have no chance against such as these. Once they taste me they cannot let go, and will ignore you, the crowd, everything until there is nothing left of me. About one minute. If you have not fled by then, they will rip you apart too. Nothing can stop them. So just please do as I ask."

"No!" shouted Lorgi.

"Please, I'm trying to save your life!" Wenji screamed. "Yes, you are a tough little dragon, brave, noble and so true it hurts. But these are giant war dogs. They have killed lions, water buffalos, giant snakes, even the rare giant *balukta*. Your only chance is escape, and only if I can draw their attention first."

"Is a *balukta* the same as a balkotar, the giant spider?"

"Yes. At least you know about that," Wenji nodded. "They drug it the night before and remove its quills, losing more than a few slaves in the process. Supposedly that makes it a fair contest. As the announcer said, these dogs always win. Always. But with me here to distract them, you have one tiny chance. One remote detail the contest planners had not thought of. Sacrifice is the only thing I can do for you now."

"NO! I'm your champion and your friend, remember?"

"Lorgi, at least one of us must die in the next few minutes. This is hardly a contest; just an execution. Do you understand? Please do as I ask!"

"No. You listen," growled Lorgi. "Just stay where you are. Always telling me what you cannot do. Now you want to do a really stupid thing. So do nothing until I say! I can take care of myself and rid the world of those war beasts."

"In a few minutes there will be nothing but bones left of either of us. Yet our names may survive."

"Give me ten minutes and I'll put a stop to this sick *hyúlem* contest!" yelled Lorgi. "You can help by staying put, out of harm's way. Then we must plan our escape. But this time you will have to run to keep up with me. Understand?"

Marveling at Lorgi's naïve confidence, Wenji shook her head. After a deep breath, she smiled and nodded to humor him. Why not let him enjoy his moment of false hope and bravado, instead of added terror, before it all hit him? At least he could go down fighting, perhaps maiming one of the dogs in the process. That might even sully the king, delight the crowd and earn the pair a bit of fame as their brief lives ended.

Wenji felt a strange lightness and calm, the kind that only assured death brought, once one ceased struggling. By embracing a dramatic end, she hoped to make the most of it. People might even recount the event, keeping its memory alive. One day it might even help inspire someone to overthrow the king. Then Shohan could become a place to live, rather than one to escape or die.

"Wenji, no matter what, just be patient. Don't move until I say. And I won't say until it's safe to open my mouth. As long as you only see red blood, it can't be mine."

"All blood is red when spilled, Lorgi."

"Álukoi blood is turquoise and deadly to others. So long as you don't see that, I'm fine."

"You come from another world entirely," sighed Wenji, her eyes red and puffy.

"Promise me that you will just stay put until I say."

"As long as my bindings are so tight, I don't really have a choice."

"Good."

"Lorgi, how long can Álukois live?"

"About 300 years, maybe. I'm not sure. How long can humans?"

"I'll never know. I'm only 22 and had hoped to at least reach 23."

"You will see many fine years if you do what I ask. Remember, I make my own luck."

"How I wish you could!"

The chosen gate opened wide, as four huge war dogs bolted from it. Each weighed more than 200 pounds of pure muscle, unrivaled in strength, speed and endurance. Coarse, patchy brown, grey to black fur of uneven length, numerous battle scars, squarish jaws and shark eyes made them profoundly ugly, as well as terrifying. The war dogs emitted terrible low growls, not unlike the screams of men charging into battle, yet their feet made almost no sound as they accelerated. All looked capable of devouring anything they chose, and faster than any land creatures Lorgi had ever seen. He did not know how anyone or anything—except giant balkotars—could possibly fight them. The team's alpha dog outpaced the others, charging straight at Lorgi.

Waiting until the last possible instant, Lorgi threw a cat-quick swipe of his right forepaw, immediately followed by his left, but the dog anticipated both and leapt aside. It circled three times before closing again. Suddenly all four enveloped Lorgi in a blurred whirlwind. He remembered Klimgu's words to always study an enemy. But these whirred too quickly to even be distinguished as four separate creatures. Having killed beasts much larger than the prey before them, the team showed little respect for Lorgi. In the eye of a war dog tornado, he would be unable to focus on anything until they actually bit him, and maybe not even then.

"Far too fast!" yelled Lorgi.

"Watch your neck!" screamed Wenji. "They always try to choke their victims. Also watch your belly. They rip out any soft parts."

"Be patient!" yelled Lorgi, through clenched teeth.

"Guard yourself. Try to get to a wall."

"Ow!"

One dog bit hard at Lorgi's neck, but found it too well armored, breaking several teeth and cutting its jowls in the attack. The crowd roared, excited by any draw of blood. Sobbing at the inevitable, Wenji jerked her head away, knowing the dogs would pin Lorgi down in seconds.

"I'm fine, Wenji. Don't believe all those sick idiots. Álukois are hard as rock. Put your faith in your friend."

"I have faith in you!" cried Wenji, inwardly cursing all humanity.

Most spectators knew it was only a matter of how little time the dogs needed to either strangle or dismember Lorgi, before turning to Wenji. Crying, she again decided to try and loosen her bonds. Feeling let down by the mismatch, some in the crowd laughed at her struggles. Lorgi noticed this but was too busy to stop her. As one dog tried to hold his neck, another latched its jaws onto his tail, in spite of the sharp spikes.

Surprised by his enemy's mistake, Lorgi opened his eyes wide and flung the tail-biter away with all his might. The beast flew halfway across the arena, spewing a fountain of blood all the way. Though mortally wounded, the beast stood up and began staggering back toward Lorgi, as the crowd exploded in cheers. To Wenji, some of them looked desperately thirsty to drink every drop of that dog's blood.

"*Guyat!*" shouted Lorgi, wanting to also repel the neck-holder. But the dogs had been trained from birth never to let go of anything until a fight had ended. As he reached to maul it with his forepaws, the two as-yet unmarked dogs tried to grab those in order to pin him down. Retracting his forepaws, Lorgi turned hard to his left, knocking the neck-biter into one of the other dogs and freeing himself. At the same time, he batted the dog on his right side with his tail.

With one member of their team dying, two others bleeding, and none with any hold on Lorgi, the dogs had lost control over their prey. Sensing they would try to pin him down or attack him from all sides at once, Lorgi refused to extend any of his paws or expose his belly.

Instead, he "made like a turtle," locking himself into a compact ball. By also digging his claws hard into the ground, he made it nearly impossible for the dogs to move him in any way. This team had been used to overturning and slaughtering beasts weighing a full ton or more. But they could not know what to do with an Álukoi. Only Lorgi's small ears remained exposed, yet almost invisible, pinned firmly against his head, and the dogs ignored them. From immediate experience, they now avoided his tail. That left only his rock hide for them to cut themselves on. Lorgi decided to "turtle" until the dogs had lost enough teeth, blood, or stamina to continue their attack. Then he would launch his own.

Angered by the sudden lack of action, most of the crowd booed. Some threw food along with a host of verbal insults. While most knew that the king's team always won, some privately wished for a different outcome, one to sting his ego. The few who had bet on the "glass dragon" screamed vehemently at him and his trainer, as if that alone could make the pair win.

To humans, a war dog's arsenal of oversized teeth were knives of death, set in incredibly powerful jaws. But to an Álukoi, even a bear's teeth were no more than enamel, harmless except to a young dragon's belly. Lorgi already knew that while most carnivore jaws held great strength, all could be broken or dislocated if struck at the proper angle. He would just have to be patient and alert until that opportunity came. For the next minute, no spectators could see what was really happening. The dogs kept breaking their teeth and cutting their jowls, gums, and paws on Lorgi's armor.

Frightened but determined, he held firm against the attack, keeping himself tightly curled into a stone ball. If the dogs should succeed in overturning him, Lorgi would make them pay for that victory with a few long, eviscerating cuts before they could pin him down for the kill. With any luck, he might sever a limb or a neck. If they punctured his belly, Lorgi hoped his blood would poison them quickly, before they did irreparable harm to him. As long as he could stay "turtled" they could only hurt themselves on his hide—or finally give up and leave him alone. Without teeth, the dogs could never hurt anyone again.

From any spectator's view, it appeared that the dogs were gnawing away at Lorgi's hide. Some wondered if he had already died, or was frozen in helpless shock, awaiting the inevitable. Only a handful of the most discerning in the crowd guessed he was just "playing stump" until the dogs finally, seriously wounded him. At that point, those spectators guessed that Lorgi would run, and only fight when cornered or pinned against a wall—where he should have been from the start.

Tiny ivory chips or whole teeth and fountains of blood sprang from what most saw as the inevitable kill. All four dogs let out ever louder growls, then painful cries, owing to severe wounds, especially to their mouths. By now, Wenji had almost freed herself of her hand restraints. Gaining the use of her hands, she set to work on her foot restraints. At the same time, she said a final prayer. But no matter how hard she tried Wenji could not shut out enough of the crowd's angry din to even think.

Some spectators stood up, refusing to sit back down, forcing those behind them to do the same or miss the end of the contest. Inevitably, the entire crowd sprang to its feet, expecting to see Lorgi ripped apart any second. Their deafening roar tortured Wenji, even as she closed her eyes to scream her prayer.

Wishing for miracles, she dared look. Through salty, stinging eyes, she saw how the dogs only bloodied themselves by gnawing at Lorgi's hide. Gallons of red, but no turquoise, poured over Lorgi and the dogs, as their mouths became toothless and broken. Trained to fight unto death, they kept at it even while choking on their own blood.

Suddenly glimpsing Wenji, free of her bindings, Lorgi panicked. In a burst of energy, he rolled over, thrust out all his limbs, and sprang to his feet, cutting all his foes in the process. He bolted a dozen yards away, but the dogs pounced. One accidentally impaled itself on Lorgi's back spikes.

A second came within easy reach of his tail. The third collapsed dead on its own. The last discovered the speed of a snowdragon's forepaws, and the battle ended. Lorgi shook himself hard to repel as much of the blood as possible. Jumping, waving, and throwing coins into the arena, the crowd screamed with delight.

Not quite aware that all of his dogs had expired, their trainer charged into the arena to retrieve any of them that he could. Turning to face that unpardonable *hyúlem*, far across the killing grounds, Lorgi swished his tail high with rage. The man froze, realizing he had just made a fatal mistake. Responding as if Lorgi were a large carnivore, the trainer began to inch himself slowly backwards, while still facing him. Eager for more drama and the prospect of human blood, the crowd hushed. Knowing the man had loosed his dogs on many others, Lorgi could not possibly restrain his hatred. Álukoi justice demanded that such evil be destroyed.

"No, Lorgi, don't!" screamed Wenji. The poles and ropes that had been suspending her in the air began to falter. "Wait!"

"Justice!" yelled Lorgi, already charging.

"Open!" shrieked the trainer, bolting for a door twenty yards behind him with the greatest athleticism of his life. Though Lorgi had begun his charge from over a hundred yards away, the man escaped only inches ahead of him, and owed his survival as much to Wenji as to his own effort. Lorgi sniffed the ground and the thick, wooden door for the man's scent. He memorized it along with the man's face, an easy task for an Álukoi.

"When I find him again, I will slay him!" Lorgi shouted in Tuzanchim.

The crowd hushed, doubly afraid of a vengeful champion who spoke their enemy's language. In seconds, The Great Arena roared with chatter. Suddenly, Autumn's heat and extreme thirst took hold of Lorgi. While he and Wenji had suffered, the audience had sat in comfort, many even laughing and taking refreshments as they watched the horror. Lorgi could not imagine what such *hyúlems* thought, or how they could view their own reflections without dying of shame. Hating the Shohaneze more than balkotars, Lorgi gazed up at 50,000 demons, wondering what horrors they would launch against him and Wenji next.

19: Lady Wenji

Measuring the arena's walls with his eyes—as only an Álukoi could—Lorgi found them no higher than those of the training grounds. With a champion effort, he just might be able to lunge over them and plow through the audience, eating and drinking his fill. Like a Tuzanchim warrior, he would punish anyone who delayed him. Because the only thing the Shohaneze seemed to respect was violence, Lorgi stretched, whipped his tail, snapped his jaws, and stood to his full height to warn them. Scanning the walls, he considered many options for his leap. Engrossed, the crowd hushed. Whoever came directly under his glare felt his rage, even with eyes closed or turned away.

Guessing Lorgi's intent, many tried to anticipate his target. Any place his eyes lingered, people scrambled aside, frantically pushing and shoving. The arena staff feared a human stampede, should he succeed. Years before, a prized tiger had managed to leap into the stands. People fled, trampling hundreds of fellow spectators. Many died, yet the tiger never touched any of them. Ever since that incident, guards had been posted every twenty feet around the first row of seats, wielding sharp pikes with blue and gold streamers. Seeing Lorgi's ears and nostrils twitch, Wenji panicked too, knowing he could not remain idle for long.

"Lorgi!" she yelled. The chair holding her sagged to the right, as the poles suspending it wobbled. Realizing she would have to jump down or fall in seconds anyway, she sat still to delay it. "Talk to me. What you are thinking?"

"I'm parched, starved and angrier than ever! What else could I be thinking?"

"Of course," said Wenji. "Please just wait. We won the contest; that proves our innocence—just like in the Castled Lands. Now I'm sure they will get you something."

"Imprisonment, torture, starvation and death. That's all they've offered to us so far," barked Lorgi. "No more! I'll have what those disgusting *hyúlems* up there are having too much of, especially near the king. And I'll have it now!"

"No, Lorgi—please! I promise you won't have to wait long. We won, but still must stay together and not break any more rules. In a moment they will escort us out of the arena, forever. If we can just leave properly, it will be into a new and better life. For once, please just do what I ask. Be patient."

"I'm done waiting for their cruel tricks. Let them spill each other's blood. They deserve it."

The handful in the crowd who understood Tuzanchim translated, their status rising with Lorgi's every word. Sniffing a breeze, he made a quick, 360-degree scan of the walls, for the easiest place to leap into the stands. Sensing this, the crowd redoubled their jostling. None remained seated. All were shouting, mostly at each other. Wherever Lorgi glanced, spectators fled in any direction they could. To Wenji, the crowd suddenly resembled the Steppe grass, mindless and helpless as Lorgi whipped them to and fro like a mean-spirited wind god.

Holding her breath, Wenji finally jumped down, just as the apparatus suspending her chair high above the ground collapsed. Desperate to avert another punishable offense, she ran to him, screaming "Lorgi" all the way. Straining not to cut herself on his bloodstained neck, she gingerly embraced him, sobbing and gasping. Both entertained and relieved to have been spared a dragon's revenge, the crowd gave a huge moan of relief. Seconds later they roared with cheers. Some began chanting "Lord Gamon, Lady Wenji!" as if the pair were nobility. In a breath, the entire mob joined in.

"Thank you, Lorgi, my champion!" cried Wenji.

"Don't thank me until we're out of this nightmare."

"Lady Wenji!" she shouted. "Lorgi, they flatter me a title—just like you. Real and proper names! Don't you see? We are still alive; your magic really works!"

With ears drooped and eyelids half-shut, he sat quietly on his haunches, frowning.

"Lady Wenji! How I have dreamed of becoming a lady before I died. You made that happen. It means that I am now a real person, a somebody, after all. Now we can actually *live*, and so very well. You will see. Oh, how I wish you could understand, Lorgi."

"Where I come from, every woman is a lady, everyone is a real person, and every person is somebody! The way it is supposed to be," yelled Lorgi. "People in my land live happy, free, and often for a very long time. No one *lives* here. Look at all those horrible people. They must spend half their lives thinking about death—by violence. Do you understand that?"

"Only too well, but we cannot help how the world is," said Wenji. "We survived the contest, witnessed by a capacity audience. They chant our names, like titles. Not even the king would dare argue that now. We have earned rewards. All that screaming is the crowd demanding to know what those will be. Can you at least be glad for that?"

"We can't help what others do, but can help how we are."

Looking as if someone had just slapped her, Wenji brought a hand to her left cheek and held her breath with her mouth open. Lorgi scowled at many eyes in the crowd, before showing his own sadness. He let out a sigh as his ears and eyes drooped again.

"You must be exhausted," guessed Wenji. "I certainly am, just from sheer terror."

"You don't have to be a grownup, a *smiley-mouth*, or in charge of anything. You just be true, a good person, and it makes you somebody. Everyone gets to know you, helps when you need it, and you help them. How we live where I come from. Now we had better help ourselves get out of here. Then we can be glad."

As Lorgi spoke, six slaves emerged from the royal gate below the announcer's podium. Bearing a gilded, blue velvet canopy on six poles, they provided the unexpected contest winners with honorary shade. Twenty palace guards followed, then servants bearing wine, a small chest, an imperial tray, and a long, narrow maroon carpet which they rolled out from the gate. As trumpets blared, the king himself waddled out, trailed by seven richly attired officials. Every one of them took care to stay on their royal carpet, which stopped twenty paces short of the canopy. Cursing the slaves for their incompetence, the king refused to budge, waiting at the end of his carpet, sweating in the sun.

Beside the king stood Satungke, looking both relieved and terrified. Giving the same false smile as he had to the Vazuk in Uxanda, the ambassador signaled Wenji to bring Lorgi to the king. In shock, neither of the pair moved. The awkward impasse made the crowd laugh.

"They need us to walk to the carpet, Lorgi," said Wenji. "I know what you're thinking, but we must not give in to violence."

"We?" asked Lorgi.

"What we choose right now, our actions at this moment, will decide our future. I'll explain later. Just please, please do as I say. Walk very slowly beside me. Our first step to leaving the arena and starting a new life."

"If you won't let me flatten *snake-man* or *hog-face*, then I'm staying right here in the shade," huffed Lorgi. "This canopy is the only nice thing anyone has done for us. Those idiots can just wait in the sun."

"Please try to forget everything that has happened to us. Never mind Satungke or the king, or all the other *smiley-mouths* as you call them. Be glad they are all staring at us."

"How can you ever forget what they've done? How can you ever forgive them?"

"I certainly did not mean that," said Wenji. "Bit by bit, I will make them *all* pay. My list of enemies could rival the king's. But for now, we must put it all aside, so that we can wring the most out of this mess."

"This is far too horrible to call a mess."

"Lorgi, there is no justice in this world. Here is our one chance. Our only chance, right now. We must not waste it by offending the king, or putting revenge before reward."

"Ignore the snakes but respect the hog?" chuckled Lorgi.

"I didn't mean that either. Now, everyone sees us as heroes. They respect that."

"No they don't, or they would not have sat by watching violence. Soon as I'm rested, we're leaving, before they do something else to us."

"Finally, we are safe, because we proved ourselves in the arena. All will be imperial for us, and quickly. I will make sure of it. You'll see. I promise. Now everyone will have to be nice to us. The court must respect us, the people will love us, and we will never hunger again."

"Just because we slew the king's war dogs?"

"And for other things, too. The mystery of your origins, your powers, and our friendship are all things we can leverage. I must make the king himself know how vital we are to his reign. Our standing, our rank, our health—everything depends on him."

"Just look at him!" huffed Lorgi. "Even shorter, smellier and more blubbery when he's standing. So disgusting and deranged and ugly. How can anyone even bear the sight of him?"

"Lorgi!" hissed Wenji.

"Nothing but another idiot fat hands, just like the Gran Vazuk, although much shorter and no beard. But more clever and dangerous."

"Hardly," said Wenji. "Everyone knows the Gran Vazuk is the most feared man on the Continent."

"Not around here! The Vazuk—and I noticed how his foes leave off the 'Gran' part—may be the most powerful man on the Continent. But hog-face here is even more cruel and dangerous. Wenji, how do you miss so much passing right before your senses?"

"A scrawny, lifelong slave like me? Who has been bought and sold like meat or furniture many times. Then starved, beaten, raped, or tortured in other ways. Deprived of any home or friends, sometimes even of my own name, and always threatened with death. Yet you expect me to match the magic dragon powers of a spoiled young prince from a fairytale realm, so far away from the world's ills. Well maybe I'm just too terrified every minute that we are about to die, Lorgi, to notice all your picky little details!"

"Sorry," he mumbled. "Moon's melt! No one ever told me off like that before! But the danger has not passed. Please find a way to get us out of here, so we can at least think."

"While we roast, the lady has such a long talk with her dragon," whined the king.

"More of an argument, I'm afraid," said Satungke.

"Good," smiled the king. "I expect you to harness even the smallest friction between those two, but keep them away from my wife. Her time will come soon. Then we can relax."

"Relax? Both the dragon and his trainer want my blood most of all, for bringing them here. And what can they think of you, or the whole court? Certainly I will never be able to influence either of them."

"And you call yourself my ambassador," jeered the king. "I noticed that you made a fortune betting on that pair of freaks."

"I had to wager on them—to show confidence in my gift to you."

"And I had to pay out, to keep confidence in the arena. A mere hundredth of your winnings can bribe even the worst courtier. It won't take much for Wenji—at least at first."

Trying to compromise, the slaves repositioned the shade halfway between their king and the contest winners, leaving both parties in the sun. This drew more threats from the king, but roaring laughter from the crowd. As Lorgi moved back under the shade, its bearers managed to deliver him to the king in five increments. Howling at each stop, the audience cheered when the honorees reached the king and his carpet. Despite the affront, he put on his biggest possible *smiley-mouth* for the crowd. Fifty thousand spectators, sacred tradition, and the king's own staggering investment in the arena all demanded it. Shouting with all the asthmatic force he could muster, the king proclaimed, "Wenji, brave lady of the stone dragons."

"First I'm glass; now I'm stone," huffed Lorgi. "Does that mean I've been elevated?"

"Lorgi, you must be quiet when the king speaks!" hissed Wenji, bowing.

Opening the chest, the king presented her with a gold necklace set with eight huge rubies as the crowd "oooh-ed." Two gaunt waiters served Lorgi a hefty tray of noodles and a jug of wine, compliments of the master chef. This was intended to keep him occupied, quiet, and make him sleepy. He inhaled it all in seconds. The arena planners always kept such things ready, in case the intended victims should actually win a contest. Handing the former concubine a beautifully written proclamation, the king officially gave Lorgi as property to "Lady Wenji, Dragon Master for the Court of Shohan, forevermore."

Ten words and a piece of paper had made her a person of rank. A high and unique rank. Suddenly Wenji had become a noble at the court of Shohan—the second largest and most powerful realm on the whole Continent. She dared not meet the king's eyes until bowing again. Yet she could not help but grin at the officials and guards all waiting behind the king, even as tears of joy and relief escaped her eyes, and those of some witnesses. Happy at this rare instant when an innocent had not only survived, but been so richly rewarded, they all mirrored her glowing expression.

"Remember me? Hello!" Lorgi nudged her with his muzzle. "Any gifts, even just words they offer you, smell their blood. It will wash away all that is good in you. Look hard. Your king has the dead hungry eyes of a balkotar."

"What does your exotic say?" pried an advisor.

"That he is very tired, hungry, and thirsty after his battle, and needs to cool off in the garden," said Wenji. She implored Lorgi with glaring eyes to be quiet and follow her game, wherever it might lead.

"The garden is not for animals, especially beasts of the arena," laughed the king, "though yours has imperial taste."

"Your Majesty, I beg you to forgive my boldness," said Wenji. "But I must state that he is no beast to be thrown into the arena."

Impressed that she seemed to be speaking up for him, Lorgi cocked his head and stared at her. His ears shot up, straining to pick up more from the conversation in Esterlan, the language of Shohan and all the Well-East.

"Perhaps this rare *exotic* has graduated from trials in the arena?" posed Satungke.

"His name is Lord Gamon of Tiefenbo, and he is no less than a young prince regent in his frozen realm!" exclaimed Wenji.

"Actually, it's Lorgámon, one word," murmured Lorgi. "I'm an Álukoi, not some *hyúlem* knight or warlord."

"Not now!" she whispered to him with blazing eyes. "Just listen quietly. I told you I'll explain later." Lorgi squatted down on all fours, with his head between his forepaws.

"Already my court infects the exotic with the urge to babble," laughed the king. "Yet Lady Wenji controls him! Maybe she can also temper that most irritating habit in my officials, advisors, courtiers and other royal beasts."

"Your Majesty," said Wenji, deeply bowing. "Lord Gamon and his kind have their own exotic ways. They take pride in ancient customs and beliefs that we must study, for the good of Shohan. We must all work very hard to erase his terrible first impression of our land. How shall we be rewarded when his enormous kin come to retrieve him one day? He will grow to be at least twelve times his present size. Maybe twenty."

"I was right!" cheered the king's doctor, clapping his hands. "If Your Majesty will recall—"

"Enough with your drivel!" the king barked at him. Turning back to Wenji, he asked, "Dearest Lady Wenji of the dragons, how can we bribe your dragon champion?"

"Of course Your Majesty sees a mighty ally in this dragon child prince," she beamed. "But only I can help you make him so. Know that he will grow far stronger than a giant *balukta*, yet wiser than we can imagine. He is loyal, fearless and true, with a genius for languages. He and I have become sworn friends and royal siblings, according to the sacred, ancient ways of his kind. Only I can manage him, tutor him for you, and negotiate when his elders finally arrive. Not even the Tuzanchim would dare attack with such powerful allies at your disposal."

The king and his entourage bristled at Wenji's lightning transformation, even as the dog blood had not quite dried on Lorgi's hide. In Shohan, only seasoned nobles of high rank dared speak boldly in front of royalty, or present such ideas. The court, as well as the crowd, still saw Lorgi as just a talking freak, with a king's temper and an armored hide. To the Shohaneze, anything west of the Tuzanchim Steppes was as safely far away as the moon.

However, a daring, young beauty of rank, with a living weapon at her command, posed a tangible threat. All eyes fixed not on Lorgi, but Wenji. She could bring endless troubles to any who might have to deal with her, long before her monster grew enough to prove his value to the kingdom. And the court of Shohan already had an infinite supply of troubles.

In fact the king spent most of his energy wrestling the myriad threats and plots against him, be they foreign, local, or imagined. He found plenty of each. With a blink and a smirk, he foresaw a tragic "accident" for the star suddenly rising before him, once he had learned enough about her dragon. Similar plans awaited his own wife, the queen. Yet the

king would commission a heroic bronze statue and give a fine speech—
written by an advisor—so that all might keep fond memories of "Lady
Wenji of the stone dragons." But no harm must ever touch Lord Gamon,
as long as there was any chance of winning him over. If not, he would
have to be buried alive under a mountain of rock to ensure his demise. In
the meantime, the pair had to be kept away from the queen, lest they
bond and hatch their own plot against the king.

"Both this exotic and his trainer sound far too clever already,"
whispered an advisor in the king's ear. Though Lorgi could not grasp the
words, the man's tight smile told that he intended to profit from them.

"I'm a full crop ahead of you," hissed the king.

"Please, Your Majesty," said Wenji. "My dragon prince must cool
off in your garden."

"We have the finest on all the Continent," boasted the king. "Your
escort stands waiting. Ask whatever you need from them."

"A bath, new clothes, and something to eat," said Wenji.

"As you wish," smiled a head servant, bowing to her and gesturing
toward a gate. "This way. Everything you need already waits."

"Go," ordered the king. "Perhaps Ambassador Satungke was right.
The arena is no place for you. Enjoy our gardens, a fine banquet, and a
well-deserved nap. We can discuss your role at court later."

He signaled the waiting entourage of *smiley-mouths* and servants
crowded under the arena's royal gate. Wenji bowed. With Lorgi beside
her, she followed them out, but in seconds was leading the group. A
dozen guards tagged after them. The last of these the king grabbed by the
arm. "Listen for your life! Keep that herd of fools together in one place
for the whole afternoon, babbling until their tongues fall off. But no
matter what they say, I want them all too stuffed to breathe, too drunk to
know their own names, too incapacitated to even dream the slightest
mischief. Follow?"

"As...as you wish, Your Majesty," stuttered the guard, sweating.

"Your Majesty," smiled Satungke, watching the group leave. "The
dragon can accomplish all that for you. Let him show them how to feast
and drink themselves to sleep. See how he holds the group tighter than
any glue. The same way that he and his lady master are inseparable."

"You mean insufferable," growled the king. "How I hate arrogant beast trainers, even more than ambitious courtiers. Wenji suddenly debuts as both. She has spoiled my lunch and may keep me from dinner. Unlike you, *I* lost a fortune on the contest, my best war dogs are gone. Their trainer has vanished. It may long, indeed, before I can punish him."

"The dragon nearly caught him," noted Satungke. "Now he suffers in hiding."

"By the fire in the beast's eyes, he would have cut the man into a million shreds of stew meat," laughed the king. "That would have been entertainment!"

"Only for an instant."

"Oh, but what an exquisite one!" rasped the king.

"We must never cross Wenji's beast or earn his hatred."

"But we have all done so repeatedly," said the king.

"Then she was right," murmured Satungke. "We must all work hard to befriend him. Especially me."

"Yes. And that is just one more thing I hate about him and Lady Wenji. Catch up with her entourage, Satungke. Take charge. A few coins here and there won't hurt, either. This is no time to hold back. See that all of them have entirely too much of the best Shohan can offer. I want them unable to even speak, let alone remain standing, after the excess. Your requests are to be king's commands. Let any workers who fail you die next week in the arena, by whatever means you choose."

* * *

"Try to notice everything about this place, Wenji," Lorgi whispered in Tuzanchim, as they entered the gardens. "You never know what may help us plan our way out of here."

"Take care. This is no place to speak in any tongue," she answered. "We must show these people that we are here to stay, and demand their respect." She glanced sternly at the entourage close behind them. Suddenly, her expression reminded Lorgi of Klimgu at his most worried.

"What does your dragon say?" asked several of them fawning over the pair.

"He loves the gardens, but needs to cool off in water." Wenji forced herself to smile. "He is also quite hungry."

"Not that hungry!" fumed Lorgi. "Now you take care, Wenji. Your smile is starting to look like theirs."

"What does he say now?" they pestered her.

"I'm not sure," she lied. "I understand him better than anyone else, but still do not always know what he means. He surprises me every day."

"Ah. A mystery to be solved!" chirped one lady, delighted to have something novel to chatter about. "We shall all help you with that. It will be our project."

"Oh, yes! Yes, indeed!" echoed the others.

The group halted when they reached an open pavilion supported by stilts over a large pond. Servants brought refreshments while the entourage sat on benches in the shade. To everyone's surprise, Lorgi ignored the food. Instead, he climbed over the pavilion's rails and dove into the pond. Washing off all the blood, he shouted a thunderous "Yes!" Refreshed at last, he sprang out of the water, crashing through the wooden rails and back into the pavilion. He gave an "oops" but declined to apologize for his damage. Far from home and his mother, Lorgi was in no mood to respect what he considered to be enemy property.

Terrified, the entourage jumped back, yet smiled with bleating laughter to cover their fear. All the while, gaunt servants raced about, struggling to produce the impromptu banquet with all possible speed. Sitting back on his haunches, Lorgi cocked his head and twitched his ears as he studied it all.

"Stop! Stop everyone," shouted Wenji. They froze silent. "Lorgi had his bath. But I will need a good hour for mine. Stay or go as you like. Thank you for your patience."

The servants nodded agreement, happy for the delay, but the guests frowned.

"She's really testing her new whip," one plump lady whispered to another.

"How long can such a foolish girl live?" asked the other.

"A few weeks?" guessed the first lady. "What a shame. Hopelessly young for her rank, and far too beautiful not to hate. Still, there is something I cannot help liking about her."

"They're talking about you," murmured Lorgi.

"Of course they are," said Wenji. "It is to be expected."

"What did your dragon say?" asked an older man among the guests.

"Why don't all of you just talk to him?" laughed Wenji, vanishing into a private room.

"Wait! Come back," shouted many in the entourage.

"You can't just leave your beast unattended," said one woman.

"Must I remind you that he is a prince, not a beast?" snapped Wenji, poking her head out. "Be nice, and you will find him quite friendly."

Lorgi began making the rounds, stopping just in front of each guest to sniff and stare them down. Kibak had once told him that a scout could not predict which observations would prove vital. So Lorgi noted every detail he could sense about them all, giving each guest in turn a long moment of fright.

"Are you quite certain he is not a carnivore?" wheezed the first guest under Lorgi's scrutiny, the woman who had lost her coat.

"And perfectly harmless, just as long as you are very nice to him—and everyone else," smiled Wenji. Feeling vindictive, she added, "He never forgets."

"What can he have to remember?" chuckled a round, middle-aged man.

"Everything about each of you," said Wenji. "Your voice, your tone, and what you say, whether he understands any of it or not. And especially your face and your scent. He was very hurt by your laughing at us when we were down in the pit cage."

The man gulped. Others sighed. Some covered their mouths with hands as they glanced at each other.

"We're so sorry," they all moaned.

"Now to my bath." Giving them all a big *smiley-mouth*, Wenji vanished, forcing them to deal with Lorgi on their own. Not daring to laugh or even speak in a normal voice, they murmured or whispered, until Lorgi began mimicking them. None dared utter the slightest insult regarding anyone or anything, lest the dragon child repeat it. Such constraints squelched all conversation. Even after Lorgi finished his rounds among the silent guests, most still reeked of adrenaline. In the next minute, he fell asleep, due to the heat and his ordeal in the arena.

Relieved, yet drained themselves, most of the guests did the same. A few tried to leave, but waiting guards stopped them. The rest snored.

"Sorry I took so long," called Wenji, returning. "Hello. Is anyone awake?"

"You look fantastic, Lady Wenji, absolutely imperial," bowed a smiling guard, as another stumbled into him.

"*Gánsi*—I mean thank you," said Wenji, smiling at the two of them.

"Absolutely imperial," repeated both guards, bowing and smiling as hard as they could.

"Thank you."

"You look different," said Lorgi, twitching his nostrils in suspicion. "I hope they didn't turn you into a *smiley-mouth*. You're still Wenji, right?"

"Yes, but *gánsi*, anyway, Lorgi. I feel much better now."

Many "ooohs" and compliments greeted her new red silk dress, pearl sandals, flowing hairstyle, and every detail of Wenji's appearance. Servants tripped over each other to assist her. Half of the men—and two of the women—in the entourage tried to flirt with her. All put on their widest false smiles, saying anything to court her favor. Suddenly feeling like a crown princess, Wenji glowed, basking in their flattery. Lorgi snorted in disgust.

Four musicians arrived and immediately began producing soft, sweet adagios on the most exquisite, refined string instruments known to the Continent. While most of the guests ignored them, Lorgi slowly approached, finally seating himself right before them so he could enjoy every note. But no one had bothered to tell the musicians about Lorgi. Terrified, they stood up to leave.

"Please don't stop!" shouted Wenji. "He loves music, like all good things. Make friends and play for him. Certainly your best audience here."

Both charmed and intimidated by Lady Wenji, they did as she requested, and everyone relaxed. Lorgi sensed a type of peace and depth in the musicians that was notably lacking in the guests. He much preferred their company and let Wenji know it.

"Music to tame the savage beast," laughed one guest.

"May it keep him occupied for a long time," added another.

"What are they saying about me, Wenji?" asked Lorgi.

"They are pleased that you like music," she answered.

"Then tell them to stop talking and listen! Maybe it can start to civilize them."

"What does your dragon say now?" begged a woman.

"That music is good for you," Wenji smiled at her.

"How nice," chirped the woman. "The king said the dragon has regal taste."

Food enough for 200 warriors arrived, though only fifty nobles would enjoy this feast. Amid trumpet fanfares, servers brought a large plate of appetizers and a glass of wine to each guest. Five minutes later, a thick soup, bread, plus a tall glass of a new wine came. Ten minutes later, servers delivered huge platters of roasted turkey, batter-fried fish, savory vegetables, noodle and rice dishes to the center of each round table—and two more types of wine. Both Lorgi and Wenji marveled that the moment any guest sipped any of the four wines before them, servers immediately refilled the glass. Like most of the guests, Lorgi wasted no time in eating his fill. But he refused any wine. Seeing nothing else to drink, he turned to leave.

"What is it, Lorgi?" asked Wenji. "I can tell when you're thinking."

"I'm thirsty, but not for wine."

"Is anything wrong with your dragon, Lady Wenji?" asked the head server, looking between her and Lorgi.

"He needs water—clean, fresh, spring water," she answered.

"We are sorry," stammered the head server. "We just have wine. But only the finest in all Shohan for Lady Wenji and her dragon. King's command."

The instant Wenji translated for Lorgi, he huffed, "Fine. I'll go visit another banquet where they have water."

"No, Lorgi, please," shouted Wenji, nervously. "You know that we have to stay together."

"Then come with me. I'm thirsty and we need to get away from all these *smiley-mouths*, so we can plan."

Sensing trouble, the musicians stopped playing, the guests hushed and the servers froze in place, all darting eyes between each other and Wenji, begging for her to resolve the situation. Two servers prostrated themselves on their knees in front of Lorgi, blocking his exit over the narrow wooden bridge linking the pavilion to dry land.

"Please bring your best water—only what the king would drink himself—as quickly as possible," asked Wenji. "But if my dragon cannot wait that long, let no one try to stop him from leaving. You must let him roam where he will in the gardens, and I must stay with him."

"As…as you wish, Lady Wenji," stuttered the head server, snapping his fingers at the two prostrate servants, who ran off to obtain her request. "I promise fresh spring water will be here in minutes—chilled, too."

Not convinced, Lorgi started across the bridge.

"Alright, Lorgi. You got your way, just like me," Wenji soothed him. "All your needs will be met and quickly, if you just stay here with me. And be patient, for once."

"What about your needs, Wenji?" asked Lorgi. "Stop talking to these smiling idiots and eat up. You're the only one here who actually needs the food. We may not get this lucky again for a very long time, and you'll need stamina for where we're going. But no wine. Last time it landed us in the arena."

"What does he say now?" chirped a short heavy woman.

"He needs water to drink," Wenji smiled.

"Water for beasts; wine for nobles," said the woman.

"How many times must I warn you that my dragon is a young prince regent in his land?" asked Wenji. "For your own good, do not ever refer to him as a beast."

"But a prince never turns down wine," said the woman.

"He likes wine, but it gave him a headache the last time."

"Aha! So he does have a weakness after all," the woman chortled.

"It would be deadly foolish to imagine so," smiled Wenji.

"Now what is he up to?" asked another woman. "How cute. Is he playing waiter?"

With all eyes on him, Lorgi took four plates, loading each with a healthy sampling of his favorite dishes. Mimicking the servers, he carried two in each forepaw, as he shuffled on his hind legs over to the musicians. Beaming genuine, wide smiles of delight, they bowed and thanked him repeatedly. But just as they began eating, a guard stepped in, ordering the musicians to set down the plates and get back to work.

"Lady Wenji," said the guard, looking unhappy with his task. "Please tell your dragon that this banquet is only for specially invited guests, and no others. Not the servants, musicians, or guards."

"I will not, and you had best not try to stop him, either," laughed Wenji. "After what he has been through, especially in Shohan, my dragon has no tolerance for any type of guards."

"The Shohaneze are so rude," muttered Lorgi. Standing to his full height, even stretching his back legs and tail, he stared down the guard at eye level, nearly touching him with his snout. The man backed away. Seizing the rare opportunity, the musicians devoured the food Lorgi had brought to them. "Look, Wenji, they're starving. I'd better get them seconds."

"What does he say?" burped one guest, a fat old man.

"He likes to feed hungry people," Wenji smiled. "We could learn much from his curious ways. But he hates guards. And mean, rude, or false people. He can smell their intent."

"Such a marvel, this talking…exotic," said a plump, middle-aged woman. "How did you ever train him to speak?"

"I did no such thing," said Wenji. "He has his own language. Perhaps one day he will teach it to me."

"Impossible," the old man shook his head. "No matter how exotic, a beast can never have its own language or customs. You or someone must have worked very hard to train him."

"For the last time, he is a prince, not a beast!" shouted Wenji. "Be very glad he does not yet understand much of our language, or you would have paid for your insult already."

"Then I suppose we shall soon have to be careful of all we say in front of him, just like a real person," giggled one woman, already drunk.

"You would be wise to take care now," said Wenji. "He learns faster than any child I have ever known."

Just then servants brought two large jugs of cold water, presenting them to Wenji. Lorgi opened one jug and drank its entire contents.

"Enough! Princess Wenji, please tell everybody to leave," Lorgi growled in Tuzanchim. "We need to talk alone. Right now."

Wenji hesitated. But suddenly she recognized the same prying eyes that had studied the pair in the garden three days before. They belonged to a short, older woman of rank and now a member of the entourage. Except for being the only other guest who was not overweight, she blended in. Wearing finer clothes than before, she also had changed her hairstyle to match the other guests. The spy still carried a small tablet and a tiny, sharp pen, which she concealed under her shawl. Rarely taking her eyes off Wenji or Lorgi, she wrote notes after everything they said.

Lorgi had spotted the agent before the group left the arena. But after all that had happened, the fact seemed not worth alarming Wenji. Noting the sudden change in her expression, Lorgi wondered why it had taken her so long to recognize the spy. Looking at her with mournful eyes, he begged her to act.

"Everyone, please excuse us; my dragon and I must leave at once," said Wenji, looking around at all of them.

"*Gánsi,*" murmured Lorgi.

"What can be wrong now?" whined the old man.

"No time to explain. Please everyone just remain here," shouted Wenji, sounding terrified. "You all must stay, and I must go before my dragon loses his temper."

"Something we said?" asked the drunken woman. "You told us he would be friendly."

Catching Lorgi's eyes, Wenji opened hers wide, pretending to fear him. Taking the cue, Lorgi stretched his limbs, whipped his tail, shook his head from side to side and snapped his jaws, as if about to fight. As an experiment, he added the growling sounds of a large carnivore, because that always seemed to frighten humans.

"I had better take my dragon away, right now," said Wenji. "You saw him in the arena, but that was nothing compared to when he lost his temper in Uxanda Palace! I must try to calm him down, find out what upset him...before...before..."

"Can we help?" asked one man. Lorgi twitched his ears in surprise.

"No, *gánsi*, I mean thank you," answered Wenji. "I must deal with him alone. It is the only way. Come along, Lorgi."

She pretended to lead him over the bridge, through strands of trees and secluded paths, until the pair found a spot safely away from people, by another shaded pond. Sitting on a stone bench, Wenji let out a sigh while shaking her head. "Satisfied?"

"How good is your smell?" asked Lorgi.

"Please! I just took a thorough bath."

"I mean, can you smell all the evil around here?"

"Every inch of this realm holds ill will, but how can you smell that?"

"I'm an Álukoi, remember?"

"Look, they are being so nice to us now. Can't we just enjoy it for a little while? Life is so short and painful as it is."

"Especially in Shohan," huffed Lorgi. "Where you said truth doesn't last a day."

"We should at least get something out of all this. A reward, a compensation. We've earned it. Besides, I think we were starting to make progress with some of those *smiley-mouths* as you call them."

"They only act nice when they want things. Bad things. Some of them hate you, especially the king."

"He hates everyone. All know it. So what?"

"He plans to harm you later," Lorgi stated dryly, gazing at Wenji the way only a child could.

"How can you possibly know that?" Wenji laughed nervously, unsure whether or not to believe him. "You are only saying that to—"

"I know. I just know. Easy to smell and easier to see. I feel it, too."

"Just because you're an Álukoi," Wenji snapped, irritated but fearful.

"Any human in Tiefenbo could tell you the same."

"That doesn't help us here, does it?"

"Everybody behaves about the same in face and body, no matter what they say, whether they're Álukois, lowland *hyúlems*, north, south, east or west. Lendish, Tuzanchim or Shohaneze. People are people."

"So now you're an expert on all peoples," snapped Wenji.

"If you are a good person, then you can know," Lorgi spoke softly. "Otherwise, you never will. That's what my mother says."

"How I wish your mother were here now," sighed Wenji.

"I wish we were both home with her right now eating pies. She says good deeds make you somebody. Then you can know. Your eyes, ears, nose—well, maybe not a human nose—but your whole feeling will tell you, and then you just know for sure."

"I can only know by all that has ever happened to me. This is the first time in my life that people have been nice to me, respected me, or at least feared me. The first time things have been given to me. And now you want me to run away from it all. I don't know, Lorgi."

"My mother says to let your spirit guide you when you must decide really big things. Like now! Mine says this is the worst place, and I don't need to be anything to know that. There is nothing good to hold onto here. Be true to yourself, Wenji. Let go of this evil place. Escape with me."

Slumping as she sat down, Wenji fondled her gold necklace, but studied her feet.

"You'll have to leave that pretty trinket," he warned.

"What?" shrieked Wenji. She shook her head. "Do you have any idea what my necklace is worth?"

"Only that it's too heavy, not worth dying for."

"You sound like a Tuzanchim," sighed Wenji. "Are you ever wrong?"

"I get in trouble almost every day at home, just trying to have fun."

"And why is that?" asked Wenji, squinting with irritation.

"I'm just a little boy, remember?" giggled Lorgi. "I can't help it."

"Good! At least that makes you human."

Surprised by her own words, Wenji gazed into Lorgi's huge eyes. He stared back, equally stunned. Both exploded with laughter. Hidden a safe distance away, the spy blinked, finally allowing herself to smile. A single tear rolled down her cheek as she took more notes.

Wenji admired her necklace again before gazing at the pond. By the water's reflection, she was able to see indirectly through a thin spot in some bushes on the other side of the pond. She glimpsed the same piercing eyes and that skillful hand, ever busy writing with a tiny pen on a tiny notepad. Once discovered, the Tuzanchim-speaking agent vanished.

"Does she ever rest?" Wenji cursed, suddenly feeling a chill. "Lorgi?"

"I saw her too. She spies more on us than on anyone else."

"How much time do you think we have, before…?"

"I don't know, but we're not staying long enough to find out!"

20: Rebellion

A horde of only 17,000 rebels should not impress the Gran Vazuk, but most of his loyal forces remained scattered in the east. Expecting trouble, he doubled the contingent normally employed to guard the capital. Like the finest castles and walled cities of the west, Uxanda could easily repel a host many times the number of her defenders, so long as a critical minimum held the walls. The ancient city at the empire's heart had always relied on stout architecture and harsh surroundings to deter foes. Having been tested only six times in history, the walls had never failed. No force or ingenuity ever came close to breaking them. Glowing red with pride in the sun's last rays, flying scores of huge banners on the incessant wind, Uxanda seemed impervious to challenge, if not time itself.

Arriving in clear sight of the capitol, Klimgu had to forcibly ignore 1,200 years of history and every military expert on the Continent. He did not have hundreds of ladders, miles of rope, or massive siege engines to overcome the walls, let alone the 50,000 warriors also needed to carry the battle to Uxanda. Any of those things would have cost months—time enough for the Vazuk to gather a huge attack force in the capital—without offering much chance of success.

Klimgu anticipated a violent reception or a dire ultimatum. Instead, Uxanda merely shut its gates. No envoys or scouts. No alarms or smoke. No force to challenge him. Either the capitol waited for a much greater foe, or just slept, as corrupt, foolish cities might, when threatened from without. Perhaps the storied capital shunned him, as if that alone could stop a rebellion. Like Chotzan before him, he stared, hoping for some visible reaction, yet now Klimgu had no expectations. Uxanda could do what it liked. Nothing would change his goal. With or without Uxanda, the Vazuk must fall, by whatever means, despite all his powers and advantages, even if Klimgu did not live to see it.

"Where should we make camp?" asked Twarejik.

"In Uxanda," quipped Serukeeba, slapping the ground with her tail. "I will scout a low point in those hideous walls."

"There are none," said Baqwam. "Twenty-five feet high, all the way around."

"I will find a weak spot to break through," said the snowdragon.

"Again, there are none," said Baqwam. "Always ten feet thick at the base. Everywhere. The dirt under them, if one can even call it that, is mean as rock. Our ancestors knew just where and how to build Uxanda. The only way in will be through one of her four Grand Gates, all heavily fortified."

"Then I will tear one down!" huffed Serukeeba.

"Not even you can do that," said Baqwam. "The attempt would kill you."

"The Vazuk won't attack without superior force," said Twarejik. "Our time is now. We must find a way in. Someone bring our clever monks."

Knowing Uxanda better than any of the others, Baqwam and Gurjik drew a crude map in the dirt, finishing just as Lutyam and Moshal arrived.

"How much rope do we have?" asked Klimgu.

"About 300 feet," said Moshal. "Allowing twelve climbers at a time."

"You'll need a thousand times that!" scoffed Lutyam. "Even then, few would reach the battlements, let alone fight their way over the top. Surely the Vazuk's best archers wait in all those towers."

"Our best can't wait to pick them off, and have far more experience," said Baqwam. "If you dare ask, people will say I am one of those."

Klimgu, his Second, Third, and all the captains furiously debated what to do. Suddenly, many found their leader too hasty to reach Uxanda without a clear plan or the impossibly massive tools needed for breaching the walls. Yet many others argued that to wait for such marvels invited disaster by giving the Vazuk time to gather his forces and crush the rebellion. Sitting back on her haunches, Serukeeba cleared her throat, waved her forepaws in the air, and asked for quiet. But the arguing raged on all around her, a battle of words all its own.

"*Yahai!*" she roared, smacking the ground with her tail. Every mouth shut. "Enough! I will need all the rope, if it can be made strong enough to hold me. Rest now. Be ready to war after dark."

"No moon tonight," said Moshal.

"Perfect," said Serukeeba. "Our advantage."

"But we won't be able to see without using fire," said Moshal.

"Then use a little, but I need none," said Serukeeba. Turning to Klimgu, she added, "I will break open this giant snake pit for you, from the inside, but only on my terms."

"No pillaging," nodded Klimgu. "I've already spoken to the captains about that."

"Before I asked?" Smiling, Serukeeba gave her best imitation of a warrior's nod in return.

"I miss the old days," sighed Twarejik. "All was much easier, simpler, quicker."

"Only in our fading memories, my friend," said Klimgu.

An hour after dark, Serukeeba led twenty scouts to a point along the walls about 300 yards north of the west gate. Stumbling in the dark, with countless tiny steps in fur-lined boots, they took pains to keep silent and unseen. Widely spaced torches along the wall's parapets and in the towers had left most of the ground below black. Only a gentle wind and the guards' muffled chatter lent the thin dry air any sound at all. Nothing above or below stirred until a loop of thick, triple-wound rope slapped against one of the wall's crenels. Serukeeba's first try made only a faint, dull thud, yet disturbed the night's usual calm. One guard asked another if he heard anything, then shrugged.

"Aim for teeth, not gums!" Serukeeba scolded herself in her mind. She focused on a single merlon, the one she had counted out to be exactly midway between two towers.

Her second attempt to lasso it also failed, but caused a guard to lean out over a crenel to scan the dark below. He sighted the Álukoi, reflected in the light of his torch, just as Baqwam's first lucky arrow impaled him through the neck. Suddenly 3,000 screaming rebels staked out firing positions along Uxanda's entire west wall, all crouching behind massive wood and leather shields, designed by Lutyam after those used for sieges in the Castled Lands. Within a minute, 2,000 rebels did the same facing the north, south and east walls. Twarejik allowed no light but a single candle for each archer behind his or her screen, giving the defenders nothing to shoot at but the night itself, compounding their fear.

On her third try, Serukeeba finally snared her chosen merlon. Instantly, she pulled her rope tight against the stone tooth and began to climb straight up, testing every fiber of the rope. A torrent of arrows pelted Serukeeba as she hoisted herself up, but just as many flew in the opposite direction. Most defenders who got a clear view of her paid for it, amid a furious crescendo of alarm bells and screaming guards racing to the battlements.

By the time Serukeeba reached the top, her rope frayed, ready to break as soldiers chopped at it with swords. As she climbed over the top and onto the battlement, she tossed the rope down to the rebels. A deafening cheer reverberated along the entire length of the west wall. Swords and a few halberds probed at her belly, but before any could cut her, Serukeeba swept all their owners off the battlement she had claimed. The battle that every expert on the Continent had said could never be waged had just begun.

A score of rebels charged in to retrieve Serukeeba's ropes. Most of those paid with their lives. Yet they delivered. Immediately, a team of skilled porters divided her triple-wound rope into a dozen pieces for the foolhardiest rebels to try and grapple over the walls the way the dragon had done. By the time volunteers started offering themselves up as easy targets in the desperate climb, Serukeeba could no longer be seen on the battlements.

On the wall walk near the West Gate, guards pummeled what they called "doom's mother" with swords and knives. The instant Serukeeba threw them off the walkway, new soldiers replaced them, frantic to protect Uxanda. Realizing their weapons had no effect, some defenders tried fire. Rather than encourage this by admitting her weakness, Serukeeba charged with extra fury at a group of ten men wielding torches, the instant they emerged from a tower door. Crushing them all against the door in one impact, she was able to snuff out most of their flames. Despite receiving minor cuts and burn blisters, she convinced any observers that she had no fear of fire. The whole tower shook as cracks appeared around the door.

Seeing that the doorway was too narrow for anything larger than a fit human, and not worth the effort of demolishing, Serukeeba quit the walls altogether and leapt down, squashing several soldiers at ground level inside the city. To reach the gate, she would have to plow through hundreds more, every one of them determined to stop her. A relentless barrage of fresh soldiers slowed her progress, as metal and wood struck against her hide from all sides. Even with her ear lids tightly shut, she winced from the sheer vibration of it all rippling through her body.

So much material flew at her that even Serukeeba could not see her goal. Four men even tried climbing onto her back. Two of them slipped, impaling themselves on her back spikes. Light as it was, she halted just long enough to throw off the dead weight, horrified by any reminder of the balkotars.

* * *

Scores of rebels raced to the walls nearest Serukeeba's point of entry. For every warrior desperately scaling the walls on one of a dozen ropes, ten more waited their turn to climb, while two or three others were being carried away, impaled by arrows. In a flash of bad luck, all three men climbing one rope fell at once. Before fresh rebels could grab hold of that rope to take their places, a quick defender snatched it away, up beyond reach. And without being shot. Now the attackers had only eleven ropes to work with.

Still, enough rebels actually made it to the top to begin carving out a foothold, because Serukeeba so completely occupied the defenders. After a brief struggle, rebels claimed the tower with the crumbling, bloody doorway. To announce their small victory, the rebels cut down the tower's huge imperial banner, set it ablaze and hurled it over the walls. Another deafening cheer erupted from the army waiting outside. Immediately the rebels set their sights on the adjacent tower to the south—closer to the west gate.

With a seemingly invincible rock monster on the loose inside the walls—and making steady progress toward the Great West Gate—one tower lost to rebels, another in play, and an army surrounding the city, Uxanda's fate suddenly became an open question.

By now the alarm had reached into the Grand Imperial Palace, many blocks away in Uxanda's center. While elite guards jolted "His Greatness" awake, everyone else demanded information that no messengers could provide. Reports and rumors of "doom's mother" and "the curse of the rock dragons" swept through the halls, chambers, and even the dungeons like a prairie fire. Deprived of facts or confident reassurances, the palace staff assumed the worst.

All rank and protocol dissolved. Servants pocketed small valuables. The highest officials did the same, also disguising themselves as peasants. The concubines, eunuchs and other slaves all seized the chance, arming themselves and cutting down abusive masters or anyone who dared hinder their escape. The Gran Vazuk screamed orders and threats, but people ran from him. Breathless, he staggered into the fountain courtyard, shunned in his own palace.

* * *

Just as Serukeeba neared the Great West Gate of Uxanda, scores of mounted defenders arrived, hurling loops of rope around her to try and immobilize the invader. One more painful reminder of her war on the balkotars. She knew the rebels desperately needed all of it. But Golármon's voice thundered "Focus!" in her mind. Shutting her eyes for a moment, Serukeeba ignored every obstacle and distraction, determined to push ahead towards where she knew the gate to be. The defenders threw everything they could at her, as well as at the handful of rebels already on the walls, determined to stop the invaders at any cost.

Despite the lines tugging around her feet, tail, and even her neck, Serukeeba reached her target. Fortunately, nothing held but a moment against her rock hide. Thick chains, iron levers and pulleys with heavy ropes operated the gate mechanism, but Serukeeba had no time to discover how any of it worked. She yanked, tore, severed, or otherwise broke every item that came within reach, until she began gnawing on the giant wooden beam that kept the gate closed. Halfway through, Serukeeba spat out arm-sized chunks of wood and stepped back twenty paces to gauge her progress.

She wanted to charge and ram the Gate, in order to snap the weakened beam, which had been more than a foot thick until she put her teeth to work on it. Once cobblestone, the ground around Serukeeba became a swamp of corpses, severed limbs, broken weapons and miles of shredded rope, swimming in blood. Not even an Álukoi could charge on that. She swept some of the mounting carnage aside so that she could run on solid stone. But bodies kept piling up as the defenders refused to leave her alone.

Sensing her goal, the defenders massed all possible force near the Great West Gate. Men in the gate towers readied boiling oil to pour down on any foe that reached the portal from either outside the walls or within. Determined to break it all open before they could stop her, Serukeeba charged.

Like her first try with the rope, her first ramming charge did not succeed. The beam splintered, yet still held. Serukeeba saw the bubbling oil start to cascade down towards her from murder holes in the gate tower. Lunging back, she barely escaped it. A too-close guard let out a yelp, while scrambling out of her way. As she turned toward him, the man thrust his torch at her as a last defense. With catlike speed, she snatched it from him, blurting out "*Gánsi!*" for his unintended help. She threw the torch right on the boiling oil, followed by anything within reach that would burn.

Taking a moment to rest on her haunches, she both praised and marveled at *hyúlem* stupidity for suddenly making her task easier. The flames jumped even beyond the gate's lofty crest, brilliantly lighting the area and roasting the tower guards. From outside the walls, thousands of rebels cheered, but could only guess what was happening within.

* * *

"What if even mighty Serukeeba cannot break Uxanda's Gates?" asked Moshal.

"Then, even she will resort to fire, as all can see," said Klimgu. "We should never have let her rush in alone, but no one offered a better plan."

"We still hold the tower nearest Serukeeba's point of entry," shouted Baqwam. "If I can get enough of my group over the walls there—"

"No!" yelled Moshal. "Let others try. You are one of our best leaders, among the very few who can read, and also probably our best shot. We need you alive, down here by Klimgu."

"We need to break open Uxanda any way we can, before they can stop us," Baqwam shouted back. "Both Serukeeba and our crumbling tower must hold, or we will all die with the moon."

"Please. Please do not do this," begged Moshal.

Grabbing the monk's cheeks in her gloved left hand, Baqwam smiled. "Then I will seize another tower. You stay here and think of a way to break open our Gate."

"No, Baqwam!"

"Dine with me tonight—in the Vazuk's palace!" She vanished.

"Baqwam!"

"It's her ride," yelled Twarejik, gripping the monk's arm. "Don't spoil her luck with doubt in the middle of a battle. Warriors can always debate choices afterwards. She is one of the sharpest captains you will ever meet. Do what she asks. Think only about how we might crack open that monstrous Gate."

Dropping to the ground, Moshal pressed an ear to it like a scout. "Listen. The struggle within recedes. Is that good or bad?"

"It is good to see you acting like a real scout," cheered Twarejik. "I think you should not have been born Laskomian or become a monk. A few battles may forge you into a warrior. A Tuzanchim warrior!"

"I'm supposed to be a monk, and work for peace," gasped Moshal, putting his ear back to the ground. "I can't tell what is going on inside anymore."

A scout only a few paces away lifted his head and shook it as he looked to Twarejik.

"Serukeeba must really be drawing them away," said Twarejik. "The rest will be up to us." Turning to thousands of mounted reserves, he yelled, "Uxanda calls to us. The Vazuk has lived too long! Be ready on Klimgu's sword!"

"Wait. I hear something," said Moshal. "The struggle returns. It nears the Gate. Serukeeba fights many at once. She lunges; they retreat. But they charge back. She throws them back again. Now she runs...toward us!"

Suddenly, Uxanda's Great West Gate burst open. Serukeeba emerged, bearing hundreds of scratches and cuts on her belly, countless bits of rope, broken lances, arrows and a few severed arms, all caught between her back spikes. No part of her body had escaped a drenching in human blood, which was itself mostly covered by ash. Such a coating made her look as if she had been roasted alive. With a pained roar, she forced the Gate completely open. The instant she finished, the great obstacle tore free of its hinges and crashed with a deafening thunderclap. For the first time in history, Uxanda lay open to conquest. Staggering out past the walls, Serukeeba groaned. "Find my son!"

"*Guyat-iha!*" yelled Klimgu, whirling his sword overhead. Six thousand screaming riders poured through the gateway. Moshal and twenty frantic porters attended to Serukeeba as the whirlwind swept past them. Two thousand rebels also harried the south, east, and north gates, to both draw away the defenders and bar any escape. With Klimgu's charge, Twarejik moved half his archers to guard the demolished Great West Gate, where he found an exhausted Serukeeba claiming to have only minor scratches and no serious injuries. Taking the dragon at her word, Moshal bolted away, in search of Baqwam.

In the next hour, the rebels killed or captured all of the Vazuk's loyal defenders. As Klimgu and Twarejik reached the palace, a dozen rebels emerged from it, laughing as they drank from gallon-size water bags filled with imperial wine. Apparently the Gran Vazuk had died of fright—in the same courtyard where he had sold the dragon child and a rejected concubine to the Shohaneze. Moments later, Serukeeba, Baqwam and Moshal arrived. They joined the rebellion's leader and his Second, just as the two reached one of the palace gates. All but Klimgu were eager to go inside. He ignored their gestures to do so.

"So falls mighty Uxanda, in far less time that it takes to ride around her!" exulted Klimgu.

"Even the slowest rebels will grasp the meaning of our victory," said Twarejik. "And celebrate long and hard into the night. Most of them will be useless tomorrow."

"Our triumph only proves that no one, no place is invincible," warned Baqwam. "Somehow, we must post enough *sober* warriors to guard Uxanda through the night. Especially at the broken West Gate."

"Already done," assured Twarejik.

Not convinced, Baqwam eyed Klimgu, saying, "Dawn will be too easy for the late Vazuk's allies to strike back. Surely our new Vazuk knows well the price for dropping one's shield, or short-sighted scouting."

"What about not fulfilling an oath?" asked Serukeeba, staggering towards them.

"*Yahai!*" shouted Twarejik. "Our wise leader spends every hour in worry. For his health, and that of all our new horde, allow Klimgu this moment of joy."

"Joy?" huffed Serukeeba, lying down on her side. Immediately she fell asleep.

"Klimgu, walk with us into the throne room," urged Twarejik. "Sit in the Vazuk's gilded chair. Take his sword. Drink his wine. Savor our triumph."

"I have no such needs," Klimgu muttered.

"Are you sure?" Twarejik held out an open hand.

"Yes." Klimgu smiled, shaking his head.

"Very well, my great friend, my new Vazuk. If you cannot relax, then we still have much to do before we rest. Things that cannot wait for the sun."

"Let us confer in the fountain courtyard," said Klimgu. "It will refresh our mighty ally. But first remove the Vazuk and all the dead in the palace. Serukeeba has seen too much already."

"Well shot, but first meet with the captains—any who are still sober," said Twarejik. "This will not concern, and may only upset our great dragon ally, she who has seen too much."

"Obviously, she is a great leader and champion among her kind. I will not risk offense by excluding her."

"But there may not be any palace doorways quite big enough to admit her," said Baqwam.

"Break one down—whichever gives the most direct access to the fountain courtyard," ordered Klimgu. He studied Serukeeba, collapsed thirty paces back, with eyes shut but mouth wide open, panting hard to cool off. "She will appreciate the gesture, even in her fevered state."

Five men pounded away at the nearest doorway with war hammers until it crumbled. Recalling Lorgi's struggles with the heat, Klimgu had porters drench Serukeeba with many buckets of water. Revived, she and seven captains, Baqwam first among them, followed the conqueror and his Second inside to the fountain courtyard.

"Now, what cannot possibly wait until morning?" asked Klimgu.

"What to do with the most important things," said Twarejik.

"Such as?" spat Klimgu.

Twarejik eyed Baqwam, gesturing for her to provide the details.

"All the gems, gold and finery, the grain stores, spices, spirits, and swords" she recited. "The Vazuk's loyal retainers, officials, his slaves, concubines and servants. Then the matter of some eighty ransomed royals from faraway lands. And so many, many horses."

"That will take weeks to sort out." Klimgu shook his head. "I can't get bogged down with it all."

"We must decide tonight, before such things vanish or are destroyed," warned Twarejik.

"What fools would pillage their own capitol?" yelled Klimgu. "I ordered all those things to be guarded—untouched—until we decide what to do with them."

"And so they are, but the sooner we deal with them, the better," said Twarejik. "Decisive leadership. Be cruel or kind, but quick above all. Because now we face the Vazuk's heir, Puchakta. He will rally the east and south parts of the empire against us, gathering a monstrous force. But now *you* rule in Uxanda. Vazuk Klimgu, what is your will?"

"Feed everyone in the city," said Klimgu. "Free all the Vazuk's prisoners, including the foreign royals."

"Very noble and generous, but then you give up fortunes in ransom," said Baqwam.

"Yet win new friends," laughed Klimgu. "Must we fight the whole Continent? Make treaties with all the royals—tonight. Clear, simple treaties. Send them home smiling tomorrow with escorts. As for the Vazuk's servants, slaves and assorted freaks, let them go. Or stay and work for us, as they choose, if their labor is honest. There. Are you happy now, Twarejik, Baqwam?"

"No. But I am!" shouted Serukeeba. "Already you have climbed much further than I ever dreamed possible. Rokímba was right. The monks, too. Good may yet grow from all this."

"Wait…about the concubines," Twarejik smiled, nudging Klimgu. Serukeeba pursed her nostrils and pinned her ears back. Baqwam scowled at him. But Twarejik looked only at his leader, murmuring, "Delicious rewards for forty of your—"

"Forty!" yelled Baqwam, disgusted.

"As I was saying," grumbled Twarejik, clearing his throat. "The perfect reward for your most heroic captains who lack mates. Or perhaps a very special one, just for—"

"No! No concubines or slaves of any kind in my horde—in our new empire," shouted Klimgu. "Whatever reminds us of the late Vazuk can only weaken and corrupt. We must never copy his vices."

"My great friend, my Vazuk," said Twarejik, in a calm, quiet voice. "I only suggest what may help you and our horde. We all understand that with the strain of leadership and war, you may have no time, energy…or inclination?"

"Enough!" Klimgu raised a hand. "Let each warrior find his or her own match in time and place, as Wind intended." Nodding to Serukeeba, hard at work sniffing the entire courtyard floor, he added, "We still also ride on her quest, which led us to Uxanda. Listen, my friends. I seek far grander rewards than what can be stolen by the sword. Our new empire must not keep what rotted the old."

Serukeeba's eyes lost focus as she rested her head in the fountain pool. She sensed Lorgi's presence, even though Álukois gave off no scent. But she also detected that of a young female human, terrified and hungry, mingled with Lorgi's energy. "She and my son became instant friends. Every decent person likes my baby. She can lead us to him. May they keep each other from harm until then." Serukeeba spoke in Álukop, her native language, oblivious to her surroundings.

"What did she say?" asked Klimgu. Baqwam and Gurjik shook their heads. "Never mind. Heat and battle fever the dragon brain in frightful ways. A hidden cost of their strength. But mighty Serukeeba will recover."

* * *

The next morning, Klimgu gathered the only sober captains and scouts to be found in his whole army—forty people. They met with Serukeeba in the same courtyard.

"Have we finally put out all the fires?" asked Klimgu.

"You promised not to start any," huffed Serukeeba.

"You lit the worst one yourself!" laughed Baqwam. "Flames to be seen for a hundred miles."

"And smoke for a thousand," warned Twarejik. "Puchakta will know in four days."

"Is he really that important?" asked Serukeeba.

"The Vazuk's nephew and sole heir," answered Twarejik. "Far more brutal and clever than his uncle. Do we ride hard to strike him before he gathers force, or hold the capitol while building our own?"

"Both," said Klimgu. "My great friend, you must hold Uxanda with only 3,000 warriors. I will lead the rest against Puchakta. Always moving, he much prefers a tent to a fortress. A worthy foe."

"You promised to complete my quest before your ambition," huffed Serukeeba. "But you have done the reverse."

"I found it!" yelled Baqwam, standing up, waving the rolled parchment she had been studying all during the conversation.

"What?" asked Serukeeba, sensing trouble.

"A record of Lorgi," said Baqwam. "Sold to Satungke, the Shohaneze ambassador. A few weeks ago. We are all very sorry, great Serukeeba."

"Sold for how much?" demanded Twarejik.

"What does that matter?" Serukeeba scowled at him. "They sold my baby, like an animal! I will have that man's head on a stick, and all who helped him!"

"We will find them," promised Twarejik. "But for how much did he sell? The more, the better for Lorgi's sake."

"And we had better be able to match it," said Klimgu.

"Five hundred horses!" gasped Baqwam.

All eyes widened in shock; heads shook in disbelief.

"Impossible," scoffed Twarejik. "What has ever fetched half that? An emperor's ransom, to be sure. But that number must be a mistake."

"No. Five hundred horses, written clear as Sun, right here," said Baqwam, pointing to the entry on the parchment, still unaware that Twarejik could not read.

"Our quests are joined, like it or not, Serukeeba," said Klimgu. "We must tread Puchakta's lands in order to reach Shohan. If we survive that, then we may have to break the kingdom of Shohan to retrieve Lorgi. Endless blood. Are you ready for such a quest?"

"I will find my son," huffed Serukeeba. "Can you possibly be ready by noon?"

"Not for a campaign this huge!" gasped Klimgu. "Puchakta keeps an army of 20,000 fiercely loyal warriors on his lands at all times. He will also gather several times that number from the late Vazuk's followers in the east and south. The King of Shohan keeps five armies of about 50,000 each—and could double that in a year. We will need many times the force we have gathered here to even consider it. All must be extremely motivated for the quest. And you must decide how much blood you can stomach."

"How dare you!" yelled Serukeeba.

"It could cost half a million lives to retrieve Lorgi. Enough to rot even the cruelest sword. Uxanda holds wealth to pay any ransom. Consider it. Yes, even we Tuzanchim have limits."

"Then I go alone," muttered Serukeeba.

"I can lead a force tomorrow morning," offered Klimgu. "If you can wait that long, you will have at least 5,000 healthy, reasonably sober warriors. Our very best. Enough to get started."

"What of Uxanda?" asked Twarejik.

"We broke her, so her magic is gone. Defend our capitol as best you can against any who oppose us, my friend."

"But I serve best by riding with you. Not waiting for enemies to attack us."

"I ride better knowing your sword guards Uxanda," Klimgu nodded.

The next morning, he assembled 8,000 warriors, 900 porters with 3,000 pack horses, 40 wagons and all the supplies to be found in the city. Sensing more history in the making, nearly everyone volunteered for the new quest. Captains had to forcibly turn away many wounded or drunken warriors, plus hundreds of youths, peasants and servants. Serukeeba patiently tolerated the mayhem, believing she needed all possible help against Puchakta and Shohan. But after enduring two hours of what seemed pure chaos, her temper boiled. Rising to her full height, she roared with enough force to shake Uxanda's Great East Gate and nearby buildings. Ten thousand mouths shut. Stunned eyes and ears gave her their complete attention.

"Enough!" Serukeeba motioned for the gate to be opened.

"This is all for the quest," said Klimgu. "We will sorely miss anything we forget to bring."

"My quest is Lorgi, not conquering Shohan. You hold Uxanda and the Vazuk is gone. But I am no closer to my baby."

"Puchakta will proclaim himself the next Gran Vazuk, plunging the Empire into civil war!" shouted Twarejik. "The Laskomians' best tactics pale beside his. He holds the Empire's easternmost quarter, and a huge advantage, fighting on his own land. Only fools, be they Tuzanchim or mighty rock dragons, dare trespass without a company of great force."

After a long breath, Serukeeba grudgingly nodded. "When can you finally be ready?"

"My advance scouts, Baqwam and her group can go with you right now," said Klimgu. "A much larger force can follow in about…half an hour."

"But they seem days from being ready," huffed Serukeeba.

"Ah, but you still have much to learn of Tuzanchim ways," said Twarejik.

"Not that I want to," grumbled Serukeeba. As she approached the gate, a frantic voice called from deep within the city. Many *"Yahai's"* begged her to stop, as two scouts rode up to Klimgu.

"An army out of the west rides on Uxanda," gasped one of them.

"How large, and how do they ride?" demanded Twarejik.

"At least 8,000—ready to fight."

"Loyalists?" guessed Klimgu.

"More rebels," huffed Serukeeba.

"How can you know?" Klimgu shook his head.

"My traveler's curse," she sighed.

"When will they reach Uxanda?" asked Twarejik.

"Two hours," said both scouts.

"Klimgu, do what you must," said Serukeeba. "I go now."

"But that army could have news relevant to your quest," said Twarejik. "At least wait to learn if they are rebels or loyalists."

Klimgu's eyes darted between Serukeeba, Twarejik and the scouts. "Twarejik, send your fastest to greet the coming force. We cannot wait to discern friend from foe. Make sure all the Vazuk's standards have been taken down. Let none think he still rules here."

"Done last night. I had hoped you noticed," said Twarejik. "But we must show that *someone* rules in Uxanda. What will Klimgu have for his new standard?"

"Right now I don't care—anything different from the Vazuk's."

Hoping for a miracle, Serukeeba waited another five minutes. Most of the warriors amassed before the Great East Gate left to prepare for battling the unknown force out of the west. Keepers began to close the gate, but Serukeeba roared again, and they opened it wide. She wasted no time in leaving the city. Only 300 choice warriors followed her, led by Baqwam, with Gurjik as her Second. One monk, twenty wagons and a hundred pack horses went with them. An hour later, Klimgu and an army of 12,000 set out in pursuit. His fastest messenger rode hard to intercept Serukeeba, who ignored all pleas to stop—for anyone or anything.

"Not even just a few minutes?" asked Baqwam. "We still ride a fisherman's hour ahead of Klimgu—a needless risk for us."

"Even crawling, I'll leave you all behind in a few days, anyway," huffed Serukeeba.

Focusing intently on the Álukoi, twice Baqwam shot her own piercing eyes up to the canopy giving shade, then back to Serukeeba. "Puchakta is deadly clever, and waits for you most of all. Not even a mighty rock dragon should face him alone. I will not let you."

"Others have said as much."

"So why can't you take their advice?"

"Most were illiterate men—warriors—so I discounted their words," said Serukeeba. "Only yours can persuade me. Baqwam, you are far too good to be a warrior."

"When I was little, my father said I was too good *not* to become one, so he taught me, and very well," said Baqwam, nodding as she rebound her ponytail. "But I know you meant that as a compliment. *Gánsi*, Serukeeba. Now mine to you, though it has been said so many times and ways by everyone last night. You are a great warrior!"

"Only by dire necessity. All I want is to bring my baby home and raise him in peace."

"But peace only exists in heaven," said Baqwam, surprised by the dragon's wishful thinking. "Earth—this life—is all about war."

"For a different perspective, visit Tiefenbo, without your horde. I promise you will enjoy it, once you can relax and think about something other than fighting."

"*Gánsi* for the invitation," Baqwam nodded, smiling. "One day I will!"

"With a smile like that, you could have any mate you want, if not a duchy or a whole kingdom, at least in the west."

"*Gánsi*, again, but I already have all that I want. Almost."

"I can see that," laughed Serukeeba. "But one can never have *all* his or her wants. At the end of my quest, we must talk at length."

"But you just said I had a lucky smile." Baqwam frowned.

"And many other qualities," said Serukeeba. "Please don't let my words or anyone's ever dampen your hopes or dreams."

"That sounds too much like something you would say to Lorgi."

"Or to anyone I really care about."

"*Gánsi*, again, Serukeeba. I am honored to ride with you."

For the next two hours, Serukeeba led her party at what she thought a stiff pace. That was all the time Klimgu needed to overtake them with his entire force. Three hours later, Twarejik and 2,000 more warriors joined them, with news that Chotzan now held Uxanda in Klimgu's name. At sunset, a greatly energized rebel horde made camp with a defensive perimeter, expecting Puchakta to attack at any time. A half-hour after dawn, they left at a stiff trot, every warrior keeping his or her weapons at the ready. They alternately rode east or southeast. Klimgu sent out only ten scouts at a time, searching for the enemy. Often they returned with a few new renegades or whole groups eager to join the quest. By the time they reached the eastern edge of the empire, the rebel force had swelled to well over 20,000 warriors. Still they found no sign of Puchakta.

"Are we chasing a ghost?" Twarejik frowned.

"So Puchakta would have us believe," said Klimgu.

"If I were him, this is where I'd fight," warned Twarejik. "In a few more days we could leave the Empire altogether."

"What dreadful place is this?" asked Serukeeba, scanning the vast, shallow valley stretching to the eastern horizon. A sea of impossibly tall yellow grass undulated in the wind, providing the sole feature and sign of life on the land.

"See the tiny clouds on the southeast horizon?" asked Baqwam. She had taken it upon herself to be Serukeeba's personal guide, which the Álukoi much appreciated.

"Of course," answered Serukeeba.

"Not clouds at all," smiled Baqwam. "But the Shirlangu Mountains, so high and sheer, already full of snow. Beyond them, the vast kingdom of Shohan. And south of that, all the other realms of the Well-East. Those are known collectively as the Forty Kingdoms of Esterlan."

Standing to her full height on just her back legs, Serukeeba focused hard on the distant mountain range. "Great snows! You have long eyes indeed! The land before us rests so flat and plain, that even I have trouble judging distance. Does this place even have a name?"

"The Near Valley."

"Near nothing," laughed Serukeeba.

"Near death," said Baqwam. "So many thousands have fallen here that one always rides close to death when traveling through it."

"Tuzanchim hospitality?" quipped Serukeeba, forgetting her audience.

"No," frowned Baqwam. "Ghosts from every battle ever fought here—even thousands of years before the Tuzanchim arrived. They say one can't even walk ten paces without stepping on bones. Layers upon layers of them. So many spirits, they outnumber the blades of grass."

"We are not looking for ghosts," said Klimgu.

"Does one ever?" asked Baqwam. "But Puchakta will have us believe so until the moment he strikes."

"This land hardly seems worth fighting over," said Serukeeba.

"Stop. This feels wrong," said Klimgu. With a signal of his raised left arm, he ordered: "Silence. Dismount. Arms ready."

"What? I sense nothing beyond our own force here," whispered Serukeeba, twitching her ears in surprise.

"Our!" Klimgu smiled as he nodded. "*Gánsi*, Serukeeba."

"I should have said *your*. But what is wrong?"

"Puchakta waits nearby, ready to strike. I feel it strongly."

Doubting her normal capabilities, Serukeeba stood up again to her full height. Everyone begged her to stay down. Those who had accompanied Lorgi looked stunned when Serukeeba did as asked. "Fine. But Klimgu, how can you know, when I am picking up nothing at all?"

"You taught me."

"I did no such thing!"

"Not intentionally," said Klimgu. "But *gánsi*, anyway."

"A rider comes from the west," hissed a captain.

"One rider?" Klimgu shook his head. "Bring the brave fool to me at once."

Four warriors did so, shaking their heads at the rider's disregard for the peril at hand. Taking a generous draught from his water bag, he dismounted and thanked them all with quick, vigorous nods and a broad smile. Three inches shorter, but huskier than Klimgu, he grabbed the leader's left arm in his own, the way lifelong Tuzanchim friends embraced.

"Kibak, still you have a death wish?" asked Klimgu, shaking his head and scowling at him.

"No, you do. A miracle that you made it this far. Riding clean through Puchakta's domain without me to guide you?" Kibak scolded him. "I know that scorpion and his lands best."

"You were supposed to be Chotzan's Second."

"Ganjaset does that far better than I, who carry glad news." Kibak smiled and nodded vigorously. "Chotzan brings 10,000 warriors to you! Only a week behind. Sacred Earth, here is Lorgi's mother!"

All conversation stopped. Kibak and Serukeeba stared at each other, under a mutual spell. For several minutes, everyone witnessed a silent communion between man and dragon. Both smiled. But then Kibak also began to feel the enemy's presence.

"We should move away from this spot, quickly but quietly," whispered Kibak, glancing in every direction. The captains nodded, but could not agree on which way to go.

"How can you be so certain?" asked Serukeeba.

"I grew up near here, while you are far from home and must also be very distraught, great Serukeeba," said Kibak. "Lorgi has told many wondrous things about you. It is a great honor to finally meet you. I hope to learn much from you, and give useful things in return."

"*Gánsi.*" Flattered, Serukeeba blinked her eyes and flapped her ears. But one look at Klimgu brought her back to the danger at hand. The leader's neck, shoulders and back muscles knotted up with tension. His forehead wrinkled as he scanned the horizon. All nearby saw the strain. In seconds, the whole army felt it. Every hand gripped a weapon, expecting an attack at any moment.

"This grass grows tall as Laskomian corn, up to my shoulders," said Klimgu. "It cannot be this high everywhere, can it?"

"Yes it can, in a good year," answered Kibak. "Except where trampled or nibbled recently."

"It could hide whole armies. We may have to burn Puchakta out."

"No!" shouted Kibak. "He may have Lorgi."

"Keep your voice down," said Klimgu. "The Vazuk sold him to Shohan."

"Puchakta may buy him back for leverage," said Kibak.

"No fire!" growled Serukeeba.

"And no arguing," hissed Baqwam, glaring at them all. "Let Puchakta show himself first."

"It's getting cloudy, hard to see at distance," said Twarejik. "More advantage to our enemy."

"Not with me here!" huffed Serukeeba, stretching her limbs, pointing her ears forward, and sitting back on her haunches.

"The last scouts I sent out won't find us in time, if we move too far from here," said Klimgu.

"We have no choice; we must move now," urged Kibak. "They will just have to find us. Send a large scouting party straight ahead east. Bring the main force close behind, in two or more separate blocks. Puchakta will ambush us no matter where we turn. You will have to sacrifice something to draw him out—in order to save the whole."

"No. We should all stay together in one solid formation," argued Twarejik.

"Which Puchakta would much prefer." Kibak shook his head.

"Send me for your scouting," offered Serukeeba. "If your foe waits ahead to the east, you can know before losing anyone."

"Let me take some volunteers along with her," asked Kibak.

"No need. I'm an Álukoi."

"Yet a foolish one, much like this man here," said Klimgu, nodding to Kibak. "Twarejik, form a diamond, with Serukeeba, Kibak and 200 warriors as the point."

"My group volunteers," said Baqwam.

"Why do you always take more than your share of risk?" asked Twarejik, echoed by Moshal.

"All take the same risk here, today," said Baqwam. "I ride with Serukeeba, who brings me dragon luck and wisdom. I try to repay by assisting her. My whole group feels the same way."

The grass never ceased undulating in the wind. Hundreds of small, swiftly moving clouds flattered the land with ever changing patterns of light and shadow. The Near Valley at its best. Only 500 paces into her advance, Serukeeba picked up many new scents, as the wind shifted. Against the advice of everyone with her, she stood to her full height, taking time to study the panorama. The instant she signaled them to do so, Klimgu's force halted. Twarejik had split it into four units, each ready for attack from any direction. Serukeeba walked a hundred more paces before stopping again. When Kibak saw her ears twitch, he stood up in his stirrups for a better look, too, because he knew rock dragons only did so for good reason.

"No wind over there, but a curious shadow from a long break in the grass," he whispered. "Unnatural. What is it?"

"Five thousand foot soldiers with black helmets, heavy iron shields and longbows," answered Serukeeba. "They stand two miles long to the east, behind a shallow trench bristling with iron-tipped stakes, determined to stop any charge. The enemy must be delighted that we have arrived squarely in their trap."

"You can see all that?" gasped Kibak.

"No time to explain. Hurry and warn Klimgu. They nock arrows to their longbows."

"Tuzanchim have never used longbows or foot soldiers outside of Uxanda," said Baqwam, signaling her group to mount up and retreat.

"Those waiting do not smell like Tuzanchim," said Serukeeba.

"But it does smell like Puchakta!" said Kibak. "Nothing is ever too low for him, using mercenaries to fight his battles."

"Listen!" Serukeeba sprawled on her belly, pressing all her paws and her left ear to the ground, to pick up any vibrations. "Large force riding far behind us, moving north...turning east...slowing, stopped."

"How can you tell? Never mind," said Kibak. "Ours?"

"No. Too far west."

Serukeeba raised up, studying all the terrain except for the entrenched foot soldiers she had already noted blocking the east. A few miles to the south, a double line of riders suddenly appeared, as they mounted up all at once. Three miles long, it contained over 10,000 warriors. Directly, a matching double line appeared to the north.

"It just keeps getting worse," said Kibak.

Puchakta's army wore black boots and sword belts, and black helmets with red stripes. They carried black shields painted with a large gold eye with a crimson pupil as their emblem. Klimgu's warriors could only be recognized by their lack of insignia. At exactly the same time, both distant enemy lines began to advance very slowly.

"Their trap is not quite set," said Kibak. "We should rejoin Klimgu. Find a way to break loose before they surround us."

"You warn Klimgu," ordered Serukeeba, "while I will test their line of foot soldiers."

"But they have sharp stakes, fire, and other war tools," said Kibak.

"And nothing to deal with the likes of me! My surprise will trump whatever they have," said Serukeeba. "Go quickly."

Alone, she approached within 400 yards of the enemy trench. Like hailstones, arrows began pelting the ground around her. A few broke on her back or bounced off of it.

* * *

"Our mighty ally makes a grand challenge, but this battle must be decided elsewhere," said Klimgu, standing up in his stirrups and looking east. "What trap waits for us back to the west?"

"Does it matter?" Twarejik grumbled. "We're hopelessly outnumbered, and about to be surrounded."

"Your specialty, Twarejik," smiled Klimgu. "Hold our main force together in the enemy's trap. Kibak, take our fastest 2,000 west, then south. Swing behind their southern line, then race to Serukeeba. I will take as many out to the north and try the same."

"That leaves us all in small groups, too easy to pick off one by one!" yelled Twarejik.

"Position first, numbers later, my friend," said Klimgu. "Just hold on. Kibak and I—and Serukeeba—will turn the battle, quick as we can."

Puchakta's lines, far apart to the north and south, began to draw slowly towards each other. What looked to be his best 10,000 warriors suddenly appeared in a tight block formation to the west. The wind, high grass, and the clouds' ever changing shadows all tended to confuse human eyes. Seeing Klimgu's army regroup, then splinter, Puchakta sent in his choice block at a full charge, desperate to close his box trap before too many rebels escaped. If they veered to intercept either of the two small, fast-moving rebel groups, then he might never be able to close his trap on the main force and their prized dragon.

Against the advice of his top aides, Puchakta insisted on holding to his original plan. Due to his own curious position on the field, he had left himself little choice.

Lutyam and Moshal frantically set dozens of "trippers" to slow the enemy's charge from the west, even knowing such devices would have little effect on the battle. Puchakta's plan was succeeding in compressing most of the rebels between his lines, while his charging 10,000 elite warriors raced to block any escape to the west. Five thousand crack Shohaneze archers held the east "fence" of the trap.

Klimgu harassed Puchakta's northern line, while working his way around it toward Serukeeba. Kibak threatened to engage the southern line head on, then bolted away. Serukeeba quickly scattered the foot soldiers. Unable to know of her success, Kibak led his group in a desperate end run to save her, well ahead of Klimgu's group. So Puchakta's southern line held firm, taking only minimal losses as Kibak's group whirred past them.

Despite using vastly superior numbers on a battlefield of his choice, Puchakta saw his plan begin to falter. Two small groups of rebels had escaped, enjoying complete mobility outside of his box trap. Something had punched through the Shohaneze line on the east. And his elite 10,000 seemed to be stumbling in their charge at the main rebel force.

Still unaware of these developments, Twarejik feared the worst. To prevent all three enemy lines from hitting him at once, he feinted a charge against the northern line, stalling its progress. Klimgu had intended to run past it, but the instant he saw a potential weakness, he abandoned his original plan. Gambling on Serukeeba's unique abilities to fend for herself, Klimgu abruptly turned and attacked the northern enemy line, breaking it.

But from the middle, Twarejik could only foresee a massacre. To three nearby captains, he screamed: "If I can just reach Puchakta and cut down that scorpion, I die happy. Gather our best swords, whoever can join me right now!"

At that instant, Serukeeba again stood to her full height, scanning the horizon. With all the mayhem, no living thing more than ten yards away could have seen or heard Twarejik. Yet his thoughts reached Serukeeba, a mile to the east, amidst thousands of screaming warriors.

While turning about to run to Twarejik's aid, she glimpsed the one all her senses told was Puchakta. On a barely perceptible rise, a mile to the southeast, thirty enemy captains and scouts watched the distant struggle, with no intention of risking themselves in it.

"Cowards!" Serukeeba roared in Tuzanchim, bolting after them. With extreme effort, she gained on Puchakta and his personal guards as they fled toward the mountains. Like a wolf, she chose him from among them; nothing could distract her.

They shot arrows, screamed and blasted retreat signals on war horns, throwing Puchakta's whole army into disarray. Despite a profound numerical advantage, his force dissolved in minutes, as the rebels outmaneuvered, slew, or captured large numbers of them.

Just as Serukeeba came within reach of Puchakta, a fanatically loyal servant rode up alongside and gave him a fresh horse. Exhausted, Serukeeba collapsed as her target and a dozen of his top aides escaped.

The servant did not. Rebels took time to make an especially gruesome example of him.

Any fleeing loyalists were run down and slaughtered. Only those who threw down their weapons and called Klimgu the new Vazuk were spared. Kibak nearly lost an arm while preventing one of his own men from killing a foot soldier trying to surrender. Once all combat ended, he put the captured Shohaneze archers to work tending the dead of both sides in the struggle.

Almost 4,000 rebels had fallen in battle. Puchakta's army lost far more; its survivors were taken prisoner or fled, never to be seen in Tuzanchim lands again. The battle had raged for less than an hour, but tending the fallen and wounded took the rest of the day. At sunset, Klimgu's army rode east for another hour, even though they were exhausted. Only then did they make camp, to avoid angering the spirits of the dead.

At dawn, Klimgu forced everyone up.

"We have only about 8,000 who are still fit for battle," said Twarejik. "Nothing by Shohaneze standards."

"They helped Puchakta; they must be punished." Klimgu threw a hand up for emphasis.

"I am not here to conquer Shohan or any other land," said Serukeeba.

"We must war on Shohan to retrieve Lorgi," said Klimgu. "After a few battles, they'll gladly hand him over, along with anyone who had the smallest part in his captivity. To save themselves, the Shohaneze will give us Puchakta and the last of his friends—dead or alive. They also will make considerable reparations, to keep us out of their lands."

"I only want my son back," said Serukeeba. "Preferably without more blood or whatever you mean by reparations."

"Far too late for that," said Baqwam. "Only great, swift force will bring Lorgi back."

"The Shohaneze only understand force, though perhaps better than any other people," said Klimgu. "We deliver only what they require."

"Thinking like that will be your doom!" roared Serukeeba.

"Wait for Chotzan, only a week behind us," urged Twarejik. "He brings many fresh warriors. Then we can launch a respectable invasion."

"I trusted you to hold Uxanda," Klimgu gazed at him. "Four hours later you join me and say Chotzan will do that. Then Kibak tells us Chotzan is on his way, too. Now who will hold Uxanda?"

"A fine captain named Jinwak," said Kibak, smiling and nodding.

"Who, by Sky, Wind, Earth, Sun and Moon, will that be?"

"Sijun's adopted son. All Chotzan's people will vouch for him," assured Kibak. "Twarejik is wise. Wait for Chotzan, who won't need a week to join us. Then you will again have a proper army with which to fight. The Shohaneze wield many times the force we saw yesterday."

"Pray the Shohaneze never learn how to war," said Klimgu.

"Now they will have Puchakta," warned Baqwam. "Plus countless resources. And be expecting us. How do we overcome all that?"

"Like his uncle, Puchakta has proven to be overrated," said Klimgu. "Yet our next battle will be the most difficult—and fascinating—that any of us have ever fought. I will lead all who can ride today. Twarejik, tend the wounded. Bring Chotzan's force along as quickly as possible. Our only chance is to strike first. And gamble everything."

21: Sanctuary

At sunset, amidst trumpet fanfares and royal banners, the king arrived on a litter, followed by advisors, servants and a dinner feast. None of the guests surrounding Wenji and her "stone dragon *prince-ling*" had recovered from lunch. Presenting all the same dishes Lorgi had inhaled at a previous banquet, the master chef added a few new ones he hoped the exotic or his trainer would like, anxiously soliciting their opinions. While most fawned over the pair, the king sat quietly observing, planning his next moves regarding many of those present. Lorgi detected plenty of scheming among the guests as well, wishing most would leave. Masking her fears, and hoping to win the king's favor, Wenji spoke only very gently about everything, even when pushed by others. Like a guard dog, Lorgi stayed right beside her, sniffing anyone who approached. When the banquet ended, unusually courteous guards escorted the pair to a luxury cottage set on its own tiny island, deep within the vast gardens.

"Few dare dream of such wonders," said Wenji. "They treat us like royalty."

"Speaking of *royals*, why haven't we seen any others besides the king?" asked Lorgi. "I heard a few people whispering about a queen, but never when the king is around. No children, no relatives. That says a lot. Where is this queen, anyway—starving in a pit cage?"

"I'm sure we'll meet her soon, and all will get even better," assured Wenji. "See how things have changed already? Gifts, banquets, flowers, imperial lodgings stocked with all we could possibly need."

"We just need to get out of here."

"Look. They strive to please us, catering to our every wish—and now I have many."

"They watch us like hawks, noting every little thing we say or do," warned Lorgi. "Getting out of here will be a lot harder than I thought."

"Suspicion rules every court. We must assure people that we are grateful to be away from the savage Tuzanchim, and keep reminding them how we are fiercely loyal to Shohan, with no intention of ever leaving. But we can still keep ourselves a mystery. Our best card. Let them all spoil us, out of fear or respect. Savor the moment, Lorgi."

"Moment is right," huffed Lorgi. "I bet even royalty die young here. Find a large bag or purse. A knapsack would be even better. If you can't find anything like that, I'll make one for you."

"What? You're going to make me a knapsack?"

"Time to pack. You'll need extra shoes, and I don't mean those flimsy party slippers. Fit, sturdy walking shoes, a scarf, a hat, gloves, a good belt and a heavy coat. Plus a container of water and any dry snacks that are not too heavy. We're leaving this nightmare."

"You're asking an awful lot," laughed Wenji. "I doubt our sweet little guest cottage will have such things."

"Just gather what you can in five minutes. No time to waste."

"Don't you need to rest after such a terrifying day—and all your feasting?"

"Rest? With their arena waiting, not four stones away? Practically everything in this place came by blood. Human blood. I hate to even touch anything."

"I know only too well. Yes, we must be careful at all hours. But no, we must not attempt to flee now. We should wait at least a week, until they get used to us and you have fully re—"

"NO!" yelled Lorgi. "Tonight may be our only chance. Are you coming with me or not?"

"Please don't shout," begged Wenji. "It will alarm the guards."

"I'll spin all five of them right now."

"No...wait. I only saw two. Lorgi, how do you know they posted five?"

"Actually, fifteen in all. Two on each end of that baby bridge to our island, a big lumpy one about thirty paces down at the trail's fork, and ten more spread out all around the pond. But those are already sleeping. They'll never see us in the dark, anyway."

"Already sleeping?" Wenji shook her head.

"Half of them snoring too," nodded Lorgi. "None of them are fit or very healthy. They have poor eyes and ears, too."

"How can you know any of that?"

Agitated, Lorgi reared his head back, pinned his ears and pursed his nostrils. "Wenji, you must learn to know friends from enemies—and believe your friends! Please hurry and pack while I put the rest of the guards to sleep."

"There is no way you can get past them all. There will be at least a hundred on duty—and awake—at any hour. It is not as simple as that, anyway. You have no idea what we are up against. I'm sorry, Lorgi. We had better just stay and make the best of our new lives here."

"There is no life here. Only death, quick or slow. Please stop arguing and get ready. I'll be right back."

"No, Lorgi. Stop. Listen to me. You cannot possibly succeed. Haven't we gotten into enough trouble here already?"

"This place is nothing but trouble, so we're leaving!" said Lorgi. "I'll just put the ones at the bridge to sleep. When they finally wake up, they won't remember anything. Don't worry. Just pack. Can you be ready in five minutes?"

"No! You just stop and think, Lorgi." She shook her head. "Shohan is far too vast, too powerful. The king has endless resources. Even if we somehow escaped the palace *and* the city—which is impossible—then whole armies will hunt us down. Cavalry, archers with tracking dogs, spies, and countless starving peasants seeking the reward posted for us— dead or alive! We have no chance."

"We have tonight. Do all the thinking you like when we're far away from this place. I hope the Tuzanchim or somebody comes and destroys it—except for the gardens."

"The Tuzanchim will never reach here, just as we will never leave. At least not for many years. How can I make you understand? We must remain here and work constantly to stay in the king's favor, just to keep our lives. What do you think all those *smiley-mouths* are doing?"

"Nice cool traveling air!" cheered Lorgi, exiting the cottage.

"Did you hear what I just said?"

"Did you know that Álukois can see even better than owls in the dark, and as well as eagles by day?"

"Lorgi!" hissed Wenji, but he had vanished into the night. Squinting at two torches lighting the footbridge sixty yards away and obscured by trees, she feared what Lorgi might do when he encountered the guards waiting there. Praying that he would find them asleep at their posts, Wenji rummaged through every closet, chest and drawer to find the things he said she would need, just in case he succeeded.

As Lorgi appeared in the torches' dim light, the two guards waiting before the bridge confronted him. Using a rare, ancient art still practiced among a few Álukois, he "spun" the variable pigments in his huge eyes. The guards could not help but stare. In four yawns, both fell into a deep sleep. Lorgi's charm worked even more quickly on the next two, yet had no effect on the "lumpy" guard, no matter how hard he tried. As the dullard inhaled to call the alarm, Lorgi smacked him unconscious with a light tap of his forepaw. He hid all five under the largest nearby shrubs. Returning to the cottage, Lorgi feared Wenji might refuse to leave.

"All done. Time to go," Lorgi said at the door. "Ready?"

"What did you do to them?" Wenji demanded.

"I just put them into a nice, deep sleep—one way or another. But they will only be out for a few hours. By then..." Lorgi sat back on his haunches and grinned, to give Wenji confidence.

"We'll be in a cage, awaiting execution," she answered. "Or dead already."

Lorgi's ears drooped and his smile vanished. "I will be far away, wishing I had a spell to make you join me. Good luck to you, Wenji, my friend. But there is no luck here. I will always miss you. Goodbye." Suddenly he disappeared, hiding just beyond the door.

"Wait! You said I could come too." Wenji lunged out, frantic to catch up with him.

"Ready now?" he giggled.

"No, you manipulative little dragon brat! Let me grab a few things."

"Is that what they mean by Tuzanchim flattery?"

"This is insane." Wenji put a hand to the side or her forehead. "Our odds are about one in a million. You do understand that?"

"I don't know that," whispered Lorgi. "But if it keeps you alert, and quick, then good!"

The pair took many devious paths and turns, through gardens, gates and shaded walkways. Whenever they met others, Wenji smiled, saying:

"Were you not told? My dragon is nocturnal. I must walk him every night or he becomes violent! You *do* know about that?" Fear made Lorgi's spell work more quickly. Finally they exited the palace complex, a small city unto itself, leaving seventy guards and officials in profoundly deep, happy sleep. Only one lay unconscious with a swollen, cut face. When others later revived him, the man had no memory of his encounter with Lorgi.

Free of the palace, the pair found the city streets dark and empty. Just as they reached the city's north wall, the palace screamed awake. Torches lit up, bells rang, horns wailed and men shrieked. A moment later, gates opened and soldiers ran out to scour the streets.

Though she had always spoken to Lorgi in Tuzanchim, Wenji suddenly spewed a host of choice words in Esterlan—harsh, stinging descriptions for the king of Shohan, his advisors, the *smiley-mouths*, Satungke, Puchakta and especially the Gran Vazuk. Lorgi could only guess what all the special adult words meant, but knew that his mother would not want him to hear them in any language.

"It won't be long now," said Wenji. "But we made a valiant try."

"We're just getting started," said Lorgi. "Come on. We reached the walls, which they make nice and low here." Finding a ladder, he added, "Perfect!" and dragged it up the last street. Bracing it at a steep angle against the wall, he motioned to Wenji.

"What about you?" she asked, already climbing.

"That wood looks too fragile for me. I better jump."

More than a dozen upper story windows on the street were open. Despite the late hour, two still glowed with candle light. Three pairs of eyes peered down at Lorgi and Wenji. But with alarms echoing in the distance and drawing closer, any candles extinguished and all the windows slammed shut. Once Wenji reached the top of the wall, Lorgi threw her ladder over to the other side. Backing up twenty paces, he charged and leapt, clearing the top of the wall. Only the very tip of his tail scratched the brickwork on the wall's outside face. Seconds later he had the tool positioned for Wenji's descent.

"Ready for you," he whispered.

"I can't see down; it's too dark on the other side."

"Half moon rising. Plenty of light for us, and soon for our enemy.

Move your left hand out about a foot...that's good. Now half again more to the left...stop. Now grip the ladder."

"Wha...got it. But I really can't see a thing. I'm sorry, Lorgi."

"You don't need to. I can talk you down." A dozen slow steps down, Wenji could just see her feet, and took the last three quickly. The instant Wenji let go of the ladder, Lorgi threw it back over the wall."

"Why did you do that?" gasped Wenji.

"So the owner won't miss it. But it might need a little fixing now."

"Now everyone on the street will know about us!"

"But be too afraid to tell," said Lorgi. "I read it in their eyes and smelled it in their blood."

"How can you?...never mind," Wenji shook her head.

The pair whisked away in the first glow of moonlight, up a dirt path climbing north into steep, pine-cloaked foothills. Instinctively, Lorgi sought high ground away from the city, something easy to defend or hide in and difficult for human travel. He wanted to hike all night, but knew Wenji was in no shape for it, either in mind or body. When the two came to a river, she rested in a tiny boat which Lorgi pulled upstream by a rope held in his mouth. But it kept breaking, so they gave up on that idea.

Suddenly Lorgi stopped, smiled and pointed up, even though steep mountains all around seemed to block any further progress. "Now we're cooking, as Jinva says. They'll never find us up there."

"Not alive!" gasped Wenji. "I'm a girl, not a mountain goat."

"Being hunted by the worst monsters in the whole, entire world— *hyúlems* with orders! If they catch up to us, I'll have to shred every one of them."

"Alright. I will try my best," promised Wenji, her voice trembling.

Lorgi guided her up a steep, rarely used footpath into the mountains. Because humans could not see in the dark, he tied the last bits of rope around his neck for Wenji to hold onto, but it kept shredding and breaking on his hide. As the trail steepened, she often stumbled in the dark. For the next hour, they made slower and slower progress, until Wenji could go no further. Lorgi sat beside her.

"Sorry, Lorgi. I'm finished. Really finished. Too tired to care if I live or die. You go ahead. Good Luck. Please remember me."

"They can't track at night, and don't know where to begin, so don't you give up on me!"

"I admire your...outlook, but I must not slow you down, or spoil your chances."

"Stone streets and rivers don't take prints. Álukois leave no scent. You would leave little of either, so we're safe for tonight." Lorgi spoke while digging a shallow depression in a level patch of ground between three pines.

"When you jumped over, I heard you scrape against the wall."

"Just the tip of my tail," said Lorgi. Turning both his neck and tail, he added: "I'm fine. See. Not a scratch. That flimsy wall will be quite a different matter."

"That is what worries me. They may know our route of escape already."

"Not until daylight, and they would have to know exactly what to look for," giggled Lorgi. "That wall had plenty of chips and cracks, anyway. I doubt the king has any Tuzanchim scouts."

"But he has so many other things," said Wenji.

"Well, I think we have at least a day's jump. Maybe much more. Plus, Nature is our ally. So we can camp here."

"I can't see a thing," said Wenji, shivering. "So cold, and it will only get worse, now that we're in the mountains. Up here, summer has long gone. May we risk a campfire?"

"No, and you know why."

"If I can't get warm, you may be the only one of us still breathing in the morning. Please, Lorgi, can we make just a tiny fire? Is that why you are gathering so many pine needles?"

"I'm making you a nice pine needle bed, the way Tundrite hunters of my village do when camping in the wilds. Now to heat it up, the way my mother showed me." By a technique known only to snowdragons, Lorgi heaved four gigantic hot breaths into the pile. "Just turtle yourself down on that. Use your sack for a pillow. Go on."

"So prickly—but warm!" Wenji smiled as she wiggled in the nest. "How did you do that?"

"Have you got yourself comfortable?"

"Too tired to move a muscle. But all things considered, yes. Thank you, Lorgi. I had no idea you were so resourceful."

"*Gánsi*, Wenji. I always knew you were clever, but had no idea you were so brave. You saved us at least a dozen times at the palace. I am proud to ride with you, as the Tuzanchim say."

"*Gánsi*, Lorgi, as your people say," Wenji laughed. "For your information, when the king resides at his Summer Palace, he keeps a small army there. Several thousand men. They will be out looking for us all night. Pouring through every street and alley. Pounding on doors or breaking them down. Terrorizing people in their search for us."

"I'm sorry about that—but only about that."

"Me, too," sighed Wenji. They'll rummage through every last room in the whole city, breaking things as they go. Then stagger out into the countryside with torches and dogs to hunt us down. All night and all day. I can't believe we're still alive! And to escape them, now we must survive the ageless unknown, the untamed wilderness!"

"You mean the real world," smiled Lorgi, his head cocked and his ears high, looking surprised by her comments.

"I suppose the savage wilds are the only real world for you. But I have never even camped outdoors."

"Really? I can't believe you have never been to the real world."

"I've been a kept slave my whole life," explained Wenji. "Usually locked up in a small room at night, to make certain I didn't *wander* off. All this…is totally alien to me."

"Welcome to the normal world, away from human workings," cheered Lorgi. "My world."

"You had to rescue me from mine. Just hope yours does not chill me to death."

"I'll put more needles and some branches on top of you, then heat it up some more. That should keep you warm—and hidden—until morning. Alright?"

Wenji was already asleep.

Only direct sunlight finally woke her the next morning. Slowly yet thoroughly, Wenji stretched and smiled, surprised at how well she had slept. Never before had the sky glowed so deep a blue, or the air smelled so sweet, or every living thing—great or small—looked so exquisitely beautiful and perfect. Not for the first time, she knew such heightened senses and perspective came from escaping death. But unable to see Lorgi, she shot up with a fright and walked about the immediate area quickly, softly calling for him. By the time he appeared five minutes later, Wenji was hysterical.

"Why did you leave me asleep, alone, defenseless against man and beast? Why didn't you answer my calls?"

Lorgi walked up to her and sat back on his haunches, his cheeks bulging like a chipmunk. Opening his mouth, he deposited a large bunch of wild berries into a forepaw and extended it toward her.

"Thank you, but I can't eat what has already been in your mouth."

"I got all these just for you, sleepy head. You won't believe how good they are, some of the best ever."

"Thank you again, but no. Sorry, I can't eat anything right now, anyway." She shook her head. "But you can enjoy them."

"We have a big long hike today and you need stamina. So eat up!"

"I can't," she sighed. "I just can't. But it was very nice of you, anyway."

"Yes you can, and yes you will!" yelled Lorgi. "No one ever caught a pox from an Álukoi." He thrust his forepaw within an inch of Wenji's mouth. "Here. Eat something, already!"

Grudgingly, she picked a berry from the center, hoping it might be cleaner. Then she saw that the whole bunch looked dry, with no trace of saliva. Thinking Lorgi must be quite dehydrated, she noted her own thirst.

Wenji had never been so out of her element, until Lorgi showed where he meant for them to hike—a ghost of a path climbing straight up into the mountains like some impossible vine. He pointed to a distant open patch of trail perhaps two thousand feet above. From Wenji's position, it looked to be most of the way up the mountain. Higher peaks towered close beyond, to the immediate west and north. Wenji imagined the trail's progress: through dense, tangled forest, past streams and waterfalls, over slippery rocks, and obstacles that only athletic young men should attempt. Few of the palace guards would qualify.

"Thrilling...but I know my limits," Wenji shook her head. "That is completely beyond mine. And probably most humans as well."

"Humans made that trail. Nice highland ones, nothing like the lowland *hyúlems* we're running away from."

"Wonderful—but impossible. I'm sorry, Lorgi. So very sorry, but—"

"How long will you wait here for the king's men?" Lorgi sat back on his haunches, folded his forepaws like Jinva, and kept up a piercing stare which had always worked before.

"Alright. I'll try." She ate a few berries. "You were right. So delicious!"

"Told you. You'll love it up there."

"But there could be wild animals, hungry dangerous beasts."

"Like me?" giggled Lorgi. "I think those are all in the king's zoo, already."

"There will be nothing to eat. How will we survive?"

"What are you doing right now? Plenty of good things up there, like most places that don't have too many humans."

"How can you know? Never mind." Wenji shook her head, unnerved that her survival depended totally on a dragon child. She knew even less about nature than she did about him. "Thank you again—I mean *gánsi*—for everything."

"So many good things wait for us up there, you'll love it! No more danger from bad *hyúlems*. No more abuse. The finest air, water, nuts and berries. Plants, animals, perhaps many things you've never seen before. *Góbo árgosang!*—a fine adventure!"

"If it doesn't kill me. You know I'm in no shape for anything like this."

"All the more reason to stop talking and start moving, as Jinva says," Lorgi nodded. "You're going to love her and everybody in Tiefenbo."

"I love them already."

Expecting problems, Lorgi set a tortuously slow pace for an Álukoi, cheering Wenji with every step. The trail proved to be nothing more than a rarely used foot path. Several hours later the pair could see that it led—eventually—to an ancient monastery looming high up, tucked into the side of an impossibly sheer mountain. The path gradually became steeper, less defined, and more precarious, just as Wenji had feared. Painfully tired, her unskilled feet began to stumble and slip. Lorgi worried that she might have a fall from which no human could recover.

"Stop," Lorgi called a halt.

"So you're finally tired too," Wenji gasped.

"Not yet, but you're done for today."

"We should have stopped at that flat spot, a half hour back. But we can't camp here, on such an exposed, steep slope. What shall we do?"

"You rest here. And I mean right here. Be patient. If anything big sees you, or you see it, then yell and I'll run right back. Otherwise—"

"Wait, I should stay with you."

"No. You better rest here and stay quiet. I'll be back as soon as I can."

"Wait. Why? Where are you going?"

"To make a bark saddle, to protect you from my back spikes."

"Are you sure you can?"

"My village had four horses. I saw how to work with them."

"Only four?" Wenji laughed. "You really do live at the end of the world."

"No. Just a nice friendly village at the mouth of the Yazutak River."

"Where is that?"

"About a million miles that way," Lorgi giggled, pointing west, "but I'm no mapmaker. Our river flows down from the Dawnwood to meet the Sea of Tundria, or what some call the Tunda-Sea, or the Sea of Ice."

"So I was right," said Wenji. "You live at the frozen end of the world."

"The world has no end because it's round and spins like a toy as it orbits the sun."

"Is that what your kind believe?" asked Wenji, "Even when you can see everything in the sky circling the earth?"

"Not if you look closely for a long time," said Lorgi. "My ancestors learned how to look many generations ago. The Delfinians helped them invent monster-size numbers to try and measure some of it. That's what my mother says."

"But the Shohaneze completed all of that work, centuries ago," Wenji frowned.

"The sky goes on forever, and not every light in it stays put, so you can never finish studying it. The Álukois call it the Grand Mystery of Time."

"I'm sorry to say, but they are mistaken. Yet how wonderful for them to try and fathom the heavens, without tools, books or humans to aid them."

"My mother has lots of books, and the Delfinians are humans. We use tools, but not nearly as much as humans do." Lorgi disappeared into the woods below. An hour later he returned, having fitted himself with a very rough, bark saddle. "Just sit on this and hang onto it. If my back spikes cut through, or it starts to tear or slip in any way, you yell and we'll stop."

"What if you slip or fall?"

"Only you can do that. This is so you don't!"

The makeshift saddle held together just until they reached the open gates of a monastery late that afternoon. Exhausted, they congratulated each other while staggering into a grand square courtyard, almost as large as the arena contest grounds. Its north side hugged a steep mountainside. The south side of the courtyard looked out over nothing but air, until one approached its stout rails to view the sharply defined river valley so far below. Lorgi and Wenji allowed themselves ten silent minutes to recover, while marveling at how far up they had come from their camp, dissolving into fog welling up from below.

"It could take the king's men weeks to find us here," Wenji laughed.

"Unless they have great trackers, or know just where to look," said Lorgi.

"Wait. I'm the pessimist, here. Of course they will try, but they have too many other places to look, too, like the whole kingdom. The people hate them."

"A few people saw us when we left the city."

"But you also saw them snuff out their candles and shutter their windows." Taking a long, deep breath of freedom, Wenji smiled. "As you said, none of them will admit to seeing or hearing anything to do with us—or anything else. People in the city know better."

"If the king's men do come, we can spot them long before they see us. Then we can take that trail, up there, deep into the mountains. I promise you they will never catch us."

"That hardly looks like a trail at all. Not that the one we climbed up here was much better." Wenji sighed, looking west. "Even if it were, it only leads deeper into the mountains and the wilderness. It must come to a dead end somewhere impassable."

"Perfect!" cheered Lorgi. "Then they can never follow us up there. We are free!"

"You have no idea what that means to me, Lorgi."

"My mother says *hyúlems* can be very barbaric and cruel to each other. She often wonders if civilization will ever reach the lowlands."

"But it has in your highlands?" asked Wenji.

"About 10,000 years ago. You must come home with me, if I can ever figure out how to get back. Everyone will be glad to see you."

"Right now we'd better see whose home all of this is. A monastery with its monks, who do not wish to be disturbed. If anyone is here at all."

Exhausted, Wenji and Lorgi forced themselves up and began exploring the premises. The courtyard's west side faced the largest structure in the complex, a massive, three-story building capable of holding several very large chambers and many small rooms. On the east side of the courtyard, an open, hexagonal pavilion reminded Lorgi of several that were used for banquets in the king's garden. Though smaller, this one had a steeper roof, thicker columns and was far better built. With sheer drop-offs on three of its six sides, it offered spectacular views. From here, one could see or even hear a bird calling from a vertical mile below. Only the distant whoosh of mountain waterfalls, the songs of birds and a constant breeze reached the quiet monastery, all sounding alien to Wenji, but comforting to Lorgi. Both visitors thought of calling out, but the monastery itself discouraged them.

"Let's explore the main building," said Wenji.

"Why? I like it out here," said Lorgi.

"We might find something to eat in there." Seeing Lorgi twitch his nostrils, Wenji smiled. "Follow me. You're in charge outside, but I'm in charge indoors."

The main building's heavy oak doors opened onto a spacious hall, curiously devoid of furniture, except against its walls. Grand staircases on opposite ends of the vast room led to corridors and many smaller rooms looking like offices and living quarters.

"Lorgi, could you please stop sniffing every inch of the floor," asked Wenji.

"That's how I find out about places, and especially people."

"I'm sorry…just that it reminds me of hounds…tracking escaped slaves—like me!"

"Gems and rainbows, I never thought of that. Sorry, Wenji. But me not sniffing would be like you exploring this place blindfolded."

"This is the only truly silent place I have ever visited. Very well kept. Probably monks only use it for a summer retreat. With that gone, so are they, maybe just before we got here. It would be too cold in winter. So I'm afraid we won't find anything to eat."

"This is a fine home, indeed!" cheered Lorgi. "No blood."

"No blood?" asked Wenji. "What do you mean?"

"Those who live here are friendly, gentle and wise. Very nice people."

"In Shohan? Are you joking? Lorgi, I hope your sniffer is not starting to fail. Maybe you have been working it too hard."

"My nose is fine. So far I count fifteen people. All vegetarians, like me! I can't wait for us to make friends with them. It will be fun."

"Lorgi, no one is here. Your vegetarians may not be back for about eight months. Next spring. This temple or monastery is some kind of retreat. Monks don't come here to be friendly. Or have any kind of fun. They are very abstract thinkers and profoundly out of touch with the world, anyway."

Sitting back on his haunches, Lorgi stared at her with a blank expression, refusing to respond to her comments.

"I do know something about monks, at least Shohaneze monks. Peaceful, but otherwise worthless."

"Follow me," said Lorgi, stretching his limbs. "This way to the pantry. They stocked plenty for us to eat."

"I think we should explore the whole place first."

"Starting with the pantry and the kitchen. We need a *góbo nóshul*—a really good snack."

"*Góbo nóshu*? Is food always your first priority?"

"We're both starving," said Lorgi. "But here we should take care to keep the kitchen clean, so they won't mind us sampling their stores."

"You didn't have to tell me that!" snapped Wenji. "I spent half my life cleaning up after witches, ogres and the worst of spoiled brats. And that was the good part."

"Sorry. Here, try some of these dried fruit things. Very tasty." Lorgi put one an inch from Wenji's mouth.

"Do I have a choice?" she laughed.

"No, because it's good for you and I'm going to keep you well."

"Thank you," she smiled, but started to cry.

"Don't worry, everything will be fine now." Lorgi sat on his haunches close by her. Gently, he patted her on the back with the soft pads of a forepaw. "We are far from danger."

"It's not that," she shook her head. "Just that you are the first…person…who has cared about me. If your hide wasn't so lethal, I'd be hugging you every minute."

"*Gánsi*, Wenji. And you are the best friend."

Checking the living quarters and offices upstairs, the two returned to the ground floor, where they discovered what looked like a school room, a book binding shop, and a grand library. Finding this last too comfortable to ignore, the pair settled down to rest.

"Time for a good, long nap," Lorgi yawned.

"About a week," sighed Wenji. "Shall I wake you later?"

"You mean the other way around. Last night you slept much longer than I did."

"But if I should wake before you," said Wenji. "Well?"

"No. I won't get up until I'm done sleeping."

"Good. Then I won't either. Late tomorrow!" said Wenji. "No more stinky, mean, stupid guards to order us around. No more ugly, wicked kings or nobles to bow and smile to. No blubber-face, snake-tongue, smiley-mouths, as you call them. We are free!"

"That's right," mumbled Lorgi, his eyes already closed. "From now on, we do what we want, when we want. What's right, and what makes good people happy."

"Thank you for making me free—and happy!" Tearfully, Wenji smiled at him, but Lorgi was already fast asleep, sprawled on his stomach.

* * *

To her surprise, Wenji arose fresh and ready for adventure early the next morning. But Lorgi lay just as he had fallen asleep the evening before. Letting him rest, she explored the grounds, gathering things they might need for their next exodus. By afternoon, she feared nothing could wake him. Yelling in his ears, lighting candles near his eyes, even wafting food under his nostrils had no effect. Alarmed, she tried prying open Lorgi's stubborn eyelids, then his ears, both without success. Even pouring a bucket of icy cold water over him caused no reaction. She found his breathing both slow and shallow. From what experience she had with dying people and animals, she knew the end was near.

"The climb was too much, even for you," Wenji sobbed, collapsing next to him. "Because of me. What have I done? You would have been better off if...I am so sorry, Lorgi. Please. You cannot leave me here alone, after what we have endured together. We reached your natural world. I need you to guide me through it. But you surely did not need me. I have been nothing but a curse upon you, spoiling your luck. Why was I even born, if it all had to come to this?"

She spent all the next day wrapped in a blanket, by his side, with the library's windows open to the wind, hoping the cold might revive him. Seeing Lorgi in a coma, Wenji reviewed her time with him. She pondered her whole life. With nothing to live for, she resolved to end her days fasting and praying for his recovery. By the next morning, her hunger pains had gone.

Though weak, light-headed and numb from the cold, she felt curiously at peace amid the awful quiet. Finding ink, a pen and paper, she wrote the longest letter of her life, to whoever lived at the monastery, explaining about herself and Lorgi. For an hour she stood at the largest pavilion's rails, gazing at the panorama below, looking for any signs of other humans. But she could find none.

"At least we beat the king, Lorgi. Shamed that bastard in his own damned arena! Rattled his court. Foiled his stupid guards and his spies. We denied him any satisfaction. Turned his Summer Palace and the whole city upside down. Now he can waste years searching for us. Even long dead, we will tax him!

"What a beautiful sunset this evening, if only you could see it. Good may yet spring from our ordeal. Maybe one day others will be able to do more, like overthrow that worst of kings. Now I just wish we were not so alone."

As if inheriting Lorgi's powers, she heard soft footsteps approaching. Suddenly Wenji had hours of explaining to do for monks who eschewed the world below. Running out to the courtyard, she surprised sixteen of them, immediately pouring out such a flood of words and tears that none dared interrupt her. Twelve monks sat down, listening intently. The others ran into the main building, but soon returned with tea, food, and a heavy blanket that they wrapped around Wenji.

"Am I speaking too fast?" she gasped, breathless. "Are you following all this? I know every bit of it sounds insane, but you can see proof of my tale sprawled in the library. This is life and death! Don't you have any questions?"

"Please continue," said one monk.

To reassure her, they nodded, regardless of comprehension. Mostly, they waited for the storm raging inside her to subside. All took turns excusing themselves for chores, one or two at a time, but always hurried back to hear more, until finally Wenji reached the end of her saga.

The Gral-Chaner, or Grand Master of the monastery, sprang to his feet, introducing everyone to Wenji. Average in height, tan and bald except for short white hair around his ears and in back, the spiritual leader seemed a remarkably fit, healthy fifty years of age. Like all the monks, he wore a green robe and a warm, smile that could not be more different from the false grins that Wenji had endured at the Summer Palace.

"Come inside. Rest your voice. Eat." He led her by the hand into the main hall. "You shared volumes in minutes. I had forgotten just how fast some young people can talk. Excuse us a moment while we confer."

"Wait. My troubles may not interest monks, but Lorgi is all I have, and close to death. Please, you must help him!"

"And you too, young lady, hardly among the living yourself," scolded the Gral-Chaner. "While you told your chronicle, we took turns visiting your Lorgi. He appears to be in a coma, but we observe in total ignorance. We will watch over him day and night. Your dragon friend may indeed be the Sign Child we have long awaited."

"What is that?" asked Wenji. "Never mind. It should not matter."

"Good. I like your path," said the Gral-Chaner. "Still, we must prepare. It will help to know when he was born."

"I can only tell you he was born—hatched—in the early spring?" Wenji guessed. "He said he is three-and-one-half years old and can hardly wait to be four."

"Good. When were you born?" he asked.

"What does that matter?" demanded Wenji.

"You traveled with him and came here," said the Gral-Chaner. "Therefore, it matters."

"Fine. I was born in the fall, on the 21st of Summerlast. Soon I'll be twenty-three, if I'm lucky."

"Good. Would you describe your nature as similar to, or different from his?"

"I'm human; he is…completely different."

"Yet you can speak with him—in two languages. Please describe his personality. How is it like or unlike yours?"

"Lorgi is fatally optimistic," Wenji shook her head, spilling more tears. "He lacks even basic self-preservation. Knows no pain, fear, inequity…or so many basic truths."

"Thank you," smiled the Gral-Chaner. Turning to a husky, bald-shaven monk of about thirty years, standing a few feet to his right, the leader asked, "Did you hear all that, Poto?"

"The Child and his guide are complementary?" guessed Poto, raising his left eyebrow.

"Our Sign Child holds a powerful spirit: free, innocent and fearless," smiled the Gral-Chaner. "A spring dragon, born in the third month, with his complement born in the ninth."

"I told you that already," said Wenji, impatient.

"And much more," said the Gral-Chaner. "Please show me your dominant hand."

"What? How can that help with anything?" she frowned. "Signs, compliments and natures may all be very interesting, if Lorgi recovers. But right now—"

"We need information, to be of help," finished Poto. A short monk stepped in front of him and pressed Wenji's left hand onto a plate covered with red ink, then onto another with paper stretched over it. All the monks compared her hand print with one made of Lorgi's left forepaw, but could find nothing conclusive or remarkable about them. None of them appeared satisfied with the results, only adding to Wenji's frustration.

"Staring at hand prints will not revive Lorgi or stop the king's men," said Wenji. She wanted to scream, but swallowed her temper. "Please, this is no time for divination. I have put you all in danger. Lorgi barely breathes. We must act now!"

"Can Lorgi write?" asked Poto calmly, still scrutinizing the prints.

"He picks up language faster than anyone, but no," said Wenji. "He did say his mother will start teaching him to read and write next year, in two languages."

"Wonderful! Can you do so, yourself?" Poto asked. "Be honest. We do not judge. Many people never learn. Many never get the chance."

"Yes, and rather well, thank you," snapped Wenji. "But that won't help anything, either. Can't you see how sick Lorgi is? Do you have any idea how brutal the king's men can be?"

"Yes we see, and yes we know—but we will not speak of those demons now," said the Gral-Chaner, giving her a stern look. Raising a hand for calm, he asked, "How does Lorgi think? Does he speak of things beyond the present, or what can be sensed?"

"Yes, but we need to think about the present, or we will all die very soon!" shouted Wenji. "If you had glimpsed only a fraction of the horrors that I have, you would be terrified."

"We understand your fears," murmured the Gral-Chaner. "To some degree, we share them. But as ill as Lorgi seems, at least he is stable. We always keep a watch on the trail below, to give us a full day's warning if the king's men venture up our way. For now, we wait, using our efforts to learn. So that when the time comes to act, we will be ready."

"How does Lorgi express ideas?" asked Poto. "Does he ask big questions to make you think?"

"I wish I knew how he thinks," Wenji moaned. "He just sees, feels, hears, smells—then suddenly knows, whether or not he can explain how. It's unnerving."

"Sensing deeply is part of good thinking," said Poto.

"Please, you must help him!" cried Wenji. "He is my only friend."

"We will try," assured the Gral-Chaner. "But he is not your only friend. Let us make a print of his right forepaw. You said he comes from the far west, where most people are right-handed. I should have thought of that before."

"Complementary," nodded Poto.

"Wenji, please take this pen and tablet," asked the Gral-Chaner. "Write anything important you can recall, regarding Lorgi, during the night, and all day tomorrow. To be of help, we must learn first. We must not harm the Sign Child by our ignorance."

"That's it? Obviously, no one saw my letter," sighed Wenji, frowning and shaking her head at the tiny pen and paper. "Just in the short weeks that I have known Lorgi, I could fill volumes."

"We do not seek quantity," said Poto.

Wenji pursed her lips, shook her head and looked away. To her, these celibate men lacked any awareness of urban female verboseness, and most other things of the real world. What could they know about children, animals, or the endless complexities, dangers, and struggles of city life? What did they know of torture, slavery, starvation, violence, or crimes against women? Perhaps they assumed that young, lay people had little or nothing to say about anything important.

Suddenly, Wenji's writing tools reminded her all too much of the old spy in the palace gardens. Demanding an explanation, she met the Gral-Chaner's sparkling eyes.

"Good!" he answered. "The size forces one to distill thoughts before writing them. We all use such tablets for observation training. May they also work for you."

"Gral-Chaner," said Wenji. "What will you do when the king's men find their way up here?"

"That is not your concern, my courageous visitor," said the Gral-Chaner. "Your responsibility—to yourself, Lorgi and everyone here—is to recall any information about him. His most important thoughts, actions and ways. Now we leave you at peace to retire to your room for thought."

"I don't need one. Let me stay in the library with Lorgi, so I can be with him if he wakes."

"No, young lady. He would seem to want cold. You must stay warm, to heal yourself before you can heal others. Lorgi needs you well."

"I'm fine, just terrified for Lorgi—and all of you."

"And dangerously ill," said the Gral-Chaner. "A person in your state would not survive a week in the city. But fortune has brought you to a place of hope. May tomorrow find you improved."

By candlelight, a tall, lean monk led her to a small, upstairs guest room. While stoking the fireplace, he asked her to ring the chime by her bed if she had any need. He warned her to promptly go down to the main hall on the ground floor when she heard the great bell early in the morning, or the Gral-Chaner would be very disappointed.

Nodding, she felt lost in the ghostly quiet, all-male environment. The monks probably had no idea how to help her, Lorgi, or anyone else, but at least they cared. Wenji thought she would rather die here than any other place, and guessed Lorgi would understand.

Only a moment past dawn, which touched the mountains early, the great bell sounded with force. Everyone scrambled down to the main hall for breakfast: a piece of fruit and a mug of tea. During the snack, the Gral-Chaner assigned chores. Two monks received the arduous labor of descending the trail all the way down to the river, to erase any footprints or other evidence that Lorgi and Wenji might have left. The others got two-hour stints at assorted tasks around the monastery. Then the Gral-Chaner turned to Wenji.

"As always, our delicious monk's bounty will only be served when all finish their contributions, giving their best effort. We wish each other joy in our work." The Gral-Chaner followed up with daily reminders, most of which Wenji suspected were stated for her benefit. But instead of hurrying off to chores, all the monks tarried.

"Why is everyone smiling at me all of a sudden?" Wenji asked.

"Do you think a monastery just runs itself, by magic?" answered the Gral-Chaner, smiling at her.

"Of course not," she said.

"Monks think and study at all hours, but are still people who must eat. Whenever possible, we much prefer our own labor to the charity of others. Monks can work and think at the same time. This nurtures peace and respect."

"I understand." Wenji nodded. "Though dressed like royalty, I'm an escaped...slave, lucky to be alive. Besides my name, and a litany of painful memories, this fancy, torn-up dress is my only possession. If you had work clothes for me, I would love to help in any way I can."

"I put some in your room a few minutes ago," said Poto. "In two hours, when the bell rings again, a hot bath will be waiting for you, and your dress will be clean and mended like new."

"Really?" she asked, surprised.

"Welcome to civilization," smiled Poto.

"And our vegetable garden," said the Gral-Chaner. "Working there will be the best medicine for you."

Once she did, she began to heal. Wenji could not recall a time without fear of instant harm if a master found the tiniest fault with her work. But gentle monks, clean mountain air and great distance from the world below loaned her peace and hope. She began to feel like a different person: generous and helpful, one who could actually take a deep breath and think. Someone not to be confused with an escaped slave. Two monks working nearby sensed the change taking place, cheering her "progress towards better worlds."

A half hour into her work, Wenji saw the Gral-Chaner scurry into the garden, exuding a child's vigor and joy as he began filling a basket with produce for the coming meal. It hardly seemed normal, fair or even acceptable that an adult had such energy so soon after sunrise, especially one claiming to be advanced in years. To Wenji, the man defied nature. Maybe he was not nearly as old as he would have others believe. Or perhaps these monks put something special in their tea to keep themselves happy, energized, and immune to the horrors of Shohan.

Whatever their secret, she wanted some for herself and many times that for Lorgi, if there were any chance it might revive him.

"Excuse me, but I must ask you something," Wenji said to him.

"Good," said the Gral-Chaner. "We love questions."

"Exactly how old are you?"

Several monks working nearby froze in shock, straining to hear the master's answer to a question none of them had ever dared to ask.

"Seventy-five years in this body, this life," said the Gral-Chaner, starting to work alongside Wenji.

"But you can't be that old!" gasped Wenji.

"Oh yes I can, *gánsi*, very much! Tell me more about Lorgi. You can talk as you work, the way we monks do."

"He's a vegetarian, never gets cold, can see in total darkness. You would not believe what he can sense, even from far away. He measures lengths and weighs things, just with his eyes. And those claws, by the heavens!—excuse me, sorry—they will cut even iron or rock. So can the ridge of spikes going down his back. His tail is a weapon like no other. He says his mother weighs either five or ten tons, depending on his audience. And he has complained of the heat and hunger ever since I met him."

"Then we had better get Lorgi home soon," chuckled the Gral-Chaner. "Our small garden won't support him through the winter. What of his kind, his people?"

"That is just how Lorgi would say it! They lack any social order. All are equals. Nobody seems to be in charge of anyone else. Yet his full name is 'Lord Gamon of Tiefenbo.' But then he says everyone is somebody in his village. Everyone there has a real name, knows everyone else and their business. They all help each other, without even being asked."

"Beautiful! I would like to visit such a place, wouldn't you?"

"If it were not so cold, I would beg to live there," said Wenji. "Because I'm an orphan, Lorgi even suggested having his mother adopt me. Can you imagine?"

"Only on my best days," laughed the Gral-Chaner. "What do you know concerning his birth, his entrance into this world?"

"Only that they hatch, apparently on a precise date, attended with great ceremony. But Lorgi was late, causing his mother extreme anguish."

"How late?" the Gral-Chaner raised his eyebrows.

"I think he said four or five days."

"About the middle of Thricemonth, or perhaps the 21st?"

"I don't know about all that."

"Yet you inform. Know that you have been uniquely blessed to walk with him—and he with you. And we, as well, because you chose to come here. A rare gift from heaven, not a day too soon, the Sign Child brings much to teach us all, even if he does not know it himself."

"But he's in a coma!" Wenji grabbed the Gral-Chaner's arm.

"Be calm. This is a place of health. Look at me."

"Do you really think Lorgi will recover?"

"The moment we are ready for him, so now it is up to us. But we must accomplish much in little time. Every helping hand and thought is needed. We must not squander this gift, lest he die in our care." With a gentle smile and nod, the master vanished into the main building.

When the bell finally sounded, Wenji really needed a break. By the time she cleaned up and reported to the main hall for the monk's bounty, it was almost noon. Two monks delivered a vegetarian feast, setting it on a very low, round table in the room's center. Following eastern monastic custom, everyone sat on the floor around the table, gazing at the food in silence. Wenji had never felt so hungry in her life. No meal had ever been so appetizing.

Suddenly all the monks raised their heads, looking to the Gral-Chaner. He smiled, giving each person slow, generous eye contact in turn as he looked around the table in counter-clockwise motion. Silently, he reminded all of their uniqueness and special gifts.

"Poto, you have outdone yourself, again!" cheered the Gral-Chaner, praising the meal.

"This is a special day," nodded Poto. Everyone murmured agreement.

"Yes, and each grows more so," said the Gral-Chaner. But he looked to the one guest with concern. "Wenji, is there anything you wish to say before we start?"

She met his kind, knowing eyes, then all the others, certain Lorgi would have enjoyed their company. Seeing the feast, she knew he would have loved it, along with the clean mountain air, pure water, and the vitally refreshing lack of heat. Since befriending him, she had used him to help herself survive, and in the end had left him in a coma. By staying at the monastery, she might also bring about its destruction, and death to all the kind, naïve monks living there. Everyone looked deep into Wenji's tearful eyes, begging her to speak. She opened her mouth to oblige, but then covered it with a hand in shame.

Like her first encounter with Lorgi, Wenji broke down, sobbing and gasping for air. Directly the Gral-Chaner escorted her out to the pavilion with the spectacular view. Lacking the monks' faith in Lorgi's recovery, or good winning out in Shohan, or anywhere else, she craved revenge against the Gran Vazuk, the king of Shohan and a host of others. Guessing her struggles, the Gral-Chaner stared silently, his expression and slightly tilted head reminding Wenji all too much of Lorgi, whenever he "just knew" something. She stepped back in shock.

"We share your pain; now share our hopes," said the Gral-Chaner. "All have been stung by the king's savagery. But we must focus on Lorgi's return and our higher, spiritual purpose."

"I just want Lorgi back," she cried.

"Call to him. Perhaps only you can wake him. Your great adventure has only begun. Both friends and enemies seek him, even as we speak."

22: Ábafosh

Glancing about the room, Jinva feared she had already spent more time in Serukeeba's kitchen than the owner ever would. Just when she finally had three sourdough loaves ready for baking, Sirwan and Brogan charged in, laughing and screaming. Nuwak had been chasing the two all over a new half-built village, especially where they were told not to run. All for a game of *pox* suddenly gripping the children of Tiefenbo. As "it," Nuwak tried to tag any other boy or girl to give away the dreaded *pox* and make them "it," but so far, was having no luck.

Thinking of the game and nothing else, Brogan jumped aside to escape him. But in so doing, he knocked over a cup of seeds Jinva had waiting on the counter to sprinkle over the loaves—the adult price of children at play. As the cup hit the floor and shattered, a startled baker ended the game with a shriek, throwing up her hands in anger. Immediately, she ordered all three children to clean up their mess. But all the noise drew Rokímba into the kitchen. Red-faced and shaking her head, Jinva did not know which bothered her more: unruly, thoughtless children at play or an elderly, psychic snowdragon with selective memory and little tact, unable to control her prophetic but often reckless words.

"Stop, don't touch a thing!" shouted the seer, her eyes wide and her ears twitching. "I must study the way those seeds landed. It could be a sign!"

"Rokímba, children must learn to respect the kitchen," said Jinva, annoyed.

"First I must take a reading," said Rokímba. "Where was the cup waiting before fate moved it?"

"Well if fate moved it, then fate can clean it up and be punished for it," huffed Jinva.

"Cleaning up and scolding mean nothing in the presence of fate!" warned the seer. Delighted by her words, the children stood close beside her and contemplated miraculous fate, hoping it could keep them from being punished for their play. "Now, where was the cup waiting?"

"Where it was supposed to be, all the way over here—*waiting* to be sprinkled on the loaves of bread, not broken on the floor. I'm here to bake, not entertain fate or wasteful games!" moaned Jinva, pointing to the countertop. "Can't children at play or the fate of nations wait 'til I'm done?"

"Sorry," said all three children.

"It was an accident," said Brogan.

"Yes, but a most telling one!" cheered Rokímba. "Oh. Yes...I'm feeling something to read here. The seeds speak to me."

"Wonderful." Jinva rolled her eyes and threw up her hands in disgust. Rokímba ignored her.

"I was just trying to get away from him," said Brogan, pretending innocence. I ran this way and didn't see the cup."

"The seeds make kind of a nice pattern, don't they?" chirped Nuwak, smiling up at Rokímba. "That means something good, right?"

"Yes—that you can help Brogan and Sirwan clean it up!" scolded Jinva.

All three children avoided her glare by keeping their eyes on the old seer.

"I didn't do anything!" protested Sirwan.

"Be calm, children," said Rokímba. "Everyone please wait quietly while I think. Oh...I'm definitely getting something potent here now."

"I'm getting a headache," said Jinva. Huffing like Serukeeba, she scowled at them all, anxious to get on with her work.

Oblivious to all else, Rokímba gazed at the floor with entranced eyes, conjuring up horrific visions of Laskomia, Tuzanchim hordes and the kingdom of Shohan."

"Oh, my!...something beautiful...something terrible...Great snows!" gasped the seer.

"Stop. For once, take motherly care what you say, especially in front of children," warned Jinva. "Tiefenbo already has far more than enough messes, great and small, to busy everyone cleaning them all up for years to come. No need to add to it, my good seer. Remember your first visit? You still have serious mending to do on *that* reading."

"I know only too well," sighed Rokímba. "But this sign is so extraordinary. Unique. Fate itself cannot decide a future or even how to guide towards one. In all my five-times-fifty snows, I have never seen anything like this. So much danger. Seri faces hard choices, loaded with possibilities and consequences. So does Lorgi and those with him. Anything could happen out there. So speak the seeds."

"In other words, we can stop wasting time on fate and start making these children clean up their wasteful mess," said Jinva, with her hands on her hips. "Of course, even minus the *gift*, you must know what Seri and I both think about your readings."

"Yes," murmured Rokímba. "Yet…perhaps Lorgi will bring doom only to those who really deserve it. But before retrieving him, Serukeeba will cause a huge *ábafosh*. Upset the Continent's whole balance. Talk about fate! Good will rise up against Tyrants. So much blood, violence and disruption—on an epic scale. But so much change. I hope for the better. Perhaps what Lorgi's shell had tried to foretell."

"If you're done 'perhapsing,' we've all got an *ábafosh* of real work to do around here, right now," snapped Jinva. "Fate or not."

"What's an *ábafosh*?" asked Brogan.

"Don't you know anything?" Sirwan teased him.

"An avalanche," said Nuwak.

23: Paths & Choices

 Once Klimgu's advance force crossed the Near Valley and reached the feet of the Shirlangu Mountains, an icy wind buffeted them. Ordering a halt—in battle formation—he sent scouts up into the foothills. He took turns pacing or gazing up at steep, giant foothills covered with dense, ancient forests. Just beyond those, a forbidding wall of rock and ice towered so far above that it formed a world of its own, between land and sky.

Vigorously grilling his captains, scouts or anyone who knew the smallest fact about this eternal boundary, Klimgu demanded all possible information regarding supplies, weather, horses, Puchakta, and the three known (or rumored) pathways into Shohan. Nothing that anyone said could satisfy him. Mostly he waited for scouts to return quickly with something—anything—to help guide his next decision. Luckily, the most skilled among them returned first.

"Grand news!" shouted Kibak, riding hard back to the army. "From several hilltops, I saw Chotzan's group—or maybe Twarejik's, only three days behind us."

"You were not sent to look back, but that is glad news indeed!" answered Klimgu. "Pray your vision does not turn into Puchakta leading a new force against us."

"Who else can it be?" posed Baqwam, shaking her head. "I am sorry to say it, but Chotzan rides a full week behind us. Twarejik will need more time, with so many wounded to care for. Only Puchakta could be so near, so soon."

"Ah, but you don't know Chotzan," laughed Kibak. "He can ride like a devil's broom, especially knowing that I race ahead of him. Never underestimate him."

"Or Puchakta," muttered Klimgu. "We must reach Shohan before he can brew something there. But by which route?"

"Southwest, around the mountains, of course," said Baqwam. "A swift, easy ride in flat open country, how the Tuzanchim have always done." Most of the captains nodded.

"Where all Shohan's armor waits?" prodded Klimgu. "At least consider our other options. Northeast, through the woods around the mountains, or the secret middle way, over them."

"No secret," Kibak shook his head. "Though direct, the middle route is known to be dangerous, while the north way is long and tedious."

"Here we go again," Klimgu groaned.

"But it may be too late in the year for either option," said Kibak. "When clouds return in a few days, you will have snow—if you're lucky."

"They say the north route is not too high, rugged, or well-guarded," posed Klimgu. "Why not ride fast that way, before snow, Puchakta or the Shohaneze can catch us?"

"Once winter descends, which could be tomorrow or a month from now, the Shohaneze will leave both routes virtually unguarded. An opportunity, if we can manage the cold."

"But we are not equipped to travel in alpine terrain, or winter weather," said Baqwam.

"Puchakta would love for us to get bogged down in snow," muttered Klimgu.

"*Yahai!*" roared Serukeeba. "Stop boring me with Puchakta or the weather. Are you flowered princesses or warriors?" Everyone froze at the slap. "I take the mountain route, where I have advantages over most enemies. With any luck, if not mercy, Lorgi's captors took him that way, to avoid summer's heat. Who can guide me?"

The captains began debating her idea, until Serukeeba roared, "Now!"

"I can take you to a village where the people all know the route," said Kibak. "But we cannot follow on our Steppe horses."

"I knew it!" huffed Serukeeba. "I must finish this alone. Klimgu, for all your trials and progressive ways, you have not brought me to my son, but across half the Continent, on a trail of blood. Goodbye. May you all finally get whatever luck you deserve." Glaring at Kibak, she pointed up toward the mountains.

He smiled with a hearty nod, yet looked to Klimgu for guidance, like everyone. Suddenly, all feared that Serukeeba was about to leave forever, taking all good fortune away with her. No Tuzanchim could allow such an ominous parting.

"Wait, great Serukeeba," shouted Klimgu. "I swore to see your quest through, and none will find teeth missing from my word! We will meet again in the heart of Shohan and celebrate your reunion with Lorgi. I promise to make that happen. If you must take the short way, then let Kibak escort you. He and a few others."

"What others? I need only one reliable guide, if such a person exists."

"Kibak, take this," yelled Klimgu, tossing a leather bag to him. "Buy all the mountain ponies and whatever else you may need up there."

Catching it, Kibak remarked, "Feels heavy enough to equip a small army." Opening the bag, Kibak gawked at five fistfuls of precious gems. "What is this, Lorgi's ransom?"

"Yes!" said Klimgu. "The Álukois have stretched your eyes as well. Take Baqwam and Gurjik with you. They speak Serukeeba's tongue best."

"*Gánsi*, but those two are far more than scouts," noted Kibak. "What of all the warriors under their command, the brave and eager 500 who first escorted Serukeeba out of Uxanda?"

"It was 300; I remember clearly," huffed Serukeeba.

"Well, yes, but it *should* have been 500, at the very least," said Kibak. "Five hundred or 5,000—how can we tear those loyal warriors away from their beloved captain and her fine Second?" Giving a look of pained sorrow, Kibak pretended to beg, yet already knew Klimgu's answer.

"Of course they can go along too," assured Klimgu. "And take all the porters you want."

"No, no, no, NO!" yelled Serukeeba. "I need but a single, competent guide, and no more. One. Only one. Alone. No others."

"You have my best, and I will sorely miss his counsel," said Klimgu, waving to Kibak. "But he needs the two who have been your faithful interpreters from the start. Two who now lead the 500 warriors I have entrusted to their command."

"May I go also?" Moshal asked, looking to Baqwam. "To assist, negotiate, map the route."

"Too dangerous," said Kibak. "Extremely hard terrain. No place for a Tuzanchim, let alone a peaceful monk of the Laskomian Plain. Why would you even want to?"

"I once read of ancient temples hidden away on the eastern parts of the Shirlangu Mountains," said Moshal, eying Serukeeba for support. "They could hold vast stores of knowledge. I must visit one before, before..."

"The Tuzanchim pillage them?" Serukeeba finished for him.

"We have no need to bother temples," said Klimgu, looking offended by the snowdragon's remark. "Go, Moshal. Visit all the temples you wish—after seeing Kibak's group through the mountains. There! Serukeeba, you take the best of everything: my best scout, interpreter, best shot *and* accounter, along with my best engineer! Enough gems for a king's ransom. And 500 outstanding warriors. A most respectable scouting party!"

"I don't want a 'most respectable scouting party.' I just want my son!"

"First we need a proper farewell," said Kibak.

"Hardly," murmured Serukeeba.

"But we must," insisted Kibak. "Vital to ensure good fortune."

"No!" moaned Serukeeba, already knowing it was useless. That moment she thought to strike out on her own, but the myriad peaks towering before her would confound even an Álukoi. Without help, she might need months to find her way. While she stared at the mountains, everyone else began preparing a farewell party.

"Great Serukeeba, you must take part," urged Kibak. "All need good fortune. Giving invites it back eightfold."

"Why the big ceremony now? We've had groups large and small coming and going all the time before."

"This time it will be dangerous! We need all the luck we can conjure by making a proper farewell. We ride on Shohan, at the end of the raiding season. They will be waiting for us."

"The *raiding* season?" huffed Serukeeba, shaking her head like a disgusted human. "Please amuse me. Explain how that is not barbaric?"

"Who is qualified to say?" chuckled Kibak.

A murmur whipped through the horde, then a deafening cheer. Gifts were exchanged along with personal goodbyes. Many gallons of liquor vanished in hundreds of toasts. Some warriors performed a ritual farewell dance, as others sang and clapped rhythmically to make good luck for Serukeeba's scouting party. Two hours later they were finally ready to leave.

"That puts a Tiefenbo farewell to shame, but my traveler's curse persists," moaned Serukeeba. "Every time I start out, someone arrives from nowhere, forcing me to halt. Kibak, if you are Lorgi's friend or mine, show me to this mountain trail at once. Please let nothing stop us. Forget all the others you asked for. We have no need of them."

Nodding, but grinning, Kibak began leading the way on horseback. Not to be left behind, Moshal instantly joined them, closely followed by Baqwam, Gurjik and all their warriors. Once her "most respectable scouting party" reached a prominent hill, Serukeeba took a long view in every direction. Horsetail cirrus clouds brushed the northern horizon, slowly growing across the autumn sky. Klimgu's army rode south at a trot—in battle formation. A large force sprouted on the western horizon, but Serukeeba said nothing, praying no one else would see it. Instead, she spurred her party on, higher into the foothills. Sighting a path climbing through rugged slopes to the east, she turned to Kibak. Already nodding and smiling, he answered her question before she had to ask.

Klimgu's army took the legendary southern way. With every mile, autumn grew younger, warmer and richer. In two days the invaders trod fertile rolling hills and valleys teeming with countless farms and dozens of small Shohaneze garrisons. Over the centuries, the Tuzanchim had raided Shohan many times by this route, each time finding the defenders slightly more clever, determined, and especially more numerous. But never yet capable of stopping them.

Without Serukeeba, Klimgu felt a gambler's anxiety about dividing his forces, though she had left him no choice. Warriors in both expeditions argued which party—the dragon's handful or the new Vazuk's army—would become the first to reach the heart of Shohan. They debated whether Lorgi waited to be rescued at the king's summer or winter palace. Privately, both Klimgu and Serukeeba guessed that the other would arrive first. And pay the ultimate price for it.

24: Mountain Trials

A chilled wind pelted the "most respectable scouting party" ascending the faint trail through a maze of foothills. Thick, hearty bushes replaced the grass, followed by strands of trees. As the path steepened, pines began to dominate. Serukeeba hummed contentment, but the steppe horses balked, hating alpine terrain. Most of the warriors feared having to abandon their horses before reaching the mountain village Kibak had promised. Silently, he prayed that either Destiny, dumb luck or his distant memory of it had set him on the right path. When Serukeeba spotted the goal, Kibak groaned with relief.

"We approach one of the main settlements of the Yimung, or Mountain People," he shouted. "They cut this route eons ago, and still maintain it—at least superficially. And take great pride in trading with both the Tuzanchim and Shohaneze. Or whoever can reach this place. The Yimung can be…difficult. But any of the villagers will guide us through the thick of the Shirlangu Mountains, gladly selling us whatever we need. Of course we will have to barter hard for everything, even buttons and boot laces."

"That sounds exhausting," said Moshal.

"And far too time-consuming," added Baqwam.

"Better I keep silent and away from your Yimung," murmured Serukeeba. "Spend as little time here as possible. Keep things simple and quiet."

"Why?" asked Kibak. "Traders are usually friendly. Often very helpful, no matter how fiercely they bargain."

"I have no patience, only so much energy, and too much baggage already," said Serukeeba. "Kibak, Baqwam and Moshal, meet me at that bend ahead. Make everyone else wait here. Not for their eyes or ears. I know you need supplies, but we must not waste Lorgi's ransom here."

"As you wish." Kibak achieved her request with a clap and a few hand signals. When the four reached Serukeeba's bend, he asked: "Excepting Lorgi's ransom, what else can we barter? The Yimung certainly have no use for our steppe horses, and we have nothing else to trade but violence—which we were saving for the Shohaneze."

"Turn this for gold to buy what you need," said Serukeeba, snapping off a spent claw from her left forepaw.

"A gem all its own, but I doubt the Yimung will give even an old pony for a stone claw, no matter how fine or rare," said Kibak, handing it to Baqwam.

"Heavy and true as any gemstone," she noted. With a smile, she handed it to Moshal.

"Looks just like a raw diamond," he noted.

"It should!" huffed Serukeeba. "Have a few warriors argue loud and hard against selling it at all. Baqwam and Moshal take the other side. Debate in front of the Yimung. A fun easy task for Tuzanchim. But in the end, only Baqwam will make the trade."

"What? Why me, when Kibak leads this party?" asked Baqwam, shaking her head and looking to Moshal for support.

"You are the only two humans in our group who can read," said Kibak. "I will pretend to referee."

"What can I expect in trade for it?" asked Baqwam. "Please take no offense, mighty Serukeeba, but when the sun sets, it is still just a claw, though unlike any other on the entire Continent."

"It is also a huge diamond," said Serukeeba. "Trade for gold. Use gold to buy mountain ponies and supplies. Though only too obvious, say nothing of its source. I wish we had a Lendishman to push the hardest bargain."

"Worry not. Who can out-argue Tuzanchim?" laughed Kibak.

"Arguing is one thing, but you all seem...well...too honest to survive a Lendish transaction." Surprised by her own words, Serukeeba reared her neck, twitching her ears. Her audience smiled and nodded at the unexpected compliment.

"A Lendish transaction?" mused Kibak, raising an eyebrow. "I should like to meet those people."

"I think not!" laughed Serukeeba. "That would end in blood."

Kibak's natural smile became a frown as he entered the village. Most of his party scattered, relaxed, or made small trades on their own. Waiting quietly outside the village, Serukeeba growled and snapped her jaws if a

Yimung came within a hundred yards of her, and that person fled. Baqwam, Moshal, and two of the party's meanest looking warriors got right to work—arguing. At first, the locals just smiled and ignored their amateur performance, having seen enough of the tactic before.

Sensing this, Baqwam widened her eyes, shouted and drew her sword to demand attention. Taking her cue, the others drew theirs. Suddenly the Yimung took interest, knowing that even the smallest Tuzanchim debate had a way of destroying villages or whole cities, once swords left their scabbards. It would not matter that the Yimung had nothing to do with the argument.

Seizing the claw, Kibak also grabbed the nearest villager, a stout older man, saying, "You must hold this for me until my captains are done fighting over it." Terrified, the man nodded, stepped back, then fled into the nearest hut, gripping the stone with both hands.

Begging peace with upraised palms, Moshal stepped between Baqwam and her opponents. Looking angry himself, Kibak pretended to keep them all from violence. Any Tuzanchim close enough to hear or see the drama turned with genuine surprise and concern, and began walking towards it. Though eager to quell tempers, the villagers showed no interest in trading until several of them confirmed that Baqwam was indeed offering a huge, uncut diamond. The Yimung bid against each other until their wealthiest emerged victorious. Within minutes, the villagers rented out all their ponies and sold all the supplies that Kibak's party needed.

Besides everything from blankets to boot strings, the Yimung also offered mountain guides, arguing with the Tuzanchim and each other over who was most qualified for the job. Amidst a rising din of voices, Kibak picked three whom he sensed were really the best guides from among twenty screaming applicants. But no matter how many times he yelled "Sorry" or "Thank you"—even in three languages—none of the rest would give up, their screams turning to threats and insults. Only when Kibak shrieked "Yahai!" with a drawn sword did they stop.

Just as the Tuzanchim prepared to leave, the three chosen guides eyed each other, swearing that no Yimung could take any group, large or small, beyond the trail's halfway point, which they adamantly refused to cross. They warned of a terrible beast in the heart of the mountains, and a curse upon all the lands beyond, owing to the king of Shohan. Hearing this in translation, Serukeeba huffed, scowled and inspected her claws. The whole group checked and readied their weapons. Weighed down by myths, rumors, mountain ponies of dubious quality, smoldering tempers and a dozen curses, the Tuzanchim left the village behind.

"Did any besides Kibak think to ask about Lorgi?" asked Serukeeba.

"At last, your voice returns," cheered Moshal. "We sorely missed it back there."

"To answer your question, none of the hill people have seen Lorgi," said Baqwam. "I am deeply sorry, great Serukeeba."

"You are a true friend. Please just call me Seri. No one else, just you."

"*Gánsi.*" Baqwam smiled with a deep nod of respect. "Now I am doubly honored to ride with you."

"Even spending less than an hour with them, surely we know the Yimung better than to trust them in any matter, great or small," laughed Kibak. "They've never seen nor heard anything until you fill their hands with coins." One of the guides overheard him and relayed the insult to the other two. All three scowled at Kibak.

"For only a few coins, they seemed sincere enough, or at least curious, when I asked about Lorgi," said Baqwam. "Yet the same villagers looked away when asked about Puchakta. None would admit to having seen him recently."

"Aha! They lie," said Kibak. "A favorite Yimung pastime. So at least we know Puchakta came this way. But even torture may not reveal a reliable *when*. The Yimung have a poor sense of time, from living in the mountains."

"Kibak, you certainly are not making friends with our guides," whispered Moshal, darting his eyes between the leader and the Yimung.

"News of Puchakta's defeat must ride before us," said Baqwam. "Perhaps they are just afraid because of that."

Hearing and understanding, one of the Yimung guides abruptly quit, handing back the advance Kibak had paid him. Immediately, the other two did the same. Nothing said by anyone could induce any of the three to reconsider. Only Serukeeba seemed happy about that development.

The alpine ponies that Baqwam and Moshal rented for the group had stout, sure legs, strong backs, thick, tough winter coats, fresh iron shoes, and a mountain goat's sure footing. But they also owned a collective stubbornness, trudging at a constant, slow pace regardless of terrain, weather, or altitude. Mindful of each other but ignoring their own riders, every hour, all of them halted at the closest, most level ground to rest. Nothing could spur their tempo or extend their short day. When the trail grew narrow or dangerous, all of the ponies required bribery before continuing. Two days of this exhausted Serukeeba's patience.

"Enough!" she shouted. "All I do is wait. A blind man on crutches, even a Lendish baker could outrun these lazy donkeys! *Gánsi*, Kibak, but I must break my own trail. Follow me if you wish. Yet if I were you, I would give up on these mountains and rejoin Klimgu with all speed."

"What of that great monster, the mountain curse, and the Shohaneze, who grow more clever each year?" asked Kibak. "What other trail can you make? It's mostly straight up or down off this one."

"My claws were made for traversing rock and ice. Not waging war. But I can manage either quite well. This is my kind of land, not yours. Try to imagine leading a group across the Steppes, but having to walk your horses, not ride them."

"Ridiculous," said Kibak, nodding. "I understand."

"In a matter of days, I can be in Shohan. At best, you will need weeks on those Yimung ponies. And to slow you even more, tomorrow will bring a taste of winter."

"The sky looks too dry to brew trouble up here, at least for a few days."

"*Kayutáve*—horsetail clouds—can bring alpine storms," Serukeeba pointed northeast. "Go as far as you can today, preferably back to that village and beyond. Because tomorrow will be much harder. Good luck."

Giving a quick group farewell, she left at an Álukoi's trot. Many warriors cried "wait!" but she closed her ear lids and vanished around a bend. Kibak tried to force a quicker pace, but the ponies balked, causing more delay. What had taken Serukeeba minutes would take the group hours. Fed up with an especially bad pony, Gurjik drew his sword. Again Kibak risked his own arm to prevent slaughter.

"Why stop me from doing all of us a favor?" asked Gurjik.

"Serukeeba would not approve," warned Baqwam. Moshal nodded in agreement.

"But this animal is totally useless," protested Gurjik. "Make dinner out of it and the others will improve."

"No," sighed Kibak. "Leave it to fend for itself, and die."

Yet the instant Gurjik removed its burden of supplies, the pony began retracing the path, back towards the village. All the ponies turned, ready to follow it home.

"Mistake!" yelled Kibak. "Seize the beast or shoot it, but don't let it get away. Good. Force it back to work. The Yimung will pay for their deceit—if we ever get through this."

* * *

Finally moving at her own pace, Serukeeba berated herself for not striking out on her own sooner. The trail wound precariously along the south face of a mountain towering over a deep river gorge twisting east by southeast. Serukeeba doubted Kibak's group could ever manage this stretch, burdened with stubborn mountain ponies, ridden by warriors used to flat ground. Late that afternoon, bursts of hard rain pelted the slopes, nearly erasing the trail. The next morning, scattered, intense salvos of hail replaced the rain, with temperatures hovering just above freezing. Only an Álukoi might travel in such weather.

The air turned "hollow," or ripe for a thunderstorm. Even Álukois had to avoid being struck by lightning. Without raising herself up, Serukeeba scanned the steep terrain for low ground or a cave to wait out nature's fury. Glorious escarpments, hardy pines gripping impossible slopes, and a hundred waterfalls spawned by sudden rain all greeted her welcoming eyes, but no good place to take shelter from a lightning strike. She would have to just keep looking until she found one.

After a few more minutes of brisk walking, Serukeeba spotted a fork in the path, an eagle's mile away but a good three by the trail, around a bottomless chasm. It was guarded by a stout round tower, shrouded in rain. With the blue, white and gold flag of Shohan fluttering on a pole atop its roof, the tower leaned hard against the mountain to keep from tumbling down into the river so far below. Thirty feet downhill from the tower waited a massive, round oak and iron gate to what looked like a carriage house, dug deep into the mountainside.

"Perfect," said Serukeeba. "They should have plenty of room. If not, then they'll just have to make some for me." Heartened, she walked faster, rousing the tower to life.

A lone sentry appeared at its crenellations. In seconds, two more joined him, running back and forth, bumping into each other, waving arms, shouting in *hyúlem* panic. A half-minute later, twelve more stood beside him, with spears and bows. Torches, helmets, and armor followed in that order. Six others scrambled out and down to the huge gate. By the time they opened it, Serukeeba had reached within 500 yards of the outpost.

She had not come to fight, but had no way of showing that until much closer to them. Sitting back on her haunches, Serukeeba raised both forepaws, clapped, then slowly drew the biggest circles she could in the air. She repeated the Álukoi greeting many times, but her intended audience never noticed.

Still, she would calm them with smiles and waves on her approach, pushing weapons aside if any blocked her progress. All she wanted was a few hours of peaceful rest and shelter. Perhaps they could tell her which trail led to Shohan. But the wind shifted, carrying the most painful odor in all her memory. The gate opened. A rare giant mountain balkotar, dwarfing any she had ever seen, slowly emerged from its cavern. Saving all energy for battle, Serukeeba walked slowly while the humans ran, coaxing their haystack-sized monster forward.

Like the mountain ponies, this balkotar could not be rushed for anything as it lumbered out, seemingly pondering what possible emergency had dared to break its long, comfortable slumber. Appearing far heavier than Serukeeba, the giant had a thick, pale grey crop of greasy, matted fur. Compared to other balkotars, this one held far fewer, yet larger and stouter quills on its back legs. On flat ground, a champion Álukoi would have to outmaneuver it and cut down its legs one by one. However, on alpine slopes this unique monster's true strengths and shortcomings could only be guessed. If the humans interfered, Serukeeba might have to slay them, too.

A dozen soldiers spread out to the sides and taunted it, as the behemoth walked at the speed of a tortoise. Serukeeba sat back on her haunches to study her foe. When it finally managed to reach within 400 yards of her, the balkotar slowly cocked its back legs. With a sudden violent whipping motion, it hurled only one quill from each. Before Serukeeba could turn her back to the missiles, both struck her in the chest with crossbow speed and force. One even chipped her rock hide.

"Golármon, what do you make of this?" Serukeeba gasped aloud.

"Take the warning," he answered in her mind. "Time and space are your only allies here. Make full use of them."

With new respect for her enemy's superior aim and throwing power, Serukeeba crouched, pressing her belly to the ground. She had to think for a moment before advancing uphill towards the tower. Two more quills struck, this time on her back spikes. She moved another fifty paces uphill. Inviting her foe to spend more quills, Serukeeba halted again, gambling that her armor could safely turn them all. A third pair of quills smacked hard against her lower back. She waited motionless for half a minute longer, and moved only when two more whirred past her eyes. This time the balkotar missed, but only by inches. Given the ample distance between foes, Serukeeba still found her enemy's throwing record to be unrivaled by human or beast.

"At this rate, the contest will take days," moaned Serukeeba.

"Destroy something dear to your enemy," said Golármon.

"Of course," shouted Serukeeba, bolting for the tower's door.

Two smacks of her tail knocked it in, sending the humans into an ant-like frenzy. But it had no effect on their balkotar. The doorway remained intact, and far too narrow to admit Serukeeba. So she doubled back around the tower and down to the balkotar's gate. Two more quills struck against her back. With all her force, she ripped the gate off its hinges and broke it to pieces. Finding nothing to destroy inside, Serukeeba turned to face her enemy. Alarmed that an intruder had entered its den, the balkotar suddenly advanced at a faster pace, still firing off two quills each minute. Serukeeba ran back up to the tower.

The balkotar matched her speed, equally bent on obtaining the higher ground. Though not suited for combat on flat, open spaces due to its bulk and slowness, the alpine giant was quite at home on steep, rugged or slippery inclines—much like an Álukoi. At last expending a full effort, it gained on Serukeeba. Alarmed, she roared with a deafening war cry. This had no effect, making her wonder if the balkotar's former slowness had been a ruse, and just how capable the beast would prove to be. Rarely missing, it refused to waste quills, and threw with such force as to chip Serukeeba's rock hide in three more places. Its mandibles seemed utterly invincible, and too huge even for the monster's overall size.

"Why die fighting a beast that would rather slumber in its hollow, pampered by guards who do the same?" muttered Serukeeba. "Not even Golármon could defeat such a monster. Now my impatience will cost me. If only I had listened to Baqwam and so many others. I must go back, endure any words they heap on me, and try to catch Klimgu before the Shohaneze do."

Suddenly a lightning flash struck the mountain's peak, nearly blinding any eyes aimed that way, be they human, balkotar or snowdragon. Seconds later, the shock hit with a deafening explosion, shaking the ground. Only this halted the beast. It contracted its legs, crouching as it raised its mandibles overhead to protect its eyes.

Enraged at her own poor judgment, and at the living fortress blocking her way, Serukeeba charged in to slice off one of the beast's giant front leg segments. She leapt aside, barely in time to escape the mandibles.

On seven legs, the monster gave a bear's chase. Fleeing, Serukeeba desperately sought stones to throw. Finding none nearby, she ran back to the tower. Five hard slaps of her tail demolished the doorway, supplying the ammunition needed. She began pelting the monster with rubble, which made it halt and raise its mandibles high to protect its eyes. Working furiously, Serukeeba smashed part of the tower walls with her tail and hurled them with her forepaws.

Just as the balkotar came within ten paces, Serukeeba threw her last salvo. Charging in, she lobbed off one of its front leg joints. Leaping aside, she snatched up two bricks that had been part of the tower wall, reusing them on her foe. She then dared to lob off another front leg segment. This time, Serukeeba felt the beast's mandibles hammer—and chip—one of her back spikes. In her entire life, no living thing had ever been able to do that. Even Álukoi spikes were not invincible.

The realization terrified her. As she fled, a dozen quills struck hard against her back. Scrambling to higher ground, Serukeeba thought the beast's newly severed front legs would slow its progress, at least uphill. Now her only intent was to escape and run back the way she had come, all the way to the Yimung village and beyond.

Ten paces and seconds from death, she led the monster around the tower and downhill. But without the use of its front legs, the balkotar slipped and stumbled when descending the slope. Serukeeba put thirty yards between herself and the beast.

"At last, a weakness!" she shouted.

"Now!" said Golármon.

Attacking the tower again, Serukeeba compelled the monster to follow. It ran back uphill at full speed. Three more tail slaps widened the crumbling doorway just enough for her to squeeze inside the tower, forcing the human defenders to act. Though terrified, they tried to discourage her with everything they had, including fire.

Risking a burn, Serukeeba lunged at them to snatch a torch away from the closest man taunting her with one. She felt the sickening squish of several humans crushed under her weight. Defeated, the others fled screaming, up a narrow spiral staircase. Serukeeba really wanted a second torch for dealing with the balkotar, and considered delving further into the structure for it.

"No time for that," said Golármon. "One will have to do. You must stay out in the open."

When the balkotar reached within ten paces, Serukeeba waved the torch to confound it. Yet just as *hyúlems* always assumed that no animal would dare steal their fire, so then did Serukeeba. With a lightning quick thrust of both mandibles, the beast snatched the torch away from her— by the burning end! Nothing the giant had done up to this point foretold such catlike speed. Or immunity to pain.

Now Serukeeba was glad she had not leaped on top of the thing to blind it. This balkotar would have killed her instantly. Yet she dared cut off a segmented leg joint from one of its middle legs. Again, she missed the death-grip of the mandibles by inches and a second. Somehow, she had to cripple the beast, so it could not hunt her down when she fled.

Hissing with pain, the monster oozed thick bubbling purple blood. All the hair on its main body stood up, making the beast appear even larger and more hideous. To confound her enemy, Serukeeba frantically circled and jumped aside, keeping beyond reach of the mandibles. She struggled to keep her mouth closed to the quills now being thrown at random. With each gallon of blood drained, the balkotar lost speed and energy. One by one, Serukeeba cut all of its legs down to bleeding stumps. Seeing this, the soldiers fled before she finished it off.

Serukeeba found three dead humans and spent an hour digging a shallow grave for them in the hard rubble, on the gentlest nearby slope. She tried to burn the balkotar, but it refused to catch fire. To warn future travelers, she gathered any unbroken lances amidst the tower ruins, propping the giant up by them right at the trail's fork. She then carved a remembrance of her duel into the nearest clean rock face, the tower's only undamaged portion of outer wall:

Serukeeba of Tiefenbo, an Álukoi
Here slew giant mountain balkotar, year 10,651
While searching for son Lorgámon.
May you read this in better times.
All justice be done.

By this ancient custom, she intended to show victory over a fierce enemy, and inspire friends, in the remote event that Álukois, Delfinians, or anyone able to read Álukop should ever find this place. Delving into the tower's remains, she claimed it for the night and consumed half its food stores. In the morning, she buried the rest in a cache, in case she had to return this way.

"If Kibak's party ever reaches here, what will they think?" mused Serukeeba. "How frustrated they will be to find only ruins, no enemy to fight or chase. No souvenirs. Nothing to destroy. Only clues to debate."

Yet barely 500 yards into this day's hike, Serukeeba felt her curse return. Baqwam and an advance party of ten scouts had appeared a half-mile back down the trail. All were on foot, dragging their ponies behind them. Screaming and waving their swords, they implored Serukeeba to wait for them. Sitting back on her haunches, she obliged for a few minutes. But on seeing their dismal pace, she vanished around a bend, closing her ear lids to their wailing.

"Alone and free is how I must find my son," she told herself.

All that day and the next, she tracked the fleeing tower guards, so that whenever a fork in the trail emerged, she knew which path led directly to Shohan. At one choice spot offering a stunning vista looking back west, Serukeeba eyed Baqwam's ten "riders," dots on a faraway slope now a full Álukoi day behind. Yet Kibak's whole party trailed only 500 yards behind them. At dusk, Serukeeba met a curious fork in the path. Most of the fleeing soldier's tracks led down the path to the right. Only one man had taken the even less used way up to the left. Unable to decide, Serukeeba camped at the fork for the night.

The next morning, she awoke under a foot of snow, yet a partly clear sky. Glad for both developments, she brushed the snow off the trail to carve a wagon-sized arrow sign. Serukeeba hoped this would point Kibak's group down the path to the right, if they ever got this far. Out of the silence, a deep bell began tolling about four times per minute, from somewhere high and distant to the east. It rang many times over the next several minutes.

"The tower guards must have signaled them," said Serukeeba. "Now I'll really have to fight my way into Shohan. Maybe Kibak and Baqwam were right. I may need help after all."

* * *

Lorgi's paws wiggled, as if he dreamt of running. His nostrils and ears twitched. His breathing grew stronger and deeper. Many audible grunts, whimpers and sighs escaped his closed mouth. His tail stretched, then suddenly whipped violently from side to side. The young monk assigned to watch him on this morning jumped to escape the weapon. Shocked, he stood against the wall, trembling. Breathing hard with his mouth wide open, he watched the "sign child" coming to life. As Lorgi drew a huge breath, the monk had to do the same. Both yawned and stretched their limbs. Finally opening his eyes, Lorgi sat up and smiled, greeting the monk with a cheerful *"Akúa. Éom Lorgi. Nómesang tum?"*

"He lives! He wakes! He speaks!" screamed the monk, bolting from the library. Not realizing that the Gral-Chaner was approaching, the monk accidentally tackled him in the hallway.

"Lorgi's recovery need not be my demise," laughed the Gral-Chaner, bruised yet overjoyed at the news.

"I am so sorry, master," gasped the monk. "I did not see—"

"Nor did I. Mortal sight is ever partial. I'll be fine. Now you may run. Get Wenji and Poto here at once. Then bring everyone."

"Lorgi wakes! He speaks!" the young man shouted joyously all the way down the hall, crashing into another monk entering it at the other end. By the time Lorgi staggered into the hall, everyone stood there, waiting to greet him.

"*Akúa...kéu?...vya?*" Lorgi mumbled sluggishly in his first language, looking at sixteen new smiling faces in the unfamiliar place. His ears twitched as he blinked his eyes and pawed his muzzle to help wake himself up.

"Lorgi!" cried Wenji. "Don't you ever do that to me again!" She lunged, grabbing him by the front of his neck. In spite of her care, she scraped both her arms as she embraced him. "Lorgi, my champion. You will be the death of me yet."

"What...where are we?" he stammered in slow Tuzanchim. "How did we get here?"

"How could you forget?" Wenji shook her head.

"Amnesia is to be expected after such trials," said the Gral-Chaner. "Full memory of his last ordeal may never return. Just be glad for his recovery and welcome him home."

"But he is so far from home," said Wenji.

"Not when among friends," said Poto. All the monks nodded.

"Wenji, who are all these smiling people and what can they want with us?" Lorgi demanded in more aggressive Tuzanchim. Several monks understood that language and grew anxious. Lorgi scrutinized them all, quickly sniffing the hands of each monk in turn. "At least they don't eat meat. They don't fight or steal. Maybe they really are friends."

"The best, Lorgi," said Wenji. "These are nice Shohaneze monks. I think most of them do not know Tuzanchim."

"A few of us do, just in case," said Poto.

"I think I forgot all of my Shohan words," burped Lorgi, inhaling a loaf of bread and a jug of water the instant Wenji handed these to him.

"All of our monks will gladly instruct him," said the Gral-Chaner.

"What's a monk?" asked Lorgi.

"They study heaven, nature, life. Ways to make the world better," said Wenji. "Like me, they have been praying for you to recover."

"How long was I asleep" asked Lorgi. "Is there more bread? Is there fruit or cheese too? Where are we? What time of day is it? What do they call this place? It feels high. How high? How much does it snow here? Is this everyone who lives here? What are all your names?"

Shaking her head, Wenji laughed. "One question at a time. First things first."

"Good," agreed Lorgi. "What's for lunch?"

"Better start his new life gently," warned the Gral-Chaner. "A monk's breakfast for now; a feast later. Perhaps tomorrow we can find a way for him to contribute, but today he should rest."

"I'm afraid to let him sleep," said Wenji.

"Of course you are," smiled the Gral-Chaner. "Today your task will be to keep him awake and engaged—yet out of mischief. Only you are qualified for this challenge."

"Since I met Lorgi, I've never been able to keep him out of trouble, though it has always served us well in the end," said Wenji.

Within minutes, Lorgi felt his normal boundless energy and curiosity return. Convincing Wenji to give him a tour of the whole monastery, he visited with all the monks in turn. Overjoyed to speak with him, none of them completed their work on this special day. All became instant friends with Lorgi, in spite of the language barrier. He learned all their names, particular skills and likes, and their schedule. His vocabulary in Esterlani, the language of Shohan, grew by the hour. Wenji's task seemed easy until Lorgi reached the monastery's Bell Pavilion.

Set just twenty paces northeast of the larger Shohan Pavilion, the Bell Pavilion had been situated in the ideal spot to achieve maximum resonance and echo. Linked to the larger pavilion by a short, covered walkway, this hexagonal structure also stood open to the wind, offering a stunning vista. Ten bells of mysterious alloys hung at eye level and seemed to fill the structure. From largest to smallest, they were tuned to C-C-G-C-E-G-Bb-C-D-E to align with the natural overtone series. Even the smallest, highest pitched of the bells weighed more than Wenji.

The Great Bell weighed five tons, more than all the rest put together, and took up half of the space in the pavilion's center. Its nine "children" circled it in divine order. With ideal conditions, the Great Bell could be heard many miles away and clear down to the river 4,000 feet below. Two large leather-tipped mallets begged for immediate use on all the smaller bells. Yet these could hardly distract Lorgi from the suspended log mallet designed for the Great Bell.

"Sweet!" cheered Lorgi, his eyes wide with delight.

"Lorgi, that is not for you to touch," scolded Wenji, as he reached for the log. "No."

"That's exactly what this is for," he giggled, pulling back the log in order to strike.

"No!"

"We should have tried this when we first got here, but we were both too tired and scared."

"No, Lorgi. I mean it."

"I'll just do a little one."

"No. Please," begged Wenji. "Stop and think about it. We are only guests here and must respect—"

As the log struck the great bell, Lorgi jumped away, with his ears momentarily pinned back, startled by its booming ring. "Great Snows!"

"What?" shouted Wenji, her hands over her ears.

"Have you ever heard anything so wondrous or fine? The tone just keeps ringing and ringing and ringing. It even makes the other bells hum. And I only gave it a baby tap."

"That was no baby tap," said Wenji. "You struck it hard, whether you realize it or not."

"Not hardly," giggled Lorgi. "But if you really hit it—"

"NO!" yelled Wenji. "I said no. For a good reason."

Yet with Lorgi holding the log and transfixed by the bell, she knew her words were useless. When the sound finally died away, Lorgi struck it again with more force. Instead of jumping back, Lorgi ran around the bells, first one way, then the other, to learn if that might change the sound. Satisfied, he sat back on his haunches and reached a forepaw within inches of the giant bell, trying to feel the sound.

Pressing her hands against her ears to save them from the intense volume, Wenji stood close beside Lorgi to shout at him. "Stop it! No more. You must respect our hosts. We are only visitors here…" she broke off, shaking her head and trying to sound angry, yet fighting back a smile.

"This has to be the grandest, biggest, bestest bell on the whole Continent!" exclaimed Lorgi, reaching to strike again.

"The bestest?" laughed Wenji.

"And now the loudest," cheered Lorgi, striking with unrestrained enthusiasm.

"Ouch! Stop! No more. Please, Lorgi."

"Come on Wenji. Have some fun for once."

"We are not supposed to…" she shook her head. "These are sacred bells, for religious purposes only."

"Here, Wenji. Use these little hammers," urged Lorgi, handing a pair of mallets to her. "They are not too heavy, even for you. You play all the small bells while I hit the big one."

"Lorgi!" she laughed. "You're just going to get us in trouble."

Like other monasteries, this one used its bells for specific rituals and signals, reserving its Great Bell for the most important of these. Enthralled with the giant toy, Lorgi kept striking it with gusto.

Responding to the emergency, every monk came running to the Bell Pavilion. Four then sprinted to the West Pavilion at the other end of the monastery, scanning the mountain trail for any sings of the Tuzanchim or Yimung bandits. Another four monks positioned themselves in the Shohan Pavilion, scanning the valley below for the king's men. The rest attended Lorgi, hard at work disturbing the peace.

Having sighted no cause for the alarm, all returned to the Bell Pavilion. Wenji screamed at Lorgi but could not be heard over the mighty bell. Several monks tried to get Lorgi's attention or induce him to stop. At the same time, others placed blankets over the hammer and the

Great Bell's crown, to at least mute the false alarm without dampening the dragon child's spirit.

"That will be heard at the guard tower to the west, if not all the way down to Shohan, even the Summer Palace!" warned Poto. "Now they will have to respond. What do we do then?"

"I am so very sorry," said Wenji. "I tried to stop him. But he's too young and knows no better."

"Why curtail such pure, harmless joy?" asked the Gral-Chaner, starting to laugh, himself. "Be honored, not sorry. And glad, all of you. The heavens speak through this child."

"What about the alarm signal?" asked Poto. "That is the volume and pacing Lorgi keeps striking. The king's men will assume the worst."

"As well they should," said the Gral-Chaner. "Lorgi brings great change, which no despot can tolerate."

"What if the Tuzanchim come this way?" asked Wenji.

"They have never reached up here, and we pray that they never will," said the Gral-Chaner. "Yimung bandits and the king's men have tried, demanding violence. But not today! Let us begin our feast. It may be the only way to distract Lorgi and spare the Great Bell, as well as our ears!"

End of Part II

25: Klimgu's Way

A fiery, late Autumn sunrise heralded Klimgu's invasion of Shohan. Gentle, rolling hills overflowed with grains, livestock, and an especially rich yield. And these were only the Wester-hills, the driest part of the vast kingdom. Each valley beyond promised greater bounty. Everywhere, countless ragged peasants bent over their fields, too busy harvesting to notice the Tuzanchim atop the highest hill. Klimgu found the distant human chatter, myriad bird calls and insects all made a calming spell, but guessed that few in his army heard such music.

"Uncover your heads," he ordered. "Sheath your weapons. We may not need them today. Make yourselves less conspicuous."

"Why?" asked a dozen captains.

"Listen and look," ordered Klimgu, waiting four deep breaths before saying more. "How many people can this valley feed? Think well, that you make a sharp guess."

"Twice our number," said one captain.

"Three times that," burped another.

"Four," yelled another.

"It's not an auction," said Twarejik. Most of the captains laughed.

Shaking his head, Klimgu looked comically disappointed. Pretending to scan the panorama for them, he smiled, tapping his left index finger to his temple. Those who knew him loved to see this behavior. It showed his confidence at its peak, and seemed to bring Klimgu great luck.

"Alright, five, ten, whatever," said the first captain. "So what?"

"This valley alone can feed a hundred thousand," boasted Klimgu.

None believed him. Twarejik laughed. Even Lutyam smiled.

"Who cares?" said the first captain. "We're just going to burn it all anyway, right?"

Klimgu frowned at him, shaking his head.

"No! We are better than that!" shouted Twarejik. Turning to Lutyam, he quietly asked, "Aren't we?"

"Interesting question," said Lutyam.

Klimgu locked eyes with Twarejik, leaned his head left and squinted at that captain. Looking again at Twarejik, Klimgu raised an eyebrow, rolled his eyes and turned his head back towards the main force waiting a half mile to the west. Twarejik nodded and obliged, reassigning that captain and his warriors to guarding the supply wagons. The new Vazuk had demoted the man without saying a word. Most who knew Klimgu admired such quiet economy.

"A brash fool, but you know he's right, my Vazuk," said Twarejik.

"On whom do we war?" asked Klimgu. "The land itself? The peasants who tend it? No. We seek the king."

"But they support him," said Twarejik. "Never mind Serukeeba. To flush out a monarch, you must destroy both land and lives."

"Not if we would keep the dragon's luck," said Klimgu. "Let the king earn the people's hatred, not us. Take only what we need from each place and ride on, until we finally reach Shohan's capitol, whatever it's called."

"Shondara," said Lutyam. "And then? What are your terms? What do you finally want? Take care, Vazuk Klimgu. Like people, empires that grow too large have a way of dying suddenly, or becoming hopelessly infirm."

"Always planning ahead, Lutyam," chuckled Klimgu. "Quick, blunt, fearless as a rock dragon."

"*Gánsi,* but dare you answer?" posed Lutyam. "Serukeeba will demand one when you meet again. She has a habit of squeezing them out of men. Consider now, while your ribs are intact."

"I already have. We seek Lorgi. Puchakta. And sufficient reparations to fund our...expedition."

"You mean invasion," said Lutyam. "What do you consider sufficient?"

"Our warriors must leave with honey in their mouths, or all Shohan will burn—dragons or not. You know only too well what Tuzanchim warriors are capable of."

"But what are *you* capable of?" demanded Lutyam, locking eyes with him and refusing to blink. "What are your terms?"

"There can be no peace until Lorgi rejoins us and Puchakta is turned to ashes. Serukeeba may have her own terms. I ride an icy, untried path between my own forces and those of Shohan. All your help is needed to avoid the worst bloodbath the Continent has yet seen."

"You have it on my word as a monk, but blood is inevitable."

* * *

The first walled city they reached threw open its gates the moment Klimgu arrived. To placate the invaders, terrified citizens offered many gifts, which he refused. Instead, he had them feed his army while the mayor showed him around. Giving a taste of Steppe justice, Klimgu ordered the city granary opened to feed the hungry, the jail emptied of political prisoners, and any held for minor offenses. But one man who seemed guilty of rape and another of corruption Klimgu had executed on the spot. Slaves were freed and their former owners put to work cleaning the streets. The Vazuk's edicts won many friends and few enemies. News of his bloodless conquest swept the Wester Hills faster than a wind-whipped prairie fire.

As Klimgu marched east, the land grew ever more crowded with towns and cities. Yet he met no resistance. Citizens either fled or welcomed the new overlord with gifts and fanfares. People began to ask Lutyam's question. None could say where Lorgi, Puchakta, or the king's fabled armies waited. Klimgu made steady progress towards the capitol, yet felt no closer to his goals. Finally he reached a city whose gates were slow to open for anyone. A delegation of twenty civic leaders marched out to negotiate, unsure whether to welcome or refuse the horde.

Impressed, Klimgu drafted his own delegation of equal number—making sure to include five Shohaneze from towns already under his control. Terrified but curious, the city leaders dared ask what life would be like under Tuzanchim rule. Even Klimgu's hand-picked captains bristled at the affront. Calming all with raised hands and a smile, Klimgu pressed the Tuzanchim limits of silence—four breaths. As if by magic, he kept both parties quiet for that long.

"Why should you join us?" he asked. Barely waiting for translation, he pressed on. "You live poorly under a king who bleeds you but cannot protect you. Peasants toil from dawn to dusk, weak from hunger, while the king's men squander labor's reward. Your streets carry filth and disease. Few of your people live long or well, most in misery. What law have you that is free of bribery?" Klimgu took a swift look back into the eyes of his own party, raising his left index finger to herald his next point. "You still have concubines, serfs and other slaves. Still allow hereditary rights, and hunger in the face of plenty. Yet you call *us* barbarians! Why should we include you?"

"Well said!" shouted an old man from the city delegation, awkwardly trying to nod like a Tuzanchim.

"Excuse us, but our council must vote on this," said another. "It is our way—or always has been until now."

"Do what you must, but before sundown," warned Klimgu.

"What if our council cannot accept your rule?" asked a less astute delegate.

"What?" gasped one of the city's own interpreters. "Do you really want that translated?"

The delegate nodded. After a quick debate amongst themselves, the interpreters did so.

"Slow learners, indeed," Klimgu shook his head. "Twarejik, why can none of these coin-counters remember their fathers? Enough talk. Prepare a classic siege, the way they do in the Castled Lands. Blood spilt here and now will spare a thousand times more later."

"Wait, they just don't understand," said Lutyam. "You must explain."

"I tried to reason with them," said Klimgu.

"Can't you try harder?" asked Lutyam.

"They can either take a generous offer or suffer the consequences of refusal. The Tuzanchim have always done what we must to keep our reputation. Even these dim, petty hens should know that." Glaring at them all, he signaled Twarejik.

"If you cannot surrender, we will take your city off the map, as if it had never existed," shouted Twarejik, scowling and shaking his head. Unlike Klimgu, he gave the translators plenty of time to finish. "We will not spare the smallest living thing, not even a kitten or a blade of grass. Wiser cities will learn from your death. They can grow and prosper in your place."

Excusing themselves to deliberate, the city leaders fled behind their walls. Within moments they witnessed a flurry of Tuzanchim industry.

The new Vazuk wanted to spare the city, but held his bluff so closely that even Twarejik failed to guess it. Not about to wait for sunset, he had warriors begin digging a series of trenches at regularly spaced intervals, all just beyond the range of anything that could be hurled or shot from the walls. Hundreds of tents sprang up, cooking fires were lit, and thousands of warriors rested as others stood alert to counter any sally the defenders might attempt. Carpenters marked four prized trees for use in building a siege engine. Porters harvested stones for its projectiles.

Estimating the invading force at more than 30,000 strong and infinitely better prepared than the city could ever be, its Council found nothing to argue about. An hour before sundown, the city threw open its gates with great fanfare. Thousands of citizens lined the streets, shouting in unison: "Welcome to Wenyasi." Not content to merely surrender, the city's hierarchy of bureaucrats and leading citizens competed for Klimgu's ear, offering diverse services to help the "new" Tuzanchim and "Emperor Vazuk" against the king of Shohan. Some in Klimgu's force spoke Esterlani, but none could match Lutyam for getting information.

"The citizens warn how the king vows to destroy any town that admits you, even the poorest village," said the monk. "He swears to hunt down and slaughter the last of you, too, etc., etc. No one I've met knows anything about his armies' real strength, where they wait, or their tactics."

"You were right, Klimgu!" cheered Twarejik. "All in our shadow must gamble and choose sides. What fool for a king do they have in Shohan?"

"Barbarians fighting barbarians," Lutyam muttered with a scowl.

"You push my tolerance hard as a rock dragon! Yet your work helps greatly, and could save many lives," Klimgu smiled. "Keep it up and you will be paid beyond dreams for it."

"My price is high," said Lutyam.

"And we all thought monks do not seek wealth," Klimgu laughed.

"Then for once, you are all actually correct. They seek grander, nobler things."

"Then what reward for your services?"

"You already know," said Lutyam. For a long silent moment the two stared at each other.

"Laskomia," Klimgu nodded.

Twarejik's eyes bulged. That his leader even voiced such an idea meant he was giving it serious thought. And anything a Vazuk said tended to become fact. "Are you well, Klimgu?"

"Never better, my friend."

* * *

At the banquet held in his honor, Klimgu aimed every word to win over the city's leaders, forcefully contrasting his own policies to those of the king. Most of them spoke of the myriad differences between Tuzanchim and Shohaneze ways. The more astute among the captains and scouts learned much about their new tenants that night, and even something about themselves. All went surprisingly well until the mayor showed Klimgu his office. Lutyam, Ganjaset and Twarejik went along. Pouring liquors for them, the mayor praised his city as translators raced to keep up with him. While the others listened, Klimgu gazed intently at a life-size portrait of Shohan's monarchs, dominating the far wall. Seeing this, the mayor hushed, Twarejik frowned, and Ganjaset squinted. Only Lutyam seemed amused.

"At last our foes appear, if only in a flat image," said Ganjaset.

"Very sorry, but with everything else, I forgot to dispose of the portrait," said the mayor, bowing and wringing his hands. "I will have it burned at once."

"No!" shouted Klimgu. "It has value."

"Such a great leader you are, not to be offended by the image of your enemies." The mayor bowed again.

"Stand up straight and stop flattering me!" ordered Klimgu. "I see but one enemy. Can you bring me the artist?"

"She is far away in another city, across the Great Ulian River. As you must know, all the bridges across it, clear down to Hangosha, have been destroyed. I am sorry."

"Only apologize for your own errors," said Klimgu, never taking his eyes off the picture. "Have you ever seen the king and queen yourself?"

"Once, briefly," said the mayor. "Of course I do not support them...anymore."

"How true are the images?"

"The king's is very flattering, as required. You would find him shorter, much wider, meaner and, well…ugly. Yet the queen's likeness is quite good. But no picture could even hint at her true beauty, her heart, or her many abilities."

"Tell me more of this queen," said Klimgu. "Starting with her name."

"Sayewin, but what can it matter?" Shohaneze law, as well as tradition, binds her forever to the king, though they despise each other. Cruel fate."

"We are Tuzanchim—mostly—building a new empire, not bound to old laws. We make our own fate, as the rock dragons say. I will meet this queen."

"Impossible." The mayor shook his head.

"I will find a way," said Klimgu, his eyes fixed on Sayewin's portrait.

"You can blink now, Klimgu," shouted Ganjaset, trying to break the spell.

"Suddenly you look like you just fell off your horse," said Twarejik, wrinkling his brow with concern. "Are you quite well, my Vazuk?"

"What you always ask when doubting my judgment," laughed Klimgu.

We can leave now," said Ganjaset, pushing them all to the door. Klimgu was the last to move. Ganjaset had to yank him out of the room. As the mayor and his aides led Klimgu and Twarejik to other offices, Lutyam turned back to catch a final glimpse of the picture. Scowling at him, Ganjaset hissed, "Stop smiling, Lutyam! Nothing funny here. Nothing a monk could understand, anyway."

"Think what you like," chuckled Lutyam.

* * *

Two days later, Klimgu began his march on Shondara, the capital of Shohan. He led an advance force of 25,000 warriors and 6,000 local partisans—Shohaneze rebelling against their own king. Many more volunteered, but Klimgu allowed only a very select group to bear arms: fit, unmarried men over the age of 20. Another 6,000 Shohaneze helped as porters, cooks, or advisors, and would be kept away from the fighting. Despite plenty of help, Klimgu found his progress maddeningly slow.

Many small but sheer mountains, dense forests, and churning rivers presented a daunting list of obstacles—the main reason the Tuzanchim had never been able to conquer Shohan. Morning fog and conflicting rumors about enemy armies also slowed the horde, forcing them to travel the same way as locals, via meandering ancient roads, bridges and causeways from town to town. Peasants usually vacated these on sighting the Tuzanchim. But often, bold or desperate ones asked to join the march. If those seemed fit, the captains found work for them. If not, the Tuzanchim gave them alms, wished them luck and sent them away.

In a few days the force reached a broad, shallow valley in the heart of Shohan. From its center rose a grand city, boasting walls rising thirty feet and looking as if they had just been white-washed. Before anyone else could offer Klimgu a map or explanation, Lutyam supplied both.

"Hangosha, first of the Three Pearls of Shohan, and its third largest city," said the monk. "Well over 100,000 people. Take it, and you will control everything east *and* north of here. About half of Shohan! The king cannot allow that. I see months or years of blood in this valley alone."

"What of the other two pearls?" asked Klimgu.

"Sangira lies a few days to the east, but across the mighty river," said Lutyam. "The capitol waits only a short day beyond that. Of course, the king will destroy Sangira's bridges before we reach them. You must build your own. It will cost many months and lives—even *without* an enemy. You can go no further until Spring."

"Unless we bypass Hangosha," agreed Klimgu. "To Sangira, like the Wind!"

The horde swept past the walled giant, as hateful eyes watched from all her towers. No warning signals or alarms came from the city. The passing horde met no resistance. Yet moments later, Hangosha burst into flames. Furious that someone had flouted his orders, Klimgu halted to seek the culprits. Countless screams issued from within the city, as flames shot up from every part of it.

"The gates are still closed and we rode no closer than a mile in passing," said Ganjaset. "We could not have burned it so fast, even putting a thousand warriors to the task."

"Those fires were lit all at once," said Lutyam. "Who would?"

"Puchakta!" yelled Twarejik. "To stain Klimgu. We must avenge this shame. At all cost."

"Yes, but not here," said Klimgu. "We see Puchakta's ugly hand at work, but he hides safely across the river. Probably by the king's side. Let us ride on the capitol with all speed."

Two days later they neared Sangira. A densely populated valley waited, framed by steep forested mountains. All level or gently sloping ground divided into fields of various crops, most ready to be harvested. Through the valley's center roared the mighty Ulian, cutting a gorge 200 feet deep, and nearly as wide. Klimgu and his force looked ahead east, as if following the water on its way to the sea. Near the valley's middle, two great bridges spanned the chasm. A thousand soldiers guarded the closer of these, while two round towers framed the other. Only a mile beyond lay Sangira, second of the Three Pearls and Shohan's second largest city. Yet just as the horde caught the sight, the whole valley began dissolving as fog rolled in from the west.

"Our first glimpse of the king's soldiers," said Ganjaset. "But now, even the land itself hides from us."

"No good," spat Twarejik. "We should backtrack to an easily defended place until the mist clears. Only a rock dragon can see in this muck."

"Smile," cheered Klimgu. "Can't you smell the salt? A grand omen."

"Blindness?" asked Twarejik.

"The Great Ocean herself, calling us to our goal! Serukeeba and Lorgi will be pleased. We camp here. At dawn, we fight."

26: Rendezvous

The morning after Lorgi's awakening, the monks discussed what he might contribute to the monastery. After one day, all knew his claws were too destructive for most chores. Ever striving to assign tasks well suited to each person, the Gral-Chaner asked Lorgi to try cutting a few stair steps into the mountainside for a new path to be made, giving him a sledgehammer and two chisels to start with. Eager to please, Lorgi attacked the project with vigor. Yet he soon found that his own claws worked better than human tools, especially when finishing an edge or keeping a cut straight. When the great bell sounded later, already he had carved seven perfect steps into the rock. This left all the claws on his forepaws spent. But he glowed with pride when the shocked monks came out to admire his work.

Adapting totally to the monastery, Lorgi woke with the monks every morning, labored furiously, and soon ate as much as all of them combined. In a week he gained thirty pounds and doubled his strength. For a child, he took great care with his claws and tail, yet scratched every floor he walked on. All knew the monastery garden and stores could not sustain his growing appetite indefinitely. One evening, as the Gral-Chaner and several monks were discussing this, a terrified soldier burst in, wide-eyed and shaking.

"Away! All must flee!" wheezed the man, gasping for air. "A terrible monster has slain the king's own. Ripped apart our stone tower like it were made of hay. The alpine trade route lies defenseless. Open to all manner of beasts and barbarians. The most demonic creature of them all marches this way. Slow but determined. Utterly invincible. Flee at once, or it will destroy you, too."

Nodding but smiling, the Gral-Chaner sat the guard down and called everyone into the great hall. "Poto, our best wine. Bring plenty. We all will be quite thirsty on this fateful night."

"What? Are you insane?" gasped the soldier. "Did you not hear me? A horrific beast comes, bent on destruction."

"No," said the Gral-Chaner. "Justice and hope, marching this way."

"If any of you understood, you would not be smiling," said the guard. "The king was right. Monasteries are for the mad. The thin mountain air has sapped your minds."

Seeing Lorgi and Wenji enter the hall, the soldier nearly fainted. Poto gave him water and a quick synopsis of the pair's tale, as the Gral-Chaner served his favorite wine. When each held a cup in his or her left hand—or forepaw—all raised them to eye level. The soldier appeared too shaken to manage his, so Poto helped him.

"Today we celebrate not one, but two miracles unfolding in our midst!" said the Gral-Chaner. "First, a mother and child finally will reunite after months of trials. Second, the long awaited fall of that...diseased soul...claiming to be the king of Shohan."

"That is what you dare to call our king?" gasped the soldier.

"I find it the gentlest, and so the least accurate reference to that deranged *entity*," answered the Gral-Chaner, locking eyes with the soldier.

"Well I call him the worst sick, evil, stinking, pox-boil, blubber hog-face!" shouted Lorgi, startling the man. "But Wenji has even better names for him. Lots of them. Right, Wenji?" He smiled at her, but she looked down and shook her head to discourage him.

"Please, speak no more of the king, anyone," begged the soldier. "He will take every life here—starting with mine—if he ever learns of this."

"No, because his time is over!" exclaimed the Gral-Chaner. "Many years have we prayed for this day. At long last, we can rejoice!"

"But I work for that diseased soul," gasped the soldier. "Look at my uniform, whatever is not covered in mud. I was a guard at the tower. What am I to do, disappear?"

"We can help with that," said Poto, holding out a set of monk's clothes. "Take a bath and throw that uniform into the fireplace. Time to grow. Transcend what shame it has brought you. Find peace. And while you are here, learn the ways of a monk."

"But I am sworn to the king."

"Who brings about his own demise, as foretold," said the Gral-Chaner. "Start a new life. You owe it to yourself."

Seeking to heal, Lorgi spun his pupils, sending the distraught guard and several monks into deep sleep. Knowing the man had seen his mother very recently, and grasping the Gral-Chaner's words, Lorgi ran outside to sniff the air and stare into the night. Wenji and two monks trailed after him, concerned that he might leave suddenly. Calming Lorgi and persuading him to return inside required extra food, wine, and many reassuring words from all, so that he—and therefore everyone else— could finally get some sleep.

* * *

Kibak halted at the last fork, kicking the snow. "Do we take the trail Serukeeba demands with her snow arrow, or where she invites with her own steps?"

"For your health, do what she asks," said Gurjik. "My ribs still hurt from when I did not."

"Obviously, she does not want to be followed," said Baqwam. "Nothing to debate here."

"I don't know," said Kibak, eying Baqwam, then Moshal. "Lorgi and his foes are still probably far away. Serukeeba may have picked up something important after drawing her sign, then had no time to return and erase it. Or else forgot. One must always adapt in war, not be a slave to plans or orders."

"War or not, take the most direct path," said Baqwam. "Where the arrow points and most of the soldiers fled. To our goal—Shohan and Lorgi. Waste no time here on Serukeeba's detour."

"But the other trail pulls me strongly," said Kibak. "No way to explain, just a dragon feeling I have about it."

"Your *dragon feeling* path is barely even a ghost, leading to nothing vital right now," said Baqwam, impatient. "Taking it may prove to be a costly delay, a mistake. The main path leads right down to northern Shohan. Our immediate goal. The fleeing soldiers' tracks prove that."

"My dragon sense has not failed me yet," assured Kibak. "I just know, as Lorgi says. Please humor me, and you will see."

"That's it?" Baqwam laughed. "A leader must be more persuasive than that. Especially one of your ambition."

"Now my ambitions ride away from leadership."

"What?" gasped Baqwam. "Now you had better explain."

"Only if you follow me," said Kibak.

"Very well," nodded Baqwam. "This will be a feast for my ears."

"Serukeeba took this way for good reason. If only I could persuade this stupid pony!"

Kibak cajoled, tugged, swore at, then slapped his pony, one that had brought the group to a halt many times. Still it refused to move. Some warriors guessed this was because the path led uphill, or appeared too little used. Sensing trouble, the other ponies balked at taking either path.

"Enough! Your time has come!" yelled Kibak, drawing his sword. "After all the treats I wasted on you."

"*Yahai!*" shouted Moshal, surprised by the commanding tone in his own voice. "Kibak, there must be another way."

"Let me try," said Baqwam, rubbing its muzzle and neck, cooing softly. Bribing it with apple slices, she got results. The other ponies turned, wanting to follow. Copying Baqwam's example, all her warriors bribed their animals and led them onto Kibak's path.

"*Gánsi*, Baqwam," said Moshal, smiling as he followed right behind her. "You taught us all a fine lesson today."

"*Gánsi* to you," Baqwam smiled back at him. "I like that you care enough to challenge a leader when it is important. Bold for a monk."

"*Gánsi* to both of you," said Kibak. "At last we are moving—on the right path."

"I hope so, or Serukeeba will be furious," said Baqwam, winking at Moshal. "Now, about those new ambitions of yours. Moshal and I demand to know."

"When we finally catch up with Serukeeba, and things calm down," said Kibak. "I don't have the fire or patience to explain twice."

* * *

Dawn found Lorgi waiting in the Shohan Pavilion, built to overlook the river valley. But at this hour, a sea of fog hid everything more than thirty yards below the monastery. Yet Lorgi kept staring down at the mist, worrying the monks. When the Great Bell sounded, he began to call out with a powerful new voice, somewhere between his fighting roar and a wolf's mournful howl. Despite the fog muffling it, his song reached everything from the mountain peaks to the thickest woods to the dark depths of the gorge. Unable to go about their chores during this phenomenon, everyone came to the pavilion. Lorgi would sound a call lasting about half a minute, wait as long, then sound it again, moving to a different spot each time. After an hour of this, his voice finally gave out. With drooped ears, he sat back on his haunches.

"We will all help, Lorgi," assured Wenji. "I promised to see you home, even if it kills me. Please come in for breakfast."

"I'll make your favorite dishes," said Poto.

Ignoring all of them, Lorgi sat gazing at the fog below.

"Let him alone," whispered the Gral-Chaner. "Leave him to his way."

"But he looks so miserable," murmured Wenji, looking sad herself.

"I know," nodded the Gral-Chaner. "We cannot help him just now."

Cold, random spurts of wind began to thin the shroud, exposing patches of the mountainsides below. Lorgi forced his spent, aching vocal chords to sound one last call. Defeated, he collapsed, limbs splayed out, ears drooping and eyelids half shut. Wenji sat down beside him.

Yet a moment later, a deep call from somewhere far below answered. Immediately, Lorgi shot up with eyes, ears and nose fully alert. Opening his mouth wide, he drew a huge breath, but had no voice left to respond. Frustrated, he paced back and forth in the pavilion, swishing his tail, inhaling through his nose and stretching his ears outward. With swollen eyes, he implored Wenji. All she could do was nod, promise to help, and assure Lorgi that his vocal cords would heal quickly. A minute later the distant call repeated, slightly closer. A haunting voice older than history, it inspired either fear or hope, but removed all other thoughts.

"Quick, someone ring the Great Bell, and hard!" said the Gral-Chaner. By now, everyone waited nearby, shivering in the cold. "Lorgi, you do that better than anyone."

"Are you sure?" Wenji and Poto asked together.

"The best thing for him, and everyone," said the Gral-Chaner. "We must answer that call promptly."

"What about Shohan, the alarm?" asked the former tower guard. As he spoke, the Great Bell began to toll, louder with each strike.

"Miracles herald the end of Shohan as we know it," said the Gral-Chaner, smiling. "Rejoice!"

"How can you be so happy about the end of Shohan?" asked the guard. "The Tuzanchim will invade. Or others. Probably both. Do you have any idea what that will mean?"

"Yes, also the end of the Tuzanchim as we have known them," cheered the Gral-Chaner. "Think on that, friend. There are far grander forces at work here than mortal greed, thank the Heavens."

"No disrespect, but I can only wish that were true." The guard shook his head.

"Poto, set lookouts in the West Pavilion to herald Serukeeba's arrival," said the Gral-Chaner. "All must meet at the gate when Serukeeba reaches it. Then we must celebrate."

"Another feast, our best wine, yes?" asked Poto, already running.

"You seem to do a lot of that," murmured the guard.

"Only the best on such a momentous day," shouted the Gral-Chaner.

"Have you no fear?" asked the guard.

"We have far more hope. Soon you will, too."

Half an hour later, two monks spotted Serukeeba far below, galloping up the trail's switchbacks. The monks redoubled their efforts to prepare a fitting welcome for the dragon prophesied to redeem Shohan. Before she reached the gate, all stood there waiting. Some took a moment for grooming, to make the best appearance. Others just stared, frozen in shock. All positioned themselves to guarantee a clear view.

"What force has Heaven brought to us?" asked Poto.

"Lorgi was not exaggerating after all," said Wenji.

"She must weigh over ten tons," said one monk.

"I would guess twelve," said another. "Maybe fifteen."

"Don't say that around my mother!" squeaked Lorgi.

"Only the main hall's ground floor can withstand her bulk," warned the Gral-Chaner. "Everything must take place there, or outdoors."

Serukeeba found the monastery's gate wide open in invitation. Eighteen smiling faces and pairs of shocked human eyes all met hers. Lorgi charged so hard that he crashed into her side, making both mother and son grunt. They rubbed muzzles and necks, while their ears fluttered and tails whipped back and forth, out of sheer joy. Álukoi eyes had no tear ducts, but all the humans shed loving tears for both of them. Lorgi had countless things to share, but no voice. A monk brought a large pot of strong herbal tea to sooth his vocal chords. Ever protective, Serukeeba would not let him drink until she had sampled the tea herself. Wenji spoke with her for two hours before Lorgi recovered his voice enough to join the conversation.

"Our banquet is ready in the main hall," announced Poto.

"Please follow me," the Gral-Chaner motioned for Serukeeba. "The best way to end a long journey. We understand that your people are also vegetarians."

Serukeeba twitched her ears and even arched her neck slightly back, overjoyed yet surprised. She knew Lorgi would have told them about some Álukoi ways. Yet she had never heard any humans outside of Tiefenbo refer to any non-humans as "people." Until now, she had only observed *hyúlems* using the word exclusively in reference to other *hyúlems*, with the assumption that only they were capable of language, culture, or "civilization." Serukeeba had never met people like these monks, and hoped they would have far more influence on Lorgi than the Tuzanchim.

At noon everyone joined at the table, eager to start the feast. Poto had made a supreme effort to include Lorgi's favorite dishes, in royal quantities. With nothing to go on but Lorgi's appetite and an estimate of his mother's size, the monks prepared enough for a hundred men. As everyone smiled at her, Serukeeba kept looking away to the entrance and the hallways, expecting many more guests to come. Then she realized this feast was just for the two Álukois and the humans already present. Lorgi beamed a cute, innocent smile to counter his mother's suspicious scowl.

"We'll discuss your dining habits later, Lorgámon of Tiefenbo."

"I didn't do anything wrong, mother."

Serukeeba spoke to him in Tuzanchim, so that at least some of the others could understand. "These are highland monks, living off their own labor at winter's dawn. How long did you expect them to keep stuffing you?"

"Just 'til you got here?" said Lorgi, trying to sound innocent.

"Very funny. Just look at it all. Enough to feed these people for a month if we were not here. Is this typical, or did you have extra big eyes for a feast today?"

"You should have seen him at the Summer Palace," said Wenji.

"Better I did not," laughed Serukeeba. "If only I had foreseen the sorcerer's plan, then we would never have disturbed any of these places, or all these people."

"The Tuzanchim Empire and the kingdom of Shohan urgently need disturbing," said the Gral-Chaner.

"Without Lorgi, I would be long dead and totally forgotten, as if I had never lived at all," said Wenji, looking up to Serukeeba with tears forming in her eyes. "Lorgi gave me a name!"

"He did *what*?" Serukeeba arched her neck, scowling at her son again.

"Don't cry, Wenji. Everything will be good now," said Lorgi. Turning to his mother, he whispered, "Told you she cries a lot."

"But for your journeys, the King of Shohan would continue unchallenged," said Wenji. "So many others would be waiting to suffer the same horrible fate he decreed for us. By foiling him, we may have weakened him and saved lives beyond our own. Time will tell."

Both Álukois drooped their ears, moved by Wenji's outpouring.

"Then I am proud, Lorgi, as your father must be." Beaming, Serukeeba glowed at her son.

"So you're not upset about my appetite, right?" asked Lorgi.

"You are starting to sound like Kibak," murmured Serukeeba. "That worries me."

Most of the conversation began in Tuzanchim, exchanging between the Gral-Chaner, Poto, the Álukois, and Wenji. The former guard and one other monk also understood, but the rest had to wait for translation. Serukeeba wanted to know all about the monastery and Lorgi's time there. But she had no interest in what most concerned everyone else: the fate of Shohan. Yet every few minutes, she caught the Gral-Chaner looking straight *into* her eyes, the way only an Álukoi seer could, as if to divine her very thoughts. When she held his eyes, he made her think about her role in bringing the Tuzanchim to Shohan.

Serukeeba looked away, unnerved and humbled at encountering such a powerful intellect. Knowing she would begin her return journey as soon as possible, the monks urgently grilled her about her homeland, her people and their ways, and especially about her ordeal crossing the

Continent. Skillful hands recorded every word the instant it had been translated. Three monks each drew up a separate map of her quest, to be combined later for the monastery archives. Her account inevitably sparked questions about Klimgu and the rebels, the Gran Vazuk, Satungke and Puchakta. No matter how brief, Serukeeba's answers always spawned more questions.

"What good can come from savage rebels?" asked the tower guard.

"Their leader slew a terrible sorcerer and his army," said Serukeeba. "In doing so, he also saved Lorgi's life, yet put him in danger repeatedly. What good may grow from them, I know not, but at least my village changed Klimgu for the better."

"How is that possible for a Tuzanchim?" asked the guard.

"Where do I begin?" laughed Serukeeba. "Manners, hygiene, conscience. His ideas on wealth, power, families, justice, happiness…all have changed. But he still has a long way to go."

"We all do," smiled the Gral-Chaner. "With your permission, we will make an imprint of your right forepaw." Two monks stood ready to do so.

"Why?" asked Serukeeba, suspicious.

"To preserve as a memento in honor of your visit here," said the Gral-Chaner, "But also to study for signs, to help direct our futures."

"I have no use for any type of prophecy or magic," huffed Serukeeba.

"Lorgi often says you make your own," noted Wenji. "He certainly brought luck to me."

"Just try it, mother. Paw prints are fun." Lorgi smiled. "Only good things can happen up here."

"Who told you that?" asked Serukeeba, scowling.

"We all did," said Poto, raising his hands to deflect her anger. "Lorgi had been in a coma for many days. Wenji was starving and despondent. Up to this very moment we have shielded both of them from any thoughts of the outside world, to help guard their fragile health."

"And I will thank you with something to help the monastery," said Serukeeba. "But please do not ask me to participate in any sort of divination."

"Come on, mother. Watch. I'll do one so you can see how fun it is. And it's art."

The monks immediately obliged, hoping Lorgi could persuade her. Serukeeba politely smiled, but only to humor her son. The instant Lorgi finished making his print, she grabbed both his forepaws and let out a frightful shriek.

"What have you done to your claws, child?"

"I carved a whole, entire new trail for the monastery. Want to see?"

"Later, *gánsi*."

"What's the matter now, mother?"

"You cannot travel without a good set of claws."

"Your claws look spent too, mother. So are your tail spikes. Even a few back spikes."

"I had to demolish a tower and fight the most gigantic balkotar on the Continent. But we are at peace now." Turning to the Gral-Chaner, she said, "It could take him a month to regrow them. I don't know what to do now."

"Stay, rest and share your wisdom," smiled the master. "You have lived long and traveled far. We can learn much from each other."

"Thank you for your kindness." Serukeeba nodded and went out to Lorgi's favorite spot for meditation, the Shohan Pavilion. Everyone began to trail after her.

"Stop," whispered the Gral-Chaner, signaling them all back into the main hall. "Leave her to think. We have plenty of work to do inside."

An hour later, he ventured out alone to speak with her. Silently, the human and the Álukoi met eyes for a long interval. Each knew the other had overcome trials and tragedies, faced death, and carried many responsibilities. Others looked to them for guidance. But what if these two needed guidance themselves? When each felt both were ready, each signaled an intent to speak. The Gral-Chaner drew a deep breath as Serukeeba twitched her ears.

"You have Lorgi back. What troubles you?" asked the master in a voice both gentle and insistent.

"I so love my son that I would do anything. Horrible deeds I only wish to forget, but..." Serukeeba halted.

"I understand," nodded the Gral-Chaner. "What matters most is that you are reunited. Among friends, in a place of healing and wisdom. Leave only when you know the time is right."

"Thank you. What terrible things will happen because of the rebels I helped? And especially how. I've become part of an avalanche that grows daily. It may engulf the whole Continent. What can I possibly tell Lorgi? You know he will ask me about everything before the night is over."

"If you have the power to see doom approaching, that lends you the power to change the outcome," said the Gral-Chaner.

"What can stop Klimgu's ambition? He sent what he called a 'most respectable scouting party' to assist me, but even more as a deception, while he invades Shohan by another route. He uses my son and his rival Puchakta for his excuse. I think we have all become unwitting pawns in his vast game. If I had not helped him..."

"You would not have found your son," finished the Gral-Chaner. "If the sorcerer had not stolen him away. If Klimgu had not found Lorgi and sped him to their Gran Vazuk. If that despot had not sold him to Shohan—along with Wenji. If the king of this land had been a human being. Has 'if' ever brought peace or solved a problem?"

"At least they brought two remarkable Laskomian monks, but only for their practical skills and cleverness, not for moral guidance. One of those *may* even reach here with that scouting party. He expressed a great desire to see a Shohaneze temple, before any Steppe warriors got to it."

"Then wait, so we can meet him together. Between all our thinkers here, we may inform your decisions."

"Why is this one named the Shohan Pavilion?" asked Serukeeba.

"It gives your first glimpse of that land below. Even amid royal horrors, countless good people live in Shohan. Many wonders await there. Perhaps the finest arts, most beautiful gardens, and longest running history on all the Continent. Magnificent rivers flowing east to the vast Sea of Esterlan, one of many sights worth every effort to reach."

"*Gánsi.* I mean thank you, but it won't work," laughed Serukeeba. "Yes, I feel terrible about the force I helped create. But my guilt will never include Shohan, after what they did to Lorgi and Wenji, and all that I have been told of their savage ways."

"You have only heard rumors from Shohan's enemy. The Shohaneze would give an equally cruel and false view of the Tuzanchim."

"That would be interesting."

"You must see for yourself to know the truth."

"*Gánsi* again, but no. Yet I respect you even more for trying. If not for Lorgi's spent claws, we would leave in the morning, just to get away from Shohan. Nothing could ever make me venture into that Hell."

"Then we monks have all misread the prophecy."

"No disrespect, but I rejected every form of it the day Lorgi began life. The oldest and most respected seer among my own people gave him the worst fortune. But I tell Lorgi we make our own luck. If only there were such a thing in this world."

"If not luck or faith, then in what can you finally believe?" asked the Gral-Chaner, frowning.

"Long eyes, sharp claws and unpredictable human nature," answered Serukeeba. "All else is wishful dreaming, if not lunacy."

At the opposite end of the courtyard, some sixty yards away, Lorgi sat on his haunches in the main hall's entrance. Serukeeba had been facing away from him and speaking to the Gral-Chaner in a quiet, sad voice. Yet with his "long ears," Lorgi heard it all. Wenji and the monks tried to comfort him as he relayed the private conversation, too distant and soft for human ears to pick up. Knowing it was against their ways to intrude, still the monks seized every word. With Lorgi's welfare at risk, they felt compelled to do so.

Everyone retreated from the doorway the instant Serukeeba turned to walk back to the main hall. Within fifteen minutes, they all retired for the night. The humans took to their rooms while Lorgi curled up beside his mother in the center of the Great Hall's floor. All slept deeply, exhausted from the day's events. Wenji and the monks had beautiful dreams of Álukois in an idyllic world. The Gral-Chaner dreamt of Shohan without a king. Lorgi adventured to exotic lands, where people were always friendly, fun-loving and ever putting on lavish banquets. But Serukeeba had nightmares about Klimgu's force being massacred in Shohan, or her own kind being terrorized by the Tierdragon of Monz.

* * *

Sunrise bathed the monastery in light, yet nothing stirred. No morning bell sounded. As on many other days at this time of year, fog drifted up from the valley below, yet stopped just short of the monastery. Finally stretching his limbs, Lorgi looked at his mother but decided he had better let her sleep.

Smelling smoke, he went to the kitchen, hoping to negotiate a pre-breakfast snack. Finding his favorite room cold and empty, Lorgi ventured outside to find the source. Just as he entered the courtyard, he saw an unknown hand raise a torch in the Bell Pavilion. Without thinking, Lorgi bolted towards it. As he charged, a dozen Shohaneze soldiers fled the structure. Wenji lay directly under the Great Bell, bound, gagged and vigorously shaking her head.

"Don't worry, I'll—"

A team of soldiers cut the ropes holding up the Great Bell, which crashed with a deafening ring, entombing the pair. All Lorgi could do was press his forepaws over Wenji's delicate human ears until the sound stopped. Total darkness and little air made both panic. Even with all his angry might, Lorgi still could not move the giant bell. He had fallen into a trap, despite Wenji's effort to warn him.

A score of soldiers quickly put up a timber barricade to the Great Hall's main door, to keep Lorgi's mother from escaping. Twice as many ran up to the building from every side, hurriedly nailing shut every window they could reach on the ground floor, as others barricaded doors. Two hundred more stood guard with swords and spears, surrounding the building. When all this had been completed, a hundred archers took aim at the hall's second and third story windows. Some of these nocked flaming arrows. The king's men intended to destroy everything—and make certain that no one survived.

Inside, the Gral-Chaner, Serukeeba and all but three of the monks conferred on the ground floor of the main hall. Two others lay unconscious upstairs. The unfortunate monk whose room was next to Wenji's had been killed by the soldiers in the course of her abduction. The former tower guard looked more terrified than anyone else.

"They mean to burn us alive in here," he screamed. "They must have 300 men."

"More than 500," said Serukeeba.

"We have no chance," cried the guard.

"Yes, we do!" said Serukeeba. "But first I must do serious damage somewhere to break out. Let me deal with those cowards outside. You must keep Lorgi safe and away from the fighting. He is just a baby—with no good claws. Where has he gone, now?"

"The king's men may know the prophecy," said the Gral-Chaner. "It is you they most want, but that won't stop them from destroying everyone and everything in their path. We must buy time while we find the best place for you to get out."

"They'll burn us all to death before then," moaned the former guard.

"This building was made to withstand fire—up to a point," said the Gral-Chaner. "Poto, did our foes think to cut off our water?"

"Not yet," he said.

"Good! Everyone up to the second floor, but stay back from the windows," ordered the Gral-Chaner. "Remember, fire can kill faster than arrows. Spend yours only when you have a clear, protected shot and no flames to put out."

All but Serukeeba and the Gral-Chaner ran upstairs, each carrying a bucket, bow and quiver of arrows.

"Where is my Lorgi?"

"They must have him; Wenji is missing, too," said the Gral-Chaner.

Outside, a commander shouted, and a volley of arrows pierced the windows, setting much of the interior ablaze. Serukeeba looked as terrified as everyone else.

"We have running water to most rooms, and have drilled many times for this day. But it gives us only minutes, at best. To the library, where the outer walls are thin. They will never guess that. Destroy whatever you need to break out; it will all burn, anyway."

"Are you sure there is no better way?" asked Serukeeba.

"Yes, I'm sure, but pray this room does not burn, too."

She found the window barricaded with a mountain of rocks and timbers. As she struggled to work through all of these, flaming arrows struck her back, followed up by sharp, iron-tipped spears that probed her hide for any weaknesses. By the time Serukeeba had broken free, a score of soldiers waited for her. Hot oil splashed over her, turning the Álukoi into a screaming, charging flame. When she rolled over to try and quell the fires, several spears found soft spots in her belly, plunging hard into her flesh. Burned and bleeding, she struggled to fight off all of those surrounding her at once. Sensing the end had finally come, she cried out, "Golármon!"

"No, it's Kibak!" yelled a distant voice.

Suddenly the attackers found themselves being cut down by Tuzanchim arrows. The Shohaneze had the advantage of cover, higher ground and greater numbers. But they were not prepared to fight off both their ancient enemy and a fully grown rock dragon at the same time. Within seconds, the king's men fled the way they had come. Chased down by Baqwam's warriors, most did not get far. Kibak took forty warriors into the Great Hall to quell the fires, but the Tuzanchim knew far more about starting them than putting them out. Before it was over, half of the grand structure had burned. To the monks' great relief, the library survived.

Fearing that Lorgi and Wenji had been lost, scouts ran out to track them. Serukeeba called them back. Though she had received serious injuries, she hobbled and sniffed her way to the Bell Pavilion, as Kibak and the Gral-Chaner followed right behind her. With a last, horrific effort, she overturned the Great Bell, then collapsed. Immediately Lorgi began to lick her wounds. Serukeeba's eyes widened in shock and her ears twitched when she saw Moshal holding a bloodied sword.

Laying on her side, wincing in pain, she asked: "What kind of day is this? Tuzanchim warriors saving Álukois and putting out fires at a temple, instead of pillaging it. If old Rokímba had predicted this, I'd have told her she'd lost her mind."

"You described your faith in the wide range of human nature," said the Gral-Chaner. "Can we now add hope to your list?"

"And luck," said Lorgi.

"Only if I can heal quickly, and stop Klimgu before it's too late."

"I am afraid the king of Shohan will be quite pleased to learn that he has hurt our dragon and flamed our monastery," sighed the Gral-Chaner.

"Take this—you've earned it," said Kibak, with a quick nod

thrusting his bag of gems at the master.

"*Gánsi*, noble warrior," said the Gral-Chaner, bowing to thank him. "Your generosity amazes us. But all the Continent's wealth cannot rebuild here without a large, highly skilled crew. We have but fourteen exhausted monks, only half still fit for work. Labor is what we need most urgently now. Perhaps you may need those gems later."

"Are you refusing our gift?" asked Kibak, looking offended.

"No, of course not!" snapped Lorgi, cocking his head and raising his ears, expecting Kibak to understand. "The Gral-Chaner is just trying to ask for your help."

All eyes darted between Lorgi, Kibak and the Gral-Chaner. Serukeeba looked as worried as everyone else. Moshal practically stepped between the two men.

"We humbly ask a favor in its place, that all may benefit," said the Gral-Chaner. "It will take us monks weeks just to clear away the rubble. But the Tuzanchim are famously efficient at...dismantling structures of all kinds. Could you stay a week and accomplish that for us?"

"We can start in an hour and be done by tomorrow night," offered Baqwam, eying Kibak and Moshal.

"I can help," cheered Lorgi. "Sounds like fun."

"No," wheezed Serukeeba. "They want to be able to save part of it. Starting the day after tomorrow, you can help with rebuilding, for learning *and* fun. I will hunt the king of Shohan to avenge what he did to you and all of us."

"You sound like an old warrior," said Baqwam. "But is that what you really want?"

"Leave Shohan to Klimgu," said the Gral-Chaner. "Your fight is over. Spend time with Lorgi. Rest. Recover. You have many wounds."

"None more than a few inches deep." Serukeeba lied. "Thanks to my son, those will heal tomorrow. I must strike Shohan before they can prepare for me. If the king's forces are half as numerous as everyone says, they will massacre Klimgu unless I draw them away first."

"With our scouting party at your side," said Baqwam. "You needed us today."

"I'm coming too," shouted Lorgi.

"No," said Serukeeba. "I need you all to stay here and rebuild this temple. Guard it until I return."

"It will be done," said Kibak.

"But most of our group will follow you, for the day you need us again," said Baqwam. "The king's men won't bother this place with a mighty rock dragon menacing the heart of Shohan. Yet the closer one gets to a king, the more violence one must expect. It will be too dangerous, even for you, great Serukeeba."

"As for my esteemed friend Klimgu," sighed Kibak, "his fate is his choice, not yours, mine, or anyone else's. Not even for Sun, Moon or Wind to decide. Like Lorgi, he will carve his own trail entirely, from beginning to end."

27: Blood of Shohan

Outside, a cold, steady rain pelted Shondara. Inside the Winter Palace, the king slumped on his throne, pouting and grinding his teeth. He had not slept since learning of Puchakta's sudden fall—one day before the late Vazuk's heir himself arrived, with only five retainers, all exhausted and in tatters. Each night brought fresh reports of Klimgu gobbling up more land and winning over more peasants. Working at all hours, royal scholars, advisors and generals weighed every shred of fact or rumor about the invaders the moment it arrived.

The king still held vast resources and armies ten times the number of his foe's. But half of his forces had been garrisoned far to the south, guarding the realm's southern borders. Even resorting to a forced march, they still would need weeks to reach Shondara. Without a miracle, the Tuzanchim would get there first. A unique cascade of events now demanded that *this* king of Shohan consider the most shameful, the impossible and the unspeakable: fleeing the capitol to keep his monarchy intact.

On this afternoon a score of advisors and the king's usual entourage joined him in the royal chambers. Here sat the same men and women Lorgi had dubbed the "smiley-mouths" at the Summer Palace less than two months earlier. Now even Lorgi would have trouble recognizing some of them. All appeared fearful, thin, tired and suddenly older. None smiled or laughed about anything. Instead, they focused every word and act on survival. With no choice but to stand or fall with their king, they gambled their lives as well as their fortunes, knowing the Tuzanchim had not lost a war in more than a century.

"A courier from the north, Your Majesties," shouted a stout, 10-year-old page. Inspired by what he guessed about the message, the boy modeled his delivery after the arena announcer.

"First bring us news from the west or the south," growled the king. "Infinitely more vital. Be quick, boy."

"Those messengers have yet to arrive, Your Majesty," said the page.

"Don't bother us until they do."

"You had best hear this one now, Your M—"

"Before you tell everyone first, you gossiping rodent?" snarled the king.

"Leave him alone!" snapped the queen, glaring at the husband she had never wanted. "Arguing wastes time."

Protocol required all to wait for the king or queen to summon them before entering, and to excuse them before leaving. The court of Shohan was not known for efficiency. Yet this haggard messenger could not wait hours or days for the king to finally grow curious and summon him, only to be punished for not reporting urgent news sooner. Bravely stomping into the royal chambers, he bowed and cleared his throat. Aching to speak, he still dared not do so until they acknowledged him in some way, if only with a threat or an insult.

"What is it?" barked the king. "Speak! Don't keep us waiting."

"The tower guarding the northern mountain road has been attacked," shouted the man, with all the speed and clarity he could deliver.

"What?" yelled the king, standing up.

"Attacked and defeated. I am sorry to have to tell you, Your Majesties."

"How can that be? My tower holds the ultimate defense in the most forbidding terrain."

"No more, Your Highness. A monster more terrible than your own has won. There is no longer any tower or guardian to speak of."

"Destroyed the tower?" asked the queen, shaking her head in disbelief.

"Only the foundation remains—more or less," said the messenger. "According to the surviving tower guards."

"I cannot believe this," hissed the king. "What of my great giant *balukta* that guarded it?"

"Dismembered, gutted and set high with lances. A sort of beastly hunting trophy. Only that grizzly sign watches the road now, like a giant scarecrow."

The king sat back down in his throne, crushed by the loss. "The finest, most terrible creature on all the Continent. Twenty years it has guarded the pass. Gentle to his handlers, yet once turned back a whole

Yimung army. I can't believe this."

"Who could possibly go to such suicidal extremes?" asked the queen.

"A monster reclaiming territory, hunting an ancient foe...or perhaps one searching for her young?" guessed the courier.

"A simple beast would only kill and move on," said the queen. "Such labor after a battle implies hatred and purpose. Thinking like a human. But why the elaborate ritual?"

"Perhaps as a warning or other signal," said the messenger.

"What of my worthless tower guards?" asked the king. Immediately he raised a hand and shook his head. "Never mind. Stupid question."

"Yet a rare flash of humanity, when the king of Shohan admits error!" said the queen, smiling at the courier. Squinting at her king, she added, "Maybe we can learn from our mistakes, after all?"

"You will regret those words by sunset, Queen Sayewin," growled the king, pouring himself another cup of wine.

"That won't help," she said. "What of this shrewd creature, mightier than the king's own?"

"A fearsome, bejeweled rock monster with a hide of stone, utterly immune to projectiles of any kind," said the courier, focusing only on the queen. "It looks to weigh twelve tons or more, yet proceeds with calm focus and efficiency, even in blizzards and hail storms."

"Another enemy to add to the king's list," sighed the queen.

Suddenly recalling Lorgi's warning, everyone in the room eyed each other with new dread. Murmuring rapidly amongst themselves, they ignored the king as he sulked and ground his teeth. Before addressing the king or his advisors, Queen Sayewin waved the page away, lest the boy hear any more bad news with which to alarm the palace staff. Yet a minute later he returned, looking more determined than ever.

"Yes?" asked the queen.

"A messenger with news from the west, Your Majesties," shouted the page.

"Hurry up with it, you scheming piglet!" growled the king. When the breathless man entered, the king shouted, "Give your full report at once."

"The invaders approach Sangira," said the messenger. "Where our vastly superior forces wait, ready to crush them in a decisive battle. Your marshal swears that he will not allow the Tuzanchim to cross the Ulian River or touch Sangira. He has every confidence."

"Did he say how he plans to keep such a noble oath?" asked the king.

"By outnumbering the Steppe savages better than four to one, and taking full advantage of local terrain and weather."

"Our fathers heard the same assurances," muttered the king. "Just before the Tuzanchim routed them."

"Your marshal also said that he will be using new battle techniques that he has been developing for some time. Novel methods for both his infantry and cavalry. As yet untested in live battle, but offering complete surprise. He says that what the Tuzanchim have never faced, they will prove too slow to comprehend, in time to save themselves."

"Well! This is glad news indeed." The king beamed. "What are these new methods?"

"I know not. The marshal would only say that he looks forward to explaining everything to Your Majesties—and only to Your Majesties—in fine detail, after his victory. We more than equal them in cavalry, and employ many times their number of foot soldiers."

"Good," hummed the king.

"One moment," said the queen, her eyes wide with alarm. "I did not know that the Tuzanchim used *any* foot soldiers. Explain."

"Until now, that has always been true, Your Majesty," said the courier. "But these new Tuzanchim also bring a well-armed peasant militia, which they train daily. It has slowed their march, but swelled their ranks with every dawn."

"Now they steal even the people from me!" shrieked the king. "And time itself. The sooner we bloody our foe, the better."

"Perhaps you are right, my king," sighed the queen. "May tomorrow bring the sun and better news."

But it rained. Late the next morning, the page trumpeted "urgent report from the north."

"We will be the judge of that, thank you," said the queen. After studying the king, who appeared to suffer from a hangover, she whispered "return in an hour," and waved the boy away. But the page stood firm, his eyes urging her to summon the courier bearing that news. "Very well. Send him in."

"I bring hard tidings from what was the Summer Palace, Your Majesties," gasped the man, drenched and shivering, yet parched and breathless after a hard ride.

"What now?" barked the king, shaking his head. "It has been closed for nearly a month already. Only a fool would disturb our vital business at a time like this. Leave us."

"Only a fool declines news carried with such effort," said the queen, motioning for the courier to stay. While the king and advisors sat quietly ignoring the man's suffering, the queen had servants bring him bread, tea, and a coat. "What of the Summer Palace?"

"It has been...er, confiscated?" said the messenger.

"But the Tuzanchim mass in the west," said the king. "Who would bother the Summer Palace, especially now?"

All eyes fixed on the messenger, already guessing his answer.

"You also have a potent new enemy to the north," said the man, forgetting to properly address the king as "Your Majesty."

Ordinarily, the slight would bring swift punishment, but everyone was too consumed with dread to care. A few feet back and to the side, the page stood frozen, soaking up as much news as possible before the king or queen thought to order him out of the room. The boy's statue technique usually made him invisible, and so privy to many of the most private and shocking words aired in the throne room. Often, other members of the palace staff, from high-ranking officials down to servants, paid him for juicy bits of information—a dangerous practice for all involved.

"Con-, continue," stuttered the king, swallowing and looking to the floor.

"An exotic wonder, a massive rock beast out of the mountains came down and stormed the Summer Palace. She has proved utterly immune to all weaponry, far more powerful than any beast known, and clever beyond kings." The man's own eyes bulged as he put a hand to his mouth. Bowing, he said, "Forgive me, Your Majesty."

"We will be the judge of all that," said the queen, fighting back a smile. She pressed the king's hand firmly against the arm rest of his throne to help focus him. "Just give us your full report, that we may quickly use it for the good of Shohan."

"The exotic speaks, long and loud, calling herself *Sedukeepa,* or *Sirkeeba,* or *Seyukeeva,* depending on which peasant you ask. She knows no fear, not even of fire. Too wily for traps. Too monstrous for knights, no matter their number. When pressed, she fights like ten lions, yet eats like a monk—a giant one."

"She?" smiled the queen.

"Yes, Your Majesty."

"Kind messenger, tell all you know of this mighty she-dragon. Enemy or not, she fascinates me."

"Gentle and kind to the innocent, hungry and dispossessed, who rally to her. They steer her safely around every possible snare or ambush the king's men set. She has strange healing powers, and the most god-like acute senses. Her following multiplies by the hour. A queen among beasts."

"A fine bedtime tale for children, with no business in Shohan!" growled the king.

"Oh, but she has deadly business, Your Majesty," warned the courier. "As mother of the rock dragon child that Satungke purchased for you. Mother of he whom you imprisoned in your zoo and starved. Mother of he whom you threw into the arena, against the advice of your own queen, astrologer and physician. Mother of he who slew your fiercest war dogs, he who—"

"Enough, already!" yelled the king, scowling at the man.

"Speak of the present, dear courier," said the queen. "What does the mother beast undertake now?"

"Revenge for every danger and every affront to her innocent son and his friend, the Lady Wenji."

"That scrawny, scheming concubine?" gasped the king. "I had so hoped we were rid of her."

"Beware, Your Majesty," said the messenger. "Lady Wenji allies with the stone dragon realm, where the child monster is a great noble: Gamon, Lord of Tiefenbo. Friends call him *Lorgi,* and his kind the *Alukyu* or

Alkoyi or *Akuloi*, again according to which peasants you ask. Both Lady Wenji and Lord Gamon are becoming legend among the masses."

"Roasting a few hundred peasants will put a stop to that!"

"Know that the mother beast has demolished your entire arena, the dungeons, and the zoo."

"What?" gasped both monarchs at once.

"Yes," nodded the messenger. "And though an herbivore, the dragon mother delights in slaying her foes. Beware, as she also possesses intellect far beyond local cap—"

"Stop," snapped the queen, cutting him off. "Please. Give us facts, not fabrications."

"Destroy the arena?" huffed the king. "Ridiculous. Impossible."

"Impossible or not, it has been done. With heroic efficiency. The arena no longer exists," stated the courier. "By whatever means, you will learn that my words are true."

Shaking his head, the king shot up and began pacing back and forth to help himself think. "Impossible. Nothing could do that. Explain."

"She did not act alone, Your Majesty."

"Who would help such a monster?" demanded the king.

"Five hundred Tuzanchim—and a few peasants."

"How many peasants?" the queen dared to ask.

"Actually, most of them," stammered the courier. "Following the dragon queen onto the palace grounds, they looted it, with infinite joy and vigor. Now they use the broken arena for a rock quarry to build new granaries, homes and roads—under the direction of the Tuzanchim who organized them."

"Granaries, homes and roads? Nonsense!" barked the king. "Why would anyone do that?"

"Because we would not," sighed the queen, looking sadly at the floor and slowly shaking her head. "They shame us."

A collective gasp went up from everyone in the room. The king collapsed in his chair. His advisors grew pale, nauseous and nearly as terrified as the victims they had once put into the arena. The muscles on their necks and backs knotted up. Their joints audibly cracked and popped from the tension. All looked to their monarchs, then to each other, pleading to be rescued from the nightmare. Knowing the time had finally come to answer for their deeds, most found themselves unable to speak. They could not know which to fear more: the Tuzanchim, a clever monster seeking revenge, or the suddenly emboldened peasants. Those who dared to consider the choices found the Tuzanchim to be the most survivable option.

"I begged you to spare Wenji and the dragon child from your arena," said the queen. "I warned you about Satungke, the Yimung, and especially Puchakta. Like so many other things. But you were always too proud and foolish to hear me."

"What of my 500 palace guards?" demanded the king, ignoring her.

"Killed, captured, or deserted, of course," said the courier, looking to both monarchs. "They…attempted a valiant defense—brief as it was."

"How brief?" asked the queen.

"What does it matter?" asked the king.

"I am sorry to bring such hard news," bowed the messenger. "Please let me spare you any further details."

"No," the queen shot back. "Tell all, so that we learn from it. What about the defense?"

"The mother beast needed only minutes to shatter the gates. The whole palace fell in just a few more."

"A few *minutes*?" gasped the king. "Did the Tuzanchim or the beast leave anything standing afterwards?"

"Well, yes. Of course."

"And? Out with it," shouted the queen.

The courier swallowed. "In truth they have begun…to make what might be considered…improvements?"

"Whose messenger are you, mine or the enemy's!" yelled the king, signaling guards to arrest him. They hesitated, looking to the queen.

"Have your wine and a nap. Let me handle this," said the queen, raising a hand for calm. She felt this courier enjoyed giving bad news, despite his portrayal of grave concern. Perhaps he *'leaned to the west'* like many other Shohaneze, especially the less fortunate, who suddenly preferred Klimgu to their own king. Even if that were so, the queen still needed to hear the man out. "Since the mother dragon owns a voice and a purpose, does she also have terms?"

"Hard terms, Your Majesty." Eyeing the floor, the courier shook his head, hoping no one would ask.

"And those are?" prodded the queen. "Out with it, man!"

"Yes, Your Majesty. The demolition of any other arenas and any *baluktas* that still exist."

"Reasonable, given the circumstances," said the queen, nodding at the king. She had never been able to influence him, yet never stopped trying.

"The beast has nearly accomplished that already," said the king. "Maybe we can buy the brute off after all."

"No, Your Majesty," said the courier. "The mother dragon also demands the immediate and permanent release of all slaves and political prisoners, an end to polygamy, and the head of every man responsible for putting her son and Lady Wenji into the arena, including he who had it built in the first place. She wants blood."

The king grimaced, swallowed and shook his head. "We must find her first."

"She swears to hunt them all down, claiming she and her son can recall the face, voice and scent of every person they have ever met. Only when all her terms are met will she end her rampage and leave Shohan."

"Impossible," screamed the king. He shot up again to pace the room. "If I can gather all my forces in one place, I will destroy the Tuzanchim, their dragon and any peasants foolish enough to have aided them. We must stall our foes until my southern armies arrive." Turning to his physician, the king ordered, "find some way to poison the rock dragons. How, I don't care. Quickly, regardless of cost."

"What?" shrieked the queen. "Madness!"

"We must destroy one of our foes before dealing with the other," said the king.

"Not that way," moaned the queen. "Yes, enemies ally against you. Yet you still discount their resolve and abilities, having such poverty of your own."

"Stop needling me!"

"Stop…everything!"

Shaking her head, Queen Sayewin stormed out of the room, drafting the page, another messenger, and whatever guards and servants crossed her path. By the time she reached her private chambers, she had gathered forty people, few with high rank but all very skilled and desperate to help save Shohan. Motioning for silence, she took a deep breath and closed her eyes to weigh several deadly gambles.

28: The Battle of Sangira

On the chosen morning, a chilled, ever dripping mist buried the fields across the river northeast of Sangira. Local partisans allied with the Tuzanchim warned of myriad clumps of woods, ponds, hedges, fences, huts and storage sheds cluttering the landscape, collectively hiding thousands of the king's soldiers. Somewhere amongst it all, on the most advantageous ground, waited the main force. But this early, anything beyond ten paces vanished in the fog. The great mist held back any sense of time, space, and the human urge to war. It also devoured sound, gave all things the same watery aspect and made noses run but unable to detect anything beyond a lance's reach.

"Worse than yesterday," said Klimgu. "Is this typical for the season?"

"Yes. Gets thicker as you near the sea," answered Tonche, a short stocky Shohaneze with a bland face. A bitter enemy of the king, he had quickly evolved into the partisans' leader. Twarejik started calling him "captain" so the rest of the horde did as well, earning Tonche that rank.

"Does the fog ever lift on a day like this?" asked Klimgu.

"One can never predict," Tonche shrugged. "Usually, at least partly."

"When?"

"Midday or early afternoon, most days this time of year. But it always returns a few hours later. By dusk sometimes you can barely see your own hands."

"A terrible omen. Forget it, Klimgu," said Twarejik. "Fight only when and where we choose. Far more to lose than gain here. Leave this place to sleep in its mist. Wait for the sun or Serukeeba."

"To reach the king, we must cross the Ulian at Sangira's bridges," said Klimgu. "Our enemy must stop us here, with or without the advantage of fog. Tuzanchim have never been slaves to weather or terrain. We will adapt. And prevail."

"Scouts can do nothing in this soup. We will lose many if we engage," warned Ganjaset. "I vote with Twarejik."

"If we avoid battle today, we will have to spend far more blood later," said Klimgu. "Our foe must answer for the atrocities at Hangosha.

Honor demands revenge, with Tuzanchim speed."

"Waste upon waste," said Lutyam. "We already hold the Wester Hills. From here we can easily maintain control over all of Shohan north of the Ulian."

"He said *We*—twice!" cheered Klimgu. "At last, Lutyam the Grumpy joins our horde!"

"I meant you, Vazuk Klimgu," snapped the monk, irritated. "Your actions have swelled your strength and appeal, while draining the king's."

"We must keep up our momentum," said Chotzan, eyeing others for support. "Attack."

"If asked, I would vote with you too," said Tonche, nodding like a warrior. "Fog hampers the king's men too, and many hail from places far to the south, nearly as foreign to this area as are you."

"*Gánsi*," said Klimgu. "Know that your vote is much needed, however you cast it."

"Puchakta may have taught our enemy how to fight," said Twarejik.

"If he has learned himself," said Klimgu. "We can only know by warring on them. I say, launch our original plan but modify during the battle. Do we fight today?"

Half the captains nodded, but few with confidence. Such a tepid response screamed for more debate, or a formal *accounter's vote*, but Klimgu had no patience for either. With a firm nod, he exercised a Vazuk's prerogative. "May the luck of the rock dragons smile upon us— and the sun when we have open fields on which to ride."

Klimgu grouped his attack force into five quivers of 5,000 warriors each, to be led by Twarejik, Chotzan, Ganjaset, Ortung and himself. From atop the middle of three hills, in the most easily defended position available, Tonche commanded 8,000 select partisans marching with the Tuzanchim as foot soldiers. They would guard the horde's base camp and line of retreat. Eight thousand more stood ready as couriers, doctors, porters, horse tenders, and engineers, while providing intelligence on local terrain and the ways of the king's army. The whole invading force took up position on and between those three hills in a north-south line.

From first light until late morning, more than a hundred scouts ventured into the mist. Despite their best efforts, and help from local partisans riding with them, many became lost. Some never returned. The captains grumbled about fog as an ill omen. A few suggested burning it away with a massive fire. Others proposed riding back to pillage towns or cities having clear weather. Klimgu politely listened but vetoed such ideas. By the time he had persuaded a majority to vote for battle, about an hour before noon, the sun showed glimpses of itself. The locals foresaw partial clearing through midafternoon.

With Tonche's help, Ganjaset drew a map in the dirt. Though determined not to have a repeat of Lake Gabriska, he found himself in a worse predicament now. Every report from returning scouts was only a blind guess. Many conflicted wildly on enemy numbers, locations, and distances. Fifteen scouts vanished. Just as many came back with nothing to report—other than becoming hopelessly lost. With all eyes upon him, Ganjaset squinted and shook his head when his time came to speak.

"Out with it!" demanded Klimgu.

"It's no good, any of it," said Ganjaset.

"Give it to us anyway," urged Klimgu.

"It reeks of a trap," said Ganjaset. "Leave this place. Do not battle today."

"Never take it upon yourself to decide for us. I wish Kibak were here."

"He could do no better!" yelled Ganjaset.

"Than what?" asked Klimgu, with outstretched hands. "Tell us something, Ganjaset!"

"Fine. Here is what I have. We know a thick, north-south infantry line waits, part way between our hills and their two bridges to the west. They may number 5,000 or 25,000. Near their middle sits a small clump of woods, packed with archers. The whole line is braced to repulse any cavalry charge with pikes, bows, and a wall of huge, interlocking shields. A second or even a third line may wait in reserve behind them. Who can even guess in this mush? We had best go around them."

"We will," said Klimgu.

"Somewhere to the east and north of that line are three more small patches of woods, packed with archers. We must avoid those."

"We will," said Klimgu. "Good work. Do you have more?"

"Beyond, a long double line of Shohaneze cavalry stretches between the river to the south and forested hills to the north. They may number only 10,000 or three times that. Again, reserve lines may wait behind them. We cannot know without sun."

"We destroy their cavalry first," said Klimgu. "Then take the bridges. Deal with their remaining archers and foot soldiers last, as needed. We shall see."

"I have more," snapped Ganjaset. "As for the two bridges, 5,000 to 10,000 infantry and as many cavalry wait by the closer one," said Ganjaset. "Only a few hundred guard the further bridge, yet it is also protected by two stone towers, one at each end. We have no idea what lurks beyond, south of the river. Local rumors put enemy strength at well over 100,000."

Afraid of interrupting Ganjaset again, Klimgu held his breath, motioning the others for silence.

"That is all I have," finished Ganjaset, scowling.

"At last, the king shows his hand!" cheered Klimgu, smiling. "*Gánsi,* my friend. Your reconnaissance astounds me. Well shot, indeed."

"*Gánsi,* but no, my Vazuk," said Ganjaset. "Some was gathered too early this morning. All distances are blind guesses. Any of those groups could have traveled far by now. A clever foe may move his pieces to confuse us. Not even a dragon can give what you need here."

"They offer up so many foot soldiers for slaughter, to make up for lean cavalry," said Twarejik. "Either they expect to stop us with that ground line or go around it into their trap."

"We should oblige them," said Klimgu.

"Forget the ground soldiers," urged Chotzan. "Put our whole force in the middle. Theirs will be too divided to hold us."

"Too bad we don't have forces on both sides of the river to start with," said Ganjaset.

"Yes, but it is the opposite side that we need," said Klimgu.

"Fog still gives the enemy long advantage on either side," said Twarejik.

"Long!" shouted Klimgu, slapping his own head. "Shohaneze longbows only reach 400 yards, to our 600. Why didn't I think of that before? Ortung, Chotzan and Twarejik will take your groups around their infantry line to form your own leading northeast. Chotzan will go the farthest, get behind their cavalry, then turn south. Ortung will turn sooner. But first…"

"Don't smile at me like that," Twarejik grimaced. He knew Klimgu had something especially dangerous in mind for him.

"Twarejik, take your group into their trap, as bait for our own. Stop only when you reach the river or an enemy line. If you can take a bridge, sweet! But not vital. Ganjaset and I will pummel the ground line so hard they may think our entire horde faces them there. If we can break it, we will meet you by the river. If not, we also will go around it. Use what fog remains to help panic our foe. Let them think we ride everywhere at once. Grand luck to all!"

"What about our partisans?" asked Ganjaset.

"Keep them guarding our hills," said Twarejik. "If the fog lifts, they can monitor the battle and relay whatever we need. Make them feel useful with less risk. But if the enemy wants one of our hills, they will have to fight their own people for it."

The leaders began to chuckle.

"No. We must steer the enemy away from our new allies," scolded Klimgu.

"We cannot keep our partisans out of battle completely and still keep them as allies," argued Chotzan. "All must sacrifice to know victory, however small their part in it may be."

"All will. None will be small," said Klimgu. "Battles never go as planned. Courage, speed and cunning are really the only advantages we have ever had. On with it. *Hatok!*"

Twarejik, Chotzan and Ortung led their groups away, as Ganjaset and Klimgu positioned their warriors in a long, double line. Silently they began to inch forward, reaching within about 600 yards of the enemy. When a few scouts found the 400-yard mark the hard way, both sides began firing. By then, Klimgu's three other generals had already led their groups around two small hills to the northeast, while Twarejik turned south. At first, the Shohaneze infantry line seemed to take heavy losses, judging by the screams and moans of the fallen.

Just as these terrible sounds began, drums tried to drown them out with a thunderous ostinato, growing steadily louder and closer. Klimgu struggled to listen only for that signal, to learn its meaning. Dismounting, he pressed his left ear hard against the ground. Countless heavy footsteps marched to the drums' rhythm. The Tuzanchim had always expected infantry to either stand fast, retreat, or panic and scatter, all of which would prove fatal in any weather but fog. They never considered that enemy foot soldiers might advance under fire.

Yet the Shohaneze determined to make effective use of their infantry against the Steppe warriors. They advanced about 200 yards and began cutting down the surprised Tuzanchim with their next volley. Several arrows missed Klimgu by inches. Immediately he pulled his line back, out of range, but the Shohaneze kept advancing. Their experiment began to repeat itself.

Ganjaset's quiver had already lost 300 warriors and many horses, plus considerable ground. In the confusion, he unintentionally pulled his line further back than Klimgu, up onto the low barren hill from which he had started this morning. Klimgu kept his line on flat ground between that one and the middle of his original three hills, now occupied by his partisans.

Suddenly, part of the Shohaneze force began ascending that hill. Terrified, yet determined, the partisans threw everything they had down on the king's men, to repulse the advance. Sweating profusely, Klimgu feared he had led his entire army into a disaster beyond any scale that his generals could imagine. Despite great victories at Uxanda and the Near Valley—which he credited mostly to Serukeeba—Klimgu had never recovered from Lake Gabriska.

* * *

Twarejik led his group around and then to the south in a quick, silent trot. Unable to even guess at his new position, he brought his force to a halt. In spite of the fog's damping effects, Twarejik plainly heard strange noises ahead to his right. Unlike the Tuzanchim, the Shohaneze boldly announced their presence with drums, to give signals among their forces. That could prove to be either an advantage or a mistake in the mist. Their sound carried farther than anything else. Only a minute later and a dozen yards closer, Twarejik also heard the tortured cries of a nearby battle in progress.

He wondered if anyone expected him so soon, so near, or at all. Had he missed the "trap" altogether? Klimgu had asked him to make for the river and the nearest bridge. But an unsuspecting enemy line ahead to his right could not be ignored. Twarejik would break it open for Klimgu, on his way to carrying out his original orders. Unlike the stricter commands of most armies on the Continent, Tuzanchim orders could be taken more as guidelines, as long as departing from them achieved worthy goals. With the fog, Twarejik seemed to be west and north of where he should be by now. Yet the deviation gave him a chance to cripple the infantry line.

The Shohaneze line consisted of thousands of longbows, protected by a double row of lances, swords and heavy shields, all to counter the Tuzanchim forces just west of them. For maximum effect, the infantry had to leave their back side unprotected, expecting nothing behind them until later in the battle. Just as the fog thinned to a bright haze, Twarejik's group fell upon the Shohaneze infantry line, shattering it. Once Klimgu and Ganjaset heard sword combat, they charged. Within minutes, half the infantry lay dead on the field.

Despite history and legend, the rest threw down their weapons, begging for mercy. Never before had the Tuzanchim stopped in mid-battle to accept prisoners. In past wars, they rarely took any, even after a battle had ended, earning their barbarous image, known throughout the Continent. But this new Rebel-Vazuk refused to waste anything. To both humiliate his foes and bolster his local allies, Klimgu made the infantry surrender to his Shohaneze partisans.

* * *

Ortung led his quiver behind Chotzan's in a long arch northeast around the hills. Before reaching the north-most patch of woods known to be infested with archers, Ortung turned his group south, aiming for the bridge with the towers, emerging from a rapidly dispersing fog. Expecting a challenge at any moment, he had his group ride in a loose, vague configuration. Suddenly a far more concentrated line of 16,000 Shohaneze heavy cavalry charged at them from the east. This line sought to broadside Ortung or push him into what had been the infantry line. Instantly, Ortung's group contracted into an ever-shifting mass, feigning a southwest retreat. They deliberately slowed, luring the Shohaneze cavalry into bow range.

The classic Tuzanchim "withdraw" began to take its toll, as Ortung's group slowly fanned out. Every few minutes they reduced their pace to allow the tiring Shohaneze to keep within firing range. Though greatly outnumbered, Ortung's warriors never doubted success with a method they had used for generations. Once his seemingly haphazard bunch reached near the river and the towers, it split into two groups. One rode east along the river as the other moved west. Learning from deadly error, the surviving Shohaneze cavalry declined to pursue either group.

* * *

From one of the towers on the riverbank, the Shohaneze general presiding over the battle let out a desperate cry. He had just ordered all his reserves, some 8,000 cavalry and 12,000 infantry waiting south of the river, to cross the bridges and engage the enemy. Only then could he see the whole field emerge from the retreating fog. While the main Shohaneze cavalry line chased one bunch of Tuzanchim, now dispersing, a second group of Tuzanchim followed behind, rapidly closing in on the cavalry. A third, larger group charged in from the west, having destroyed the main infantry line.

* * *

Chotzan's group helped Ortung's finish the main cavalry line. Ganjaset captured the reserve infantry almost as soon as they crossed the bridge. Twarejik dealt with the reserve cavalry.

Before turning back west toward the first bridge, Klimgu discovered another clump of woods stuffed with archers. Impatient to end the struggle, he sent a messenger to offer them surrender. In the roaring confusion of battle, the archers did not understand. Out of fear more than duty, they shot down the rider and his horse. Enraged, Klimgu let his group surround the strand of woods, set it ablaze and slay every man that emerged from it, even if they threw down their weapons and begged for mercy. Moments later, every clump of woods hiding archers met the same fate.

From his perch in the tower, the Shohaneze general saw the battle's terrible endgame. His surviving cavalry fled. All that remained of his huge army seemed to be the 150 tower guards. Even if he escaped the Tuzanchim, the general knew the king would have him executed for such a colossal failure. Only minutes after giving his last order, the general stood on the tower wall's edge. Calling out, he waved his arms vigorously to draw attention. Once he had it, he threw himself down, striking the rocks of the riverbank.

Most of the tower guards plunged into the river, knowing that they would drown in the cold, swift current even before reaching the cataracts a mile downstream. Only a handful tried to surrender, flinging open the gates to the bridge and kneeling on the ground to await whatever fate the Tuzanchim chose for them. Several angry warriors leapt from their horses with swords drawn, but Klimgu stopped them with a resounding "*Yahai*," ending the horrific battle. Twelve thousand prisoners set to work burying the dead. Klimgu's army had lost 3,000, with triple that number wounded. The Shohaneze army had utterly dissolved.

* * *

All knew Shohan's king could still muster an army to defend Shondara, and that two huge armies were marching north to rally there. But those were weeks away, and the king's best had already fallen at Sangira. For now, very little stood between Klimgu and the capitol. The king and his court would have to flee hundreds of miles south before making another stand, with less experienced forces and no time to plan. Each battle would become less of a challenge for the Tuzanchim.

In his heart, Klimgu feared the aftermath of an easy conquest. For him, like most Tuzanchim, war remained second nature. Without enemies to fight, he did not know how he and his force—tiny as it was by eastern standards—could manage in this vast and complex new territory. But for the fog, Klimgu and his horde already might be far closer to the capitol and the terrifying mysteries of peace.

"What troubles you, my Vazuk?" asked Twarejik.

"I wonder what Serukeeba would think," said Klimgu. "Maybe the land owns itself, after all, and we are no more than fleas tickling its skin when we fight over it."

"You have won a great victory; Shohan will be yours!" cheered his friend.

"For a while," murmured Klimgu.

Only three hours past noon, the fog returned, diluting the myriad pools of blood and muffling the cries of the dying. Within an hour it reclaimed all the land.

29: Of Counsels and Parleys

A tired, exasperated Vazuk held court at his new temporary headquarters, Sangira's town hall, joined by Chotzan, Ganjaset, Lutyam, and Tonche. Twelve captains, the city's mayor and his staff assisted him. Klimgu tried to work with the local system, but whenever things got too frustrating, he resorted to blunt Tuzanchim ways. Just as he called a well-earned midday break, envoys from the kingdoms of Pechon and Zanchor burst in, frantic to see him at once. Both had ridden hard from Shondara the instant news of Klimgu's victory had reached them. Arguing with the mayor's bailiffs and each other, they fought for the first audience with the conqueror. Amused, he invited both to speak at the same time. Both tried to flatter Klimgu while discrediting each other.

"But I must confer with you in private," wheezed the Pechon envoy.

"My report holds far more urgency," crowed the Zanchor envoy.

"If only Serukeeba could witness this," he laughed. Pointing to the envoys, he asked the mayor, "Have you a quiet place to calm these pestering hens?"

"Our city jail?" guessed the mayor, a stout, balding man.

Klimgu grinned with a nod.

"Done," said the mayor, signaling his bailiffs. Awkwardly, he tried nodding like a Tuzanchim.

"*Gánsi*," said Klimgu.

The mayor looked puzzled.

"*Thank you* in Lorgi's tongue, dragon-speak. Quicker, more song-like than the Tuzanchim word, *tekursedim*, so we stole it."

"Taking words is a good thing," said the mayor. "Take all the words you like from Shohan."

"Already our spy returns," yelled a scout, running into the hall.

"So soon?" said Klimgu, surprised. "Show Natiqua in the instant she is ready."

"How can that old woman ride like a young warrior?" asked Ganjaset, starting to squint.

"By playing both sides at once," said Klimgu. "Don't frown, Ganjaset. Natiqua always brings truth and luck—despite her conflicting liaisons."

Seizing Klimgu's arm and his eyes, Ganjaset warned, "We must finally know where her heart rides, before going any further. Now it is critical."

"That may be a mystery even to her, being half Shohaneze. One need not be even part Tuzanchim—or human—to ride with us. If only Serukeeba were here, to sense Natiqua's heart, and so many other things."

"Please...use my private office for such important council," said the mayor, gesturing to an adjoining room. Bowing, he stepped back.

"*Gánsi*, again," nodded Klimgu. "Your hospitality matches the best. You should ride far in life, and do great things."

"*Gánsi*, said the mayor, trying to nod like a warrior, yet bowing like a Shohaneze. "*Gánsi.*"

"Tonche, Lutyam, Ganjaset, Chotzan, join me. No others unless Twarejik shows," said Klimgu.

The mayor turned to leave, certain he had no place at a conqueror's meeting. But Klimgu signaled Chotzan with just his eyes. Instantly, Chotzan grabbed the mayor by the arm and yanked him into the office. Jostled but honored, the mayor smiled, managing to nod like a real Tuzanchim.

"While we await our spy, what of those scheming chickens, the envoys?" asked Klimgu.

"The kingdom of Pechon has long coveted part of Shohan, as does Zanchor," said Tonche. "Everyone knows this. See how they wasted no time in abandoning the king for a winner."

"Vultures," huffed Ganjaset. "Reject their envoys."

"Tolerating them implies weakness, begging war," said Chotzan. "Throw them out. Let them sweat in ignorance."

"A bold and noble gesture, but both kingdoms wield large, efficient armies, and use them often," said Tonche. "Together, they could easily drive you out of Shohan."

The Tuzanchim seated around the table bristled. The two Shohaneze present did not blink, yet looked to Klimgu for direction.

"They try crude gambits like this regularly," said the mayor.

"Let Twarejik deal with the envoys," laughed Chotzan. "His penalty for being late. He has a way with irksome people."

A knock at the door halted discussion.

Natiqua entered, dressed like a royal Shohaneze courier, yet wearing Tuzanchim boots. Her left ear was red from pressing it against the door, yet she asked, "What do you debate?" When none answered, she smiled. "No harm. I have tasty news, my Vazuk!"

"You always do," said Klimgu. Chotzan and Lutyam smiled and nodded. Tonche and the mayor kept still. Ganjaset put on a stone face.

"Your demands come to life," she said. "At first, panic, looting and fires swept the capitol. But Queen Sayewin has restored order, and with almost no blood! She opens the granaries, ends slavery and polygamy, forgives debts, and brings justice. Having arrested Puchakta, she hunts Satungke.

"Puchakta!" cheered the Tuzanchim in the room, demanding wine to celebrate.

"Don't gallop on ice!" shouted Natiqua. "All the Ulian's bridges are destroyed, except what you hold at Sangira. And though weeks away, two armies march north to challenge us—in a pincers movement. What force remains in this region musters in the capitol."

"Good," said Chotzan. "We can finish them in one blow."

"Not so." Pulling a tiny notebook from her sleeve, Natiqua opened it to review a long list. "They have considerable resources, both military and intellectual. Shondara will not be easy. The queen stands ready to talk—or fight like a rock dragon!"

"At last, a respectable foe," said Klimgu. "But my dear wily Natiqua, how did you accomplish all this?"

"I didn't," said Natiqua. "Thank the king of Shohan. Died from a poison he made his doctor brew for the dragons. I had no part in any of that madness."

"But you certainly know who did," pried Lutyam.

"It hardly matters now." She smiled, giving a slow, subtle nod. "The king bred fear and hatred far and wide across his realm. A wonder he lived this long. None spoke a word of him after his death. No bells, no mourners, not even a peasant's candle."

"Shohan has never been ruled by a queen," said Tonche. "She won't last a day."

"Two, and the people adore her," said Natiqua. "Most of our success in Shohan has been due to a common enemy—the king. With him gone, all is changed."

While others tried to guess the spy's allegiance, Klimgu focused on Tonche.

"The people like anyone opposed to the king," answered Tonche. The mayor agreed.

"Klimgu's first real political competition?" prodded Lutyam. Klimgu scowled at him.

"The Queen says that Shohan has suffered long without a good leader," said Natiqua.

"But what good can she do?" asked Tonche. "The court, the nobles, the army won't support her. She has no heirs, and may not be able to produce any. She may be dead already. Other kingdoms will devour what remains of Shohan, if the horde does not."

"She has potent allies at court and in the army," said Natiqua. "Sharp as swords, she has learned to speak flawless Tuzanchim and figures math in her head quick as arrows."

"Sounds like you," huffed Ganjaset, narrowing his eyelids.

"Stop glaring at me," said Natiqua. "The Queen need not be our enemy."

"Which *our* do you mean?" demanded Ganjaset.

Motioning for calm, Klimgu asked, "What sort of person is this Queen? How does she think?"

"She asked the very same about you!" shouted the spy. "In truth, you fit each other perfectly, each excelling where the other struggles. She copies your ways, determined to learn from you. She asks for a truce, saying war is a waste. A tragic, foolish waste."

"I did not journey all this way to war on a decent ruler," said Klimgu.

"Try explaining that to your captains," said Lutyam.

Ignoring him, Klimgu asked, "Natiqua, tell me more about this Queen Sayewin. Everything. Describe her voice."

"Sweet or powerful, as needed," said the spy. "Beware. It could melt you."

"Her likeness seems to have done that already," muttered Ganjaset.

"I will meet this Queen," said Klimgu. "It may be productive."

"She said the same about you!" gasped Natiqua.

"How convenient," huffed Ganjaset.

"Consider her position," said Lutyam. "High time to negotiate."

"Chotzan?" asked Klimgu.

"We must meet at some point," he answered. "The sooner the better for all."

"I could arrange it," offered Natiqua.

"Send our best courier at once," ordered Klimgu. "We have a truce."

"No. The queen requires me to deliver your reply," nodded the spy, standing up to leave.

"You are tired and old for such a hard ride," scolded Klimgu.

"Not yet," shouted Natiqua. "Challenge revives me, and the Queen wants her answer tonight!"

"Then may your ride be grand," said Klimgu. "For my health, I have learned not to question the powers of older women." Amid a round of chuckles and nods, Natiqua whirled out of the room.

"Have her tailed by a respectable escort, at least 500," said Klimgu. Immediately Chotzan relayed orders to scouts waiting outside.

The door burst open with Twarejik. "Klimgu, did you stay up all night again?"

"What? Oh. Yes, in a way. Friends, we reach a curious fork in the trail. I need quiet to think."

"Rest on it. You look like you just drank too much Laskomian ale," said Twarejik.

Nodding, Klimgu stumbled out of the room. Turning to the others, Twarejik said, "He was fine last night. What hit him today?"

"A spy with honeyed words," said Ganjaset. "You have acquired dragon sight, Twarejik. Maybe just in time."

"For being late, you must deal with squabbling chickens," said Chotzan, slapping him on the back, then signaling guards to bring the envoys. "Lutyam and Tonche can assist, to the limits of human patience.

Do whatever you think is best. Use your new dragon powers."

"And see me the instant you are rid of the envoys," said Ganjaset. "I must tend to our Vazuk before he does something fatally beyond foolish."

With a sour nod and a grunt, Twarejik summoned the envoys. Repulsed by their chatter, he had them put in separate rooms while he shared a flask of wine and snacks with Tonche, Lutyam and the mayor. Not to be rushed, he took time to get their views on the health of Klimgu and his government. An hour later, Twarejik called the Pechon envoy into the mayor's office, drafting all three drinking companions for his advisors and translators.

"Tell Pechon's king that we claim all of Shohan, no more and no less," said Twarejik. "Whoever trespasses here becomes our enemy, forfeiting their own lands. If you need blood, fight Zanchor or others. But why war when you can trade in peace with us?"

"How do we know you will not seek to conquer Pechon?" asked the envoy.

"Are we enemies?"

"Well… no," said the envoy.

"We only conquer the lands of enemies. We trade with friends. Shall we be friends?"

"Yes, we will be your friends," agreed the envoy.

The moment that man left, Twarejik offered the same to Zanchor's envoy.

Afterwards, Lutyam frowned. "How can you expect anyone to swallow that?"

"I wanted both to leave quickly, with insults for souvenirs," laughed Twarejik, slapping the monk on the back. "What do you think?"

Lutyam smiled and nodded, but had no intention of sharing his thoughts. Like Serukeeba, he could not decide if Twarejik was simple, clever—or a mixture of both.

* * *

Serukeeba made slow progress on roads shadowing the Princess River down to the coast. She discouraged people from joining her, until they began warning of ambushes and traps waiting along the way. Each day her following doubled, becoming a horde of its own. The people and the king's men saw her as clairvoyant, magical and invincible. Overnight, such rumors became legend. When people actually met Serukeeba, they found her far too small for some of the deeds ascribed to her.

So many garrisons, traps and obstacles waited on the coast that she chose the sea over spilling any more blood on land. Reaching the mouth of the mighty Ulian, she forged upriver along increasingly rugged shores. Crossing it entailed swimming more than two miles down a raging torrent before she could gain the southern bank. To finally reach Shondara, she had to scale the steep, twisted gorge cut by the Ulian, trudging over densely wooded hills, then flat, intensely cultivated land under a slowly dissipating mist.

Despite traversing one of the Continent's most crowded areas, Serukeeba met no one, owing to the terrors of war. She stood up to her full height to glimpse the spires of Shondara. Smoke rising from many places told her that Klimgu had arrived first—and broken his promise. For that, she would have to kill him. For all she knew, Serukeeba had failed to prevent a bloodbath. Reaching the edge of an open field, she studied several hundred cavalry practicing. They rode like Tuzanchim, but smelled and sounded like Shohaneze. Confused, Serukeeba hid herself among a stand of trees to study them further.

Klimgu and a tiny scouting party halted at the opposite end of the same field.

"They ride too well. Puchakta must have trained them," said Chotzan. "But they are only about 400."

"And we are only twelve," quipped Lutyam.

"Puchakta's remnants must ride among them," said Ganjaset. "What if the queen made him a general instead of a prisoner? We should not blindly trust Natiqua, nor be here like this, naked, without force."

"Of course, we should not be here at all," added Lutyam.

"Pretend we are traders who lost our way in the fog," said Klimgu. "Let Tonche speak for us. But if we find the chance to negotiate—"

"Then do it properly, in front of an army," said Ganjaset. "This is suicide. They will just throw us in a dungeon and sell tickets to our executions, laughing the whole time. The Shohaneze do not ransom prisoners like in the Castled Lands."

"I wager all on the honorable Queen that Natiqua described," said Klimgu.

"We may know soon enough," said Chotzan. "Twelve riders on that rise to the left."

"Excellent. That will be the Queen's delegation, numbered to match our own," cheered Klimgu.

"Or an idiot's trap," warned Ganjaset.

* * *

Seeing Klimgu's delegation, the queen and a dozen knights turned to ride toward them. But her lead knight begged her to wait while he had the cavalry encircle the foreigners.

"No," ordered Queen Sayewin. "We will bring grace, dignity and an equal number, just as Klimgu did before every city he claimed. Our challenge now is to win over the conquerors. By persuasion, not force. We must greet them with all possible civility."

"Greeting barbarians as equals would pain any monarch," said the knight. "What good can follow that?"

"Peace, if Natiqua's magic has had any effect on Klimgu," said Sayewin. "He holds the power of a hundred kings. We must all listen and observe, for the good of Shohan. Make his scouts relax, so that they reveal things useful to us. They seek the same of us, certainly more clever than they like to appear."

"Such a strange, motley delegation, if one can even call it that," said the lead knight dismissively, as the groups approached.

"Stars! Why does he have to be so...?" gasped Queen Sayewin, staring at Klimgu with her mouth open. Once their eyes met, even at a distance, neither could look away. Something long repressed suddenly gripped both of them. While the rulers gazed into each other's dazed, hopeful eyes, their delegations looked on in horror.

"Be so what, my Queen?' asked her lead knight.

For a moment, Sayewin held her breath. "Far more than Natiqua had warned. It will make negotiating even harder."

"More what, my Queen?"

In the next moment, the groups met.

"We are traders, my lady," Tonche bowed, as if to address a lady of rank at court, but not a queen. Because Sayewin never wore her crown while riding, all had to excuse Tonche's pretended ignorance. "We bring fine things from Sangira and points further west."

"Much further west, I would say," laughed the Queen, pointing to Lutyam, the only Caucasian in the group. Smiling at Klimgu, she asked, "Traders? What trade requires twelve nervous men for a single wagon?"

"Good things, vital and…useful things," Klimgu stammered in broken Esterlani, too awkward not to be sincere. For days he only had been able to think about Sayewin, having firmly etched her image and words in his mind. He had lost sleep, forgotten many important things and not heard his advisors. Abruptly dropping pretense, he spoke in Tuzanchim. "The first mayor was quite right. No portrait could ever do your beauty and honor justice."

"*Gánsi* for such kind and flattering words," said Sayewin, in flawless Tuzanchim, also nodding like one. Natiqua had taught her queen well, and kept her informed during Lorgi's days at the Summer Palace. Surprised expressions told all that the spy's work now could bear fruit.

Sayewin and Klimgu held each other's eyes and smiled, alarming everyone in both delegations. Ganjaset and the lead knight sounded unhappy grunts, while frowning and nodding to each other in agreement. All but Lutyam struggled to adjust to the incredible development, frantic eyes darting between the love-struck enemy rulers.

Finally rousing herself, Sayewin asked, "What important and useful things?"

"Maps, gifts and an honorable proposal," said Klimgu.

"Maps and a proposal—for carving up Shohan?" she asked. "Or do you still pretend to be lost?"

"No, Great Queen. I have just found a treasure that few dare dream of," said Klimgu. "Your very presence transforms everything."

"*Gánsi*, again," said Sayewin, nodding like a Tuzanchim. "I could offer you the same flattery. But what good can grow here? Our peoples have always been enemies. How can we change that?"

"People always war over land, but never keep it long. Maybe the land owns itself after all. My enemies are mostly dead or in irons. I am done fighting. Now I seek friends." Giving a hand signal, Klimgu and all in his group dismounted, a Tuzanchim sign of peace. Immediately the queen made her delegation do the same.

"Then you are both courageous and wise, Vazuk Klimgu," said Sayewin. "In spite of everything, I am honored to meet you."

"The honor is mine, as you are the bravest and wisest and…" Klimgu halted before stumbling over his words, trying to bow like a Shohaneze. "I did not set out to conquer this land. I only swore an oath to amend wrongs. We drove one evil from power, then chased another all the way here, in search of two innocents sold against their will."

"All that is long known to me," said Sayewin. "But what now? What happens to Shohan? What are your terms? In the end, what do you finally want, Klimgu, if you really are done fighting?"

Klimgu's eyes darted between Sayewin and Lutyam, as the monk's question assailed him yet again. This time, he felt compelled to answer. "What I have taken already is too much to govern. I want no more and will swear to it. But I need your help. And you need mine, against enemies to the south."

"Noble gestures, but first I must tame some fools, even in my own capital, as I'm sure you are aware," said Sayewin. "The land you seized north of the Ulian has always been part of Shohan. It is wrong to be held by any foreigners, however gently they may try to do so."

"You are right, but—" began Klimgu.

"The mother rock dragon approaches, looking to fight!" yelled a knight, riding up to the meeting. The cavalry that had been training stopped and turned. After forming up, they gave chase, but were too slow and far away to catch up with Serukeeba.

"Klimgu!" roared Serukeeba, charging. "Your time has come!"

"We thought she was your ally?" gasped Sayewin.

"There has been a fatal misunderstanding!" yelled Klimgu, stomping away from the group and signaling for them to leave. "Ride off, all of you. Be gone! None need die with me."

"No!" yelled Sayewin, running to him.

She deliberately put herself between Klimgu and a charging Serukeeba, gambling her life on the dragon's rumored distaste for innocent blood. Klimgu grabbed her, intent on forcing her out of harm's way. But before he could do so, she embraced him tightly. Only Serukeeba's quick reflexes saved the two. Digging her claws into the dirt, she jolted to a halt just two feet from the rulers, kicking up barrels of dirt and christening the whole group. Her eyes, ears, nose and tail all twitched in agitated confusion. Snorting at irrational human behavior, she still sighed in relief at the sudden peace.

"We fought but once, and never pillaged in Shohan, mighty Serukeeba," shouted Klimgu, stretching out an open hand to beg for calm. "We fed everyone in our reach and burned nothing. The king and his ways are gone. Your demands are being met. Until yesterday, we kept searching for Lorgi as we conquered."

"He studies at the Temple of the Gral-Chaner until I fetch him," said Serukeeba. "As should all of you! But you have come far, Klimgu. For that, I am glad."

"Certainly farther than I ever thought possible," chuckled Lutyam.

"But how far can he go, an illiterate warrior?" Serukeeba asked the monk.

"He is learning to read Esterlani—slowly," said Lutyam. "Between them, these two love-struck rulers have just banished the most disgusting practices of both their realms. How they will live without such barbarisms, I cannot imagine." All but Serukeeba looked to the monk with hurt eyes, stung by his words.

"You must visit Tiefenbo, Lutyam," said Serukeeba. "But Klimgu, what will you do now? And don't make me squeeze the truth out of you."

"I will not make the same mistakes as the last Vazuk," said Klimgu. "But I fear the peace, not knowing how to run a government in such a state." He looked to Sayewin, her eyes mesmerizing him.

"Great Snows, she's spinning him!" huffed Serukeeba. "Did Lorgi teach her that?"

"I fear war, and welcome a friend, as any should," said Sayewin. "Once we declare peace between Shohan and the Tuzanchim, the other kingdoms of Esterlan will set upon us both—regardless of your reputation, Klimgu."

"The solution is obvious," laughed Serukeeba. "As the sun needs the moon, the sea needs the land, and the stars need the sky, so too do you need each other. Neither of you will survive on your own. Can't you sense that? Combine your lands and rule together, as equal partners. But Klimgu, get out of Laskomia and leave the West alone, or I will have to squash you after all."

"Thank you, great heavenly dragon!" shouted Lutyam.

"I was going to part with Laskomia anyway," said Klimgu. "Besides, it is nothing but grass and bitter memories. I already offered that as a reward to Lutyam."

"Now to Lorgi, before he eats that poor temple out of existence," sighed his mother.

"They will be snowed in by now, and the trails impassible," said Sayewin.

"Good!" cheered Serukeeba. "Then none can follow me. Best I go now. Terrible things brew in the West."

"How can you possibly know that, Serukeeba?" Klimgu shook his head.

"Enjoy your new peace," she smiled. "If you work hard enough, you may even keep it. I return to lands ever in danger, and usually at war. Wish me all the luck on the Continent."

"But you are luck itself," said Klimgu. Most in his delegation nodded agreement.

"Not against plagues, lowlanders or the Tierdragon of Monz," said Serukeeba. "Keeping my son and village safe are about all the luck that I dare ask of this life—if even there is such a thing."

* * *

A snowy afternoon brought Serukeeba within sight of the monastery, still 1,200 feet up and three snaking miles away. Trumpeting her loudest call, she hoped it would cut through the falling snow. Only Lorgi heard it, though he dozed in the just-rebuilt main hall, bored by Poto's attempted lesson for the day. Bolting from the room, Lorgi stopped in the Shohan Pavilion to sound his own call before running to his favorite spot. Wenji trailed behind him. Even before he began pounding the Great Bell, Lorgi had roused the whole monastery. Everyone dropped whatever they had been doing to prepare for Serukeeba's return.

"Shall I...?" asked Poto.

"Of course!" cheered the Gral-Chaner, running past him to catch up to Wenji. "Our very, very best. All can help."

"I had best pack Lorgi's mementos," said Wenji, already crying as she stopped and turned to the Gral-Chaner. "I have always dreaded this last day."

"This is not that day," smiled the Gral-Chaner. "No packing today. Stay with Lorgi and share his joy."

Serukeeba had anticipated waking a broken outpost, struggling to heal itself and ration meager provisions to last the winter. Instead, she found the monastery completely renovated, bursting with activity and preparing for an imperial feast. By the time she reached the gate, many people waited for her, all smiling but shivering in the cold. Most were new faces. Giving her son a suspicious look, Serukeeba wondered how the temple could feed all of them. Lorgi just smiled back, as the crowd poured out a joyful welcome. She could never scold her son in the midst of such loving friendship, and he knew it.

"And now, the ultimate feast!" shouted Poto, emerging from the main hall.

Hungry and eager to celebrate, everyone urged Serukeeba indoors. Special places had been set for her and Lorgi several days before, in anticipation of the reunion. She met sixty pairs of human eyes, glowing with happiness. Wenji managed to smile and cry at the same time. The monks beamed with confidence, looking like they planned to trek all the way to Tiefenbo. In contrast, Baqwam and Moshal seemed to have reached their journey's end, grinning as they sat arm-in-arm. Kibak and a dozen Tuzanchim all smiled at the bewildered mother Álukoi.

Lorgi introduced everyone to Serukeeba, starting with the former head chef for the Summer Palace, three of the king's former concubines, the "rooster man" who had been the arena announcer, then a host of others who had sought refuge or wisdom at the monastery. He informed his mother that all of them had become his friends.

"How can you afford all this on my spent claw?" gasped Serukeeba.

"We saved it and also the one you had offered the Yimung," answered the Gral-Chaner. "May both bring good fortune on your return journey."

"Then how do you manage, especially with all these guests?" wondered Serukeeba. "And Lorgi, who has gained a hundred pounds?"

"Kibak supplies us from what was formerly the Summer Palace," smiled the Gral-Chaner. "Now he even accomplishes it in our traditional way, through donations."

"*Right*," chuckled Serukeeba, not believing it.

"I also made the Yimung give us a full refund for their evil ponies," said Kibak. "With interest! Something I learned from Shohaneze business ways. It is all very interesting."

"That I can believe," laughed Serukeeba. "Kibak, what are you really doing here?"

"I wanted to prove that the Tuzanchim can build, as well as destroy. I think Klimgu, Lutyam and the others will be proud. How do you like this new hall, built in record time, partly by our most respectable scouting party?"

"Impressive, but it looks to me like Shohaneze work."

"It should. We worked alongside the monks and many Shohaneze carpenters," said Kibak. "They have taught us many clever new ways. And at night, Lorgi teaches all of us Lendish."

"What!" yelled Serukeeba, alarmed. "Lorgi, what were you thinking?"

"To share our good luck, mother," he answered. "Kibak and others will need to know Lendish."

"For trading with Tiefenbo, the Stonelaw, and all of the exotic west," explained Kibak. "Trade makes the world grow. It is the future. I will lead the first caravan. Queen Sayewin and Vazuk Klimgu love my idea and promise to sponsor it."

"How is this possible?" gasped Serukeeba. "I have just run all the way from Shondara, in wind, rain and snow, yet you already trump my news."

"Ah, but now Tuzanchim news can travel faster than ever, thanks to Shohaneze wizardry," said Kibak. "But one must read in order to use it. So Wenji teaches us all that."

"Wenji!" shrieked Serukeeba. "Why?"

"Baqwam is also training me to fight like a Tuzanchim warrior," she cheered. "I will never be passive again."

"What monsters have I wrought?" moaned Serukeeba, looking to the Gral-Chaner for help as well as forgiveness.

"Progress," laughed the Gral-Chaner. "Not your choice, but your destiny. Our destiny."

"And you, Moshal?" asked Serukeeba, her eyes pleading for stability in him. "You will return to Laskomia with this caravan…and join Lutyam in rebuilding Laskomia?"

"Um…well…so much has happened, changed," Moshal began. Baqwam smiled at him and squeezed his hand for support, yet made no offer to speak. The two of them sat so close that they appeared to be glued together. "Actually, Baqwam and I want to get married."

"But I thought Laskomian monks do not take mates," said Serukeeba.

"True, but I do not wish to remain a monk," he stated.

"You can do that?" asked Serukeeba. "Didn't you have to swear an oath, make a vow?"

"Long ago. But these are new and different times," said Moshal. "Lorgi says we can all make our own luck, choose our own destinies."

"Is that so?" Serukeeba threw a quick scowl at Lorgi to stem his giggling. She then focused entirely on the Gral-Chaner, as did everyone else.

"Good follows you," said the master. "May you travel far, in peace and joy. May you bring to the Castled Lands what you have brought to the Well-East, what we here call the Esterlans. May you change and improve the destinies of others as you create your own."

"You do me far too much honor, Gral-Chaner. I only wish to return home to a quiet, simple life with my Lorgi and forget the world. That is about all the peace and joy I can imagine." She lied. Serukeeba could never be truly free, at peace or capable of joy while the Tierdragon of Monz still lived. Looking around the hall, full of smiling faces, she mused, "I wish we could just stay here."

"Most people who visit us say that," said the Gral-Chaner.

"Can we, mother?" asked Lorgi.

"Many friends in need await your return home," said the master.

"So do my enemies," muttered Serukeeba.

"What fools would make enemies of the Álukois?" asked Kibak.

"You don't want to know," warned Serukeeba.

* * *

The next morning, as snow silently floated down, everyone gathered in the main hall, saying tearful farewells to Serukeeba, Lorgi, and several others leaving the monastery. The monks chanted a twenty-minute prayer, whose ritual included gongs, candles and incense. Then the Tuzanchim launched into a "proper farewell" with their own song and dance to conjure good luck for all, exchanging gifts, toasts and encouraging words with everyone. When this seemed about done, an hour later, two monks approached the snowdragons, carrying what looked like a giant and a small set of saddle bags.

"We tried to make these exactly according to your instructions," said Poto. "We packed each with dried fruit, nuts, two books, a few mementos, and a compass—in case your *pahápkoltam* ever fails again. Also a replacement chain for the day when the first gives out on your back spikes."

"*Méni Gánsi*," said Serukeeba, echoed by Lorgi.

"May your packs see you all the way home," Poto smiled.

"That would be several miracles, especially for Lorgi's," said Serukeeba. "But know that every mile we carry them will help us reach home that much sooner."

"Please stay until spring," begged Wenji. "Why must you brave winter?"

"Nothing brave about it," laughed Serukeeba. "Our favorite season. No balkotars, tierdragons, or lowlander dragon hunters. For a few precious months, we have the wild all to ourselves. Healthy quiet, cold and peace. What Álukois dream of."

"How will you cover any distance in snow and ice...or mud?" asked Wenji. "Would it not be much easier to travel in spring?"

"We were made for arctic and alpine terrains. But *gánsi* for asking us to stay longer. How I wish we could. But in spring, our journey would become dangerous, hindered at every step by humans."

"What will you eat?" Wenji began shedding tears.

Lorgi's eyes widened in panic, recalling all the hunger and misery he had endured on his journey east. He looked to his mother for assurance.

"Be glad for yesterday, Lorgi," said Serukeeba. "No feasting again until we reach home. But we won't starve either. While trekking with Klimgu, your mother took care to bury small caches of food along the way."

Wenji sobbed. "The first real friend I ever had, leaving after only a few months, and we will never see each other again."

"Of course we will," cheered Lorgi.

"How can you say that?" cried Wenji.

"I just know," he answered.

The Gral-Chaner smiled at Wenji before glancing at everyone else. Only the Álukois had dry eyes, but their ears drooped with sadness.

"I'm sorry, Gral-Chaner," sobbed Wenji. "No amount of your training could prepare me for this. Suddenly I feel all alone."

"We are all sad at parting, but you will always be among friends," assured Kibak, putting an arm around her shoulder to comfort her. Wenji melted into his embrace. Instantly Kibak's expression changed from sorrow to awkward panic. With his eyes, he told Serukeeba of his sudden dilemma.

"Oh, the human realm's incessant turmoil!" moaned Serukeeba. "Lorgi, we need time away from it to gather our wits, and our true strength. Best we leave at once, before parting grows too painful for all."

"Wait! Not before our gift," shouted Poto, presenting Lorgi with a hexagonal wooden box, large enough to hold a teapot. Opening it, Poto displayed a bronze miniature of the Great Bell. "Exact in all proportions. Tiny, but anything larger would add too much bulk and weight on your journey. May it remind you of peace here, giving focus and luck when most needed."

"Méni Gánsi!" shouted Lorgi, nodding like a Tuzanchim. "I have gifts for you, too." Opening a large, burlap sack, he began handing out rolled parchments, one to every person at the monastery. "I made these myself."

"What extravagance is this?" asked Serukeeba.

"Paw prints with friendship letters, written in Esterlani," cheered Lorgi. "Wenji and the monks showed me how."

"Parchment is quite expensive," said Serukeeba, her ears twitching.

"I hope you got permission."

The Gral-Chaner nodded to her with a smile.

"You said to learn how to write, mother," Lorgi reminded her.

"*Gánsi*, Lorgi—I almost forgot!" shouted Kibak. "Serukeeba, this is for you. An Imperial writ, by order of Queen Sayewin and Vazuk Klimgu, with both their official seals. It entitles you to anything you ask, anywhere in their combined realm."

"And I had thought you were illiterate," gasped Serukeeba, rearing her neck back in surprise.

"He still is," said Baqwam, laughing.

"Well, partly—but you will be proud of my learning efforts." Kibak nodded, beaming.

"He still has an epic ride ahead of him, before he can call himself literate," chuckled Baqwam. "Yet Kibak is wise to have had the writ drawn up, in case you ever need it."

"*Gánsi*," said Serukeeba. "This monastery, what has taken place here, trumps all other marvels I have seen. We will always remember everyone here, and miss you beyond stars. Thank you all for everything."

"*Méni Gánsi* to you too!" said the Gral-Chaner. "A younger *I* would journey west to your village and witness the progress of your destiny."

"Far healthier to stay here and think the best, at any age," said Serukeeba. "If this paradise were my home, I'd keep it hidden forever."

"We have a wonderful home too, mother," said Lorgi.

"The best. When we return to it, we will work hard to make it so once again," said Serukeeba.

30: Yómgolin

On one of winter's shortest days, in a blizzard, the Álukoi Yómgolin struggled to find Tiefenbo. He had memorized Rokímba's directions, and owned the sharpest *pahápkoltam* of any living snowdragon, yet began to doubt both. Fearing he might miss the storied village altogether, he sat down, letting the snow pile up on him as he waited for something to show him the way. Winter storms had cleared his trail of any live hindrances, but did the same for help. Alone, hungry, and far from home, he pondered the foolishness of his goals, seeing no chance of ever reaching them. Just as he turned to go back, the weather calmed. Salt and smoke spiced the air. A moment later the sweet, lilting chatter of Delfinians restored the youth's confidence. Either Tiefenbo itself or Yómgolin's spirit guide had called to him.

He found the coastal village just where Rokímba had said it would be, but looking nothing like her description. No "sleepy jumble of curious, misshapen huts, a lodge, and a mill." Only a high granite wall topped with crenellations worthy of a castle—standing hundreds of miles away from any need for one. Bulging from the wall and just to the right of a massive iron gate stood a burly round tower rising to thirty feet. There, two Delfinian bowmen scanned the horizon. Sighting Yómgolin, they waved, cheered and sounded a large bell. In four breaths, the gate opened. Seven human children wearing snowshoes marched out, screaming with joy as they raced toward the visitor much faster than Yómgolin had thought possible.

"You're not Serukeeba," yelled Nuwak, still fifty yards away. "Where is she? Who are you?" The other children caught up with him, all shouting the same questions.

"I am Yómgolin. Serukeeba and her son Lorgámon are my quest."

"You came to find Seri and Lorgi?" asked Brogan.

"Serukeeba and Lorgámon," corrected Yómgolin. Shocked that human children used the personal, familiar name forms, he reared back, twitching his ears and nostrils. In his view, either these children lacked manners or Serukeeba had lost all dignity when she severed her cultural roots. "Have any of you heard of an old Álukoi, a soothsayer named Rokímba?"

"About time you got here!" scolded Sirwan, with her hands on her hips. "She has been expecting you for *weeks.*"

"What?" gasped Yómgolin. "How could she be?"

"Every time somebody spills or breaks anything, Roki gets a premonition," said Sirwan.

"Roki?" moaned Yómgolin. "Has all the Continent sunk to Lendish slang? Please use the seer's real name, Rokímba. But how can she be expecting me?"

"Other people's accidents are signs to her," said Brogan. "She knew you were on your way when I spilled my oatmeal one morning. So all the children love her."

"But if no one spills or breaks anything," explained Sirwan, "and Roki needs to see into the future or really far away, she has people make a mess on the floor so she can take one of her readings."

Yómgolin twitched his ears. "I knew she was eccentric, but..."

"Hurry up and follow us," ordered Sirwan.

Uneasy around these assertive human children, Yómgolin mutely trailed them through the gate, into the village, then to Serukeeba's hall, where the old seer waited by the door. Greeting each other in the traditional way, the two Álukois said *"Akúa"* while lightly tapping muzzles. Within seconds, the whole village gathered around them. But then Rokímba raised her left forepaw to eye level, asking that Yómgolin do the same and grasp hers with his own.

"What lowland barbarism is this?" gasped Yómgolin, his eyes wide, his nostrils pinched and his ears twitching like butterfly wings.

"Tuzanchim, a Steppe greeting," said Rokímba.

"Why?" begged Yómgolin, with pained revulsion.

"Because a curious Tuzanchim warrior arrived some moons ago. We taught him some Tundrish and he showed us a few things. A week later he left with Seri to help find Lorgi."

"What became of them?"

"We hope you can find out," sighed Rokímba. "At least you have Golármon's profile—almost—though lacking his other qualities."

"Best to go easy on your flattery, Roki," said Jinva, smiling nervously at both Álukois. "Give all our visitors a chance to prove themselves. Klimgu taught us that much. I'm sure Yómgolin will show us something new as well."

"Now that I take a good look at you, it seems you are barely of age," said Rokímba. "Too lean, soft and empty-eyed. Unfit for a runt's quest, let alone one screaming for a champion."

"But it was you who gave me the idea, just before leaving for Tiefenbo yourself!" huffed Yómgolin. "An urgent and noble quest for the right person coming of age, you said."

"What is *of age*?" asked Sirwan, echoed by others.

"About 25 years for an Álukoi, which is like 18 to 20 for a human," said Yómgolin. "I will prove myself on a vital but dangerous quest. Then all the Álukois must respect me as an adult. An ancient custom, once shared by many peoples."

"The Council of Elders should have discouraged you," muttered Rokímba.

"They tried. But I kept arguing. So they granted my quest, laughing at my folly. Proving them wrong will be the greatest joy."

"There are much greater joys," said Rokímba. "At the last Winter Gathering, I met three young ladies nearly of age. Have you no interest in any of them?"

"Selinéa," sighed Yómgolin. "But I doubt she holds the smallest thought of me. Her parents want mighty Zortríton, or at least a proven adult for her mate. Not a young, untested orphan from the quiet wooded banks of the Zárong Kórzel."

"What's a Zárong Kórzel?" demanded Sirwan.

"The Quartz River," said Yómgolin. "One of the coldest, calmest, most beautiful places in the world. So yes, I will have to prove myself in the most difficult way."

"Thank your stars the tierdragon sleeps," said Rokímba. "At least Seri had a veteran Tuzanchim warrior to guide her through hellish territory. You won't even have that. Be glad for winter. Summer would kill you. How good is your Tundrish?"

"I have always lived too far away from them to speak any."

"By some miracle do you know any Laskomian or Tuzanchim?"

"Of course not," said Yómgolin, surprised that she asked. "I only speak Álukop and Lendish."

"Seri journeyed deep into savage, warring human lands to the east. How will you speak with anyone to learn her whereabouts?"

"I hope to find her in spite of the *hyúlems.*"

"Look around you," said the seer. "Already you tread far from the Stonelaw. These are all Seri and Lorgi's dearest human friends. Mine too, I am honored to say. Stay but a day and they become yours as well."

"I meant no offense to anyone here," murmured Yómgolin. " I know nothing about…things outside the mountains of the Stonelaw."

"Most of the Continent is a human realm. The world does not spare even the mightiest fool. Return to your hall by the quiet, wooded banks of the Zárong Kórzel, deep in the heart of the Stonelaw, before the plague or a gang of clever bandits finds you. Dare not dream of questing until you have learned enough to survive, and to speak the tongue of a people beyond your wood!"

"I can run, climb and fight just as well as Zortríton. Who else can say that?"

"A mere handful of scrawny, dim-wit thugs butchered him—inside the Stonelaw!" shouted Rokímba, angry. "Our strongest living champion, young though he was. Go home with the snows, before tragedy takes you, like some helpless, stranded calf, a meal for wolves. Or a brainless buck, destined for a trophy collection on some grease-stained castle wall."

"Why are you trying to discourage him, when you suggested he come here in the first place?" asked Jinva. "We need all the help we can get."

Every villager glared at the seer.

"I want Seri and Lorgi home more than anyone, so that I may return to mine," said Rokímba. "But another young idiot throwing his life away won't bring them back. It will only deepen the pain. A deadly pain that erodes the Álukoi people. And the whole Stonelaw."

"I can learn nothing, prove nothing, attain nothing by staying home," said Yómgolin. "If I must face death to grow clever and skilled, so be it. Avoiding peril has rotted several old Álukois of the west. Yet they sit on the Council of Elders, giving worthless advice to others. My foolishness pales beside theirs."

"Well shot!—as Klimgu would say," cheered Kamwa. "Yómgolin sounds a lot like me."

"Are you going, too?" asked Birentak, his uncle. All the villagers suddenly looked horrified.

"If Yómgolin can wait until spring, I will be his guide, the way Klimgu did for Seri." The children all grabbed hold of Kamwa, determined to stop him.

"Thank you, but no," said Yómgolin. "I must trek as far as I can before spring thaws and humans—or others—claim the land. Then we will see just how much of a fool I really am."

"I see it with tragic clarity right now," said Rokímba.

"Stay the week, learn some Tuzanchim phrases, and what we've been told about their frightful Steppes," said Jinva. "You will need it all, I'm sure."

"Thank you," said Yómgolin.

"You mean *gánsi*," said Sirwan, raising a finger for emphasis. "The Tuzanchim say that now, because of Lorgi. So you already know the most important word."

Dumbfounded, Yómgolin met eyes with Rokímba and every villager in turn. All smiled back, delighted by his amazement. "Now I'm doubly curious. Honored Rokímba, no words can keep me from my chosen quest. You can only choose to help me or not."

"Then learn, and so prepare," said the seer. "Before spring, you will see strange and wondrous things. You should live so long. But be alert! You may be severely tested in battle. May you prevail, that we meet again. Fool or not, know that we all wish you success and long for your safe return."

"*Gánsi*," said Yómgolin, looking at everyone.

But only three days later, Rokímba suddenly got an ominous reading from gazing into the fireplace. She made Yómgolin leave at once, pushing him out the hall's door. Everyone ran out to wish him luck. Fearing that he, like Seri and Lorgi, might never return, some children cried. No words could comfort them. Though working hard not to show it, most of the adults ached the same way. After that, whenever Rokímba seized upon a "founding" or spill to take one of her readings, all held their breath. Most of her visions seemed to bode ill. Taking extreme care not to drop or break anything, the villagers made sure to clean up even the smallest mess before Rokímba could discover it. Constantly aware of the seer's whereabouts, they shied away from her.

Despite heavy snow, Yómgolin quickly retraced Serukeeba's path to the Sorcerer's Bluff. He headed south for three more days before turning southeast, for the Laskomian plains. But something on the horizon caught his eye and drew him toward the heart of the Dawnwood. Without knowing how or why, he sensed that he would have violent work to do there.

He took far too long to reach sleep that moon-graced night. In the timeless fog between sleep and wakefulness, Yómgolin glimpsed a Lendish thief making away with his neck pack. The bandit ran as no human could, light and swift in the snow. But Yómgolin struggled like an ox, falling more and more behind until the man dove into a distant cave.

With all the force of his will, a sluggish young Álukoi threw himself down into the abyss after him. Sliding, tumbling and screaming, he hit every part of his body against progressively narrower tunnel walls as he fell. Suddenly, a host of flaming torches replaced the darkness, as a bruised and bloodied Yómgolin crashed into an underground lake of gold coins, enough for all the realms of the Continent. From above, the *hyúlem* thief laughed long and hard, certain the Álukoi would never be able to catch him.

Angered to violence, Yómgolin ignored his own property, only three yards away, to hunt the bandit. Taunting insults, the man led a chase through a maze of caverns. This time, Yómgolin gained on him. After many forks, turns and loops, the young warrior-to-be cornered the pest at a dead end. The man cried out in terror before Yómgolin even reached to punish him. Suddenly the wall behind the man crumbled, revealing death itself.

The Tierdragon of Monz. Her eyes, nostrils and gaping mouth glowed like molten iron. Her head alone had nearly the mass of Yómgolin's entire body. Only the tiny human separated the two eternal enemies. Snatching the pawn in her jaws, the tierdragon chewed four times and swallowed. Then she threw a wall of fire, burning away Yómgolin's face, his spikes, then his limbs and even his tail. Blind, paralyzed, and suffocating, he cursed a fate shared by champions of many peoples, and countless fleeing innocents.

But Yómgolin woke up screaming, in a fine snowdrift nestled between stout, ancient pines. His neck pack waited patiently, dangling from a rope between two of them, safely out of bear reach. The moon had sailed clear across the sky. The horizon started to lighten in the east. Shaken by his nightmare, Yómgolin faced the morning with dread. What lesson or warning should he take from the dream? How could he or anyone survive if such a monster waited in the Dawnwood?

"Not even the Monz Tierdragon could be *that* big," Yómgolin told himself. "Or could it? Why was Rokímba so frantic to be rid of me? And what would she make of my dream? No, better not to even ask."

Resuming his quest, but with slow, unsure steps, Yómgolin suddenly saw himself as the fool that the Council of Elders and Rokímba had described. From far to the east, a mournful howl broke the silence. Was it Álukoi? Or the worst tierdragon ever known, luring him to his death. Too distant and faint for him to be sure, the call still told Yómgolin that he was no longer alone. Fate had cast him into a deadly adventure, whether he was fit for it or not.

31: The Dawnwood

Two quiet days brought mother and son to the tower ruins, already forgotten under three feet of snow. Since Seri's duel, the giant mountain balkotar corpse had profoundly withered and broken apart, looking ancient or unreal. Everything else within view spoke of peace and beauty. Robust pine forests graced the gentler slopes, to the longest eye's reach. Silent, frozen air and a heavy sky promised more snow. Icicles hung like glass crystals from every tree and ledge, while thick, fluffy drifts blanketed any slopes that could hold them. Serukeeba retold her battle against the monster, as Lorgi studied it from a safe distance. Digging up her first cache so they could have a snack, she also dusted off her remembrance carving. While explaining it to Lorgi, she added three more lines at the bottom, which read:

Mother and son reunited at Temple of the Gral-Chaner.
Leaving lands better than they found them.
May Good triumph, and Peace be yours.

"Do Álukois usually carve their words all over the place?" asked Lorgi.

"Only when it seems important," answered his mother.

"But we're thousands of miles from home. Even further from the Stonelaw. You said most Álukois never go past its borders, and nobody outside it can read our language, anyway. So why bother?"

"Never forget the Delfinian traders," cheered Serukeeba. "One day, some may reach even here. Think what a nice surprise our carving will be, to read familiar words so far from home."

"That's a mighty long *may*," giggled Lorgi.

"Don't laugh. No one knows what the future holds."

Two weeks of plowing through drifts, climbing over rock, ice, and an occasional fallen tree brought them out of the Shirlangu Mountains to the Near Valley. For many reasons, Serukeeba had not dared to leave a cache there. She and Lorgi had to trek several days before their next snack, with their stomachs grumbling most of the way. Serukeeba kept warning Lorgi not to expect anything when they reached Uxanda, many days to the west. But to her surprise, a completely restored and thriving city treated them to a fabulous banquet. A week after leaving the former capital, Serukeeba turned slightly northwest.

"This is not how I remember coming," said Lorgi. "Are you sure?"

"Good. You noticed. We can reach Tiefenbo faster by angling northwest, treading less of Laskomia and more of the Dawnwood."

"Jinva and Weliben tell frightful stories of it," said Lorgi.

"To keep children like you from wandering off," laughed his mother. "Be glad humans fear the Great Woods, or nothing would be left of them. Still, they have chipped away at all the Continent's forests. Our ancestors would weep, seeing how much less remains today."

"I thought only humans weep," said Lorgi, twitching his ears in confusion.

"With their eyes. But Volpings, Álukois, or anyone with a caring heart also weeps inside. Revere the forests, a source of strength, wisdom and peace. By legend, in ancient times an Álukoi might trek from the Stonelaw clear south to Akromilot, or cross the whole Continent— entirely in shade. A squirrel could do the same, and never touch the ground, so thick were the trees."

"I don't believe that!" shouted Lorgi.

"After suffering the Steppes, nor do I."

"Do you have any legends about the Dawnwood?"

"The Delfinians call it the Firstwood, oldest and wildest of all forests. One of the few places left where humans fear to tread, where explorers have vanished without trace. Said to host the longest winters, biggest mosquitoes, and fiercest monsters anywhere on the Continent."

"No more monsters," said Lorgi.

"Most humans ignorant of Álukois would call us monsters."

"That is stupid," huffed Lorgi.

"Some Álukois only see humans as monsters. We may have to argue with those at the next Winter Gathering."

"I'm not sure I want to go," said Lorgi. "I feel much more like a monk or a warrior than an Álukoi. At least those people like me, and say I bring *good* luck."

"The Álukois, the whole Stonelaw, in fact peoples everywhere hunger for good luck, no matter what they believe," said Serukeeba. "Think of the Winter Gathering as an adventure. Vital to your education, and that of Álukois we will meet, young or old."

"No more adventures for me," said Lorgi.

"Never mind. Let us enjoy the end of this one. When the dancing ghost lights grace the sky, they will be more beautiful than anything we can see from Tiefenbo."

"But at home it's usually cloudy, raining or snowing," said Lorgi.

"Exactly. Savor whatever is special about any place we visit."

"I could really savor another banquet."

"Once we get home," laughed Serukeeba.

After weeks of marching through parched, windswept Steppe, the pair finally met robust hills, covered in many layers of snow. Though thinly populated with gnarled, vanguard trees, the former mountains welcomed the Álukois to the Dawnwood. For half an hour, a pack of wolves shadowed them, wondering if Lorgi just might be edible. Warning yawns from Serukeeba and a dozen well aimed snowballs from Lorgi sent them away. A white sky pressed down, nearly touching the trees, promising yet more snow and silence to an already quiet forest. At this, Serukeeba heaved a long sigh of relief.

"What were you worried about, mother?"

"Everything. But no more. Here we walk far from enemies, and only weeks from home. Nothing can go wrong now. At last our ordeal has ended. We are at peace, making us free!"

"I'm so hungry it hurts," said Lorgi.

"Of course you are. I am, too."

"I can't wait to have one of Jinva's pies!"

"Tiefenbo may not be up to pies for a while."

"But you promised!" Lorgi shouted.

"We'll just have to see once we get home."

"I smell salt and sulfur, that way." Lorgi pointed to a massive, barren hill, curiously removed from the forest.

"Hot springs," sighed his mother. "Useful only if we had shivering humans in tow."

"What are hot springs? Let's go see."

"Nothing worth delaying us, Lorgi," said Serukeeba, struggling to keep her ears and nose still. "I know some much better ones we can see on our way to the next Winter Gathering."

"What are you worried about now, mother?"

"Well, this far north, in winter, any springs are bound to be...occupied."

"Good!" cheered Lorgi, starting to run ahead. "They can feed us."

"No. Nothing hospitable could exist there. Stop!"

"Can you hear that, coming from the hilltop?" asked Lorgi. "Only big, fat humans snore like that. Let's wake them up and make friends. Then we can all have something to eat."

"No friends or food here. If you're so hungry, don't waste time that could bring us home all the sooner. Forget the springs. Come back down."

"Such slobs," said Lorgi, already a thousand yards uphill. "Garbage all over the place. I'll go explore that big, steaming cave on the hillside."

"NO!" yelled his mother.

But Lorgi had already vanished into it.

Seeing refuse and discarded human tools leading up to the cave, Serukeeba guessed a handful of third-rate bandits had claimed it. Until she found a Laskomian shield rusting amidst broken pottery. Ten paces further, she spotted a war lance, its iron tip still sharp and hardly rusted, but its long wooden shaft charred. Near the cave's mouth, an assortment of Kitrian, Laskomian and Tuzanchim weapons and artifacts covered the ground like discarded shoes. Some had lain in the same spot for years, while others had dropped only recently. Suddenly recognizing the signs, Serukeeba charged after her son, frantic to stop him before he awakened a terrible, ancient foe.

"Lorgi, get back here this instant!"

He let out a scream that quickly trailed off. This told Serukeeba that her child had fallen into an abyss.

Deep within the hill, a murderous screech welled up. The ground shook. Great puffs of steam escaped the cave's mouth, as if the earth itself were smoking. When Serukeeba reached the entrance, she was hit by a noxious brew of smoke, steam and hot, poisonous fumes, enough to flatten even an Álukoi. Yet she charged blindly into the dark, holding her breath and shutting her eyes against the corrosive mix. With only her ears, paws, and *pahápkoltam* to guide her, she rumbled down through a hopelessly random chain of caverns. At times, a human skull or piles of them crunched under her feet. Just as the air began to clear, Serukeeba heard Lorgi give a quick scream. A furious, deafening roar answered, so violent that the cavern walls trembled.

"Lorgi!" shrieked his mother, before she could stop herself. Now the resident beast would guess many things about her, including her location. With all the force of her mind, Serukeeba begged her son *not* to answer, or do anything to give away his position. At a fork in the caverns, she quietly darted down the smaller passage on her left. At the next branch, she took the rightmost of three tunnels, praying the cave's monster would not be too clever.

"Louurrghhiii," rumbled a gigantic voice from below, rolling throughout the cave system like thunder. Only a tierdragon could emit such a powerful sound. Only a tierdragon could destroy an enemy's resolve by voice alone.

Silence.

For a torturously long minute, nothing alive dared move. In another chamber, not far below, a single drop of water struck the middle of an underground lake every quarter minute, telling Serukeeba that she was getting close. Every eight seconds, the beast wheezed to inhale. Both sounds would be too faint, above ground. But in the caverns they swelled and echoed like Dunhala war horns. The time between wheezes tortured Serukeeba, desperate to find her baby.

Knowing that even a dozen champion Álukois stood no chance against a tierdragon, Serukeeba prayed that Lorgi had somehow escaped injury, found a place the beast could not reach, and that it would have to guard more than one entrance to its favorite chamber. Far too much to wish for. Like a skilled predator, Serukeeba crept toward her nemesis' most prized cavern, assured that no tierdragon could suffer trespassers into its sleeping area, its treasure, or its nest if it was tending eggs. Finding a horse's skull, Serukeeba affixed it to one of her back spikes, in case she might need it later.

Light and smoke from six torches filled the vast chamber, whose floor sparkled with all the human talismans of wealth and war, in obscene quantities. Even a tierdragon that never slept would need centuries to amass such plunder—unless it had vanquished many packs of bandits or several of its own kind. Only sheer terror kept Serukeeba from gasping at the sight, which dwarfed even Uxanda's treasury vaults. Hundreds of royal swords, helms and shields swam or drowned in a sea of gold and silver coins from every realm on the Continent. So did scores of chests, both great and small, all brimming with gems, pearls and jewelry.

Countless banners and standards from far-flung kingdoms had been carefully arranged and propped up against the walls, as mementos of the endless hunt. Yet no bones, hides or shells of any kind littered the treasure chamber, and no trace of blood either. This particular tierdragon kept meals and plunder carefully separated.

From the shadows behind three natural pillars, Serukeeba finally saw her nemesis—or part of it. Due to the chamber's uneven shape and its arrays of stalactites, stalagmites and other features, she could not view all of the monster at once from her hiding place. By luck, the tierdragon had its back to her and gazed out into the yawning black of the large tunnel at the far end of the chamber. For several minutes, it stood motionless, wheezing loudly and slightly more quickly as its ribs bellowed. Its nose and ears visibly strained to detect anything.

The behemoth's massive back resembled the upturned hull of a king's longboat. Shining like polished armor, it's plate-sized scales reflected gold in the dim firelight, giving no hint of their color by daylight. When the beast turned its neck, the scales creaked like thick leather saddles and changed hues, depending on their angles. Forty yards away, they shined like new shields, looking just as stubborn. But when the creature opened its gigantic, bat-like wings, those seemed remarkably delicate, even translucent in places. Rows of teeth longer than Jinva's rolling pin and talons bigger than a giant balkotar's mandibles made anyone ignore the wings, which the beast suddenly closed tightly against its sides. A patch of violet glowed, hissed and bubbled, as blood trickled down one side of its head. Serukeeba knew that such an injury had to have been sustained in the last few minutes.

"Clumsy old brute, hitting her head in her own caves," thought Serukeeba. "Hear me, Golármon. While the monster's scales look new and invincible, her lungs rot. May her brain rot as well. May patience and cunning triumph over sheer size and power."

"Away, my love," answered Golármon in her mind. "This is not your battle."

"It has always been our battle," thought Serukeeba. "If ever such magic as luck or justice could work, let it be now!"

As she had wished, the tierdragon needed to mind three entrances to its treasure room, only one of which proved large enough for itself. Serukeeba hid close to the second one, ample for her, but far too small for the beast. A third opening poured into the chamber from a high angle, looking just big enough for Lorgi or humans, yet too steep and slippery. Swishing its long, thin tail, the tierdragon kept its body motionless and pressed to the ground, to detect vibrations. Bobbing and craning its long neck, it continually looked between the three entrances, twitching its nostrils.

Unable to locate either intruder, the tierdragon vented its frustration with an angry roar, so forceful it shook the cavern walls again. Serukeeba's ear lids slammed shut; she had trouble coaxing them back open. Turning toward the smallest, human-sized entrance, the monster pressed its snout against the opening and inhaled deeply. It stepped back, grabbed the nearest torch in a forepaw and held the tool up to the tunnel. Serukeeba watched as the tierdragon worked its jaws and stomach, looking as if it were about to vomit. Drawing a huge breath, it exhaled with intense force, spewing a ball of fire up that passageway.

From far up that tunnel, Lorgi emitted another frightful yelp. Having found the first intruder, the monster rumbled out of the chamber to hunt him, carrying the torch as it went. At first the ground shook from the tierdragon's thunderous steps. Serukeeba wondered that it did not bring down the whole cave system with all the shaking. A creature of the air, the tierdragon made awkward progress by ground, even in its own lair, moving no faster than an old human. Still, the sound faded quickly once the beast vanished into the dark, lumbering steadily away from the main chamber and towards the source of the yelp.

Desperate, Serukeeba hissed, "Lorgi!"

With a rolling, whooshing sound, he tumbled into the main chamber, landing in the sea of coins with a jingle, like new treasure piling on top of the old. Covered in soot, he sighed with relief.

"Sorry, mother," murmured Lorgi. "What do we do now?"

"Oh, my baby!" gasped Serukeeba. "We must put you in water before the burns kill you."

"I'm fine, just smoky," whispered Lorgi. "The dragon won't be able to spot me like this, but we better get out before it returns."

"First we snuff out the torches. Make the beast spend its own fire just to see. They can only spew so much of it in a day. Like humans, tierdragons lack night eyes. Our one advantage here."

"But won't it just relight the torches?" asked Lorgi.

"Not this one," whispered Serukeeba, chewing the first torch to bits.

"That's making too much noise," said Lorgi.

"Too bad," huffed his mother. "The beast already knows we're here. But we can make it blind. Snuff out and break apart that one on the left while I get the others."

"How do we slay such a beast?"

"Lorgi, only a team of champion Álukois would dare even attempt it."

"We are that!"

"Many champions. A whole host of them. Golármon and four other very experienced champions all died trying. We are fools for waking the beast and will be lucky beyond stars just to escape. When it returns, you run up that mid-sized tunnel to the left. I will be right behind you. Do not stop until you reach the thick of the woods, no matter what happens—to either of us. Do you hear me?"

"Mother!" Lorgi cried aloud.

"Mother's orders for your survival! Our one chance. If you had obeyed me instead of feeding your curiosity…"

The ground shook as the tierdragon stomped back into the main cavern. With a push from his mother, Lorgi did as told, scurrying up the tunnel. Serukeeba threw the horse skull to the far end of the chamber, where it bounced off a stalactite with a loud, echoing pop. Confused, the tierdragon lunged toward the sound and missed Serukeeba's exit. With all the chamber's torches destroyed, the beast could only see by the one it still carried, greatly slowing its progress. At the cave's mouth, Serukeeba found Lorgi tinkering with a dozen lances.

"Not now!" she screamed.

"We need Moshal's wagon breaker if we are to reach the woods!" yelled Lorgi. He braced the lances at angles, between several boulders near the entrance. "Done. Hard to spot in the dark, but an easy trip."

Seconds after they escaped the caves, its owner charged straight into the obstacle, tripping even as the lances broke under its weight. Screaming in pain, the tierdragon stopped at the entrance to pick several of them out of its bleeding feet, like so many thorns. In that breath, the Álukois fled a hundred yards. But taking to the air, the beast caught up to them in seconds. Lorgi and his mother barely entered the woods ahead of giant talons. Hovering just above the treetops, the tierdragon lashed down every possible way with its tail, but could never quite reach the Álukois. In a minute, winter's freezing wind drove the beast back down into its lair.

"We made it!" cheered Lorgi.

"You were right about your wagon breaker as Klimgu was right about the monks," gasped Serukeeba, breathless. "Perhaps your travels with barbarians have been useful, after all."

"Most of them are just people, not barbarians," corrected Lorgi.

"We woke the tierdragon. Left alone, it might have slept for years. Now it will not rest until it has slain us. I am sorry, Lorgi, but I do not know how we can survive this."

"No, mother. I am sorry. But we'll find a way, like Klimgu says. I wish Kibak, Baqwam, Moshal and all the Tuzanchim were here to help."

"They know nothing of tierdragons. Not that it would make any difference."

"Well, they would find out fast and think of something," said Lorgi.

"This is no *hyúlem* contest, not a matter of which side holds the better ground or has more ants."

"Ants?" asked Lorgi, puzzled.

"Lowlanders muster huge armies. From great distance, they look like warring ant queendoms. But they only know how to fight each other."

"Not true, mother. I saw Tuzanchim fight balkotars and win. They can help us, just like we helped them. They have to try. For their honor."

"I only helped them to find you," admitted Serukeeba.

"I know. But now it's their turn. We should go back and get them to help us."

"We must not leave the Dawnwood. Besides, humans are helpless in winter."

"We're not much good in the summer."

"Lorgi, we may have to stay in this forest a long time."

"How long, mother?"

"Until the beast dies or gives up and leaves us alone."

"When will that be?"

"I cannot guess." Serukeeba lied, to avoid saying "never."

She ached to show Lorgi the wonders of the west: Gruneborg's fabled hospitality; the Stonelaw's mountains, glaciers and rivers; the rugged Host coastlines of the northwest; the 100 kingdoms' countless charms and "painted" shores; Duncheza's royal gardens; the Mitersea; 500 Lakes region; all the great rivers, woods, and mountains; perhaps even Akromilot and the Dolanzia Islands during a long winter. Now mother and son could only hide like rodents in the forest, ever watching the sky for death. Suddenly all that Serukeeba—or anyone—had ever done for good or ill meant nothing, with a tierdragon waiting to strike.

"If you had just minded me…" Serukeeba trailed off, shaking her head like a human, sitting on her haunches with her forepaws crossed.

"How was I supposed to know the tierdragon was sleeping here?" cried Lorgi. "You said she can hibernate for years and had her own mountain, far away, deep in the Castled Lands."

"I also told you that she had more than one lair! But who knew she kept one this far east—or north? And why so far from the livestock and treasure she craves?"

"So her enemies cannot hunt her where she hibernates," guessed Lorgi. "We found her secret and now she will have to move or risk attack."

"No one attacks a tierdragon!" uttered Serukeeba.

"Wasn't that your biggest wish, to avenge Golármon and find peace?" asked Lorgi.

"I never told you that!" gasped his mother.

"Or other things. But you said so to Jinva and Weli, and to the Gral-Chaner. I understand."

"How could you?" Serukeeba drooped her ears.

"Kibak says a good warrior sees things from many sides to understand."

"Suddenly you are growing up too fast, and not even four."

"I'm not a baby. Our adventures made me a warrior!"

"Warrior or not, you are still my precious child. We must keep impossibly alert and careful, just to survive. No place on all the Continent will be safe for us. Not the stoutest human fortress or Álukoi hall. For over 200 years, the Monz Tierdragon has been felling the greatest champions, even whole armies, of every race. We have slim chance of escape and food only for a few days."

"We have the whole Dawnwood to forage and hide in," said Lorgi. "We have experience with the Tuzanchim, the Continent's best fighters. The dragon doesn't like the cold wind, and you said she cannot see in the dark, which leaves only a few hours of daylight to worry about. We also have luck and hope on our side."

"Perhaps that lofty, ever smiling monastery was not a healthy influence on you, after all," sighed Serukeeba. "It may become impossible to hide from our foe, try as we must. By day, the tierdragon holds the most powerful eyes known."

"Make that one eye," said Lorgi.

"I saw the blood running down one side of her head. How did the beast manage to lose an eye in her own lair?"

"When I fell into the big chamber, I bumped into the tierdragon and woke her up. She growled like she was going to eat me, so I swatted her across the face."

"You did *that*, and survived?" gasped Serukeeba.

"I dove into a tunnel too small for the monster. But it only went up to a dead end. As soon as I turned around, the dragon blasted me with a stinky fire, so now I'm charcoal all over. Is that permanent?"

"A miracle you are still alive, child," moaned his mother. "We must treat your burns at once. I wish we had something for your pain."

"I'm not hurt, mother."

"Of course you are, but terror always trumps pain. Where does it hurt most?" Gingerly, Serukeeba used the soft pads of her forepaws to touch Lorgi on his muzzle, neck, and chest. "Lorgi, you are not helping by keeping silent. No time to be brave. I need to know where it hurts to touch."

"Nowhere, mother. I'm fine, just dirty. And terrified!"

"How could you survive the fire unscathed? By overcoming the balkotar venom, or the Steppes in summer? Lucky, indeed! Come along. I smell a squirrel's cache nearby."

"But if we take it, the squirrel may starve," said Lorgi.

"A tiny morsel for us, and the squirrel will have buried many similar caches in case one is discovered. I'm far too tired to forage. Like knights on campaign, we must tax the land until our ordeal is ended."

Two days later, near sunset, the tierdragon delayed its search for the Álukois to hunt a bull elk. Awkward in the fading light and a gusty wind, and missing an eye, the beast failed to make a kill, allowing the prey to strike with its antlers. Suddenly, both cried out in pain. While Serukeeba and Lorgi hid among the trees, the tierdragon struggled. A torn wing made it unable to carry the prize back to its lair. Instead of ripping the elk apart and devouring raw flesh, the tierdragon repeatedly yawned, belched flammable gas, puffed its cheeks, and smacked its jaws hard, the way tierdragons made their fire. Yet none ever came. Looking hungry yet inept, the tierdragon stared at its kill, rolled it over, and tried at least a dozen more times to spark a flame. Stretching its long neck, the monster scanned its surroundings, worried that other predators might steal the kill. In the dim light, it could not spot the Álukois.

"The fire has really gone out of her," Serukeeba whispered, while holding Lorgi's mouth shut. "Even the Monz Tierdragon ages, after all. She has bad teeth, or she would have devoured the elk by now. That wheezing must tax her flying range. May the plague find her at last. Wish her to choke on her dinner."

Lorgi motioned his readiness to attack.

"Have you lost your mind?" hissed his mother. "No! We can do no more than observe—if we want to survive."

"But it has a cut wing," whispered Lorgi.

"Hardly enough to ground her. That will heal tomorrow, just the way our cuts do."

"Then what about her right eye? Does that have to heal too?"

"No, thank the stars!" smiled Serukeeba. "Lorgi, you have done the world a great service in damaging the beast. Only Álukois can regrow sight. It is a cruel turn of Nature that humans do not share our gift."

Resigned to eating cold, raw flesh, the beast used its talons instead of its teeth to laboriously shred the kill. For its immense size, the tierdragon proved remarkably dainty, needing twenty minutes to consume most of the meat, but leaving the hide, entrails and bones. Surrendering to a frozen, windy dusk, it flew back to its lair.

"Are tierdragons poisonous?" asked Lorgi.

"No. Nothing a tenth their size would ever need to be."

"Are they rock-hard like us?"

"Again, no. But they are so much stronger than anything else, with scales far too thick for any weapons. By day they see better than we do, and their sense of smell is keener, too. They can fly at horrific speed and cover impossible distances. And of course they spew deadly fire."

"Not this one!" cheered Lorgi.

"It almost roasted you in the cave."

"But it had a torch. It can't burn us out here. And it's not ten times your size, mother."

"Closer to six. But did you see its claws and tail? Respect your enemy, Lorgi. That is what your father and all your Tuzanchim friends would say."

"When we're done respecting, we better find a way to beat it. That's what Kibak would say."

"Only a team of champions," muttered Serukeeba. "Many, many champions."

Two days later, they spotted the tierdragon carrying a dead horse in its clutches, the victim still giving a steady rain of blood.

"Don't look, Lorgi," said his mother, tapping his chin with a forepaw. "You have seen far too many horrors already."

"You said to observe, mother. That's a Laskomian horse, the biggest kind."

"How can you know that?"

"I fought at the Battle of Lake Gabriska!" bragged Lorgi.

With a moan and a shake of her head, Serukeeba stopped him. "You had been kidnapped, poisoned and bartered. You should never have been within a thousand miles of that savage *hyúlem* battle—a mindless tragedy, not a thing to boast of."

"What was I supposed to do, just sit there when they were trying to kill my friends?"

"Never mind. We await our own battle. After gorging itself, the tierdragon must rest."

"Good." Lorgi perked his ears up. "Our attack will give it indigestion."

"This is no game! Patience. We must learn all its habits. Everything we can about it. Only when the most opportune moment arrives do we attack, if at all."

Frightened and hungry, Lorgi gazed at the landscape. Forest alternated with meadow, granite outcroppings, and shallow frozen lakes or ponds. In spite of the latitude and elevation, snow had been only modest so far this winter, offering few good drifts to hide in. Under other circumstances, the land begged for Álukoi sport. But mother and son had to always take care to stay in the thick of the wood, except at night. This tierdragon hunted for food every other day, and would be gone for as long as light glowed in the sky, or about four hours. Only twice did it return with nothing. Every night it snored as loud as thunder, but Serukeeba dared not attack, fearing for her son.

One night Lorgi could stand the waiting no longer and devised his own plan. While his mother slept, he crept out onto the ice of a frozen lake. By the time Serukeeba found him at dawn, he had completed his work.

"Lorgi, get back over here under the trees!" Serukeeba ordered. "What do you think you are doing playing out there in the open?"

"That's me," Lorgi pointed to a life-sized ice sculpture he had made at the center of the frozen lake. "Good thing we made lots of art at the monastery."

"Worlds away and of no use to us now, son."

"You're wrong," said Lorgi. "If the tierdragon pounces on that, it can crash through the ice or get stuck on Kibak's fish hook."

"Kibak's fish hook?"

"A giant, wooden version of it with three swords for a tip," explained Lorgi, smiling with pride in his work. "Then we attack!"

"No! What if the beast only swats at your bait, or just grazes it with her tail? Or does not land hard enough to break through the ice?"

"What if it flies away and never returns?" asked Lorgi. "How long do we wait here?"

Stung, Serukeeba gazed at her son. He smiled back with confidence, but his ribs were starting to show. Without better nutrition, injuries did not heal. Nothing would replace spent claws. No "second wind" after great exertion. And neither of them had slept well since waking the monster. As long as winter held, not even a tierdragon could spot Álukois sitting among shaded drifts. No matter how late it came, spring would melt it all away, bringing ever longer days for the beast to hunt them. Though aching for revenge, Serukeeba had lost the strength and courage to attempt it. She wanted to strike when the beast snored in its lair. But it was proving to be a light sleeper. Serukeeba had no alternative plan, and Lorgi argued like a Tuzanchim.

"What's wrong now, mother? You look like Klimgu, before the Battle of Lake Gabriska."

"Please don't say that." Serukeeba winced.

"Don't be superstitious, mother. We make our own luck. Kibak says great peril and doubt usually precede great victory."

"Forget Kibak. Forget Klimgu, Baqwam, Moshal and all the rest. I wish you had asked me before making your ice carving, Lorgi. Or before falling into the cave and waking the beast in the first place! Now the tierdragon will never rest until it has slaughtered us. Do you understand?"

"You said it would keep hunting us anyway. If we can't sleep, why should we let the enemy?"

"I was hoping that if the beast lost track of us for long enough, then it would tire of this hunt and look for another."

"Want me to break it up? I can make it look natural."

"Too many tracks, too light already," said Serukeeba. "Back into the woods and stay there. Our lives depend on it."

"Fine," mumbled Lorgi. "But I have to see how my hook works."

"Only from the safety of the wood. I hope this will teach you a lesson. Nothing stops the Tierdragon of Monz. Absolutely nothing!"

Just as they hid under short trees to observe, their nemesis entered the sky, making large circles from a thousand feet up. Suddenly diving at falcon speed, it leveled out just a yard above the lake. With talons spread wide as a man's arms, eager to crush its prey, the terror pounced on Lorgi's carving.

Despite cracking and heaving, the long frozen lake refused to break, even under the impact. Out of rage or pain, the creature emitted such a long, deafening screech that both Álukois shut their ear lids. Lorgi's ruined work started to glow a pale violet, soaking up tierdragon blood. With all possible vigor, it flapped its wings and worked all but one limb, caught on something within the former ice sculpture. The monster had not broken through the ice as Lorgi had wished, but Kibak's design held fast.

"Yes!" shouted Lorgi. "I knew it would work."

"It seems you have taught me the lesson, here," said Serukeeba.

"No time to lose. Charge!" roared Lorgi, breaking into a gallop.

"NO! Get back here!" shrieked his mother. "We have no chance. You must come back. Lorgi! NO!"

"Hurry up," he shouted back. "Attaaaaaack!"

Lorgi had already run halfway to the beast and refused to stop. Knowing both would die in the attempt, Serukeeba chased after her son, praying for impossible luck. The tierdragon kept arching its back, then yanking or twisting a bleeding foot impaled on something thick and stubborn in the ice. Caught in a snare for the first time in its life, the beast emitted horrific screams and ignored everything but its foot until Lorgi came too close. Serukeeba roared her own war cry, hoping to draw the beast's attention away from her son.

Yet Lorgi kept silent like a general, focused only on his goal, intent on harming the enemy in the most efficient way possible. Just as he reached the tierdragon, it managed to free itself. Unwilling to risk a bleeding foot on the tiny but sharp-edged pest, the monster opted for a lash of its tail. Seeing doom, Lorgi turtled just in time.

Gasping in horror, Serukeeba heard a loud smack and saw a glistening white ball fly, bounce, then roll at terrible speed across to the far end of the lake—and beyond. When it finally came to rest, the tight bundle that had been Lorgi did not unravel, bleed or make any sound. It did not move at all. Both his mother and the tierdragon guessed that Lorgi had died from the trauma.

"Lorgi!" cried Serukeeba, aching to run to her son. But the tierdragon stood in her way.

"Lourghii," the beast mimicked her. Its tail bled from where it had struck Lorgi. Thinking, the beast eyed both Álukois. It turned to deal with the mother first.

"So this is how it ends," cursed Serukeeba. "For you, my Lorgi, my Golármon."

Rather than prolong the inevitable, she charged, desperate to inflict some type of injury before the beast took to the air and finished her off. Serukeeba was only able to grab the end of its tail in her forepaws as the tierdragon left the ground. Biting hard into the reptile, all that Serukeeba got for her efforts were a few bitter, leathery scales and a sore jaw. No blood, no injury.

In seconds, the beast swooped down upon Lorgi, half a mile away and still tightly rolled into a protective ball. In spite of its bleeding foot, the tierdragon seized the bundle with all its limbs, just in case the child still lived. Instantly it carried the prize back to the lair, as a distant, roaring Serukeeba chased after them on the ground. From a terrible height above the cave's entrance, the monster dropped its cargo, to ensure that it broke and died.

Lorgi hit the ground with a resounding smack. Sparks and chips from his back spikes flew off his body. Bouncing twice, he rolled down into the caves. Knowing all was lost, Serukeeba kept charging, in total rage. Expecting her, the tierdragon grabbed a torch to help flame the mother Álukoi when she arrived at the lair. Because it could not fly and keep the tool lit at the same time, the beast marched out on foot to battle its only *potential* natural enemy.

Serukeeba threw rock and ice in a desperate attempt to extinguish the torch, while making herself an evasive foe. Against a younger tierdragon, she could do nothing. But this beast had only one eye, lacked the ability to spark its own fire, and still bled from one foot and its tail. It would require both a torch and a stationary target to make its flame work. Serukeeba kept circling or darting from side to side to keep the giant off balance.

In a few minutes, the beast grew apathetic, waiting for the Álukoi to wear herself down. As long as Serukeeba could move freely among the boulders surrounding the cave's entrance, the stalemate persisted. But something began to stir from deep within the lair. For only a second, the foes stopped to listen.

Seeing the only opportunity she would have to injure the giant, Serukeeba lunged in. With all the speed and force of a young champion, she mauled the tierdragon's right wing with two quick slashes of both forepaws. The beast should have been quick enough to punish her for the surprise move, but Serukeeba's many duels against balkotars had given her unique skills. She escaped with only a tinge of heat on her back spikes.

The tierdragon lashed back, yet missed with its tail, its talons and even its fire. Daring the beast to expend its fire or risk tearing its wing more, Serukeeba backed away, but just to the maximum range of the beast's flame, about sixteen feet. Taking the gambit, the monster threw a lightning quick burst of fire at her.

Leaping aside, Serukeeba escaped the brunt of it. Yet several of her largest back spikes and half of her tail glowed from the heat. As that searing light faded, they turned a purple-grey and ached with pain from the burn. Putting an extra two feet between herself and the tierdragon, Serukeeba stopped again, ready to charge or jump aside with the next fireball. Not about to repeat the same mistake, the tierdragon waited, holding the torch directly in front of its huge mouth.

Serukeeba had to make her foe move before it stopped bleeding. She gathered a paw-full of dirt and tiny rocks as the tierdragon watched.

Aiming for the torch's fire, she threw with more speed than care, spraying the beast's whole face as well as the torch. The fire remained lit, but the monster pulled both the torch and its head back, also turning to the left and blinking to protect its good eye.

Out of ideas or the will to prolong the contest, Serukeeba charged in again. This time she slashed the beast's same wing with three more cuts, each as long as a man. She also snapped one of its vital bones in her jaws. Suddenly, the whole right wing looked like a ship's broken mast, its sail ripped apart by horrific winds or the most clever human enemy. This tierdragon would not fly again for months, if ever. But the effort had landed Serukeeba hard against the side of a beast many times her size, too close to escape its wrath this time.

Finding the Álukoi too close to hurt in any other way, the tierdragon made a gambit of its own. Sacrificing an already broken wing, the beast opted to roll its body on top of and over the foe, in order to crush her before the too clever Álukoi escaped again. Sudden, crushing weight broke some of Serukeeba's ribs and forced all the air out of her lungs. After completing its roll, the tierdragon bled in many places, while hundreds of its scales lay on the ground. But Serukeeba lay sprawled on her stomach, barely breathing.

Seeing its torch still lit after all that had just happened, the tierdragon opted for fire to finish off its enemy. Holding the torch inches before its mouth, the beast drew one long breath that swelled its belly. Wringing and squeezing all the fire it had left to throw on this day, the tierdragon puffed its cheeks to their maximum. When these could hold no more, the monster blew hard and long, sending out a flame that scorched most of Serukeeba's left side. Knowing that the Álukoi would soon die from that anyway—assuming that it still lived at all—the tierdragon slowly backed away. Anxious to deal with its own serious wounds, it began to stagger back towards its cave.

Despite subfreezing temperatures outside, steam from a natural hot spring kept the tierdragon's lair as warm as a tropical swamp. Unconscious, Lorgi dreamed he was home in the village lodge as the Tundrites were performing one of their more extreme cures. But the terrible sounds of warring dragons above jarred him awake. Finding his way out of the caverns, Lorgi reached the entrance only in time to see the end result. Both foes bled from many wounds. Serukeeba had inflicted far more severe cuts, but her own left side and belly glowed from burns, making those areas vulnerable. With several broken ribs, and unarmored areas completely exposed, she lay almost lifeless on her side. All hope and energy gone, she could only wait for the beast to finish her off.

"Run, Lorgi, or you die too!" she gasped, spitting blood as she spoke.

"NO!" screamed Lorgi, charging a beast many times his size.

Knowing that burnt armor offered the least resistance, the tierdragon raised its huge talons to strike the mother Álukoi's charred side. Desperate to stop the giant, Lorgi bit hard into its tail, but got no reaction. Frantic to stop the beast from killing his mother, Lorgi leapt onto its back, climbing all the way up to the base of its long neck. Surprised, the tierdragon froze, unsure whether to deal with the nuisance on its back first, or to kill the mother while she lay helpless.

With all his strength, Lorgi bit into the beast's neck, but only got his teeth stuck in the leathery hide. Immediately he discovered it was far easier to pry the tierdragon's scales away than to try and bite through them. The beast lost nine good ones, each larger than a man's hand, before deciding it had to remove the child nuisance first. The scales all over its body had always protected the tierdragon better than any armor. But once exposed, the softer tissue under them proved no match for Lorgi's teeth.

Shrieking in pain, the tierdragon suddenly bled from the neck. It lashed with its tail, but Lorgi dug his claws hard into the beast and could not be removed. Using all its uninjured limbs, the tierdragon struggled to force Lorgi off, but he anticipated every move and kept repositioning himself. After a few minutes, the beast realized it would have to strain its bleeding neck and risk breaking its own teeth on the foe.

Seeing her son about to die in the jaws of a tierdragon, Serukeeba forced herself back to life. In spite of her wounds and loss of blood, she regained a standing position. With one final burst of energy, she charged. Just before impact, she threw her body in such a way as to gore the tierdragon in the belly with her largest back spikes. The beast roared in agony, its blood pouring all over Serukeeba.

Lorgi kept prying more scales away and biting at the tierdragon's neck until it sprouted a fountain of blood. He only stopped when the great beast faltered and swayed. Fearing the behemoth would collapse on his mother, Lorgi jumped down and struggled to pull, push, then roll his mother out of the way. He barely succeeded when the giant crashed on its side, dead.

Lorgi's plan had succeeded, but at a horrible cost. His mother lay unconscious, breathing with the gurgling sound of mortal wounds. Suddenly Lorgi knew why she had to destroy his shell. Though a thousand miles from the nearest help, he still cried out, emitting a deep, mournful howl. Nothing stirred in the Dawnwood. Already the sun prepared to set, as a dry, frozen wind gained speed. Lorgi began to lick his mother's wounds, ignoring his own, and kept at it until exhaustion forced him to sleep.

32: A World Changed

Soon after Yómgolin began marching toward the unknown call, tierdragon screams shattered the air, even from many miles away. Moments later, those clashed with Álukoi roars for several minutes. Silence followed as Yómgolin continued, using his *pahápkoltam* to help find the source. At first, time and distance eluded the youth on his quest. But when those roars trumpeted again minutes later, Yómgolin stood to his maximum height, even stretching his ears to help locate the battle.

The instant he knew, he broke into a gallop. Suddenly more terrified than he had thought possible, Yómgolin had no idea what he could do when he finally got there. After what seemed like an hour, when he stopped to catch his breath, he heard a child's desperate cry for help. Only then did he realize just how far away the struggle had been.

The next morning, Yómgolin finally reached the spot, but no Álukois were to be found. All he could see was a massive tierdragon sprawled on its belly, framed in a muddy lake of its own dried blood. Much Álukoi blood had crystallized nearby. Away from the corpse, Yómgolin found two sets of Álukoi prints, one adult and one child. Only the mother's had come from a lake, and at a hard gallop. Both sets staggered down into the lair. Yómgolin wondered how either of them could have survived a battle with the tierdragon. Horrified yet curious, he ventured into the cave, expecting to find only charred corpses, countless bones—and two dead Álukois.

"Who enters?" Lorgi barked in Lendish, expecting a human.

"Yómgolin, of the Stonelaw," he gasped, surprised.

"Who is Yómgolin? Show yourself!" demanded Lorgi.

"I will when I can find you, whoever you are. What can you tell me of the battle above?"

"You don't sound like a Delfinian," said Lorgi, suspicious.

"I'm not! I am Yómgolin of the Zárong Kórzel, an Álukoi on a quest. What brave souls fought here?" When he reached the main chamber, Lorgi was waiting for him. Yet the instant they saw each other, both dropped their fighting stances. Necks reared back, ears shot up and eyes widened. Lorgi had never seen any other Álukoi but his mother.

"You don't even sound like a Lendishman," said Lorgi, confused.

"You hardly sound like an Álukoi," replied Yómgolin. "Why do you stay in this foul cave?"

"Only to hide from tierdragons. The one outside had been hunting us for weeks. Please help us."

"I'm sorry," Yómgolin gasped, seeing Lorgi's mother. "If only I had come earlier. Is she even...?"

"Barely. Only wakes for a few minutes at a time. I licked her cuts until they stopped bleeding. When she woke up, I helped her down here. But I don't know what else to do."

"Nor do I, except that she needs air, food, and a skilled healer," said Yómgolin. "The Stonelaw still has a few, if we can just get her to one. What of your own wounds, Lorgámon?"

"How do you know my name?"

"You both are well known—especially to me—despite living outside the Stonelaw," said Yómgolin. "Serukeeba as the *Recluse of Tiefenbo*, and you as the *Doom Child* which the seer Rokímba foretold. But now, you are also my quest."

"My mother and I just slew the Tierdragon of Monz! So don't call me a *doom* child!"

"No time to argue," said Yómgolin. "I will cut two saplings, trim them into poles, and fasten a choice portion of the dragon's hide to them, while you gather things we can use."

Confused, Lorgi wiggled his ears.

"A travois for your mother. I need all the help you can give, whatever your own injuries will allow, Lorgámon."

"Call me Lorgi. What can I do?"

"Bring any rope, chain, leather, and all the round shields you can find. Then we must get your mother out of the lair. Its fumes are not helping her. Then far away from here before... never mind."

"Before what?" demanded Lorgi.

"Others discover your deed. In my 25 years, no one has ever slain a tierdragon. Do you have any idea what you have achieved here?"

"A disaster," said Lorgi. "Please hurry."

While Yómgolin harvested two young pines just strong enough to support Serukeeba's weight, Lorgi gathered what he could find quickly. Done in ten minutes, he sat down by Yómgolin as the young adult finished making poles out of the saplings. At that moment, Lorgi wished he had a big brother or sister, as did several human children of Tiefenbo who also lacked them. He mutely waited for as long as he could, but had spent months with the Tuzanchim and feared for his mother's survival.

"What are you doing and how long will it take?"

"I'm working as fast as I can," said Yómgolin.

"How soon can we go?"

"That depends. How many round shields did you find?"

"Five," shouted Lorgi, hoping that would speed their departure.

"Only five?" Yómgolin frowned.

"How many do we need?"

"All that there are. Even the best shields make poor wheels, lasting only minutes under an Álukoi's weight. Find more while I skin the dragon. If there are none, then grab anything round and sturdy. Round enough to roll like a wheel. Understand?"

"Of course I do," barked Lorgi. "You don't have to talk to me like a baby or a drunken human!"

"You sound like a champion to me," Yómgolin smiled, keeping his true thoughts to himself: *Not even four and already your wayward mother has turned you into a lowlander hyúlem barbarian! You sound like a desperate young man of the Miter Kingdoms, or an angry rogue from The Claim looking for a fight, or even a bloodthirsty Tuzanchim! The price for Álukois living outside the Stonelaw, ignoring the ways of their own people.*

"Gánsi," chirped Lorgi. "The Tuzanchim made me a warrior after I fought at the Battle of Lake Gabriska."

"Uuph," moaned Yómgolin, holding his belly with both forepaws. "The thought makes me nauseous."

"My mother said it was nothing to be proud of, but I had to protect my friends. You would have done the same."

"Let us bring you home, to the Continent's only real civilization. Know that by fighting the Tuzanchim, savages with no honor, you have done a good deed, even if you still shout like one."

"No, I fought with them. We were ambushed."

"Say no more," begged Yómgolin, waving his forepaws to make sure Lorgi stopped. His ears drooped and his face grimaced with a look of pained disgust.

"The Tuzanchim have honor, hospitality and traditions, just like us," said Lorgi. "They saved me from a wicked sorcerer who was raising balkotars."

"That was *you*?" gasped Yómgolin. "I have misjudged you. You must tell me all about your adventures, once we are safely away from here. But time to check on your mother."

Lorgi ran back into the lair. Only a moment later he returned, frantic. "She's not breathing!"

"Serukeeba was stable when I checked a few minutes ago," said Yómgolin. "You have been too long among *hyúlems*. Maybe you think an Álukoi needs a breath every few seconds."

Yet both ran straight down to the main chamber where she lay. After a long pause, Yómgolin still could not be sure if she lived. But he knew nothing of the healing arts. To keep Lorgi's hopes up, as well as his own, Yómgolin insisted on removing Serukeeba from the lair at once to get fresh air, saying it could help her. Running back up to the entrance, he lobbed off a portion of the tierdragon's good wing, folded it to double thickness, then returned to gently roll Serukeeba onto it. With Lorgi's help, he dragged her most of the way before the wing ripped apart. Once they had gotten Serukeeba into the open, they sat staring at her and each other.

"At least she's breathing now," said Lorgi.

"Good. Hurry and see what else you can find while I finish the travois."

Scouring the lair for anything that might be useful, Lorgi collected a dozen more shields that were not round, thinking that Yómgolin could easily make them so. The mighty quester tried, but discovered that *hyúlem* metalwork had improved since he had been a child of Lorgi's age. These shields would rather break than surrender their form. Lorgi brought out a dozen good war lances and a chest overflowing with gems and pearls. At first Yómgolin saw no use for any of it. But after a long silent pause, he started making a second, much smaller travois for Lorgi.

"Before we go, Lorgi, I have a favor to ask."

"Only if it's quick."

"Find something small, able to hold fifty Dunhala Crowns."

"But the Tuzanchim say gold outweighs its worth for travelers," said Lorgi, pinching his nostrils and twitching his ears with suspicion. "My mother says to avoid gold for all its ills and evils."

"These are ill and evil times, young Lorgi. A paw-full of gold—even a king's boatload—will make no difference, except as a great bargaining tool. Coins from the kingdom of Dunhala out-value any other in the West. A mere fifty of them will not be too weighty for us."

"But a chest of gems can be worth twelve filled with gold."

"Yes, but *hyúlems* will do anything for gold," said Yómgolin. "It will come in handy if we meet up with any."

"Alright, but only if I can find it quickly so we can go."

"*Gánsi*, Lorgi."

When they were ready to leave, Serukeeba opened her eyes halfway, murmuring "Golármon?"

"No, mother," said Lorgi. "This is Yómgolin. Yómgolin of the Zárong Kórzel, here to help us."

"Golármon, where are you?" moaned Serukeeba, gazing up at the sky. "I will rejoin you very soon. Be ready for me."

"Mother, it's me. Lorgi. Father died before I hatched."

"Golármon, know that I have partly avenged..." Serukeeba trailed off.

"She is far away from us now," said Yómgolin. "Too far to reach. I am very sorry, Lorgi."

"She was like that last night," said Lorgi. "Every few hours she seemed to wake, only to talk to herself, like she could not hear me, see me, or anything."

"The tierdragon's fire must have fevered her mind," guessed Yómgolin.

"Weliben said she was like that when they found her after she fought the balkotars. We should go straight home to Tiefenbo. Jinva and

Weliben and Ubwan and others in our village will know what to do."

"I doubt it," sighed Yómgolin.

With eyes closed, Serukeeba mumbled. "As the Tierdragon of Monz took you from me, my Golármon, so have we taken from her. You can be proud...I named our son Lorgámon, not of the Stonelaw that failed us, but of Tiefenbo, our dear home."

"Lorgi, people only speak like that when very close to death, be they Álukoi, Volping or even *hyúlem*," murmured Yómgolin. "There is nothing anyone can—"

"NO! Don't you dare give up on my mother!" screamed Lorgi. "She was like this once before, and so was I. With our help she will get well. We make our own luck. And you are supposed to be the quester. So don't tell me what you can't do. Be a warrior!"

Yómgolin reared his neck back, drooped his ears and swallowed hard. "Of course I will do all I can, and we are both—I mean, all three of us—on the same quest now. No need to argue. You must have had terrible adventures indeed, and not even four years old!"

"I'm fine, and will be four when the snow starts to melt. It smells ready now, so stop talking down to me."

Raising both forepaws as a sign of truce, Yómgolin kept silent. What could he or anyone possibly say to an angry, frightened child? He had to evacuate Serukeeba, and yet she should not be moved at all for at least a week, due to her injuries. The journey home would kill her. Yet camping anywhere near a fallen tierdragon's lair begged a violent death. Countless human bandits, perhaps a rival tierdragon, and various other savage beasts would seek its plunder, and kill anyone—even a child—whom they only guessed might have had a chance to see it.

Hating his choices, Yómgolin knew he must sacrifice the mother to save her son. He dreaded the moment when she no longer lived, and would do all he could to postpone it, though that could only add to her suffering.

Struggling to bring a delirious Serukeeba home, Yómgolin and Lorgi made slow progress through the rugged hills of the western Dawnwood. All their shields gave out within the first hour. By strapping the buckling shields against each other, Lorgi was able to make them last an hour more. But from that point on, the pair had to drag their loads the hard way, the ancient way. Serukeeba's travois began to give out, requiring ever more frequent repairs. Three or four times per hour they stopped to check on her.

Whenever anything edible came into view, it became their priority. If they could get Serukeeba to swallow it, Lorgi cheered. But he and Yómgolin went hungry most of the time. Each day they seemed to cover less ground, until it seemed that even *hyúlems* with snowshoes could do better. By the time they reached the Yazutak River, it swelled from snowmelt as the days were growing longer and warmer.

Suddenly, Serukeeba's nostrils flared, then began to twitch. Familiar aromas made her inhale deeply. With a yawn and a stretch that broke her travois, she stood on all fours. Still too weak to walk, she waited patiently while her son and Yómgolin repaired her travois yet again. Sitting back on her haunches, she perked her ears up, sniffed hard and looked all around. Knowing she was near home, she smiled. Now she recognized her son, who finally succeeded in introducing her to Yómgolin.

Two days later, the trio came within sight of Tiefenbo. Yómgolin sighed with relief, but Lorgi gasped in shock at what he saw. Serukeeba rose from her travois, breaking it beyond any hope of repair. With her eyes, ears and nostrils working hard to make sense of it all, she stood to her full height for the first time since her battle. What she saw horrified her, yet brought her fully back to life.

Two Delfinian bowmen in the village's new tower scanned the southern horizon. A dozen more looked ready to do so from Tiefenbo's wall walk. Demanding all eyes with its steep conical roof set with glazed red tiles, the tower dared to fly the great banner of the Stonelaw. The sight made Yómgolin sigh with gladness. Serukeeba snorted her disdain, but Lorgi delighted in its red, white and brilliant gold colors standing out against the grey sky.

"The Stonelaw's banner screams louder than any other on the Continent," huffed Serukeeba. "Nothing but foolish vanity to fly it here. I would have advised Tiefenbo against such needless risk."

"Big as the banners at Uxanda," said Lorgi. "Flying from the tower's steep roof, it all looks like a giant hat with a feather on top."

"A sad day it is, when lowland *flumpetry* reaches Tiefenbo," moaned Serukeeba. "I always admired Klimgu for avoiding it."

"What is *flumpetry*, mother?"

"Blatant displays of self-flattery, usually wasting much resources," she answered. "You will need to see a bit of the Castled Lands to really understand."

"Hasn't young Lorgi seen too much already?" asked Yómgolin.

"Perhaps the rest of us Álukois have not seen enough," said Serukeeba.

Smoke from a dozen chimneys wafted into the air, some with the enchanting aromas of savory stews, fresh baked pies, breads, muffins and pastries, all carried toward the hungry Álukois by a gentle sea breeze. First Lorgi, then his mother and Yómgolin stood up to their full heights to savor them, and for the best view of the strange new village-turned-fortress. All three gave audible groans of hunger.

"Still smells like Tiefenbo," said Lorgi, unnerved. "But it looks like a castle."

"Rokímba had described a sleepy village, so I was shocked when I first arrived," said Yómgolin. "But it has changed, even since then. Now their tower has a roof and a banner. What next?"

"When I left, people were many miles and moons away from any plan beyond starting over from scratch," said Serukeeba. "Yet all promised to see the village rebuilt before we returned. 'Stout and thriving' they said. Maybe they went too far."

"This is no village of seventy people," laughed Yómgolin. "Three hundred at least. And ready as Miters to turn away any unwanted visitors."

"Who can blame them?" huffed Serukeeba. "If only that wall and tower had been up before the sorcerer came, it would have spared us from many long and bloody journeys."

"But then so many good things would not get to happen, mother," said Lorgi. "We saved lives and spun great luck. And made so many friends in the east."

"He makes friends as quickly as a Volping!" laughed Serukeeba, speaking to Yómgolin.

"What's a Volping?" asked Lorgi.

"The most lovable, furry little friend you ever could have," smiled his mother. "We must visit one of their towns on our way back from the next Winter Gathering."

"And they must come and visit us here, too," insisted Lorgi.

"We can talk about that later," said Serukeeba, urging him to walk ahead while she and Yómgolin paused.

"His speech hardly sounds Álukoi," said Yómgolin. "It may be hard for him at his first Gathering. Lorgi knows so little about the Stonelaw."

"Why should he? It failed him and everyone dear to him. But now he speaks five languages and can write in Esterlani. May his gift help us all. The Tuzanchim taught him to think like a Steppe warrior. But he also studied with the Gral-Chaner, a holy man of Shohan. Don't ask me how, but he has learned to spin. If only I could! Even now he has a bit of the seer in him, as well as the champion. At all of four years. How am I to parent him?"

"You must be only too proud," sighed Yómgolin, looking glum.

"Take cheer," Serukeeba smiled. "You will become fast friends and achieve great things together, Yómgolin of the Zárong Kórzel."

"How can you even guess?"

"Because a bit of the seer runs in me too," laughed Serukeeba.

"I hope you won't take to spilling food or breaking things to make your prophecies, when you grow old," chuckled Yómgolin.

"Nor will I offend people the first time I meet them. Only Rokímba has such ways, despite her good heart. But know that I am old now, long before my time, thanks to the tierdragon."

"The Stonelaw's best healers may be able to help you," said Yómgolin.

"I doubt it, and we are still far from the Stonelaw, by a trail rife with bandits. Far better for me to rest at home among friends."

"Nuwak!" shouted Lorgi, waving to a boy in the tower.

"Lorgi!" screamed the Tundrite boy, from a quarter mile away.

Lorgi broke into a run. His mother and Yómgolin walked.

Adult voices shouted. All the soldiers scurried to the walls. Bells rang. Horns sounded. Every voice within the town screamed with joy. Seconds later, the iron gate burst open and the town's residents poured out to greet their long-lost champions. When calm was restored an hour later, the Delfinian soldiers finally convinced everyone to return to the safety within the walls.

At sundown Tiefenbo held the most lavish feast in its history. For three hours, people devoured every word as Serukeeba and Lorgi retold their adventures. The moment Lorgi finished, the Delfinians made music and danced to celebrate. Most people took turns grilling the Álukois about details of their travels. The Tundrites made certain that all had too much to eat, were up to date on local matters and always in good humor.

Awkward at being around so many humans, Yómgolin just observed. He spoke only to answer direct questions. Within minutes, even the Tundrites left him alone. Lorgi talked with his young friends, especially Brogan, Nuwak, and Sirwan. All three children had grown an inch or two, and carried a twinge of sadness in their eyes. Brogan's voice sounded deeper. But Lorgi had changed the most, having "earned" several scars on his belly and gained 150 pounds.

The festivities would have lasted all night but for Serukeeba. Though in fine spirits, she was still healing from deep wounds and burns. Dozing off, she woke a few minutes later but soon fell asleep again. Excusing herself, she urged everyone to keep celebrating while she retired. Concerned, Rokímba trailed after her, followed by Lorgi and Jinva. Weliben came next, then most of the villagers. Without any of the talkative Álukois to sustain it, the party ended.

The next morning, all four Álukois met to discuss the treasure brought from the tierdragon's lair. As Lorgi, his mother and Yómgolin watched, Rokímba scattered the chest's contents randomly about the solarium floor. Gesturing for silence, she divined order from her chaotic "founding" of the riches gleaming and sparkling before them. The old seer tried to remain neutral and detached, but a frown came over her face. Her eyes narrowed and her ears pulled back, the way she had looked when divining Lorgi's shell. Just as Rokímba began to speak, Jinva and Weliben knocked at the door. Thankful for the interruption, Serukeeba hoped it would spare all of them from another dire prediction.

"Far beyond fifty crowns, master Lorgi!" chuckled Yómgolin.

"I had no time to be picky; we had to get away from the tierdragon's cave," said Lorgi. "So I just grabbed the nearest chest and stuffed it with whatever was handy."

"A king's ransom!" gasped Jinva and Weliben together.

"Quite a terrible dragon indeed," said Yómgolin. 'Perhaps the longest-lived tierdragon ever, by the sea of riches we found."

"The Tierdragon of Monz had rotting teeth and lungs," said Lorgi. "And she needed torches to make fire."

"Actually, it was a *he*, but a terrible dragon just the same," said Yómgolin.

Puzzled and irked, Lorgi looked to his mother for an explanation.

"By *dragon*, Yómgolin means a pirate, a bandit on a grand scale," Serukeeba told him. "I guess we never got around to using that word at home. What the word *drágon* means in Álukop, and why Álukois take great offense when *hyúlems* apply the word to us."

"How are they supposed to know that?" asked Lorgi. "Human people would also take offence by how we use the words *hyúlem* and *lowlander*."

"The most important thing is that we take great care with this treasure," said Rokímba.

"I'll toast that," cheered Weliben.

"You'll toast anything," Jinva laughed. "Just think what it could buy for our village."

"Trouble beyond anything Tiefenbo has ever seen," warned the seer.

"I have no stores, no spent claws to trade," said Serukeeba. "After what happened to me, I may never have any again."

"Our Delfinian soldiers say Zortríton was done in by lances tipped with spent Álukoi claws," said Weliben.

"None of us should ever trade in claws again," said Rokímba. "I see it becoming a law."

"All the more reason to enjoy this wealth," argued Serukeeba. "How else will I ever restock my hall? We could all use this treasure."

"The tierdragon hoarded these riches after devouring their owners," said the seer. "Only by careful restraint may any dare touch them— without bringing terrible curses upon us all."

"And what might those be, that we have not tasted already?"

demanded Serukeeba, growing angrier with each word.

"First, last and foremost, lowlander greed, beyond anything you can imagine," answered Rokímba. "Even now it tugs at us."

"After what all of us have suffered, we need this reward," said Serukeeba. "I think our whole village should vote on it."

"Weli and I heartily agree," said Jinva, as her husband nodded.

"But Lorgi found the treasures," said Yómgolin. "He packed them onto his travois and carried them all the way home. Spoils of a battle he fought and won. They are rightfully his to do with as he sees fit."

All eyes bored in on the seer, demanding her reaction. Ears and nostrils twitching, Rokímba looked shocked for not having predicted Yómgolin's suggestion. By every feudal law and custom known to the Continent, he was right. Lorgi found the plunder, helped slay the tierdragon, saved his mother's life and brought the spoils home. He had also helped Yómgolin in his quest, and Yómgolin supported his claim. So Lorgi could do what he liked with the treasure, despite being far too young to make such decisions.

For once, the seer found no words with which to respond. Her fluttering ears, blinking eyes and pinched nostrils showed her agitation. A mere youth by the name of Yómgolin had just bested Rokímba, the oldest seer of the Álukois.

Smiling hugely, Lorgi decided right then that Yómgolin would be his new, big brother. Glaring at Yómgolin to keep him from going to extremes to influence her son, Serukeeba then gave her harshest look to Rokímba, to try and stop her from making any more dire predictions. Studying all four Álukois, Jinva and Weliben found their expressions just as telling as any humans. Lorgi met all eyes before focusing on his mother, expecting her to give the final word. Yómgolin looked between the mother and the seer, wondering who would prevail.

"If we don't know what to do with this treasure, we had best sit on it quietly until we do," muttered Serukeeba.

"A secret half this rich is hard to keep," said Jinva.

"Make that impossible," said Weliben, looking sternly at his wife.

Resenting his implication, she scowled back at him.

"Once travelers learn of this tierdragon's fall, greed and desperation will drive untold thousands to seek its plunder," warned Rokímba. "I see endless trails of blood."

"Stop!" roared Serukeeba. After a long breath, she asked, "How long before it can be traced here?"

"We took almost nothing of what there was," said Lorgi. "All the Continent's wagons could not hold it. You saw the treasure room, mother. Remember?"

"Actually, I cannot," sighed Serukeeba.

"As is to be expected," said Rokímba.

"What do you remember, mother?" asked Lorgi.

"Our nightmare on the frozen lake," she answered. "Then being dragged along on a travois of wood and tierdragon hide, beside our dear Yazutak, welcoming us home."

"Divide the treasure now," said the seer. "You can keep the pearls here. At least they are of the sea that salts this hamlet. Safe to trade here—a handful at a time. But the gold must go. Yómgolin can take it back to the Stonelaw as proof of his quest. May it irk the Council of Elders, yet help him win favor with people vital to his happiness. The gems can be safely traded when a large caravan from the east arrives this summer."

"Kibak!" cheered Lorgi. "Is Wenji coming too?"

"Lorgi, don't interrupt," scolded his mother.

"None can see that far, Lorgi," chuckled Rokímba. "But take great care with every barter using this haunted wealth. If any of you trade too directly with the lowlanders, it will destroy Tiefenbo—and any who whisper the name."

"All that from spilling things on the floor?" wondered Jinva, shaking her head.

"No. Sadly, I have more," moaned the seer. "The plague ends. It will hibernate for at least several years. Perhaps a decade."

"Cause for cheer, I'd say," shouted Jinva.

"No! Without plague, all the Castled Lands race to war!" shouted Rokímba. "This will be the bloodiest year ever. We must work hard to stay clear of it all. Ever beware the lowlanders."

"We've always been far enough away," said Jinva.

"No more," said the seer. "The world shrinks. New evils supplant the old. They will find ways to extend their reach further than ever before."

"So the lowlanders have gotten more clever. Well so have we," assured Weliben, with a nod.

"Ruthless fortune hunters, whole companies of brigands will test the Stonelaw," said Rokímba. "Some may find Tiefenbo."

"How can you…never mind," Weliben stopped himself.

"I was sent a warning dream last night," sighed Rokímba. "One might as well travel the lowlands. No place is safe. Dragon hunters may soon ply the furthest reaches of the Stonelaw. The most wicked *hyúlem* ambitions know no limits. Only plague and tierdragons keep them in check. Yet both now sleep."

"But the tierdragon is dead," said Lorgi. "And we can make friends with the lowlanders."

"I'll turn back the dragon hunters for you," boasted Yómgolin.

"Before you charge into their nets, know that they are a new breed, far more skilled in the crime," snapped Rokímba.

"Nets? Why would you think they use nets?" laughed Yómgolin.

Jinva and Weliben shook their heads. Their eyes told the youth to be quiet.

"Because I'm the oldest and most practiced seer of the Álukois. You are but a young, love-smitten fool trying to become a warrior. I cannot imagine easier prey for the clever. Those who would not listen to me are all dead. Wake up, Yómgolin!"

"No lowlander hunters will ever catch me dozing."

"Only thirteen of them made quick work of Zortríton," warned the seer. "You found a tierdragon miraculously slain by two Álukois, a burned mother and her child. Whole empires have been toppled by surprisingly small armies, or even a mere handful of individuals. The future belongs to the swift and the clever—good or not."

"If Zortríton had been awake, if any had fought him in an honorable contest, none would have defeated him," argued Yómgolin, still smarting from the seer's put downs. "If that dragon still had the means to spark its own fire, none could have defeated it, or dared to try in the first place."

"Wrong again," snapped Rokímba, meeting everyone's eyes. "Lorgi felt compelled to attack. If the tierdragon still had its spark, it certainly would have roasted him—and broken through the ice, frozen its wings and drowned. So Lorgi's plan would have worked anyway." Rokímba gazed at Lorgi before adding, "I believe he considered that."

Glowing with pride, Serukeeba opened her mouth to speak, but Rokímba stopped her.

"I know Lorgi to be the doom child, but for whom?" asked the seer. "He and his mother have a curious way of bringing doom to those most needing it. Seri, if only you still had his shell, I would study it again today, and take it to the next Winter Gathering to confer with other seers."

"You just had to bring that up now!" muttered Serukeeba, scowling at her.

"What was so wrong with my shell?" asked Lorgi, casting a hurt look between his mother and Rokímba. "Why did you have to destroy it, mother?"

Swallowed hard, Serukeeba took a long breath. Her most dreaded moment had suddenly arrived. "Lorgi, I have lived with hard luck my whole life, as if under a curse."

"Did you have a bad shell too?" he asked.

"No, but the seer at my hatching party hardly predicted my destiny. We Álukois are always being visited by tragedy. Over-hibernation. War. Dragon hunters. And now plague. For all its Councils, Winter Gatherings and finely brushed words, the Stonelaw has not been able to help its people, or reverse our decline. What good is it? Doom doesn't surprise me, after everything else."

"What about my shell?" asked Lorgi. "What about all the good luck you say we make?"

"After all that had happened before your hatching, I could stand no more." Serukeeba looked only at her son, who cocked his head and raised his ears, trying to understand. "Rokímba's words only doomed your shell, Lorgi. I just…with all the loss, pain and despair…I refused to listen or accept any more of it. I just had to drive away all the bad luck, for both our sakes. For everyone else too."

"What did Rokímba say to you on my first day?" demanded Lorgi.

"I can tell you later, in private," murmured Serukeeba.

"No. I'm tired of people telling me how they are going to explain things later!" yelled Lorgi. "Later never comes. I want to know right now. Rokímba, do you remember what you said?"

Swallowing, the seer nodded. She tried to look away, but Lorgi began to spin her. Rokímba fought it, yet Lorgi forced her to lock eyes with him, like the most skilled in that rare art. She opened her mouth to speak, but struggled. "I…it…so long ago…" Rokímba felt like she was going to faint.

After a grueling pause, Serukeeba tapped her son on the side of his head to break the spell. "Perhaps now you can understand how I feel about all this."

Rokímba sighed with a nod of admission. "Whatever you think of me, the Stonelaw, or the world, you both must come to the next Winter Gathering. It may be our last. With what you have been through, you carry great influence. We desperately need your voice, Serukeeba. Stop hiding and use it. Terrible wars are coming. We must prepare if we are to survive."

"We just defeated the Tierdragon of Monz!" shouted Lorgi. "We helped overthrow the Gran Vazuk of the Tuzanchim Empire and the horrible king of Shohan. We got rid of that sorcerer and his whole army of balkotars. Who would dare bother us now?"

"You certainly rid the world of powerful evils," sighed Rokímba. "But not the Monz Tierdragon."

"You were not even there!" yelled Lorgi. "For weeks, we had to stay hidden in the woods near her lair. My mother got very little sleep. We had almost no food. But we waited and studied our enemy, like good warriors. When the chance came, we risked everything and fought her to the death."

"Unfortunately that was an old male," said Yómgolin. "Hopefully too old to ever have nested with the real Tierdragon of Monz."

"How could you know, Yómgolin?" shouted Lorgi. "You had never even been outside the Stonelaw until your quest."

"I am sorry to tell you, Lorgi, but the female tierdragon is even larger and more violent than the male," said Yómgolin.

"Nothing in all the world could be bigger or worse than what we met," screamed Lorgi. "And since you never fought anything, you could not possibly know."

"There are other differences between genders of the tierdragon," murmured Yómgolin, looking to Serukeeba or the seer to steer the conversation.

"Like what?" snapped Lorgi. "I don't believe you."

Yómgolin shook his head. "That I will let your mother explain later."

"No more later!" yelled Lorgi. "Everyone stop talking to me like a baby! I'm a warrior, and I want everything explained right now."

"I do remember fighting the beast, and never had a second to worry about its gender!" huffed Serukeeba. "Both Lorgi and I were too terrified to notice such details. We should all just be glad that the Continent has one less tierdragon."

"Yómgolin, how well did you close its lair when you left?" asked Rokímba.

"We were too worried about getting Seri out alive to care about anything else," he admitted.

"Pray that no one else finds it before you return to seal the lair," said the seer. "Every scoundrel on the Continent—whole armies of them— will seek the treasure the instant rumors sprout. As for Lorgi, the real Monz Tierdragon will seek revenge, if that old male ever belonged to her. You will never be safe anywhere."

"Stop it!" yelled Serukeeba. "No more doom, blood, curses or avalanches. Not in my hall. We have all suffered enough. Don't you dare feed more fear to my son."

"I'm not afraid," assured Lorgi. "We beat all our enemies. We are strong. We are free. And blessed with friends from here all the way to Shohan."

"I am sorry, but the tierdragon you slew has spawned dangerous new quests," said Rokímba. "This is only the beginning. Of Doom. But for whom, I cannot say. If we are to survive, we must be more clever, fierce, and better able to work with *hyúlems*. Something I learned from Tiefenbo. What must be said at the next Gathering. I will need all your support to make the old ones listen—and the young ones think."

"In other words, we must change our ways," said Serukeeba. "What many people fear most."

"The Stonelaw will have to crumble before our doting Council of Elders dare consider it," warned Yómgolin.

"What's so hard about change?" asked Lorgi.

"You will be the key to it, child," sighed the seer.

defín lebék yo

gánsi méni, góbo nóshuls yi árgosangs
kámur góbo tirfúm; kámur páu túzin vir
Lorgi-zin árgosang tudá katínu!

Many thanks, fine snacks and adventures.
May good triumph; may peace be yours.
Lorgi's adventure will continue!

End of Book One

Character Glossary

Aterwak (**Ăt**erwăk) Tundrite man of Tiefenbo.

Baqwam (**Bôk**wôm) Gifted female Tuzanchim captain, imperial *accounter*, and one of the few literate Tuzanchim.

Birentak (**Bĭr**entăk) Tundrite elder of Tiefenbo and Kamwa's uncle.

Brogan (**Brō**găn) Far-sighted Delfinian boy of Tiefenbo, seven years older than Lorgi.

Chotzan (Chōt**săn**) Tuzanchim, Second for Klimgu until Battle at Lake Gabriska.

Chumga (**Chūm**gah) Old Tuzanchim, Lorgi's wagon driver on journey to Uxanda.

Ganjaset (**Gôn**jôset) Stern, cautious Tuzanchim, lead scout and Third for Klimgu.

Glomin (**Glō**mĭn**)** Cynical, worldly Delfinian trader of Tiefenbo.

Golármon (Gō**lôr**môn) Serukeeba's late husband, Lorgi's father, and great Álukoi champion. Died fighting a tierdragon.

Gral-Chaner (Grăl-**Chă**ner) Spiritual monastery leader, who saw the Álukois as heaven-sent to help overthrow the king of Shohan.

Gran Vazuk (Grăn Va**zūk**) Emperor, "His Greatness," supreme ruler of the Tuzanchim Empire, residing in the capital, Uxanda. Uncle of Puchakta, his sole heir.

Gurjik (Gur**jĭk**) Tuzanchim rebel fluent in Tundrish; Second for Baqwam, and one of Serukeeba's interpreters.

Jinva (**Jĭn**va) Middle-aged Delfinian woman of Tiefenbo and Weliben's wife.

Jinwak (**Jĭn**wăk) Captain of the Guard (one of many in Uxanda). Sijun's adopted son. He was born a Tundrite.

Kamwa   (**Kăm**wa) Tundrite adolescent of Tiefenbo and
              Birentak's nephew.

Kibak   (**Kee**bôk) Outspoken Tuzanchim lead scout, gambler,
              adventurer and entrepreneur.

Klimgu   (**Klĭm**gū) Charismatic Tuzanchim quiver leader, whose
              destiny (and that of the Tuzanchim Empire) changed by
              meeting Lorgi.

Lorgámon (Lor**găm**ôn) Nicknamed "**Lorgi**." Lorgámon of
              Tiefenbo, son of Serukeeba and Golármon. Álukoi child
              with a gift for languages, making friends, getting into
              trouble, feasting and *spinning*.

Lutyam   (**Lŭt**yăm) Cynical Laskomian monk/linguist, working to
              remove the Tuzanchim from his homeland, while nagging
              their leaders with questions of conscience.

Moshal   (**Mō**shal) Laskomian monk/engineer from Lutyam's
              village, also working to remove the Tuzanchim from his
              homeland. But then he fell in love with one.

Natiqua   (Nă**tee**kwah) Old yet spry Tuzanchim/Shohaneze double
              agent working for Queen Sayewin (but not the king), *and*
              for Klimgu at the same time.

Nuwak   (**Nū**wăk) far-sighted Tundrite boy of Tiefenbo, six
              months younger than Brogan, and grandson of Ubwan.

Ortung   (**Ō**r**tūng**) One of five Tuzanchim generals who fought
              in the Battle of Sangira.

Palitéa   (Pă**lĭte**-ah) Old Álukoi and Rokímba's best friend, who
              tried to help at Lorgi's hatching.

Porzan   (**Pō**r**zăn**) Tuzanchim healer/herbalist who treated Lorgi
              on the journey to Uxanda.

Poto   (**Pō**tō) Gral-Chaner's main assistant at monastery in the
              Shirlangu Mountains; also its gourmet cook.

Puchakta (Pū**chôk**tô) Nephew and sole heir of the Gran Vazuk.
              Personally owned the Near Valley.

Rauben (**Rau**ben) Delfinian tradesman of Tiefenbo.

Rokímba (Rŏ**kĭm**bah) Eldest Álukoi seer, predicted doom from Lorgi's shell. She obtained most of her prophecies by *founding*, or spills, accidents, and chance.

Satungke (Sô**tūng**ke) Shohaneze ambassador to the Tuzanchim Empire under the Gran Vazuk. Bought Lorgi and Wenji, for use in his king's arena, then regretted it. At one time the richest man in Shohan.

Sayewin (**Sā**ewĭn) Queen of Shohan. Capable, beautiful, and miserable as wife to the king. Employed Natiqua as spy.

Serukeeba (Serū**kee**bah) Nicknamed "**Seri**." Tiefenbo's protector, Lorgi's mother and Golármon's wife. Dubbed the "Recluse of Tiefenbo" for making her hall outside the Stonelaw. Also called "doom's mother."

Sijun (Sĭ**jūn**) Wise old Tuzanchim *wagoner*, who helped care for Lorgi on the journey to Uxanda. Advised Klimgu, then Chotsan. Jinwak's adoptive mother.

Sirwan (**Sĭr**wăn) Tundrite girl of Tiefenbo, six years older than Lorgi. Liked to tease Brogan.

Spider Sorcerer (spider shaman) Grew army of balkotars at his stronghold in west Dawnwood. Attacked Serukeeba, Tiefenbo, and abducted Lorgi, who burned his house down while playing in his laboratory.

Temsuji (Tem**sū**jee) Tuzanchim *wagoner* and Sijun's friend.

Tonche (**Tōn**che) Lead Shohaneze partisan, allied with Klimgu against Shohan's king. Quickly earned rank in horde.

Twarejik (**Twôr**ejeek – OR – Twôre**jeek**) Tuzanchim quiver leader, skilled at defensive warfare, swaying difficult people, and Klimgu's lifelong friend.

Ubwan (**Ūb**wăn) Tundrite, Nuwak's grandmother, and oldest human resident of Tiefenbo.

Weliben   (**Wel**ĭben) Middle-aged Delfinian. Jinva's husband and Tiefenbo's informal mayor.

Wenji   (**Wen**jee) Beautiful, clever Shohaneze orphan, slave, concubine, and Lorgi's friend.

Yómgolin   (**Yôm**gōlĭn) Álukoi adolescent on his coming-of-age quest to find Lorgi and Serukeeba.

Zikurjam   (Zĭ**kūr**jăm) Corrupt, freakish "special envoy" to the Gran Vazuk in Uxanda.

Ziteng   (**Zee**teng) Tuzanchim scout for Klimgu until he perished in the Battle of Lake Gabriska.

Zortríton   (Zōr**trī**tôn) Overconfident young Álukoi champion slain by human bandits.

Glossary of Places & Peoples

Álukois (**Ăl**ūkoys) Snowdragons, or "rock dragons" who migrated to the Continent over 10,000 years ago. {* the Wembrish pronounce it *Ălūqwahs* *}

Castled Lands (**Că**sld **Lă**nds) Everything west of the Deadwood and south of the Stonelaw. Also called the (West) Lowlands by residents of the Highlands, or Stonelaw.

Dawnwood (**Dôn**wood) Largest and oldest of the Continent's "Great Woods" or ancient forests, stretching from Kitria in the West to the extreme northeast reaches of the Tuzanchim Empire in the East.

Delfinians (Delf**ĭn**ians) A short, hearty (human) people originally from the West Delfinian Islands. They settled in the Stonelaw about 4,000 years after the Álukois.

Esterlans (**Es**terlans) The Well-East: Everything south of the Shirlangu Mountains and east of the Chompra Mountains. All these lands, including Shohan, speak Esterlani.

Great Ulian River (**Ū**lian) Longest, mightiest river of the East, winding through much of Shohan, forming most of its border with Pechon, and Pechon's border with Zanchor.

Hyúlems (**Hyū**lems) Álukoi term for humans of the lowlands: anywhere outside the mountains or tundra (all human cultures, except the Delfinians and Tundrites).

Kitria (**Kĭ**tria) North-most kingdom of the Castled Lands.

Laskomia (Lă**skō**mia) Kingdom forming a vast plain bordered by the Dawnwood, Deadwood, Tharidun, and the Tuzanchim Empire. Homeland of Lutyam and Moshal. Its most famous landmark is Lake Gabriska.

Lendish (**Len**dĭsh) The enterprising people and culture of Lendria, and the language they gave to most of the Castled Lands. Most Álukois also speak Lendish.

Monz   (Mônz) Dormant volcano, crater lake and surrounding "wilds," and for over 200 years, the home of the largest tierdragon ever known to the Continent.

Near Valley   Huge, flat grassland northwest of Shirlangu Mountains, and Puchakta's slice of the Tuzanchim Empire, said to have "hosted" more battles than any other place.

Pechon   (Pechōn) Land-locked kingdom south of Shohan and second largest in the "Well-East" or Esterlans.

Shirlangu Mountains   (Shĭrlôngū) Natural border between Shohan and Tuzanchim Empire, from southwest to northeast, boasting some of the highest peaks on the Continent.

Shohan   (Shōhôn) The Continent's second largest, yet by far its most populous realm. One of the many kingdoms of the "Well-East" or Esterlans, and perhaps the oldest.

Snowdragon   The *hyúlem* or lowlander term for an Álukoi. It is considered acceptable for the ignorant.

Stonelaw   Ancient confederacy formed by the Delfinians, Álukois, and Volpings in the sparsely populated mountain region north of the Castled Lands. Some consider the Stonelaw to be the only civilized place on the Continent.

The Claim   A Vast, fertile plain, but divided among thousands of tiny, ever-changing feudal states, where "No law has even the range of an arrow," and anarchy runs wild!

Tunda-Host   (Tundria or "Frozen North") The Continent's tundra lands, north coast and "ice-ways," or everything north of the Stonelaw and Dawnwood. Home of the Tundrites.

Tiefenbo   (Teefenbō) Lorgi's remote village on the Yazutak, not claimed by, or owing allegiance to any king or realm. Visitors may place the accent on any syllable, as the villagers are most tolerant. Half are Delfinian, half are Tundrite. Two Álukois also live there.

Tundrites   (Tundrīts) Peaceful nomads of the tundra and arctic, with no written language, and no word for war. Half of Tiefenbo's residents are Tundrites.

Tuzanchim (Tūz**ôn**chĭm) The people, language and culture of the Tuzanchim Steppes and Empire, known for superior equestrian, military, and debating skills, savagery in war, yet democratic ways and social mobility.

Volpings (**Vōl**pĭngs) Race of highly intelligent, marmot-like creatures living in underground cities in the Galatin Mountains, speaking a high-pitched language only fathomable to their own kind.

Well-East The Esterlans: everything south of the Shirlangu Mountains and east of Chompra Mountains. The whole region, including Shohan, speaks Esterlani.

Wembrish (**Wem**brĭsh) "dwarf" Delfinians, having the longest human lifespan, they dwell in huge granshire trees, found only in the Granshire- and Wembry-woods.

Wenyasi (Wen**yô**si) Major city on the Ulian River in west-central Shohan, where Klimgu became mesmerized by the queen's portrait.

Wester Hills Region of Northeast Shohan with few natural obstacles, hence the Tuzanchim's choice route to invading Shohan.

Yazutak River (**Yă**zutak) runs south through Kitria, turns east, then north through Dawnwood until reaching the Sea of Tundria (or Tunda-Sea), where stands Tiefenbo.

Yimung (**Yĭ**mūng) "mountain people" of the Shirlangus, who trade with the Tuzanchim and Shohaneze.

Zanchor (Zan**chōr)** Coastal kingdom south of Shohan, and largest in the "Well-East" or Esterlans.

Zárong Kórzel (**Zô**rong **Kōr**zel) The Quartz River, the Stonelaw's main river. Lowlanders consider this wilderness area uninhabitable for its severe winters, lack of potential farmland, and snowdragon "tree vigilantes." Yómgolin's quiet, beloved, home.

Álukop & Tuzanchim Words *(used in this tale)*

Álukop *(Yes, "Dragon-Speak" has many cognates with Lendish)*

Álukois	snowdragons
ábafosh	avalanche
ánter	other
akúa	hello
éom	am (I am)
gánsi	thank you
góbo	good, superb
góbo nóshul	generous, gourmet snack
hyúlem	a lowlander human, one not of the Stonelaw or tundra
Íye	me
kayutáve	horsetails (high clouds)
kéu	who
komenónda	coming
méni gánsi	many thanks (or *gánsi méni*)
mústar	mustard
myit	with
nómesang	name (for a person)
nóshul	snack
pahápkoltam	(Lit. "middle-finder") Álukoi location-sensing organ
pyar	for
syaz	sauce
tum	you, your
vat	wait
vya	what
yi	and
yoih(!)	oi (a mental "ouch")
Zárong Kórzel	Quartz River
zeeblut	honey
Zoténdok	The Stonelaw

(For more about Álukop, visit **www.snowdragontale.com/***)*

Tuzanchim *(same word means language, people and culture)*

banchugit	scatter or stagger
gánsi	thank you (adopted from Álukop)
guyat	go
guyat-iha!	charge
guyat par hatok	take up battle formations
hatok	take up, form
hatok banchugit	take up defensive, staggered formation
hai	yes
nok	no
karmchugtai	a fierce animal possessed by a vengeful human ghost
tekursedim	thank you (word supplanted by *gánsi* in Lorgi's time)
Yahai!	Stop!

www.ingramcontent.com/pod-product-compliance
Lightning Source LLC
Chambersburg PA
CBHW051429260626
47162CB00001B/12